THE
HORROR OF THE HEIGHTS

& OTHER TALES OF SUSPENSE

SIR ARTHUR CONAN DOYLE

THE HORROR OF THE HEIGHTS

& OTHER TALES OF SUSPENSE

Chronicle Books
San Francisco

Printed in the United States of America.

Library of Congress Cataloging-in-Publication Data

Doyle, Arthur Conan, Sir. 1859–1930.
   The horror of the heights and other tales of suspense / by Sir Arthur Conan Doyle.
      p.   cm.
   ISBN 0-8118-0144-6 (paperback)
   1. Horror tales, English.   I Title.
PR4621   1992a
823'.8—dc20   91–30040
                                                                           CIP

Cover design: Alex Laurant
Composition: Words & Deeds

Distributed in Canada by Raincoast Books,
112 East Third Avenue, Vancouver, B.C. V5T 1C8

10 9 8 7 6 5 4 3 2 1

Chronicle Books
275 Fifth Street
San Francisco, CA 94103

CONTENTS

PREFACE — viii

THE HORROR OF THE HEIGHTS — I

LOT NO. 249 — 16

THE LOS AMIGOS FIASCO — 47

THE PARASITE — 54

OUR MIDNIGHT VISITOR — 92

THROUGH THE VEIL — 112

DE PROFUNDIS — 117

THE GREAT KEINPLATZ EXPERIMENT — 126

DANGER! — 141

THE AMERICAN'S TALE — 167

SELECTING A GHOST — 174

THE GREAT BROWN-PERICORD MOTOR — 190

THE TERROR OF BLUE JOHN GAP — 198

THE WINNING SHOT — 213

PREFACE

I CARE NOT HOW HUMBLE your bookshelf may be, nor how lowly the room which it adorns. Close the door of that room behind you, shut off with it all the cares of the outer world, plunge back into the soothing company of the great dead, and then you are through the magic portal into that fair land wither worry and vexation can follow you no more. You have left all that is vulgar and all that is sordid behind you. There stand your noble, silent comrades, waiting in their ranks. Pass your eye down their files. Choose your man. And then you have but to hold up your hand to him and away you go together into dreamland. Surely there would be something eerie about a line of books were it not that familiarity has deadened our sense of it. Each is a mummified soul embalmed in cerecloth and natron of leather and printer's ink. Each cover of a true book enfolds the concentrated essence of a man. The personalities of the writers have faded into the thinnest shadows, as their bodies into impalpable dust, yet here are their very spirits at your command.

It is our familiarity also which has lessened our perception of the miraculous good fortune which we enjoy. Let us suppose that we were suddenly to learn that Shakespeare had returned to earth, and that he would favor any of us with an hour of his wit and his fancy. How eagerly we would seek him out! And yet we have him—the very best of him—at our elbows from week to week, and hardly trouble ourselves to put out our hands to beckon him down. No matter what mood a man may be in, when once he has passed through the magic door he can summon the world's greatest to sympathize with him in it. If he be thoughtful, here are the kings of thought. If he be dreamy, here are the masters of fancy. Or is it amusement that he lacks? He can signal to any one of the world's great storytellers, and out comes the dead man and holds him enthralled by the hour. The dead are such good company that one may come to think too little of the living. It is a real and a pressing danger with many of us, that we should never find our own thoughts and our own souls, but be ever obsessed by the dead. Yet secondhand romance and secondhand emotion are surely better than the dull, soul-killing monotony which life brings to most of the human race. But best of all when the dead man's wisdom and the dead man's example give us guidance and strength in the living of our own strenuous days.

Come through the magic door with me, and sit here on the green settee, where you can see the old oak case with its untidy lines of volumes. Smoking is not forbidden. Would you care to hear me talk of them? Well, I ask nothing better, for there is no volume there which is not a dear, personal friend, and what can a man talk of more pleasantly than that? The other books are over yonder, but these are my own favorites—the ones I care to reread and to have near my elbow. There is not a tattered cover which does not bring its mellow memories to me....

Sir Arthur Conan Doyle
from *Through the Magic Door*

THE HORROR OF THE HEIGHTS

T he idea that the extraordinary narrative which has been called the Joyce-Armstrong Fragment is an elaborate practical joke, evolved by some unknown person cursed by a perverted and sinister sense of humor, has now been abandoned by all who have examined the facts. The most *macabre* and imaginative of plotters would hesitate before linking his morbid fancies with the unquestioned and tragic facts which reinforce the statement. Though the assertions contained in it are amazing and even monstrous, it is nonetheless forcing itself upon the general intelligence that they are true, and that we must readjust our ideas to the new situation.

This world of ours appears to be separated by a slight and precarious margin of safety from a most singular and unexpected danger. I will endeavor in this narrative, which reproduces the original document in its necessarily somewhat fragmentary form, to lay before the reader the whole of the facts up to date, prefacing my statement by saying that if there be any who doubt the narrative of Joyce-Armstrong there can be no question at all as to the facts concerning Lieutenant Myrtle, R. N., and Mr. Hay Connor, who undoubtedly met their end in the manner described.

The Joyce-Armstrong Fragment was found in the field which is called Lower Haycock, lying one mile to the westward of the village of Withyham upon the Kent and Sussex border. It was on the fifteenth of

September last that an agricultural laborer, James Flynn, in the employment of Matthew Dodd, farmer of the Chauntry Farm, Withyham,
perceived a brier pipe lying near the footpath which skirts the hedge in
Lower Haycock. A few paces farther on he picked up a pair of broken
binocular glasses. Finally, among some nettles in the ditch, he caught
sight of a flat canvas-backed book which proved to be a notebook with
detachable leaves, some of which had come loose and were fluttering
along the base of the hedge. These he collected, but some, including the
first, were never recovered and leave a deplorable hiatus in this all-
important statement.

The notebook was taken by the laborer to his master, who in turn
showed it to Dr. J. H. Atherton of Hartfield. This gentleman at once
recognized the need for an expert examination, and the manuscript was
forwarded to the Obro Club in London, where it now lies.

The first two pages of the manuscript are missing. There is also one
torn away at the end of the narrative, though none of these affects the
general coherence of the story. It is conjectured that the missing
opening is concerned with the record of Mr. Joyce-Armstrong's qualifications as an aeronaut, which can be gathered from other sources and
are admitted to be unsurpassed among the air pilots of England. For
many years he has been looked upon as among the most daring and the
most intellectual of flying men, a combination which has enabled him
both to invent and to test several new devices, including the common
gyroscopic attachment which is by his known name.

The main body of the manuscript is written neatly in ink, but the last
few lines are in pencil and are so ragged as to be hardly legible—exactly,
in fact, as they might be expected to appear if they were scribbled off
hurriedly from the seat of a moving airplane.

There are, it may be added, several stains both on the last page and on
the outside cover which have been pronounced by the Home Office
experts to be blood—probably human and certainly mammalian. The
fact that something closely resembling the organism of malaria was
discovered in this blood, and that Joyce-Armstrong is known to have
suffered from intermittent fever, is a remarkable example of the new
weapons which modern science has placed in the hands of our detectives.

And now a word as to the personality of the author of this epoch-
making statement. Joyce-Armstrong, according to the few friends who
really knew something of the man, was a poet and a dreamer as well as a
mechanic and an inventor. He was a man of considerable wealth, much

of which he had spent in the pursuit of his aeronautical hobby. He had four private airplanes in his hangars near Devizes, and is said to have made no less than one hundred and seventy ascents in the course of last year.

He was a retiring man, with dark moods in which he would avoid the society of his fellows. Captain Dangerfield, who knew him better than anyone else, says that there were times when his eccentricity threatened to develop into something more serious. His habit of carrying a shotgun with him in his airplane was one manifestation of it. Another was the morbid effect which the fall of Lieutenant Myrtle had upon his mind.

Myrtle, who was attempting the height record, fell from an altitude of something over thirty thousand feet. Horrible to narrate, his head was entirely obliterated, though his body and limbs preserved their configuration. At every gathering of airmen, Joyce-Armstrong, according to Dangerfield, would ask with an enigmatic smile: "And where, pray, is Myrtle's head?" This dreadful question, and the strange fashion in which it was asked, froze the blood of men who were callous to the dangers of their perilous calling.

On another occasion, after dinner at the mess of the Flying School on Salisbury Plain, he started a debate as to what will be the most permanent danger which airmen will have to encounter. Having listened to successive opinions as to air pockets, faulty engines, and overbanking, he ended by shrugging his shoulders and refusing to put forward his own views, though he gave the impression that they differed from any advanced by his companions. It is worth remarking that after his own complete disappearance it was found that his private affairs were arranged with a precision which may show that he had a strong premonition of disaster.

With these essential explanations I will now give the narrative exactly as it stands, beginning at page three of the blood-soaked notebook.

"Nevertheless, when I dined at Rheims with Coselli and Gustav Raymond I found that neither of them was aware of any particular danger in the higher layers of the atmosphere. I did not actually say what was in my thoughts, but I got so near it that if they had had any corresponding idea they could not have failed to express it. But then they are two empty, vain-glorious fellows with no thought beyond seeing their silly names in the newspaper. It is interesting to note that neither of them had ever been much beyond the twenty-thousand-foot level. Of course, men have been higher than this both in balloons and in the ascent of mountains. It must be well above that point that the airplane enters the danger zone—always presuming that my premonitions are correct.

"Airplaning has been with us now for more than twenty years, and one might well ask, why should this peril be only revealing itself in our day? The answer is obvious. In the old days of weak engines, when a hundred-horsepower Gnome was considered ample for every need, the flights were very restricted. Now that three hundred horsepower is the rule rather than the exception, visits to the upper layers have become easier and more common. Some of us can remember how in our youth Garros made a worldwide reputation by attaining nineteen thousand feet, and it was considered a remarkable achievement to fly over the Alps.

"Our standard now has been immeasurably raised, and there are twenty high flights for one in former years. Many of them have been undertaken with impunity. The thirty-thousand-foot level has been reached time after time with no discomfort beyond cold and asthma.

"What does this prove? A visitor might descend upon this planet a thousand times and never see a tiger. Yet tigers exist, and if he chanced to come down into a jungle he might be devoured. There are jungles of the upper air, and there are worse things than tigers which inhabit them. I believe in time these jungles will be accurately mapped out. Even at the present moment I could name two of them. One of them lies over the Pau-Biarritz district of France. Another is just over my head as I write here in my house in Wiltshire. I rather think there is a third in the Homburg-Wiesbaden district.

"It was the disappearance of the airmen that first set me thinking. Of course, everyone said that they had fallen into the sea, but that did not satisfy me at all. First, there was Verrier in France; his machine was found near Bayonne, but they never got his body.

"There was the case of Baxter also, who vanished, though his engine and some of the iron fixings were found in a wood in Leicestershire. In that case, Dr. Middleton of Amesbury, who was watching the flight with a telescope, declares that just before the clouds obscured the view he saw the machine, which was at an enormous height, suddenly rise perpendicularly upward in a succession of jerks, in a manner that he would have thought to be impossible. That was the last seen of Baxter. There was a correspondence in the papers, but it never led to anything.

"There were several other similar cases, and then there was the death of Hay Connor. What a crackle there was about an unsolved mystery of the air, and what columns in the halfpenny papers, and yet how little was ever done to get at the bottom of the business! He came down in a tremendous volplane from an unknown height. He never got off his machine, and died in his pilot's seat.

"Died of what? 'Heart disease,' said the doctors. Rubbish! Hay Connor's heart was as sound as mine is. What did Venables say? Venables was the only man who was at his side when he died. He said that he was shivering and looked like a man who had been badly scared. 'Died of fright,' said Venables, but could not imagine what he was frightened about. Only said one word to Venables, which sounded like 'Monstrous.' They could make nothing of that at the inquest. But I could make something of it.

"Monsters! That was the last word of poor Harry Hay Connor. And he *did* die of fright, just as Venables thought.

"And then there was Myrtle's head. Do you really believe—does anybody really believe—that a man's head could be driven clean into his body by the force of a fall? Well, perhaps it may be possible, but I for one have never believed that it was so with Myrtle. And the grease upon his clothes—'all slimy with grease,' said somebody at the inquest. Queer that nobody got thinking after that! I did—but then I had been thinking for a good long time.

"I've made three ascents—how Dangerfield used to chaff me about my shotgun!—but I've never been high enough! Now, with this new, light Paul Veroner machine and its one hundred seventy-five Robur, I should easily touch the thirty thousand tomorrow. I'll have a shot at the record. Maybe I shall have a shot at something else as well. Of course, it's dangerous. If a fellow wants to avoid danger he had best keep out of flying altogether and subside finally into flannel slippers and a dressing gown. But I'll visit the air jungle tomorrow—and if there's anything there I shall know it.

"If I return, I'll find myself a bit of a celebrity. If I don't, this notebook may explain what I am trying to do, and how I lost my life in doing it. But no drivel about accidents or mysteries, if *you* please.

"I chose my Paul Veroner monoplane for the job. There's nothing like a monoplane when real work is to be done. Beaumont found that out in very early days. For one thing, it doesn't mind damp, and the weather looks as if we should be in the clouds all the time. It's a bonny little model, and answers my hand like a tender-mouthed horse. The engine is a ten-cylinder rotary Robur, working up to one hundred seventy-five. It has all the modern improvements, enclosed fuselage, high-curved landing skids, brakes, gyroscopic steadiers, and three speeds worked by an alteration of the angle of the planes, upon the Venetian-blind principle.

"I took a shotgun with me, with a dozen cartridges filled with buckshot. You should have seen the face of Perkins, my old mechanic, when I directed him to put them in. I was dressed like an Arctic explorer, with two jerseys under my overalls, thick socks inside my padded boots, a storm cap with flaps, and my talc goggles. It was stifling outside the hangars, but I was going for the summit of the Himalayas, and had to dress for the part.

"Of course, I took an oxygen bag; the man who goes for the altitude record without one will either be frozen or smothered—or both.

"I had a good look at the planes, the rudder bar, and the elevating lever before I got in. Everything was in order so far as I could see. Then I switched on my engine and found that she was running sweetly. When they let her go she rose almost at once, upon the lowest speed. I circled my home field once or twice just to warm her up, and then with a wave to the others I flattened out my planes and put her on her highest. She skimmed like a swallow down wind for eight or ten miles until I turned her nose up a little and she began to climb in a great spiral for the cloud bank above me. It's all important to rise slowly and adapt yourself to the pressure as you go.

"It was a close, warm day for an English September, and there was the hush and heaviness of impending rain. Now and then there came sudden puffs of wind from the southwest—one of them so gusty and unexpected that it caught me napping and turned me half-round for an instant. I remember the time when gusts and whirls and air pockets used to be things of danger—before we learned to put an overmastering power into our engines. Just as I reached the cloud banks, with the altimeter marking three thousand, down came the rain.

"My word, how it poured! It drummed upon my wings, and lashed against my face, blurring my glasses so that I could hardly see. I got down on to a low speed, for it was painful to travel against it. As I got higher it became hail, and I had to turn tail to it. One of my cylinders was out of action—a dirty plug, I should imagine; but still I was rising steadily with plenty of power.

"After a bit the trouble passed, whatever it was, and I heard the full, deep-throated purr—then ten singing as one. That's where the beauty of our modern silencers comes in. We can at last control our engines by ear. How they squeal and squeak and sob when they are in trouble! All those cries for help were wasted in the old days when every sound was swallowed up by the monstrous racket of the machine. If only the early aviators could come back to see the beauty and perfection of the mechanism which has been bought at the cost of their lives!

"About 9:30 I was nearing the clouds. Down below me, all blurred and shadowed with rain, lay the vast expanse of Salisbury Plain. Half a dozen flying machines were doing hackwork at the thousand-foot level, looking like little black swallows against the green background. I dare say they were wondering what I was doing up in cloudland.

"Suddenly a gray curtain drew across beneath me, and the wet folds of vapor were swirling round my face. It was clammily cold and miserable. But I was above the hailstorm and that was something gained. The cloud was as dark and thick as a London fog. In my anxiety to get clear, I cocked her nose up until the automatic alarm bell rang and I actually began to slide backward. My sopped and dripping wings had made me heavier than I thought, but presently I was in lighter cloud and soon had cleared the first layer.

"There was a second—opal-colored and fleecy—at a great height above my head; a white, unbroken ceiling above, and a dark, unbroken floor below, with the monoplane laboring upward upon a vast spiral between them. It is deadly lonely in these cloud spaces. Once a great flight of some small water bird went past me, flying very fast to the westward. The quick whir of their wings and their musical cry were cheery to my ear. I fancy that they were teal, but I am a wretched zoologist. Now that we humans have become birds, we must really learn to know our brethren by sight.

"The wind down beneath me whirled and swayed the broad cloud plain. Once a great eddy formed in it, a whirlpool of vapor, and through it, as down a funnel, I caught sight of the distant world. A large white biplane was passing at a vast depth beneath me. I fancy it was the morning mail service between Bristol and London. Then the drift swirled inward again and the great solitude was unbroken.

"Just after ten I touched the lower edge of the upper-cloud stratum. It consisted of fine, diaphanous vapor drifting swiftly from the westward. The wind had been steadily rising all this time, and it was now blowing a sharp breeze—twenty-eight an hour by my gaze. Already it was very cold, though my altimeter marked only nine thousand. The engines were working beautifully, and we went droning steadily upward. The cloud bank was thicker than I had expected, but at last it thinned out into a golden mist before me, and then in an instant I had shot out from it, and there was an unclouded sky and a brilliant sun over my head—all blue and gold above, all shining silver below, one vast, glimmering plain as far as my eyes could reach.

"It was quarter past ten o'clock, and the barograph needle pointed to twelve thousand eight hundred. Up I went and up, my ears concentrated upon the deep purring of my motor, my eyes busy always with the watch, the revolution indicator, the petrol lever, and the oil pump. No wonder aviators are said to be a fearless race. With so many things to think of there is no time to trouble about oneself. About this time I noted how unreliable is the compass when above a certain height from earth. At fifteen thousand feet mine was pointing east and a point south. The sun and the wind gave me my true bearings.

"I rose steadily, reflecting the sun like a gilded dragonfly between earth and heaven, soaring higher and higher from the silver fleece beneath me.

"But a mighty wind was flowing like a great, smooth river across these empty solitudes of air. I had hoped to reach an eternal stillness in these high altitudes, but with every thousand feet of ascent the gale grew stronger. My machine groaned and trembled in every joint and rivet as she faced it, and swept away like a sheet of paper when I banked her on the turn, skimming down wind at a greater pace, perhaps, than ever mortal man has moved. Yet I had always to turn again and tack up in the wind's eye, for it was not merely a height record that I was after. By all my calculations it was above Wiltshire that my air jungle lay, and all my labor might be lost if I struck the outer layers at some farther point.

"When I reached the nineteen-thousand-foot level, which was about midday, the wind was so severe that I looked with some anxiety to the stays of my wings, expecting momentarily to see them snap or slacken. I even cast loose the parachute behind me, and fastened its hook into the ring of my leathern belt so as to ready for the worst. This is the time when a bit of scamped work by the mechanic is paid for by the life of the aeronaut. But she held together bravely. Every cord and strut was humming and vibrating like a harp string; but it was glorious to see how, for all the beating and the buffeting, she was still the mistress of the sky.

"This is surely something divine in man himself that he should rise so superior to the limitations which Creation seems to impose—rise, too, by such unselfish, heroic devotion as this air conquest has shown. Talk of human degeneration! When has such a story as this been written in the annals of our race!

"These were the thoughts in my head as I climbed that monstrous inclined plane, with the wind sometimes beating in my face and sometimes whistling behind my ears, while the cloudland beneath me fell away to such a distance that the folds and hummocks of silver had all smoothed out into one flat, shining plain.

"But suddenly I had a horrible and unprecedented experience. I have known before what it is to be in what our neighbors have called a '*tourbillon*,' but never on such a scale as this. That huge, sweeping river of wind of which I have spoken had, as it appears, whirlpools within it which were as monstrous as itself. Without a moment's warning I was dragged suddenly into the heart of one. I spun round for a minute or two with such velocity that I almost lost my senses, and then fell suddenly, left wing foremost, down the vacuum funnel in the center. I dropped like a stone, and lost nearly a thousand feet in about twenty seconds. It was only my belt that kept me in my seat, and the shock and breathlessness left me hanging half-insensible over the side of the fuselage.

"But I am always capable of a supreme effort—it is my one great merit as an aviator. I was conscious that the descent was slower. The whirlpool was a cone rather than a funnel, and I had come to the apex. With a terrific wrench, throwing my weight all to one side, I leveled my planes and brought her head away from the wind. In an instant I had shot out of the eddies and was skimming down the sky.

"Then, shaken but victorious, I turned her nose up and began once more my steady grind on the upward spiral. I took a large sweep to avoid the danger spot of the whirlpool, and soon I was safely above it. Just after one o'clock I was twenty-one thousand feet above the sea level. To my great joy I had topped the gale, and with every hundred feet of ascent the air grew stiller. On the other hand, it was very cold, and I was conscious of that peculiar nausea which goes with rarefication of air. For the first time I unscrewed the mouth of my oxygen bag and took an occasional whiff of the glorious bag. I could feel it running like a cordial through my veins, and I was exhilarated almost to the point of drunkenness. I shouted and sang as I soared upward into the cold, still outer world.

"It was very clear to me that the insensibility which came upon Glaisher, and in a lesser degree upon Coxwell, when in 1862 they ascended in a balloon to the height of thirty thousand feet, was due to the extreme speed with which a perpendicular ascent is made. Doing it at an easy gradient and accustoming oneself to the lessened barometric pressure by slow degrees, there are no such dreadful symptoms. At the same great height I found that even without my oxygen inhaler I could breathe without undue distress.

"It was bitterly cold, however, and my thermometer was at zero Fahrenheit. At 1:30, I was nearly seven miles above the surface of the earth, and still ascending steadily. I found, however, that the rarefied air was giving markedly less support to my planes, and that my angle of ascent had to be considerably lowered in consequence. It was already clear that even with my light weight and strong engine power there was a point in front of me where I should be held. To make matters worse, one of my sparking plugs was in trouble again and there was intermittent misfiring in the engine. My heart was heavy with the fear of failure.

"It was about that time that I had a most extraordinary experience. Something whizzed past me in a trail of smoke and exploded with a loud hissing sound, sending forth a cloud of steam. For the instant I could not imagine what had happened. Then I remembered that the earth is forever being bombarded by meteor stones and would be hardly inhabitable were they not in nearly every case turned to vapor in the outer layers of the atmosphere. Here is a new danger for the high-altitude man, for two others passed me when I was nearing the forty-thousand-foot mark. I cannot doubt that at the edge of the earth's envelope the risk would be a very real one.

"My barograph needle marked forty-one thousand three hundred when I became aware that I could go no farther. Physically, the strain was not as yet greater than I could bear, but my machine had reached its limit. The attenuated air gave no firm support to the wings, and the least tilt developed into sideslip, while she seemed sluggish on her controls. Possibly, had the engine been at its best, another thousand feet might have been within our capacity; but it was still misfiring, and two out of the ten cylinders appeared to be out of action. If I had not already reached the zone for which I was searching, then I should never see it upon this journey.

"But was it not possible that I had attained it? Soaring in circles like a monstrous hawk upon the forty-thousand-foot level, I let the mono-plane guide herself, and with my Mannheim glass I made a careful observation of my surroundings. The heavens were perfectly clear; there was no indication of those dangers which I had imagined.

"I have said I was soaring in circles. It struck me suddenly that I should do well to take a wider sweep and open up a new air tract. If the hunter entered an earth jungle he would drive through it if he wished find his game. My reasoning had led me to believe that the air jungle which I had imagined lay somewhere over Wiltshire. This should be to the south and west of me. I took my bearings from the sun, for the compass was hopeless and no trace of earth was to be seen—nothing but the distant silver cloud plain. However, I got my direction as best I might and kept her head straight to the mark. I reckoned more that my petrol supply would not last for more than another hour or so, but I could afford to use it to the last drop, since a single magnificent volplane would at anytime take me to the earth.

"Suddenly I was aware of something new. The air in front of me had lost its crystal clearness. It was full of long, ragged wisps of something which I can only compare to very fine cigarette smoke. It hung about in wreaths and coils, turning and twisting slowly in the sunlight. As the monoplane shot through it, I was aware of a faint taste of oil upon my lips, and there was a greasy scum upon the woodwork of the machine. Some infinitely fine organic matter appeared to be suspended in the atmosphere.

"There was no life there. It was inchoate and diffuse, extending for many square acres and then fringing off into the void. No, it was not life. But might it not be the remains of life? Above all, might it not be the food of life, of monstrous life, even as the humble grease of the ocean is the food for the mighty whale? The thought was in my mind when my eyes looked upward and I saw the most wonderful vision that ever man has seen. Can I hope to convey it to you, even as I saw it myself last Thursday!

"Conceive a jellyfish such as sails in our summer seas, bell-shaped and of enormous size—far larger, I should judge, than the dome of Saint Paul's. It was of a light pink color veined with a delicate green, but the whole huge fabric so tenuous that it was but a fairy outline against the dark blue sky. It pulsated with a delicate and regular rhythm. From it there depended two long, drooping green tentacles which swayed slowly backward and forward. This gorgeous vision passed gently with noiseless dignity over my head, as light and fragile as a soap bubble, and drifted upon its stately way.

"I had half-turned my monoplane that I might look after this beautiful creature, when in a moment I found myself amidst a perfect fleet of them, of all sizes, but none so large as the first. Some were quite small, but the majority about as big as an average balloon, and with much the same curvature at the top. There was in them a delicacy of texture and coloring which reminded me of the finest Venetian glass. Pale shades of pink and green were the prevailing tints, but all had a lovely iridescence where the sun shimmered through their dainty forms. Some hundreds of them drifted past me, a wonderful fairy squadron of strange, unknown argosies of sky—creatures whose forms and substance were so attuned to these pure heights that one could not conceive anything so delicate within actual sight or sound of earth.

"But soon my attention was drawn to a new phenomenon—the serpents of the outer air. These were long, thin, fantastic coils of vaporlike material, which turned and twisted with great speed, flying round and round so fast that the eyes could hardly follow them. Some of these ghostlike creatures were twenty or thirty feet long; but it was difficult to tell their girth, for their outline was so hazy that it seemed to fade away into the air around them. These air snakes were of a very light gray or smoke color, with some darker lines within which gave the impression of a definite organism. One of them whisked past my very face, and I was conscious of a cold, clammy contact; but their composition was so unsubstantial that I could not connect them with any thought of physical danger, any more than the beautiful belllike creatures which had preceded them. There was no more solidity in their frames than in the floating spume from a broken wave.

"But a more terrible experience was in store for me. Floating downward from a great height, there came a purplish patch of vapor, small as I saw it first, but rapidly enlarging as it approached me, until it appeared to be hundreds of square feet in size. Though fashioned of some transparent jellylike substance, it was nonetheless of much more definite outline and solid consistence than anything which I had seen before.

"There were more traces, too, of a physical organization, especially two vast, shadowy, circular plates upon either side, which may have been eyes, and a perfectly solid white projection between them which was as curved and cruel as the beak of a vulture. The whole aspect of this monster was formidable and threatening, and it kept changing its color from a very light mauve to a dark, angry purple so thick that it cast a shadow as it drifted between my monoplane and the sun. On the upper curve of its huge body there were three great projections which I can only describe as enormous bubbles, and I was convinced as I looked at them that they were charged with some extremely light gas which served to buoy up the misshapen and semisolid mass in the rarefied air.

"The creature moved swiftly along, keeping pace easily with the monoplane, and for twenty miles or more it formed my horrible escort, hovering over me like a bird of prey which is waiting to pounce. Its method of progression—done so swiftly that it was not easy to follow—was to throw out a long, glutinous streamer in front of it, which in turn seemed to draw forward the rest of the writhing body. So elastic and gelatinous was it that never for two successive minutes was it the same shape, and yet each change made it more threatening and loathsome than the last.

"I knew that it meant mischief. Every purple flush of its hideous body told me so. The vague, goggling eyes, which were turned always upon me, were cold and merciless in their viscid hatred. I dipped the nose of my monoplane downward to escape it. As I did so, as quick as a flash, there shot out a long tentacle from this mass of floating blubber, and it fell as light and sinuous as a whiplash across the front of my machine. There was a loud hiss as it lay for a moment across the hot engine, and it whisked itself into the air again while the huge, flat body drew itself together as if in sudden pain.

"I dipped to a vol-piqué, but again a tentacle fell over the monoplane, and was shorn off by the propeller as easily as it might have cut through a smoke wreath. A long, gliding, sticky, serpentlike coil came from behind and caught me round the waist, dragging me out of the fuselage. I tore at it, my fingers sinking into the smooth, gluelike surface, and for an instant I disengaged myself, but only to be caught round the boot by another coil, which gave me a jerk that tilted me almost on my back.

"As I fell over I blazed off both barrels of my gun, though indeed it was like attacking an elephant with a peashooter to imagine that any human weapon could cripple that mighty bulk. And yet I aimed better than I knew, for with a loud report one of the great blisters upon the creature's back exploded with the puncture of the buckshot. It was very clear that my conjecture was right, and that these vast, clear bladders were distended with some lifting gas, for in an instant the huge, cloudlike body turned sideways, writhing desperately to find its balance, while the white beak snapped and gaped in horrible fury.

"But already I had shot away on the steepest glide that I dared to attempt, my engine still full on, the flying propeller and the force of gravity shooting me downward like an aerolite. Far behind me I saw a dull purplish smudge growing swiftly smaller and merging into the blue sky behind it.

"I was safe out of the deadly jungle of the outer air.

"Once out of danger I throttled my engine, for nothing tears a machine to pieces quicker than running on full power from a height. It was a glorious spiral volplane from nearly eight miles in altitude, first to the level of the silver cloud bank, then to that of the storm cloud beneath it, and finally in beating rain to the surface of the earth. I saw the Bristol Channel beneath me as I broke from the clouds; but having still some petrol in my tank I got twenty miles inland before I found myself stranded in a field near the village of Ashcombe.

"There I got three tins of petrol from a passing motorcar, and at ten minutes past six that evening I alighted gently in my own home meadow at Devizes after such a journey as no mortal upon earth has ever yet taken and lived to tell the tale. I have seen the beauty and I have seen the horror of the heights—and greater beauty or greater horror than that is not within the ken of man.

"And now it is my plan to go once again before I give my results to the world.

"My reason for this is that I must surely have something to show by the way of proof before I lay such a tale before my fellow men. It is true that others will soon follow and will confirm what I have said, and yet I should wish to carry conviction from the first. Those lovely iridescent bubbles of the air should not be hard to capture. They drift slowly upon their way, and the swift monoplane could intercept their leisurely course. It is likely enough that they would dissolve in the heavier layers of the atmosphere, and that some small heap of amorphous jelly might be all that I should bring to earth with me. And yet something there would surely be, by which I could substantiate my story.

"Yes, I will go, even if I run a risk by doing so. These purple horrors would not seem to be numerous. It is probable that I shall not see one. If I do I shall dive at once. At the worst there is always the shotgun and my knowledge of . . . "

(Here a page of the manuscript is unfortunately missing.) On the next page is written in large, struggling writing:

Forty-three thousand feet. I shall never see earth again. They are beneath me, three of them. God help me, it is a dreadful death to die!

Such in its entirety is the Joyce-Armstrong Statement.

Of the man nothing has since been seen. Pieces of his shattered monoplane have been picked up in the preserves of Mr. Budd-

Lushington upon the borders of Kent and Sussex, within a few miles of the spot where the notebook was discovered.

If the unfortunate aviator's theory is correct that this air jungle, as he called it, existed only over the southwest of England, then it would seem that he had fled from it at the full speed of his monoplane, but had been overtaken and devoured by these horrible creatures at some spot in the outer atmosphere above the place where the grim relics were found. The picture of that monoplane skimming down the sky, with the nameless terrors flying swiftly beneath it and cutting it off always from the earth, while they gradually closed in upon their victim, is one upon which a man who valued his sanity would prefer not to dwell.

There are many, as I am aware, who still jeer at the facts which I have here set down, but even they must admit that Joyce-Armstrong has disappeared, and I would commend to them his own words:

"This notebook may explain what I am trying to do, and how I lost my life in doing it. But no drivel about accidents or mysteries, if *you* please."

LOT NO. 249

Of the dealings of Edward Bellingham with William Monkhouse Lee, and of the cause of the great terror of Abercrombie Smith, it may be that no absolute and final judgment will ever be delivered. It is true that we have the full and clear narrative of Smith himself, and such corroboration as he could look for from Thomas Styles, the servant, from the Reverend Plumptree Peterson, Fellow of Old's, and from such other people as chanced to gain some passing glance at this or that incident in a singular chain of events. Yet, in the main, the story must rest upon Smith alone, and the most will think that it is more likely that one brain, however outwardly sane, has some subtle warp in its texture, some strange flaw in its workings, than that path of nature has been overstepped in open day in so famed a center of learning and light as the University of Oxford. Yet when we think how narrow and how devious this path of nature is, how dimly we can trace it, for all our lamps of science, and how from the darkness which girds it round great and terrible possibilities loom ever shadowly upward, it is a bold and confident man who will put a limit to the strange bypaths into which the human spirit may wander.

In a certain wing of what we will call Old College in Oxford there is a corner turret of an exceeding great age. The heavy arch which spans the open door has bent downward in the center under the weight of its years, and the gray lichen-blotched blocks of stone are bound and knitted together with withes and strands of ivy, as though the old mother had set herself to brace them up against wind and weather. From the door a stone stair curves upward spirally, passing two landings, and terminating in a third one, its steps all shapeless and hollowed by the tread of so many generations of the seekers after knowledge. Life has flowed like water down this winding stair, and, waterlike, has left these smooth-worn grooves behind it. From the long-gowned pedantic scholars of Plantagenet days down to the young bloods of a later age, how full and strong had been that tide of young English life! And what was left now of all those hopes, those strivings, those fiery energies, save here and there in some old-world churchyard a few scratches upon a stone, and perchance a handful of dust in a moldering coffin? Yet here were the silent stair and the gray old wall, with a bend and saltire and many another heraldic device still to be read upon its surface, like grotesque shadows thrown back from the days that had passed.

In the month of May, in the year 1884, three young men occupied the sets of rooms which opened on to the separate landing of the old stair. Each set consisted simply of a sitting room and of a bedroom, while the two corresponding rooms upon the ground floor were used, the one as a coal cellar, and the other as the living room of the servant, or gyp, Thomas Styles, whose duty it was to wait upon the three men above him. To right and to left was a line of lecture rooms and of offices, so that the dwellers in the old turret enjoyed a certain seclusion, which made the chambers popular among the more studious undergraduates. Such were the three who occupied them now—Abercrombie Smith above, Edward Bellingham beneath him, and William Monkhouse Lee upon the lowest story.

It was ten o'clock on a bright spring night, and Abercrombie Smith lay back in his armchair, his feet upon the fender, and his brierroot pipe between his lips. In a similar chair, and equally at his ease, there lounged on the other side of the fireplace his old school friend Jephro Hastie. Both men were in flannels, for they had spent their evening upon the river, but apart from their dress no one could look at their hard-cut alert faces without seeing that they were open-air men—men whose minds and tastes turned naturally to all that was manly and robust. Hastie, indeed, was stroke of his college boat, and Smith was an even better oar, but a coming examination had already cast its shadow over him and held him to his work, save for the few hours a week which health demanded. A litter of medical books upon the table, with scattered bones, models, and anatomical plates, pointed to the extent as well as the nature of his studies, while a couple of singlesticks and a set of boxing gloves above the mantelpiece hinted at the means by which, with Hastie's help, he might take his exercise in its most compressed and least distant form. They knew each other very well—so well that they could sit now in that soothing silence which is the very highest development of companionship.

"Have some whiskey," said Abercrombie Smith at last, between two cloudbursts. "Scotch in the jug and Irish in the bottle."

"No, thanks. I'm in for the sculls. I don't liquor when I'm training. How about you?"

"I'm reading hard. I think it best to leave it alone."

Hastie nodded, and they relapsed into a contented silence.

"By the way, Smith," asked Hastie, presently, "have you made the acquaintance of either of the fellows on your stair yet?"

"Just a nod when we pass. Nothing more."

"Hum! I should be inclined to let it stand at that. I know something of them both. Not much, but as much as I want. I don't think I should take them to my bosom if I were you. Not that there's much amiss with Monkhouse Lee."

"Meaning the thin one?"

"Precisely. He is a gentlemanly little fellow. I don't think there is any vice in him. But then you can't know him without knowing Bellingham."

"Meaning the fat one?"

"Yes, the fat one. And he's a man whom I for one would rather not know."

Abercrombie Smith raised his eyebrows and glanced across at his companion. "What's up, then?" he asked. "Drink? Cards? Cad? You used not to be censorious."

"Ah! you evidently don't know the man, or you wouldn't ask. There's something damnable about him, something reptilian. My gorge always rises at him. I should put him down as a man with secret vices— an evil liver. He's no fool, though. They say that he is one of the best men in his line that they have ever had in the college."

"Medicine or classics?"

"Eastern languages. He's a demon at them. Chillingworth met him somewhere above the second cataract last long, and he told me that he just prattled to the Arabs as if he had been born and nursed and weaned among them. He talked Coptic to the Copts, and Hebrew to the Jews, and Arabic to the Bedouins, and they were all ready to kiss the hem of his frock coat. There are some old hermit Johnnies up in those parts who sit on rocks and scowl and spit at the casual stranger. Well, when they saw this chap Bellingham, before he had said five words they just lay down on their bellies and wriggled. Chillingworth said that he never saw anything like it. Bellingham seemed to take it as his right too, and strutted about among them and talked down to them like a Dutch uncle. Pretty good for an undergrad of Old's, wasn't it?"

"That sort of thing doesn't mean much in the East, though. It was just their way of saying that they were surprised and pleased to find a foreigner who knew something of their history and language. But how do you come to know this fellow?"

"Well, I come from Applesford, you know, and so does young Monkhouse Lee. His father is vicar there, and he has a sister, Eveline Lee, who is as nice a little girl as you would wish to see. When Lee began to be chummy with Bellingham, he asked him down to stay at the vicarage, and I saw something of him. The mischief of it is that he's managed in some way to get the better of little Eveline, and she is engaged to him. What she can see in the fellow! But it's my belief that there are many women, and Eveline Lee is among them, who are so unselfish, and so gentle, and so frightened of giving pain, that if their fathers' gardeners were to propose to them, they would accept them for fear of hurting their feelings if they refused. Well, I suppose they know their own business best, but it makes a man grind his teeth. A dove and a toad—that's what I always think of."

Abercrombie Smith grinned and knocked his ashes out against the side of the grate. "You show every card in your hand, old chap," said he. "What a prejudiced, green-eyed, evil-thinking old man it is! You have really nothing against the fellow except that."

"Well, I've known her ever since she was as long as that cherry-wood pipe, and I don't like to see her taking risks. And it is a risk. He looks beastly. And he has a beastly temper, a venomous temper. You remember his row with Long Norton?"

"No; you always forget that I am a freshman."

"Ah, it was last winter. Of course. Well, you know the towpath along by the river. There were several fellows going along it, Bellingham in front, when they came on an old market woman coming the other way. It had been raining—you know what those fields are like when it has rained—and the path ran between the river and a great puddle that was nearly as broad. Well, what does this swine do but keep the path, and push the old girl into the mud, where she and her marketings came to terrible grief. It was a blackguard thing to do, and Long Norton, who is as gentle a fellow as ever stepped, told him what he thought of it. One word led to another, and it ended in Norton laying his stick across the fellow's shoulders. There was the deuce of a fuss about it, and it's a treat to see the way in which Bellingham looks at Norton when they meet now. By Jove, Smith, it's nearly eleven o'clock."

"No hurry. Light your pipe again."

"Not I. I'm supposed to be in training. Here I've been sitting gossiping like a ———— old woman when I ought to have been safely tucked up. I'll borrow your skull, if you can spare it. Williams has had mine for a month. I'll take the little bones of your ear too, if you are sure you won't need them. Thanks very much. Never mind a bag, I can carry them very well under my arm. Good-night, my son, and take my tip as to your neighbor."

When Hastie, bearing his anatomical plunder, had clattered off down the winding stair, Abercrombie Smith hurled his pipe into the waste-paper basket, and drawing his chair nearer to the lamp, plunged into a formidable green-covered volume, adorned with great colored maps of that strange internal kingdom of which we are the hapless and helpless monarchs. Though a freshman at Oxford, the student was not so in medicine, for he had worked for four years at Glasgow and at Berlin, and this coming examination would place him finally as a member of his profession. With his firm mouth, broad forehead, and clear-cut, somewhat hard-featured face, he was a man who, if he had no brilliant talent, was yet so dogged, so patient, and so strong that he might in the end overtop a more showy genius. A man who can hold his own among Scotchmen and North Germans is not a man to be easily set back. Smith had left a name at Glasgow and at Berlin, and he was bent now upon doing as much at Oxford, if hard work and devotion could accomplish it.

He had sat reading for about an hour, and the hands of the noisy carriage clock upon the side table were rapidly closing together upon the twelve, when a sudden sound fell upon the student's ear, a sharp, rather shrill sound, like the hissing intake of a man's breath who gasps under some strong emotion. Smith laid down his book and slanted his ear to listen. There was no one on either side or above him, so that the interruption came certainly from the neighbor beneath him—the same neighbor of whom Hastie had given so unsavory an account. Smith knew him only as a flabby pale-faced man of silent and studious habits, a man whose lamp threw a golden bar from the old turret even after he had extinguished his own. This community in lateness had formed a certain silent bond between them. It was soothing to Smith when the hours stole on toward dawning to feel that there was another so close who set as small a value upon his sleep as he did. He could even see him at times, for when the moon lay behind the turret, and cast its black length across the green quadrangle lawn, each window stood out upon the shadow as a yellow glimmering square, and there, in the center of this golden frame, Smith could sometimes see the blurred outline of the sunken head and rounded shoulders of the worker beneath him. Even now, as his thoughts turned toward him, Smith's feelings were kindly. Hastie was a good fellow, but he was rough, strong-fibered, with no imagination or sympathy. He could not tolerate departures from what he looked upon as the model type of manliness. If a man could not be measured by a public-school standard, then he was beyond the pale with Hastie. Like so many who are themselves robust, he was apt to confuse the constitution with the character, to ascribe to want of principle what was really a want of circulation. Smith, with his stronger mind, knew his friend's habit, and made allowance for it now as his thoughts turned toward the man beneath him.

There was no return of the singular sound, and Smith was about to turn to his work once more, when suddenly there broke out in the silence of the night a hoarse cry, a positive scream, the call of a man who is moved and shaken beyond all control. Smith sprang out of his chair and dropped his book. He was a man of fairly firm fiber, but there was something in this sudden uncontrollable shriek of horror which chilled his blood and pringled in his skin. Coming in such a place and at such an hour, it brought a thousand fantastic possibilities into his head. Should he rush down, or was it better to wait? He had all the national hatred of making a scene, and he knew so little of his neighbor that he would not lightly intrude upon his affairs. For a moment he stood in doubt, and even as he balanced the matter there was a quick rattle of footsteps upon the stairs, and young Monkhouse Lee, half dressed and as white as ashes, burst into his room.

"Come down!" he gasped. "Bellingham's ill."

Abercrombie Smith followed him closely down the stairs into the sitting room which was beneath his own, and intent as he was upon the matter in hand, he could not but take an amazed glance around him as he crossed the threshold. It was such a chamber as he had never seen before—a museum rather than a study. Walls and ceiling were thickly covered with a thousand strange relics from Egypt and the East. Tall angular figures bearing burdens or weapons stalked in an uncouth frieze round the apartments. Above were bull-headed, stork-headed, cat-headed, owl-headed statues, with viper-crowned, almond-eyed monarchs, and strange beetlelike deities cut out of the blue Egyptian lapis lazuli. Horus and Isis and Osiris peeped down from every niche and shelf, while across the ceiling a true son of Old Nile, a great hanging-jawed crocodile, was hung in a double noose.

In the center of this singular chamber was a large square table, littered with papers, bottles, and the dried leaves of some graceful palmlike plant. These varied objects had all been heaped together in order to make room for a mummy case, which had been conveyed from the wall, as was evident from the gap there, and laid across the front of the table. The mummy itself, a horrid, black, withered thing, like a charred head on a gnarled bush, was lying half out of the case, with its clawlike hand and bony forearm resting upon the table. Propped up against the sarcophagus was an old yellow scroll of papyrus, and in front of it, in a wooden armchair, sat the owner of the room, his head thrown back, his widely opened eyes directed in a horrified stare to the crocodile above him, and his blue thick lips puffing loudly with every expiration.

"My God! he's dying!" cried Monkhouse Lee, distractedly. He was a slim, handsome young fellow, olive-skinned and dark-eyed, of a Spanish rather than of an English type, with a Celtic intensity of manner which contrasted with the Saxon phlegm of Abercrombie Smith.

"Only a faint, I think," said the medical student. "Just give me a hand with him. You take his feet. Now on to the sofa. Can you kick all those little wooden devils off? What a litter it is! Now he will be all right if we undo his collar and give him some water. What has he been up to at all?"

"I don't know. I heard him cry out as I ran up. I know him pretty well, you know. It is very good of you to come down."

"His heart is going like a pair of castanets," said Smith, laying his hand on the breast of the unconscious man. "He seems to me to be frightened all to pieces. Chuck the water on him! What a face he has got on him!"

It was indeed a strange and most repellent face, for color and outline were equally unnatural. It was white, not with the ordinary pallor of fear, but with an absolutely bloodless white, like the underside of a sole. He was very fat, but gave the impression of having at sometime been considerably fatter, for his skin hung loosely in creases and folds, and was shot with a meshwork of wrinkles. Short stubbly brown hair bristled up from his scalp, with a pair of thick wrinkled ears protruding on either side. His light gray eyes were still open, the pupils dilated, and the balls projecting in a fixed and horrid stare. It seemed to Smith as he looked down upon him that he had never seen nature's danger signals flying so plainly upon a man's countenance, and his thoughts turned more seriously to the warning which Hastie had given him an hour before.

"What the deuce can have frightened him so?" he asked.

"It's the mummy."

"The mummy? How, then?"

"I don't know. It's beastly and morbid. I wish he would drop it. It's the second fright he has given me. It was the same last winter. I found him just like this, with that horrid thing in front of him."

"What does he want with the mummy, then?"

"Oh, he's a crank, you know. It's his hobby. He knows more about these things than any man in England. But I wish he wouldn't! Ah, he's beginning to come to."

A faint tinge of color had begun to steal back into Bellingham's ghastly cheeks, and his eyelids shivered like a sail after a calm. He clasped and unclasped his hands, drew a long thin breath between his teeth, and suddenly jerking up his head, threw a glance of recognition around him. As his eyes fell upon the mummy, he sprang off the sofa, seized the roll of papyrus, thrust it into a drawer, locked the drawer, and then staggered back onto the sofa.

"What's up?" he asked. "What do you chaps want?"

"You've been shrieking out and making no end of a fuss," said Monkhouse Lee. "If our neighbor here from above hadn't come down, I'm sure I don't know what I should have done with you."

"Ah, it's Mr. Abercrombie Smith," said Bellingham, glancing up at him. "How very good of you to come in! What a fool I am! Oh, my God, what a fool I am!" He sunk his head on to his hands, and burst into peal after peal of hysterical laughter.

"Look here! Drop it!" cried Smith, shaking him roughly by the shoulder. "Your nerves are all in a jangle. You must drop these little midnight games with mummies, or you'll be going off your chump. You're all on wires now."

"I wonder," said Bellingham, "whether you would be as cool as I am if you had seen—"

"What, then?"

"Oh, nothing. I meant that I wonder if you could sit up at night with a mummy without trying your nerves. I have no doubt that you are quite right. I dare say that I have been taking it out of myself too much lately. But I am all right now. Please don't go, though. Just wait for a few minutes until I am quite myself."

"The room is very close," remarked Lee, throwing open the window and letting in the cool night air.

"It's balsamic resin," said Bellingham. He lifted up one of the dried palmate leaves from the table and frizzled it up over the chimney of the lamp. It broke away into heavy smoke wreaths, and a pungent biting odor filled the chamber. "It's the sacred plant—the plant of the priests," he remarked. "Do you know anything of Eastern languages, Mr. Smith?"

"Nothing at all. Not a word."

The answer seemed to lift a weight from the Egyptologist's mind. "By the way," he continued, "how long was it from the time that you came down until I came to my senses?"

"Not long. Some four or five minutes."

"I thought it could not be very long," said he, drawing a long breath. "But what a strange thing unconsciousness is! There is no measurement to it. I could not tell from my own sensations if it were seconds or weeks. Now that gentleman on the table was packed up in the days of the eleventh dynasty, some forty centuries ago, and yet if he could find his tongue, he would tell us that this lapse of time has been but a closing of the eyes and a reopening of them. He is a singularly fine mummy, Mr. Smith."

Smith stepped over to the table and looked down with a professional eye at the black and twisted form in front of him. The features, though horribly discolored, were perfect, and two little nutlike eyes still lurked in the depths of the black hollow sockets. The blotched skin was drawn tightly from bone to bone, and a tangled wrap of black coarse hair fell over the ears. Two thin teeth, like those of a rat, overlay the shriveled lower lip. In its crouching position, with bent joints and craned head, there was a suggestion of energy about the horrid thing which made Smith's gorge rise. The gaunt ribs, with their parchmentlike covering, were exposed, and the sunken, leaden-hued abdomen, with the long slit where the embalmer had left his mark; but the lower limbs were wrapped round with coarse yellow bandages. A number of little clovelike pieces of myrrh and of cassia were sprinkled over the body, and lay scattered on the inside of the case.

"I don't know his name," said Billingham, passing his hand over the shriveled head. "You see the outer sarcophagus with the inscriptions is missing. Lot 249 is all the title he has now. You see it printed on his case. That was his number in the auction at which I picked him up."

"He has been a very pretty sort of fellow in his day," remarked Abercrombie Smith.

"He has been a giant. His mummy is six feet seven in length, and that would be a giant over there, for they were never a very robust race. Feel these great knotted bones too. He would be a nasty fellow to tackle."

"Perhaps these very hands helped to build the stones into the pyramids," suggested Monkhouse Lee, looking down with disgust in his eyes at the crooked, unclean talons.

"No fear. This fellow has been pickled in natron, and looked after in the most approved style. They did not serve hodsmen in that fashion. Salt or bitumen was enough for them. It has been calculated that this sort of thing cost about seven hundred and thirty pounds in our money. Our friend was a noble at the least. What do you make of that small inscription near his feet, Mr. Smith?"

"I told you that I know no Eastern tongue."

"Ah, so you did! It is the name of the embalmer, I take it. A very conscientious worker he must have been. I wonder how many modern works will survive four thousand years?"

He kept on speaking lightly and rapidly, but it was evident to Abercrombie Smith that he was still palpitating with fear. His hands shook, his lower lip trembled, and look where he would, his eye always came sliding round to his gruesome companion. Through all his fear, however, there was a suspicion of triumph in his tone and manner. His eye shone, and his footstep, as he paced the room, was brisk and jaunty. He gave the impression of a man who has gone through an ordeal the marks of which he still bears upon him, but which has helped him to his end.

"You're not going yet?" he cried as Smith rose from the sofa. At the prospect of solitude, his fears seemed to crowd back upon him, and he stretched out a hand to detain him.

"Yes, I must go. I have my work to do. You are all right now. I think that with your nervous system you should take up some less morbid study."

"Oh, I am not nervous as a rule; and I have unwrapped mummies before."

"You fainted last time," observed Monkhouse Lee.

"Ah yes, so I did. Well, I must have a nerve tonic or a course of electricity. You are not going, Lee?"

"I'll do whatever you wish, Ned."

"Then I'll come down with you and have a shakedown on your sofa. Good-night, Mr. Smith. I am so sorry to have disturbed you with my foolishness."

They shook hands, and as the medical student stumbled up the spiral and irregular stair he heard a key turn in a door, and the steps of his two new acquaintances as they descended to the lower floor.

In this strange way began the acquaintance between Edward Bellingham and Abercrombie Smith, an acquaintance which the latter, at least, had no desire to push further. Bellingham, however, appeared to have taken a fancy to his rough-spoken neighbor, and made his advances in such a way that he could hardly be repulsed without absolute brutality. Twice he called to thank Smith for his assistance, and many times afterward he looked in with books, papers, and such other civilities as two bachelor neighbors can offer each other. He was, as Smith soon found, a man of wide reading, with catholic tastes and an extraordinary memory. His manner, too, was so pleasing and suave that one came, after a time, to overlook his repellent appearance. For a jaded and wearied man he was no unpleasant companion, and Smith found himself, after a time, looking forward to his visits, and even returning them.

Clever as he undoubtedly was, however, the medical student seemed to detect a dash of insanity in the man. He broke out at times into a high inflated style of talk which was in contrast with the simplicity of his life.

"It is a wonderful thing," he cried, "to feel that one can command powers of good and evil—a ministering angel or a demon of vengeance." And again, of Monkhouse Lee he said: "Lee is a good fellow, an honest fellow, but he is without strength or ambition. He would not make a fit partner for a man with a great enterprise. He would not make a fit partner for me."

At such hints and innuendos stolid Smith, puffing solemnly at his pipe, would simply raise his eyebrows and shake his head, with little interjections of medical wisdom as to earlier hours and fresher air.

One habit Bellingham had developed of late which Smith knew to be a frequent herald of a weakening mind. He appeared to be forever talking to himself. At late hours of the night, when there could be no visitor with him, Smith could still hear his voice beneath him in a low muffled monologue, sunk almost to a whisper, and yet very audible in the silence. This solitary babbling annoyed and distracted the student, so that he spoke more than once to his neighbor about it. Bellingham, however, flushed up at the charge, and denied curtly that he had uttered a sound; indeed, he showed more annoyance over the matter than the occasion seemed to demand.

Had Abercrombie Smith had any doubt as to his own ears he had not to go far to find corroboration. Tom Styles, the little wrinkled manservant who had attended to the wants of the lodgers in the turret for a longer time than any man's memory could carry him, was sorely put to it over the same matter.

"If you please, sir," said he, as he tidied down the top chamber one morning, "do you think Mr. Bellingham is all right, sir?"

"All right, Styles?"

"Yes, sir. Right in the head, sir."

"Why should he not be, then?"

"Well, I don't know, sir. His habits has changed of late. He's not the same man he used to be, though I make free to say that he was never quite one of my gentlemen, like Mr. Hastie or yourself, sir. He's took to talkin' to himself something awful. I wonder it don't disturb you. And for days sometimes he'll keep his door locked, so as I can't even make the bed; and then again he'll have it open the same as ever—wide open so as all who pass can see his mummies and things. I don't know what to make of him, sir."

"I don't know what business it is of yours, Styles."

"Well, I takes an interest, Mr. Smith. It may be forward of me, but I can't help it. I feel sometimes as if I was mother and father to my young gentlemen. It all falls on me when things go wrong and the relations come. There was poor Mr. Williams, who went mad in '47. And Mr. McAlister in '62. Brain softening from overwork, they said. He lived in this very room. I don't speak of the delirium tremenses which I've had, three on each floor, and four on the lowest. But Mr. Bellingham, sir. I want to know what it is that walks about his room sometimes when he's out and when the door's locked on the outside."

"Eh? You're talking nonsense, Styles."

"Maybe so, sir; but I heard it more'n once with my own ears."

"Rubbish, Styles."

"Very good, sir. You'll ring the bell if you want me."

Abercrombie Smith gave little heed to the gossip of the old manservant, but a small incident occurred a few days later which left an unpleasant effect upon his mind, and brought the words of Styles forcibly to his memory.

Bellingham had come up to see him late one night, and was entertaining him with an interesting account of the rock tombs of Beni Hassan in Upper Egypt, when Smith, whose hearing was remarkably acute, distinctly heard the sound of a door opening on the landing below.

"There's some fellow gone in or out of your room," he remarked.

Bellingham sprang up and stood helpless for a moment, with the expression of a man who is half incredulous and half afraid.

"I surely locked it. I am almost positive that I locked it," he stammered. "No one could have opened it."

"Why, I hear someone coming up the steps now," said Smith.

Bellingham rushed out through the door, slammed it loudly behind him, and hurried down the stairs. About halfway down Smith heard him stop, and thought he caught the sound of whispering. A moment later the door beneath him shut, a key creaked in a lock, and Bellingham, with beads of moisture upon his pale face, ascended the stairs once more, and reentered the room.

"It's all right," he said, throwing himself down in a chair. "It was that fool of a dog. He had pushed the door open. I don't know how I came to forget to lock it."

"I didn't know you kept a dog," said Smith, looking very thoughtfully at the disturbed face of his companion.

"Yes. I haven't had him long. I must get rid of him. He's a great nuisance."

"He must be, if you find it so hard to shut him up. I should have thought that shutting the door would have been enough without locking it."

"I want to prevent old Styles from letting him out. He's of some value, you know, and it would be awkward to lose him."

"I am a bit of a dog fancier myself," said Smith, still gazing hard at his companion from the corner of his eyes. "Perhaps you'll let me have a look at it."

"Certainly. But I am afraid it cannot be tonight; I have an appointment. Is that clock right? Then I am a quarter of an hour late already. You'll excuse me, I am sure." He picked up his cap and hurried from the room. In spite of his appointment, Smith heard him reenter his own chamber and lock his door upon the inside.

This interview left a disagreeable impression upon the medical student's mind. Bellingham had lied to him, and lied so clumsily that it looked as if he had desperate reasons for concealing the truth. Smith knew that his neighbor had no dog. He knew, also, that the step which he had heard upon the stairs was not the step of an animal. But if it were not, then what could it be? There was old Styles's statement about the something which used to pace the room at times when the owner was absent. Could it be a woman? Smith rather inclined to the view. If so, it would mean disgrace and expulsion to Bellingham if it were discovered by the authorities, so that his anxiety and falsehoods might be accounted for. And yet it was inconceivable that an undergraduate could keep a woman in his rooms without being instantly detected. Be the explanation what it might, there was something ugly about it, and Smith determined, as he turned to his books, to discourage all further attempts at intimacy on the part of his soft-spoken and ill-favored neighbor.

But his work was destined to interruption that night. He had hardly caught up the broken threads when a firm heavy footfall came three steps at a time from below, and Hastie, in blazer and flannels, burst into the room.

"Still at it!" said he, plumping down into his wonted armchair. "What a chap you are to stew! I believe an earthquake might come and knock Oxford into a cocked hat, and you would sit perfectly placid with your books among the ruins. However, I won't bore you long. Three whiffs of baccy, and I am off."

"What's the news, then?" asked Smith, cramming a plug of bird's-eye into his brier with his forefinger.

"Nothing very much. Wilson made seventy for the freshmen against the eleven. They say that they will play him instead of Buddicomb, for Buddicomb is clean off color. He used to be able to bowl a little, but it's nothing but half volleys and long hops now."

"Medium right," suggested Smith, with the intense gravity which comes upon a 'varsity man when he speaks of athletics.

"Inclining to fast with a work from leg. Comes with the arm about three inches or so. He used to be nasty on a wet wicket. Oh, by the way, have you heard about Long Norton?"

"What's that?"

"He's been attacked."

"Attacked?"

"Yes, just as he was turning out of the High Street, and within a hundred yards of the gate of Old's."

"But who—"

"Ah, that's the rub! If you said 'what,' you would be more grammatical. Norton swears that it was not human, and, indeed, from the scratches on his throat, I should be inclined to agree with him."

"What, then? Have we come down to spooks?" Abercrombie Smith puffed his scientific contempt.

"Well, no; I don't think that is quite the idea, either. I am inclined to think that if any showman has lost a great ape lately, and the brute is in these parts, a jury would find a true bill against it. Norton passes that way every night, you know, about the same hour. There's a big elm from Rainy's garden. Norton thinks the thing dropped on him out of the tree. Anyhow, he was nearly strangled by two arms, which, he says, were as strong and as thin as steel bands. He saw nothing; only these beastly arms that tightened and tightened on him. He yelled his head nearly off, and a couple of chaps came running, and the thing went over the wall like a cat. He never got a fair sight of it the whole time. It gave Norton a shake up, I can tell you. I tell him it has been as good as a change at the seaside for him."

"A garroter, most likely," said Smith.

"Very possibly. Norton says not; but we don't mind what he says. The garroter had long nails, and was pretty smart at swinging himself over walls. By the way, your beautiful neighbor would be pleased if he heard about it. He had a grudge against Norton, and he's not a man, from what I know of him, to forget his little debts. But hullo, old chap, what have you got in your noddle?"

"Nothing," Smith answered, curtly. He had started in his chair, and the look had flashed over his face which comes upon a man who is struck suddenly by some unpleasant idea.

"You looked as if something I had said had taken you on the raw. By the way, you have made the acquaintance of Master B. since I looked in last, have you not? Young Monkhouse Lee told me something to that effect."

"Yes; I know him slightly. He has been up here once or twice."

"Well, you're big enough and ugly enough to take care of yourself. He's not what I should call exactly a healthy sort of Johnny, though, no doubt, he's very clever, and all that. But you'll soon find out for yourself. Lee is all right; he's a very decent little fellow. Well, so long, old chap! I row Mullins for the Vice-Chancellor's pot on Wednesday week, so mind you come down, in case I don't see you before."

He clattered off, with a trail of smoke behind him like a steamer, while bovine Smith laid down his pipe and turned stolidly to his books once more. But with all the will in the world, he found it very hard to keep his mind upon his work. It would slip away to brood upon the man beneath him, and upon the little mystery which seemed to hang round his chambers. Then his thoughts turned to this singular attack of which Hastie had spoken, and to the grudge which Bellingham was said to owe the object of it. The two ideas would persist in rising together in his mind, as though there were some close and intimate connection between them. And yet the suspicion was so dim and vague that it could not be put down in words.

"Confound the chap!" cried Smith, as he shied his book on pathology across the room. "He has spoiled my night's reading, and that's reason enough, if there were no other, why I should steer clear of him in the future."

For ten days the medical student confined himself so closely to his studies that he neither saw nor heard anything of either of the men beneath him. At the hours when Bellingham had been accustomed to visit him, he took care to sport his oak, and though he more than once heard a knocking at his outer door, he resolutely refused to answer it. One afternoon, however, he was descending the stairs when, just as he was passing it, Bellingham's door flew open, and young Monkhouse Lee came out with his eyes sparkling and a dark flush of anger upon his olive cheeks. Close at his heels followed Bellingham, his fat, unhealthy face all quivering with malignant passion.

"You fool!" he hissed. "You'll be sorry."

"Very likely," cried the other. "Mind what I say. It's off! I won't hear of it!"

"You've promised, anyhow."

"Oh, I'll keep that! I won't speak. But I'd rather little Eva was in her grave. Once for all, it's off. She'll do what I say. We don't want to see you again."

So much Smith could not avoid hearing, but he hurried on, for he had no wish to be involved in their dispute. There had been a serious breach between them, that was clear enough, and Lee was going to cause the engagement with his sister to be broken off. Smith thought of Hastie's comparison of the toad and the dove, and was glad to think that the matter was at an end. Bellingham's face when he was in a passion was not pleasant to look upon. He was not a man to whom an innocent girl could be trusted for life. As he walked, Smith wondered languidly what could have caused the quarrel, and what the promise might be which Bellingham had been so anxious that Monkhouse Lee should keep.

It was the day of the sculling match between Hastie and Mullins, and a stream of men were making their way down to the banks of the Isis. A May sun was shining brightly, and the yellow path was barred with the black shadows of the tall elm trees. On either side the gray colleges lay back from the road, the hoary old mothers of minds looking out from their high mullioned windows at the tide of young life which swept so merrily past them. Black-clad tutors, prim officials, pale reading men, brown-faced, straw-hatted young athletes in white sweaters or many-colored blazers, all were hurrying toward the blue winding river which curves through the Oxford meadows.

Abercrombie Smith, with the intuition of an old oarsman, chose his position at the point where he knew that the struggle, if there were a struggle, would come. Far off he heard the hum which announced the start, the gathering roar of the approach, the thunder of running feet, and the shouts of the men in the boats beneath him. A spray of half-clad, deep-breathing runners shot past him, and craning over their shoulders, he saw Hastie pulling a steady thirty-six, while his opponent, with a jerky forty, was a good boat's length behind him. Smith gave a bellow of approval, and pulling out his watch, was starting off again for his chambers, when he felt a touch upon his shoulder, and found that young Monkhouse Lee was beside him.

"I saw you there," he said in a timid, deprecating way. "I wanted to speak to you, if you could spare me a half hour. This cottage is mine. I share it with Harrington of King's. Come in and have a cup of tea."

"I must be back presently," said Smith. "I am hard on the grind at present. But I'll come in for a few minutes with pleasure. I wouldn't have come out only Hastie is a friend of mine."

"So he is of mine. Hasn't he a beautiful style? Mullins wasn't in it. But come into the cottage. It's a little den of a place, but it is pleasant to work in during the summer months."

It was a little square white building with green doors and shutters, and a rustic trelliswork porch, with a drapery of creepers over it, standing back some fifty yards from the river's bank. Inside, the main room was roughly fitted up as a study—deal table, unpainted shelves with books, and a few cheap oleographs upon the wall. A kettle sang upon a spirit stove, and there were tea things upon a tray on the table.

"Try that chair and have a cigarette," said Lee. "Let me pour you out a cup of tea. It's so good of you to come in, for I know that your time is a good deal taken up. I wanted to say to you that if I were you I would change my rooms at once."

"Eh?" Smith sat staring with a lighted match in one hand and his unlit cigarette in the other.

"Yes; it must seem very extraordinary, and the worst of it is that I cannot give my reasons, for I am under a solemn promise—a very solemn promise. But I may go as far as to say that I don't think Bellingham is a very safe man to live near. I intend to camp out here as much as I can for a time."

"Not safe? What do you mean?"

"Ah, that's what I mustn't say. But do take my advice, and move your rooms. We had a grand row today. You must have heard us, for you came down the stairs."

"I saw that you had fallen out."

"He's a horrible chap, Mr. Smith. That is the only word for him. I have had my doubts about him ever since that night when he fainted—you remember, when you came down. I taxed him today, and he told me things that made my hair rise, and wanted me to stand in with him. I'm not straitlaced, but I am a clergyman's son, you know, and I think there are some things which are quite beyond the pale. I only thank God that I found him out before it was too late, for he was to have married into my family."

"This is all very fine, Lee," said Abercrombie Smith, curtly. "But either you are saying a great deal too much or a great deal too little."

"I give you a warning."

"If there is real reason for warning, no promise can bind you. If I see a rascal about to blow a place up with dynamite, no pledge will stand in my way of preventing him."

"Ah, but I cannot prevent him, and I can do nothing but warn you."

"Without saying what you warn me against."

"Against Bellingham."

"But that is childish. Why should I fear him, or any man?"

"I can't tell you. I can only entreat you to change your rooms. You are in danger where you are. I don't even say that Bellingham would wish to injure you. But it might happen, for he is a dangerous neighbor just now."

"Perhaps I know more than you think," said Smith, looking keenly at the young man's boyish, earnest face. "Suppose I tell you that someone else shares Bellingham's rooms."

Monkhouse Lee sprang from his chair in uncontrollable excitement. "You know, then?" he gasped.

"A woman."

Lee dropped back again with a groan. "My lips are sealed," he said. "I must not speak."

"Well, anyhow," said Smith, rising, "it is not likely that I would allow myself to be frightened out of rooms which suit me very nicely. It would be a little too feeble for me to move out all my goods and chattels because you say that Bellingham might in some unexplained way do me an injury. I think that I'll just take my chance, and stay where I am, and as I see that it's nearly five o'clock, I must ask you to excuse me." He bade the young student adieu in a few curt words, and made his way homeward through the sweet spring evening, feeling half ruffled, half amused, as any other strong, unimaginative man might who has been menaced by a vague and shadowy danger.

There was one little indulgence which Abercrombie Smith always allowed himself, however closely his work might press upon him. Twice a week, on the Tuesday and the Friday, it was his invariable custom to walk over to Farlingford, the residence of the Reverend Plumptree Peterson, situated about a mile and a half out of Oxford. Peterson had been a close friend of Smith's elder brother Francis, and as he was a bachelor, fairly well-to-do, with a good cellar and a better library, his house was a pleasant goal for a man who was in need of a brisk walk. Twice a week, then, the medical student would swing out there along the dark country roads, and spend a pleasant hour in Peterson's comfortable study, discussing, over a glass of old port, the gossip of the 'varsity or the latest black letter which the book dealers had sent to his host.

On the day which followed his interview with Monkhouse Lee, Smith shut up his books at a quarter past eight, the hour when he usually started for his friend's house. As he was leaving his room, however, his eyes happened to fall upon one of the books which Bellingham had lent him, and his conscience pricked him for not having returned it. However repellent the man might be, he should not be treated with discourtesy. Taking the book, he walked down stairs and knocked at his neighbor's door. There was no answer; but on turning the handle he found that it was unlocked. Pleased at the thought of avoiding an interview, he stepped inside, and placed the book with his card upon the table.

The lamp was turned half down, but Smith could see the details of the room plainly enough. It was all much as he had seen it before—the frieze, the animal-headed gods, the hanging crocodile, and the table littered over with papers and dried leaves. The mummy case stood upright against the wall, but the mummy itself was missing. There was no sign of any second occupant of the room, and he felt as he withdrew that he had probably done Bellingham an injustice. Had he a guilty secret to preserve, he would hardly leave his door open so that all the world might enter.

The spiral stair was as black as pitch, and Smith was slowly making his way down its irregular steps, when he was suddenly conscious that something had passed him in the darkness. There was a faint sound, a whiff of air, a light brushing past his elbow, but so slight that he could scarcely be certain of it. He stopped and listened, but the wind was rustling among the ivy outside, and he could hear nothing else.

"Is that you, Styles?" he shouted.

There was no answer, and all was still behind him. It must have been a sudden gust of air, for there were crannies and cracks in the old turret. And yet he could almost have sworn that he heard a footfall by his very side. He had emerged into the quadrangle, still turning the matter over in his head, when a man came running swiftly across the smooth-cropped lawn.

"Is that you, Smith?"

"Hullo, Hastie!"

"For God's sake come at once! Young Lee is drowned! Here's Harrington of King's with the news. The doctor is out. You'll do, but come along at once. There may be life in him."

"Have you brandy?"

"No."

"I'll bring some. There's a flask on my table."

Smith bounded up the stairs, taking three at a time, seized the flask, and was rushing down with it, when, as he passed Bellingham's room, his eyes fell upon something which left him gasping and staring upon the landing.

The door, which he had closed behind him, was now open, and right in front of him, with the lamplight shining upon it, was the mummy case. Three minutes ago it had been empty. He could swear to that. Now it framed the lank body of its horrible occupant, who stood, grim and stark, with his black shriveled face toward the door. The form was lifeless and inert, but it seemed to Smith as he gazed that there still lingered a lurid spark of vitality, some faint sign of consciousness in the little eyes which lurked in the depths of the hollow sockets. So astounded and shaken was he that he had forgotten his errand, and still stood staring at the lean sunken figure when the voice of his friend below recalled him to himself.

"Come on, Smith!" he shouted. "It's life and death, you know. Hurry up! Now, then," he added, as the medical student reappeared, "let us do a sprint. It is well under a mile, and we should do it in five minutes. A human life is better worth running for than a pot."

Away they dashed, neck and neck, through the darkness, and did not pull up until, panting and spent, they had reached the little cottage by the river. Young Lee, limp and dripping like a broken water plant, was stretched upon the sofa, the green scum of the river upon his black hair, and a fringe of white foam upon his leaden-hued lips. Beside him knelt his fellow student Harrington and their old housekeeper, endeavoring to chafe some warmth back into his rigid limbs.

"I think there's life in him," said Smith, with his hand to his side. "Put your watch glass to his lips. Yes, there's dimming on it. You take one arm, Hastie. Now work it as I do, and we'll soon pull him round."

For ten minutes they worked in silence, inflating and depressing the chest of the unconscious man. At the end of that time a shiver ran through his body, his lips trembled, and he opened his eyes. The three students burst out into an irrepressible cheer.

"Wake up, old chap. You've frightened us quite enough."

"Have some brandy. Take a sip from the flask."

"He's all right now," said his companion Harrington. "Heavens, what a fright I got! I was reading here, and he went out for a stroll as far as the river, when I heard a scream and a splash. Out I ran, and by the time I could find him and fish him out, all life seemed to have gone out of him. Then Mrs. Simpson couldn't get a doctor, for she has a game leg, and I had to run, and I don't know what I'd have done without you fellows. That's right, old chap. Sit up."

Monkhouse Lee had raised himself on his hands and looked wildly about him. "What's up?" he asked. "I've been in the water. Ah, yes; I remember." A look of fear came into his eyes, and he sank his face in his hands.

"How did you fall in?"

"I didn't fall in."

"How, then?"

"I was thrown in. I was standing by the bank, and something from behind picked me up like a feather and hurled me in. I heard nothing, and I saw nothing. But I know what it was for all that."

"And so do I," whispered Smith.

Lee looked up with a quick glance of surprise. "You've learned, then?" he said. "You remember the advice I gave you?"

"Yes, and I begin to think that I shall take it."

"I don't know what the deuce you fellows are talking about," said Hastie, "but I think if I were you, Harrington, I would get Lee to bed at once. It will be time enough to discuss why and the wherefore when he is a little stronger. I think, Smith, you and I can leave him alone now. I am walking back to college; if you are coming in that direction, we can have a chat."

But it was little chat that they had upon their homeward path. Smith's mind was too full of the incidents of the evening, the absence of the mummy from from his neighbor's rooms, the step that passed him on the stair, the reappearance—the extraordinary, inexplicable reappearance of the grisly thing—and then this attack upon Lee, corresponding so closely to the previous outrage upon another man against whom Bellingham bore a grudge. All this settled in his thoughts, together with the many little incidents which had previously turned him against his neighbor, and the singular circumstances under which he was first called to him. What had been a dim suspicion, a vague fantastic conjecture, had suddenly taken form, and stood out in his mind as a grim fact, a thing not to be denied. And yet how monstrous it was! how unheard of! how entirely beyond all bounds of human experience. An impartial judge, or even the friend who walked by his side would simply tell him that his eyes had deceived him, that the mummy had been there all the time, that young Lee had tumbled into the river as any other man tumbles into a river, and that a blue pill was the best thing for a disordered liver. He felt that he would have said as much if the positions had been reversed. And yet he could swear that Bellingham was a murderer at heart, and that he wielded a weapon such as no man had ever used in all the grim history of crime.

Hastie had branched off to his rooms with a few crisp and emphatic comments upon his friend's unsociability, and Abercrombie Smith crossed the quadrangle to his corner turret with a strong feeling of repulsion for his chambers and their associations. He would take Lee's advice, and move his quarters as soon as possible, for how could a man study when his ear was ever straining for every murmur or footstep in the room below? He observed, as he crossed over the lawn, the light was still shining in Bellingham's window, and as he passed up the staircase the door opened, and the man himself looked out at him. With his fat evil face he was like some bloated spider fresh from the weaving of his poisonous web.

"Good-evening," said he. "Won't you come in?"

"No," cried Smith, fiercely.

"No? You are busy as ever? I wanted to ask you about Lee. I was sorry to hear that there was a rumor that something was amiss with him." His features were grave, but there was the gleam of a hidden laugh in his eyes as he spoke. Smith saw it, and he could have knocked him down for it.

"You'll be sorrier still to hear that Mr. Monkhouse Lee is doing very well, and is out of all danger," he answered. "Your hellish tricks have not come off this time. Oh, you needn't try to brazen it out. I know all about it."

Bellingham took a step back from the angry student, and half closed the door as if to protect himself. "You are mad," he said. "What do you mean? Do you assert that I had anything to do with Lee's accident?"

"Yes," thundered Smith. "You and that bag of bones behind you; you worked it out between you. I tell you what it is, Master B., they have given up burning folk like you, but we still keep a hangman, and, by George! if any man in this college meets his death while you are here, I'll have you up, and if you don't swing for it, it won't be my fault. You'll find that your filthy Egyptian tricks won't answer in England."

"You're a raving lunatic," said Bellingham.

"All right. You just remember what I say, for you'll find that I'll be better than my word."

The door slammed, and Smith went fuming up to his chamber, where he locked the door upon the inside, and spent half the night in smoking his old brier and brooding over the strange events of the evening.

On the next day Abercrombie Smith heard nothing of his neighbor, but Harrington called upon him in the afternoon to say that Lee was almost himself again. All day Smith stuck fast to his work, but in the evening he determined to pay the visit to his friend Peterson which he had started upon the night before. It was the first time that he had ever failed to put in an appearance, and he knew that Peterson would be expecting an explanation for his absence the previous evening. A good walk and a friendly chat would be welcome to his jangled nerves after all that occurred.

Bellingham's door was shut as he passed, but glancing back when he was some distance from the turret, he saw his neighbor's head at the window outlined against the lamplight, his face pressed apparently against the glass as he gazed out into the darkness. It was a blessing to be away from all contact with him, if but for a few hours, and Smith stepped out briskly, and breathed the soft spring air into his lungs. The half-moon lay in the west between two Gothic pinnacles, and threw upon the silvered street a dark tracery from the stonework above. There was a brisk breeze, and light fleecy clouds drifted swiftly across the sky. Old's was on the very border of the town, and in five minutes Smith found himself beyond the houses and between the hedges of a May-scented Oxfordshire lane.

It was a lonely and little-frequented road which led to his friend's house. Early as it was, Smith did not meet a single soul upon his way. He walked briskly along until he came to the avenue gate, which opened into the long gravel drive leading up to Farlingford. In front of him he could see the cozy red light of the windows glimmering through the foliage. He stood with his hand upon the iron latch of the swinging gate, and he glanced back at the road along which he had come. Something was coming swiftly down it.

It moved in the shadow of the hedge, silently and furtively, a dark crouching figure, dimly visible against the black background. Even as he gazed back at it it had lessened its distance by twenty paces, and was fast closing upon him. Out of the darkness he had a glimpse of a scraggy neck, and of two eyes that will ever haunt him in his dreams. He turned, and with a cry of terror he ran for his life up the avenue. There were the red lights, the signals of safety, almost within a stone's throw of him. He was a famous runner, but never had he run as he ran that night.

The heavy gate had swung into place behind him, but he heard it dash open again before his pursuer. As he rushed madly and wildly through the night he could hear a swift dry patter behind him, and could see, as he threw back a glance, that this horror was bounding like a tiger at his heels, with blazing eyes and stringy arms outthrown. Thank God, the door was ajar. He could see the thin bar of light which shot from the lamp in the hall. Nearer yet sounded the clatter from behind. He heard a hoarse gurgling at his very shoulder. With a shriek he flung himself against the door, slammed and bolted it behind him, and sank half-fainting on to the hall chair.

"My goodness, Smith, what's the matter?" asked Peterson, appearing at the door of his study.

"Give me some brandy!"

Peterson disappeared, and came rushing out again with a glass and a decanter.

"You need it," he said, as his visitor drank off what he poured out for him. "Why, man, you are as white as a cheese."

Smith laid down his glass, rose up, and took a deep breath. "I am my own man again now," said he. "I was never so unmanned before. But, with your leave, Peterson, I will sleep here tonight, for I don't think I could face that road again except by daylight. It's weak, I know, but I can't help it."

Peterson looked at his visitor with a very questioning eye. "Of course you shall sleep here if you wish. I'll tell Mrs. Burney to make up the spare bed. Where are you off to now?"

"Come up with me to the window that overlooks the door. I want you to see what I have seen."

They went up to the window of the upper hall, whence they could overlook the whole front of the house. The drive and the fields on either side lay quiet and still, bathed in the peaceful moonlight.

"Well, really, Smith," remarked Peterson, "it is well that I know you to be an abstemious man. What in the world can have frightened you?"

"I'll tell you presently. But where can it have gone? Ah, now look, look! See the curve of the road just beyond your gate."

"Yes, I see; you needn't pinch my arm off. I saw someone pass. I should say a man, rather thin apparently, and tall, very tall. But what of him? And what of yourself? You are still shaking like an aspen leaf."

"I have been within handgrip of the devil, that's all. But come down to your study, and I shall tell you the whole story."

He did so. Under the cheery lamplight, with a glass of wine on the table beside him, and the portly form and florid face of his friend in front, he narrated, in their order, all the events, great and small, which had formed so singular a chain, from the night on which he had found Bellingham fainting in front of the mummy case until his horrid experience of an hour ago.

"There, now," he said, as he concluded, "that's the whole black business. It is monstrous and incredible, but it is true."

The Reverend Plumptree Peterson sat for sometime in silence with a very puzzled expression upon his face.

"I never heard of such a thing in my life, never!" he said at last. "You have told me the facts. Now tell me your inferences."

"You can draw your own."

"But I should like to hear yours. You have thought over the matter, and I have not."

"Well, it must be a little vague in detail, but the main points seem to me to be clear enough. This fellow Bellingham in his Eastern studies has got hold of some infernal secret by which a mummy—or possibly only this particular mummy—can be temporarily brought to life. He was trying this disgusting business on the night when he fainted. No doubt the sight of the creature moving had shaken his nerve, even though he had expected it. You remember that almost the first words he said was to call out upon himself as a fool. Well, he got more hardened afterward, and carried the matter through without fainting. The vitality which he could put into it was evidently only a passing thing, for I have seen it continually in its case as dead as this table. He has some elaborate process, I fancy, by which he brings the thing to pass. Having done it, he naturally bethought him that he might use the creature as an agent. It has intelligence and it has strength. For some purpose he took Lee into his confidence; but Lee, like a decent Christian, would have nothing to do with such a business. Then they had a row, and Lee vowed that he would tell his sister of Bellingham's true character. Bellingham's game was to prevent him, and he nearly managed it, by setting this creature of his on his track. He had already tried its powers upon another man—Norton—toward whom he had a grudge. It is the merest chance that he has not two murders upon his soul. Then, when I taxed him with the matter, he had the strongest reason for wishing to get me out of the way before I could convey my knowledge to anyone else. He got his chance when I went out, for he knew my habits, and where I was bound for. I have had a narrow shave, Peterson, and it is mere luck you didn't find me on your doorstep in the morning. I'm not a nervous man as a rule, and I never thought to have the fear of death put upon me as it was tonight."

"My dear boy, you take the matter too seriously," said his companion. "Your nerves are out of order with your work, and you make too much of it. How could such a thing as this stride out about the streets of Oxford, even at night, without being seen?"

"It has been seen. There is quite a scare in the town about an escaped ape, as they imagine the creature to be. It is the talk of the place."

"Well, it's a striking chain of events. And yet, my dear fellow, you must allow that each incident in itself is capable of a more natural explanation."

"What! even my adventure of tonight?"

"Certainly. You come out with your nerves all unstrung, and your head full of this theory of yours. Some gaunt, half-famished tramp steals after you, and seeing you run, is emboldened to pursue you. Your fears and imagination do the rest."

"It won't do, Peterson; it won't do."

"And again in the instance of your finding the mummy case empty, and then a few moments later with an occupant, you know that it was lamplight, that the lamp was half turned down, and that you had no special reason to look hard at the case. It is quite possible that you may have overlooked the creature in the first instance."

"No, no; it is out of the question."

"And then Lee may have fallen into the river, and Norton been garroted. It is certainly a formidable indictment that you have against Bellingham; but if you were to place it before a police magistrate, he would simply laugh in your face."

"I know he would. That is why I mean to take the matter into my own hands."

"Eh?"

"Yes; I feel that a public duty rests upon me. And besides, I must do it for my own safety, unless I choose to allow myself to be hunted by this beast out of the college, and that would be a little too feeble. I have quite made up my mind what I shall do. And first of all, may I use your paper and pens for an hour?"

"Most certainly. You will find all that you want upon that side table."

Abercrombie Smith sat down before a sheet of fool'scap, and for an hour, and then for a second hour, his pen traveled swiftly over it. Page after page was finished and tossed aside, while his friend leaned back in his armchair, looking across at him with patient curiosity. At last, with an exclamation of satisfaction, Smith sprang to his feet, gathered his papers up into order, and laid the last one upon Peterson's desk.

"Kindly sign this as a witness," he said.

"A witness? Of what?"

"Of my signature, and of the date. The date is the most important. Why, Peterson, my life might hang upon it."

"My dear Smith, you are talking wildly. Let me beg you to go to bed."

"On the contrary, I never spoke so deliberately in my life. And I will promise to go to bed the moment you have signed it."

"But what is it?"

"It is a statement of all that I have been telling you tonight. I wish you to witness it."

"Certainly," said Peterson, signing his name under that of his companion. "There you are! But what is the idea?"

"You will kindly retain it, and produce it in case I am arrested."

"Arrested? For what?"

"For murder. It is quite on the cards. I wish to be ready for every event. There is only one course open to me, and I am determined to take it."

"For Heaven's sake, don't do anything rash!"

"Believe me, it would be far more rash to adopt any other course. I hope that we won't need to bother you, but it will ease my mind to know that you have this statement of my motives. And now I am ready to take your advice and to go to roost, for I want to be at my best in the morning."

Abercrombie Smith was not an entirely pleasant man to have as an enemy. Slow and easy-tempered, he was formidable when driven to action. He brought to every purpose in life the same deliberate resoluteness which had distinguished him as a scientific student. He had laid his studies aside for a day, but he intended that the day should not be wasted. Not a word did he say to his host as to his plans, but by nine o'clock he was well on his way to Oxford.

In the High Street he stopped at Clifford's, the gun maker's, and bought a heavy revolver, with a box of central fire cartridges. Six of them he slipped into the chambers, and half cocking the weapon, placed it in the pocket of his coat. He then made his way to Hastie's rooms, where the big oarsman was lounging over his breakfast, with the *Sporting Times* propped up against the coffee pot.

"Hullo! What's up?" he asked. "Have some coffee?"

"No, thank you. I want you to come with me, Hastie, and do what I ask you."

"Certainly, my boy."

"And bring a heavy stick with you."

"Hullo!" Hastie stared. "Here's a hunting crop that would fell an ox."

"One other thing. You have a box of amputating knives. Give me the longest of them."

"There you are. You seem to be fairly on the war trail. Anything else?"

"No; that will do." Smith placed the knife inside his coat, and led the way to the quadrangle. "We are neither of us chickens, Hastie," said he. "I think I can do this job alone, but I take you as a precaution. I am going to have a little talk with Bellingham. If I have only him to deal with, I won't, of course, need you. If I shout, however, up you come, and lam out with your whip as hard as you can lick. Do you understand?"

"All right. I'll come if I hear you bellow."

"Stay here, then. I may be a little time, but don't budge until I come down."

"I'm a fixture."

Smith ascended the stairs, opened Bellingham's door, and stepped in. Bellingham was seated behind his table, writing. Beside him, among his litter of strange possessions, towered the mummy case, with its sale number 249 still stuck upon its front, and its hideous occupant stiff and stark within it. Smith looked very deliberately round him, closed the door, locked it, and then stepping across to the fireplace, struck a match and set the fire alight. Bellingham sat staring, with amazement and rage upon his bloated face.

"Well, really now. You make yourself at home," he gasped.

Smith sat himself deliberately down, placed his watch upon the table, drew out his pistol, cocked it, and laid it in his lap. Then he took the long amputating knife from his bosom, and threw it down in front of Bellingham. "Now, then," said he. "Just get to work and cut up that mummy."

"Oh, is that it?" said Bellingham, with a sneer.

"Yes, that is it. They tell me that the law can't touch you. But I have a law that will set matters straight. If in five minutes you have not set to work, I swear by the God who made me that I will put a bullet through your brain."

"You would murder me?" Bellingham had half risen, and his face was then color of clay.

"Yes."

"And for what?"

"To stop your mischief. One minute has gone."

"But what have I done?"

"I know and you know."

"This is mere bullying."

"Two minutes are gone."

"But you must give reasons. You are a madman—a dangerous

madman. Why should I destroy my own property? It is a valuable mummy."

"You must cut it up, and you must burn it."

"I will do no such thing."

"Four minutes are gone." Smith took up the pistol, and he looked toward Bellingham with an inexorable face. As the second-hand stole round, he raised his hand, and the finger twitched upon the trigger.

"There! there! I'll do it!" screamed Bellingham. In frantic haste he caught up the knife and hacked at the figure of the mummy, ever glancing round to see the eye and the weapon of his terrible visitor bent upon him. The creature crackled and snapped under every stab of the keen blade. A thick yellow dust rose up from it. Spices and dried essences rained down upon the floor. Suddenly, with a rending crack, its backbone snapped asunder, and it fell, a brown heap of sprawling limbs, upon the floor.

"Now into the fire!" said Smith.

The flames leaped and roared as the dried and tinderlike debris was piled upon it. The little room was like the stokehole of a steamer, and the sweat ran down the faces of the two men; but still the one stooped and worked, while the other sat watching him with a set face. A thick fat smoke oozed out from the fire, and a heavy smell of burned rosin and singed hair filled the air. In a quarter of an hour a few charred and brittle sticks were all that was left of Lot No. 249.

"Perhaps that will satisfy you," snarled Bellingham, with hate and fear in his little gray eyes as he glanced back at his tormentor.

"No; I must make a clean sweep of all your materials. We must have no more devil's tricks. In with all these leaves! They may have something to do with it."

"And what now?" asked Bellingham, when the leaves also had been added to the blaze.

"Now the roll of papyrus which you had on the table that night. It is in that drawer, I think."

"No, no," shouted Bellingham. "Don't burn that! Why, man, you don't know what you do! It is unique; it contains wisdom which is nowhere else to be found."

"Out with it!"

"But look here, Smith, you can't really mean it. I'll share the knowledge with you. I'll teach you all that is in it. Or, stay, let me only copy it before you burn it!"

Smith stepped forward and turned the key in the drawer. Taking out the yellow curled roll of paper, he threw it into the fire, and pressed it down with his heel. Bellingham screamed, and grabbed at it; but Smith pushed him back, and stood over it until it was reduced to a formless gray ash.

"Now, Master B.," said he, "I think I have pretty well drawn your teeth. You'll hear from me again, if you go back to your old tricks. And now, good-morning, for I must go back to my studies."

And such is the narrative of Abercrombie Smith as to the singular events which occurred in Old College, Oxford, in the spring of '81. As Bellingham left the university immediately afterward, and was last heard of in the Sudan, there is no one who can contradict his statement. But the wisdom of men is small, and the ways of nature are strange, and who shall put a bound to the dark things which may be found by those who seek for them?

THE LOS AMIGOS FIASCO

I used to be the leading practitioner of Los Amigos. Of course, everyone has heard of the great electrical generating gear there. The town is widespread, and there are dozens of little townlets and villages all round, which receive their supply from the same center, so that the works are on a very large scale. The Los Amigos folk say that they are the largest upon earth, but then we claim that for everything in Los Amigos except the gaol and the death rate. Those are said to be the smallest.

Now, with so fine an electrical supply, it seemed to be a sinful waste of hemp that the Los Amigos criminals should perish in the old-fashioned manner. And then came the news of the electrocutions in the East, and how the results had not after all been so instantaneous as had been hoped. The Western Engineers raised their eyebrows when they read of the puny shocks by which these men had perished, and they vowed in Los Amigos that when an irreclaimable came their way he should be dealt handsomely by, and have the run of all the big dynamos. There should be no reserve, said the engineers, but he should have all that they had got. And what the result of that would be none could predict, save that it must be absolutely blasting and deadly. Never before had a man been so charged with electricity as they would charge him. He was to be smitten by the essence of ten thunderbolts. Some prophesied combustion, and some disintegration and disappearance. They were waiting eagerly to settle the question by actual demonstration, and it was just at that moment that Duncan Warner came that way.

Warner had been wanted by the law, and by nobody else, for many years. Desperado, murderer, train robber, and road agent, he was a man beyond the pale of human pity. He had deserved a dozen deaths, and the Los Amigos folk grudged him so gaudy a one as that. He seemed to feel himself to be unworthy of it, for he made two frenzied attempts at escape. He was a powerful, muscular man, with a lion head, tangled black locks, and a sweeping beard which covered his broad chest. When he was tried, there was no finer head in all the crowded court. It's no new thing to find the best face looking from the dock. But his good looks could not balance his bad deeds. His advocate did all he knew, but the cards lay against him, and Duncan Warner was handed over to the mercy of the big Los Amigos dynamos.

I was there at the committee meeting when the matter was discussed. The town council had chosen four experts to look after the arrangements. Three of them were admirable. There was Joseph M'Connor, the very man who had designed the dynamos, and there was Joshua Westmacott, the chairman of the Los Amigos Electrical Supply Company, Limited. Then there was myself as the chief medical man, and lastly an old German of the name of Peter Stulpnagel. The Germans were a strong body at Los Amigos, and they all voted for their man. That was how he got on the committee. It was said that he had been a wonderful electrician at home, and he was eternally working with wires and insulators and Leyden jars; but, as he never seemed to get any further, or to have any results worth publishing, he came at last to be regarded as a harmless crank, who had made science his hobby. We three practical men smiled when we heard that he had been elected as our colleague, and at the meeting we fixed it all up very nicely among ourselves without much thought of the old fellow who sat with his ears scooped forward in his hands, for he was a trifle hard of hearing, taking no more part in the proceedings than the gentlemen of the Press who scribbled their notes on the back benches.

We did not take long to settle it all. In New York a strength of some two thousand volts had been used, and death had not been instantaneous. Evidently their shock had been too weak. Los Amigos should not fall into that error. The charge should be six times greater, and therefore, of course, it would be six times more effective. Nothing could possibly be more logical. The whole concentrated force of the great dynamos should be employed on Duncan Warner.

So we three settled it, and had already risen to break up the meeting, when our silent companion opened his mouth for the first time.

"Gentlemen," said he, "you appear to me to show an extraordinary ignorance upon the subject of electricity. You have not mastered the first principles of its actions upon a human being."

The committee was about to break into an angry reply to this brusque comment, but the chairman of the Electrical Company tapped his forehead to claim its indulgence for the crankiness of the speaker.

"Pray tell us, sir," said he, with an ironical smile, "what is there in our conclusions with which you find fault?"

"With your assumption that a large dose of electricity will merely increase the effect of a small dose. Do you not think it possible that it might have an entirely different result? Do you know anything, by actual experiment, of the effect of such powerful shocks?"

"We know it by analogy," said the chairman, pompously. "All drugs increase their effect when they increase their dose; for example—for example—"

"Whiskey," said Joseph M'Connor.

"Quite so. Whiskey. You see it there."

Peter Stulpnagel smiled and shook his head.

"Your argument is not very good," said he. "When I used to take whiskey, I used to find that one glass would excite me, but that six would send me to sleep, which is just the opposite. Now, suppose that electricity were to act in just the opposite way also, what then?"

We three practical men burst out laughing. We had known that our colleague was queer, but we never had thought that he would be as queer as this.

"What, then?" repeated Peter Stulpnagel.

"We'll take our chances," said the chairman.

"Pray consider," said Peter, "that workmen who have touched the wires, and who have received shocks of only a few hundred volts, have died instantly. The fact is well known. And yet when a much greater force was used upon a criminal in New York, the man struggled for some little time. Do you not clearly see that the smaller dose is the more deadly?"

"I think, gentlemen, that this discussion had been carried on quite long enough," said the chairman, rising again. "The point, I take it, has already been decided by the majority of the committee, and Duncan Warner shall be electrocuted on Tuesday by the full strength of the Los Amigos dynamos. Is it not so?"

"I agree," said Joseph M'Connor.

"I agree," said I.

"And I protest," said Peter Stulpnagel.

"Then the motion is carried, and your protest will be duly entered in the minutes," said the chairman, and so the sitting was dissolved.

The attendance at the electrocution was a very small one. We four members of the committee were, of course, present with the executioner, who was to act under their orders. The others were the United States Marshal, the governor of the gaol, the chaplain, and three members of the Press. The room was a small brick chamber, forming an outhouse to the Central Electrical station. It had been used as a laundry, and had an oven and copper at one side, but no other furniture save a single chair for the condemned man. A metal plate for his feet was placed in front of it, to which ran a thick, insulated wire. Above, another wire depended from the ceiling, which could be connected with a small metallic rod projecting from a cap which was to be placed upon his head. When the connection was established Duncan Warner's hour was come.

There was a solemn hush as we waited for the coming of the prisoner. The practical engineers looked a little pale, and fidgeted nervously with the wires. Even the hardened Marshal was ill at ease, for a mere hanging was one thing, and this blasting of the flesh and blood a very different one. As to the Pressmen, their faces were whiter than the sheets which lay before them. The only man who appeared to feel none of the influence of these preparations was the little German crank, who strolled from one to the other with a smile on his lips and mischief in his eyes. More than once he even went so far as to burst into a shout of laughter, until the chaplain sternly rebuked him for his ill-timed levity.

"How can you so far forget yourself, Mr. Stulpnagel," said he, "as to jest in the presence of death?"

But the German was quite unabashed.

"If I were in the presence of death I should not jest," said he, "but since I am not I may do what I choose."

This flippant reply was about to draw another and a sterner reproof from the chaplain, when the door was swung open and two warders entered leading Duncan Warner between them. He glanced round him with a set face, stepped resolutely forward, and seated himself upon the chair.

"Touch her off!" said he.

It was barbarous to keep him in suspense. The chaplain murmured a few words in his ear, the attendant placed the cap upon his head, and then, while we all held our breath, the wire and the metal were brought in contact.

"Great Scott!" shouted Duncan Warner.

He had bounded in his chair as the frightful shock crashed through his system. But he was not dead. On the contrary, his eyes gleamed far more brightly than they had done before. There was only one change, but it was a singular one. The black had passed from his hair and beard as the shadow passes from a landscape. They were both as white as snow. And yet there was no other sign of decay. His skin was smooth and plump and lustrous as a child's.

The Marshal looked at the committee with a reproachful eye.

"There seems to be some hitch here, gentlemen," said he.

We three practical men looked at each other.

Peter Stulpnagel smiled pensively.

"I think that another should do it," said I.

Again the connection was made, and again Duncan Warner sprang in his chair and shouted, but, indeed, were it not that he still remained in the chair none of us would have recognized him. His hair and his beard had shredded off in an instant, and the room looked like a barber's shop on a Saturday night. There he sat, his eyes still shining, his skin radiant with the glow of perfect health, but with a scalp as bald as a Dutch cheese, and a chin without so much as a trace of down. He began to revolve one of his arms, slowly and doubtfully at first, but with more confidence as he went on.

"That jint," said he, "has puzzled half the doctors on the Pacific Slope. It's as good as new, and as limber as a hickory twig."

"You are feeling pretty well?" asked the old German.

"Never better in my life," said Duncan Warner cheerily.

The situation was a painful one. The Marshal glared at the committee. Peter Stulpnagel grinned and rubbed his hands. The engineers scratched their heads. The bald-headed prisoner revolved his arms and looked pleased.

"I think that one more shock—" began the chairman.

"No, sir," said the Marshal; "we've had foolery enough for one morning. We are here for an execution, and a execution we'll have."

"What do you propose?"

"There's a hook handy upon the ceiling. Fetch in a rope, and we'll soon set this matter straight."

There was another awkward delay while the warders departed for the cord. Peter Stulpnagel bent over Duncan Warner, and whispered something in his ear. The desperado started in surprise.

"You don't say?" he asked.

The German nodded.

"What! No ways?"

Peter shook his head, and the two began to laugh as though they shared some huge joke between them.

The rope was brought, and the Marshal himself slipped the noose over the criminal's neck. Then the two warders, the assistant, and he swung their victim into the air. For half an hour he hung—a dreadful sight—from the ceiling. Then in solemn silence they lowered him down, and one of the warders went out to order the shell to be brought round. But as he touched ground again what was our amazement when Duncan Warner put his hands up to his neck, loosened the noose, and took a long, deep breath.

"Paul Jefferson's sale is goin' well," he remarked, "I could see the crowd from up yonder," and he nodded at the hook in the ceiling.

"Up with him again!" shouted the Marshal, "we'll get the life out of him somehow."

In an instant the victim was up at the hook once more.

They kept him there for an hour, but when he came down he was perfectly garrulous.

"Old man Plunket goes too much to the Arcady Saloon," said he. "Three times he's been there in an hour; and him with a family. Old man Plunket would do well to swear off."

It was monstrous and incredible, but there it was. There was no getting round it. The man was there talking when he ought to have been dead. We all sat staring in amazement, but United States Marshal Carpenter was not a man to be euchred so easily. He motioned the others to one side, so that the prisoner was left standing alone.

"Duncan Warner," said he, slowly, "you are here to play your part, and I am here to play mine. Your game is to live if you can, and my game is to carry out the sentence of the law. You've beat us on electricity. I'll give you one there. And you've beaten us on hanging, for you seem to thrive on it. But it's my turn to beat you now, for my duty has to be done."

He pulled a six-shooter from his coat as he spoke, and fired all the shots through the body of the prisoner. The room was so filled with smoke that we could see nothing, but when it cleared the prisoner was still standing there, looking down in disgust at the front of his coat.

"Coats must be cheap where you come from," said he. "Thirty dollars it cost me, and look at it now. The six holes in front are bad enough, but four of the balls have passed out, and a pretty state the back must be in."

The Marshal's revolver fell from his hand, and he dropped his arms to his sides, a beaten man.

"Maybe some of you gentlemen can tell me what this means," said he, looking helplessly at the committee.

Peter Stulpnagel took a step forward.

"I'll tell you all about it," said he.

"You seem to be the only person who knows anything."

"I *am* the only person who knows anything. I should have warned these gentlemen; but, as they would not listen to me, I have allowed them to learn by experience. What you have done with your electricity is that you have increased this man's vitality until he can defy death for centuries."

"Centuries!"

"Yes, it will take the wear of hundreds of years to exhaust the enormous nervous energy with which you have drenched him. Electricity is life, and you have charged him with it to the utmost. Perhaps in fifty years you might execute him, but I am not sanguine about it."

"Great Scott! What shall I do with him?" cried the unhappy Marshal.

Peter Stulpnagel shrugged his shoulders.

"It seems to me that it does not much matter what you do with him now," said he.

"Maybe we could drain the electricity out of him again. Suppose we hang him up by the heels?"

"No, no, it's out of the question."

"Well, well, he shall do no more mischief in Los Amigos, anyhow," said the Marshal, with decision. "He shall go into the new gaol. The prison will wear him out."

"On the contrary," said Peter Stulpnagel, "I think that it is much more probable that he will wear out the prison."

It was rather a fiasco, and for years we didn't talk more about it than we could help, but it's no secret now, and I thought you might like to jot down the facts in your casebook.

THE PARASITE

March 24th.—The spring is fairly with us now. Outside my laboratory window the great chestnut tree is all covered with the big glutinous gummy buds, some of which have already begun to break into little green shuttlecocks. As you walk down the lanes you are conscious of the rich silent forces of Nature working all around you. The wet earth smells fruitful and luscious. Green shoots are peeping out everywhere. The twigs are stiff with their sap, and the moist heavy English air is laden with a faintly resinous perfume. Buds in the hedges, lambs beneath them—everywhere the work of reproduction going forward!

I can see it without and I can feel it within. We also have our spring, when the little arterioles dilate, the lymph glands in a brisker stream, the glands work harder, winnowing and straining. Every nature readjusts the whole machine. I can feel the ferment in my blood at this very moment, and as the cool sunshine pours through my window I could dance about in it like a gnat. So I should, only Charles Sadler would rush upstairs to know what was the matter. Besides, I must remember that I am Professor Gilroy. An old professor may afford to be natural, but when fortune has given one of the first chairs in the university to a man of four-and-thirty, he must try and act the part consistently.

What a fellow Wilson is! If I could only throw the same enthusiasm into physiology that he does into psychology. I should become a Claude

Bernard, at the least. His whole life and soul and energy work to one end. He drops to sleep collating his results of the past day, and he wakes to plan his researches for the coming one. And yet outside the narrow circle who follow his proceedings he gets so little credit for it. Physiology is a recognized science. If I add even a brick to the edifice, everyone sees and applauds it. But Wilson is trying to dig the foundations for a science of the future. His work is underground, and does not show. Yet he goes on uncomplainingly, corresponding with a hundred semimaniacs in the hope of finding one reliable little speck of truth, collating old books, devouring new ones, experimenting, lecturing, trying to light up in others the fiery interest which is consuming him. I am filled with wonder and admiration when I think of him, and yet when he asks me to associate myself with his researches I am compelled to tell him that in their present state they offer little attraction to a man who is devoted to exact science. If he could show me something positive and objective I might then be tempted to approach the question from its physiological side. So long as half his subjects are tainted with charlatanry and the other half with hysteria we physiologists must content ourselves with the body, and leave the mind to our descendants.

No doubt I am a materialist. Agatha says that I am a rank one. I tell her that is an excellent reason for shortening our engagement, since I am in such urgent need of her spirituality. And yet I may claim to be a curious example of the effect of education upon temperament, for by nature I am, unless I deceive myself, a highly psychic man. I was a nervous, sensitive boy, a dreamer, a somnambulist, full of impressions and intuitions. My black hair, my dark eyes, my thin olive face, my tapering fingers, are all characteristic of my real temperament, and cause experts like Wilson to claim me as their own. But my brain is soaked with exact knowledge. I have trained myself to deal only with fact and with proof. Surmise and fancy have no place in my scheme of thought. Show me what I can see with my microscope, cut with my scalpel, weigh in my balance, and I will devote a lifetime to its investigation. But when you ask me to study feelings, impressions, suggestions, you ask me to do what is distasteful, and even demoralizing. A departure from pure reason affects me like an evil smell or a musical discord.

Which is a very sufficient reason why I am a little loath to go to Professor Wilson's tonight. Still, I feel that I could hardly get out of the invitation without positive rudeness—and now that Mrs. Marden and Agatha are going, of course I would not if I could. But I had rather meet them anywhere else. I know that Wilson would draw me into this nebulous semiscience of his if he could. In his enthusiasm he is perfectly impervious to hints or remonstrances. Nothing short of a positive quarrel will make him realize my aversion to the whole business. I have no doubt that he has some new mesmerist or clairvoyant or medium or trickster of some sort whom he is going to exhibit to us, for even his entertainments bear upon his hobby. Well, it will be a treat for Agatha, at any rate. She is interested in it as a woman usually is in whatever is vague and mystical and indefinite.

10:50 P.M.—This diary-keeping of mine is, I fancy, the outcome of that scientific habit of mind about which I wrote this morning. I like to register impressions while they are fresh. Once a day, at least, I endeavor to define my own mental position. It is a useful piece of self-analysis, and has, I fancy, a steadying effect upon the character. Frankly, I must confess that my own needs what stiffening I can give it. I fear that, after all, much of my neurotic temperament survives, and that I am far from that cool, calm precision which characterizes Murdoch or Pratt-Haldane. Otherwise, why should the tomfoolery which I have witnessed this evening have set my nerves thrilling so that even now I am all unstrung? My only comfort is that neither Wilson nor Miss Penclosa, nor even Agatha, could have possibly known my weakness.

And what in the world was there to excite me? Nothing; or so little that it will seem ludicrous when I set it down.

The Mardens got to Wilson's before me. In fact, I was one of the last to arrive, and found the room crowded. I had hardly time to say a word to Mrs. Marden and to Agatha, who was looking charming in white and pink, with glittering wheatears in her hair, when Wilson came twitching at my sleeve.

"You want something positive, Gilroy," said he, drawing me apart into a corner. "My dear fellow, I have a phenomenon—a phenomenon."

I should have been more impressed had I not heard the same before. His sanguine spirit turns every firefly into a star.

"No possible question about the *bona fides* this time," said he, in answer, perhaps, to some little gleam of amusement in my eyes. "My wife has known her for many years. They both came from Trinidad, you know. Miss Penclosa has only been in England a month or two, and knows no one outside the university circle, but I assure you that the things she has told us suffice in themselves to establish clairvoyance upon an absolutely scientific basis. There is nothing like her, amateur or professional. Come and be introduced."

I like none of these mystery mongers, but the amateur least of all.

With the paid performer you may pounce upon him and expose him the instant that you have seen through his trick. He is there to deceive you, and you are there to find him out. But what are you to do with the friend of your host's wife? Are you to turn on a light suddenly, expose her slapping a surreptitious banjo? Or are you to hurl cochineal over her evening frock when she steals round with her phosphorous bottle and her supernatural platitude? There would be a scene, and you would be looked upon as a brute. So you have your choice of being that or a dupe. I was in no very good humor as I followed Wilson to the lady.

Anyone less like my idea of a West Indian could not be imagined. She was a small frail creature, well over forty, I should say, with a pale peaky face, and hair of a very light shade of chestnut. Her presence was insignificant, and her manner retiring. In any group of ten women she would have been the last woman whom one would have picked out. Her eyes were perhaps her most remarkable, and also, I am compelled to say, her least pleasant, feature. They were gray in color—gray with a shade of green—and their expression struck me as being decidedly furtive. I wonder if furtive is the word, or should I have said fierce? On second thoughts feline would have expressed it better. A crutch leaning against the wall told me, what was painfully evident when she rose, that one of her legs was crippled.

So I was introduced to Miss Penclosa, and it did not escape me that as my name was mentioned she glanced across at Agatha. Wilson had evidently been talking. And presently, no doubt, thought I, she will inform me by occult means that I am engaged to a young lady with wheatears in her hair. I wondered how much more Wilson had been telling her about me.

"Professor Gilroy is a terrible skeptic," said he. "I hope, Miss Penclosa, that you will be able to convert him."

She looked keenly up at me.

"Professor Gilroy is quite right to be skeptical if he has not seen anything convincing," said she. "I should have thought," she added, "that you would yourself have been an excellent subject."

"For what, may I ask?" said I.

"Well, for mesmerism, for example,"

"My experience has been that mesmerists go for their subjects to those who are mentally unsound. All their results are vitiated, as it seems to me, by the fact that they are dealing with abnormal organisms."

"Which of these ladies would you say possessed a normal organism?" she asked. "I should like you to select the one who seems to you to have

the best-balanced mind. Should we say the girl in pink and white?—
Miss Agatha Marden, I think the name is."

"Yes, I should attach weight to any results from her."

"I have never tried how far she is impressionable. Of course some
people respond much more rapidly than others. May I ask how far your
skepticism extends? I suppose that you admit the mesmeric sleep and the
power of suggestion?"

"I admit nothing, Miss Penclosa."

"Dear me, I though science had got further than that. Of course I
know nothing about the scientific side of it. I only know what I can do.
You see the girl in red, for example, over near the Japanese jar. I shall
will that she come across to us."

She bent forward as she spoke and dropped her fan upon the floor.
The girl whisked round and came straight toward us with an inquiring
look upon her face, as if someone had called her.

"What do you think of that, Gilroy?" cried Wilson, in a kind of
ecstasy.

I did not dare to tell him what I thought of it. To me it was the most
barefaced shameless piece of imposture that I had ever witnessed. The
collusion and the signal had really been too obvious.

"Professor Gilroy is not satisfied," said she, glancing up at me with
her strange little eyes. "My poor fan is to get the credit of that experiment. Well, we must try something else. Miss Marden, would you have
any objection to my putting you off?"

"Oh, I should love it!" cried Agatha. By this time all the company
had gathered round us in a circle—the shirtfronted men and the white-
throated women, some awed, some critical, as though it were something between a religious ceremony and a conjurer's entertainment. A
red-velvet armchair had been pushed into the center, and Agatha lay
back in it, a little flushed, and trembling slightly from excitement. I
could see it from the vibration of the wheatears. Miss Penclosa rose from
her seat and stood over her, leaning upon her crutch.

And there was a change in the woman. She no longer seemed small
or insignificant. Twenty years were gone from her age. Her eyes were
shining; a tinge of color had come into her sallow cheeks; her whole
figure had expanded. So I have seen a dull-eyed, listless lad change in an
instant into briskness and life when given a task of which he felt himself
master. She looked down at Agatha with an expression which I resented
from the bottom of my soul—the expression with which a Roman
empress might have looked at her kneeling slave. Then, with a quick,

commanding gesture, she tossed up her arms and swept them slowly down in front of her.

I was watching Agatha narrowly. During these passes she seemed to be simply amused. At the fourth I observed a slight glazing of her eyes, accompanied by some dilation of her pupils. At the sixth there was a momentary rigor. At the seventh her lids began to droop. At the tenth her eyes were closed, and her breathing was slower and fuller than usual. I tried, as I watched, to preserve my scientific calm, but a foolish, causeless agitation convulsed me. I trust that I hid it, but I felt as a child feels in the dark. I could not have believed that I was still open to such weakness.

"She is in the trance," said Miss Penclosa.

"She is sleeping!" I cried.

"Wake her, then!"

I pulled her by the arm and shouted in her ear. She might have been dead for all the impression that I could make. Her body was there on the velvet chair. Her organs were acting, her heart, her lungs. But her soul! It had slipped from beyond our ken. Whither had it gone? What power had dispossessed it? I was puzzled and disconcerted.

"So much for the mesmeric sleep," said Mrs. Penclosa. "As regards suggestion—whatever I may suggest Miss Marden will infallibly do, whether it be now or after she has awakened from her trance. Do you demand proof of it?"

"Certainly," said I

"You shall have it." I saw a smile pass over her face, as though an amusing thought had struck her. She stooped and whispered earnestly into the subject's ear. Agatha, who had been so deaf to me, nodded her head as she listened.

"Awake!" cried Miss Penclosa, with a sharp tap of her crutch upon the floor. The eyes opened, the glazing cleared slowly away, and the soul looked out once more after its strange eclipse.

We went away early. Agatha was none the worse for her strange excursion, but I was nervous and unstrung, unable to listen to or answer the stream of comments which Wilson was pouring out for my benefit. As I bade her good-night, Miss Penclosa slipped a piece of paper into my hand.

"Pray forgive me," said she, "if I take means to overcome your skepticism. Open this note at ten o'clock tomorrow morning. It is a little private test."

I can't imagine what she means, but there is the note, and it shall be opened as she directs. My head is aching, and I have written enough for tonight. Tomorrow I dare say that what seems so inexplicable will take quite another complexion. I shall not surrender my convictions without a struggle.

March 25th.—I am amazed, confounded. It is clear that I must reconsider my opinion upon this matter. But first let me place on record what has occurred.

I had finished breakfast, and was looking over some diagrams with which my lecture is to be illustrated, when my housekeeper entered to tell me that Agatha was in my study and wished to see me immediately. I glanced at the clock, and saw with surprise that it was only half past nine.

When I entered the room she was standing on the hearthrug facing me. Something in her pose chilled me, and checked the words which were rising to my lips. Her veil was half down, but I could see that she was pale, and that her expression was constrained.

"Austin," she said, "I have come to tell you that our engagement is at an end."

I staggered. I believe that I literally did stagger. I know that I found myself leaning against the bookcase for support.

"But—but," I stammered—"this is very sudden, Agatha."

"Yes, Austin, I have come here to tell you that our engagement is at an end."

"But surely," I cried, "you will give me some reason. This is unlike you, Agatha. Tell me how I have been unfortunate enough to offend you."

"It is all over, Austin."

"But why? You must be under some delusion, Agatha. Perhaps you have been told some falsehood about me. Or you may have misunderstood something that I have said to you. Only let me know what it is, and a word may set it all right."

"We must consider it all at an end."

"But you left me last night without a hint at any disagreement. What could have occurred in the interval to change you so? It must have been something that happened last night. You have been thinking it over, and you have disapproved of my conduct. Was it the mesmerism? Did you blame me for letting that woman exercise her power over you? You know that at the least sign I should have interfered."

"It is useless, Austin. All is over."

Her voice was cold and measured, her manner strangely formal and hard. It seemed to me that she was absolutely resolved not to be drawn into any argument or explanation. As for me, I was shaking with agitation, and I turned my face aside, so ashamed was I that she should see my want of control.

"You must know what this means to me," I cried. "It is the blasting of all my hopes and the ruin of my life. You surely will not inflict such a punishment upon me unheard. You will let me know what is the matter. Consider how impossible it would be for me under any circumstances to treat you so. For God's sake, Agatha, let me know what I have done."

She walked past me without a word and opened the door.

"It is quite useless, Austin," said she. "You must consider our engagement at an end." An instant later she was gone, and before I could recover myself sufficiently to follow her I heard the hall door close behind her.

I rushed into my room to change my coat, with the idea of hurrying round to Mrs. Marden's to learn from her what the cause of my misfortune might be. So shaken was I that I could hardly lace my boots. Never shall I forget those horrible ten minutes. I had just pulled on my overcoat when the clock upon the mantelpiece struck ten.

Ten! I associated the idea with Miss Penclosa's note. It was lying before me on the table, and I tore it open. It was scribbled in pencil in a peculiarly angular handwriting.

MY DEAR PROFESSOR GILROY [it said].—Pray excuse the personal nature of the test which I am giving you. Professor Wilson happened to mention the relations between you and my subject of this evening, and it struck me that nothing could be more convincing to you than if I were to suggest to Miss Marden that she should call upon you at half past nine tomorrow morning and suspend your engagement for half an hour or so. Science is so exacting that it is difficult to give a satisfying test, but I am convinced that this at least will be an action which she would be most unlikely to do of her own free will. Forget anything that she may have said, as she has really nothing whatever to do with it, and will certainly not recollect anything about it. I write this note to shorten your anxiety, and to beg you to forgive me for the momentary unhappiness which my suggestion must have caused you.

Yours faithfully,   HELEN PENCLOSA

Really, when I had read the note, I was too relieved to be angry. It was a liberty. Certainly it was a very great liberty indeed on the part of a lady whom I had only met once. But, after all, I had challenged her by my skepticism. It may have been, as she said, a little difficult to devise a test which would satisfy me.

And she had done that. There could be no question at all upon the point. For me hypnotic suggestion was finally established. It took its place from now onward as one of the facts of life. That Agatha, who of all women of my acquaintance had the best-balanced mind, had been reduced to a condition of automatism appeared to be certain. A person at a distance had worked her as an engineer on the shore might guide a Brennan torpedo. A second soul had stepped in, as it were, had pushed her own aside, and had seized her nervous mechanism, saying, "I will work this for half an hour." And Agatha must have been unconscious as she came and as she returned. Could she make her way in safety through the streets in such a state? I put on my hat and hurried round to see if all was well with her.

Yes. She was at home. I was shown into the drawing room, and found her sitting with a book upon her lap.

"You are an early visitor, Austin," she said, smiling.

"And you have been an even earlier one," I answered. She looked puzzled. "What do you mean?" she asked.

"You have not been out today?"

"No, certainly not."

"Agatha," said I seriously, "would you mind telling me exactly what you have done this morning?"

She laughed at my earnestness. "You've got on your professional look, Austin. See what comes of being engaged to a man of science! However, I will tell you, though I can't imagine what you want to know for. I got up at eight. I breakfasted at half past. I came into this room at ten minutes past nine, and began to read *The Memoirs of Madame de Rémusat*. In a few minutes I did the French lady the bad compliment of dropping to sleep over her pages; and I did you, sir, the flattering one of dreaming about you. It is only a few minutes since I woke up."

"And found yourself where you had been before?"

"Why, where else should I find myself?"

"Would you mind telling me, Agatha, what it was that you dreamed about me? It really is not mere curiosity on my part."

"I merely had a vague impression that you came into it. I cannot recall really anything definite."

"If you have not been out today, Agatha, how is it that your shoes are dusty?"

A pained look came over her face.

"Really, Austin, I do not know what is the matter with you this morning. One would almost think that you doubted my word. If my boots are dusty it must be, of course, that I have put on a pair which the maid had not cleaned."

It was perfectly evident that she knew nothing whatever about the matter, and I reflected that, after all, perhaps it was better that I should not enlighten her. It might frighten her, and could serve no good purpose that I could see. I said no more about it, therefore, and left shortly afterward to give my lecture.

But I am immensely impressed. My horizon of scientific possibilities has suddenly been enormously extended. I no longer wonder at Wilson's demonic energy and enthusiasm. Who would not work hard who had a vast virgin field ready to his hand? Why, I have known the novel shape of a nucleolus, or a trifling peculiarity of striped muscular fiber seen under a three-hundred-diameter lens, fill me with exultation. How petty do such researches seem when compared with this one, which strikes at the very roots of life and the nature of the soul! I had always looked upon spirit as a product of matter. The brain, I thought, secreted the mind, as the liver does the bile. But how can this be, when I see mind working from a distance, and playing upon matter as a musician might upon a violin? The body does not give rise to the soul, then, but is rather the rough instrument by which the spirit manifests itself. The windmill does not give rise to the wind, but only indicates it. It was opposed to my whole habit of thought, and yet it was undeniably possible and worthy of investigation.

And why should I not investigate it? I see that under yesterday's date I said, "If I could see something positive and objective I might be tempted to approach it from the physiological aspect." Well, I have got my test. I shall be as good as my word. The investigation would, I am sure, be of immense interest. Some of my colleagues might look askance at it, for science is full of unreasoning prejudices, but if Wilson has the courage of his convictions I can afford to have it also. I shall go to him tomorrow morning—to him and to Miss Penclosa. If she can show us so much it is probable that she can show us more.

March 26th.—Wilson was, as I had anticipated, very exultant over my conversion, and Miss Penclosa was also demurely pleased at the result of her experiment. Strange what a silent, colorless creature she is, save only when she exercises her power! When talking about it gives her color and life. She seems to take a singular interest in me. I cannot help observing how her eyes follow me about the room.

We had the most interesting conversation about her own powers. It is just as well to put her views on record, though they cannot, of course, claim any scientific weight.

"You are on the very fringe of the subject," said she, when I had expressed wonder at the remarkable instance of suggestion which she had shown me. "I had no direct influence upon Miss Marden when she came round to you. I was not even thinking of her that morning. What I did was to set her mind, as I might set the alarm of a clock, so that at the hour named it would go off of its own accord. If six months instead of twelve hours had been suggested, it would have been the same."

"And if the suggestion had been to assassinate me?"

"She would have most inevitably have done so."

"But this is a terrible power," I cried.

"It is, as you say, a terrible power," she answered, gravely; "and the more you know of it, the more terrible will it seem to you."

"May I ask," said I, "what you meant when you said that this matter of suggestion is only at the fringe of it? What do you consider the essential?"

"I had rather not tell you."

I was surprised at the decision of her answer.

"You understand," said I, "that it is not out of curiosity I ask, but in hope that I may find some scientific explanation for the facts with which you furnish me."

"Frankly, Professor Gilroy," said she, "I am not at all interested in science, nor do I care whether it can or cannot classify these powers."

"But I was hoping—"

"Ah, that is quite another thing. If you make it a personal matter," said she, with the pleasantest of smiles, "I shall be only too happy to tell you anything you wish to know. Let me see. What was it you asked me? Oh, about the further powers. Professor Wilson won't believe in them, but they are quite true all the same. For example, it is possible for an operator to gain complete command over his subject—presuming that the latter is a good one. Without any previous suggestion he may make him do whatever he likes."

"Without the subject's knowledge?"

"That depends. If the force were strongly exerted, he would know no more about it than Miss Marden did when she came round and frightened you so. Or, if the influence was less powerful, he might be conscious of what he was doing, but be quite unable to prevent himself from doing it."

"Would he have lost his own will power, then?"

"It would be overridden by another stronger one."

"Have you ever exercised this power yourself?"

"Several times."

"Is your own will so strong, then?"

"Well, it does not entirely depend on that. Many have strong wills which are not detachable from themselves. The thing is to have the gift of projecting it into another person, and superseding their own. I feel that the power varies with my own strength and health."

"Practically you send your soul into another person's body."

"Well, you might put it that way."

"And what does your own body do?"

"It merely feels lethargic."

"Well, but is there no danger to your own health?" I asked.

"There might be a little. You have to be careful never to let your own consciousness absolutely go, otherwise you might experience some difficulty in finding your way back in. You must always preserve the connection, as it were. I am afraid I express myself very badly, Professor Gilroy, but of course I don't know how to put these things in a scientific way. I am just giving you my own experiences and my own explanations."

Well, I read this over now at my leisure, and I marvel at myself. Is this Austin Gilroy, the man who has won his way to the front by his hard reasoning power and by his devotion to fact? Here I am, gravely retailing the gossip of a woman who tells me how her soul may be projected from her body, and how, while she lies in a lethargy, she can control the actions of people at a distance. Do I accept it? Certainly not. She must prove and reprove before I yield a point. But if I am a still a skeptic, I have at least ceased to be a scoffer. We are to have a sitting this evening, and she is to try if she can produce any mesmeric effect upon me. If she can it will make an excellent starting point for our investigation. No one can accuse *me*, at any rate, of complicity. If she cannot, we must try and find some subject who will be like Caesar's wife. Wilson is perfectly impervious.

10 P.M.—I believe that I am on the threshold of an epoch-making investigation. To have the power of examining these phenomena from

inside—to have an organism which will respond, and at the same time a brain which will appreciate and criticize—that is surely a unique advantage. I am quite sure that Wilson would give five years of his life to be as susceptible as I have proved myself to be.

There was no one present except Wilson and his wife. I was seated with my head leaning back; and Miss Penclosa, standing in front, and a little to the left, used the same long sweeping strokes as with Agatha. At each of them a warm current of air seemed to strike me, and to suffuse a thrill and glow all through me, from head to foot. My eyes were fixed upon Miss Penclosa's face; but as I gazed, the features seemed to blur and to fade away. I was conscious only of her own eyes looking down at me, gray, deep, inscrutable. Larger they grew, and larger, until they changed suddenly into two mountain lakes, toward which I seemed to be falling with horrible rapidity. I shuddered; and as I did so, some deeper stratum of thought told me that the shudder represented the rigor which I had observed in Agatha. An instant later, I struck the surface of the lakes, now joined into one, and down I went beneath the water, with a fullness in my head and a buzzing in my ears. Down I went, down, down, and then with a swoop up again, until I could see the light streaming brightly through the green water. I was almost at the surface, when the word "Awake!" rang through my head, and with a start I found myself back in the armchair, with Miss Penclosa leaning on her crutch, and Wilson, his notebook in his hand, peeping over her shoulder. No heaviness or weariness was left behind. On the contrary, though it is only an hour or so since the experiment, I feel so wakeful that I am more inclined for my study than my bedroom. I see quite a vista of interesting experiments extending before us, and am all impatience to begin upon them.

March 27th.—A blank day, as Miss Penclosa goes with Wilson and his wife to the Suttons. Have begun Binet and Ferré's *Animal Magnetism.* What strange deep waters these are! Results, results, results—and the cause an absolute mystery! It is stimulating to the imagination, but I must be on my guard against that. Let us have no inferences nor deductions, and nothing but solid facts. I *know* that the mesmeric trance is true; I *know* that mesmeric suggestion is true; I *know* that I am myself sensitive to this force. That is my present position. I have a large new notebook, which shall be devoted entirely to scientific detail.

Long talk with Agatha and Mrs. Marden in the evening about our marriage. We think that the summer vac. (the beginning of it) would be the best time for the wedding. Why should we delay? I grudge even those few months. Still, as Mrs. Marden says, there are a good many things to be arranged.

March 28th.—Mesmerized again by Miss Penclosa. Experience much the same as before, save that insensibility came on more quickly. See Notebook A for temperature of room, barometric pressure, pulse, and respiration, as taken by Professor Wilson.

March 29th.—Mesmerized again. Details in Notebook A.

March 30th.—Sunday, and a blank day. I grudge any interruption of our experiments. At present they merely embrace the physical signs, which go with slight, with complete, and with extreme insensibility. Afterward we hope to pass on to the phenomena of suggestion and of lucidity. Professors have demonstrated these things upon women at Nancy and the Salpêtrière. It will be more convincing when a woman demonstrates them upon a professor, with a second professor as a witness. And that I should be the subject—I, the skeptic, the materialist! At least, I have shown that my devotion to science is greater than to my own personal consistency. The defeating of our own words is the greatest sacrifice which truth ever requires of us.

My neighbor, Charles Sadler, the handsome young demonstrator of anatomy, came in this evening to return a volume of Virchow's *Archives*, which I had lent him. I call him young, but, as a matter of fact, he is a year older than I am.

"I understand, Gilroy," said he, "that you are being experimented upon by Miss Penclosa? Well," he went on, when I had acknowledged it, "if I were you, I should not let it go any further. You will think me very impertinent, no doubt; but, nonetheless I feel it to be my duty to advise you to have no more to do with her."

Of course I asked him why.

"I am so placed that I cannot enter into particulars as freely as I could wish," said he. "Miss Penclosa is the friend of my friend, and my position is a delicate one. I can only say this, that I have myself been the subject of some of the woman's experiments, and that they have left a most unpleasant impression on my mind."

He could hardly expect me to be satisfied with that, and I tried hard to get something more definite out of him, but without success. Is it conceivable that he could be jealous at my having superseded him? Or is he one of those men of science who feel personally injured when facts run counter to their preconceived opinions? He cannot seriously suppose that because he has some vague grievance, I am therefore to abandon a series of experiments which promise to be so fruitful of results. He appeared to be annoyed at the light way in which I treated his shadowy warnings, and we parted with some little coldness on both sides.

March 31st.—Mesmerized by Miss P.

April 1st.—Mesmerized by Miss P. (Notebook A.)

April 2nd.—Mesmerized by Miss P. (Sphygmographic chart by Professor Wilson.)

April 3rd.—It is possible that this course of mesmerism may be a little trying to the general constitution. Agatha says that I am thinner, and darker under the eyes. I am conscious of a nervous irritability which I had not observed in myself before. The least noise, for example, makes me start, and the stupidity of a student causes me exasperation instead of amusement. Agatha wishes me to stop, but I tell her that every course of study is trying, and that one can never attain a result without paying some price for it. When she sees the sensation which my forthcoming paper on "The relation between mind and matter" may make she will understand that it is worth a little nervous wear and tear. I should not be surprised if I got my F.R.S. over it.

Mesmerized again in the evening. The effect is produced more rapidly now, and the subjective visions are less marked. I keep full notes of each sitting. Wilson is leaving for town for a week or ten days, but we shall not interrupt the experiments, which depend for their value as much upon my sensations as on his observations.

April 4th.—I must be carefully on my guard. A complication has crept into our experiments which I had not reckoned upon. In my eagerness for scientific facts, I have been foolishly blind to the human relations between Miss Penclosa and myself. I can write here what I would not breathe to a living soul. The unhappy woman appears to have formed an attachment for me.

I should not say such a thing, even in the privacy of my own intimate journal, if it had not come to such a pass that it is impossible to ignore it. For some time—that is, for the last week—there have been signs which I have brushed aside and refused to think of. Her brightness when I come, her dejection when I go, her eagerness that I should come often, the expression of her eyes, the tone of her voice—I tried to think that they meant nothing, and were perhaps only her ardent West Indian manner. But last night, as I awoke from the mesmeric sleep, I put out my hand, unconsciously, involuntarily, and clasped hers. When I came fully to myself we were sitting with them locked, she looking up at me with an expectant smile. And the horrible thing was that I felt impelled

to say what she expected me to say. What a false wretch I should have
been! How I should have loathed myself today had I yielded to the
temptation of that moment! But, thank God, I was strong enough to
spring up and hurry from the room. I was rude, I fear, but I could not—
no, I *could* not—trust myself another moment. I, a gentleman, a man of
honor, engaged to one of the sweetest girls in England—and yet in a
moment of reasonless passion I nearly professed my love for this woman,
whom I hardly know. She is far older than myself, and a cripple. It is
monstrous, odious, and yet the impulse was so strong that had I stayed
another minute in her presence I should have committed myself. What
was it? I have to teach others the workings of our organism, and what do
I know of it myself? Was it the sudden uncropping of some lower
stratum in my nature—a brutal primitive instinct suddenly asserting
itself? I could almost believe the tales of obsession by evil spirits so
overmastering was the feeling.

Well, the incident places me in a most unfortunate position. On the
one hand, I am very loath to abandon a series of experiments which
have already gone so far, and which promise such brilliant results. On
the other, if this unhappy woman has conceived a passion for me— But
surely even now I must have made some hideous mistake. She, with her
age and her deformity! It is impossible. And then she knew about
Agatha. She understood how I was placed. She only smiled out of
amusement, perhaps, when in my dazed state I seized her hand. It was
my half-mesmerized brain which gave it a meaning, and sprang with
such bestial swiftness to meet it. I wish I could persuade myself that it
was indeed so. On the whole, perhaps, my wisest plan would be to
postpone our other experiments until Wilson's return. I have written a
note to Miss Penclosa, therefore, making no allusion to last night, but
saying that a press of work would cause me to interrupt our sittings for a
few days. She has answered, formally enough, to say that if I should
change my mind I should find her at home at the usual hour.

10 P.M.—Well, well, what a thing of straw I am! I am coming to
know myself better of late, and the more I know, the lower I fall in my
own estimation. Surely I was not always so weak as this. At four o'clock
I should have smiled had anyone told me that I should go to Miss
Penclosa's tonight, and yet at eight I was at Wilson's door as usual. I
don't know how it occurred. The influence of habit, I suppose. Perhaps
there is a mesmeric craze, as there is an opium craze, and I am a victim to
it. I only know that as I worked in my study I became more and more
uneasy. I fidgeted. I worried. I could not concentrate my mind upon the

papers in front of me. And then at last, almost before I knew what I was doing, I seized my hat, and hurried round to keep my usual appointment.

We had an interesting evening. Mrs. Wilson was present during most of the time, which prevented the embarrassment which one at least of us must have felt. Miss Penclosa's manner was quite the same as usual, and she expressed no surprise at my having come in spite of my note. There was nothing in her bearing to show that yesterday's incident had made any impression upon her, and so I am inclined to hope that I overrated it.

April 6th.—No, no, no, I did not overrate it. I can no longer attempt to conceal from myself that this woman has conceived a passion for me. It is monstrous, but it is true. Again tonight I awoke from the mesmeric trance to find my hand in hers, and to suffer that odious feeling which urges me to throw away my honor, my career, everything, for the sake of this creature, who, as I can plainly see when I am away from her influence, possesses no single charm upon earth. But when I am near her I do not feel this. She rouses something in me—something evil— something I had rather not think of. She paralyzes my better nature, too, at the moment when she stimulates my worse. Decidedly it is not good for me to be near her.

Last night was worse than before. Instead of flying, I actually sat for some time with my hand in hers, talking over the most intimate subjects with her. We spoke of Agatha among other things. What could I have been dreaming of? Miss Penclosa said that she was conventional, and I agreed with her. She spoke once or twice in a disparaging way of her, and I did not protest. What a creature I have been!

Weak as I have proved myself to be, I am still strong enough to bring this sort of thing to an end. It shall not happen again. I have sense enough to fly when I cannot fight. From this Sunday night onward I shall never sit with Miss Penclosa again. Never! Let the experiments go; let the research come to an end; anything is better than facing this monstrous temptation which drags me so low. I have said nothing to Miss Penclosa, but I shall simply stay away. She can tell the reason without any words of mine.

April 7th.—Have stayed away as I said. It is a pity to ruin such an interesting investigation, but it would be a greater pity still to ruin my life, and I *know* that I cannot trust myself with that woman.

11 P.M.—God help me! What is the matter with me? Am I going

mad? Let me try and be calm and reason with myself. First of all I shall set down exactly what occurred.

It was nearly eight when I wrote the lines with which this day begins. Feeling strangely restless and uneasy, I left my rooms and walked round to spend the evening with Agatha and her mother. They both remarked that I was pale and haggard. About nine Professor Pratt-Haldane came in, and we played a game of whist. I tried hard to concentrate my attention upon the cards, but the feeling of restlessness grew and grew until I found it impossible to struggle against it. I simply *could* not sit still at the table. At last, in the very middle of a hand, I threw my cards down, and with some sort of an incoherent apology about having an appointment, I rushed from the room. As if in a dream, I have a vague recollection of tearing through the hall, snatching my hat from the stand, and slamming the door behind me. As in a dream, too, I have the impression of the double line of gas lamps, and my bespattered boots tell me that I must have run down the middle of the road. It was all misty and strange and unnatural. I came to Wilson's house; I saw Mrs. Wilson, and I saw Miss Penclosa. I hardly recall what we talked about, but I do remember that Miss P. shook the head of her crutch at me in a playful way, and accused me of being late and of losing interest in our experiments. There was no mesmerism, but I stayed some time, and have only just returned.

My brain is quite clear again now, and I can think over what has occurred. It is absurd to suppose that it is merely weakness and force of habit. I tried to explain it in that way the other night, but it will no longer suffice. It is something much deeper and more terrible than that. Why, when I was at the Mardens' whist table I was dragged away as if the noose of a rope had been cast round me. I can no longer disguise it from myself. The woman has her grip upon me. I am in her clutch. But I must keep my head and reason it out, and see what is best to be done.

But what a blind fool I have been! In my enthusiasm over my research I have walked straight into the pit, although it lay gaping before me. Did she not herself warn me? Did she not tell me, as I can read in my own journal, that when she has acquired power over a subject she can make him do her will? And she has acquired that power over me, and I am for the moment at the beck and call of this creature with the crutch. I must come when she wills it. I must do as she wills. Worst of all, I must feel as she wills. I loathe her and fear her, yet while I am under the spell she can doubtless make me love her.

There is some consolation in the thought, then, that these odious impulses for which I have blamed myself do not really come from me at all. They are all transferred from her, little as I could have guessed it at the time. I feel cleaner and lighter for the thought.

April 8th.—Yes, now in broad daylight, writing coolly and with time for reflection, I am compelled to confirm everything which I find in my journal of last night. I am in a horrible position; but, above all, I must not lose my head. I must pit my intellect against her powers. After all, I am no silly puppet to dance at the end of a string. I have energy, brains, courage. For all her devil's tricks I may beat her yet. May! I *must* or what is to become of me?

Let me try to reason it out. This woman, by her own explanation, can dominate my nervous organism. She can project herself into my body and take command of it. She has a parasite soul—yes, she is a parasite, a monstrous parasite. She creeps into my frame as the hermit crab does into the whelk's shell. I am powerless. What can I do? I am dealing with forces of which I know nothing. And I can tell no one of my trouble. They would set me down as a madman. Certainly if it got noised abroad, the university would say that they had no need of a devil-ridden professor. And Agatha! No, no; I must face it alone.

I read over my notes of what the woman said when she spoke of her powers. There is one point which fills me with dismay. She implies that when the influence is slight the subject knows what he is doing, but cannot control himself, whereas when it is strongly exerted he is absolutely unconscious. Now I have always known what I did, though less so last night than on the previous occasion. That seems to mean that she has never yet exerted her full powers upon me. Was ever a man so placed before?

Yes, perhaps there was, and very near me, too. Charles Sadler must know something of this. His vague words of warning take a meaning now. Oh, if I had only listened to him then before I helped by these repeated sittings to forge the links of the chain which binds me! But I will see him today. I will apologize to him for having treated his warning so lightly. I will see if he can advise me.

4 P.M.—No, he cannot. I have talked with him, and he showed some surprise at the first words in which I tried to express my unspeakable secret that I went no further. As far as I can gather—by hints and inferences rather than by any statement—his own experience was limited to some words or looks such as I have myself endured. His abandonment of Miss Penclosa is in itself a sign that he was never really

in her toils. Oh, if he only knew his escape! He has to thank his phlegmatic Saxon temperament for it. I am black and Celtic, and this hag's clutch is deep in my nerves. Shall I ever get it out? Shall I ever be the same man that I was just one short fortnight ago?

Let me consider what I had better do. I cannot leave the university in the middle of the term. If I were free, my course would be obvious. I should start at once and travel in Persia. But would she allow me to start? And could her influence not reach me in Persia, and bring me back to within touch of her crutch? I can only find out the limits of this hellish power by my own bitter experience. I will fight and fight and fight— and what can I do more?

I know very well that about eight o'clock tonight that craving for her society—that irresistible restlessness—will come upon me. How shall I overcome it? What shall I do? I must make it impossible for me to leave the room. I shall lock the door and throw the key out of the window. But then what am I to do in the morning? Never mind about the morning. I must at all costs break this chain which holds me.

April 9th.—Victory! I have done splendidly! At seven o'clock last night I took a hasty dinner, and then locked myself up in my bedroom and dropped the key into the garden. I chose a cheery novel and lay in bed for three hours trying to read it, but really in a horrible state of trepidation, expecting every instant that I should become conscious of the impulse. Nothing of the sort occurred, however, and I woke this morning with the feeling that a black nightmare had been lifted off me. Perhaps the creature realized what I had done, and understood that it was useless to try to influence me. At any rate, I have beaten her once, and if I can do it once I can do it again.

It was most awkward about the key in the morning. Luckily there was an undergraduate below, and I asked him to throw it up. No doubt he thought I had just dropped it. I will have doors and windows screwed up, and six stout men to hold me down in my bed, before I will surrender myself to be hag-ridden in this way.

I had a note from Mrs. Marden this afternoon, asking me to go round and see her. I intended to do so in any case, but had not expected to find bad news waiting for me. It seems that the Armstrongs, from whom Agatha has expectations, are due home from Adelaide in the *Aurora*, and that they have written to Mrs. Marden and her to meet them in town. They will probably be away for a month or six weeks, and as the *Aurora* is due on Wednesday, they must go at once—tomorrow if they are ready in time. My consolation is that when we meet again there will be no more parting between Agatha and me.

"I want you to do one thing, Agatha," said I, when we were alone together; "if you should happen to meet Miss Penclosa, either in town or here, you must promise me never again to allow her to mesmerize you."

Agatha opened her eyes.

"Why, it was only the other day that you were saying how interesting it all was, and how determined you were to finish your experiments."

"I know. But I have changed my mind since then."

"And you won't have it any more?"

"No."

"I am so glad, Austin. You can't think how pale and worn you have been lately. It was really our principal objection to going to London now, that we did not wish to leave you, when you were so pulled down. And your manner has been so strange occasionally—especially that night when you left poor Professor Pratt-Haldane to play dummy. I am convinced that these experiments are very bad for your nerves."

"I think so too, dear."

"And for Miss Penclosa's nerves as well. You have heard that she is ill?"

"No."

"Mrs. Wilson told us so last night. She described it as nervous fever. Professor Wilson is coming back this week, and of course Mrs. Wilson is very anxious that Miss Penclosa should be well again then, for he has quite a program of experiments which he is anxious to carry out."

I was glad to have Agatha's promise, for it was enough that this woman should have one of us in her clutch. On the other hand, I was disturbed to hear about Miss Penclosa's illness. It rather discounts the victory which I appeared to win last night. I remember that she said that loss of health interfered with her power. That may be why I was able to hold my own so easily. Well, well, I must take the same precautions tonight, and see what comes of it. I am childishly frightened when I think of her.

April 10th.—All went very well last night. I was amused at the gardener's face when I had again to hail him this morning and ask him to throw up my key. I shall get the same among the servants if this sort of thing goes on. But the great point is that I stayed in my room without the slightest inclination to leave it. I do believe that I am getting myself clear of this incredible bond—or is it only that the woman's power is in abeyance until she recovers her strength? I can but pray for the best.

The Mardens left this morning, and the brightness seems to have gone out of the spring sunshine. And yet it is very beautiful also, as it gleams on the green chestnuts opposite my windows, and gives a touch of gaiety to the heavy lichen-mottled walls of the old colleges. How sweet and gentle and soothing is Nature! Who would think that there lurked in her also such vile forces, such odious possibilities? For of course I understand that this dreadful thing which has sprung out at me is neither supernatural nor even preternatural. No; it is a natural force which this woman can use, and society is ignorant of. The mere fact that it ebbs with her strength shows how entirely it is subject to physical laws. If I had time I might probe it to the bottom, and lay my hands upon its antidote. But you cannot tame the tiger when you are beneath his claws. You can but try to writhe away from him. Ah! when I look in the glass and see my own dark eyes and clear-cut Spanish face, I long for a vitriol splash or a bout of the smallpox. One or the other might have saved me from this calamity.

I am inclined to think that I may have trouble tonight. There are two things which make me fear so. One is that I met Mrs. Wilson in the street, and that she tells me that Miss Penclosa is better, though still weak. I find myself wishing in my heart that the illness had been her last. The other is that Professor Wilson comes back in a day or two, and his presence would act as a constraint upon her. I should not fear our interviews if a third person were present. For both these reasons I have a presentiment of trouble tonight, and I shall take the same precautions as before.

April 11th.—No, thank God, all went well last night. I really could not face the gardener again. I locked my door and thrust the key underneath it so that I had to ask the maid to let me out in the morning. But the precaution was really not needed, for I never had any inclination to go out at all. Three evenings in succession at home! I am surely near the end of my troubles, for Wilson will be home again either today or tomorrow. Shall I tell him of what I have gone through or not? I am convinced that I should not have the slightest sympathy from him. He would look upon me as an interesting case, and read a paper about me at the next meeting of the Psychical Society, in which he would gravely discuss the possibility of my being a deliberate liar, and weigh it against the chances of my being in an early stage of lunacy. No, I shall get no comfort out of Wilson.

I am feeling wonderfully fit and well. I don't think I ever lectured with greater spirit. Oh, if I could only get this shadow off my life, how happy I should be! Young, fairly wealthy, in the front rank of my profession, engaged to a beautiful and charming girl—have I not everything which a man could ask for? Only one thing to trouble me; but what a thing it is!

Midnight.—I shall go mad. Yes, that will be the end of it. I shall go mad. I am not far from it now. My head throbs as I rest it on my hot hand. I am quivering all over like a scared horse. Oh, what a night I have had! And yet I have some cause to be satisfied also.

At the risk of becoming the laughing stock of my own servant, I again slipped my key under the door, imprisoning myself for the night. Then, finding it too early to go to bed, I lay down with my clothes on and began to read one of Dumas's novels. Suddenly I was gripped—gripped and dragged from the couch. It is only thus that I can describe the overpowering nature of the force which pounced upon me. I clawed at the coverlet. I clung to the woodwork. I believe that I screamed out in my frenzy. It was all useless—hopeless. I *must* go. There was no way out of it. It was only at the outset that I resisted. The force soon became too overmastering for that. I thank goodness that there were no watchers there to interfere with me. I could not have answered for myself if there had been. And besides the determination to get out, there came to me also the keenest and coolest judgment in choosing my means. I lit a candle and endeavored, kneeling in front of the door, to pull the key through with the feather end of a quill pen. It was just too short, and pushed it further away. Then with quiet persistence I got a paper knife out of one of the drawers, and with that I managed to draw the key back. I opened the door, stepped into my study, took a photograph of myself from the bureau, wrote something across it, placed it in the inside pocket of my coat, and then started off for Wilson's.

It was all wonderfully clear, and yet disassociated from the rest of my life, as the incidents of even the most vivid dream might be. A peculiar double consciousness possessed me. There was the predominant alien will which was bent upon drawing me to the side of its owner, and there was the feebler protesting personality, which I recognized as being myself, tugging feebly at the overmastering impulse as a led terrier might at its chain. I can remember recognizing these two conflicting forces, but I recall nothing of my walk, nor of how I was admitted to the house.

Very vivid, however, is my recollection of how I met Miss Penclosa. She was reclining on the sofa in the little boudoir in which our experiments had usually been carried out. Her head was rested on her hand, and a tiger-skin rug had been partly drawn over her. She looked up expectantly as I entered, and as the lamplight fell upon her face I could see that she was very pale and thin, with dark hollows under her eyes. She smiled at me, and pointed to a stool beside her. It was with her left hand that she pointed, and I, running eagerly forward, seized it—I loathe myself as I think of it—and pressed it passionately to my lips. Then seating myself upon the stool, and still retaining her hand, I gave her the photograph which I had brought with me, and talked and talked and talked, of my love for her, of my grief over her illness, of my joy at her recovery, of the misery it was to me to be absent a single evening from her side. She lay quietly looking down at me with imperious eyes and her provocative smile. Once I remember that she passed her hand over my hair, as one caresses a dog; and it gave me pleasure—the caress. I thrilled under it. I was her slave, body and soul, and for the moment I rejoiced in my slavery.

And then came the blessed change. Never tell me that there is not a Providence. I was on the brink of perdition. My feet were on the edge. Was it a coincidence that at that very instant help should come? No, no, no; there is a Providence, and Its hand has drawn me back. There is something in the universe stronger than this devil woman with her tricks. Ah, what a balm to my heart it is to think so!

As I looked up at her I was conscious of a change in her. Her face which had been pale before, was now ghastly. Her eyes were dull, and the lids drooped heavily over them. Above all, the look of serene confidence had gone from her features. Her mouth had weakened. Her forehead had puckered. She was frightened and undecided. And as I watched the change my own spirit fluttered and struggled, trying hard to clear itself from the grip which held it—a grip which from moment to moment grew less secure.

"Austin," she whispered. "I have tried to do too much. I was not strong enough. I have not recovered yet from my illness. But I could not live longer without seeing you. You won't leave me, Austin. This is only a passing weakness. If you will only give me five minutes, I shall be myself again. Give me the small decanter from the table in the window."

But I had regained my soul. With her waning strength the influence had cleared away from me and left me free. And I was aggressive—bitterly, fiercely aggressive. For once, at least, I could make this woman understand what my real feelings toward her were. My soul was filled with a hatred as bestial as the love against which it was a reaction. It was the savage murderous passion of the revolted serf. I could have taken the crutch from her side and beaten her face in with it. She threw her hands up as if to avoid a blow, and cowered away from me into the corner of the settee.

"The brandy!" she gasped. "The brandy!"

I took the decanter and poured it over the roots of a palm in the window. Then I snatched the photograph from her hands and tore it into a hundred pieces.

"You vile woman!" I said. "If I did my duty to society you would never leave this room alive."

"I love you, Austin—I love you," she wailed.

"Yes," I cried, "and Charles Sadler before. And how many others before that?"

"Charles Sadler!" she gasped. "He has spoken to you! So, Charles Sadler—Charles Sadler!" Her voice came through her white lips like a snake hiss.

"Yes, I know you, and others shall know you too. You shameless creature! You knew how I stood. And yet you used your vile power to bring me to your side. You may perhaps do so again, but at least you will remember that you have heard me say that I love Miss Marden from the bottom of my soul, and that I loathe you, abhor you. The very sight of you and the sound of your voice fill me with horror and disgust. The thought of you is repulsive. That is how I feel toward you, and if it pleases you by your tricks to draw me again to your side as you have done tonight you will at least, I should think, have little satisfaction in trying to make a lover out of a man who has told you his real opinion of you. You may put what words you will into my mouth, but you cannot help remembering."

I stopped, for the woman's head had fallen back, and she had fainted. She could not bear to hear what I had to say to her. What a glow of satisfaction it gives me to think that, come what may, in the future she can never misunderstand my true feelings toward her! But what will occur in the future? What will she do next? I dare not think of it. Oh, if only I could hope that she will leave me alone! But when I think of what I said to her— Never mind: I have been stronger than she for once.

April 12th.—I hardly slept last night and found myself in the morning so unstrung and feverish that I was compelled to ask Pratt-Haldane to do my lecture for me. It is the first I have ever missed. I rose at midday, but my head is aching, my hands quivering, and my nerves in a pitiable state.

Who should come round this evening but Wilson! He has just come back from London, where he has lectured, read papers, convened meetings, exposed a medium, conducted a series of experiments on thought transference, entertained Professor Richet of Paris, spent hours gazing into a crystal, and obtained some evidence as to the passage of matter through matter. All this he poured into my ears in a single gust.

"But you?" he cried at last. "You are not looking well. And Miss Penclosa is quite prostrated today. How about the experiments?"

"I have abandoned them."

"Tut, tut! Why?"

"The subject seems to me to be a dangerous one."

Out came his big brown notebook.

"This is of great interest," said he. "What are your grounds for saying that it is a dangerous one? Please give me your facts in chronological order, with approximate dates, and names of reliable witnesses, with their permanent addresses."

"First of all," I asked, "would you tell me whether you have collected any cases where the mesmerist has gained a command over the subject and has used it for evil purposes?"

"Dozens!" he cried, exultantly. "Crime by suggestion——"

"I don't mean suggestion. I mean where a sudden impulse comes from a person at a distance—an uncontrollable impulse."

"Obsession!" he shrieked, in an ecstasy of delight. "It is the rarest condition. We have eight cases, five well attested. You don't mean to say——" his exultation made him hardly articulate.

"No, I don't," said I. "Good evening. You will excuse me, but I am not very well tonight." And so at last I got rid of him, still brandishing his pencil and his notebook. My troubles may be hard to bear, but at least it is better to hug them to myself than to have myself exhibited by Wilson like a freak at a fair. He has lost sight of human beings. Everything to him is a case and a phenomenon. I will die before I speak to him again upon the matter.

April 14th.—My nerves have quite recovered their tone. I really believe that I have conquered the creature. But I must confess to living in some suspense. She is well again, for I hear that she was driving with Mrs. Wilson in the High Street in the afternoon.

April 15th.—I do wish I could get away from the place altogether. I shall fly to Agatha's side the very day that the term closes. I suppose it is pitiably weak of me, but this woman gets upon my nerves most terribly. I have seen her again, and I have spoken with her.

It was just after lunch, and I was smoking a cigarette in my study, when I heard the step of my servant Murray in the passage. I was languidly conscious that a second step was audible behind, and had hardly troubled myself to speculate who it might be, when suddenly a slight noise brought me out of my chair with my skin creeping with apprehension. I had never particularly observed before what sort of sound the tapping of a crutch was, but my quivering nerves told me that I heard it now in the sharp wooden clacks which alternated with the muffled thud of the foot fall. Another instant and my servant had shown her in.

I did not attempt the usual conventions of society, nor did she. I simply stood with the smoldering cigarette in my hand and gazed at her. She in turn looked silently at me, and at her look I remembered how in these very pages I had tried to define the expression of her eyes, whether they were furtive or fierce. Today they were fierce, coldly and inexorably so.

"Well," said she at last, "are you still of the same mind as when I saw you last?"

"I have always been of the same mind."

"Let us understand each other, Professor Gilroy," said she slowly. "I am not a very safe person to trifle with, as you should realize by now. It was you who asked me to enter into a series of experiments with you, it was you who won my affections, it was you who professed your love for me, it was you who brought me your own photograph with words of affection upon it, and finally, it was you who on the very same evening thought fit to insult me most outrageously, addressing me as no man has ever dared to speak to me yet. Tell me that those words came from you in a moment of passion, and I am prepared to forget and to forgive them. You did not mean what you said, Austin. You do not really hate me?"

I might have pitied this deformed woman—such a longing for love broke suddenly through the menace of her eyes. But then I thought of what I had gone through and my heart set like flint.

"If ever you heard me speak of love," said I, "you knew very well that it was your voice which spoke, and not mine. The only words of truth which I have ever been able to say to you are those which you heard when last we met."

"I know. Someone has set you against me. It was he." She tapped with her crutch upon the floor. "Well, you know very well that I could bring you this instant crouching like a spaniel to my feet. You will not find me again in my hour of weakness when you can insult me with impunity. Have a care what you are doing, Professor Gilroy. You stand in a terrible position. You have not yet really felt the hold which I have upon you."

I shrugged my shoulders and turned away.

"Well," said she, after a pause, "if you despise my love I must see what can be done with fear. You smile, but the day will come when you will come screaming to me for pardon. Yes, you will grovel on the ground before me, proud as you are, and you will curse the day that ever you turned me from your best friend into your most bitter enemy. Have a care, Professor Gilroy." I saw a white hand shaking in the air, and a face which was scarcely human, so convulsed was it with passion. An instant later she was gone, and I heard the quick hobble and tap receding down the passage.

But she has left a weight upon my heart. Vague presentiments of coming misfortune lie heavily upon me. I try in vain to persuade myself that these are only words of empty anger. I can remember those relentless eyes too clearly to think so. What shall I do?—ah, what shall I do? I am no longer master of my own soul. At any moment this loathsome parasite may creep into me, and then—? I must tell someone of my hideous secret—I must tell it or go mad. If I had someone to sympathize and advise! Wilson is out of the question. Charles Sadler would understand me only so far as his own experience carries him. Pratt-Haldane! he is a well-balanced man, a man of great common sense and resource. I will go to him. I will tell him everything. God grant that he may be able to advise me!

6:45 P.M.—No, it is useless. There is no human help for me. I must fight this out single-handed. Two courses lie before me. I might become this woman's lover. Or I must endure such persecutions as she can inflict upon me. Even if none come, I shall live in a hell of apprehension. But she may torture me, she may drive me mad, she may kill me—I will never, never, never give in. What can she inflict which would be worse than the loss of Agatha, and the knowledge that I am a perjured liar and have forfeited the name of gentleman?

Pratt-Haldane was most amiable, and listened with all politeness to my story. But when I looked at his heavy-set features, his slow eyes, and the ponderous study furniture which surrounded him, I could hardly tell him what I had come to say. It was all so substantial, so material. And besides, what would I myself have said, a short month ago, if one of my colleagues had come to me with a story of demoniac possession. Perhaps I should have been less patient than he was. As it was, he took notes of my statement, asked me how much tea I drink, how many hours I slept, whether I had been overworking much, had I had sudden pains in the head, evil dreams, singing in the ears, flashes before the eyes—all questions which pointed to his belief that brain congestion was at the bottom of my trouble. Finally he dismissed me with a great many platitudes about open-air exercise and avoidance of nervous excitement. His prescription, which was for chloral and bromide, I rolled up and threw into the gutter.

No, I can look for no help from any human being. If I consult any more, they may put their heads together, and I may find myself in an asylum. I can but grip my courage with both hands and pray that an honest man may not be abandoned.

April 15th.—It is the sweetest spring within the memory of man—so green, so mild, so beautiful! Ah, what a contrast between nature without, and my own soul so torn with doubt and terror! It has been an uneventful day, but I know that I am on the edge of an abyss. I know it, and yet I go on with the routine of my life. The one bright spot is that Agatha is happy and well, and out of all danger. If this creature had a hand on each of us, what might she not do?

April 16th.—The woman is ingenious in her torments. She knows how fond I am of my work, and how highly my lectures are thought of. So it is from that point that she now attacks me. It will end, I can see, in my losing my professorship, but I will fight it to the finish. She shall not drive me out of it without a struggle.

I was not conscious of any change during my lecture this morning save that for a minute or two I had a dizziness and swimminess, which rapidly passed away. On the contrary, I congratulated myself upon having made my subject (the functions of the red corpuscles) both interesting and clear. I was surprised, therefore, when a student came into my laboratory immediately after the lecture and complained of being puzzled by the discrepancy between my statements and those in the textbooks. He showed me his notebook, in which I was reported as having in one portion of the lecture championed the most outrageous and unscientific heresies. Of course, I denied it, and declared that he had misunderstood me; but on comparing his notes with those of his companions, it became clear that he was right, and that I really had made some most preposterous statements. Of course, I shall explain it away as being the result of a moment of aberration, but I feel only too sure that it will be the first of a series. It is but a month now to the end of the session, and I pray that I may be able to hold out till then.

April 26th.—Ten days have elapsed since I have had the heart to make any entry in my journal. Why should I record my own humiliation and degradation? I had vowed never to open it again. And yet the force of habit is strong, and here I find myself taking up once more the record of my own dreadful experiences—in much the same spirit in which a suicide has been known to take notes of the effects of the poison which killed him.

Well, the crash which I had foreseen has come—and that no further back than yesterday. The university authorities have taken my lecture-ship from me. It has been done in the most delicate way, purporting to be a temporary measure to relieve me from the effects of overwork, and to give me the opportunity of recovering my health. Nonetheless it has been done, and I am no longer Professor Gilroy. The laboratory is still in my charge, but I have little doubt that that also will soon go.

The fact is that my lectures had become the laughingstock of the university. My class was crowded with students who came to see and hear what the eccentric professor would do or say next. I cannot go into the detail of my humiliation. Oh, that devilish woman! There is no depth of buffoonery and imbecility to which she has not forced me. I would begin my lecture clearly and well—but always with a sense of a coming eclipse. Then, as I felt the influence, I would struggle against it, striving with clinched hands and beads of sweat upon my brow to get the better of it, while the students, hearing my incoherent words and watching my contortions, would roar with laughter at the antics of their professor. And then, when she had once fairly mastered me, out would come the most outrageous things: silly jokes, sentiments as though I were proposing a toast, snatches of ballads, personal abuse even against some member of my class. And then, in a moment my brain would clear again, and my lecture would proceed decorously to the end. No wonder that my conduct has been the talk of colleges! No wonder that the university senate has been compelled to take official notice of such a scandal! Oh, that devilish woman!

And the most dreadful part of it all is my own loneliness. Here I sit in a commonplace English bow window looking out upon a common-place English street, with its garish 'buses and its lounging policeman, and behind me there hangs a shadow which is out of all keeping with the age and place. In the home of knowledge I am weighed down and tortured by a power of which science knows nothing. No magistrate would listen to me. No paper would discuss my case. No doctor would believe my symptoms. My own most intimate friends would only look upon it as a sign of brain derangement. I am out of all touch with my kind. Oh, that devilish woman! Let her have a care! She may push me too far. When the law cannot help a man, he may make a law for himself.

She met me in the High Street yesterday evening and spoke to me. It was as well for her perhaps that it was not between the hedges of a lonely country road. She asked me with her cold smile whether I had been chastened yet. I did not deign to answer her. "We must try another turn of the screw," said she. Have a care, my lady—have a care! I had her at my mercy once. Perhaps another chance may come.

April 28th.—The suspension of my lectureship has had the effect also of taking away her means of annoying me, and so I have enjoyed two blessed days of peace. After all, there is no reason to despair. Sympathy pours in to me from all sides, and every one agrees that it is my devotion to science and the arduous nature of my researches which have shaken my nervous system. I have had the kindest message from the council, advising me to travel abroad, and expressing the confident hope that I may be able to resume all my duties by the beginning of the summer term. Nothing could be more flattering than their allusions to my career and to my services to the university. It is only in misfortune that one can test one's own popularity. This creature may weary of tormenting me, and then all may yet be well. May God grant it!

April 29th.—Our sleepy little town has had a small sensation. The only knowledge of crime which we ever have is when a rowdy undergraduate breaks a few lamps or comes to blows with a policeman. Last night, however, there was an attempt to break into the branch of the Bank of England, and we are all in a flutter in consequence.

Parkenson the manager is an intimate friend of mine, and I found him very much excited when I walked round there after breakfast. Had the thieves broken into the countinghouse they would still have had the safes to reckon with, so that the defence was considerably stronger than the attack. Indeed, the latter does not appear to have been very formidable. Two of the lower windows have marks as if a chisel or some such instrument had been pushed under them to force them open. The police should have a good clue, for the woodwork had been done with green paint only the day before, and from the smears it is evident that some of it has found its way onto the criminal's hands or clothes.

4:30 P.M.—Ah, that accursed woman! That thrice-accursed woman! Never mind! She shall not beat me! No, she shall not! But oh, the she-devil! She has taken my professorship. Now she would take my honor. Is there nothing I can do against her, nothing save— Ah, but hard pushed as I am, I cannot bring myself to think of that!

It was about an hour ago that I went into my bedroom, and was brushing my hair before the glass, when suddenly my eyes lit upon something which left me so sick and cold that I sat down upon the edge of the bed and began to cry. It is many a long year since I shed tears, but all my nerve was gone, and I could but sob and sob in impotent grief and anger. There was my house jacket, the coat I usually wear after dinner, hanging on its peg by the wardrobe, with the right sleeve thickly crusted from wrist to elbow with daubs of green paint.

So this was what she meant by another turn of the screw! She had made a public imbecile of me. Now she would brand me as a criminal. This time she has failed. But how about the next? I dare not think of it— and of Agatha and my poor old mother! I wish that I were dead!

Yes, this is the other turn of the screw. And this is also what she meant, no doubt, when she said that I had not realized yet the power she has over me. I look back at my account of my conversation with her, and I see how she declared that with a slight exertion of her will her subject would be conscious, and with a stronger one unconscious. Last night I was unconscious. I could have sworn I slept soundly in my bed without so much as a dream. And yet those stains tell me that I dressed, made my way out, attempted to open the bank windows, and returned. Was I observed? Is it possible that someone saw me do it and followed me home? Ah, what a hell my life has become! I have no peace, no rest. But my patience is nearing its end.

10 P.M.—I have cleaned my coat with turpentine. I do not think that any one could have seen me. It was with my screwdriver that I made the marks. I found it all crusted with paint, and I have cleaned it. My head aches as if it would burst, and I have taken five grains of antipyrine. If it were not for Agatha, I should have taken fifty and had an end of it.

May 3rd.—Three quiet days. This hell fiend is like a cat with a mouse. She lets me loose only to pounce upon me again. I am never so frightened as when everything is still. My physical state is deplorable— perpetual hiccough and ptosis of the left eyelid.

I have heard from the Mardens that they will be back the day after tomorrow. I do not know whether I am glad or sorry. They were safe in London. Once here, they may be drawn into the miserable network in which I am myself struggling. And I must tell them of it. I cannot marry Agatha so long as I know that I am not responsible for my own actions. Yes, I must tell them, even if it brings everything to an end between us.

Tonight is the university ball, and I must go. God knows I never felt less in the humor for festivity, but I must not have it said that I am unfit to appear in public. If I am seen there, and have speech with some of the elders of the university, it will go a long way toward showing them that it would be unjust to take my chair away from me.

11:30 P.M.—I have been to the ball. Charles Sadler and I went together, but I have come away before him. I shall wait up for him, however, for, indeed, I fear to go to sleep these nights. He is a cheery, practical fellow, and a chat with him will steady my nerves. On the whole, the evening was a great success. I talked to everyone who has influence, and I think that I made them realize that my chair is not vacant quite yet. The creature was at the ball—unable to dance, of course, but sitting with Mrs. Wilson. Again and again her eyes rested upon me. They were almost the last things I saw before I left the room. Once as I sat sideways to her I watched her, and saw that her gaze was following someone else. It was Sadler, who was dancing at the time with the second Miss Thurston. To judge by her expression, it is well for him that he is not in her grip as I am. He does not know the escape he has had. I think I hear his step in the street now, and I will go down and let him in. If he will—

May 4th.—Why did I break off in this way last night? I never went downstairs after all—at least, I have no recollection of doing so. But, on the other hand, I cannot remember going to bed. One of my hands is greatly swollen this morning, and yet I have no remembrance of injuring it yesterday. Otherwise, I am feeling all the better for last night's festivity. But I cannot understand how it is that I did not meet Charles Sadler when I so fully intended to do so. Is it possible—my God, it is only too probable! Has she been leading me in some devil's dance again? I will go down to Sadler and ask him.

Midday.—The thing has come to a crisis. My life is not worth living. But, if I am to die, then she shall come also. I will not leave her behind to drive some other man mad as she has me. No, I have come to the limit of my endurance. She has made me as desperate and dangerous a man as walks the earth. God knows I have never had the heart to hurt a fly, and yet if I had my hands now upon that woman she should never leave this room alive. I shall see her this very day, and she shall learn what she has to expect from me.

I went to Sadler, and found him to my surprise in bed. As I entered he sat up and turned a face toward me which sickened me as I looked at it.

"Why, Sadler, what has happened?" I cried, but my heart turned cold as I said it.

"Gilroy," he answered, mumbling with his swollen lips, "I have for some weeks been under the impression that you are a madman. Now I know it, and that you are a dangerous one as well. If it were not that I am unwilling to make a scandal in the college, you would now be in the hands of the police."

"Do you mean——" I cried.

"I mean that as I opened the door last night you rushed out upon me, struck me with both of your fists in the face, knocked me down, kicked me furiously in the side, and left me lying almost unconscious in the street. Look at your own hand bearing witness against you."

Yes, there it was, puffed up with spongelike knuckles as after some terrific blow. What could I do? Though he put me down as a madman, I must tell him all. I sat by his bed, and went over all my troubles from the beginning. I poured them out with quivering hands and burning words, which might have carried conviction to the most skeptical.

"She hates you and she hates me," I cried. "She revenged herself last night on both of us at once. She saw me leave the ball, and she must have seen you also. She knew how long it would take you to reach home. Then she had but to use her wicked will. Ah, your bruised face is a small thing beside my bruised soul!"

He was struck by my story. That was evident. "Yes, yes; she watched me out of the room," he muttered. "She is capable of it. But is it possible that she has really reduced you to this? What do you intend to do?"

"To stop it," I cried. "I am perfectly desperate; I shall give her fair warning today, and the next time will be the last."

"Do nothing rash," said he.

"Rash!" I cried. "The only rash thing is that I should postpone it another hour." With that I rushed to my room, and here I am on the eve of what may be the great crisis of my life. I shall start at once. I have gained one thing today, for I have made one man, at least, realize the truth of this monstrous experience of mine. And, if the worst should happen, this diary remains as proof of the good that has driven me.

Evening.—When I came to Wilson's I was shown up, and found that he was sitting with Miss Penclosa. For half an hour I had to endure his fussy talk about his recent research into the exact nature of the spiritualistic rap, while the creature and I sat in silence looking across the room at each other. I read a sinister amusement in her eyes, and she must have seen hatred and menace in mine. I had almost despaired of having speech with her, when he was called from the room and we were left for a few minutes together.

"Well, Professor Gilroy—or is it Mr. Gilroy?" said she, with that bitter smile of hers. "How is your friend Mr. Charles Sadler after the ball?"

"You fiend!" I cried. "You have come to the end of your tricks now. I will have no more of them. Listen to what I say"—I strode across and shook her roughly by the shoulder—"as sure as there is a God in heaven, I swear that if you try another of your devilries upon me I will have your life for it. Come what may, I will have your life. I have come to the end of what a man can endure."

"Accounts are not quite settled between us," said she, with a passion that equaled my own; "I can love and I can hate. You had your choice. You chose to spurn the first; now you must test the other. It will take a little more to break your spirit, I see, but broken it shall be. Miss Marden comes back tomorrow, as I understand."

"What has that to do with you?" I cried. "It is a pollution that you should dare even to think of her. If I thought that you would harm her—"

She was frightened, I could see, though she tried to brazen it out. She read the black thought in my mind, and cowered away from me.

"She is fortunate in having such a companion," said she. "He actually dares to threaten a lonely woman. I must really congratulate Miss Marden upon her protector."

The words were bitter, but the voice and manner were more acid still.

"There is no use talking," said I. "I only came here to tell you, and to tell you most solemnly, that your next outrage upon me will be your last." With that, as I heard Wilson's step upon the stair, I walked from the room. Ay, she may look venomous and deadly, but for all that, she is beginning to see now that she has as much to fear from me as I can have from her. Murder! It has an ugly sound. But you don't talk of murdering a snake or of murdering a tiger. Let her have a care now.

May 5th.—I met Agatha and her mother at the station at eleven o'clock. She is looking so bright, so happy, so beautiful. And was so overjoyed to see me. What have I done to deserve such love! I went back home with them, and we lunched together. All the troubles seem in a moment to have been shredded back from my life. She tells me that I am looking pale and worried and ill. The dear child puts it down to my loneliness, and the perfunctory attentions of a housekeeper. I pray that she may never know the truth! May the shadow, if shadow there must be, lie ever black across my life, and leave hers in the sunshine! I have just come back from them, feeling a new man. With her by my side I think that I could show a bold face to anything which life might send.

5 P.M.—Now let me try to be accurate. Let me try to say exactly how it occurred. It is fresh in my mind, and I can set it down correctly, though it is not likely that the time will ever come when I shall forget the doings of today.

I had returned from the Mardens' after lunch, and was cutting some microscopic sections in my freezing microtome when in an instant I lost consciousness in the sudden hateful fashion which has become only too familiar to me of late.

When my senses came back to me I was sitting in a small chamber, very different from the one in which I had been working. It was cozy and bright, with chintz-covered settees, colored hangings, and a thousand pretty little trifles upon the wall. A small ornamental clock ticked in front of me, and the hands pointed to half past three. It was all quite familiar to me, and yet I stared about for a moment in a half-dazed way until my eyes fell upon a cabinet photograph of myself upon the top of the piano. On the other side stood one of Mrs. Marden. Then, of course, I remembered where I was. It was Agatha's boudoir.

But how came I there, and what did I want? A horrible sinking came to my heart. Had I been sent here on some devilish errand? Had the errand already been done? Surely it must, otherwise why should I be allowed to come back to consciousness? Oh, the agony of that moment! What had I done? I sprang to my feet in my despair, and as I did so a small glass bottle fell from my knees on to the carpet.

It was unbroken, and I picked it up. Outside was written "Sulphuric Acid, Fort." When I drew the round glass stopper a thick fume rose slowly up, and a pungent, choking smell pervaded the room. I recognized it as one which I kept for chemical testing in my chambers. But why had I brought a bottle of vitriol into Agatha's chamber? Was it not this thick reeking liquid with which jealous women had been known to mar the beauty of their rivals? My heart stood still as I held the bottle to the light. Thank God, it was full! No mischief had been done as yet. But had Agatha come in a minute sooner, was it not certain that the hellish parasite within me would have dashed the stuff onto her? Ah, it will not bear to be thought of. But it must have been for that. Why else should I have brought it? At the thought of what I might have done my worn nerves broke down, and I sat shivering and twitching, the pitiable wreck of a man.

It was the sound of Agatha's voice and the rustle of her dress which restored me. I looked up and saw her blue eyes, so full of tenderness and pity, gazing down at me.

"We must take you away to the country, Austin," she said. "You want rest and quiet. You look wretchedly ill."

"Oh, it is nothing," said I, trying to smile. "It was only a momentary weakness. I am all right again now."

"I am sorry to keep you waiting. Poor boy, you must have been here for quite half an hour! The vicar was in the drawing room, and as I knew that you did not care for him I thought it better that Jane should show you up here. I thought the man would never go."

"Thank God he stayed!—thank God he stayed!" I cried, hysterically.

"Why, what is the matter with you, Austin?" she asked, holding my arm as I staggered up from the chair. "Why are you glad that the vicar stayed? And what is this little bottle in your hand?"

"Nothing," I cried, thrusting it into my pocket. "But I must go. I have something important to do."

"How stern you look, Austin. I have never seen your face like that. You are angry?"

"Yes, I am angry."

"But not with me?"

"No, no, my darling. You would not understand."

"But you have not told me why you came."

"I came to ask you whether you would always love me—no matter what I did or what shadow might fall on my name. Would you believe in me and trust me, however black appearances might be against me?"

"You know I would, Austin."

"Yes, I know that you would. What I do I shall do for you. I am driven to it. There is no other way out, my darling!" I kissed her and rushed from the room.

The time for indecision was at an end. As long as the creature threatened my own prospects and my honor there might be a question as to what I should do. But now when Agatha—my innocent Agatha— was endangered, my duty lay before me like a turnpike road. I had no weapon, but I never paused for that. What weapon should I need, when I felt every muscle quivering with the strength of a frenzied man? I ran through the streets so set upon what I had to do that I was only dimly conscious of the faces of friends whom I met—dimly conscious also that Professor Wilson met me, running with equal precipitance in the opposite direction. Breathless but resolute I reached the house and rang the bell. A white-cheeked maid opened the door, and turned whiter yet when she saw the face that looked in at her.

"Show me up at once to Miss Penclosa," I demanded.

"Sir," she gasped, "Miss Penclosa died this afternoon at half past three."

OUR MIDNIGHT VISITOR

On the western side of the island of Arran, seldom visited, and almost unknown to tourists, is the little island named Uffa. Between the two lies a strait or roost, two miles and a half broad, with a dangerous current which sets in from the north. Even on the calmest day there are ripples, and swirls, and dimples on the surface of the roost, which suggest hidden influences, but when the wind blows from the west, and the great Atlantic waves choke up the inlet and meet their brethren which have raced round the other side of the island, there is such seething and turmoil that old sailors say they have never seen the like. God help the boat that is caught there on such a day!

My father owned one third part of the island of Uffa, and I was born and bred there. Our farm or croft was a small one enough, for if a good thrower were to pick up a stone on the shore at Carracuil (which was our place) he could manage, in three shies, to clear all our arable land, and it was hardly longer than it was broad. Behind this narrow track, on which we grew corn and potatoes, was the homesteading of Carracuil—a rather bleak-looking gray stone house with a red-tiled byre buttressed against one side of it, and behind this again the barren undulating moorland stretched away up to Beh-na-sacher and Beg-na-phail, two rugged knowes which marked the center of the island. We had grazing ground for a couple of cows, and eight or ten sheep, and we had our boat anchored down in Carravoe. When the fishing failed, there was more time to devote to the crops, and if the season was bad, as likely as not the herring would be thick on the coast. Taking one thing with another a crofter in Uffa had as much chance of laying by a penny or two as most men on the mainland.

Besides our own family, the McDonalds of Carracuil, there were two others on the island. These were the Gibbs of Arden and the Fullartons of Corriemains. There was no priority claimed among us, for none had any legend of the coming of the others. We had all three held our farms by direct descent for many generations, paying rent to the Duke of Hamilton and all prospering in a moderate way. My father had been enabled to send me to begin the study of medicine at the University of Glasgow, and I had attended lectures there for two winter sessions, but whether from caprice or from some lessening in his funds, he had recalled me, and in the year 1865 I found myself cribbed up in this island with just education enough to wish for more, and with no associate at home but the grim, stern old man, for my mother had been dead some years, and I had neither brother nor sister.

There were two youths about my own age in the island, Geordie and Jock Gibbs, but they were rough, loutish fellows, good-hearted enough, but with no ideas above fishing and farming. More to my taste was the society of Minnie Fullarton, the pretty daughter of old Fullarton of Corriemains. We had been children together, and it was natural that when she blossomed into a buxom, fresh-faced girl, and I into a square-shouldered, long-legged youth there should be something warmer than friendship between us. Her elder brother was a corn chandler in Ardrossan, and was said to be doing well, so that the match was an eligible one, but for some reason my father objected very strongly to our intimacy and even forbade me entirely to meet her. I laughed at his commands, for I was a hot-headed, irreverent youngster, and continued to see Minnie, but when it came to his ears, it caused many violent scenes between us, which nearly went the length of blows. We had a quarrel of this sort just before the equinoctial gales in the spring of the year in which my story begins, and I left the old man with his face flushed, and his great bony hands shaking with passion, while I went jauntily off to our usual trysting place. I have often regretted since that I was not more submissive, but how was I to guess the dark things which were to come upon us?

I can remember that day well. Many bitter thoughts rose in my heart as I strode along the narrow pathway, cutting savagely at the thistles on either side with my stick. One side of our little estate was bordered by the Combera cliffs, which rose straight out of the water to the height of a couple of hundred feet. The top of these cliffs was covered with green sward and commanded a noble view on every side. I stretched myself on the turf there and watched the breakers dancing over the Winners sands and listened to the gurgling of the water down beneath me in the caves of Combera. We faced the western side of the island, and from where I lay I could see the whole stretch of the Irish Sea, right across to where a long hazy line upon the horizon marked the northern coast of the sister isle. The wind was blowing freshly from the northwest and the great Atlantic rollers were racing merrily in, one behind the other, dark brown below, light green above, and breaking with a sullen roar at the base of the cliffs. Now and again a sluggish one would be overtaken by its successor, and the two would come crashing in together and send the spray right over me as I lay. The whole air was prickly with the smack of the sea. Away to the north there was a piling up of clouds, and the peak of Goatfell in Arran looked lurid and distinct. There were no craft in the offing except one little eager, panting steamer making for the shelter of the Clyde, and a trim brigantine tacking along the coast. I was speculating as to her destination when I heard a light spring footstep, and Minnie Fullarton was standing beside me, her face rosy with exercise and her brown hair floating behind her.

"Wha's been vexing you, Archie?" she asked with the quick intuition of womanhood. "The auld man has been speaking aboot me again; has he no'?"

It was strange how pretty and mellow the accents were in her mouth which came so raspingly from my father. We sat down on a little green hillock together, her hand in mine, while I told her of our quarrel in the morning.

"You see they're bent on parting us," I said; "but indeed they'll find they have the wrong man to deal with if they try to frighten me away from you."

"I'm no' worth it, Archie," she answered, sighing. "I'm ower hamely and simple for one like you that speaks well and is a scholar forbye."

"You're too good and true for any one, Minnie," I answered, though in my heart I thought there was some truth in what she said.

"I'll no' trouble anyone lang," she continued, looking earnestly into my face. "I got my call last night; I saw a ghaist, Archie."

"Saw a ghost!" I ejaculated.

"Yes, and I doubt it was a call for me. When my cousin Steevie deed he saw one the same way."

"Tell me about it, dear," I said, impressed by her solemnity.

"There's no' much to tell: it was last nicht aboot twelve, or maybe one o'clock. I was lying awake thinking o' this and that wi' my een fixed on the window. Suddenly I saw a face looking in at me through the glass—an awfu'like face, Archie. It was na the face of anyone on the island. I canna tell what it was like—it was just awfu'. It was there maybe a minute looking tae way and tither into the room. I could see the glint o' his very een—for it was a man's face—and his nose was white where it was pressed against the glass. My very blood ran cauld and I couldna scream for fright. Then it went awa' as quickly and as sudden as it came."

"Who could it have been?" I exclaimed.

"A wraith or a bogle," said Minnie positively.

"Are you sure it wasn't Tommy Gibbs?" I suggested.

"Na, na, it wasna Tammy. It was a dark, hard, dour sort of face."

"Well," I said, laughing, "I hope the fellow will give me a look up, whoever he is. I'll soon learn who he is and where he comes from. But we won't talk of it, or you'll be frightening yourself tonight again. It'll be a dreary night as it is."

"A bad night for the puir sailors," she answered sadly, glancing at the dark wrack hurrying up from the northward, and at the white line of breakers on the Winners sands. "I wonder what yon brig is after! Unless it gets roond to Lamlash or Brodick Bay, it'll find itself on a nasty coast."

She was watching the trim brigantine which had already attracted my attention. She was still standing off the coast, and evidently expected rough weather, for her foresail had been taken in and her topsail reefed down.

"It's too cold for you up here!" I exclaimed at last, as the clouds covered the sun, and the keen north wind came in more frequent gusts. We walked back together, until we were close to Carracuil, when she left me, taking the footpath to Corriemains, which was about a mile from our bothy. I hoped that my father had not observed us together, but he met me at the door, fuming with passion. His face was quite livid with rage, and he held his shotgun in his hands. I forget if I mentioned that in spite of his age he was one of the most powerful men I ever met in my life.

"So you've come!" he roared, shaking the gun at me. "You great gowk—" I did not wait for the string of adjectives which I knew was coming.

"You keep a civil tongue in your head," I said.

"You dare!" he shouted, raising his arm as if to strike me. "You wunna come in here. You can gang back where you come frae!"

"You can go to the devil!" I answered, losing my temper completely, on which he jabbed at me with the butt end of the gun, but I warded it off with my stick. For a moment the devil was busy in me, and my throat was full of oaths, but I choked them down, and, turning on my heel, walked back to Corriemains, where I spent the day with the Fullartons. It seemed to me that my father, who had long been a miser, was rapidly becoming a madman—and a dangerous one to boot.

My mind was so busy with my grievance that I was poor company, I fear, and drank perhaps more whisky than was good for me. I remember that I stumbled over a stool once and that Minnie looked surprised and tearful, while old Fullarton sniggered to himself and coughed to hide it. I did not set out for home till half past nine, which was a very late hour for the island. I knew my father would be asleep, and that if I climbed through my bedroom window I should have one night in peace.

It was blowing great guns by this time, and I had put my shoulder against the gale as I came along the winding path which led down to Carracuil. I must still have been under the influence of liquor, for I remember that I sang uproariously and joined my feeble pipe to the howling of the wind. I had just got to the enclosure of our croft when a little incident occurred which helped to sober me.

White is a color so rare in nature that in an island like ours, where even paper was a precious commodity, it would arrest the attention at once. Something white fluttered across my path and stuck flapping upon a furze bush. I lifted it up and discovered, to my very great surprise, that it was a linen pocket-handkerchief—and scented. Now I was very sure that beyond my own there was no such thing as a white pocket-handkerchief in the island. A small community like ours knew each other's wardrobes to a nicety. But as to scent in Uffa—it was preposterous! Who did the handkerchief belong to then? Was Minnie right, and was there really a stranger in the island? I walked on very thoughtfully, holding my discovery in my hand and thinking of what Minnie had seen the night before.

When I got into my bedroom and lit my rushlight I examined it again. It was clean and new, with the initials A. W. worked in red silk in the corner. There was no other indication as to who it might belong to, though from its size it was evidently a man's. The incident struck me as so extraordinary that I sat for some time on the side of my bed turning it

over in my befuddled mind, but without getting any nearer a conclusion. I might even have taken my father into confidence, but his hoarse
snoring in the adjoining room showed that he was fast asleep. It is as well
that it was so, for I was in no humor to be bullied, and we might have
had words. The old man had little longer to live, and it is some solace to
me now that that little was unmarred by any further strife between us.

I did not take my clothes off, for my brain was getting swimmy after
its temporary clearness, so I dropped my head upon the pillow and sank
into profound slumber. I must have slept about four hours when I woke
with a violent start. To this day I have never known what it was that
roused me. Everything was perfectly still, and yet I found all my faculties
in a state of extreme tension. Was there someone in the room? It was
very dark, but I peered about, leaning on my elbow. There was nothing
to be seen, but still that eerie feeling haunted me. At that moment the
flying scud passed away from the face of the moon and a flood of cold
light was poured into my chamber. I turned my eyes up instinctively,
and—good God!—there at the window was the face, an evil, malicious
face, hard-cut, and distinct against the silvery radiance, glaring in at me
as Minnie had seen it the night before. For one moment I tingled and
palpitated like a frightened child, the next both glass and sash were gone
and I was rolling over and over on the gravel path with my arms round
a tall strong man—the two of us worrying each other like a pair of dogs.
Almost by intuition I knew as we went down together that he had
slipped his hand into his side pocket, and I clung to that wrist like grim
death. He tried hard to free it but I was too strong for him, and we
staggered on to our feet again in the same position, panting and snarling.

"Let go my hand, damn you!" he said.

"Let go the pistol then," I gasped.

We looked hard at each other in the moonlight and then he laughed
and opened his fingers. A heavy glittering object, which I could see was
a revolver, dropped with a clink on to the gravel. I put my foot on it and
let go my grip of him.

"Well, matey, how now?" he said with another laugh. "Is that an end
of a round, or the end of the battle? You islanders seem a hospitable lot.
You're so ready to welcome a stranger, that you can't wait to find the
door, but must come flying through the window like infernal fire-
works."

"What do you want to come prowling round people's houses at night
for, with weapons in your pocket?" I asked sternly.

"I should think I needed a weapon," he answered, "when there are young devils like you knocking around. Hullo! here's another of the family."

I turned my head, and there was my father, almost at my elbow. He had come round from the front door. His gray woolen nightdress and grizzled hair were streaming in the wind, and he was evidently much excited. He had in his hand the double-barreled gun with which he had threatened me in the morning. He put this to his shoulder, and would most certainly have blown out either my brains or those of the stranger, had I not turned away the barrel with my hand.

"Wait a bit, father," I said, "let us hear what he has to say for himself. And you," I continued, turning to the stranger, "can come inside with us and justify yourself if you can. But remember we are in a majority, so keep your tongue between your teeth."

"Not so fast, my young bantam," he grumbled; "you've got my six-shooter, but I have a Derringer in my pocket. I learned in Colorado to carry them both. However, come along into this shanty of yours, and let us get the damned palaver over. I'm wet through, and most infernally hungry."

My father was still mumbling to himself, and fidgeting with his gun, but he did not oppose my taking the stranger into the house. I struck a match, and lit the oil lamp in the kitchen, on which our prisoner stooped down to it and began smoking a cigarette. As the light fell full on his face, both my father and I took a good look at him. He was a man of about forty, remarkably handsome, of rather a Spanish type, with blue-black hair and beard, and sunburned features. His eyes were very bright, and their gaze so intense that you would think they projected somewhat, unless you saw him in profile. There was a dash of recklessness and devilry about them, which, with his wiry, powerful frame and jaunty manner, gave the impression of a man whose past had been an adventurous one. He was elegantly dressed in a velveteen jacket, and grayish trousers of a foreign cut. Without in the least resenting our prolonged scrutiny, he seated himself upon the dresser, swinging his legs, and blowing little blue wreaths from his cigarette. His appearance seemed to reassure my father, or perhaps it was the sight of the rings which flashed on the stranger's left hand every time he raised it to his lips.

"Ye munna mind Archie, sir," he said in a cringing voice. "He was aye a fashious bairn, ower quick wi' his hands, and wi' mair muscle than brains. I was fashed mysel' wi' the sudden stour, but as tae shootin' at ye, sir, that was a' an auld man's havers. Nae doobt ye're a veesitor, or maybe it's a shipwreck—it's no a shipwreck, is't?" The idea awoke the covetous devil in my father's soul, and it looked out through his glistening eyes, and set his long stringy hands a-shaking.

"I came here in a boat," said the stranger shortly. "This was the first house I came to after I left the shore, and I'm not likely to forget the reception you have given me. That young hopeful of yours has nearly broken my back."

"A good job too!" I interrupted hotly, "why couldn't you come up to the door like a man, instead of skulking at the window?"

"Hush, Archie, hush!" said my father imploringly; while our visitor grinned across at me as amicably as if my speech had been most conciliatory.

"I don't blame you," he said—he spoke with a strange mixture of accents, sometimes with a foreign lisp, sometimes with a slight Yankee intonation, and at other times very purely indeed. "I have done the same, mate. Maybe you noticed a brigantine standing on and off the shore yesterday?"

I nodded my head.

"That was mine," he said. "I'm owner, skipper, and everything else. Why shouldn't a man spend his money in his own way? I like cruising about, and I like new experiences. I suppose there's no harm in that. I was in the Mediterranean last month, but I'm sick of blue skies and fine weather. Chios is a damnable paradise of a place. I've come up here for a little fresh air and freedom. I cruised all down the western isles, and when we came abreast of this place of yours it rather took my fancy, so I hauled the foreyard aback and came ashore last night to prospect. It wasn't this house I struck, but another farther to the west'ard; however, I saw enough to be sure it was a place after my own heart—a real quiet corner. So I went back and set everything straight aboard yesterday, and now here I am. You can put me up for a few weeks, I suppose. I'm not hard to please, and I can pay my way; suppose we say ten dollars a week for board and lodging, and a fortnight to be paid in advance."

He put his hand in his pocket and produced four shining napoleons, which he pushed along the dresser to my father, who grabbed them up eagerly.

"I'm sorry I gave such a rough reception," I said, rather awkwardly. "I was hardly awake at the time."

"Say no more, mate, say no more!" he shouted heartily, holding out his hand and clasping mine. "Hard knocks are nothing new to me. I suppose we may consider the bargain settled then?"

"Ye can bide as lang as ye wull, sir," answered my father, still fingering the four coins. "Archie and me'll do a' we can to mak' your veesit a pleasant ane. It's no' such a dreary place as ye might think. When the Lamlash boats come in we get the papers and a' the news."

It struck me that the stranger looked anything but overjoyed by this piece of information. "You don't mean to say that you get the papers here," he said.

"'Oo aye, the *Scotsman* an' the *Glasgey Herald*. But maybe you would like Archie and me to row ower to your ship in the morn, an' fetch your luggage."

"The brig is fifty miles away by this time," said our visitor. "She is running before the wind of Marseilles. I told the mate to bring her round again in a month or so. As to the luggage, I always travel light in that matter. If a man's purse is only full he can do with very little else. All I have is in a bundle under your window. By the way, my name is Digby—Charles Digby."

"I thought your initials were A. W.," I remarked.

He sprang off the dresser as if he had been stung, and his face turned quite gray for a moment. "What the devil do you mean by that?" he said.

"I thought this might be yours," I answered, handing him the handkerchief I had found.

"Oh, is that all!" he said with rather a forced laugh. "I didn't quite see what you were driving at. That's all right. It belongs to Whittingdale, my second officer. I'll keep it until I see him again. And now suppose you give me something to eat, for I'm about famished."

We brought him out such rough fare as was to be found in our larder, and he ate ravenously, and tossed off a stiff glass of whisky and water. Afterward my father showed him into the solitary spare bedroom, with which he professed himself well pleased, and we all settled down for the night. As I went back to my couch I noticed that the gale had freshened up, and I saw long streamers of seaweed flying past my broken window in the moonlight. A great bat fluttered into the room, which is reckoned a sure sign of misfortune in the islands—but I was never superstitious, and let the poor thing find its way out again unmolested.

In the morning it was still blowing a whole gale, though the sky was blue for the most part. Our guest was up betimes and we walked down to the beach together. It was a sight to see the great rollers sweeping in, overtopping one another like a herd of oxen, and then bursting with a roar, sending the Carracuil pebbles flying before them like grapeshot, and filling the whole air with drifting spume.

We were standing together watching the scene, when looking round I saw my father hurrying toward us. He had been up and out since early dawn. When he saw us looking, he began waving his hands and shouting, but the wind carried his voice away. We ran toward him however, seeing that he was heavy with news.

"The brig's wrecked, and they're a' drowned!" he cried as we met him.

"What!" roared our visitor.

If ever I heard exceedingly great joy compressed into a monosyllable it vibrated in that one.

"They're a' drowned and naething saved!" repeated my father. "Come yoursel' and see."

We followed him across the Combera to the level sands on the other side. They were strewn with wreckage, broken pieces of bulwark and handrail, paneling of a cabin, and an occasional cask. A single large spar was tossing in the waves close to the shore, occasionally shooting up toward the sky like some giant's javelin, then sinking and disappearing in the trough of the great scooping seas. Digby hurried up to the nearest pieces of timber, and stooping over it examined it intently.

"By God!" he said at last, taking in a long breath between his teeth, "you are right. It's the *Proserpine*, and all hands are lost. What a terrible thing!"

His face was very solemn as he spoke, but his eyes danced and glittered. I was beginning to conceive a great repugnance and distrust toward this man.

"Is there no chance of anyone having got ashore?" he said.

"Na, na, nor cargo neither," my father answered with real grief in his voice. "Ye dinna ken this coast. There's an awful undertow outside the Winners, and it's a' swept round to Holy Isle. De'il take it, if there was to be a shipwreck what for should they no' run their ship aground to the east'ard o' the point and let an honest mun have the pickings instead o' the rascally loons in Arran? An empty barrel might float in here, but there's no chance o' a seachest, let alane a body."

"Poor fellows!" said Digby. "But there—we must meet it some day, and why not here and now? I've lost my ship, but thank Heaven I can buy another. It is sad about them, though—very sad. I warned Lamarck that he was waiting too long with a low barometer and an ugly shore under his lee. He has himself to thank. He was my first officer, a prying, covetous, meddlesome hound."

"Don't call him names," I said. "He's dead."

"Well said, my young prig!" he answered. "Perhaps you wouldn't be so mealymouthed yourself if you lost five thousand pounds before breakfast. But there—there's no use crying over spilt milk. *Vogue la galère!* as the French say. Things are never so bad that they might be worse."

My father and Digby stayed at the scene of the wreck, but I walked over to Corriemains to reassure Minnie's mind as to the apparition at the window. Her opinion, when I had told her all, coincided with mine, that perhaps the crew of the brig knew more about the stranger than he cared for. We agreed that I should keep a close eye upon him without letting him know that he was watched.

"But oh, Archie," she said, "ye munna cross him or anger him while he carries them awfu' weapons. Ye maun be douce and saft, and no' gainsay him."

I laughed, and promised her to be very prudent, which reassured her a little. Old Fullarton walked back with me in the hope of picking a piece of timber, and both he and my father patroled the shore for many days, without, however, finding any prize of importance, for the undercurrent off the Winners was very strong, and everything had probably drifted right round to Lamlash Bay in Arran.

It was wonderful how quickly the stranger accommodated himself to our insular ways, and how useful he made himself about the homesteading. Within a fortnight he knew the island almost as well as I did myself. Had it not been for that one unpleasant recollection of the shipwreck which rankled in my remembrance, I could have found it in my heart to become fond of him. His nature was a tropical one—fiercely depressed at times, but sunny as a rule, bursting continually into jest and song from pure instinct, in a manner which is unknown among us Northerners. In his graver moments he was a most interesting companion, talking shrewdly and eloquently of men and manners, and his own innumerable and strange adventures. I have seldom heard a more brilliant conversationalist. Of an evening he would keep my father and myself spellbound by the kitchen fire for hours and hours, while he chatted away in a desultory fashion and smoked his cigarettes. It seemed to me that the packet he had brought with him on the first night must have consisted entirely of tobacco. I noticed that in these conversations, which were mostly addressed to my father, he used, unconsciously perhaps, to play upon the weak side of the old man's nature. Tales of cunning, of smartness, of various ways in which mankind had been cheated and money gained, came most readily to his lips, and were relished by an eager listener. I could not help one night remarking upon it, when my father had gone out of the room, laughing hoarsely, and vibrating with amusement over some story of how the Biscayan peasants will strap lanterns to a bullock's horns, and taking the beast some distance inland on a stormy night, will make it prance and rear so that the ships at sea may imagine it to be the lights of a vessel, and steer fearlessly in that direction, only to find themselves on a rockbound coast.

"You shouldn't tell such tales to an old man," I said.

"My dear fellow," he answered very kindly, "you have seen nothing of the world yet. You have formed fine ideas no doubt, and notions of delicacy and such things, and you are very dogmatic about them, as clever men of your age always are. I had notions of the right and wrong once, but it has been all knocked out of me. It's just a sort of varnish which the rough friction of the world soon rubs off. I started with a whole soul, but there are more gashes and seams and scars in it now than there are in my body, and that's pretty fair as you'll allow"—with which he pulled open his tunic and showed me his chest.

"Good heavens!" I said, "How on earth did you get those?"

"This was a bullet," he said, pointing to a deep bluish pucker underneath his collarbone. "I got it behind the barricades in Berlin in '48. Langenback said it just missed the subclavian artery. And this," he went on, indicating a pair of curious elliptical scars upon his throat, "was a bite from a Sioux chief, when I was under Custer on the plains—I've got an arrow wound on my leg from the same party. This is from a mutinous Lascar aboard ship, and the others are mere scratches— Californian vaccination marks. You can excuse my being a little ready with my own irons, though, when I've been dropped so often."

"What's this?" I asked, pointing to a little chamois leather bag which was hung by a strong cord round his neck. "It looks like a charm."

He buttoned up his tunic again hastily, looking extremely disconcerted. "It is nothing," he said brusquely. "I am a Roman Catholic, and it is what we call a scapular." I could hardly get another word out of him that night, and even next day he was reserved and appeared to avoid me. This little incident made me very thoughtful, the more so as I noticed shortly afterward when standing over him, that the string was no longer round his neck. Apparently he had taken it off after my remark about it.

What could there be in that leather bag which needed such secrecy and precaution! Had I but known it, I would sooner have put my left hand in the fire than have pursued that inquiry.

One of the peculiarities of our visitor was that in all his plans for the future, with which he often regaled us, he seemed entirely untrammeled by any monetary considerations. He would talk in the lightest and most offhand way of schemes which would involve the outlay of much wealth. My father's eyes would glisten as he heard him talk carelessly of sums which to our frugal minds appeared enormous. It seemed strange to both of us that a man who by his own confession had been a vagabond and adventurer all his life, should be in possession of such a fortune. My father was inclined to put it down to some stroke of luck on the American goldfields. I had my own ideas even then—chaotic and half-formed as yet, but tending in the right direction.

It was not long before these suspicions began to assume a more definite shape, which came about in this way. Minnie and I made the summit of the Combera cliff a favorite trysting place, as I think I mentioned before, and it was rare for a day to pass without our spending two or three hours there. One morning, not long after my chat with our guest, we were seated together in a little nook there, which we had chosen as sheltering us from the wind as well as my father's observation, when Minnie caught sight of Digby walking along the Carracuil beach. He sauntered up to the base of the cliff, which was boulder studded and slimy from the receding tide, but instead of turning back he kept on climbing over the great green slippery stones, and threading his way among the pools until he was standing immediately beneath us so that we looked straight down at him. To him the spot must have seemed the very acme of seclusion, with the great sea in front, the rocks on each side, and the precipice behind. Even had he looked up, he could hardly have made out the two human faces, which peered down at him from the distant ledge. He gave a hurried glance round, and then slipping his hand into his pocket, he pulled out the leather bag which I had noticed, and took out of it a small object which he held in the palm of his hand and looked at long, and, as it were, lovingly. We both had an excellent view of it from where we lay. He then replaced it in the bag, and shoving it down to the very bottom of his pocket picked his way back more cheerily than he had come.

Minnie and I looked at each other. She was smiling; I was serious.

"Did you see it?" I asked.

"Yon? Aye, I saw it."

"What did you think it was, then?"

"A wee bit of glass," she answered, looking at me with wondering eyes.

"No," I cried excitedly, "glass could never catch the sun's rays so. It was a diamond, and if I mistake not, one of extraordinary value. It was as large as all I have seen put together, and must be worth a fortune."

A diamond was a mere name to poor, simple Minnie, who had never seen one before, nor had any conception of their value, and she prattled away to me about this and that, but I hardly heard her. In vain she exhausted all her little wiles in attempting to recall my attention. My mind was full of what I had seen. Look where I would, the glistening of the breakers, or the sparkling of the mica-laden rocks, recalled the brilliant facets of the gem which I had seen. I was moody and distraught, and eventually let Minnie walk back to Corriemains by herself, while I made my way to the homesteading. My father and Digby were just sitting down to the midday meal, and the latter hailed me cheerily.

"Come along, mate," he cried, pushing over a stool, "we were just wondering what had become of you. Ah! you rogue, I'll bet my bottom dollar it was that pretty wench I saw the other day who kept you."

"Mind your own affairs," I answered angrily.

"Don't be thin-skinned," he said; "young people should control their tempers, and you've got a mighty bad one, my lad. Have you heard that I am going to leave you?"

"I'm sorry to hear it," I said frankly; "when do you intend to go?"

"Next week," he answered, "but don't be afraid; you'll see me again. I've had too good a time here to forget you easily. I'm going to buy a good steam yacht—250 tons or thereabouts—and I'll bring her round in a few months and give you a cruise."

"What would be a fair price for a craft of that sort?" I asked.

"Forty thousand dollars," said our visitor, carelessly.

"You must be very rich," I remarked, "to throw away so much money on pleasure."

"Rich!" echoed my companion, his Southern blood mantling up for a moment. "Rich, why man, there is hardly a limit—but there, I was romancing a bit. I'm fairly well off, or shall be very shortly."

"How did you make your money?" I asked. The question came so glibly to my lips that I had no time to check it, though I felt the moment afterward that I had made a mistake. Our guest drew himself into himself at once, and took no notice of my query, while my father said:

"Hush, Archie laddie, ye munna speer they questions o' the gentleman!" I could see, however, from the old man's eager gray eyes, looking out from under the great thatch of his brows, that he was meditating over the same problem himself.

During the next couple of days I hesitated very often as to whether I should tell my father of what I had seen and the opinions I had formed about our visitor; but he forestalled me by making a discovery himself which supplemented mine and explained all that had been dark. It was one day when the stranger was out for a ramble, that, entering the kitchen, I found my father sitting by the fire deeply engaged in perusing a newspaper, spelling out the words laboriously, and following the lines with his great forefinger. As I came in he crumpled up the paper as if his instinct were to conceal it, but then spreading it out again on his knee he beckoned me over to him.

"What d'ye think this chiel Digby is?" he asked. I could see by his manner that he was much excited.

"No good," I answered.

"Come here, laddie, come here!" he croaked. "You're a braw scholar. Read this tae me alood—read it and tell me if you dinna think I've fitted the cap on the right heid. It's a *Glasgey Herald* only four days auld—a Loch Ranza feeshin' boat brought it in the morn. Begin frae here—'Oor Paris Letter.' Here it is, 'Fuller details;' read it a' to me."

I began at the spot indicated, which was a paragraph of the ordinary French correspondence of the Glasgow paper. It ran in this way. "Fuller details have now come before the public of the diamond robbery by which the Duchesse de Rochevieille lost her celebrated gem. The diamond is a pure brilliant weighing eighty three and a half carats, and is supposed to be the third largest in France, and the seventeenth in Europe. It came into the possession of the family through the great grand-uncle of the Duchess, who fought under Bussy in India, and brought it back to Europe with him. It represented a fortune then, but its value now is simply enormous. It was taken, as will be remembered, from the jewel case of the Duchess two months ago during the night, and though the police have made every effort, no real clue has been obtained as to the thief. They are very reticent upon the subject, but it seems that they have reason to suspect one Achille Wolff, an American-ized native of Lorraine, who had called at the Château a short time before. He is an eccentric man, of Bohemian habits, and it is just possible that his sudden disappearance at the time of the robbery may have been a coincidence. In appearance he is described as romantic looking, with an artistic face, dark eyes and hair, and a brusque manner. A large reward is offered for his capture."

When I finished reading this, my father and I sat looking at each other in silence for a minute or so. Then my father jerked his finger over his shoulder. "Yon's him," he said.

"Yes, it must be he," I answered, thinking of the initials on the handkerchief.

Again we were silent for a time. My father took one of the faggots out of the grate and twisted it about in his hands. "It maun be a muckle stane" he said. "He canna hae it aboot him. Likely he's left it in France."

"No, he has it with him," I said, like a cursed fool as I was.

"Hoo d'ye ken that?" asked the old man, looking up quickly with eager eyes.

"Because I have seen it."

The faggot which he held broke in two in his grip, but he said nothing more. Shortly afterward our guest came in, and we had dinner, but neither of us alluded to the arrival of the paper.

I have often been amused, when reading stories told in the first person, to see how the narrator makes himself out as a matter of course to be a perfect and spotless man. All around may have their passions and weaknesses, and vices, but he remains a cold and blameless nonentity, running like a colorless thread through the tangled skein of the story. I shall not fall into this error. I see myself as I was in those days, shallow-hearted, hot-headed, and with little principle of any kind. Such I was, and such I depict myself.

From the time that I finally identified our visitor Digby with Achille Wolff the diamond robber, my resolution was taken. Some might have been squeamish in the matter, and thought that because he had shaken their hand and broken their bread he had earned some sort of grace from them. I was not troubled with sentimentality of this sort. He was a criminal escaping from justice. Some providence had thrown him into our hands, and an enormous reward awaited his betrayers. I never hesitated for a moment as to what was to be done.

The more I thought of it the more I admired the cleverness with which he had managed the whole business. It was clear that he had had a vessel ready, manned either by confederates or by unsuspecting fishermen. Hence he would be independent of all those parts where the police would be on the lookout for him. Again, if he had made for

England or for America, he could hardly have escaped ultimate capture, but by choosing one of the most desolate and lonely spots in Europe he had thrown them off his track for a time, while the destruction of the brig seemed to destroy the last clue as to his whereabouts. At present he was entirely at our mercy, since he could not move from the island without our help. There was no necessity for us to hurry therefore, and we could mature our plans at our leisure.

Both my father and I showed no change in our manner toward our guest, and he himself was as cheery and lighthearted as ever. It was pleasant to hear him singing as we mended the nets or caulked the boat. His voice was a very high tenor and one of the most melodious I ever listened to. I am convinced that he could have made a name upon the operatic stage, but like most versatile scoundrels, he placed small account upon the genuine talents which he possessed, and cultivated the worse portion of his nature. My father used sometimes to eye him sideways in a strange manner, and I thought I knew what he was thinking about—but there I made a mistake.

One day, about a week after our conversation, I was fixing up one of the rails of our fence which had been snapped in the gale, when my father came long the seashore, plodding heavily among the pebbles, and sat down on a stone at my elbow. I went on knocking in the nails, but looked at him from the corner of my eye, as he pulled away at his short black pipe. I could see that he had something weighty on his mind, for he knitted his brows, and his lips projected.

"D'ye mind what was in yon paper?" he said at last, knocking his ashes out against the stone.

"Yes," I answered shortly.

"Well, what's your opeenion?" he asked.

"Why, that we should have the reward, of course!" I replied.

"The reward!" he said, with a fierce snarl. "You would tak' the reward. You'd let the stane that's worth thoosands an' thoosands gang awa' back tae some furrin Papist, an' a' for the sake o' a few pund that they'd fling till ye, as they fling a bane to a dog when the meat's a' gone. It's a clean flingin' awa' o' the gifts o' Providence."

"Well, father," I said, laying down the hammer, "you must be satisfied with what you can get. You can only have what is offered."

"But if we got the stone itsel'," whispered my father, with a leer on his face.

"He'd never give it up," I said.

"But if he deed while he's here—if he was suddenly—"

"Drop it, father, drop it!" I cried, for the old man looked like a fiend out of the pit. I saw now what he was aiming at.

"If he deed," he shouted, "wha saw him come, and wha was speer where he'd ganged till? If an accident happened, if he came by a dud on the heid, or woke some nicht to find a knife at his thrapple, wha wad be the wiser?"

"You mustn't speak so, father," I said, though I was thinking many things at the same time.

"It may as well be oot as in," he answered, and went away rather sulkily, turning round after a few yards and holding up his finger toward me to impress the necessity of caution.

My father did not speak of this matter to me again, but what he said rankled in my mind. I could hardly realize that he meant his words, for he had always, as far as I knew, been an upright, righteous man, hard in his ways, and grasping in his nature, but guiltless of any great sin. Perhaps it was that he was removed from temptation, for isothermal lines of crime might be drawn on the map through places where it is hard to walk straight, and there are others where it is as hard to fall. It was easy to be a saint in the island of Uffa.

One day we were finishing breakfast when our guest asked if the boat was mended (one of the tholepins had been broken). I answered that it was.

"I want you two," he said, "to take me round to Lamlash today. You shall have a couple of sovereigns for the job. I don't know that I may not come back with you—but I may stay."

My eyes met those of my father for a flash. "There's no' vera much wind," he said.

"What there is, is in the right direction," returned Digby, as I must call him.

"The new foresail has no' been bent," persisted my father.

"There's no use throwing difficulties in the way," said our visitor angrily. "If you won't come, I'll get Tommy Gibbs and his father, but go I shall. Is it a bargain or not?"

"I'll gang," my father replied sullenly, and went down to get the boat ready. I followed, and helped him to bend on the new foresail. I felt nervous and excited.

"What do you intend to do?" I asked.

"I dinna ken," he said irritably. "Gin the worst come to the worst we can gie him up at Lamlash—but oh, it wad be a peety, an awfu' peety. You're young an' strong, laddie; can we no' master him between us?"

"No," I said, "I'm ready to give him up, but I'm damned if I lay a hand on him."

"You're a cooardly, white-livered loon!" he cried, but I was not to be moved by taunts, and left him mumbling to himself and picking at the sail with nervous fingers.

It was about two o'clock before the boat was ready, but as there was a slight breeze from the north we reckoned on reaching Lamlash before nightfall. There was just a pleasant ripple upon the dark blue water, and as we stood on the beach before shoving off, we could see the Carlin's leap and Goatfell bathed in a purple mist, while beyond them along the horizon loomed the long line of the Argyleshire hills. Away to the south the great bald summit of Ailsa crag glittered in the sun, and a single white fleck showed where a fishing boat was beating up from the Scotch coast. Digby and I stepped into the boat, but my father ran back to where I had been mending the rails, and came back with the hatchet in his hand, which he stowed away under the thwarts.

"What d'ye want with the axe?" our visitor asked.

"It's a handy thing to hae aboot a boat," my father answered with averted eyes, and shoved us off. We set the foresail, jib, and mainsail, and shot away across the Roost, with blue water splashing merrily under our bows. Looking back, I saw the coastline of our little island extend rapidly on either side. There was Carravoe which we had left, and our own beach of Carracuil and the steep brown face of the Combera, and away behind the rugged crests of Beg-na-phail and Beg-na-sacher. I could see the red tiles of the byre of our homesteading, and across the moor a thin blue reek in the air which marked the position of Corriemains. My heart warmed toward the place which had been my home since childhood.

We were about halfway across the Roost when it fell a dead calm, and the sails flapped against the mast. We were perfectly motionless except for the drift of the current, which runs from north to south. I had been steering and my father managing the sails, while the stranger smoked his eternal cigarettes and admired the scenery; but at his suggestion we now got the sculls out to row. I shall never know how it began, but as I was stooping down to pick up an oar I heard our visitor give a great scream that he was murdered, and looking up I saw him with his face all in a sputter of blood leaning against the mast, while my father made at him with the hatchet. Before I could move hand or foot Digby rushed at the old man and caught him round the waist. "You gray-headed devil," he cried in a husky voice. "I feel that you have done

for me. But you'll never get what you want. No—never! never! never!"
Nothing can ever erase from my memory the intense and concentrated
malice of those words. My father gave a raucous cry, they swayed and
balanced for a moment and then over they went into the sea. I rushed to
the side, boathook in hand, but they never came up. As the long rings
caused by the splash widened out however and left an unruffled space in
the center, I saw them once again. The water was very clear, and far
down I could see the shimmer of two white faces coming and going,
faces which seemed to look up at me with an expression of unutterable
horror. Slowly they went down, revolving in each other's embrace until
they were nothing but a dark loom, and then faded from my view
forever. There they shall lie, the Frenchman and the Scot, till the great
trumpet shall sound and the sea give up its dead. Storms may rage above
them and great ships labor and creak, but their slumber shall be dream-
less and unruffled in the silent green depths of the Roost of Uffa. I trust
when the great day shall come that they will bring up the cursed stone
with them, that they may show the sore temptation which the devil had
placed in their way, as some slight extenuation of their errors while in
this mortal flesh.

It was a weary and waesome journey back to Carravoe. I remember
tug-tugging at the oars as though to snap them in trying to relieve the
tension in my mind. Toward evening a breeze sprang up and helped me
on my way, and before nightfall I was back in the lonely homesteading
once more, and all that had passed that spring afternoon lay behind me
like some horrible nightmare.

I did not remain in Uffa. The croft and the boat were sold by public
roup in the marketplace of Ardrossan, and the sum realized was sufficient to enable me to continue my medical studies at the University. I
fled from the island as from a cursed place, nor did I ever set foot on it
again. Gibbs and his son, and even Minnie Fullarton too, passed out of
my life completely and for ever. She missed me for a time, no doubt, but
I have heard that young McBane, who took the farm, went a-wooing to
Corriemains after the white fishing, and as he was a comely fellow
enough he may have consoled her for my loss. As for myself, I have
settled quietly down into a large middle-class practice in Paisley. It has
been in the brief intervals of professional work that I have jotted down
these reminiscences of the events which led up to my father's death.
Achille Wolff and the Rochevieille diamond are things of the past now,
but there may be some who will care to hear of how they visited the
island of Uffa.

THROUGH THE VEIL

He was a great shock-headed, freckle-faced Borderer, the lineal descendant of a cattle-thieving clan in Liddesdale. In spite of his ancestry he was as solid and sober a citizen as one would wish to see, a town councillor of Melrose, an elder of the Church, and the chairman of the local branch of the Young Men's Christian Association. Brown was his name—and you saw it printed up as "Brown and Handiside" over the great grocery stores in the High Street. His wife, Maggie Brown, was an Armstrong before her marriage, and came from an old farming stock in the wilds of Teviothead. She was small, swarthy, and dark-eyed, with a strangely nervous temperament for a Scotch woman. No greater contrast could be found than the big tawny man and the dark little woman, but both were of the soil as far back as any memory could extend.

One day—it was the first anniversary of their wedding—they had driven over together to see the excavations of the Roman Fort at Newstead. It was not a particularly picturesque spot. From the northern bank of the Tweed, just where the river forms a loop, there extends a gentle slope of arable land. Across it run the trenches of the excavators, with here and there an exposure of old stonework to show the foundation of the ancient walls. It had been a huge place, for the camp was fifty acres in extent, and the fort fifteen. However, it was all made easy for

THROUGH THE VEIL 113

them since Mr. Brown knew the farmer to whom the land belonged. Under his guidance they spent a long summer evening inspecting the trenches, the pits, the ramparts, and all the strange variety of objects which were waiting to be transported to the Edinburgh Museum of Antiquities. The buckle of a woman's belt had been dug up that very day, and the farmer was discoursing upon it when his eyes fell upon Mrs. Brown's face.

"Your good leddy's tired," said he. "Maybe you'd best rest a wee before we gang further."

Brown looked at his wife. She was certainly very pale, and her dark eyes were bright and wild.

"What is it, Maggie? I've wearied you. I'm thinkin' it's time we went back."

"No, no, John, let us go on. It's wonderful! It's like a dreamland place. It all seems so close and so near to me. How long were the Romans here, Mr. Cunningham?"

"A fair time, mam. If you saw the kitchen midden pits you would guess it took a long time to fill them."

"And why did they leave?"

"Well, mam, by all accounts they left because they had to. The folk round could thole them no longer, so they just up and burned the fort aboot their lugs. You can see the fire marks on the stanes."

The woman gave a quick little shudder. "A wild night—a fearsome night," said she. "The sky must have been red that night—and these gray stones, they may have been red also."

"Aye, I think they were red," said her husband. "It's a queer thing, Maggie, and it may be your words that have done it; but I seem to see that business aboot as clear as ever I saw anything in my life. The light shone on the water."

"Aye, the light shone on the water. And the smoke gripped you by the throat. And all the savages were yelling."

The old farmer began to laugh. "The leddy will be writin' a story aboot the old fort," said he. "I've shown many a one ower it, but I never heard it put so clear afore. Some folk have the gift."

They had strolled along the edge of the foss, and a pit yawned upon the right of them.

"That pit was fourteen foot deep," said the farmer. "What d'ye think we dug oot from the bottom o't? Weel, it was just the skeleton of a man wi' a spear by his side. I'm thinkin' he was grippin' it when he died.

Now, how cam' a man wi' a spear doon a hole fourteen foot deep. He wasna' buried there, for they aye burned their dead. What make ye o' that, mam?"

"He sprang doon to get clear of the savages," said the woman.

"Weel, it's likely enough, and a' the professors from Edinburgh coulda gie a better reason. I wish you were aye here, mam, to answer a' oor deeficulties sae readily. Now, here's the altar that we foond last week. There's an inscreeption. They tell me it's Latin, and it means that the men o' this fort give thanks to God for their safety."

They examined the old worn stone. There was a large deeply-cut "VV" upon the top of it.

"What does 'VV' stand for?" asked Brown.

"Naebody kens," the guide answered.

"*Valeria Victrix,*" said the lady softly. Her face was paler than ever, her eyes far away, as one who peers down the dim aisles of overarching centuries.

"What's that?" asked her husband sharply.

She started as one who wakes from sleep. "What were we talking about?" she asked.

"About this 'VV' upon the stone."

"No doubt it was just the name of the Legion which put the altar up."

"Aye, but you gave some special name."

"Did I? How absurd! How should I ken what the name was?"

"You said something—'*Victrix,*' I think."

"I suppose I was guessing. It gives me the queerest feeling, this place, as if I were not myself, but someone else."

"Aye, it's an uncanny place," said her husband, looking round with an expression almost of fear in his bold gray eyes. "I feel it mysel'. I think we'll just be wishin' you good-evenin', Mr. Cunningham, and get back to Melrose before the dark sets in."

Neither of them could shake off the strange impression which had been left upon them by their visit to the excavations. It was as if some miasma had risen from those damp trenches and passed into their blood. All the evening they were silent and thoughtful, but such remarks as they did make showed that the same subject was in the minds of each. Brown had a restless night, in which he dreamed a strange connected dream, so vivid that he woke sweating and shivering like a frightened horse. He tried to convey it all to his wife as they sat together at breakfast in the morning.

"It was the clearest thing, Maggie," said he. "Nothing that has ever come to me in my waking life has been more clear than that. I feel as if these hands were sticky with blood."

"Tell me of it—tell me slow," said she.

"When it began, I was oot on a braeside. I was laying flat on the ground. It was rough, and there were clumps of heather. All round me was just darkness, but I could hear the rustle and the breathin' of men. There seemed a great multitude on every side of me, but I could see no one. There was a low chink of steel sometimes, and then a number of voices would whisper 'Hush!' I had a ragged club in my hand, and it had spikes o' iron near the end of it. My heart was beatin' quickly, and I felt that a moment of great danger and excitement was at hand. Once I dropped my club, and again from all round me the voices in the darkness cried, 'Hush!' I put oot my hand, and it touched the foot of another man lying in front of me. There was someone at my very elbow on either side. But they said nothin'.

"Then we all began to move. The whole braeside seemed to be crawlin' downward. There was a river at the bottom and a high-arched wooden bridge. Beyond the bridges were many lights—torches on a wall. The creepin' men all flowed toward the bridge. There had been no sound of any kind, just a velvet stillness. And then there was a cry in the darkness, the cry of a man who has been stabbed suddenly to the hairt. That one cry swelled out for a moment, and then the roar of a thoosand furious voices. I was runnin'. Every one was runnin'. A bright red light shone out, and the river was a scarlet streak. I could see my companions now. They were all mad with rage, jumpin' as they ran, their mouths open, their arms wavin', the red light beatin' on their faces. I ran, too, and yelled out curses like the rest. Then I heard a great cracklin' of wood, and I knew that the palisades were doon. There was a loud whistlin' in my ears, and I was aware that arrows were flyin' past me. I got to the bottom of a dyke, and I saw a hand stretched doon from above. I took it, and was dragged to the top. We looked doon, and there were silver men beneath us holdin' up their spears. Some of our folk sprang on to the spears. Then we others followed, and we killed the soldiers before they could draw the spears oot again. They shouted loud in some foreign tongue, but no mercy was shown them. We went ower them like a wave, and trampled them doon into the mud, for they were few, and there was no end to our numbers.

"I found myself among buildings, and one of them was on fire. I saw the flames spoutin' through the roof. I ran on, and then I was alone among the buildings. Someone ran across in front o' me. It was a woman. I caught her by the arm, and I took her chin and turned her face so as the light of the fire would strike it. Whom think you that it was, Maggie?"

His wife moistened her dry lips. "It was I," she said.

He looked at her in surprise. "That's a good guess," said he. "Yes, it was just you. Not merely like you, you understand. It was you—you yourself. I saw the same soul in your frightened eyes. You looked white and bonny and wonderful in the firelight. I had just one thought in my head—to get you awa' with me; to keep you all to mysel' in my own home somewhere beyond the hills. You clawed at my face with your nails. I heaved you over my shoulder, and I tried to find a way oot of the light of the burning hoose and back into the darkness.

"Then came the thing that I mind best of all. You're ill, Maggie. Shall I stop? My God! you have the very look on your face that you had last night in my dream. You screamed. He came runnin' in the firelight. His head was bare; his hair was black and curled; he had a naked sword in his hand, short and broad, little more than a dagger. He stabbed at me, but he tripped and fell. I held you with one hand, and with the other—"

His wife had sprung to her feet with writhing features.

"Marcus!" she cried. "My beautiful Marcus! Oh, you brute! you brute! you brute!" There was a clatter of tea cups as she fell forward senseless upon the table.

They never talk about that strange isolated incident in their married life. For an instant the curtain of the past had swung aside, and some strange glimpse of a forgotten life had come to them. But it closed down; never to open again. They live their narrow round—he in his shop, she in her household—and yet new and wider horizons have vaguely formed themselves around them since that summer evening by the crumbling Roman fort.

DE PROFUNDIS

As long as the oceans are the ligaments which bind together the great broad-cast British Empire, so long there will be a dash of romance in our slow old Frisian minds. For the soul is swayed by the waters, as the waters are by the moon, and when the great highways of an Empire are along such roads as those, so full of strange sights and sounds, with danger ever running like a hedge on either side of the course, it is a dull mind indeed which does not bear away with it some trace of such a passage. And now, Britain lies far beyond herself, for in truth the three-mile limit of every seaboard is her frontier, which has been won by hammer and loom and pick, rather than by arts of war. For it is written in history that neither a king in his might, nor an army with banners, can bar the path to the man who having twopence in his strongbox, and knowing well where he can turn it to threepence, sets his mind to that one end. And as the Empire has broadened, the mind of Britain has broadened too, spreading out into free speech, free press, free trade, until all men can see that the ways of the island are Continental, even as those of the Continent are insular.

But for this a price must be paid, and the price is a grievous one. As the beast of old must have one young human life as a tribute every year, so to our Empire we throw from day to day the pick and flower of our youth. The engine is worldwide and strong, but the only fuel that will drive it is the lives of British men. Thus it is that in the gray old cathedrals, as we look round upon the brasses on the walls, we see strange names, such names as they who reared those walls had never heard, for it is in Peshawur, and Umballah, and Korti, and Fort Pearson that the youngsters die, leaving only a precedent and a brass behind them. But if every man had his obelisk, even where he lay, then no frontier line need be drawn, for a cordon of British graves would ever show how high the Anglo-Saxon tide had lapped.

And this too, as well as the waters which separate us from France, and join us to the world, has done something to tinge us with romance. For when so many have their loved ones over the seas, walking amid hillman's bullets, or swamp malaria, where death is sudden and distance great, then mind communes with mind, and strange stories arise of dream, presentiment or vision, where the mother sees her dying son, and is past the first bitterness of her grief ere the message comes which should have broke the news. The learned have of late looked into the matter, and have even labeled it with a name, but what can we know more of it save that a poor stricken soul, when hard-pressed and driven, can shoot across the earth some ten-thousand-mile-long picture of its trouble to the mind which is most akin to it. Far be it from me to say that there lies no such power within us, for of all things which the brain will grasp the last will be itself, but yet it is well to be very cautious over such matters, for once at least I have known that which was within the laws of nature to seem to be far upon the further side of them.

John Vansittart was the younger partner of the firm of Hudson and Vansittart, coffee exporters of the Island of Ceylon, three-quarters Dutchmen by descent, but wholly English in his sympathies. For years I had been his agent in London, and when in '72 he came over to England for a three months' holiday, he turned to me for the introductions which would enable him to see something of town and country life. Armed with seven letters he left my offices, and for many weeks scrappy notes from different parts of the country let me know that he had found favor in the eyes of my friends. Then came word of his engagement to Emily Lawson, of a cadet branch of the Hereford Lawsons, and at the very tail of the first flying rumor the news of his absolute marriage, for the wooing of a wanderer must be short, and the days were already crowding on toward the date when he must be upon his homeward journey. They were to return together to Colombo in one of the firm's own thousand ton barque-rigged sailing ships, and this was to be their princely honeymoon, at once a necessity and a delight.

Those were the royal days of coffee planting in Ceylon, before a single season and a rotting fungus drove a whole community through years of despair to one of the greatest commercial victories which pluck and ingenuity ever won. Not often is it that men have the heart when their one great industry is withered to rear up in a few years another as rich to take its place, and the tea fields of Ceylon are as true a monument to courage as is the lion at Waterloo. But in '72 there was no cloud yet above the skyline, and the hopes of the planters were as high and as bright as the hillsides on which they reared their crops. Vansittart came down to London with his young and beautiful wife. I was introduced, dined with them, and it was finally arranged that I, since business called me also to Ceylon, should be a fellow passenger with them on the *Eastern Star*, which was timed to sail upon the following Monday.

It was on the Sunday evening that I saw him again. He was shown up into my rooms about nine o'clock at night, with the air of a man who is bothered and out of sorts. His hand, as I shook it, was hot and dry.

"I wish, Atkinson," said he, "that you could give me a little lime juice and water. I have a beastly thirst upon me, and the more I take the more I seem to want."

I rang and ordered in a carafe and glasses. "You are flushed," said I. "You don't look the thing."

"No, I'm clean off color. Got a touch of rheumatism in my back, and don't seem to taste my food. It is this vile London that is choking me. I'm not used to breathing air which has been used up by four million lungs all sucking away on every side of you." He flapped his crooked hands before his face, like a man who really struggles for his breath.

"A touch of the sea will soon set you right."

"Yes, I'm of one mind with you there. That's the thing for me. I want no other doctor. If I don't get to sea tomorrow I'll have an illness. There are no two ways about it." He drank off a tumbler of lime juice, and clapped his two hands with his knuckles doubled up into the small of his back.

"That seems to ease me," said he, looking at me with a filmy eye. "Now I want your help, Atkinson, for I am rather awkwardly placed."

"As how?"

"This way. My wife's mother got ill and wired for her. I couldn't go—you know best yourself how tied I have been—so she had to go alone. Now I've had another wire to say that she can't come tomorrow, but that she will pick up the ship at Falmouth on Wednesday. We put in there, you know, and in, and in, though I count it hard, Atkinson, that a man should be asked to believe in a mystery, and cursed if he can't do it. Cursed, mind you, no less." He leaned forward and began to draw a catchy breath like a man who is poised on the very edge of a sob.

Then first it came into my mind that I had heard much of the hard drinking life of the island, and that from brandy came these wild words and fevered hands. The flushed cheek and the glazing eye were those of one whose drink is strong upon him. Sad it was to see so noble a young man in the grip of that most bestial of all the devils.

"You should lie down," I said, with some severity.

He screwed up his eyes, like a man who is striving to wake himself, and looked up with an air of surprise.

"So I shall presently," said he, quite rationally. "I felt quite swimmy just now, but I am my own man again now. Let me see, what was I talking about? Oh ah, of course, about the wife. She joins the ship at Falmouth. Now I want to go round by water. I believe my health depends upon it. I just want a little clean firsthand air to set me on my feet again. Now I want you, like a good fellow, to go to Falmouth by rail, so that in case we should be late you may be there to look after the wife. Put up at the Royal Hotel, and I will wire her that you are there. Her sister will bring her down, so that it will be all plain sailing."

"I'll do it with pleasure," said I. "In fact, I should rather go by rail, for we shall have enough and to spare of the sea before we reach Colombo. I believe too that you badly need a change. Now I should go and turn in, if I were you."

"Yes, I will. I sleep aboard tonight. You know," he continued, as the film settled down again over his eyes, "I've not slept well the last few nights. I've been troubled with theolololog—that is to say, theologi-cal—hang it," with a desperate effort, "with the doubts of theolologicians. Wondering why the Almighty made us, you know, and why He made our heads swimmy, and fixed little pains into the small of our backs. Maybe I'll do better tonight." He rose, and steadied himself with an effort against the corner of the chair back.

"Look here, Vansittart," said I gravely, stepping up to him, and laying my hand upon his sleeve, "I can give you a shakedown here. You are not fit to go out. You are all over the place. You've been mixing your drinks."

"Drinks!" he stared at me stupidly.

"You used to carry your liquor better than this."

"I give you my word, Atkinson, that I have not had a drain for two days. It's not drink. I don't know what it is. I suppose you think this is drink." He took up my hand in his burning grasp, and passed it over his own forehead.

"Great Lord!" said I.

His skin felt like a thin sheet of velvet beneath which lies a close packed layer of small shot. It was smooth to the touch at any one place, but, to a finger passed along it, rough as a nutmeg grater.

"It's all right," said he, smiling at my startled face. "I've had the prickly heat nearly as bad."

"But this is never prickly heat."

"No, it's London. It's breathing bad air. But tomorrow it'll be all right. There's a surgeon aboard, so I shall be in safe hands. I must be off now."

"Not you," said I, pushing him back into a chair. "This is past a joke. You don't move from here until a doctor sees you. Just stay where you are." I caught up my hat, and rushing round to the house of a neighboring physician, I brought him back with me. The room was empty and Vansittart gone. I rang the bell. The servant said that the gentleman had ordered a cab the instant that I had left, and had gone off in it. He had told the cabman to drive to the docks.

"Did the gentleman seem ill?" I asked.

"Ill!" The man smiled. "No, sir, he was singin' his 'ardest all the time."

The information was not as reassuring as my servant seemed to think, but I reflected that he was going straight back to the *Eastern Star*, and that there was a doctor aboard of her, so that there was nothing which I could do in the matter. Nonetheless, when I thought of his thirst, his burning hands, his heavy eye, his tripping speech, and lastly, of that leprous forehead, I carried with me to bed an unpleasant memory of my visitor and his visit.

At eleven o'clock next day I was at the docks, but the *Eastern Star* had already moved down the river, and was nearly at Gravesend. To Gravesend I went by train, but only to see her topmasts far off, with a plume of smoke from a tug in front of her. I would hear no more of my friend until I rejoined him at Falmouth. When I got back to my offices a telegram was awaiting for me from Mrs. Vansittart, asking me to meet her, and next evening found us both at the Royal Hotel, Falmouth, where we were to wait for the *Eastern Star*. Ten days passed, and there came no news of her.

They were ten days which I am not likely to forget. On the very day that the *Eastern Star* had cleared from the Thames, a furious easterly gale had sprung up, and blew on from day to day for the greater part of a week without the sign of a lull. Such a screaming, raving, long-drawn storm has never been known on the southerly coast. From our hotel windows the sea view was all banked in with haze, with a little rain-swept half circle under our very eyes, churned and lashed into one tossing stretch of foam. So heavy was the wind upon the waves that little sea could rise, for the crest of each billow was torn shrieking from it, and lashed broadcast over the bay. Clouds, wind, sea, all were rushing to the west, and there, looking down at this mad jumble of elements, I waited on day after day, my sole companion a white, silent woman, with terror in her eyes, her forehead pressed ever against the bar of the window, her gaze from early morning to the fall of night fixed upon the wall of gray haze through which the loom of a vessel might come. She said nothing, but that face of hers was one long wail of fear.

On the fifth day I took counsel with an old seaman. I should have preferred to have done so alone, but she saw me speak with him, and was at our side in an instant, with parted lips and a prayer in her eyes.

"Seven days out from London," said he, "and five in the gale. Well, the Channel's swept as clear as clear by this wind. There's three things for it. She may have popped into port on the French side. That's like enough."

"No, no, he knew we were here. He would have telegraphed."

"Ah, yes, so he would. Well then, he might have run for it, and if he did that he won't be very far from Madeira by now. That'll be it, marm, you may depend."

"Or else? You said there was a third chance."

"Did I, marm? No, only two, I think. I don't think I said anything of a third. Your ship's out there, depend upon it, away out in the Atlantic, and you'll hear of it time enough, for the weather is breaking; now don't you fret, marm, and wait quiet, and you'll find a real blue Cornish sky tomorrow."

The old seaman was right in his surmise, for the next day broke calm and bright, with only a low dwindling cloud in the west to mark the last trailing wreaths of the storm wrack. But still there came no word from the sea, and no sign of the ship. Three more weary days had passed, the weariest that I have ever spent, when there came a seafaring man to the hotel with a letter. I gave a shout of joy. It was from the Captain of the *Eastern Star*. As I read the first lines of it I whisked my hand over it, but she laid her own upon it and drew it away. "I have seen it," said she, in a cold, quiet voice; "I may as well see the rest, too."

Dear Sir [said the letter], Mr. Vansittart is down with the smallpox, and we are blown so far on our course that we don't know what to do, he being off his head and unfit to tell us. By dead reckoning we are but three hundred miles from Funchal, so I take it that it is best that we should push on there, get Mr. V. into hospital, and wait in the Bay until you come. There's a sailing ship due from Falmouth to Funchal in a few days time, as I understand. This goes by the brig *Marian*, of Falmouth, and five pounds is due to the master.

Yours respectfully,   JNO HINES.

She was a wonderful woman that, only a chit of a girl fresh from school, but as quiet and strong as a man. She said nothing—only pressed her lips together tight, and put on her bonnet.

"You are going out?" I asked.

"Yes."

"Can I be of use?"

"No, I am going to the Doctor's."

"To the Doctor's?"

"Yes. To learn how to nurse a smallpox case."

She was busy at that all evening, and next morning we were off with a fine ten-knot breeze in the barque *Rose of Sharon* for Madeira. For five days we made good time, and were no great way from the island, but on the sixth there fell a calm, and we lay without motion on a sea of oil, heaving slowly, but making not a foot of weigh.

At ten o'clock that night Emily Vansittart and I stood leaning on the starboard railing of the poop, with a full moon shining at our backs, and casting a black shadow of the barque, and of our own two heads upon the shining water. From the shadow on, a broadening path of moon-shine stretched away to the lonely skyline, flickering and shimmering in the gentle heave of the swell. We were talking with bent heads, chatting of the calm, of the chances of wind, of the look of the sky, when there came a sudden plop, like a rising salmon, and there in the clear light John Vansittart sprang out of the water and looked up at us.

I never saw anything clearer in my life than I saw that man. The moon shone full upon him, and he was but three oars' lengths away. His face was more puffed than when I had seen him last, mottled here and there with dark scabs, his mouth and eyes open as one who is struck with some overpowering surprise. He had some white stuff streaming from his shoulders, and one hand was raised to his ear, the other crooked across his breast. I saw him leap from the water into the air, and in the dead calm the waves of his coming lapped up against the sides of the vessel. Then his figure sank back into the waters again, and I heard a rending, crackling sound like a bundle of brushwood snapping in the fire upon a frosty night. There were no signs of him when I looked again, but a swift swirl and eddy on the still sea still marked the spot where he had been. How long I stood there, tingling to my fingertips, holding up an unconscious woman with one hand, clutching at the rail of the vessel with the other, was more than I could afterward tell. I had been noted as a man of slow and unresponsive emotions, but this time at least I was shaken to the core. Once and twice I struck my foot upon the deck to be certain that I was indeed the master of my own senses, and that this was not some mad prank of an unruly brain. As I stood, still marveling, the woman shivered, opened her eyes, gasped, and then standing erect with her hands upon the rail, looked out over the moonlit sea with a face which had aged ten years in a summer night.

"You saw his vision?" she murmured.

"I saw something."

"It was he. It was John. He is dead."

I muttered some lame words of doubt.

"Doubtless he died at this hour," she whispered. "In hospital at Madeira. I have read of such things. His thoughts were with me. His vision came to me. Oh, my John, my dear, dear, lost John!"

She broke out suddenly in a storm of weeping, and I led her down into her cabin, where I left her with her sorrow. That night a brisk breeze blew up from the east, and in the evening of the next day we passed the two islets of Los Desertos, and dropped anchor at sundown in the Bay of Funchal. The *Eastern Star* lay no great distance from us, with the quarantine flag flying from her main, and her Jack halfway up her peak.

"You see," said Mrs. Vansittart quickly. She was dry-eyed now, for she had known how it would be.

That night we received permission from the authorities to move on board the *Eastern Star*. The Captain, Hines, was waiting upon deck with confusion and grief contending upon his bluff face as he sought for words with which to break this heavy tidings, but she took the story from his lips.

"I know that my husband is dead," she said. "He died yesterday night, about ten o'clock, in hospital at Madeira, did he not?"

The seaman stared aghast. "No, marm, he died eight days ago at sea, and we had to bury him out there, for we lay in a belt of calm, and could not say when we might make the land."

Well, those are the main facts about the death of John Vansittart, and his appearance to his wife somewhere about latitude 35° N. and longitude. 15° W. A clearer case of a wraith has seldom been made out, and since then it has been told as such, and put into print as such, and endorsed by a learned society as such, and so floated off with many others to support the recent theory of telepathy. For myself I hold telepathy to be proved, but I would snatch this one case from amid the evidence, and say that I do not think that it was the wraith of John Vansittart, but John Vansittart himself whom we saw that night leaping into the moonlight out of the depths of the Atlantic. It has ever been my belief that some strange chance, one of these chances which seem so improbable and yet so constantly occur, had becalmed us over the very spot where the man had been buried a week before. For the rest the surgeon tells me that the leaden weight was not too firmly fixed and that seven days bring about changes which are wont to fetch a body to the surface. Coming from the depth which the weight would have sunk it to, he explains that it might well attain such a velocity as to carry it clear of the water. Such is my own explanation of the matter, and if you ask me what then became of the body, I must recall to you that snapping, crackling sound, with the swirl in the water. The shark is a surface feeder and is plentiful in those parts.

THE GREAT KEINPLATZ EXPERIMENT

Of all the the sciences which have puzzled sons of men, none had such an attraction for the learned Professor von Baumgarten as those which relate to psychology and the ill-defined relations between mind and matter. A celebrated anatomist, a profound chemist, and one of the first physiologists in Europe, it was a relief for him to turn from these subjects and to bring his varied knowledge to bear upon the study of the soul and the mysterious relationship of spirits. At first, when as a young man he began to dip into the secrets of mesmerism, his mind seemed to be wandering in a strange land where all was chaos and darkness, save that here and there some great unexplainable and disconnected fact loomed out in front of him. As the years passed, however, and as the worthy Professor's stock of knowledge increased, for knowledge begets knowledge as money bears interest, much which had seemed strange and unaccountable began to take another shape in his eyes. New trains of reasoning became familiar to him, and he perceived connecting links where all had been incomprehensible and startling. By experiments which extended over twenty years, he obtained a basis of facts upon which it was his ambition to build up a new exact science which should embrace mesmerism, spiritualism, and all cognate subjects. In this he was much helped by his intimate knowledge of the more intricate parts of animal physiology which treat of nerve currents and the working of the brain; for Alexis von Baumgarten was Regius Professor of Physiology at the University of Keinplatz, and had all the resources of the laboratory to aid him in his profound researches.

Professor von Baumgarten was tall and thin, with a hatchet face and steel-gray eyes, which were singularly bright and penetrating. Much thought had furrowed his forehead and contracted his heavy eyebrows, so that he appeared to wear a perpetual frown, which often misled people as to his character, for though austere he was tenderhearted. He was popular among the students, who would gather round him after his lectures and listen eagerly to his strange theories. Often he would call for volunteers from amongst them in order to conduct some experiment, so that eventually there was hardly a lad in the class who had not, at one time or another, been thrown into a mesmeric trance by his Professor.

Of all these young devotees of science there was none who equaled in enthusiasm Fritz von Hartmann. It had often seemed strange to his fellow students that wild, reckless Fritz, as dashing a young fellow as ever hailed from the Rhinelands, should devote the time and trouble which he did in reading up abstruse works and in assisting the Professor in his strange experiments. The fact was, however, that Fritz was a knowing and long-headed fellow. Months before he had lost his heart to young Elise, the blue-eyed, yellow-haired daughter of the lecturer. Although he had succeeded in learning from her lips that she was not indifferent to his suit, he had never dared to announce himself to her family as a formal suitor. Hence he would have found it a difficult matter to see his young lady had he not adopted the expedient of making himself useful to the Professor. By this means he frequently was asked to the old man's house, where he willingly submitted to be experimented upon in any way as long as there was the chance of his receiving one bright glance from the eyes of Elise or one touch of her little hand.

Young Fritz von Hartmann was a handsome lad enough. There were broad acres, too, which would descend to him when his father died. To many he would have seemed an eligible suitor; but Madame frowned upon his presence in the house, and lectured the Professor at times on his allowing such a wolf to prowl around their lamb. To tell the truth, Fritz had an evil name in Keinplatz. Never was there a riot or a duel, or any other mischief aloof, but the young Rhinelander figured as a ringleader in it. No one used more free and violent language, no one drank more, no one played cards more habitually, no one was more idle, save in the one solitary subject. No wonder, then, that the good Frau Professorin gathered her Fräulein under her wing, and resented the attentions of such a *mauvais sujet*. As to the worthy lecturer, he was too much engrossed by his strange studies to form an opinion upon the subject one way or the other.

For many years there was one question which had continually obtruded itself upon his thoughts. All his experiments and his theories turned upon a single point. A hundred times a day the Professor asked himself whether it was possible for the human spirit to exist apart from the body for a time and then to return to it once again. When the possibility first suggested itself to him his scientific mind had revolted from it. It clashed too violently with preconceived ideas and the prejudices of his early training. Gradually, however, as he proceeded farther and farther along the pathway of original research, his mind shook off its old fetters and became ready to face any conclusion which could reconcile the facts. There were many things which made him believe that it was possible for mind to exist apart from matter. At last it occurred to him that by a daring and original experiment the question might be definitely decided.

"It is evident," he remarked in his celebrated article upon invisible entities, which appeared in the *Keinplatz wochenliche Medicalschrift* about this time, and which surprised the whole scientific world—"it is evident that under certain conditions the soul or mind does separate itself from the body. In the case of a mesmerized person, the body lies in a cataleptic condition, but the spirit has left it. Perhaps you reply that the soul is there, but in a dormant condition. I answer that this is not so, otherwise how can one account for the condition of clairvoyance, which has fallen into disrepute through the knavery of certain scoundrels, but which can easily be shown to be an undoubted fact. I have been able myself, with a sensitive subject, to obtain an accurate description of what was going on in another room or another house. How can such knowledge be accounted for on any hypothesis save that the soul of the subject has left the body and is wandering through space? For a moment it is recalled by the voice of the operator and says what it has seen, and then wings its way once more through the air. Since the spirit is by its very nature invisible, we cannot see these comings and goings, but we see their effect in the body of the subject, now rigid and inert, now struggling to narrate impressions which could never have come to it by natural means. There is only one way which I can see by which the fact can be demonstrated. Although we in the flesh are unable to see these spirits, yet our own spirits, could we separate them from the body, would be conscious of the presence of others. It is my intention, therefore, shortly to mesmerize one of my pupils. I shall then mesmerize myself in a manner which has become easy to me. After that, if my theory holds good, my spirit will have no difficulty in meeting and communing with the spirit of my pupil, both being separated from the body. I hope to be able to communicate the result of this interesting experiment in an early number of the *Keinplatz wochenliche Medicalschrift.*"

When the good Professor finally fulfilled his promise, and published an account of what occurred, the narrative was so extraordinary that it was received with general incredulity. The tone of some of the papers was so offensive in their comments upon the matter that the angry savant declared that he would never open his mouth again or refer to the subject in anyway—a promise which he has faithfully kept. This narrative has been compiled, however, from the most authentic sources, and the events cited in it may be relied upon as substantially correct.

It happened, then, that shortly after the time when Professor von Baumgarten conceived the idea of the above-mentioned experiment, he was walking thoughtfully homeward after a long day in the laboratory, when he met a crowd of roistering students who had just streamed out from a beerhouse. At the head of them, half-intoxicated and very noisy, was young Fritz von Hartmann. The Professor would have passed them, but his pupil ran across and intercepted him.

"Heh ! my worthy master," he said, taking the old man by the sleeve, and leading him down the road with him. "There is something that I have to say to you, and it is easier for me to say it now, when the good beer is humming in my head, than at another time."

"What is it, then, Fritz?" the physiologist asked, looking at him in mild surprise.

"I hear, mein herr, that you are about to do some wondrous experiment in which you hope to take a man's soul out of his body, and then to put it back again. Is it not so?"

"It is true, Fritz."

"And have you considered, my dear sir, that you may have some difficulty in finding someone on whom to try this? Potztausend! Suppose that the soul went out and would not come back. That would be a bad business. Who is to take the risk?"

"But, Fritz," the Professor cried, very much startled by this view of the matter, "I had relied upon your assistance in the attempt. Surely you will not desert me. Consider the honor and glory."

"Consider the fiddlesticks!" the student cried angrily. "Am I to be paid always thus? Did I not stand two hours upon a glass insulator while you poured electricity into my body? Have you not stimulated my phrenic nerves, besides ruining my digestion with a galvanic current round my stomach? Four-and-thirty times you have mesmerized me, and what have I got from all this? Nothing. And now you wish to take my soul out, as you would take the works from a watch. It is more than flesh and blood can stand."

"Dear, dear!" the Professor cried in great distress. "That is very true, Fritz. I never thought of it before. If you can but suggest how I can compensate you, you will find me ready and willing."

"Then listen," said Fritz solemnly. "If you will pledge your word that after this experiment I may have the hand of your daughter, then I am willing to assist you; but if not, I shall have nothing to do with it. These are my only terms."

"And what would my daughter say to this?" the Professor exclaimed, after a pause of astonishment.

"Elise would welcome it," the young man replied. "We have loved each other long."

"Then she shall be yours," the physiologist said with decision, "for you are a good-hearted man, and one of the best neurotic subjects that I have ever known—that is when you are not under the influence of alcohol. My experiment is to be performed upon the fourth of next month. You will attend at the physiological laboratory at twelve o'clock. It will be a great occasion, Fritz. Von Gruben is coming from Jena, and Hinterstein from Basle. The chief men of science of all South Germany will be there."

"I shall be punctual," the student said briefly; and so the two parted. The Professor plodded homeward, thinking of the great coming event, while the young man staggered along after his noisy companions, with his mind full of the blue-eyed Elise, and of the bargain which he had concluded with her father.

The Professor did not exaggerate when he spoke of the widespread interest excited by his novel psycho-physiological experiment. Long before the hour had arrived the room was filled by a galaxy of talent. Besides the celebrities whom he had mentioned, there had come from London the great Professor Lurcher, who had just established his reputation by a remarkable treatise upon cerebral centers. Several great lights of the Spiritualistic body had also come a long distance to be present, as had a Swedenborgian minister, who considered that the proceedings might throw some light upon the doctrines of the Rosy Cross.

There was considerable applause from this eminent assembly upon the appearance of Professor von Baumgarten and his subject upon the platform. The lecturer, in a few well-chosen words, explained what his views were, and how he proposed to test them. "I hold," he said, "that when a person is under the influence of mesmerism, his spirit is for the time released from his body, and I challenge anyone to put forward any other hypothesis which will account for the fact of clairvoyance. I therefore hope that upon mesmerizing my young friend here, and then putting myself into a trance, our spirits may be able to commune together, though our bodies lie still and inert. After a time nature will resume her sway, our spirits will return into our respective bodies, and all will be as before. With your kind permission, we shall now proceed to attempt the experiment."

The applause was renewed at this speech, and the audience settled down in expectant silence. With a few rapid passes the Professor mesmerized the young man, who sank back in his chair, pale and rigid. He then took a bright globe of glass from his pocket, and by concentrating his gaze upon it and making a strong mental effort, he succeeded in throwing himself into the same condition. It was a strange and impressive sight to see the old man and the young sitting together in the same cataleptic condition. Whither, then, had their souls fled? That was the question which presented itself to each and every one of the spectators.

Five minutes passed, and then ten, and then fifteen, and then fifteen more, while the Professor and his pupil sat stiff and stark upon the platform. During that time not a sound was heard from the assembled savants, but every eye was bent upon the two pale faces, in search of the first signs of returning consciousness. Nearly an hour had elapsed before the patient watchers were rewarded. A faint flush came back to the cheeks of Professor von Baumgarten. The soul was coming back once more to its earthly tenement. Suddenly he stretched out his long thin arms, as one awaking from sleep, and rubbing his eyes, stood up from his chair and gazed about him as though he hardly realized where he was. "Tausend Teufel!" he exclaimed, rapping out a tremendous South German oath, to the great astonishment of his audience and to the disgust of the Swedenborgian. "Where the Henker am I then, and what in thunder has occurred? Oh yes, I remember now. One of these nonsensical mesmeric experiments. There is no result this time, for I remember nothing at all since I became unconscious; so you have had all your long journeys for nothing, my learned friends, and a very good joke too;" at which the Regius Professor of Physiology burst into a roar of laughter and slapped his thigh in a highly indecorous fashion. The audience were so enraged at this unseemly behavior on the part of their host, that there might have been a considerable disturbance, had it not been for the judicious interference of young Fritz von Hartmann, who had now recovered from his lethargy. Stepping to the front of the platform, the young man apologized for the conduct of his companion. "I am sorry to say," he said, "that this is a harum-scarum sort of fellow, although he appeared so grave at the commencement of this experiment. He is still suffering from mesmeric reaction, and is hardly accountable for his words. As to the experiment itself, I do not consider it to be a failure. It is very possible that our spirits may have been communing in space during this hour; but, unfortunately, our gross bodily memory is distinct from our spirit, and we cannot recall what has occurred. My energies shall now be devoted to devising some means by which spirits may be able to recollect what occurs to them in their free state, and I trust that when I have worked this out, I may have the pleasure of meeting you all once again in this hall, and demonstrating to you the result." This address, coming from so young a student, caused considerable astonishment among the audience, and some were inclined to be offended, thinking that he assumed rather too much importance. The majority, however, looked upon him as a young man of great promise, and many comparisons were made as they left the hall between his dignified conduct and the levity of his professor, who during the above remarks was laughing heartily in a corner, by no means abashed at the failure of the experiment.

Now although all these learned men were filing out of the lecture room under the impression that they had seen nothing of note, as a matter of fact one of the most wonderful things in the whole history of the world had just occurred before their very eyes. Professor von Baumgarten had been so far correct in his theory that both his spirit and that of his pupil had been for a time absent from his body. But here a strange and unforeseen complication had occurred. In their return the spirit of Fritz von Hartmann had entered into the body of Alexis von Baumgarten, and that of Alexis von Baumgarten had taken up its abode in the frame of Fritz von Hartmann. Hence the slang and scurrility which issued from the lips of the serious Professor, and hence also the weighty words and grave statements which fell from the careless student. It was an unprecedented event, yet no one knew of it, least of all those whom it concerned.

The body of the Professor, feeling conscious suddenly of a great dryness about the back of the throat, sallied out into the street, still chuckling to himself over the result of the experiment, for the soul of Fritz within was reckless at the thought of the bride whom he had won so easily. His first impulse was to go up to the house and see her, but on second thoughts he came to the conclusion that it would be best to stay away until Madame Baumgarten should be informed by her husband of the agreement which had been made. He therefore made his way down to the Grüner Mann, which was one of the favorite trysting places of the wilder students, and ran, boisterously waving his cane in the air, into the little parlor, where sat Spiegler and Müller and half a dozen other boon companions.

"Ha, ha! my boys," he shouted. "I knew I should find you here. Drink up, everyone of you, and call for what you like, for I'm going to stand treat today."

Had the green man who is depicted upon the signpost of that well-known inn suddenly marched into the room and called for a bottle of wine, the students could not have been more amazed than they were by this unexpected entry of their revered professor. They were so astonished that for a minute or two they glared at him in utter bewilderment without being able to make any reply to his hearty invitation.

"Donner und Blitzen!" shouted the Professor angrily. "What the deuce is the matter with you, then? You sit there like a set of stuck pigs staring at me. What is it, then?"

"It is the unexpected honor," stammered Spiegel, who was in the chair.

"Honor—rubbish!" said the Professor testily. "Do you think that just because I happen to have been exhibiting mesmerism to a parcel of old fossils, I am therefore too proud to associate with dear old friends like you? Come out of that chair, Spiegel my boy, for I shall preside now. Beer, or wine, or schnapps, my lads—call for what you like, and put it all down to me."

Never was there such an afternoon in the Grüner Mann. The foaming flagons of lager and the green-necked bottles of Rhenish circulated merrily. By degrees the students lost their shyness in the presence of their Professor. As for him, he shouted, he sang, he roared, he balanced a long tobacco pipe upon his nose, and offered to run a hundred yards against any member of the company. The Kellner and the barmaid whispered to each other outside the door their astonishment at such proceedings on the part of a Regius Professor of the ancient university of Keinplatz. They had still more to whisper about afterward, for the learned man cracked the Kellner's crown, and kissed the barmaid behind the kitchen door.

"Gentleman," said the Professor, standing up, albeit somewhat totteringly, at the end of the table, and balancing his high old-fashioned wineglass in his bony hand, "I must now explain to you what is the cause of this festivity."

"Hear! hear!" roared the students, hammering their beer glasses against the table; "a speech, a speech—silence for the speech!"

"That fact is, my friends," said the Professor, beaming through his spectacles, "I hope very soon to be married."

"Married!" cried a student, bolder than the others. "Is Madame dead, then?"

"Madame who?"

"Why, Madame von Baumgarten, of course."

"Ha, ha!" laughed the Professor; "I can see, then, that you know all about my former difficulties. No, she is not dead, but I have reason to believe that she will not oppose my marriage."

"That is very accommodating of her," remarked one of the company.

"In fact," said the Professor, "I hope that she will now be induced to aid me in getting a wife. She and I never took to each other very much; but now I hope all that may be ended, and when I marry she will come and stay with me."

"What a happy family!" exclaimed some wag.

"Yes, indeed; and I hope you will come to my wedding, all of you. I won't mention names, but here is to my little bride!" and the Professor waved his glass in the air.

"Here's to his little bride!" roared the roisterers, with shouts of laughter. "Here's her health. Sie soll leben—Hoch!" And so the fun waxed still more fast and furious, while each young fellow followed the Professor's example, and drank a toast to the girl of his heart.

While all this festivity had been going on at the Grüner Mann, a very different scene had been enacted elsewhere. Young Fritz von Hartmann, with a solemn face and a reserved manner, had, after the experiment, consulted and adjusted some mathematical instruments; after which with a few peremptory words to the janitors, he had walked out into the street and wended his way slowly in the direction of the house of the Professor. As he walked he saw Von Althaus, the professor of anatomy, in front of him, and quickening his pace he overtook him.

"I say, Von Althaus," he exclaimed, tapping him on the sleeve, "you were asking me for some information the other day concerning the middle coat of the cerebral arteries. Now I find—"

"Donnerwetter!" shouted Von Althaus, who was a peppery old fellow. "What the deuce do you mean by your impertinence! I'll have you up before the Academical Senate for this, sir;" with which threat he turned on his heel and hurried away. Von Hartmann was much surprised at this reception. "It's on account of this failure of my experiment," he said to himself, and continued moodily on his way.

Fresh surprises were in store for him, however. He was hurrying along when he was overtaken by two students. These youths, instead of raising their caps or showing any other sign of respect, gave a wild whoop of delight the instant that they saw him, and rushing at him, seized him by each arm and commenced dragging him along with them.

"Gott in himmel!" roared Von Hartmann. "What is the meaning of this unparalleled insult? Where are you taking me?"

"To crack a bottle of wine with us," said the two students. "Come along! That is an invitation which you have never refused."

"I never heard of such insolence in my life!" cried Von Hartmann. "Let go my arms! I shall certainly have you resticated for this. Let me go, I say!" and he kicked furiously at his captors.

"Oh, if you choose to turn ill-tempered, you may go where you like," the students said, releasing him. "We can do very well without you."

"I know you. I'll pay you out," said Von Hartmann furiously, and continued in the direction which he imagined to be his own home, much incensed at the two episodes which had occurred to him on the way.

Now, Madame von Baumgarten, who was looking out of the window and wondering why her husband was late for dinner, was considerably astonished to see the young student come stalking down the road. As already remarked, she had a great antipathy to him, and if ever he ventured into the house it was on sufferance, and under the protection of the Professor. Still more astonished was she, therefore, when she beheld him undo the wicket gate and stride up the garden path with the air of one who is master of the situation. She could hardly believe her eyes, and hastened to the door with all her maternal instincts up in arms. From the upper windows the fair Elise had also observed this daring move upon the part of her lover, and her heart beat quick with mingled pride and consternation.

"Good day, sir," Madame Baumgarten remarked to the intruder, as she stood in gloomy majesty in the open doorway.

"A very fine day, indeed, Martha," returned the other. "Now, don't stand there like a statue of Juno, but bustle about and get the dinner ready, for I am well-nigh starved."

"Martha! Dinner!" ejaculated the lady, falling back in astonishment.

"Yes, dinner, Martha, dinner!" howled Von Hartmann, who was becoming irritable. "Is there anything wonderful in that request when a man has been out all day? I'll wait in the dining room. Anything will do. Schinken, and sausage, and prunes—any little thing that happens to be about. There you are, standing staring again. Woman, will you or will you not stir your legs?"

This last address, delivered with a perfect shriek of rage, had the effect of sending good Madame Baumgarten flying along the passage and through the kitchen, where she locked herself up in the scullery and went into violent hysterics. In the meantime Von Hartmann strode into the room and threw himself down upon the sofa in the worst of tempers.

"Elise!" he shouted. "Confound the girl! Elise!"

Thus roughly summoned, the young lady came timidly downstairs and into the presence of her lover. "Dearest!" she cried, throwing her arms round him, "I know this is all done for my sake! It is a *ruse* in order to see me."

Von Hartmann's indignation at this fresh attack upon him was so great that he became speechless for a minute with rage, and could only glare and shake his fists, while he struggled in her embrace. When he at last regained his utterance, he indulged in such a bellow of passion that the young lady dropped back, petrified with fear, into an armchair.

"Never have I passed such a day in my life," Von Hartmann cried, stamping upon the floor. "My experiment failed. Von Althaus has insulted me. Two students have dragged me along the public road. My wife nearly faints when I ask her for dinner, and my daughter flies at me and hugs me like a grizzly bear."

"You are ill, dear," the young lady cried. "Your mind is wandering. You have not even kissed me once."

"No, and I don't intend to either," Von Hartmann said with decision. "You ought to be ashamed of yourself. Why don't you go and fetch my slippers, and help your mother to dish the dinner?"

"And is it for this," Elise cried, burying her face in her handkerchief—"is it for this that I have loved you passionately for upward of ten months? Is it for this that I have braved my mother's wrath? Oh, you have broken my heart; I am sure you have!" and she sobbed hysterically.

"I can't stand much more of this," roared Von Hartmann furiously. "What the deuce does the girl mean? What did I do ten months ago which inspired you with such a particular affection for me? If you are really so very fond, you would do better to run away down and find the schinken and some bread, instead of talking all this nonsense."

"Oh, my darling!" cried the unhappy maiden, throwing herself into the arms of what she imagined to be her lover, "you do but joke in order to frighten your little Elise."

Now it chanced that at the moment of this unexpected embrace Von Hartmann was still leaning back against the end of the sofa, which, like much German furniture, was in a somewhat rickety condition. It also chanced that beneath this end of the sofa there stood a tank full of water in which the physiologist was conducting certain experiments upon the ova of fish, and which he kept in his drawing room in order to insure an equable temperature. The additional weight of the maiden, combined with the impetus with which she hurled herself upon him, caused the precarious piece of furniture to give way, and the body of the unfortunate student was hurled backward into the tank, in which his head and shoulders were firmly wedged, while his lower extremities flapped helplessly about in the air. This was the last straw. Extricating himself with some difficulty from his unpleasant position, Von Hartmann gave an inarticulate yell of fury, and dashing out of the room, in spite of the entreaties of Elise, he seized his hat and rushed off into the town, all dripping and disheveled, with the intention of seeking in some inn the food and comfort which he could not find at home.

As the spirit of Von Baumgarten encased in the body of Von Hartmann strode down the winding pathway which led down to the little town, brooding angrily over his many wrongs, he became aware that an elderly man was approaching him who appeared to be in an advanced state of intoxication. Von Hartmann waited by the side of the road and watched this individual, who came stumbling along, reeling from one side of the road to the other, and singing a student song in a very husky and drunken voice. At first his interest was merely excited by the fact of seeing a man of so venerable an appearance in such a disgraceful condition, but as he approached nearer, he became convinced that he knew the other well, though he could not recall when or where he had met him. This impression became so strong with him, that when the stranger came abreast of him he stepped in front of him and took a good look at his features.

"Well, sonny," said the drunken man, surveying Von Hartmann and swaying about in front of him, "where the Henker have I seen you before? I know you as well as I know myself. Who the deuce are you?"

"I am Professor von Baumgarten," said the student. "May I ask who you are? I am strongly familiar with your features."

"You should never tell lies, young man," said the other. "You're certainly not the Professor, for he is an ugly snuffy old chap, and you are a big broad-shouldered young fellow. As to myself, I am Fritz von Hartmann at your service."

"That you certainly are not," exclaimed the body of Von Hartmann. "You might very well be his father. But hullo, sir, are you aware that you are wearing my studs and my watch chain?"

"Donnerwetter!" hiccoughed the other. "If those are not the trousers for which my tailor is about to sue me, may I never taste beer again."

Now as Von Hartmann, overwhelmed by the many strange things which had occurred to him that day, passed his hand over his forehead and cast his eyes downward, he chanced to catch the reflection of his own face in a pool which the rain had left upon the road. To his utter astonishment he perceived that his face was that of a youth, that his dress was that of a fashionable young student, and that in every way he was the antithesis of the grave and scholarly figure in which his mind was wont to dwell. In an instant his active brain ran over the series of events which had occurred and sprang to the conclusion. He fairly reeled under the blow.

"Himmel!" he cried, "I see it all. Our souls are in the wrong bodies. I am you and you are I. My theory is proved—but at what an expense! Is the most scholarly mind in Europe to go about with this frivolous exterior? Oh the labors of a lifetime are ruined!" and he smote his breast in his despair.

"I say," remarked the real Von Hartmann from the body of the Professor, "I quite see the force of your remarks, but don't go knocking my body about like that. You received it in excellent condition, but I perceive that you have wet it and bruised it, and spilled snuff over my ruffled shirtfront."

"It matters little," the other said moodily. "Such as we are so must we stay. My theory is triumphantly proved, but the cost is terrible."

"If I thought so," said the spirit of the student, "it would be hard indeed. What could I do with these stiff old limbs, and how could I woo Elise and persuade her that I was not her father? No, thank Heaven, in spite of the beer which has upset me more than ever it could upset my real self, I can see a way out of it."

"How?" gasped the Professor.

"Why, by repeating the experiment. Liberate our souls once more, and the chances are that they will find their way back into their respective bodies."

No drowning man could clutch more eagerly to a straw than did Von Baumgarten's spirit at this suggestion. In feverish haste he dragged his own frame to the side of the road and threw it into a mesmeric trance; he then extracted the crystal ball from the pocket, and managed to bring himself into the same condition.

Some students and peasants who chanced to pass during the next hour were much astonished to see the worthy Professor of Physiology and his favorite student both sitting upon a very muddy bank and both completely insensible. Before the hour was up quite a crowd had assembled, and they were discussing the advisability of sending for an ambulance to convey the pair to hospital, when the learned savant opened his eyes and gazed vacantly around him. For an instant he seemed to forget how he had come there, but next moment he astonished his audience by waving his skinny arms above his head and crying in a voice of rapture, "Gott sei gedanket! I am myself again. I feel I am!" Nor was the amazement lessened when the student, springing to his feet, burst into the same cry, and the two performed a sort of *pas de joie* in the middle of the road.

For sometime after that people had some suspicion of the sanity of both the actors in this strange episode. When the Professor published his experiences in the *Medicalschrift* as he had promised, he was met by an intimation, even from his colleagues, that he would do well to have his mind cared for, and that another such publication would certainly consign him to a madhouse. The student also found by experience that it was wisest to be silent about the matter.

When the worthy lecturer returned home that night he did not receive the cordial welcome which he might have looked for after his strange adventures. On the contrary, he was roundly upbraided by both his female relatives for smelling of drink and tobacco, and also for being absent while a young scapegrace invaded the house and insulted its occupants. It was long before the domestic atmosphere of the lecturer's house resumed its normal quiet, and longer still before the genial face of

Von Hartmann was seen beneath its roof. Perseverance, however, conquers every obstacle, and the student eventually succeeded in pacifying the enraged ladies and in establishing himself upon the old footing. He has now no longer any cause to fear the enmity of Madame, for he is Hauptmann von Hartmann of the Emperor's own Uhlans, and his loving wife Elise has already presented him with two little Uhlans as a visible sign and token of her affection.

DANGER!

It is an amazing thing that the English, who have the reputation of being a practical nation, never saw the danger to which they were exposed. For many years they had been spending nearly a hundred millions a year upon their army and their fleet. Squadrons of dreadnoughts costing two millions each had been launched. They had spent enormous sums upon cruisers, and both their torpedo and their submarine squadrons were exceptionally strong. They were also by no means weak in their aerial power, especially in the matter of hydroplanes. Besides all this, their army was very efficient in spite of its limited numbers, and it was the most expensive in Europe. Yet when the day of trial came, all this imposing force was of no use whatever, and might as well have not existed. Their ruin could not have been more complete or more rapid if they had not possessed an ironclad or a regiment. And all this was accomplished by me, Captain John Sirius, belonging to the navy of one of the smallest powers in Europe, and having under my command a flotilla of eight vessels, the collective cost of which was eighteen hundred thousand pounds. No one has a better right to tell the story than I.

I will not trouble you about the dispute concerning the Colonial frontier, embittered, as it was, by the subsequent death of the two missionaries. A naval officer has nothing to do with politics. I only came upon the scene after the ultimatum had been actually received. Admiral

Horli had been summoned to the Presence, and he asked that I should be allowed to accompany him, because he happened to know that I had some clear ideas as to the weak points of England and also some schemes as to how to take advantage of them. There were only four of us present at this meeting—the King, the Foreign Secretary, Admiral Horli, and myself. The time allowed by the ultimatum expired in forty-eight hours.

I am not breaking any confidence when I say that both the King and the Minister were in favor of a surrender. They saw no possibility of standing up against the colossal power of Great Britain. The Minister had drawn up an acceptance of the British terms, and the King sat with it before him on the table. I saw the tears of anger and humiliation run down his cheeks as he looked at it.

"I fear that there is no possible alternative, Sire," said the Minister. "Our envoy in London has just sent this report, which shows that the public and the Press are more united than he has ever known them. The feeling is intense, especially since the rash act of Malort in desecrating the flag. We must give way."

The King looked sadly at Admiral Horli.

"What is your effective fleet, Admiral?" he asked.

"Two battleships, four cruisers, twenty torpedo boats, and eight submarines," said the Admiral.

The King shook his head.

"It would be madness to resist," said he.

"And yet, Sire," said the Admiral, "before you come to a decision I should wish you to hear Captain Sirius, who has a very definite plan of campaign against the English."

"Absurd!" said the King, impatiently. "What is the use? Do you imagine that you could defeat their vast armada?"

"Sire," I answered, "I will stake my life that if you will follow my advice you will, within a month or six weeks at the utmost, bring proud England to her knees." There was an assurance in my voice which arrested the attention of the King.

"You seem self-confident, Captain Sirius."

"I have no doubt at all, Sire."

"What then would you advise?"

"I would advise, Sire, that the whole fleet be gathered under the forts of Blankenberg and be protected from attack by booms and piles. There they can stay till the war is over. The eight submarines, however, you will leave in my charge to use as I think fit."

"Ah, you would attack the English battleships with submarines?"

"Sire, I would never go near an English battleship."

"And why not?"

"Because they might injure me, Sire."

"What, a sailor and afraid?"

"My life belongs to the country, Sire. It is nothing. But these eight ships—everything depends upon them. I could not risk them. Nothing would induce me to fight."

"Then what will you do?"

"I will tell you, Sire."

And I did so. For half an hour I spoke. I was clear and strong and definite, for many an hour on a lonely watch I had spent in thinking out every detail. I held them enthralled. The King never took his eyes from my face. The Minister sat as if turned to stone.

"Are you sure of all this?"

"Perfectly, Sire."

The King rose from the table.

"Send no answer to the ultimatum," said he. "Announce in both Houses that we stand firm in the face of menace. Admiral Horli, you will in all respects carry out that which Captain Sirius may demand in furtherance of his plan. Captain Sirius, the field is clear. Go forth and do as you have said. A grateful King will know how to reward you."

I need not trouble you by telling you the measures which were taken at Blankenberg, since, as you are aware, the fortress and the entire fleet were destroyed by the British within a week of the declaration of war. I will confine myself to my own plans, which had so glorious and final a result.

The fame of my eight submarines, *Alpha*, *Beta*, *Gamma*, *Theta*, *Delta*, *Epsilon*, *Iota*, and *Kappa*, has spread through the world to such an extent that people have begun to think that there was something peculiar in their form and capabilities. This is not so. Four of them, the *Delta*, *Epsilon*, *Iota*, and *Kappa*, were, it is true, of the very latest model, but had their equals (though not their superiors) in the navies of all the great powers. As to *Alpha*, *Beta*, *Gamma*, and *Theta*, they were by no means modern vessels, and found their prototypes in the old F class of British boats, having a submerged displacement of eight hundred tons, with heavy oil engines of sixteen hundred horsepower, giving them a speed of eighteen knots on the surface and of twelve knots submerged. Their length was one hundred and eighty-six and their breadth twenty-four feet. They had a radius of action of four thousand miles and a submerged endurance of nine hours. These were considered the latest word in 1915, but the four new boats exceeded them in all respects. Without troubling you with precise figures, I may say that they represented roughly a 25 percent advance upon the older boats, and were fitted with several auxiliary engines which were wanting in the others. At my suggestion, instead of carrying eight of the very large Bakdorf torpedoes, which are nineteen feet long, weigh half a ton, and are charged with two hundred pounds of wet guncotton, we had tubes designed for eighteen of less than half the size. It was my design to make myself independent of my base.

And yet it was clear that I must have a base, so I made arrangements at once with that object. Blankenberg was the last place I would have chosen. Why should I have a *port* of any kind? Ports would be watched or occupied. Anyplace would do for me. I finally chose a small villa standing alone nearly five miles from any village and thirty miles from any port. To this I ordered them to convey, secretly by night, oil, spare parts, extra torpedoes, storage batteries, reserve periscopes, and everything that I could need for refitting. The little whitewashed villa of a retired confectioner—that was the base from which I operated against England.

The boats lay at Blankenberg, and thither I went. They were working frantically at the defenses, and they had only to look seaward to be spurred to fresh exertions. The British fleet was assembling. The ultimatum had not yet expired, but it was evident that a blow would be struck the instant that it did. Four of their airplanes, circling at an immense height, were surveying our defences. From the top of the lighthouse I counted thirty battleships and cruisers in the offing, with a number of the trawlers with which in the British service they break through the minefields. The approaches were actually sown with two hundred mines, half contact and half observation, but the result showed that they were insufficient to hold off the enemy, since three days later both town and fleet were speedily destroyed.

However, I am not here to tell you the incidents of the war, but to explain my own part in it, which had such a decisive effect upon the result. My first action was to send my four second-class boats away instantly to the point which I had chosen for my base. There they were to wait submerged, lying with negative buoyancy upon the sands in twenty feet of water, and rising only at night. My strict orders were that they were to attempt nothing upon the enemy, however tempting the opportunity. All they had to do was to remain intact and unseen until they received further orders. Having made this clear to Commander Panza, who had charge of this reserve flotilla, I shook him by the hand and bade him farewell, leaving with him a sheet of notepaper upon which I had explained the tactics to be used and given him certain general principles which he could apply as circumstances demanded.

My whole attention was now given to my own flotilla, which I divided into two divisions, keeping *Iota* and *Kappa* under my own command, while Captain Miriam had *Delta* and *Epsilon*. He was to operate separately in the British Channel, while my station was the Straits of Dover. I made the whole plan of campaign clear to him. Then I saw that each ship was provided with all it could carry. Each had forty tons of heavy oil for surface propulsion and charging the dynamo which supplied the electric engines under water. Each had also eighteen torpedoes, as explained, and five hundred rounds for the collapsible quick-firing twelve-pounder which we carried on deck, and which, of course, disappeared into a watertight tank when we were submerged. We carried spare periscopes and a wireless mast, which could be elevated above the conning tower when necessary. There were provisions for sixteen days for the ten men who manned each craft. Such was the equipment of the four boats which were destined to bring to naught all the navies and armies of Britain. At sundown that day—it was April 10th—we set forth upon our historic voyage.

Miriam had got away in the afternoon, since he had so much farther to go to reach his station. Stephan of the *Kappa* started with me; but, of course, we realized that we must work independently, and that from that moment when we shut the sliding hatches of our conning towers on the still waters of Blankenberg Harbor it was unlikely that we should ever see each other again, though consorts in the same waters. I waved to Stephan from the side of my conning tower, and he to me. Then I called through the tube to my engineer (our water tanks were already filled and all Kingstons and vents closed) to put her full speed ahead.

Just as we came abreast of the end of the pier and saw the white-capped waves rolling in upon us, I put the horizontal rudder hard down and she slid under water. Through my glass portholes I saw its light green change to a dark blue, while the manometer in front of me indicated twenty feet. I let her go to forty, because I should then be under the warships of the English, though I took the chance of fouling the moorings of our own floating contact mines. Then I brought her on an even keel, and it was music to my ear to hear the gentle, even ticking of my electric engines and to know that I was speeding at twelve miles an hour on my great task.

At that moment, as I stood controling my levers in my tower, I could have seen, had my cupola been of glass, the vast shadows of the British blockaders hovering above me. I held my course due westward for ninety minutes, and then, by shutting off the electric engine without blowing out the water tanks, I brought her to the surface. There was a rolling sea and the wind was freshening, so I did not think it safe to keep my hatch open long, for so small is the margin of buoyancy that one must run no risks. But from the crests of the rollers I had a look backward at Blankenberg, and saw the black funnels and upper works of the enemy's fleet with the lighthouse and the castle behind them, all flushed with the pink glow of the setting sun. Even as I looked there was the boom of the great gun, and then another. I glanced at my watch. It was six o'clock. The time of the ultimatum had expired. We were at war.

There was no craft near us, and our surface speed is nearly twice that of our submerged, so I blew out the tanks and our whaleback came over the surface. All night we were steering southwest, making an average of eighteen knots. At about five in the morning, as I stood alone upon my tiny bridge, I saw, low down in the west, the scattered lights of the Norfolk coast. "Ah, Johnny, Johnny Bull," I said, as I looked at them, "you are going to have your lesson, and I am to be your master. It is I who have been chosen to teach you that one cannot live under artificial conditions and yet act as if they were natural ones. More foresight, Johnny, and less party politics—that is my lesson to you." And then I had a wave of pity, too, when I thought of those vast droves of helpless people, Yorkshire miners, Lancashire spinners, Birmingham metal-workers, the dockers and workers of London, over whose little homes I would bring the shadow of starvation. I seemed to see all those wasted, eager hands held out for food and I, John Sirius, dashing it aside. Ah, well! war is war, and if one is foolish one must pay the price. Just before daybreak I saw the lights of a considerable town, which must have been Yarmouth, bearing about ten miles west-southwest on our starboard bow. I took her farther out, for it is a sandy, dangerous coast, with many shoals. At 5:30 we were abreast of the Lowestoft lightship. A coastguard was sending up flash signals which faded into a pale twinkle as the white dawn crept over the water. There was a good deal of shipping about, mostly fishing boats and small coasting craft, with one large steamer hull down to the west, and a torpedo destroyer between us and the land. It could not harm us, and yet I thought it as well that there should be no word of our presence, so I filled my tanks again and went down to ten feet. I was pleased to find that we got under in one hundred and fifty seconds. The life of one's boat may depend upon this when a swift craft comes suddenly upon you.

We were now within a few hours of our cruising ground, so I determined to snatch a rest, leaving Vornal in charge. When he woke me at ten o'clock we were running on the surface, and had reached the Essex coast off the Maplin Sands. With that charming frankness which is one of their characteristics, our friends of England had informed us by their Press that they had put a cordon of torpedo boats across the Straits of Dover to prevent the passage of submarines, which is about as sensible as to lay a wooden plank across a stream to keep the eels from passing. I knew that Stephan, whose station lay at the western end of the Solent, would have no difficulty in reaching it. My own cruising ground was to be the mouth of the Thames, and here I was at the very spot with my tiny *Iota*, my eighteen torpedoes, my quick-firing gun, and, above all, a brain that knew what should be done and how to do it.

When I resumed my place in the conning tower I saw in the periscope (for we had dived) that a lightship was within a few hundred yards of us upon the port bow. Two men were sitting on her bulwarks, but neither of them cast an eye upon the little rod that clove the water so close to them. It was an ideal day for submarine action, with enough ripple upon the surface to make us difficult to detect, and yet smooth enough to give me a clear view. Each of my three periscopes had an angle of sixty degrees, so that between them I commanded a complete semicircle of the horizon. Two British cruisers were steaming north from the Thames within half a mile of me. I could easily have cut them off and attacked them had I allowed myself to be diverted from my great plan. Farther south a destroyer was passing westward to Sheerness. A dozen small steamers were moving about. None of these were worthy of my notice. Great countries are not provisioned by small steamers. I kept the engines running at the lowest pace which would hold our position under water, and, moving slowly across the estuary, I waited for what must assuredly come. I had not long to wait.

Shortly after one o'clock I perceived in the periscope a cloud of smoke to the south. Half an hour later a large steamer raised her hull, making for the mouth of the Thames. I ordered Vornal to stand by the starboard torpedo tube, having the other also loaded in case of a miss. Then I advanced slowly, for though the steamer was going very swiftly we could easily cut her off. Presently I laid the *Iota* in a position near which she must pass, and would very gladly have lain to, but could not for fear of rising to the surface. I therefore steered out in the direction from which she was coming. She was a very large ship, fifteen thousand tons at the least, painted black above and red below, with two cream-colored funnels. She lay so low in the water that it was clear she had a full cargo. At her bows were a cluster of men, some of them looking, I dare say, for the first time at the mother country. How little could they have guessed the welcome that was waiting them!

On she came with the great plumes of smoke floating from her funnels, and two white waves foaming from her cutwater. She was within a quarter of a mile. My moment had arrived. I signaled full speed ahead and steered straight for her course. My timing was exact. At a hundred yards I gave the signal, and heard the clank and swish of the discharge. At the same instant I put the helm hard down and flew off at an angle. There was a terrific lurch, which came from the distant explosion. For a moment we were almost on our side. Then, after staggering and trembling, the *Iota* came on an even keel. I stopped the engines, brought her to the surface, and opened the conning, while all my excited crew came crowding to the hatch to know what had happened.

The ship lay within two yards of us, and it was easy to see that she had her deathblow. She was already settling down by the stern. There was a sound of shouting and people running wildly about her decks. Her name was visible, the *Adela* of London, bound, as we afterward learned, from New Zealand with frozen mutton. Strange as it may seem to you, the notion of a submarine had never even now occurred to her people, and all were convinced that they had struck a floating mine. The starboard quarter had been blown in by the explosion, and the ship was sinking rapidly. Their discipline was admirable. We saw boat after boat slip down crowded with people as swiftly and quietly as if it were part of their daily drill. And suddenly, as one of the boats lay off waiting for the others, they caught a glimpse for the first time of my conning tower so close to them. I saw them shouting and pointing, while the men in the other boats got up to have a better look at us. For my part, I cared nothing, for I took it for granted that they already knew that a submarine had destroyed them. One of them clambered back into the sinking ship. I was sure that he was about to send a wireless message as to our presence. It mattered nothing, since, in any case, it must be known; otherwise I could easily have brought him down with a rifle. As it was, I waved my hand to them, and they waved back at me. War is too big a thing to leave room for personal ill feeling, but it must be remorseless all the same.

I was still looking at the sinking *Adela* when Vornal, who was beside me, gave a sudden cry of warning and surprise, gripping me by the shoulder and turning my head. There behind us, coming up the fairway, was a huge black vessel with black funnels, flying the well-known house flag of the P. and O. Company. She was not a mile distant, and I calculated in an instant that even if she had seen us she would not have time to turn and get away before we could reach her. We went straight for her, therefore, keeping awash just as we were. They saw the sinking vessel in front of them and that little dark speck moving over the surface, and they suddenly understood their danger. I saw a number of men rush to the bows, and there was a rattle of rifle fire. Two bullets were flattened upon our four-inch armor. You might as well try to stop a charging bull with paper pellets as the *Iota* with rifle fire. I had learned my lesson from the *Adela*, and this time I had the torpedo discharged at a safer distance—two hundred and fifty yards. We caught her amidships and the explosion was tremendous, but we were well outside its area. She sank almost instantaneously.

I am sorry for her people, of whom I hear that more than two hundred, including seventy Lascars and forty passengers, were drowned. Yes, I am sorry for them. But when I think of the huge floating granary that went to the bottom, I rejoice as a man does who has carried out that which he plans.

It was a bad afternoon that for the P. and O. Company. The second ship which we destroyed was, as we have since learned, the *Moldavia*, of fifteen thousand tons, one of their finest vessels; but about half past three we blew up the *Cusco*, of eight thousand, of the same line, also from Eastern ports, and laden with corn. Why she came on in face of the wireless messages, which must have warned her of danger, I cannot imagine. The other two steamers which we blew up that day, the *Maid of Athens* (Robson Line) and the *Cormorant*, were neither of them provided with apparatus, and came blindly to their destruction. Both were small boats of from five thousand to seven thousand tons. In the case of the second, I had to rise to the surface and fire six twelve-pound shells under her waterline before she would sink. In each case the crew took to the boats, and so far as I know no casualties occurred.

After that no more steamers came along, nor did I expect them. Warnings must by this time have been flying in all directions. But we had no reason to be dissatisfied with our first day. Between the Maplin Sands and Nore we had sunk five ships of a total tonnage of about fifty thousand tons. Already the London markets would begin to feel the pinch. And Lloyd's—poor old Lloyd's—what a demented state it would be in! I could imagine the London evening papers and the howling in Fleet Street. We saw the result of our actions, for it was quite laughable to see the torpedo boats buzzing like angry wasps out of Sheerness in the evening. They were darting in every direction across the estuary, and the airplanes and hydroplanes were like flights of crows, black dots against the red western sky. They quartered the whole river mouth, until they discovered us at last. Some sharp-sighted fellow with a telescope on board of a destroyer got a sight of our periscope, and came for us full speed. No doubt he would very gladly have rammed us, even if it had meant his own destruction, but that was not part of our program at all. I sank her and ran her east-southeast with an occasional rise. Finally we brought her to, not very far from the Kentish coast, and the searchlights of our pursuers were far on the western skyline. There we lay quietly all night, for a submarine at night is nothing more than a very third-rate surface torpedo boat. Besides, we were all weary and needed rest. Do not forget, you captains of men, when you grease and trim your pumps and compressors and rotators, that the human machine needs some tending also.

I had put up the wireless mast above the conning tower, and had no difficulty in calling up Captain Stephan. He was lying, he said, off Ventnor, and had been unable to reach his station on account of engine trouble, which he had now set right. Next morning he proposed to block the Southampton approach. He had destroyed one large Indian boat on his way down Channel. We exchanged good wishes. Like myself, he needed rest. I was up at four in the morning, however, and called all hands to overhaul the boat. She was somewhat up by the head, owing to the forward torpedoes having been used, so we trimmed her by opening the forward compensating tank, admitting as much water as the torpedoes had weighed. We also overhauled the starboard air compressor and one of the periscope motors which had been jarred by the shock of the first explosion. We had hardly got ourselves shipshape when the morning dawned.

I have no doubt that a good many ships which had taken refuge in the French ports at the first alarm had run across and got safely up the river in the night. Of course I could have attacked them, but I do not care to take risks—and there are always risks at night. But one had miscalculated his time, and there she was, just abreast of Warden Point, when the daylight disclosed her to us. In an instant we were after her. It was a near thing, for she was a flyer, and could do two miles to our one; but we just reached her as she went swashing by. She saw us at the last moment, for I attacked her awash, since otherwise we could not have had the pace to reach her. She swung away and the first torpedo missed, but the second took her full under the counter. Heavens, what a smash! The whole stern seemed to go aloft. I drew off and watched her sink. She went down in seven minutes, leaving her masts and funnels over the water and a cluster of her people holding on to them. She was the *Virginia* of the Bibby Line—twelve thousand tons—and laden, like the others, with foodstuffs from the East. The whole surface of the sea was covered with the floating grain. "John Bull will have to take up a hole or two of his belt if this goes on," said Vornal, as we watched the scene.

And it was at that moment that the very worst danger occurred that could befall us. I tremble now when I think how our glorious voyage might have been nipped in the bud. I had freed the hatch of my tower and was looking at the boats of the *Virginia* with Vornal beside me, when there was a swish and a terrific splash in the water beside us, which covered us both with spray. We looked up, and you can imagine our feelings when we saw an airplane hovering a few hundred feet above us like a hawk. With its silencer, it was perfectly noiseless, and had its bomb not fallen into the sea we should never have known what had destroyed us. She was circling round in the hope of dropping a second one, but we shoved on all speed ahead, crammed down the rudders, and vanished into the side of a roller. I kept the deflection indicator falling until I had put fifty good feet of water between the airplane and ourselves, for I knew well how deep they can see under the surface. However, we soon threw her off our track, and when we came to the surface near Margate there was no sign of her, unless she was one of several which we saw hovering over Herne Bay.

There was not a ship in the offing save a few small coasters and little thousand-ton steamers, which were beneath my notice. For several hours I lay submerged with a blank periscope. Then I had an inspiration. Orders had been Marconied to every food ship to lie in French waters and dash across after dark. I was as sure of it as if they had been recorded in our own receiver. Well, if they were there, that was where I should be also. I blew out the tanks and rose, for there was no sign of any warship near. They had some good system of signaling from the shore, however, for I had not got the North Foreland before three destroyers came foaming after me, all converging from different directions. They had about as good a chance of catching me as three spaniels would of overtaking a porpoise. Out of pure bravado—I know it was very wrong—I waited until they were actually within gunshot. Then I sank and we saw each other no more.

It is, as I have said, a shallow, sandy coast, and submarine navigation is very difficult. The worst mishap that can befall a boat is to bury its nose in the side of a sand drift and be held there. Such an accident might have been the end of our boat, though with our Fluess cylinders and electric lamps we should have found no difficulty in getting out at the air lock and in walking ashore across the bed of the ocean. As it was, however, I was able, thanks to our excellent charts, to keep the channel and so to gain the open straits. There we rose about midday, but, observing a hydroplane at no great distance, we sank again for half an hour. When we came up for the second time, all was peaceful around us, and the English coast was lining the whole western horizon. We kept outside the Goodwins and straight down Channel until we saw a line of black dots in front of us, which I knew to be the Dover-Calais torpedo-boat cordon. When two miles distant we dived and came up again seven miles to the southwest, without one of them dreaming that we had been within thirty feet of their keels.

When we rose, a large steamer flying the German flag was within half a mile of us. It was the North German Lloyd *Altona*, from New York to Bremen. I raised our whole hull and dipped our flag to her. It was amusing to see the amazement of her people at what they must have regarded as our unparalleled impudence in those English-swept waters. They cheered us heartily, and the tricolor flag was dipped in greeting as they went roaring past us. Then I stood in to the French coast.

It was exactly as I had expected. There were three great British steamers lying at anchor in Boulogne, outer harbor. They were the *Cæsar*, the *King of the East*, and the *Pathfinder*, none less than ten thousand tons. I suppose they thought they were safe in French waters, but what did I care about three-mile limits and international law! The view of my Government was that England was blockaded, food contraband, and vessels carrying it to be destroyed. The lawyers could argue about it afterward. My business was to starve the enemy anyway I could. Within an hour the three ships were under the waves and the *Iota* was steaming down the Picardy coast, looking for fresh victims. The Channel was covered with English torpedo boats buzzing and whirling like a cloud of midges. How they thought they could hurt me I cannot imagine, unless by accident I were to come up underneath one of them. More dangerous were the airplanes which circled here and there.

The water being calm, I had several times to descend as deep as a hundred feet before I was sure that I was out of their sight. After I had blown up the three ships at Boulogne I saw two airplanes flying down Channel, and I knew that they would head off any vessels which were coming up. There was one very large white steamer lying off Havre, but she steamed west before I could reach her. I dare say Stephan or one of the others would get her before long. But those infernal airplanes spoiled our sport for that day. Not another steamer did I see, save the never-ending torpedo boats. I consoled myself with the reflection, however, that no food was passing me on its way to London. That was what I was there for, after all. If I could do it without spending my torpedoes, all the better. Up to date I had fired ten of them and sunk nine steamers, so I had not wasted my weapons. That night I came back to the Kent coast and lay upon the bottom in shallow water near Dungeness.

We were all trimmed and ready at the first break of day, for I expected to catch some ships which had tried to make the Thames in the darkness and had miscalculated their time. Sure enough, there was a great steamer coming up Channel and flying the American flag. It was all the same to me what flag she flew so long as she was engaged in conveying contraband of war to the British Isles. There were no torpedo boats about at the moment, so I ran out on the surface and fired a shot across at her bows. She seemed inclined to go on, so I put a second one just above her waterline on her port bow. She stopped then and a very angry man began to gesticulate from the bridge. I ran the *Iota* almost alongside. "Are you the captain?" I asked.

"What the———" I won't attempt to reproduce his language.

"You have foodstuffs on board?" I said.

"It's an American ship, you blind beetle!" he cried. "Can't you see the flag? It's the *Vermondia* of Boston."

"Sorry, Captain," I answered. "I have really no time for words. Those shots of mine will bring the torpedo boats, and I dare say at this very moment your wireless is making trouble for me. Get your people into the boats."

I had to show him I was not bluffing, so I drew off and began putting shells into him just on the waterline. When I had knocked six holes in his ship he was very busy on his boats. I fired twenty shots altogether, and no torpedo was needed, for she was lying over with a terrible list to port, and presently came right onto her side. There she lay for two or three minutes before she foundered. There were eight boats crammed with people lying round her when she went down. I believe everybody was saved, but I could not wait to inquire. From all quarters the poor old panting, useless war vessels were hurrying. I filled my tanks, ran our bows under, and came up fifteen miles to the south. Of course, I knew there would be a big row afterward—as there was—but that did not help the starving crowds round the London bakers, who only saved their skins, poor devils, by explaining to the mob that they had nothing to bake.

By this time I was becoming rather anxious, as you can imagine, to know what was going on in the world and what England was thinking about it all. I ran alongside a fishing boat, therefore, and ordered them to give up their papers. Unfortunately, they had none, except a rag of an evening paper, which was full of nothing but betting news. In a second attempt I came alongside a small yachting party from Eastbourne, who were frightened to death at our sudden appearance out of the depths. From them we were lucky enough to get the London *Courier* of that very morning.

It was interesting reading—so interesting that I had to announce it all to the crew. Of course, you know the British style of headline, which gives you all the news at a glance. It seemed to me that the whole paper was headlines, it was in such a state of excitement. Hardly a word about me and my flotilla. We were on the second page. The first one began something like this:

CAPTURE OF BLANKENBERG!

DESTRUCTION OF ENEMY'S FLEET

BURNING OF TOWN

TRAWLERS DESTROY MINEFIELD
LOSS OF TWO BATTLESHIPS

IS IT THE END?

Of course, what I had foreseen had occurred. The town was actually occupied by the British. And they thought it was the end! We would see about that.

On the round-the-corner page, at the back of the glorious resonant leaders, there was a little column which read like this:

HOSTILE SUBMARINES

Several of the enemy's submarines are at sea, and have inflicted some appreciable damage upon our merchant ships. The danger spots upon Monday and the greater part of Tuesday appear to have been the mouth of the Thames and the western entrance to the Solent. On Monday, between the Nore and Margate, there were sunk five large steamers, the *Adela, Moldavia, Cuso, Cormorant,* and *Maid of Athens*, particulars of which will be found below. Near Ventnor on the same day was sunk the *Verulam*, from Bombay. On Tuesday the *Virginia, Cæsar, King of the East,* and *Pathfinder* were destroyed between the Foreland and Boulogne. The latter three were actually lying in French waters, and the most energetic representations have been made by the Government of the Repub- lic. On the same day *The Queen of Sheba, Orontes, Diana,* and *Atalanta* were destroyed near the Needles. Wireless messages have stopped all ingoing cargo ships from coming up Channel, but unfortunately there is evidence that at least two of the enemy's submarines are in the west. Four cattle ships from Dublin to Liverpool were sunk yesterday evening, while three Bristol-bound steamers, *The Hilda, Mercury,* and *Maria Toser*, were blown up in the neigh- borhood of Lundy Island. Commerce has, so far as possible, been diverted into safer channels, but in the meantime, however vexa- tious these incidents may be, and however grievous the loss both to the owners and to Lloyd's, we may console ourselves by the reflection that since a submarine cannot keep the sea for more than ten days without refitting, and since the base has been captured, there must come a speedy term to these depredations.

So much for the *Courier's* account of our proceedings. Another small paragraph was, however, more eloquent:

The price of wheat [it said], which stood at thirty-five shillings a week before the declaration of war, was quoted yesterday on the Baltic at fifty-two. Maize has gone from twenty-one to thirty-seven, barley from nineteen to thirty-five, sugar (foreign granulated) from eleven shillings and threepence to nineteen shillings and sixpence.

"Good, my lads!" I said when I read it to the crew. "I can assure you that those few lines will prove to mean more than the whole page about the fall of Blankenberg. Now let us get down Channel and send those prices up a little higher."

All traffic had stopped from London—not so bad for the little *Iota*—and we did not see a steamer that was worth a torpedo between Dungeness and the Isle of Wight. There I called Stephan up by wireless, and by seven o'clock we were actually lying side by side in a smooth, rolling sea—Hengistbury Head bearing N.N.W. and about five miles distant. The two crews clustered on the whalebacks and shouted their joy at seeing friendly faces once more. Stephan had done extraordinarily well. I had, of course, read in the London paper of his four ships on Tuesday, but he had sunk no fewer than seven since, for many of those which should have come to the Thames had tried to make Southampton. Of the seven, one was of twenty thousand tons, a grain ship from America; a second was a grain ship from the Black Sea; and two others were great liners from South Africa. I congratulated Stephan with all my heart upon his splendid achievement. Then, as we had been seen by a destroyer which was approaching at a great pace, we both dived, coming up again off the Needles, where we spent the night in company. We could not visit each other, since we had no boat, but we lay so nearly alongside that we were able, Stephan and I, to talk from hatch to hatch and so make our plans.

He had shot away more than half his torpedoes and so had I, and yet we were very averse from returning to our base so long as our oil held out. I told him of my experience with the Boston steamer, and we mutually agreed to sink the ships by gunfire in future so far as possible. I remember old Horli saying: "What use is a gun aboard a submarine?" We were about to show. I read the English paper to Stephan by the light of my electric torch, and we both agreed that few ships would now come up the Channel. That sentence about diverting commerce to safer routes could only mean that the ships would go round the north of Ireland and unload at Glasgow. Oh, for two more ships to stop that entrance! Heavens, what *would* England have done against a foe with thirty or forty submarines, since we only needed six instead of four to complete her destruction!

After much talk we decided that the best plan would be that I should dispatch a cipher telegram next morning from a French port to tell them to send the four second-rate boats to cruise off the north of Ireland and west of Scotland. Then when I had done this I should move down Channel with Stephan and operate at the mouth, while the other two boats could work in the Irish Sea. Having made these plans, I set off across the Channel in the early morning, reaching the small village of Etretat, in Brittany. There I got off my telegram and then laid my course for Falmouth, passing under the keels of two British cruisers which were making eagerly for Etretat, having heard by wireless that we were there.

Halfway down Channel we had trouble with a short circuit in our electric engines, and were compelled to run on the surface for several hours while we replaced one of the camshafts and renewed some washers. It was a ticklish time, for had a torpedo boat come upon us we could not have dived. The perfect submarine of the future will surely have some alternative engines for such an emergency. However, by the skill of Engineer Morrow we got things going once more. All the time we lay there I saw a hydroplane floating between us and the British coast. I can understand how a mouse feels when it is in a tuft of grass and sees a hawk high up in the heavens. However, all went well; the mouse became a water rat, it wagged its tail in derision at the poor blind old hawk, and it dived down into a nice, safe, green, quiet world where there was nothing to injure it.

It was on Wednesday night that the *Iota* crossed to Etretat. It was Friday afternoon before we had reached our new cruising ground. Only one large steamer did I see upon our way. The terror we had caused had cleared the Channel. This big boat had a clever captain on board. His tactics were excellent and took him in safety to the Thames. He came zigzagging up Channel at twenty-five knots, shooting off from his course at all sorts of unexpected angles. With our slow pace we could not catch him, nor could we calculate his line so as to cut him off. Of course, he had never seen us, but he judged, and judged rightly, that wherever we were those were the tactics by which he had the best chance of getting past. He deserved his success.

But, of course, it is only in a wide channel that such things can be done. Had I met him in the mouth of the Thames there would have been a different story to tell. As I approached Falmouth I destroyed a three-thousand-ton boat from Cork, laden with butter and cheese. It was my only success for three days.

That night (Friday, April 16th) I called up Stephan, but received no reply. As I was within a few miles of our rendezvous, and as he would not be cruising after dark, I was puzzled to account for his silence. I could only imagine that his wireless was deranged. But, alas! I was soon to find the true reason from a copy of the *Western Morning News*, which I obtained from a Brixham trawler. The *Kappa*, with her gallant commander and crew, were at the bottom of the English Channel.

It appeared from this account that after I had parted from him he had met and sunk no fewer than five vessels. I gathered this to be his work, since all of them were by gunfire and all were on the south coast of Dorset or Devon. How he met his fate was stated in a short telegram which was headed "Sinking of Hostile Submarine." It was marked "Falmouth," and ran thus:

The P. and O. mail steamer *Macedonia* came into this port last night with five shell holes between wind and water. She reports having been attacked by a hostile submarine ten miles to the southeast of the Lizard. Instead of using her torpedoes, the submarine for some reason approached upon the surface and fired five shots from a semiautomatic twelve-pounder gun. She was evidently under the impression that the *Macedonia* was unarmed. As a matter of fact, being warned of the presence of submarines in the Channel, the *Macedonia* had mounted her armament as an auxiliary cruiser. She opened fire with two quick-firers and blew away the conning tower of the submarine. It is probable that the shells went right through her, as she sank at once with her hatches open. The *Macedonia* was only kept afloat by her pumps.

Such was the end of the *Kappa* and my gallant friend, Commander Stephan. His best epitaph was in a corner of the same paper, and was headed, "Mark Lane." It ran: "Wheat (average) 66, maize 48, barley 50."

Well, if Stephan was gone there was the more need for me to show energy. My plans were quickly taken, but they were comprehensive. All that day (Saturday) I passed down the Cornish coast and round Land's End, getting two steamers on the way. I had learned from Stephan's fate that it was better to torpedo the large craft, but I was aware that the auxiliary cruisers of the British Government were all over ten thousand tons, so that for all ships under that size it was safe to use my gun. Both these craft, the *Yelland* and the *Playboy*—the latter an American ship— were perfectly harmless, so I came up within a hundred yards of them and speedily sank them, after allowing their people to get into the boats. Some other steamers lay farther out, but I was so eager to make my new arrangements that I did not go out of my course to molest them. Just before sunset, however, so magnificent a prey came within my radius of action that I could not possibly refuse her.

No sailor could fail to recognize that glorious monarch of the sea, with her four cream funnels tipped with black, her huge black sides, her red bilges, and her high white top hamper, roaring up channel at twenty-three knots and carrying her forty-five thousand tons as lightly as if she were a five-ton motor boat. It was the queenly *Olympic* of the White Star Line—once the largest and still the comeliest of liners. What a picture she made, with the blue Cornish sea creaming round her giant forefoot, and the pink western sky with one evening star forming the background to her noble lines!

She was about five miles off when we dived to cut her off. My calculation was exact. As we came abreast we loosed our torpedo and struck her fair. We swirled round with the concussion of the water. I saw her in my periscope list over on her side, and I knew that she had her deathblow. She settled down slowly, and there was plenty of time to save her people. The sea was dotted with her boats. When I got about three miles off I rose to the surface, and the whole crew clustered up to see the wonderful sight. She dived bow foremost, and there was a terrific explosion, which sent one of the funnels into the air. I suppose we should have cheered—somehow none of us felt like cheering. We were all keen sailors, and it went to our hearts to see such a ship go down like a broken eggshell. I gave a gruff order, and all were at their posts again while we headed northwest. Once round the Land's End I called up my two consorts, and we met next day at Hartland Point, the south end of Bideford Bay. For the moment the Channel was clear, but the English could not know it, and I reckoned that the loss of the *Olympic* would stop all ships for a day or two at least.

Having assembled the *Delta* and *Epsilon*, one on each side of me, I received reports from Miriam and Var, the respective commanders. Each had expended twelve torpedoes, and between them they had sunk twenty-two steamers. One man had been killed by the machinery on board of the *Delta*, and two had been burned by the ignition of some oil on the *Epsilon*. I took these injured men on board, and I gave each of the boats one of my crew. I also divided my spare oil, my provisions, and my torpedoes among them, though we had the greatest possible difficulty in those crank vessels in transferring them from one to the other. However, by ten o'clock it was done, and the two vessels were in condition to keep the sea for another ten days. For my part, with only two torpedoes left, I headed north up the Irish Sea. One of my torpedoes I expended that evening upon a cattle ship making for Milford Haven. Late at night, being abreast of Holyhead, I called upon my four northern boats, but without reply. Their Marconi range is very limited. About three in the afternoon of the next day I had a feeble answer. It was a great relief to me to find that my telegraphic instructions had reached them and that they were on their station. Before evening we all assembled in the lee of Sanda Island, in the Mull of Kintyre. I felt an admiral indeed when I saw my five whalebacks all in a row. Panza's report was excellent. They had come round by the Pentland Firth and reached their cruising ground on the fourth day. Already they had destroyed twenty vessels without any mishap. I ordered the *Beta* to divide her oil and torpedoes among the other three, so that they were in good condition to continue their cruise. Then the *Beta* and I headed for home, reaching our base upon Sunday, April 25th. Off Cape Wrath I picked up a paper from a small schooner.

"Wheat, 84; maize, 60; barley, 62." What were battles and bombardments compared to that!

The whole coast of Norland was closely blockaded by cordon within cordon, and every port, even the smallest, held by the British. But why should they suspect my modest confectioner's villa more than any other of the ten thousand houses that face the sea? I was glad when I picked up its homely white front in my periscope. That night I landed and found my stores intact. Before morning the *Beta* reported itself, for we had the windows lit as a guide.

It is not for me to recount the messages which I found waiting for me at my humble headquarters. They shall ever remain as the patents of nobility of my family. Among others was that never-to-be-forgotten salutation from my King. He desired me to present myself at Hauptville, but for once I took it upon myself to disobey his commands. It took me two days—or rather two nights, for we sank ourselves during the daylight hours—to get all our stores on board, but my presence was needful every minute of the time. On the third morning, at four o'clock, the *Beta* and my own little flagship were at sea once more, bound for our original station off the mouth of the Thames.

I had no time to read our papers while I was refitting, but I gathered the news after we got under way. The British occupied all our ports, but otherwise we had not suffered at all, since we have excellent railway communications with Europe. Prices had altered little, and our industries continued as before. There was talk of a British invasion, but this I knew to be absolute nonsense, for the British must have learned by this time that it would be sheer murder to send transports full of soldiers to sea in the face of submarines. When they have a tunnel they can use their fine expeditionary force upon the Continent, but until then it might just as well not exist so far as Europe is concerned. My own country, therefore, was in good case and had nothing to fear. Great Britain, however, was already feeling my grip upon her throat. As in normal times four fifths of her food is imported, prices were rising by leaps and bounds. The supplies in the country were beginning to show signs of depletion, while little was coming in to replace them. The insurance at Lloyd's had risen to a figure which made the price of food prohibitive to the mass of the people by the time it had reached the market. The loaf, which under ordinary circumstances stood at fivepence, was already at one and twopence. Beef was three shillings and fourpence a pound, and mutton two shillings and ninepence. Everything else was in proportion. The Government had acted with energy and offered a big bounty for corn to be planted at once. It could only be reaped five months hence, however, and long before then, as the papers pointed out, half the island would be dead from starvation.

Strong appeals had been made to the patriotism of the people, and they were assured that the interference with trade was temporary, and that with a little patience all would be well. But already there was a marked rise in the death rate, especially among children, who suffered from want of milk, the cattle being slaughtered for food. There was serious rioting in the Lanarkshire coalfields and in the Midlands, together with a Socialistic upheaval in the East of London, which had assumed the proportions of a civil war. Already there were responsible papers which declared that England was in an impossible position, and that an immediate peace was necessary to prevent one of the greatest tragedies in history. It was my task now to prove to them that they were right.

It was May 2 when I found myself back at the Maplin Sands to the north of the estuary of the Thames. The *Beta* was sent on to the Solent to block it and take the place of the lamented *Kappa*. And now I was throttling Britain indeed—London, Southampton, the Bristol Channel, Liverpool, the North Channel, the Glasgow approaches, each was guarded by my boats. Great liners were, as we learned afterward, pouring their supplies into Galway and the west of Ireland, where provisions were cheaper than has ever been known. Tens of thousands were embarking from Britain for Ireland in order to save themselves from starvation. But you cannot transplant a whole dense population. The main body of the people, by the middle of May, were actually starving. At that date wheat was at a hundred, maize and barley at eighty. Even the most obstinate had begun to see that the situation could not possibly continue.

In the great towns starving crowds clamored for bread before the municipal offices, and public officials everywhere were attacked and often murdered by frantic mobs, composed largely of desperate women who had seen their infants perish before their eyes. In the country, roots, bark, and weeds of every sort were used as food. In London the private mansions of Ministers were guarded by strong pickets of soldiers, while a battalion of Guards was camped permanently round the Houses of Parliament. The lives of the Prime Minister and of the Foreign Secretary were continually threatened and occasionally attempted. Yet the Government had entered upon the war with the full assent of every party in the state. The true culprits were those, be they politicians or journalists, who had not the foresight to understand that unless Britain grew her own supplies, or unless by means of a tunnel she had some way of conveying them into the island, all her mighty expenditure upon her army and her fleet was a mere waste of money so long as her antagonist had a few submarines and men who could use them. England has often been stupid, but has got off scot free.

This time she was stupid and had to pay the price. You can't expect luck to be your savior always.

It would be a mere repetition of what I have already described if I were to recount all our proceedings during that first ten days after I resumed my station. During my absence the ships had taken heart and had begun to come up again. In the first day I got four. After that I had to go farther afield, and again I picked up several in French waters. Once I had a narrow escape through one of my Kingston valves getting some grit into it and refusing to act when I was below the surface. Our margin of buoyancy just carried us through. By the end of that week the channel was clear again, and both *Beta* and my own boat were down west once more. There we had encouraging messages from our Bristol consort, who in turn had heard from *Delta* at Liverpool. Our task was completely done. We could not prevent all food from passing into the British Islands, but at least we had raised what did get in to a price which put it far beyond the means of the penniless, workless multitudes. In vain Government commandeered it all and doled it out as a general feeds the garrison of a fortress. The task was too great—the responsibility too horrible. Even the proud and stubborn English could not face it any longer.

I remember well how the news came to me. I was lying at the time off Selsey Bill when I saw a small war vessel coming down channel. It had never been my policy to attack any vessel coming down. My torpedoes and even my shells were too precious for that. I could not help being attracted, however, by the movements of this ship, which came slowly zigzagging in my direction.

"Looking for me," thought I. "What on earth does the foolish thing hope to do if she could find me?"

I was lying awash at the time and got ready to go below in case she should come for me. But at that moment—she was about half a mile away—she turned her quarter, and there, to my amazement, was the red flag with the blue circle, our own beloved flag, flying from her peak. For a moment I though that this was some clever dodge of the enemy to tempt me within range. I snatched up my glasses and called on Vornal.

Then we both recognized the vessel. It was the *Juno*, the only one left intact of our own cruisers. What could she be doing flying the flag in the enemy's waters? Then I understood it, and, turning to Vornal, we threw ourselves into each other's arms. It could only mean an armistice—or peace!

And it was peace. We learned the glad news when we had risen alongside the *Juno*, and the ringing cheers which greeted us had at last died away. Our orders were to report ourselves at once at Blankenberg. Then she passed on down channel to collect the others. We returned to port upon the surface, steaming through the whole British fleet as we passed up the North Sea. The crews clustered thick along the sides of the vessels to watch us. I can see now their sullen, angry faces. Many shook their fists and cursed us as we went by. It was not that we had damaged them—I will do them the justice to say that the English, as the old Boer War has proved, bear no resentment against a brave enemy—but that they thought us cowardly to attack merchant ships and avoid the warships. It is like the Arabs, who think that flank attack is a mean, unmanly device. War is not merely a big game, my English friends. It is a desperate business to gain the upper hand, and one must use one's brain in order to find the weak spot of one's enemy. It is not fair to blame me if I have found yours. It was my duty. Perhaps those officers and sailors who scowled at the little *Iota* that May morning have by this time done me justice when the first bitterness of undeserved defeat was past.

Let others describe my entrance into Blankenberg; the mad enthusiasm of the crowds and the magnificent public reception of each successive boat as it arrived. Surely the men deserved the grant made them by the State which has enabled each of them to be independent for life. As a feat of endurance, that long residence in such a state of mental tension in cramped quarters, breathing an unnatural atmosphere, will long remain as a record. The country may well be proud of such sailors.

The terms of peace were not made onerous, for we were in no condition to make Great Britain our permanent enemy. We knew well that we had won the war by circumstances which would never be allowed to occur again, and that in a few years the island power would be as strong as ever—stronger, perhaps—for the lesson that she had learned. It would be madness to provoke such an antagonist. A mutual salute of flags was arranged, the colonial boundary was adjusted by arbitration, and we claimed no indemnity beyond an undertaking on the part of Britain that she would pay any damages which an international court might award to France or to the United States for injury received through the operations of our submarines. So ended the war.

Of course England will not be caught napping in such a fashion again! Her foolish blindness is partly explained by her delusion that her enemy would not torpedo merchant vessels. Common sense should have told her that her enemy would play the game that suited them best—that they would not inquire what they could do, but they would do it first and talk about it afterward. The opinion of the whole world now is that if a blockade were proclaimed one might do what one could with those who tried to break it, and that it was as reasonable to prevent food from reaching England in wartime as it would be for a besieger to prevent the victualing of a beleaguered fortress.

I cannot end this account better than by quoting the first few paragraphs of a leader in the *Times*, which appeared shortly after the declaration of peace. It may be taken to epitomize the saner public opinion of England upon the meaning and lessons of the episode:

> In all this miserable business [said the writer], which has cost the loss of a considerable portion of our merchant fleet, and more than fifty thousand civilian lives, there is just one consolation to be found. It lies in the fact that our temporary conqueror is a power which is not strong enough to reap the fruits of her victory. Had we endured this humiliation at the hands of any of the first-class powers, it would certainly have entailed the loss of all our Crown colonies and tropical possessions, besides the payment of a huge indemnity. We were absolutely at the feet of our conqueror, and had no possible alternative but to submit to her terms, however onerous. Norland has had the good sense to understand that she must not abuse her temporary advantage, and has been generous in her dealings. In the grip of any other power we should have ceased to exist as an empire.
>
> Even now we are not out of the wood. Someone may maliciously pick a quarrel with us before we get our house in order and use the easy weapon which has been demonstrated. It is to meet such a contingency that the Government has rushed enormous stores of food at the public expense into the country. In a very few months the new harvest will have appeared. On the whole we can

face the immediate future without undue depression, though there remain some causes for anxiety. These will no doubt be energetically handled by this new and efficient Government which has taken the place of those discredited politicians who led us into a war without having foreseen how helpless we were against an obvious form of attack.

Already the lines of our reconstruction are evident. The first and most important is that our party men realize that there is something more vital than their academic disputes about free trade or protection, and that all theory must give way to the fact that a country is in an artificial and dangerous condition if she does not produce within her own borders sufficient food at least to keep life in her population. Whether this should be brought about by a tax upon foreign foodstuffs, or by a bounty upon home products, or by a combination of the two, is now under discussion. But all parties are combined upon the principle, and, though it will undoubtedly entail either a rise in prices or a deterioration in quality in the food of the working classes, they will at least be insured against so terrible a visitation as that which is fresh in our memories. At any rate, we have got past the stage of argument. It *must* be so. The increased prosperity of the farming interest, and, as we will hope, the cessation of agricultural emigration, will be benefits to be counted against the obvious advantages.

The second lesson is the immediate construction of not one but two double-lined railways under the channel. We stand in a white sheet over the matter, since the project has always been discouraged in these columns, but we are prepared to admit that, had such railway communication been combined with adequate arrangements for forwarding supplies from Marseilles, we should have avoided our recent surrender. We still insist that we cannot trust entirely to a tunnel, since our enemy might have allies in the Mediterranean; but in a single contest with any power of the north of Europe it would certainly be of inestimable benefit. There may be dangers attendant upon the existence of a tunnel, but it must now be admitted that they are trivial compared to those which come from its absence. As to the building of large fleets of merchant submarines for the carriage of food, that is a new departure which will be an additional insurance against the danger which has left so dark a page in the history of our country.

THE AMERICAN'S TALE

I t air strange, it air," he was saying as I opened the door of the room where our social little semiliterary society met; "but I could tell you queerer things than that 'ere—almighty queer things. You can't learn everything out of books, sirs, nohow. You see it ain't the men as can string English together and as has had good eddications as find themselves in the queer places I've been in. They're mostly rough men, sirs, as can scarce speak aright, far less tell with pen and ink the things they've seen; but if they could they'd make some of your European's har riz with astonishment. They would, sirs, you bet!"

His name was Jefferson Adams, I believe; I know his initials were J. A., for you may see them yet deeply whittled on the right-hand upper panel of our smoking-room door. He left us this legacy, and also some artistic patterns done in tobacco juice upon our Turkey carpet; but beyond these reminiscences our American storyteller has vanished from our ken. He gleamed across our ordinary quiet conviviality like some brilliant meteor, and then was lost in the outer darkness. That night, however, our Nevada friend was in full swing; and I quietly lit my pipe and dropped into the nearest chair, anxious not to interrupt his story.

"Mind you," he continued, "I hain't got no grudge against your men of science. I likes and respects a chap as can match every beast and plant, from a huckleberry to a grizzly with a jaw-breakin' name; but if you wants real interestin' facts, something a bit juicy, you go to your whalers and your frontiersmen, and your scouts and Hudson Bay men, chaps who mostly can scarce sign their names."

There was a pause here, as Mr. Jefferson Adams produced a long cheroot and lit it. We preserved a strict silence in the room, for we had already learned that on the slightest interruption our Yankee drew himself into his shell again. He glanced round with a self-satisfied smile as he remarked our expectant looks, and continued through a halo of smoke.

"Now which of you gentlemen has ever been in Arizona? None, I'll warrant. And of all English or Americans as can put pen to paper, how many has been in Arizona? Precious few, I calc'late. I've been there, sirs, lived there for years; and when I think of what I've seen there, why, I can scarce get myself to believe it now.

"Ah, there's a country! I was one of Walker's filibusters, as they chose to call us; and after we'd busted up, and the chief was shot, some of us made tracks and located down there. A reg'lar English and American colony, we was, with our wives and children, and all complete. I reckon there's some of the old folk there yet, and that they hain't forgotten what I'm agoing to tell you. No, I warrant they hain't, never on this side of the grave, sirs.

"I've was talking about the country, though; and I guess I could astonish you considerable if I spoke of nothing else. To think of such a land being built for a few "Greasers" and half-breeds! It's a misusing of the gifts of Providence, that's what I calls it. Grass as hung over a chap's head as he rode through it, and trees so thick that you couldn't catch a glimpse of blue sky for leagues and leagues, and orchids like umbrellas! Maybe some on you has seen a plant as they calls the "fly-catcher," in some parts of the States?"

"Diancea muscipula," murmured Dawson, our scientific man *par excellence*.

"Ah, 'Die near a municipal,' that's him! You'll see a fly stand on that 'ere plant, and then you'll see the two sides of a leaf snap up together and catch it between them, and grind it up and mash it to bits, for all the world like some great sea squid with its beak; and hours after, if you open the leaf, you'll see the body lying half-digested, and in bits. Well, I've seen those flytraps in Arizona with leaves eight and ten feet long, and thorns or teeth a foot or more; why, they could—— But darn it, I'm going too fast!

"It's about the death of Joe Hawkins I was going to tell you; 'bout as queer a thing, I reckon, as ever you heard tell on. There wasn't nobody in Montana as didn't know of Joe Hawkins—'Alabama' Joe, as he was called there. A reg'lar out and outer, he was, 'bout the darndest skunk as ever man clapt eyes on. He was a good chap enough, mind ye, as long as you stroked him the right way; but rile him anyhow, and he were worse nor a wildcat. I've seen him empty his six-shooter into a crowd as chanced to jostle him agoing into Simpson's bar when there was a dance on; and he bowied Tom Hooper 'cause he spilt his liquor over his weskit by mistake. No, he didn't stick at murder, Joe didn't; and he weren't a man to be trusted further nor you could see him.

"Now at the time I tell on, when Joe Hawkins was swaggerin' about the town and layin' down the law with his shootin' irons, there was an Englishman there of the name of Scott—Tom Scott, if I rec'lects aright. This chap Scott was a thorough Britisher (beggin' the present company's pardon), and yet he didn't freeze much to the British set there, or they didn't freeze much to him. He was a quiet simple man, Scott was—rather too quiet for a rough set like that; sneakin' they called him, but he weren't that. He kept hisself mostly apart, an' didn't interfere with nobody as long as he were left alone. Some said as how he'd been kinder ill-treated at home—been a Chartist, or something of that sort, and had to up stick and run; but he never spoke of it hisself, an' never complained. Bad luck or good, that chap kept a stiff lip on him.

"This chap Scott was a sort o' butt among the men about Montana, for he was so quiet an' simplelike. There was no party either to take up his grievances; for, as I've been saying, the Britishers hardly counted him one of them, and many a rough joke they played on him. He never cut up rough, but was polite to all hisself. I think the boys got to think he hadn't much grit in him till he showed 'em their mistake.

"It was in Simpson's bar as the row got up, an' that led to the queer thing I was going to tell you of. Alabama Joe and one or two other rowdies were dead on the Britishers in those days, and they spoke their opinions pretty free, though I warned them as there'd be an almighty muss. That partic'lar night Joe was nigh half drunk, an' he swaggered about the town with his six-shooter, lookin' out for a quarrel. Then he turned into the bar where he know'd he'd find some o' the English as ready for one as he was hisself. Sure enough, there was half a dozen lounging about, an' Tom Scott standin' alone before the stove. Joe sat down by the table, and put his revolver and bowie down in front of him. 'Them's my arguments, Jeff,' he says to me, 'if any white-livered Britisher dares give me the lie.' I tried to stop him, sirs; but he weren't a man as you could easily turn, an' he began to speak in a way as no chap

could stand. Why, even a 'Greaser' would flare up if you said as much of
Greaser-land! There was a commotion at the bar, an' every man laid his
hands on his wepin's; but afore they could draw we heard a quiet voice
from the stove: 'Say your prayers, Joe Hawkins; for, by Heaven, you're
a dead man!' Joe turned round, and looked like grabbin' at his iron; but
it weren't no manner of use. Tom Scott was standing up, covering him
with his Derringer; a smile on his white face, but the very devil shining
in his eye. 'It ain't that the old country has used me overwell,' he says,
'but no man shall speak agin it afore me, and live.' For a second or two
I could see his finger tighten round the trigger, an' then he gave a laugh,
an' threw the pistol on the floor. 'No,' he says, 'I can't shoot a half-
drunk man. Take your dirty life, Joe, an' use it better nor you have
done. You've been nearer the grave this night than you will be agin
until your time comes. You'd best make tracks now, I guess. Nay, never
look black at me, man; I'm not afeard at your shootin' iron. A bully's
nigh always a coward." And he swung contemptuously round, and relit
his half-smoked pipe from the stove; while Alabama slunk out o' the
bar, with laughs of the Britishers ringing in his ears. I saw his face as he
passed me, and on it I saw murder, sirs—murder, as plain as ever I seed
anything in my life.

"I stayed in the bar after the row, and watched Tom Scott as he shook
hands with the men about. It seemed kinder queer to me to see him
smilin' and cheerfullike; for I knew Joe's bloodthirsty mind, and that the
Englishman had small chance of ever seeing the morning. He lived in an
out-of-the-way sort of place, you see, clean off the trail, and had to pass
through the Flytrap Gulch to get to it. This here gulch was a marshy
gloomy place, lonely enough during the day even; for it were always a
creepy sort o' thing to see the great eight- and ten-foot leaves snapping
up if aught touched them; but at night there were never a soul near.
Some parts of the marsh, too, were soft and deep, and a body thrown in
would be gone in the morning. I could see Alabama Joe crouchin'
under the leaves of the great Flytrap in the darkest part of the gulch,
with a scowl on his face and a revolver in his hand; I could see it, sirs, as
plain as with my two eyes.

"'Bout midnight Simpson shuts up his bar, so out we had to go. Tom
Scott started off for his three-mile walk at a slashing pace. I just dropped
him a hint as he passed me, for I kinder liked the chap. 'Keep your
Derringer loose in your belt, sir,' I says, 'for you might chance to need
it.' He looked round at me with his quiet smile, and then I lost sight of
him in the gloom. I never thought to see him again. He'd hardly gone

afore Simpson comes up to me and says, 'There'll be a nice job in the Flytrap Gulch tonight, Jeff; the boys say that Hawkins started half an hour ago to wait for Scott and shoot him on sight. I calc'late the coroner'll be wanted tomorrow.'

"What passed in the gulch that night? It were a question as were asked pretty free next morning. A half-breed was in Ferguson's store after daybreak, and he said as he'd chanced to be near the gulch 'bout one in the morning. It warn't easy to get at his story, he seemed so uncommon scared; but he told us, at last, as he'd heard the fearfulest screams in the stillness of the night. There weren't no shots, he said, but scream after scream, kinder muffled, like a man with a serapé over his head, an' in mortal pain. Abner Brandon and me, and a few more, was in the store at the time; so we mounted and rode out to Scott's house, passing through the gulch on the way. There weren't nothing partic'lar to be seen there—no blood nor marks of a fight, nor nothing; and when we gets up to Scott's house, out he comes to meet us as fresh as a lark. 'Hullo, Jeff!' says he, 'no need for the pistols after all. Come in an' have a cocktail, boys.' 'Did ye see or hear nothing as ye came home last night?' says I. 'No,' says he; 'all was quiet enough. An owl kinder moaning in the Flytrap Gulch—that was all. Come, jump off and have a glass.' 'Thank ye,' says Abner. So off we gets, and Tom Scott rode into the settlement with us when we went back.

"An allfired commotion was on in Main Street as we rode into it. The 'Merican party seemed to have gone clean crazed. Alabama Joe was gone, not a darned particle of him left. Since he went out to the gulch nary eye had seen him. As we got off our horses there was a considerable crowd in front of Simpson's, and some ugly looks at Tom Scott, I can tell you. There was a clickin' of pistols, and I saw as Scott had his hand in his bosom too. There weren't a single English face about. 'Stand aside, Jeff Adams,' says Zebb Humphrey, as great a scoundrel as ever lived, 'you hain't got no hand in this game. Say, boys, are we, free Americans, to be murdered by any darned Britisher?' It was the quickest thing as ever I seed. There was a rush an' a crack; Zebb was down, with Scott's ball in his thigh, and Scott hisself was on the ground with a dozen men holding him. It weren't no use struggling, so he lay quiet. They seemed a bit uncertain what to do with him at first, but then one of Alabama's special chums put them up to it. 'Joe's gone,' he said; 'nothing ain't never surer nor that, an' there lies the man as killed him. Some on you knows as Joe went on business to the gulch last night; he never came back. That 'ere Britisher passed through after he'd gone;

they'd had a row, screams is heard 'mong the great flytraps. I say agin he has played poor Joe some o' his sneakin' tricks, an' thrown him into the swamp. It ain't no wonder as the body is gone. But air we to stan' by and see English murderin' our own chums? I guess not. Let Judge Lynch try him, that's what I say.' 'Lynch him!' shouted a hundred angry voices— for all the ragtag an' bobtail o' the settlement was round us by this time. 'Here, boys, fetch a rope, and swing him up. Up with him over Simpson's door!' 'See here though,' says another, coming forward; 'let's hang him by the great flytrap in the gulch. Let Joe see as he's revenged, if so be as he's buried 'bout theer.' There was a shout for this, an' away they went, with Scott tied on his mustang in the middle, and a mounted guard, with cocked revolvers, round him; for we knew as there was a score or so Britishers about, as didn't seem to recognize Judge Lynch, and was dead on a free fight."

"I went out with them, my heart bleedin' for Scott, though he didn't seem a cent put out, he didn't. He were game to the backbone. Seems kinder queer, sirs, hangin' a man to a flytrap; but our'n were a reg'lar tree, and the leaves like a brace of boats with a hinge between 'em and thorns at the bottom.

"We passed down the gulch to the place where the great one grows, and there we seed it with the leaves, some open, some shut. But we seed something worse nor that. Standin' round the tree was some thirty men, Britishers all, an' armed to the teeth. They was waitin' for us evidently, an' had a businesslike look about 'em, as if they'd come for something and meant to have it. There was the raw material there for about as warm a scrimmidge as ever I seed. As we rode up, a great red-bearded Scotchman—Cameron were his name—stood out afore the rest, his revolver cocked in his hand. 'See here, boys,' he says, 'you've got no call to hurt a hair of that man's head. You hain't proved as Joe is dead yet; and if you had, you hain't proved as Scott killed him. Anyhow, it were in self-defence; for you all know as he was lying in wait for Scott, to shoot him on sight; so I say agin, you hain't got no call to hurt that man; and what's more, I've got thirty six-barreled arguments against your doin' it.' 'It's an interestin' pint, and worth arguin' out,' said the man as was Alabama Joe's special chum. There was a clickin' of pistols, and a loosenin' of knives, and the two parties began to draw up to one another, an' it looked like a rise in the mortality of Montana. Scott was standing behind with a pistol at his ear if he stirred, lookin' quiet and composed as having no money on the table, when sudden he gives a start an' a shout as rang in our ears like a trumpet. 'Joe!' he cried, 'Joe!

Look at him! In the Flytrap!' We all turned an' looked where he was pointin'. Jerusalem! I think we won't get that picter out of our minds agin. One of the great leaves of the Flytrap, that had been shut and touchin' the ground as it lay, was slowly rolling back upon its hinges. There, lying like a child in its cradle, was Alabama Joe in the hollow of the leaf. The great thorns had been slowly driven through his heart as it shut upon him. We could see as he'd tried to cut his way out, for there was a slit in the thick fleshy leaf, an' his bowie was in his hand; but it had smothered him first. He'd lain down on it likely to keep the damp off while he were awaitin' for Scott, and it had closed on him as you've seen your little hothouse ones do on a fly; an' there he were as we found him, torn and crushed into pulp by the great jagged teeth of the man-eatin' plant. There, sirs, I think you'll own as that's a curious story."

"And what became of Scott?" asked Jack Sinclair.

"Why, we carried him back on our shoulders, we did, to Simpson's bar, and he stood us liquors round. Made a speech too—a darned fine speech—from the counter. Somethin' about the British lion an' the 'Merican eagle walkin' arm in arm forever an' a day. And now, sirs, that yarn was long and my cheroot's out, so I reckon I'll make tracks afore it's later;" and with a "Good-night!" he left the room.

"A most extraordinary narrative!" said Dawson. "Who should have thought a Dianœa had such power!"

"Deuced rum yarn!" said young Sinclair.

"Evidently a matter-of-fact truthful man," said the doctor.

"Or the most original liar that ever lived," said I.

I wonder which he was.

SELECTING A GHOST

I am sure that Nature never intended me to be a self-made man. There are times when I can hardly bring myself to realize that twenty years of my life were spent behind the counter of a grocer's shop in the East End of London, and that it was through such an avenue that I reached a wealthy independence and the possession of Goresthorpe Grange. My habits are Conservative, and my tastes refined and aristocratic. I have a soul which spurns the vulgar herd. Our family, the D'Odds, date back to a prehistoric era, as is to be inferred from the fact that their advent into British history is not commented on by any trustworthy historian. Some instinct tells me that the blood of a Crusader runs in my veins. Even now, after the lapse of so many years, such exclamations as 'By'r Lady!' rise naturally to my lips, and I feel that, should circumstances require it, I am capable of rising in my stirrups and dealing an infidel a blow—say with a mace—which would considerably astonish him.

Goresthorpe Grange is a feudal mansion—or so it was termed in the advertisement which originally brought it under my notice. Its right to this adjective had a most remarkable effect upon its price, and the advantages gained may possibly be more sentimental than real. Still, it is soothing to me to know that I have slits in my staircase through which I can discharge arrows; and there is a sense of power in the fact of possessing a complicated apparatus by means of which I am enabled to pour molten lead upon the head of the casual visitor. These things chime in with my peculiar humor, and I do not grudge to pay for them. I am proud of my battlements and of the circular uncovered sewer which girds me round. I am proud of my portcullis and donjon and keep. There is but one thing wanting to round off the mediævalism of my abode, and to render it symmetrically and completely antique. Goresthorpe Grange is not provided with a ghost.

Any man with old-fashioned tastes and ideas as to how such establishments should be conducted would have been disappointed at the omission. In my case it was particularly unfortunate. From my childhood I had been an earnest student of the supernatural, and a firm believer in it. I have reveled in ghostly literature until there is hardly a tale bearing upon the subject which I have not perused. I learned the German language for the sole purpose of mastering a book upon demonology. When an infant I have secreted myself in dark rooms in the hope of seeing some of those bogies with which my nurse used to threaten me; and the same feeling is as strong in me now as then. It was a proud moment when I felt that a ghost was one of the luxuries which my money might command.

It is true that there was no mention of an apparition in the advertisement. On reviewing the mildewed walls, however, and the shadowy corridors, I had taken it for granted that there was such a thing on the premises. As the presence of a kennel presupposes that of a dog, so I imagined that it was impossible that such desirable quarters should be untenanted by one or more restless shades. Good heavens, what can the noble family from whom I purchased it have been doing during these hundreds of years! Was there no member of it spirited enough to make away with his sweetheart, or take some other steps calculated to establish a hereditary specter? Even now I can hardly write with patience upon the subject.

For a long time I hoped against hope. Never did rat squeak behind the wainscot, or rain drip upon the attic floor, without a wild thrill shooting through me as I thought that at last I had come upon traces of some unquiet soul. I felt no touch of fear upon these occasions. If it occurred in the nighttime, I would send Mrs. D'Odd—who is a strong-minded woman—to investigate the matter while I covered up my head with the bedclothes and indulged in an ecstasy of expectation. Alas, the result was always the same! The suspicious sound would be traced to some cause so absurdly natural and commonplace that the most fervid imagination could not clothe it with any of the glamour of romance.

I might have reconciled myself to this state of things had it not been for Jorrocks of Havistock Farm. Jorrocks is a coarse, burly, matter-of-fact fellow whom I only happen to know through the accidental circumstances of his fields adjoining my demesne. Yet this man, though utterly devoid of all appreciation of archæological unities, is in possession of a well authenticated and undeniable specter. Its existence only dates back, I believe, to the reign of the Second George, when a young lady cut her throat upon hearing of the death of her lover at the battle of Dettingen. Still, even that gives the house an air of respectability, especially when coupled with bloodstains upon the floor. Jorrocks is densely unconscious of his good fortune; and his language when he reverts to the apparition is painful to listen to. He little dreams how I covet everyone of those moans and nocturnal wails which he describes with unnecessary objurgation. Things are indeed coming to a pretty pass when democratic specters are allowed to desert the landed proprietors and annul every social distinction by taking refuge in the house of the great unrecognized.

I have a large amount of perseverance. Nothing else could have raised me into my rightful sphere, considering the uncongenial atmosphere in which I spent the earlier part of my life. I felt now that a ghost must be secured, but how to set about securing one was more than either Mrs. D'Odd or myself was able to determine. My reading taught me that such phenomena are usually the outcome of crime. What crime was to be done, then, and who was to do it? A wild idea entered my mind that Watkins, the house steward, might be prevailed upon—for a consideration—to immolate himself or someone else in the interests of the establishment. I put the matter to him in a half-jesting manner; but it did not seem to strike him in a favorable light. The other servants sympathized with him in his opinion—at least, I cannot account in any other way for their having left the house in a body the same afternoon.

"My dear," Mrs. D'Odd remarked to me one day after dinner, as I sat moodily sipping a cup of sack—I love the good old names—"my dear, that odious ghost of Jorrocks's has been gibbering again."

"Let it gibber," I answered recklessly.

Mrs. D'Odd struck a few chords on her virginal and looked thoughtfully into the fire.

"I'll tell you what it is, Argentine," she said at last, using the pet name which we usually substituted for Silas, "we must have a ghost sent down from London."

"How can you be so idiotic, Matilda?" I remarked severely. "Who could get us such a thing?"

"My cousin, Jack Brocket, could," she answered confidently.

Now, this cousin of Matilda's was rather a sore subject between us. He was rakish clever young fellow, who had tried his hand at many things, but wanted perseverance to succeed at any. He was, at that time, in chambers in London, professing to be a general agent, and really living, to a great extent, upon his wits. Matilda managed so that most of our business should pass through his hands, which certainly saved me a great deal of trouble; but I found that Jack's commission was generally considerably larger than all the other items of the bill put together. It was this fact which made me feel inclined to rebel against any further negotiations with the young gentleman.

"Oh yes, he could," insisted Mrs. D., seeing the look of disapprobation upon my face. "You remember how well he managed that business about the crest?"

"It was only a resuscitation of the old family coat-of-arms, my dear," I protested.

Matilda smiled in an irritating manner. "There was a resuscitation of the family portraits, too, dear," she remarked. "You must allow that Jack selected them very judiciously."

I thought of the long line of faces which adorned two walls of my banqueting hall, from the burly Norman robber, through every graduation of casque, plume, and ruff, to the somber Chesterfieldian individual who appears to have staggered against a pillar in his agony at the return of a maiden MS. which he grips convulsively in his right hand. I was fain to confess that in that instance he had done his work well, and that it was only fair to give him an order—with the usual commission—for a family specter, should such a thing be attainable.

It is one of my maxims to act promptly when once my mind is made up. Noon of the next day found me ascending the spiral stone staircase which leads to Mr. Brocket's chambers, and admiring the succession of arrows and fingers upon the whitewashed wall, all indicating the direction of that gentleman's sanctum. As it happened, artificial aid of the sort were entirely unnecessary, as an animated flap dance overhead could proceed from no other quarter, though it was replaced by a deathly silence as I groped my way up the stair. The door was opened by a youth evidently astounded at the appearance of a client, and I was ushered into the presence of my young friend, who was writing furiously in a large ledger—upside down, as I afterward discovered.

After the first greetings, I plunged into business at once.

"Look here, Jack," I said, "I want you to get me a spirit, if you can."

"Spirits you mean!" shouted my wife's cousin, plunging his hand into the wastepaper basket and producing a bottle with the celerity of a conjuring trick. "Let's have a drink!"

I held up my hand as a mute appeal against such a proceeding so early in the day; but on lowering it again I found that I had almost involuntarily closed my fingers round the tumbler which my adviser had pressed upon me. I drank the contents hastily off, lest anyone should come in upon us and set me down as a toper. After all, there was something very amusing about the young fellow's eccentricities.

"Not spirits," I explained smilingly; "an apparition—a ghost. If such a thing is to be had, I should be very willing to negotiate."

"A ghost for Goresthorpe Grange?" inquired Mr. Brocket, with as much coolness as if I had asked for a drawing room suite.

"Quite so," I answered.

"Easiest thing in the world," said my companion, filling up my glass again in spite of my remonstrance. "Let us see!" Here he took down a large red notebook, with all the letters of the alphabet in a fringe down the edge. "A ghost you said, didn't you? That's G. G—gems—gimlets—gaspipes—gauntlets—guns—galleys. Ah, here we are. Ghosts. Volume nine, section six, page forty-one. Excuse me." And Jack ran up a ladder and began rummaging among a pile of ledgers on a high shelf. I felt half inclined to empty my glass into the spittoon when his back was turned; but on second thoughts I disposed of it in a legitimate way.

"Here it is!" cried my London agent, jumping off the ladder with a crash, and depositing an enormous volume of manuscript upon the table. "I have all these things tabulated, so that I may lay my hands upon them in a moment. It's all right—it's quite weak" (here he filled our glasses again). "What were we looking up, again?"

"Ghosts," I suggested.

"Of course; page forty-one. Here we are. 'J. H. Fowler & Son, Dunkel Street, suppliers of mediums to nobility and gentry; charms sold—horoscopes cast.' Nothing in your line there, I suppose?"

I shook my head despondingly.

"Frederick Tabb," continued my wife's cousin, "sole channel of communications between the living and the dead. Proprietor of the spirits of Byron, Kirke White, Grimaldi, Tom Cribb, and Inigo Jones. That's about the figure!"

"Nothing romantic enough there," I objected. "Good heavens! Fancy a ghost with a black eye and a handkerchief tied round its waist, or turning sommersaults, and saying, "How are you tomorrow?" The very idea made me so warm that I emptied my glass and filled it again.

"Here is another," said my companion, " 'Christopher McCarthy; biweekly séances—attended by all the eminent spirits of ancient and modern times. Nativities—charms—abracadabras, messages from the dead.' He might be able to help us. However, I shall have a hunt round myself tomorrow, and see some of these fellows. I know their haunts, and it's odd if I can't pick up something cheap. So there's an end of business," he concluded, hurling the ledger into the corner, "and now we'll have something to drink."

We had several things to drink—so many that my inventive faculties were dulled next morning, and I had some little difficulty in explaining to Mrs. D'Odd why it was that I hung my boots and spectacles upon a peg along with my other garments before retiring to rest. The new hopes excited by the confident manner in which my agent had under-taken the commission caused me to rise superior to alcoholic reaction, and I paced about the rambling corridors and old-fashioned rooms, picturing to myself the appearance of my expected acquisition, and deciding what part of the building would harmonize best with its presence. After much consideration, I pitched upon the banqueting hall as being, on the whole, most suitable for its reception. It was a long low room, hung round with valuable tapestry and interesting relics of the old family to whom it had belonged. Coats of mail and implements of war glimmered fitfully as the light of the fire played over them, and the wind crept under the door, moving the hangings to and fro with a ghastly rustling. At one end there was the raised dais, on which in ancient times the host and his guests used to spread their table, while a descent of a couple of steps led to the lower part of the hall, where the vassals and retainers held wassail. The floor was uncovered by any sort of carpet, but a layer of rushes had been scattered over it by my direction. In the whole room there was nothing to remind one of the nineteenth century; except, indeed, my own solid silver plate, stamped with the resuscitated family arms, which was laid out upon an oak table in the center. This, I determined, should be the haunted room, supposing my wife's cousin to succeed in his negotiation with the spirit mongers. There was nothing for it now but to wait patiently until I heard some news of the result of his inquiries.

A letter came in the course of a few days, which, if it was short, was at least encouraging. It was scribbled in pencil on the back of a playbill, and sealed apparently with a tobacco stopper. "Am on the track," it said. "Nothing of the sort to be had from any professional spiritualist, but picked up a fellow in a pub yesterday who says he can manage it for you. Will send him down unless you wire to the contrary. Abrahams is his name, and he has done one or two of these jobs before." The letter wound up with some incoherent allusions to a cheque, and was signed by my affectionate cousin, John Brocket.

I need hardly say that I did not wire, but awaited the arrival of Mr. Abrahams with all impatience. In spite of my belief in the supernatural, I could scarcely credit the fact that any mortal could have such a command over the spirit world as to deal in them and barter them against mere earthly gold. Still, I had Jack's word for it that such a trade existed; and here was a gentleman with a Judaical name ready to demonstrate it by proof positive. How vulgar and commonplace Jorrocks's eighteenth-century ghost would appear should I succeed in securing a real mediæval apparition! I almost thought that one had been sent down in advance, for, as I walked round the moat that night before retiring to rest, I came upon a dark figure engaged in surveying the machinery of my portcullis and drawbridge. His start of surprise, however, and the manner in which he hurried off into the darkness, speedily convinced me of his earthly origin, and I put him down as some admirer of one of my female retainers mourning over the muddy Hellespont which divided him from his love. Whoever he may have been, he disappeared and did not return, though I loitered about for some time in the hope of catching a glimpse of him and exercising my feudal rights upon his person.

Jack Brocket was as good as his word. The shades of another evening were beginning to darken round Goresthorpe Grange, when a peal at the outer bell, and the sound of a fly pulling up, announced the arrival of Mr. Abrahams. I hurried down to meet him, half expecting to see a choice assortment of ghosts crowding in at his rear. Instead, however, of being the sallow-faced melancholy-eyed man that I had pictured to myself, the ghost dealer was a sturdy little podgy fellow, with a pair of wonderfully keen sparkling eyes and a mouth which was constantly stretched in a good-humored, if somewhat artificial grin. His sole stock-in-trade seemed to consist of a small leather bag jealously locked and strapped, which emitted a metallic chink upon being placed on the stone flags of the hall.

"And how are you, sir?" he asked, wringing my hand with the utmost effusion. "And the missis, how is she? And all the others—'ow's all their 'ealth?"

I intimated that we were all as well as could reasonably be expected; but Mr. Abrahams happened to catch a glimpse of Mrs. D'Odd in the distance, and at once plunged at her with another string of inquiries as to her health, delivered so volubly and with such an intense earnestness that I half expected to see him terminate his cross-examination by feeling her pulse and demanding a sight of her tongue. All this time his little eyes rolled round and round, shifting perpetually from the floor to the ceiling, and from the ceiling to the walls, taking in apparently every article of furniture in a single comprehensive glance.

Having satisfied himself that neither of us was in a pathological condition, Mr. Abrahams suffered me to lead him upstairs, where a repast had been laid out for him to which he did ample justice. The mysterious little bag he carried along with him, and deposited it under his chair during the meal. It was not until the table had been cleared and we were left together that he broached the matter on which he had come down.

"I understand," he remarked, puffing at a trichinopoly, "that you want my 'elp in fitting up this 'ere 'ouse with a happarition."

I acknowledged the correctness of his surmise, while mentally wondering at those restless eyes of his, which still danced about the room as if he were making an inventory of the contents.

"And you won't find a better man for the job, though I says it as shouldn't," continued my companion. "Wot did I say to the young gent wot spoke to me in the bar of the Lame Dog? 'Can you do it?' says he. 'Try me,' says I, 'Me and my bag. Just try me.' I couldn't say fairer than that."

My respect for Jack Brocket's business capacities began to go up very considerably. He certainly seemed to have managed the matter wonderfully well. "You don't mean to say that you carry ghosts about in bags!" I remarked, with diffidence.

Mr. Abrahams smiled a smile of superior knowledge. "You wait," he said; "give me the right place and the right hour, with a little of the essence of Lucoptolycus"—here he produced a small bottle from his waistcoat pocket—"and you won't find no ghost that I ain't up to.

You'll see them yourself, and pick your own, and I can't say fairer than that."

As all Mr. Abraham's protestations of fairness were accompanied by a cunning leer and a wink from one or other of his wicked little eyes, the impression of candor was somewhat weakened.

"When you going to do it?" I asked reverentially.

"Ten minutes to one in the morning," said Mr. Abrahams, with decision. "Some says midnight, but I says ten to one, when there ain't such a crowd, and you can pick your own ghost. And now," he continued, rising to his feet, "suppose you trot me round the premises, and let me see where you wants it; for there's some places as attracts 'em, and some as they won't hear of—not if there was no other place in the world."

Mr. Abrahams inspected our corridors and chambers with a most critical and observant eye, fingering the old tapestry with the air of a connoisseur, and remarking in an undertone that it would, "match uncommon nice." It was not until he reached the banqueting hall, however, which I had myself picked out, that his admiration reached the pitch of enthusiasm. "'Ere's the place!" he shouted, dancing, bag in hand, round the table on which my plate was lying, and looking not unlike some quaint little goblin himself. " 'Ere's the place; we won't get nothin' to beat this! A fine room—noble, solid, none of your electroplate trash! That's the way as things ought to be done, sir. Plenty of room for 'em to glide here. Send up some brandy and the box of weeds; I'll sit here by the fire and do the preliminaries, which is more trouble than you'd think; for them ghosts carries on hawful at times, before they finds out who they've got to deal with. If you wait in the room they'd tear you to pieces as like as not. You leave me alone to tackle them, and at half past twelve come in, and I bet they'll be quiet enough by then."

Mr. Abrahams's request struck me as a reasonable one, so I left him with his feet upon the mantelpiece, and his chair in front of the fire, fortifying himself with stimulants against his refractory visitors. From the room beneath, in which I sat with Mrs. D'Odd, I could hear that after sitting for some time he rose up, and paced about the hall with quiet impatient steps. We then heard him try the lock of the door, and afterward drag some heavy article of furniture in the direction of the window, on which, apparently, he mounted, for I heard the creaking of the rusty hinges of the diamond-paned casement folded backward, and I knew it to be situated several feet above the little man's reach. Mrs. D'Odd says that she could distinguish his voice speaking in low and rapid whispers after this, but that may have been her imagination. I confess that I began to feel more impressed than I had deemed it possible to be. There was something awesome in the thought of the solitary mortal standing by the open window and summoning in from the gloom outside the spirits of the netherworld. It was with a trepidation which I could hardly disguise from Matilda that I observed that the clock was pointing to half past twelve, and that the time had come for me to share the vigil of my visitor.

He was sitting in his old position when I entered, and there were no signs of the mysterious movements which I had overheard, though his chubby face was flushed as with recent exertion.

"Are you succeeding all right?" I asked as I came in, putting on as careless an air as possible, but glancing involuntarily round the room to see if we were alone.

"Only your help is needed to complete the matter," said Mr. Abrahams, in a solemn voice. "You shall sit by me and partake of the essence of Lucoptolycus, which removes the scales from our earthly eyes. Whatever you may chance to see, speak not and make no movement, lest you break the spell." His manner was subdued, and his usual cockney vulgarity had entirely disappeared. I took the chair which he indicated, and awaited the result.

My companion cleared the rushes from the floor in our neighborhood, and, going down upon his hands and knees, described a half circle with chalk, which enclosed the fireplace and ourselves. Round the edge of this half circle he drew several hieroglyphics, not unlike the signs of the zodiac. He then stood up and uttered a long invocation, delivered so rapidly that it sounded like a single gigantic word in some uncouth guttural language. Having finished this prayer, if prayer it was, he pulled out the small bottle which he had produced before, and poured a couple of teaspoonfuls of clear transparent fluid into a phial, which he handed to me with an intimation that I should drink it.

The liquid had a faintly sweet odor, not unlike the aroma of certain sorts of apples. I hesitated a moment before applying it to my lips, but an impatient gesture from my companion overcame my scruples, and I tossed it off. The taste was not unpleasant; and, as it gave rise to no immediate effects, I leaned back in my chair and composed myself for what was to come. Mr. Abrahams seated himself beside me, and I felt that he was watching my face from time to time while repeating some more of the invocations in which he had indulged before.

A sense of delicious warmth and languor began gradually to steal over me, partly, perhaps, from the heat of the fire, and partly from some unexplained cause. An uncontrollable impulse to sleep weighed down my eyelids, while, at the same time, my brain worked actively, and a hundred beautiful and pleasing ideas flitted through it. So utterly lethargic did I feel that, though I was aware that my companion put his hand over the region of my heart, as if to feel how it were beating, I did not attempt to prevent him, nor did I even ask him for the reason of his action. Everything in the room appeared to be reeling slowly, round in a drowsy dance, of which I was the center. The great elk's head at the far end wagged solemnly backward and forward, while the massive salvers on the tables performed cotillions with the claret cooler and the epergne. My head fell upon my breast from sheer heaviness, and I should have become unconscious had I not been recalled to myself by the opening of the door at the other end of the hall.

This door led on to the raised dais, which, as I mentioned, the heads of the house used to reserve for their own use. As it swung slowly back upon its hinges, I sat up in my chair, clutching at the arms, and staring with a horrified glare at the dark passage outside. Something was coming down it—something unformed and intangible, but still a *something*. Dim and shadowy, I saw it flit across the threshold, while a blast of ice-cold air swept down the room, which seemed to blow through me, chilling my very heart. I was aware of the mysterious presence, and then I heard it speak in a voice like the sighing of an east wind among pine trees on the banks of a desolate sea.

It said: "I am the invisible nonentity. I have affinities and am subtle. I am electric, magnetic, and spiritualistic. I am the great ethereal sigh heaver. I kill dogs. Mortal, wilt thou choose me?"

I was about to speak, but the words seemed to be choked in my throat; and, before I could get them out, the shadow flitted across the hall and vanished in the darkness at the other side, while a long-drawn melancholy sigh quivered through the apartment.

I turned my eyes toward the door once more, and beheld, to my astonishment, a very small old woman, who hobbled along the corridor and into the hall. She passed backward and forward several times, and then, crouching down at the very edge of the circle upon the floor, she disclosed a face the horrible malignity of which shall never be banished from my recollection. Every foul passion appeared to have left its mark upon that hideous countenance.

"Ha! ha!" she screamed, holding out her wizened hands like the talons of an unclean bird. "You see what I am. I am the fiendish old woman. I wear snuff-colored silks. My curse descends on people. Sir Walter was partial to me. Shall I be thine, mortal?"

I endeavored to shake my head in horror; on which she aimed a blow at me with her crutch, and vanished with an eldritch scream.

By this time my eyes turned naturally toward the open door, and I was hardly surprised to see a man walk in of tall and noble stature. His face was deadly pale, but was surmounted by a fringe of dark hair which fell in ringlets down his back. A short pointed beard covered his chin. He was dressed in loose-fitting clothes, made apparently of yellow satin, and a large white ruff surrounded his neck. He paced across the room with slow and majestic strides. When turning, he addressed me in a sweet, exquisitely modulated voice.

"I am the cavalier," he remarked. "I pierce and am pierced. Here is my rapier. I clink steel. This is a bloodstain over my heart. I can emit hollow groans. I am patronized by many old Conservative families. I am the original manor house apparition. I work alone, or in company with shrieking damsels."

He bent his head courteously, as though awaiting my reply, but the same choking sensation prevented me from speaking; and, with a deep bow, he disappeared.

He had hardly gone before a feeling of intense horror stole over me and I was aware of the presence of a ghastly creature in the room of dim outlines and uncertain proportions. One moment it seemed to pervade the entire apartment, while at another it would become invisible, but always leaving behind it a distinct consciousness of its presence. Its voice, when it spoke, was quavering and gusty. It said, "I am the leaver of footsteps and the spiller of gouts of blood. I tramp upon corridors. Charles Dickens has alluded to me. I make strange and disagreeable noises. I snatch letters and place invisible hands on people's wrists. I am cheerful. I burst into peals of hideous laughter. Shall I do one now?" I raised my hand in a deprecating way, but too late to prevent one discordant outbreak which echoed through the room. Before I could lower it the apparition was gone.

I turned my head toward the door in time to see a man come hastily and stealthily into the chamber. He was a sunburned powerfully built fellow, with earrings in his ears and a Barcelona handkerchief tied loosely round his neck. His head was bent upon his chest, and his whole aspect was that of one afflicted by intolerable remorse. He paced rapidly backward and forward like a caged tiger, and I observed that a drawn knife glittered in one of his hands, while he grasped what appeared to be a piece of parchment in the other. His voice, when he spoke, was deep and sonorous. He said, "I am a murderer. I am a ruffian. I crouch when I walk. I step noiselessly. I know something of the Spanish Main. I can do the lost treasure business. I have charts. Am able-bodied and a good walker. Capable of haunting a large park." He looked toward me beseechingly, but before I could make a sign I was paralyzed by the horrible sight which appeared at the door.

It was a very tall man, if indeed, it might be called a man, for the gaunt bones were protruding though the corroding flesh, and the features were of leaden hue. A winding sheet was wrapped round the figure, and formed a hood over the head, from under the shadow of which two fiendish eyes, deep set in their grisly sockets, blazed and sparkled like red hot coals. The lower jaw had fallen upon the breast, disclosing a withered shriveled tongue and two lines of black and jagged fangs. I shuddered and drew back as this fearful apparition advanced to the edge of the circle.

"I am the American blood curdler," it said, in a voice which seemed to come in a hollow murmur from the earth beneath it. "None other is genuine. I am the embodiment of Edgar Allan Poe. I am circumstantial and horrible. I am a low-caste spirit-subduing specter. Observe my blood and my bones. I am gristly and nauseous. No depending on artificial aid. Work with grave clothes, a coffin lid, and a galvanic battery. Turn hair white in a night." The creature stretched out its fleshless arms to me as if in entreaty, but I shook my head; and it vanished, leaving a low sickening repulsive odor behind it. I sank back in my chair, so overcome by terror and disgust that I would have very willingly resigned myself to dispensing with a ghost altogether, could I have been sure that this was the last of the hideous procession.

A faint sound of trailing garments warned me that it was not so. I looked up, and beheld a white figure emerging from the corridor into the light. As it stepped across the threshold I saw that it was that of a young and beautiful woman dressed in the fashion of a bygone day. Her hands were clasped in front of her, and her pale proud face bore traces of passion and of suffering. She crossed the hall with a gentle sound, like the rustling of autumn leaves, and then, turning her lovely and unutterably sad eyes upon me, she said,

"I am the plaintive and sentimental, the beautiful and ill-used. I have been forsaken and betrayed. I shriek in the nighttime and glide down passages. My antecedents are highly respectable and generally aristocratic. My tastes are aesthetic. Old oak furniture like this would do, with a few more coats of mail and plenty of tapestry. Will you not take me?"

Her voice died away in a beautiful cadence as she concluded, and she held out her hands as if in supplication. I am always sensitive to female influences. Besides, what would Jorrocks's ghost be to this! Could anything be in better taste? Would I not be exposing myself to the chance of injuring my nervous system by interviews with such creatures as my last visitor, unless I decided at once? She gave me a seraphic smile, as if she knew what was passing in my mind. That smile settled the matter. "She will do," I cried; "I choose this one;" and as, in my enthusiasm, I took a step toward her I passed over the magic circle which had girdled me round.

"Argentine, we have been robbed!"

I had an indistinct consciousness of these words being spoken, or rather screamed, in my ear a great number of times without me being able to grasp their meaning. A violent throbbing in my head seemed to adapt itself to their rhythm, and I closed my eyes to the lullaby of "Robbed, robbed, robbed." A vigorous shake caused me to open them again, however, and the sight of Mrs. D'Odd in the scantiest of costumes and most furious of tempers was sufficiently impressive to recall all my scattered thoughts, and make me realize that I was lying on my back on the floor, with my head among the ashes which had fallen from last night's fire, and a small glass phial in my hand.

I staggered to my feet, but felt so weak and giddy that I was compelled to fall back into a chair. As my brain became clearer, stimulated by the exclamations of Matilda, I began gradually to recollect the events of the night. There was the door through which my supernatural visitors had filed. There was the circle of chalk with the hieroglyphics round the edge. There was the cigar box and brandy bottle which had been honored by the attentions of Mr. Abrahams. But the seer himself—where was he? And what was this open window with a rope running out of it? And where, O where, was the pride of Goresthorpe Grange, the glorious plate which was to have been the delectation of generations of D'Odds? And why was Mrs. D'Odd standing in the gray light of dawn, wringing her hands and repeating her monotonous refrain? It was only very gradually that my misty brain took these things in, and grasped the connection between them.

Reader, I have never seen Mr. Abrahams since, and have never seen the plate stamped with the resuscitated family crest; hardest of all, I have never caught a glimpse of the melancholy specter with the trailing garments, nor do I expect that I ever shall. In fact my night's experiences have cured me of my mania for the supernatural and quite reconciled me to inhabiting the humdrum nineteenth century edifice on the outskirts of London which Mrs. D. has long had in her mind's eye.

As to the explanation of all that occurred—that is a matter which is open to several surmises. That Mr. Abrahams, the ghost hunter, was identical with Jemmy Wilson, *alias* the Nottingham crackster, is considered more than probable at Scotland Yard, and certainly the description of that remarkable burglar tallied very well with the appearance of my visitor. The small bag which I have described was picked up in a neighboring field next day, and found to contain a choice assortment of jemmies and centerbits. Footmarks deeply imprinted in the mud on either side of the moat showed that an accomplice from below had received the sack of precious metals which had been let down through the open window. No doubt the pair of scoundrels, while looking round for a job, had overheard Jack Brocket's indiscreet inquiries, and had promptly availed themselves of the tempting opening.

And now as to my less substantial visitors, and the curious grotesque vision which I had enjoyed—am I to lay it down to any real power over occult matters possessed by my Nottingham friend? For a long time I was doubtful upon the point, and eventually endeavored to solve it by consulting a well-known analyst and medical man, sending him the few drops of the so-called essence of Lucoptolycus which remained in my phial. I append the letter which I received from him, only too happy to have the opportunity of winding up my little narrative by the weighty words of a man of learning.

Arundel Street

Dear Sir,—Your very singular case has interested me extremely. The bottle which you sent contained a strong solution of chloral, and the quantity which you describe yourself as having swallowed must have amounted to at least eighty grains of the pure hydrate. This would of course have reduced you to a partial state of insensibility, gradually going on to complete coma. In this semiunconscious state of chloralism it is not unusual for circumstantial and *bizarre* visions to present themselves—more especially to individuals unaccustomed to the use of the drug. You tell me in your note that your mind was saturated with ghostly literature, and that you had long taken a morbid interest in classifying and recalling the various forms in which apparitions have been said to appear. You must also remember that you were expecting to see something of that very nature, and that your nervous system was worked up to an unnatural state of tension. Under the circumstances, I think that, far from the sequel being an astonishing one, it would have been very surprising indeed to anyone versed in narcotics had you not experienced some such effects.—I remain, dear sir, sincerely yours,

T. E. Stube, M.D.

Argentine D'Odd, Esq.,
The Elms, Brixton

THE GREAT BROWN-PERICORD MOTOR

It was a cold, foggy, dreary evening in May. Along the Strand blurred patches of light marked the position of the lamps. The flaring shop windows flickered vaguely with steamy brightness through the thick and heavy atmosphere.

The high lines of houses which lead down to the Embankment were all dark and deserted, or illuminated only by the glimmering lamp of the caretaker. At one point, however, there shone out from three windows upon the second floor a rich flood of light, which broke the somber monotony of the terrace. Passersby glanced up curiously, and drew each other's attention to the ruddy glare, for it marked the chambers of Francis Pericord, the inventor and electrical engineer. Long into the watches of the night the gleam of his lamps bore witness to the untiring energy and restless industry which was rapidly carrying him to the first rank in his profession.

Within the chamber sat two men. The one was Pericord himself—hawk-faced and angular, with the black hair and brisk bearing which spoke of his Celtic origin. The other—thick, sturdy, and blue-eyed, was Jeremy Brown, the well-known mechanician. They had been partners in many an invention, in which the creative genius of the one had been aided by the practical abilities of the other. It was a question among their friends as to which was the better man.

It was no chance visit which had brought Brown into Pericord's workshop at so late an hour. Business was to be done—business which was to decide the failure or success of months of work, and which might affect their whole careers. Between them lay a long brown table, stained and corroded by strong acids, and littered with giant carboys, Faure's accumulators, voltaic piles, coils of wire, and great blocks of nonconducting porcelain. In the midst of all this lumber there stood a singular whizzing, whirring machine, upon which the eyes of both partners were riveted.

A small square metal receptacle was connected by numerous wires to a broad steel girdle, furnished on either side with two powerful projecting joints. The girdle was motionless, but the joints with the short arms attached to them flashed round every few seconds, with a pause between each rhythmic turn. The power which moved them came evidently from the metal box. A subtle odor of ozone was in the air.

"How about the flanges, Brown?" asked the inventor.

"They were too large to bring. They are seven foot by three. There is power enough there to work them however. I will answer for that."

"Aluminum with an alloy of copper?"

"Yes."

"See how beautifully it works." Pericord stretched out a thin, nervous hand, and pressed a button upon the machine. The joints revolved more slowly, and came presently to a dead stop. Again he touched a spring and the arms shivered and woke up again into their crisp metallic life. "The experimenter need not exert his muscular powers," he remarked. "He has only to be passive, and use his intelligence."

"Thanks to my motor," said Brown.

"*Our* motor," the other broke in sharply.

"Oh, of course," said his colleague impatiently. "The motor which you thought of, and which I reduced to practice—call it what you like."

"I call it the Brown-Pericord Motor," cried the inventor, with an angry flash of his dark eyes. "You worked out the details, but the abstract thought is mine, and mine alone."

"An abstract thought won't turn an engine," said Brown, doggedly.

"That was why I took you into partnership," the other retorted, drumming nervously with his fingers upon the table. "I invent, you build. It is a fair division of labor."

Brown pursed his lips, as though by no means satisfied upon the point. Seeing, however, that further argument was useless, he turned his attention to the machine, which was shivering and rocking with each swing of its arms, as though a very little more would send it skimming from the table.

"Is it not splendid?" cried Pericord.

"It is satisfactory," said the more phlegmatic Anglo-Saxon.

"There's immortality in it!"

"There's money in it!"

"Our names will go down with Montgolfier's."

"With Rothschild's, I hope."

"No, no, Brown; you take too material a view," cried the inventor, raising his gleaming eyes from the machine to his companion. "Our fortunes are a mere detail. Money is a thing which every heavy-witted plutocrat in the country shares with us. My hopes rise to something higher than that. Our true reward will come in the gratitude and goodwill of the human race."

Brown shrugged his shoulders. "You may have my share of that," he said. "I am a practical man. We must test our invention."

"Where can we do it?"

"That is what I wanted to speak about. It must be absolutely secret. If we had private grounds of our own it would be an easy matter, but there is no privacy in London."

"We must take it into the country."

"I have a suggestion to offer," said Brown. "My brother has a place in Sussex on the high land near Beachy Head. There is, I remember, a large and lofty barn near the house. Will is in Scotland, but the key is always at my disposal. Why not take the machine down tomorrow and test it in the barn?"

"Nothing could be better."

"There is a train to Eastbourne at one."

"I shall be at the station."

"Bring the gear with you, and I will bring the flanges," said the mechanician, rising. "Tomorrow will prove whether we have been following a shadow, or whether fortune is at our feet. One o'clock at Victoria." He walked swiftly down the stair and was quickly reabsorbed into the flood of comfortless clammy humanity which ebbed and flowed along the Strand.

The morning was bright and springlike. A pale blue sky arched over London, with a few gauzy white clouds drifting lazily across it. At eleven o'clock Brown might have been seen entering the Patent Office with a great roll of parchment, diagrams, and plans under his arm. At twelve he emerged again smiling, and, opening his pocketbook, he packed away very carefully a small slip of official blue paper. At five minutes to one his cab rolled into Victoria Station. Two giant canvas-covered parcels, like enormous kites, were handed down by the cabman from the top, and consigned to the care of a guard. On the platform Pericord was pacing up and down, with long eager steps and swinging arms, a tinge of pink upon his sunken and sallow cheeks.

"All right?" he asked.

Brown pointed in answer to his baggage.

"I have the motor and the girdle already packed away in the guard's van. Be careful, guard, for it is delicate machinery of great value. So! Now we can start with an easy conscience."

At Eastbourne the precious motor was carried to a four-wheeler, and the great flanges hoisted on the top. A long drive took them to the house where the keys were kept, whence they set off across the barren Downs. The building which was their destination was a commonplace white-washed structure, with straggling stables and outhouses, standing in a grassy hollow which sloped down from the edge of the chalk cliffs. It was a cheerless house even when in use, but now with its smokeless chimneys and shuttered windows it looked doubly dreary. The owner had planted a grove of young larches and firs around it, but the sweeping spray had blighted them, and they hung their withered heads in melancholy groups. It was a gloomy and forbidding spot.

But the inventors were in no mood to be moved by such trifles. The lonelier the place, the more fitted for their purpose. With the help of the cabman they carried their packages down the footpath, and laid them in the darkened dining room. The sun was setting as the distant murmur of wheels told them that they were finally alone.

Pericord had thrown open the shutters and the mellow evening light streamed in through the discolored windows. Brown drew a knife from his pocket and cut the packthread with which the canvas was secured. As the brown covering fell away it disclosed two great yellow metal fans. These he leaned carefully against the wall. The girdle, the connecting bands, and the motor were then in turn unpacked. It was dark before all was set out in order. A lamp was lit, and by its light the two men continued to tighten screws, clinch rivets, and make the last preparations for their experiment.

"That finishes it," said Brown at last, stepping back and surveying the machine.

Pericord said nothing, but his face glowed with pride and expectation.

"We must have something to eat," Brown remarked, laying out some provisions which he had brought with him.

"Afterward."

"No, now," said the stolid mechanician. "I am half starved." He pulled up to the table and made a hearty meal, while his Celtic companion strode impatiently up and down, with twitching fingers and restless eyes.

"Now then," said Brown, facing round, and brushing the crumbs from his lap, "who is to put it on?"

"I shall," cried his companion eagerly. "What we do tonight is likely to be historic."

"But there is some danger," suggested Brown. "We cannot quite tell how it may act."

"That is nothing," said Pericord, with a wave of his hand.

"But there is no use our going out of our way to incur danger."

"What then? One of us must do it."

"Not at all. The motor would act equally well if attached to any inanimate object."

"That is true," said Pericord, thoughtfully.

"There are bricks by the barn. I have a sack here. Why should not a bagful of them take your place?"

"It is a good idea. I see no objection."

"Come on then," and the two sallied out, bearing with them the various sections of their machine. The moon was shining cold and clear though an occasional ragged cloud drifted across her face. All was still and silent upon the Downs. They stood and listened before they entered the barn, but not a sound came to their ears, save the dull murmur of the sea and the distant barking of a dog. Pericord journeyed backward and forward with all that they might need, while Brown filled a long narrow sack with bricks.

When all was ready, the door of the barn was closed, and the lamp balanced upon an empty packing case. The bag of bricks was laid upon two trestles, and the broad steel girdle was buckled round it. Then the great flanges, the wires, and the metal box containing the motor were in turn attached to the girdle. Last of all a flat steel rudder, shaped like a fish's tail, was secured to the bottom of the sack.

"We must make it travel in a small circle," said Pericord, glancing round at the bare high walls.

"Tie the rudder down at one side," suggested Brown. "Now it is ready. Press the connection and off she goes!"

Pericord leaned forward, his long sallow face quivering with excitement. His white nervous hands darted here and there among the wires. Brown stood impassive with critical eyes. There was a sharp burr from the machine. The huge yellow wings gave a convulsive flap. Then another. Then a third, slower and stronger, with a fuller sweep. Then a fourth which filled the barn with a blast of driven air. At the fifth the bag of bricks began to dance upon the trestles. At the sixth it sprang into the air, and would have fallen to the ground, but the seventh came to save it, and fluttered it forward through the air. Slowly rising, it flapped heavily round in a circle, like some great clumsy bird, filling the barn with its buzzing and whirring. In the uncertain yellow light of the single lamp it was strange to see the loom of the ungainly thing, flapping off into the shadows, and then circling back into the narrow zone of light.

The two men stood for a while in silence. Then Pericord threw his long arms up into the air.

"It acts!" he cried. "The Brown-Pericord Motor acts!" He danced about like a madman in his delight. Brown's eyes twinkled, and he began to whistle.

"See how smoothly it goes, Brown!" cried the inventor. "And the rudder—how well it acts! We must register it tomorrow."

His comrade's face darkened and set. "It is registered," he said, with a forced laugh.

"Registered?" said Pericord. "Registered?" He repeated the word first in a whisper, and then in a kind of scream. "Who has dared to register my invention?"

"I did this morning. There is nothing to be excited about. It is all right."

"You registered the motor! Under whose name?"

"Under my own," said Brown, sullenly. "I consider that I have the best right to it."

"And my name does not appear?"

"No, but—"

"You villain!" screamed Pericord. "You thief and villain! You would steal my work! You would filch my credit! I will have that patent back if I have to tear your throat out!" A somber fire burned in his black eyes, and his hands writhed themselves together with passion. Brown was no coward, but he shrank back as the other advanced upon him.

"Keep your hands off!" he said, drawing a knife from his pocket. "I will defend myself if you attack me."

"You threaten me?" cried Pericord, whose face was livid with anger. "You are a bully as well as a cheat. Will you give up the patent?"

"No, I will not."

"Brown, I say, give it up!"

"I will not. I did the work."

Pericord sprang madly forward with blazing eyes and clutching fingers. His companion writhed out of his grasp, but was dashed against the packing case, over which he fell. The lamp was extinguished, and the whole barn plunged into darkness. A single ray of moonlight shining through a narrow chink flickered over the great waving fans as they came and went.

"Will you give up the patent, Brown?"

There was no answer.

"Will you give it up?"

Again no answer. Not a sound save the humming and creaking overhead. A cold pang of fear and doubt struck through Pericord's heart. He felt aimlessly about in the dark and his fingers closed upon a hand. It was cold and unresponsive. With all his anger turned to icy horror he struck a match, set the lamp up, and lit it.

Brown lay huddled up on the other side of the packing case. Pericord seized him in his arms, and with convulsive strength lifted him across. Then the mystery of his silence was explained. He had fallen with his right arm doubled up under him, and his own weight had driven the knife deeply into his body. He had died without a groan. The tragedy had been sudden, horrible, and complete.

Pericord sat silently on the edge of the case, staring blankly down, and shivering like one with the ague, while the great Pericord-Brown Motor boomed and hurtled above him. How long he sat there can never be known. It might have been minutes or it might have been hours. A thousand mad schemes flashed through his dazed brain. It was true that he had been only the indirect cause. But who would believe that? He glanced down at his blood-spattered clothing. Everything was against him. It would be better to fly than to give himself up, relying upon his innocence. No one in London knew where they were. If he could dispose of the body he might have a few days clear before any suspicion would be aroused.

Suddenly a loud crash recalled him to himself. The flying sack had gradually risen with each successive circle until it had struck against the rafters. The blow displaced the connecting gear, and the machine fell heavily to the ground. Pericord undid the girdle. The motor was uninjured. A sudden, strange thought flashed upon him as he looked at it. The machine had become hateful to him. He might dispose both of it and the body in a way that would baffle all human search.

He threw open the barn door, and carried his companion out into the moonlight. There was a hillock outside, and on the summit of this he laid him reverently down. Then he brought from the barn the motor, the girdle, and the flanges. With trembling fingers he fastened the broad steel belt round the dead man's waist. Then he screwed the wings into the sockets. Beneath he slung the motor box, fastened the wires, and switched on the connection. For a minute or two the huge yellow fans flapped and flickered. Then the body began to move in little jumps down the side of the hillock, gathering a gradual momentum, until at last it heaved up into the air and soared heavily off in the moonlight. He had not used the rudder, but had turned the head for the south. Gradually the weird thing rose higher, and sped faster, until it passed over the line of cliff, and was sweeping over the silent sea. Pericord watched it with a white drawn face, until it looked like a black bird with golden wings half shrouded in the mist which lay over the waters.

In the New York State Lunatic Asylum there is a wild-eyed man whose name and birthplace are alike unknown. His reason has been unseated by some sudden shock, the doctors say, though of what nature they are unable to determine. "It is the most delicate machine which is most readily put out of gear," they remark, and point, in proof of their axiom, to the complicated electric engines, and remarkable aeronautic machines which the patient is fond of devising in his more lucid moments.

THE TERROR OF BLUE JOHN GAP

The following narrative was found among the papers of Dr. James Hardcastle, who died of phthisis on February 4th, 1908, at 36, Upper Coventry Flats, South Kensington. Those who knew him best, while refusing to express an opinion upon this particular statement, are unanimous in asserting that he was a man of a sober and scientific turn of mind, absolutely devoid of imagination, and most unlikely to invent any abnormal series of events. The paper was contained in an envelope, which was docketed, "A Short Account of the Circumstances which Occurred near Miss Allerton's Farm in Northwest Derbyshire in the Spring of Last Year." The envelope was sealed, and on the other side was written in pencil:

> DEAR SEATON,—It may interest, and perhaps pain, you to know that the incredulity with which you met my story has prevented me from ever opening my mouth upon the subject again. I leave this record after my death, and perhaps strangers may be found to have more confidence in me than my friend.

Inquiry has failed to elicit who this Seaton may have been. I may add that the visit of the deceased to Allerton's Farm, and the general nature of the alarm there, apart from his particular explanation, have been absolutely established. With this foreword I append his account exactly as he left it. It is in the form of a diary, some entries in which have been expanded, while a few have been erased.

April 17th.—Already I feel the benefit of this wonderful upland air. The farm of the Allertons lies fourteen hundred and twenty feet above sea-level, so it may well be a bracing climate. Beyond the usual morning cough I have very little discomfort, and, what with the fresh milk and the home-grown mutton, I have every chance of putting on weight. I think Saunderson will be pleased.

The two Miss Allertons are charmingly quaint and kind, two dear little hard-working old maids, who are ready to lavish all the heart which might have gone out to husband and to children upon an invalid stranger. Truly, the old maid is a most useful person, one of the reserve forces of the community. They talk of the superfluous woman, but what would the poor superfluous man do without her kindly presence? By the way, in their simplicity they very quickly let out the reason why Saunderson recommended their farm. The Professor rose from the ranks himself, and I believe that in his youth he was not above scaring cows in those very fields.

It is a most lonely spot, and the walks are picturesque in the extreme. The farm consists of grazing land lying at the bottom of an irregular valley. On each side are the fantastic limestone hills, formed of rock so soft that you can break it away with your hands. All this country is hollow. Could you strike it with some gigantic hammer it would boom like a drum, or possibly cave in altogether and expose some huge subterranean sea. A great sea there must surely be, for on all sides the streams run into the mountain itself, never to reappear. There are gaps everywhere amid the rocks, and when you pass through them you find yourself in great caverns, which wind down into the bowels of the earth. I have a small bicycle lamp, and it is a perpetual joy to me to carry it into these weird solitudes, and to see the wonderful silver and black effects when I throw its light upon the stalactites which drape the lofty roofs. Shut off the lamp, and you are in the blackest darkness. Turn it on, and it is a scene from the Arabian Nights.

But there is one of these strange openings in the earth which has special interest, for it is the handiwork, not of Nature, but of Man. I had never heard of Blue John when I came to these parts. It is the name given to a peculiar mineral of a beautiful purplish shade, which is only found at one or two places in the world. It is so rare that an ordinary vase of Blue John would be valued at a great price. The Romans, with that extraordinary instinct of theirs, discovered that it was to be found in this valley, and sank a horizontal shaft deep into the mountain side. The opening of their mine has been called Blue John Gap, a clean cut arch in the rock, the mouth all overgrown with bushes. It is a goodly passage which the Roman miners have cut, and it intersects some of the great water-worn caves, so that if you enter Blue John Gap you would do well to mark your steps and to have a good store of candles, or you may never make your way back to the daylight again. I have not yet gone deeply into it, but this very day I stood at the mouth of the arched tunnel, and peering down into the black recesses beyond I vowed that when my health returned I would devote some holiday to exploring those mysterious depths and finding out for myself how far the Roman had penetrated into the Derbyshire hills.

Strange how superstitious these countrymen are! I should have thought better of young Armitage, for he is a man of some education and character, and a very fine fellow for his station in life. I was standing at the Blue John Gap when he came across the field to me.

"Well, doctor," said he, "you're not afraid, anyhow."

"Afraid!" I answered. "Afraid of what?"

"Of it," said he, with a jerk of his thumb toward the black vault; "of the Terror that lives in the Blue John Cave."

How absurdly easy it is for a legend to arise in a lonely countryside! I examined him as to the reasons for his weird belief. It seems that from time to time sheep have been missing from the fields, carried bodily away, according to Armitage. That they could have wandered away of their own accord and disappeared among the mountains was an explanation to which he would not listen. On one occasion a pool of blood had been found, and some tufts of wool. That also, I pointed out, could be explained in a perfectly natural way. Further, the nights upon which sheep disappeared were invariably very dark, cloudy nights, with no moon. This I met with the obvious retort that those were the nights which a commonplace sheep stealer would naturally choose for his work. On one occasion a gap had been made in a wall, and some of the stones scattered for a considerable distance. Human agency again, in my opinion. Finally, Armitage clinched all his arguments by telling me that he had actually heard the Creature—indeed, that anyone could hear it who remained long enough at the Gap. It was a distant roaring of an immense volume. I could not but smile at this, knowing, as I do, the strange reverberations which come out of an underground water system running amid the chasms of a limestone formation. My incredulity annoyed Armitage, so that he turned and left me with some abruptness.

And now comes the queer point about the whole business. I was still standing near the mouth of the cave, turning over in my mind the various statements of Armitage and reflecting how readily they could be explained away, when suddenly, from the depth of the tunnel beside me, there issued a most extraordinary sound. How shall I describe it? First of all, it seemed to be a great distance away, far down in the bowels of the earth. Secondly, in spite of this suggestion of distance, it was very loud. Lastly, it was not a boom, nor a crash, such as one would associate with falling water or tumbling rock; but it was a high whine, tremulous and vibrating, almost like the whinnying of a horse. It was certainly a most remarkable experience, and one which for a moment, I must admit, gave a new significance to Armitage's words. I waited by the Blue John Gap for half an hour or more, but there was no return of the sound, so at last I wandered back to the farmhouse, rather mystified by what had occurred. Decidedly, I shall explore that cavern when my strength is restored. Of course, Armitage's explanation is too absurd for discussion, and yet that sound was certainly very strange. It still rings in my ears as I write.

April 20th.—In the last three days I have made several expeditions to the Blue John Gap, and have even penetrated some short distance, but my bicycle lantern is so small and weak that I dare not trust myself very far. I shall do the thing more systematically. I have heard no sound at all, and could almost believe that I had been the victim of some hallucination, suggested, perhaps, by Armitage's conversation. Of course, the whole idea is absurd, and yet I must confess that those bushes at the entrance of the cave do present an appearance as if some heavy creature had forced its way through them. I begin to be keenly interested. I have said nothing to the Miss Allertons, for they are quite superstitious enough already, but I have bought some candles, and mean to investigate for myself.

I observed this morning that among the numerous tufts of sheep's wool which lay among the bushes near the cavern there was one which was smeared with blood. Of course, my reason tells me that if sheep wander into such rocky places they are likely to injure themselves, and yet somehow that splash of crimson gave me a sudden shock, and for a moment I found myself shrinking back in horror from the old Roman arch. A fetid breath seemed to ooze from the black depths into which I peered. Could it indeed be possible that some nameless thing, some dreadful presence, was lurking down yonder? I should have been incapable of such feelings in the days of my strength, but one grows more nervous and fanciful when one's health is shaken.

For the moment I weakened in my resolution, and was ready to leave the secret of the old mine, if one exists, forever unsolved. But tonight my interest has returned and my nerves grown more steady. Tomorrow I trust that I shall have gone more deeply into this matter.

April 22nd.—Let me try and set down as accurately as I can my extraordinary experience of yesterday. I started in the afternoon, and made my way to the Blue John Gap. I confess that my misgivings returned as I gazed into its depths, and I wished that I had brought a companion to share my exploration. Finally, with a return of resolution, I lit my candle, pushed my way through the briers, and descended into the rocky shaft.

It went down at an acute angle for some fifty feet, the floor being covered with broken stone. Thence there extended a long, straight passage cut in the solid rock. I am no geologist, but the lining of this corridor was certainly of some harder material than limestone, for there were points where I could actually see the toolmarks which the old miners had left in their excavation, as fresh as if they had been done yesterday. Down this strange, old-world corridor I stumbled, my feeble flame throwing a dim circle of light around me, which made the shadows beyond the more threatening and obscure. Finally, I came to a spot where the Roman tunnel opened into a water-worn cavern—a huge hall, hung with long white icicles of lime deposit. From this central chamber I could dimly perceive that a number of passages worn by the subterranean streams wound away into the depths of the earth. I was standing there wondering whether I had better return, or whether I dare venture farther into this dangerous labyrinth, when my eyes fell upon something at my feet which strongly arrested my attention.

The greater part of the floor of the cavern was covered with boulders of rock or with hard incrustations of lime; but at this particular point there had been a drip from the distant roof, which had left a patch of soft mud. In the very center of this there was a huge mark—an ill-defined blotch, deep, broad, and irregular, as if a great boulder had fallen upon it. No loose stone lay near, however, nor was there anything to account for the impression. It was far too large to be caused by any possible animal, and , besides, there was only the one, and the patch of mud was of such a size that no reasonable stride could have covered it. As I rose from the examination of that singular mark and then looked round into the black shadows which hemmed me in, I must confess that I felt for a moment a most unpleasant sinking of my heart, and that, do what I would, the candle trembled in my outstretched hand.

I soon recovered my nerve, however, when I reflected how absurd it was to associate so huge and shapeless a mark with the track of any known animal. Even an elephant could not have produced it. I determined, therefore, that I would not be scared by vague and senseless fears from carrying out my exploration. Before proceeding I took good note of a curious rock formation in the wall by which I could recognize the entrance of the Roman tunnel. The precaution was very necessary, for the great cave, so far as I could see it, was intersected by passages. Having made sure of my position, and reassured myself by examining my spare candles and my matches, I advanced slowly over the rocky and uneven surface of the cavern.

And now I come to the point where I met with such sudden and desperate disaster. A stream, some twenty feet broad, ran across my path, and I walked for some little distance along the bank to find a spot where I could cross dry-shod. Finally, I came to a place where a single flat boulder lay near the center, which I could reach in a stride. As it chanced, however, the rock had been cut away and made top-heavy by the rush of the stream, so that it tilted over as I landed on it, and shot me into the ice-cold water. My candle went out, and I found myself floundering about in an utter and absolute darkness.

I staggered to my feet again, more amused than alarmed by my adventure. The candle had fallen from my hand, and was lost in the stream; but I had two others in my pocket, so that it was of no importance. I got one of them ready, and drew out my box of matches to light it. Only then did I realize my position. The box had been soaked in my fall into the river. It was impossible to strike the matches.

A cold hand seemed to close round my heart as I realized my position. The darkness was opaque and horrible. It was so utter that one put one's hand up to one's face as if to press off something solid. I stood still, and by an effort I steadied myself. I tried to reconstruct in my mind a map of the floor of the cavern as I had last seen it. Alas! the bearings which had impressed themselves upon my mind were high on the wall, and not to be found by touch. Still, I remembered in a general way how the sides were situated, and I hoped that by groping my way along them I would at last come to the opening of the Roman tunnel. Moving very slowly, and continually striking against the rocks, I set out on this desperate quest.

But I very soon realized how impossible it was. In that black, velvety darkness one lost all one's bearings in an instant. Before I had made a dozen paces I was utterly bewildered as to my whereabouts. The rippling of the stream, which was the one sound audible, showed me where it lay, but the moment that I left its bank I was utterly lost. The idea of finding my way back in absolute darkness through that limestone labyrinth was clearly an impossible one.

I sat down upon a boulder and reflected upon my unfortunate plight. I had not told anyone that I proposed to come to the Blue John mine, and it was unlikely that a search party would come after me. Therefore, I must trust to my own resources to get clear of the danger. There was only one hope, and that was the matches might dry. When I fell into the river only half of me had got thoroughly wet. My left shoulder had remained above the water. I took the box of matches, therefore, and put it in my left armpit. The moist air of the cavern might possibly be counteracted by the heat of my body, but even so I knew that I could not hope to get a light for many hours. Meanwhile there was nothing for it but to wait.

By good luck I had slipped several biscuits into my pocket before I had left the farmhouse. These I now devoured, and washed them down with a draught from that wretched stream which had been the cause of all my misfortunes. Then I felt about for a comfortable seat among the rocks, and, having discovered a place where I could get a support for my back, I stretched out my legs and settled myself down to wait. I was wretchedly damp and cold, but I tried to cheer myself with the reflection that modern science prescribed open windows and walks in all weather for my disease. Gradually, lulled by the absolute darkness, I sank into an uneasy slumber.

How long this lasted I cannot say. It may have been for one hour, it may have been for several. Suddenly I sat up on my rock couch, with every nerve thrilling and every sense acutely on the alert. Beyond all doubt I had heard a sound—some sound very distinct from the gurgling of the waters. It had passed, but the reverberation of it still lingered in my ear. Was it a search party? They would most certainly have shouted, and vague as this sound was which had wakened me, it was very distinct from the human voice. I sat palpitating and hardly daring to breathe. There it was again! And again! Now it had become continuous. It was a tread—yes, surely it was the tread of some living creature. But what a tread it was! It gave one the impression of enormous weight carried upon spongelike feet, which gave forth a muffled but ear-filling sound. The darkness was as complete as ever, but the tread was regular and decisive. And it was coming beyond all question in my direction.

My skin grew cold, and my hair stood on end as I listened to that steady and ponderous footfall. There was some creature there, and surely, by the speed of its advance, it was one who could see in the dark. I crouched low on my rock and tried to blend myself into it. The steps grew nearer still, then stopped, and presently I was aware of a loud lapping and gurgling. The creature was drinking at the stream. Then again there was silence, broken by a succession of long sniffs and snorts, of tremendous volume and energy. Had it caught the scent of me? My own nostrils were filled by a low fetid odor, mephitic and abominable. Then I heard the steps again. They were on my side of the stream now. The stones rattled within a few yards of where I lay. Hardly daring to breathe, I crouched upon my rock. Then the steps drew away. I heard the splash as it returned across the river, and the sound died away in the distance in the direction from which it had come.

For a long time I lay upon the rock, too much horrified to move. I thought of the sound which I had heard coming from the depths of the cave, of Armitage's fears, of the strange impression in the mud, and now came this final and absolute proof that there was indeed some inconceivable monster, something utterly un-English and dreadful, which lurked in the hollow of the mountain. Of its nature or form I could frame no conception, save that it was both light-footed and gigantic. The combat between my reason, which told me that such things could not be, and my senses, which told me that they were, raged within me as I lay. Finally, I was almost ready to persuade myself that this experience had been part of some evil dream, and that my abnormal condition might have conjured up an hallucination. But there remained one final experience which removed the last possibility of doubt from my mind.

I had taken my matches from my armpit and felt them. They seemed perfectly hard and dry. Stooping down into a crevice of the rocks, I tried one of them. To my delight it took fire at once. I lit the candle, and, with a terrified backward glance into the obscure depths of the cavern, I hurried in the direction of the Roman passage. As I did so I passed the patch of mud on which I had seen the huge imprint. Now I stood astonished before it, for there were three similar imprints upon its surface, enormous in size, irregular in outline, of a depth which indicated the ponderous weight which had left them. Then a great terror surged over me. Stooping and shading my candle with my hand, I ran in a frenzy of fear to the rocky archway, hastened down it, and never stopped until, with weary feet and panting lungs, I rushed up the final slope of stones, broke through the tangle of briers, and flung myself exhausted upon the soft grass under the peaceful light of the stars. It was three in the morning when I reached the farmhouse, and today I am all unstrung and quivering after my terrific adventure. As yet I have told no one. I must move warily in the matter. What would the poor lonely women, or the uneducated yokels here, think of it if I were to tell them my experience? Let me go to someone who can understand and advise.

April 25th.—I was laid up in bed for two days after my incredible adventure in the cavern. I use the adjective with a very definite meaning, for I have had an experience since which has shocked me almost as much as the other. I have said that I was looking round for someone who could advise me. There is a Dr. Mark Johnson who practices some few miles away, to whom I had a note of recommendation from Professor Saunderson. To him I drove, when I was strong enough to get about, and I recounted to him my whole strange experience. He listened intently, and then carefully examined me, paying special attention to my reflexes and to the pupils of my eyes. When he had finished he refused to discuss my adventure, saying that it was entirely beyond him, but he gave me the card of a Mr. Picton at Castleton, with the advice that I should instantly go to him and tell him the story exactly as I had done it to himself. He was, according to my adviser, the very man who was preeminently suited to help me. I went on to the station, therefore, and made my way to the little town, which is some ten miles away. Mr. Picton appeared to be a man of importance, as his brass plate was displayed upon the door of a considerable building on the outskirts of the town. I was about to ring his bell, when some misgiving came into my mind, and, crossing to a neighboring shop, I asked the man behind the counter if he could tell me anything of Mr. Picton. "Why," said he, "he is the best mad doctor in Derbyshire, and yonder is his asylum." You can imagine that it was not long before I had shaken the dust of Castleton from my feet and returned to the farm, cursing all unimaginative pedants who cannot conceive that there may be things in creation which have never yet chanced to come across their mole's vision. After all, now that I am cooler, I can afford to admit that I have been no more sympathetic to Armitage than Dr. Johnson has been to me.

April 27th.—When I was a student I had the reputation of being a man of courage and enterprise. I remember that when there was a ghosthunt at Coltbridge it was I who sat up in the haunted house. Is it advancing years (after all, I am only thirty-five), or is it this physical malady which has caused degeneration? Certainly my heart quails when I think of that horrible cavern in the hill, and the certainty that it has some monstrous occupant. What shall I do? There is not an hour in the day that I do not debate the question. If I say nothing, then, the mystery remains unsolved. If I do say anything, then I have the alternative of mad alarm over the whole countryside, or of absolute incredulity which may end in consigning me to an asylum. On the whole, I think that my best course is to wait, and to prepare for some expedition which shall be more deliberate and better thought-out than the last. As a first step I have been to Castleton and obtained a few essentials—a large acetylene lantern for one thing, and a good double-barreled sporting rifle for another. The latter I have hired, but I have bought a dozen heavy game cartridges, which would bring down a rhinoceros. Now I am ready for my troglodyte friend. Give me better health and a little spate of energy, and I shall try conclusions with him yet. But who and what is he? Ah! there is the question which stands between me and my sleep. How many theories do I form, only to discard each in turn! It is all so utterly unthinkable. And yet the cry, the footmark, the tread in the cavern—no reasoning can get past these. I think of the old world legends of dragons and of monsters. Were they, perhaps not such fairytales as we have thought? Can it be that there is some fact which underlies them, and am I, of all mortals, the one who is chosen to expose it?

May 3rd.—For several days I have been laid up by the vagaries of an English spring, and during those days there have been developments, the true and sinister meaning of which no one can appreciate save myself. I may say that we have had cloudy and moonless nights of late, which according to my information were the seasons upon which sheep disappeared. Well, sheep *have* disappeared. Two of Miss Allerton's, one of old Pearson's of the Cat Walk, and one of Mrs. Moulton's. Four in all, during three nights. No trace is left of them at all, and the countryside is buzzing with rumors of Gypsies and of sheep stealers.

But there is something more serious than that. Young Armitage has disappeared also. He left his moorland cottage early on Wednesday night, and has never been heard of since. He was an unattached man, so there is less sensation than would otherwise be the case. The popular explanation is that he owes money, and has found a situation in some other part of the country, whence he will presently write for his belongings. But I have grave misgivings. Is it not much more likely that the recent tragedy of the sheep has caused him to take some steps which may have ended in his own destruction? He may, for example, have lain wait for the creature, and been carried off by it into the recesses of the mountains. What an inconceivable fate for a civilized Englishman of the twentieth century! And yet I feel that it is possible and even probable. But in that case, how far am I answerable both for his death and for any other mishap which may occur? Surely with the knowledge I already possess it must be my duty to see that something is done, or if necessary to do it myself. It must be the latter, for this morning I went down to the local police station and told my story. The inspector entered it all in a large book and bowed me out with commendable gravity, but I heard a burst of laughter before I had got down his garden path. No doubt he was recounting my adventure to his family.

June 10th.—I am writing this, propped up in bed, six weeks after my last entry in this journal. I have gone through a terrible shock both to mind and body, arising from such an experience as has seldom befallen a human being before. But I have attained my end. The danger from the Terror which dwells in the Blue John Gap has passed, never to return. This much at least I, a broken invalid, have done for the common good. Let me now recount what occurred, as clearly as I may.

The night of Friday, May 3rd, was dark and cloudy—the very night for the monster to walk. About eleven o'clock I went from the farm-house with my lantern and my rifle, having first left a note upon the table of my bedroom in which I said that if I were missing search should be made for me in the direction of the Gap. I made my way to the mouth of the Roman shaft, and, having perched myself among the rocks close to the opening, I shut off my lantern and waited patiently with my loaded rifle ready to my hand.

It was a melancholy vigil. All down the winding valley I could see the scattered lights of the farmhouses, and the church clock of Chapel-le-Dale tolling the hours came faintly to my ears. These tokens of my fellowmen served only to make my own position seem the more lonely, and to call for a greater effort to overcome the terror which tempted me continually to get back to the farm, and abandon forever this dangerous quest. And yet there lies deep in every man a rooted self-respect which makes it hard for him to turn back from that which he has once undertaken. This feeling of personal pride was my salvation now, and it was that alone which held me fast when every instinct of my nature was dragging me away. I am glad now that I had the strength. In spite of all that it has cost me, my manhood is at least above reproach.

Twelve o'clock struck in the distant church, then one, then two. It was the darkest hour of the night. The clouds were drifting low, and there was not a star in the sky. An owl was hooting somewhere among the rocks, but no other sound, save the gentle sough of the wind, came to my ears. And then suddenly I heard it! From far away down the tunnel came those muffled steps, so soft and yet so ponderous. I heard also the rattle of stones as they gave way under that giant tread. They drew nearer. They were close upon me. I heard the crashing of the bushes round the entrance, and then dimly through the darkness I was conscious of the loom of some enormous shape, some monstrous inchoate creature, passing swiftly and very silently out from the tunnel. I was paralyzed with fear and amazement. Long as I had waited, now that it had actually come I was unprepared for the shock. I lay motionless and breathless, whilst the great dark mass whisked by me and was swallowed up in the night.

But now I nerved myself for its return. No sound came from the sleeping countryside to tell of the horror which was loose. In no way could I judge how far off it was, what it was doing, or when it might be back. But not a second time should my nerve fail me, not a second time should it pass unchallenged. I swore it between my clenched teeth as I laid my cocked rifle across the rock.

And yet it nearly happened. There was no warning of approach now as the creature passed over the grass. Suddenly, like a dark, drifting shadow, the huge bulk loomed up once more before me, making for the entrance of the cave. Again came that paralysis of volition, which held my crooked forefinger impotent upon the trigger. But with a desperate effort I shook it off. Even as the brushwood rustled, and the monstrous beast blended with the shadow of the Gap, I fired at the retreating form. In the blaze of the gun I caught a glimpse of a great shaggy mass, something with rough and bristling hair of a withered gray color, fading away to white in its lower parts, the huge body supported upon short, thick, curving legs. I had just that glance, and then I heard the rattle of the stones as the creature tore down into its burrow. In an instant, with a triumphant revulsion of feeling, I had cast my fears to the wind, and uncovering my powerful lantern, with my rifle in my hand, I sprang down from my rock and rushed after the monster down the old Roman shaft.

My splendid lamp cast a brilliant flood of vivid light in front of me, very different from the yellow glimmer which had aided me down this same passage only twelve days before. As I ran I saw the great beast lurching along before me, its huge bulk filling up the whole space from wall to wall. Its hair looked like coarse faded oakum, and hung down in long, dense masses which swayed as it moved. It was like an enormous unclippped sheep in its fleece, but in size it was far larger than the largest elephant, and its breadth seemed to be nearly as great as its height. It fills me with amazement now to think that I should have dared to follow such a horror into the bowels of the earth, but when one's blood is up, and when one's quarry seems to be flying, the old primeval hunting spirit awakes and prudence is cast to the wind. Rifle in hand, I ran at the top of my speed upon the trail of the monster.

I had seen the creature was swift. Now I was to find out to my cost that it was also very cunning. I had imagined that it was in panic flight, and that I had only to pursue it. The idea that it might turn upon me never entered my excited brain. I have already explained that the passage down which I was racing opened into a great central cave. Into this I rushed, fearful lest I should lose all trace of the beast. But he had turned upon his own traces, and in a moment we were face to face.

That picture, seen in the brilliant white light of the lantern, is etched forever upon my brain. He had reared up on his hind legs as a bear would do, and stood above me, enormous, menacing—such a creature as no nightmare had ever brought to my imagination. I have said that he reared like a bear, and there was something bearlike—if one could conceive a bear which was tenfold the bulk of any bear seen upon earth—in his whole pose and attitude, in his great crooked forelegs with their ivory-white claws, in his rugged skin, and in his red, gaping mouth, fringed with monstrous fangs. Only in one point did he differ from the bear, or from any other creature which walks the earth, and even at that supreme moment a shudder of horror passed over me as I observed that the eyes which glistened in the glow of the lantern were huge, projecting bulbs, white and sightless. For a moment his great paws swung over my head. The next he fell forward upon me, I and my broken lantern crashed to the earth, and I remember no more.

When I came to myself I was back in the farmhouse of the Allertons. Two days had passed since my terrible adventure in the Blue John Gap. It seems that I had lain all night in the cave insensible from concussion of the brain, with my left arm and two ribs badly fractured. In the morning my note had been found, a search party of a dozen farmers assembled, and I had been tracked down and carried back to my bedroom, where I had lain in high delirium ever since. There was, it seems, no sign of the creature, and no bloodstain which would show that my bullet had found him as he passed. Save for my own plight and the marks upon the mud, there was nothing to prove that what I said was true.

Six weeks have now elapsed, and I am able to sit out once more in the sunshine. Just opposite me is the steep hillside, gray with shaly rock, and yonder on its flank is the dark cleft which marks the opening of the Blue John Gap. But it is no longer a source of terror. Never again through that ill-omened tunnel shall any strange shape flit out into the world of men. The educated and the scientific, the Dr. Johnsons and the like, may smile at my narrative, but the poorer folk of the countryside had never a doubt as to its truth. On the day after my recovering consciousness they assembled in their hundreds round the Blue John Gap. As the *Castleton Courier* said:

> It was useless for our correspondent, or for any of the adventurous gentlemen who had come from Matlock, Buxton, and other parts, to offer to descend, to explore the cave to the end, and to finally test the extraordinary narrative of Dr. James Hardcastle. The country people had taken the matter into their own hands, and from an early hour of the morning they had worked hard in stopping up the entrance of the tunnel. There is a sharp slope where the shaft begins, and great boulders, rolled along by many willing hands, were thrust down it until the Gap was absolutely sealed. So ends the episode which has caused such excitement throughout the country. Local opinion is fiercely divided upon the subject. On the one hand are those who point to Dr. Hardcastle's impaired health, and to the possibility of cerebral lesions of tuber-cular origin giving rise to strange hallucinations. Some *idée fixe*, according to these gentlemen, caused the doctor to wander down the tunnel, and a fall among the rocks was sufficient to account for his injuries. On the other hand, a legend of a strange creature in the Gap has existed for some months back, and the farmers look upon Dr. Hardcastle's narrative and his personal injuries as a final corroboration. So the matter stands, and so the matter will con-tinue to stand, for no definite solution seems to us to be now possible. It transcends human wit to give any scientific explanation which could cover the alleged facts.

Perhaps before the *Courier* published these words they would have been wise to send their representative to me. I have thought the matter out, as no one else has had occasion to do, and it is possible that I might have removed some of the more obvious difficulties of the narrative and brought it one degree nearer to scientific acceptance. Let me then write down the only explanation which seems to me to elucidate what I know to my cost to have been a series of facts. My theory may seem to be wildly improbable, but at least no one can venture to say that it is impossible.

My view is—and it was formed, as is shown by my diary, before my personal adventure—that in this part of England there is a vast subterranean lake or sea, which is fed by the great number of streams which pass down through the limestone. Where there is a large collection of water there must also be some evaporation, mists or rain, and a possibility of vegetation. This in turn suggests that there may be animal life, arising, as the vegetable life would also do, from those seeds and types which had been introduced at an early period of the world's history, when communication with the outer air was more easy. This place had then developed a fauna and flora of its own, including such monsters as the one which I had seen, which may well have been the old cave bear, enormously enlarged and modified by its new environment. For countless æons the internal and the external creation had kept apart, growing steadily away from each other. Then there had come some rift in the depths of the mountain which had enabled one creature to wander up and, by means of the Roman tunnel, to reach the open air. Like all subterranean life, it had lost the power of sight, but this had no doubt been compensated for by Nature in other directions. Certainly it had some means of finding its way about, and of hunting down the sheep upon the hillside. As to its choice of dark nights, it is part of my theory that light was painful to those great white eyeballs, and that it was only a pitch-black world which it could tolerate. Perhaps, indeed, it was the glare of my lantern which saved my life at that awful moment when we were face to face. So I read the riddle. I leave these facts behind me, and if you can explain them, do so; or if you choose to doubt them, do so. Neither your belief nor your incredulity can alter them, nor affect one whose task is nearly over.

So ended the strange narrative of Dr. James Hardcastle.

THE WINNING SHOT

Caution.—The public are hereby cautioned against a man calling himself Octavius Gaster. He is to be recognized by his great height, his flaxen hair, and by a deep scar upon his left cheek, extending from the eye to the angle of the mouth. His predilection for bright colors—green neckties, and the like—may help to identify him. A slightly foreign accent is to be detected in his speech. This man is beyond the reach of the law, but is more dangerous than a mad dog. Shun him as you would shun the pestilence that walketh at noonday. Any communication as to his whereabouts will be thankfully acknowledged by A. C. U., Lincoln's Inn, London.

This is a copy of an advertisement which may have been noticed by many readers in the columns of the London morning papers during the early part of the present year. It has, I believe, excited considerable curiosity in certain quarters, and many guesses have been hazarded as to the identity of Octavius Gaster and the nature of the charge brought against him. When I state that the "caution" has been inserted by my elder brother, Arthur Cooper Underwood, barrister-at-law, upon my representations, it will be acknowledged that I am the most fitting person to enter upon an authentic explanation.

Hitherto the horror and vagueness of my suspicion, combined with my grief at the loss of my poor darling on the very eve of our wedding, have prevented me from revealing the events of last August to anyone save my brother.

Now, however, looking back, I can fit in many little facts almost unnoticed at the time, which form a chain of evidence that, though worthless in a court of law, may yet have some effect upon the mind of the public.

I shall therefore relate, without exaggeration or prejudice, all that occurred from the day upon which this man, Octavius Gaster, entered Toynby Hall up to the great rifle competition. I know that many people will always ridicule the supernatural, or what our poor intellects choose to regard as supernatural, and that the fact of my being a woman will be thought to weaken my evidence. I can only plead that I have never been weak-minded or impressionable, and that other people formed the same opinion of Octavius Gaster that I did.

Now to the story.

It was at Colonel Pillar's place at Roborough, in the pleasant county of Devon, that we spent our autumn holidays. For some months I had been engaged to his eldest son Charley, and it was hoped that the marriage might take place before the termination of the Long Vacation.

Charley was considered "safe" for his degree, and in any case was rich enough to be practically independent, while I was by no means penniless.

The old Colonel was delighted at the prospect of the match, and so was my mother; so that look what way we would, there seemed to be no cloud above our horizon.

It was no wonder, then, that that August was a happy one. Even the most miserable of mankind would have laid his woes aside under the genial influence of the merry household at Toynby Hall.

There was Lieutenant Daseby, or "Jack," as he was invariably called, fresh home from Japan in Her Majesty's ship Shark, who was on the same interesting footing with Fanny Pillar, Charley's sister, as Charley was with me, so that we were able to lend each other a certain moral support.

Then there was Harry, Charley's younger brother, and Trevor, his bosom friend at Cambridge.

Finally there was my mother, dearest of old ladies, beaming at us through her gold-rimmed spectacles, anxiously smoothing every little difficulty in the way of the two young couples, and never weary of detailing to them *her* own doubts and fears and perplexities when that gay young blood, Mr. Nicholas Underwood, came a-wooing into the provinces, and forswore Crockford's and Tattersall's for the sake of the country parson's daughter.

I must not, however, forget the gallant old warrior who was our host; with his time-honored jokes, and his gout, and his harmless affectation of ferocity.

"I don't know what's come over the governor lately," Charley used to say. "He has never cursed the Liberal Administration since you've been here, Lottie; and my belief is that unless he has a good blow off, that Irish question will get into his system and finish him."

Perhaps in the privacy of his own apartment the veteran used to make up for his self-abnegation during the day.

He seemed to have taken a special fancy to me, which he showed in a hundred little attentions.

"You're a good lass," he remarked one evening, in a very port-winy whisper. "Charley's a lucky dog, egad! and has more discrimination than I thought. Mark my words, Miss Underwood, you'll find that young gentleman isn't such a fool as he looks!"

With which equivocal complaint the Colonel solemnly covered his face with his handkerchief and went off into the land of dreams.

How well I remember the day that was the commencement of all our miseries!

Dinner was over, and we were in the drawing room, with the windows open to admit the balmy southern breeze.

My mother was sitting in the corner, engaged on a piece of fancy-work, and occasionally purring forth some truism which the dear old soul believed to be an entirely original remark, and founded exclusively upon her own individual experiences.

Fanny and the young lieutenant were billing and cooing upon the sofa, while Charley paced restlessly about the room.

I was sitting by the window, gazing out dreamily at the great wilderness of Dartmoor, which stretched away to the horizon, ruddy and glowing in the light of the sinking sun, save where some rugged tor stood out in bold relief against the scarlet background.

"I say," remarked Charley, coming over to join me at the window, "it seems a positive shame to waste an evening like this."

"Confound the evening!" said Jack Daseby.

"You're always victimizing yourself to the weather. Fan and I ar'n't going to move off this sofa—are we, Fan?"

That young lady announced her intention of remaining by nestling among the cushions, and glancing defiantly at her brother.

"Spooning is a demoralizing thing—isn't it, Lottie?" said Charley, appealing laughingly to me.

"Shockingly so," I answered.

"Why, I can remember Daseby here when he was as active a young fellow as any in Devon; and just look at him now! Fanny, Fanny, you've got a lot to answer for!"

"Never mind him, my dear," said my mother, from the corner. "Still, my experience has always shown me that moderation is an excellent thing for young people. Poor dear Nicholas used to think so too. He would never go to bed of a night until he had jumped the length of the hearthrug. I often told him it was dangerous; but he *would* do it, until one night he fell on the fender and snapped the muscle of his leg, which made him limp till the day of his death, for Doctor Pearson mistook it for a fracture of the bone, and put him in splints, which had the effect of stiffening his knee. They did say that the doctor was almost out of his mind at the time from anxiety, brought on by his younger daughter swallowing a halfpenny, and that that was what caused him to make the mistake."

My mother had a curious way of drifting along in her conversation, and occasionally rushing off at a tangent, which made it rather difficult to remember her original proposition. On this occasion Charley had, however, stowed it away in his mind as likely to admit of immediate application.

"An excellent thing, as you say, Mrs. Underwood," he remarked; "and we have not been out today. Look here, Lottie, we have an hour of daylight yet. Suppose we go down and have a try for a trout, if your mamma does not object."

"Put something round your throat, dear," said my mother, feeling that she had been outmaneuvered.

"All right, dear," I answered; "I'll just run up and put on my hat."

"And we'll have a walk back in the gloaming," said Charley, as I made for the door.

When I came down, I found my lover waiting impatiently with his fishing basket in the hall.

We crossed the lawn together, and passed the open drawing room windows, where three mischievous faces were looking out at us.

"Spooning is a terribly demoralizing thing," remarked Jack, reflectively staring up at the clouds.

"Shocking," said Fan; and all three laughed until they woke the sleeping Colonel, and we could hear them endeavoring to explain the joke to that ill-used veteran, who apparently obstinately refused to appreciate it.

We passed down the winding lane together, and through the little wooden gate, which opens on to the Tavistock road.

Charley paused for a moment after we had emerged and seemed irresolute which way to turn.

Had we but known it, our fate depended upon that trivial question.

"Shall we go down to the river, dear," he said, "or shall we try one of the brooks upon the moor?"

"Whichever you like?" I answered.

"Well, I vote that we cross the moor. We'll have a longer walk back that way," he added, looking down lovingly at the little white-shawled figure beside him.

The brook in question runs through a most desolate part of the country. By the path it is several miles from Toynby Hall; but we were both young and active, and struck out across the moor, regardless of rocks and furze bushes.

Not a living creature did we meet upon our solitary walk, save a few scraggy Devonshire sheep, who looked at us wistfully, and followed us for some distance, as if curious as to what could possibly have induced us to trespass upon their domains.

It was almost dark before we reached the little stream, which comes gurgling down through a precipitous glen, and meanders away to help to form the Plymouth "leat."

Above us towered two great columns of rock, between which the water trickled to form a deep, still pool at the bottom. This pool had always been a favorite spot of Charley's, and was a pretty cheerful place by day; but now, with the rising moon reflected upon its glassy waters, and throwing dark shadows from the overhanging rocks, it seemed anything rather than the haunt of a pleasure-seeker.

"I don't think, darling, that I'll fish, after all," said Charley, as we sat down together on a mossy bank. "It's a dismal sort of place, isn't it?"

"Very," said I, shuddering.

"We'll just have a rest, and then we will walk back by the pathway. You're shivering. You're not cold, are you?"

"No," said I, trying to keep up my courage; "I'm not cold, but I'm rather frightened, though it's very silly of me."

"By Jove!" said my lover, "I can't wonder at it, for I feel a bit depressed myself. The noise that water makes is like the gurgling in the throat of a dying man."

"Don't, Charley; you frighten me!"

"Come, dear, we mustn't get the blues," he said, with a laugh trying to reassure me. "Let's run away from this charnel-house place, and— Look!—see!—good gracious! what is that?"

Charley had staggered back, and was gazing upwards with a pallid face.

I followed the direction of his eyes, and could scarcely suppress a scream.

I have already mentioned that the pool by which we were standing lay at the foot of a rough mound of rocks. On the top of this mound, about sixty feet above our heads, a tall dark figure was standing, peering down, apparently, into the rugged hollow in which we were.

The moon was just topping the ridge behind, and the gaunt, angular outlines of the stranger stood out hard and clear against its silvery radiance.

There was something ghastly in the sudden and silent appearance of this solitary wanderer, especially when coupled with the weird nature of the scene.

I clung to my lover in speechless terror, and glared up at the dark figure above us.

"Hullo, you sir!" cried Charley, passing from fear into anger, as Englishmen generally do. "Who are you, and what the devil are you doing?"

"Oh! I thought it, I thought it!" said the man who was overlooking us, and disappeared from the top of the hill.

We heard him scrambling about among the loose stones, and in another moment he emerged upon the banks of the brook and stood facing us.

Weird as his appearance had been when we first caught sight of him, the impression was intensified rather than removed by a closer acquaintance.

The moon shining full upon him revealed a long, thin face of ghastly pallor, the effect being increased by its contrast with the flaring green necktie which he wore.

A scar upon his cheek had healed badly and caused a nasty pucker at the side of his mouth, which gave his whole countenance a most distorted expression, more particularly when he smiled.

The knapsack on his back and stout staff in his hand announced him to be a tourist, while the easy grace with which he raised his hat on perceiving the presence of a lady showed that he could lay claim to the *savoir faire* of a man of the world.

There was something in his angular proportions and bloodless face which, taken in conjunction with the black cloak which fluttered from his shoulders, irresistibly reminded me of a blood-sucking species of bat which Jack Daseby had brought from Japan upon his previous voyage, and which was the bugbear of the servants' hall at Toynby.

"Excuse my intrusion," he said, with a slightly foreign lisp, which imparted a peculiar beauty to his voice. "I should have had to sleep on the moor had I not had the good fortune to fall in with you."

"Confound it, man!" said Charley; "why couldn't you shout out, or give us some warning? You quite frightened Miss Underwood when you suddenly appeared up there."

The stranger once more raised his hat as he apologized to me for having given me such a start.

"I am a gentleman from Sweden," he continued, in that peculiar intonation of his, "and am viewing this beautiful land of yours. Allow me to introduce myself as Doctor Octavius Gaster. Perhaps you could tell me where I may sleep, and how I can get from this place, which is truly of great size?"

"You're very lucky in falling in with us," said Charley. "It is no easy matter to find your way upon the moor."

"That can I well believe," remarked our new acquaintance.

"Strangers have been found dead on it before now," continued Charley. "They lose themselves, and then wander in a circle until they fall from fatigue."

"Ha, ha!" laughed the Swede; "it is not I, who have drifted in an open boat from Cape Blanco to Canary, that will starve upon an English moor. But how may I turn to seek an inn?"

"Look here!" said Charley, whose interest was excited by the stranger's allusion, and who was at all times the most openhearted of men. "There's no an inn for many a mile round; and I daresay you have had a long day's walk already. Come home with us, and my father, the Colonel, will be delighted to see you and find you a spare bed."

"For this great kindness how can I thank you?" returned the traveler. "Truly, when I return to Sweden, I shall have strange stories to tell of the English and their hospitality!"

"Nonsense!" said Charley. "Come, we will start at once, for Miss

Underwood is cold. Wrap the shawl well round your neck, Lottie, and we will be home in no time."

We stumbled along in silence, keeping as far as we could to the rugged pathway, sometimes losing it as a cloud drifted over the face of the moon, and then regaining it further on with the return of the light.

The stranger seemed buried in thought, but once or twice I had the impression that he was looking hard at me through the darkness as we strode along together.

"So," said Charley at last, breaking the silence, "you drifted about in an open boat, did you?"

"Ah, yes," answered the stranger; "many strange sights have I seen, and many perils undergone, but none worse than that. It is, however, too sad a subject for a lady's ears. She has been frightened once tonight."

"Oh, you needn't be afraid of frightening me now," said I, as I leaned on Charley's arm.

"Indeed there is but little to tell, and yet is it sorrowful.

"A friend of mine, Karl Osgood, of Upsale, and myself started on a trading venture. Few white men had been among the wandering Moors at Cape Blanco, but nevertheless we went, and for some months lived well, selling this and that, and gathering much ivory and gold.

"'Tis a strange country, where is neither wood nor stone, so that the huts are made from the weeds of the sea.

"At last, just as we had what we thought was a sufficiency, the Moors conspired to kill us, and came down against us in the night.

"Short was our warning, but we fled to the beach, launched a canoe, and put out to sea, leaving everything behind.

"The Moors chased us, but lost us in the darkness; and when day dawned the land was out of sight.

"There was no country where we could hope for food nearer than Canary, and for that we made.

"I reached it alive, though very weak and mad, but poor Karl died the day before we sighted the islands.

"I gave him warning!

"I cannot blame myself in the matter.

"I said, 'Karl, the strength that you might gain by eating them would be more than made up for by the blood that you would lose!'

"He laughed at my words, caught the knife from my belt, cut them off, and eat them; and he died."

"Eat what?" asked Charley.

"His ears!" said the stranger.

We both looked round at him in horror.

There was no suspicion of a smile or joke upon his ghastly face.

"He was what you call headstrong," he continued, "but he should have known better than to do a thing like that. Had he but used his will he would have lived as I did."

"And you think a man's will can prevent him from feeling hungry?" said Charley.

"What can it not do?" returned Octavius Gaster, and relapsed into a silence which was not broken until our arrival at Toynby Hall.

Considerable alarm had been caused by our nonappearance, and Jack Daseby was just setting off with Charley's friend Trevor in search of us. They were delighted, therefore, when we marched in upon them, and considerably astonished at the appearance of our companion.

"Where the deuce did you pick up that secondhand corpse?" asked Jack, drawing Charley aside into the smoking room.

"Shut up, man; he'll hear you," growled Charley. "He's a Swedish doctor on a tour, and a deuced good fellow. He went in an open boat from What's-it's-name to another place. I've offered him a bed for the night."

"Well, all I can say is," remarked Jack, "that his face will never be his fortune."

"Ha, ha! Very good! very good!" laughed the subject of the remark, walking calmly into the room, to the complete discomfiture of the sailor. "No, it will never, as you say, in this country be my fortune,"—and he grinned until the hideous gash across the angle of his mouth made him look more like the reflection in a broken mirror than anything else.

"Come upstairs and have a wash; I can lend you a pair of slippers," said Charley; and hurried the visitor out of the room to put an end to a somewhat embarrassing situation.

Colonel Pillar was the soul of hospitality, and welcomed Doctor Gaster as effusively as if he had been an old friend of the family.

"Egad, sir," he said, "the place is your own; and as long as you care to stop you are very welcome. We're pretty quiet down here, and a visitor is an acquisition."

My mother was a little more distant. "A very well informed young man, Lottie," she remarked to me; "but I wish he would wink his eyes more. I don't like to see people who never wink their eyes. Still, my dear, my life has taught me one great lesson, and that is that a man's looks are of very little importance compared with his actions."

With which brand new and eminently original remark, my mother kissed me and left me to my meditations.

Whatever Doctor Octavius Gaster might be physically, he was certainly a social success.

By next day he had so completely installed himself as a member of the household that the Colonel would not hear of his departure.

He astonished everybody with the extent and variety of his knowledge. He could tell the veteran considerably more about the Crimea than he knew himself; he gave the sailor information about the coast of Japan; and even tackled my athletic lover upon the subject of rowing, discoursing about levers of the first order, and fixed points and fulcra, until the unhappy Cantab was fain to drop the subject.

Yet all this was done so modestly and even deferentially, that no one could possibly feel offended at being beaten upon their own ground. There was a quiet power about everything he said and did which was very striking.

I remember one example of this, which impressed us all at the time.

Trevor had a remarkably savage bulldog, which, however fond of its master, fiercely resented any liberties from the rest of us. This animal was, it may be imagined, rather unpopular, but as it was the pride of the student's heart, it was agreed not to banish it entirely, but to lock it up in the stable and give it a wide berth.

From the first it seemed to have taken a decided aversion to our visitor, and showed every fang in its head whenever he approached it.

On the second day of his visit, we were passing the stable in a body, when the growls of the creature inside arrested Doctor Gaster's attention.

"Ha!" he said. "There is that dog of yours, Mr. Trevor, is it not?"

"Yes; that's Towzer," assented Trevor.

"He is a bulldog, I think? What they call the national animal of England on the Continent?"

"Purebred," said the student, proudly.

"They are ugly animals—very ugly. Would you come into the stable and unchain him, that I may see him to advantage. It is a pity to keep an animal so powerful and full of life in captivity."

"He's rather a nipper," said Trevor, with a mischievous expression in his eye; "but I suppose you are not afraid of a dog?"

"Afraid?—no. Why should I be afraid?"

The mischievous look on Trevor's face increased as he opened the stable door. I heard Charley mutter something to him about its being past a joke, but the other's answer was drowned by the hollow growling from inside.

The rest of us retreated to a respectable distance, while Octavius Gaster stood in the open doorway with a look of mild curiosity upon his pallid face.

"And those," he said, "that I see so bright and red in the darkness—are those his eyes?"

"Those are they," said the student, as he stooped down and unbuckled the strap.

"Come here!" said Octavius Gaster.

The growling of the dog suddenly subsided into a long whimper, and instead of making the furious rush that we expected, he rustled among the straw as if trying to huddle into a corner.

"What the deuce is the matter with him?" exclaimed his perplexed owner.

"Come here!" repeated Gaster, in sharp metallic accents, with an indescribable air of command in them. "Come here!"

To our astonishment, the dog trotted out and stood at his side, but looking as unlike the usually pugnacious Towzer as it is possible to conceive. His ears were drooping, his tail limp, and he altogether presented the very picture of canine humiliation.

"A very fine dog, but singularly quiet," remarked the Swede, as he stroked him down. "Now, sir, go back!"

The brute turned and slunk back into its corner. We heard the rattling of its chain as it was being fastened, and next moment Trevor came out of the stable door with blood dripping from his finger.

"Confound the beast!" he said. "I don't know what can have come over him. I've had him three years, and he never bit me before."

I fancy—I cannot say it for certain—but I fancy that there was a spasmodic twitching of the cicatrix upon our visitor's face, which betokened an inclination to laugh.

Looking back, I think that it was from that moment that I began to have a strange indefinable fear and dislike of the man.

Week followed week, and the day fixed for my marriage began to draw near.

Octavius Gaster was still a guest at Toynby Hall, and, indeed, had so ingratiated himself with the proprietor that any hint at departure was laughed to scorn by that worthy soldier.

"Here you've come, sir, and here you'll stay; you shall, by Jove."

Whereat Octavius would smile and shrug his shoulders, and mutter something about the attractions of Devon, which would put the Colonel in a good humor for the whole day afterward.

My darling and I were too much engrossed with each other to pay very much attention to the traveler's occupations. We used to come upon him sometimes in our rambles through the woods, sitting reading in the most lonely situations.

He always placed the book in his pocket when he saw us approaching. I remember on one occasion, however, that we stumbled upon him so suddenly that the volume was still lying open before him.

"Ah, Gaster," said Charley, "studying as usual! What an old bookworm you are! What's the book? Ah, a foreign language; Swedish, I suppose?"

"No, it is not Swedish," said Gaster; "it is Arabic."

"You don't mean to say you know Arabic?"

"Oh, very well—very well indeed!"

"And what's it about?" I asked, turning over the leaves of the musty old volume.

"Nothing that would interest one so young and fair as yourself, Miss Underwood," he answered, looking at me in a way which had become habitual to him of late. "It treats of the days when mind was stronger than what you call matter; when great spirits lived that were able to exist without these coarse bodies of ours, and could mold all things to their so-powerful wills."

"Oh, I see; a kind of ghost story," said Charley. "Well, adieu; we won't keep you from your studies."

We left him sitting in the little glen still absorbed in his mystical treatise. It must have been imagination which induced me, on turning suddenly round half an hour later, to think that I saw his familiar figure glide rapidly behind a tree.

I mentioned it to Charley at the time, but he laughed my idea to scorn.

I alluded just now to a peculiar manner which this man Gaster had of looking at me. His eyes seemed to lose their usual steely expression when he did so, and soften into something which might be almost called caressing. They seemed to influence me strangely, for I could always tell, without looking at him, when his gaze was fixed upon me.

Sometimes I fancied that this idea was simply due to a disordered nervous system or morbid imagination; but my mother dispelled that delusion from my mind.

"Do you know," she said, coming into my bedroom one night, and carefully shutting the door behind her, "if the idea was not so utterly preposterous, Lottie, I should say that that Doctor was madly in love with you?"

"Nonsense, 'ma!" said I, nearly dropping my candle in my consternation at the thought.

"I really think so, Lottie," continued my mother. "He's got a way of looking which is very like that of your poor dear father, Nicholas, before we were married. Something of this sort, you know."

And the old lady cast an utterly heartbroken glance at the bedpost.

"Now, go to bed," said I, "and don't have such funny ideas. Why, poor Doctor Gaster knows that I am engaged as well as you do."

"Time will show," said the old lady, as she left the room; and I went to bed with the words still ringing in my ears.

Certainly, it is a strange thing that on that very night a thrill which I had come to know well ran through me, and awakened me from my slumbers.

I stole softly to the window, and peered out through the bars of the Venetian blinds, and there was the gaunt, vampirelike figure of our Swedish visitor standing upon the gravel walk, and apparently gazing up at my window.

It may have been that he detected the movement of the blind, for, lighting a cigarette, he began pacing up and down the avenue.

I noticed that at breakfast next morning he went out of his way to explain the fact that he had been restless during the night, and had steadied his nerves by a short stroll and a smoke.

After all, when I came to consider it calmly, the aversion which I had against the man and my distrust of him were founded on very scanty grounds. A man might have a strange face, and be fond of curious literature, and even look approvingly at an engaged young lady, without being a very dangerous member of society.

I say this to show that even up to that point I was perfectly unbiased and free from prejudice in my opinion of Octavius Gaster.

"I say!" remarked Lieutenant Daseby, one morning; "what do you think of having a picnic today?"

"Capital!" ejaculated everybody.

"You see, they are talking of commissioning the old Shark soon, and Trevor here will have to go back to the mill. We may as well compress as much fun as we can into the time."

"What is it that you call nicpic?" asked Doctor Gaster.

"It's another of our English institutions for you to study," said Charley. "It's our version of a *fête champêtre*."

"Ah, I see! That will be very jolly!" acquiesced the Swede.

"There are half a dozen places we might go to," continued the Lieutenant. "There's the Lover's Leap, or Black Tor, or Beer Ferris Abbey."

"That's the best," said Charley. "Nothing like ruins for a picnic."

"Well, the Abbey be it. How far is it?"

"Six miles," said Trevor.

"Seven by the road," remarked the Colonel, with military exactness. "Mrs. Underwood and I shall stay at home, and the rest of you can fit into a wagonette. You'll all have to chaperon each other."

I need hardly say that this motion was carried also without a division.

"Well," said Charley, "I'll order the trap to be round in half an hour, so you'd better all make the best of your time. We'll want salmon, and salad, and hard-boiled eggs, and liquor, and any number of things. I'll look after the liquor department. What will you do, Lottie?"

"I'll take charge of the china," I said.

"I'll bring the fish," said Daseby.

"And I the vegetables," added Fan.

"What will you do, Gaster?" asked Charley.

"Truly," said the Swede, in his strange, musical accents, "but little is left for me to do. I can, however, wait upon the ladies, and I can make what you call a salad."

"You'll be more popular in the latter capacity than in the former," said I, laughingly.

"Ah, you say so," he said, turning sharp round upon me, and flushing up to his flaxen hair. "Yes. Ha! ha! Very good!"

And with a discordant laugh, he strode out of the room.

"I say, Lottie," remonstrated my lover, "you've hurt the fellow's feelings."

"I'm sure I didn't mean to," I answered. "If you like, I'll go after him and tell him so."

"Oh, leave him alone," said Daseby. "A man with a mug like that has no right to be so touchy. He'll come round right enough."

It was true that I had not had the slightest intention of offending Gaster, still I felt pained at having annoyed him.

After I had stowed away the knives and plates into a hamper, I found that the others were still busy at their various departments. The moment seemed a favorable one for apologizing for my thoughtless remark, so without saying anything to anyone, I slipped away and ran down the corridor in the direction of our visitor's room.

I suppose I must have tripped along very lightly, or it may have been the rich thick matting of Toynby Hall—certain it is that. Mr. Gaster seemed unconscious of my approach.

His door was open, and as I came up to it and caught sight of him inside, there was something so strange in his appearance that I paused, literally petrified for the moment with astonishment.

He had in his hand a small slip from a newspaper which he was reading, and which seemed to afford him considerable amusement. There was something horrible too in this mirth of his, for though he writhed his body about as if with laughter, no sound was emitted from his lips.

His face, which was half-turned toward me, wore an expression upon it which I had never seen on it before; I can only describe it as one of savage exultation.

Just as I was recovering myself sufficiently to step forward and knock at the door, he suddenly, with a last convulsive spasm of merriment, dashed down the piece of paper upon the table, and hurried out by the other door of his room, which led through the billiard room to the hall.

I heard his steps dying away in the distance, and peeped once more into his room.

What could be the joke that had moved this stern man to mirth? Surely some masterpiece of humor.

Was there a woman whose principles were strong enough to overcome her curiosity?

Looking cautiously round to make sure that the passage was empty, I slipped into the room and examined the paper which he had been reading.

It was a cutting from an English journal, and had evidently been long carried about and frequently perused, for it was almost illegible in places. There was, however, as far as I could see, very little to provoke laughter in its contents. It ran, as well as I can remember, in this way:

SUDDEN DEATH IN THE DOCKS.—The master of the bark-rigged steamer *Olga*, from Tromsberg, was found lying dead in his cabin on Wednesday afternoon. Deceased was, it seems, of a violent disposition, and had had frequent altercations with the surgeon of the vessel. On this particular day he had been more than usually offensive, declaring that the surgeon was a necromancer and worshipper of the devil. The latter retired on deck to avoid further persecution. Shortly afterward the steward had occasion to enter the cabin, and found the captain lying across the table quite dead. Death is attributed to heart disease, accelerated by excessive passion. An inquest will be held today.

And this was the paragraph which this strange man had regarded as the height of humor!

I hurried downstairs, astonishment, not unmixed with repugnance, predominating in my mind. So just was I, however, that the dark inference which has so often occurred to me since never for one moment crossed my mind. I looked upon him as a curious and rather repulsive enigma—nothing more.

When I met him at the picnic, all remembrance of my unfortunate speech seemed to have vanished from his mind. He made himself agreeable as usual, and his salad was pronounced a *chef-d'œuvre*, while his quaint little Swedish songs and his tales of all climes and countries alternately thrilled and amused us. It was after luncheon, however, that the conversation turned upon a subject which seemed to have special charms for his daring mind.

I forget who it was that broached the question of the supernatural. I think it was Trevor, by some story of a hoax which he had perpetrated at Cambridge. The story seemed to have a strange effect upon Octavius Gaster, who tossed his long arms about in impassioned invective as he ridiculed those who dared to doubt about the existence of the unseen.

"Tell me," he said, standing up in his excitement, "which among you has ever known what you call an instinct to fail? The wild bird has an instinct which tells it of the solitary rock upon the so boundless sea on which it may lay its egg, and is it disappointed? The swallow turns to the south when the winter is coming, and has its instinct led it astray? And shall this instinct which tells us of the unknown spirits around us, and which pervades every untaught child and every race so savage, be wrong? I say, never!"

"Go it, Gaster!" cried Charley.

"Take your wind and have another spell," said the sailor.

"No, never," repeated the Swede, disregarding our amusement. "We can see that matter exists apart from mind; then why should not mind exist apart from matter?"

"Give it up," said Daseby.

"Have we not proofs of it?" continued Gaster, his gray eyes gleaming with excitement. "Who that has read Steinberg's book upon spirits, or that by the eminent American, Madame Crowe, can doubt it? Did not Gustav von Spee meet his brother Leopold in the streets of Strasburg, the same brother having been drowned three months before in the Pacific? Did not Home, the spiritualist, in open daylight, float above the housetops of Paris? Who has not heard the voices of the dead around him? I myself—"

"Well, what of yourself?" asked half a dozen of us, in a breath.

"Bah! it matters nothing," he said, passing his hand over his forehead, and evidently controling himself with difficulty. "Truly, our talk is too sad for such an occasion." And, in spite of all our efforts, we were unable to extract from Gaster any relation of his own experiences of the supernatural.

It was a merry day. Our approaching dissolution seemed to cause each one to contribute his utmost to the general amusement. It was settled that after the coming rifle match Jack was to return to his ship and Trevor to his university. As to Charley and myself, we were to settle down into a staid respectable couple.

The match was one of our principal topics of conversation. Shooting had always been a hobby of Charley's, and he was the captain of the Roborough company of Devon volunteers, which boasted some of the crack shots of the county. The match was to be against a picked team of regulars from Plymouth, and as they were no despicable opponents, the issue was considered doubtful. Charley had evidently set his heart on winning, and descanted long and loudly on the chances.

"The range is only a mile from Toynby Hall," he said, "and we'll all drive over, and you shall see the fun. You'll bring me luck, Lottie," he whispered, "I know you will."

Oh, my poor lost darling, to think of the luck that I brought you!

There was one dark cloud to mar the brightness of that happy day.

I could not hide from myself any longer the fact that my mother's suspicions were correct, and that Octavius Gaster loved me.

Throughout the whole of the excursion his attentions had been most assiduous, and his eyes hardly ever wandered away from me. There was a manner, too, in all that he said which spoke louder than words.

I was on thorns lest Charley should perceive it, for I knew his fiery temper; but the thought of such treachery never entered the honest heart of my lover.

He did once look up with mild surprise when the Swede insisted on relieving me of a fern which I was carrying; but the expression faded away into a smile at what he regarded as Gaster's effusive good nature. My own only feeling in the matter was pity for the unfortunate foreigner, and sorrow that I should have been the means of rendering him unhappy.

I thought of the torture it must be for a wild, fierce spirit like his to have a passion gnawing at his heart which honor and pride would alike prevent him from ever expressing in words. Alas! I had not counted upon the utter recklessness and want of principle of the man; but it was not long before I was undeceived.

There was a little arbor at the bottom of the garden, overgrown with honeysuckle and ivy, which had long been a favorite haunt of Charley and myself. It was doubly dear to us from the fact that it was here, on the occasion of my former visit, that words of love had first passed between us.

After dinner on the day following the picnic I sauntered down to this little summer house, as was my custom. Here I used to wait until Charley, having finished his cigar with the other gentlemen, would come down and join me.

On that particular evening he seemed to be longer away than usual. I waited impatiently for his coming, going to the door every now and then to see if there were any signs of his approach.

I had just sat down again after one of those fruitless excursions, when I heard the tread of a male foot upon the gravel, and a figure emerged from among the bushes.

I sprang up with glad smile, which changed to an expression of bewilderment, and even fear, when I saw the gaunt, pallid face of Octavius Gaster peering in at me.

There was certainly something about his actions which would have inspired distrust in the mind of anyone in my position. Instead of greeting me, he looked up and down the garden, as if to make sure that we were entirely alone. He then stealthily entered the arbor, and seated himself upon a chair, in such a position that he was between me and the doorway.

"Do not be afraid," he said, as he noticed my scared expression.

"There is nothing to fear. I do but come that I may have talk with you."

"Have you seen Mr. Pillar?" I asked, trying hard to seem at my ease.

"Ha! Have I seen your Charley?" he answered, with a sneer upon the last words. "Are you so anxious that he come? Can no one speak to thee but Charley, little one?"

"Mr. Gaster," I said, "you are forgetting yourself."

"It is Charley, Charley, ever Charley!" continued the Swede, disregarding my interruption. "Yes, I have seen Charley. I have told him that you wait upon the bank of the river, and he has gone thither upon the wings of love."

"Why have you told him this lie?" I asked, still trying not to lose my self-control.

"That I might see you; that I might speak to you. Do you, then, love him so? Cannot the thought of glory, and riches, and power, above all that the mind can conceive, win you from this first maiden fancy of yours? Fly with me, Charlotte, and all this, and more, shall be yours! Come!"

And he stretched his long arms out in passionate entreaty.

Even at that moment the thought flashed through my mind of how like they were to tentacles of some poisonous insect.

"You insult me, sir!" I cried, rising to my feet. "You shall pay heavily for this treatment of an unprotected girl!"

"Ah, you say it," he cried, "but you mean it not. In your heart so tender there is pity left for the most miserable of men. Nay, you shall not pass me—you shall hear me first!"

"Let me go, sir!"

"Nay; you shall not go until you tell me nothing that I can do may win your love."

"How dare you speak so?" I almost screamed, losing all fear in my indignation. "You, who are the guest of my future husband! Let me tell you, once and for all, that I had no feeling toward you before save one of repugnance and contempt, which you have now converted into positive hatred."

"And is it so?" he gasped, tottering backward toward the doorway, and putting his hand up to his throat as if he found a difficulty in uttering the words. "And has my love won hatred in return? Ha!" he continued, advancing his face within a foot of mine as I cowered away from his glassy eyes, "I know it now. It is this—it is this!" and he struck the horrible cicatrix on his face with his clenched hand. "Maids love not such faces as this! I am not smooth, and brown, and curly like this Charley—this brainless schoolboy; this human brute who cares but for his sport and his—"

"Let me pass!" I cried, rushing at the door.

"No; you shall not go—you shall not!" he hissed, pushing me backward.

I struggled furiously to escape from his grasp. His long arms seemed to clasp me like bars of steel. I felt my strength going, and was making one last despairing effort to shake myself loose, when some irresistible power from behind tore my persecutor away from me and hurled him backward onto the gravel walk.

Looking up, I saw Charley's towering figure and square shoulders in the doorway.

"My poor darling!" he said, catching me in his arms. "Sit here—here in the angle. There is no danger now. I shall be with you in a minute."

"Don't Charley, don't!" I murmured, as he turned to leave me.

But he was deaf to my entreaties, and strode out of the arbor.

I could not see either him or his opponent from the position in which he had placed me, but I heard every word that was spoken.

"You villain!" said a voice that I could hardly recognize as my lover's. "So this is why you put me on a wrong scent?"

"That is why," answered the foreigner, in a tone of easy indifference.

"And this is how you repay our hospitality, you infernal scoundrel!"

"Yes; we amuse ourselves in your so beautiful summerhouse."

"We! You are still on my ground and my guest, and I would wish to keep my hands from you; but, by heavens—"

Charley was speaking very low and in gasps now.

"Why do you swear? What is it, then?" asked the languid voice of Octavius Gaster.

"If you dare to couple Miss Underwood's name with this business, and insinuate that—"

I heard the sound of a heavy blow, and a great rattling of the gravel.

I was too weak to rise from where I lay, and could only clasp my hands together and utter a faint scream.

"You cur!" said Charley. "Say as much again, and I'll stop your mouth for all eternity!"

There was a silence, and then I heard Gaster speaking in a husky, strange voice.

"You have struck me!" he said; "you have drawn my blood!"

"Yes; I'll strike you again if you show your cursed face within these grounds. Don't look at me so! You don't suppose your hanky-panky tricks can frighten me?"

An indefinable dread came over me as my lover spoke. I staggered to my feet and looked out at them, leaning against the doorway for support.

Charley was standing erect and defiant, with his young head in the air, like one who glories in the cause for which he battles.

Octavius Gaster was opposite to him, surveying him with pinched lips and a baleful look in his cruel eyes. The blood was running freely from a deep gash on his lip, and spotting the front of his green necktie and white waistcoat. He perceived me the instant I emerged from the arbor.

"Ha, ha!" he cried, with a demoniacal burst of laughter. "She comes! The bride! She comes! Room for the bride! Oh, happy pair, happy pair!"

And with another fiendish burst of merriment he turned and disappeared over the crumbling wall of the garden with such rapidity that he was gone before we had realized what it was that he was about to do.

"Oh, Charley," I said, as my lover came back to my side, "you've hurt him!"

"Hurt him! I should hope I have! Come, darling, you are frightened and tired. He did not injure you, did he?"

"No; but I feel rather faint and sick."

"Come, we'll walk slowly to the house together. The rascal! It was cunningly and deliberately planned, too. He told me he had seen you down by the river, and I was going down when I met young Stokes, the keeper's son, coming back from fishing, and he told me that there was nobody there. Somehow, when Stokes said that, a thousand little things flashed into my mind at once, and I became in a moment so convinced of Gaster's villainy that I ran as hard as I could to the arbor."

"Charley," I said, clinging to my lover's arm, "I fear he will injure you in some way. Did you see the look in his eyes before he leaped the wall?"

"Pshaw!" said Charley. "All these foreigners have a way of scowling and glaring when they are angry, but it never comes to much."

"Still, I am afraid of him," said I, mournfully, as we went up the steps together, "and I wish you had not struck him."

"So do I," Charley answered; "for he was our guest, you know, in spite of his rascality. However, it's done now and it can't be helped, as the cook says in 'Pickwick,' and really it was more than flesh and blood could stand."

I must run rapidly over the events of the next few days. For me, at least, it was a period of absolute happiness. With Gaster's departure a cloud seemed to be lifted off my soul, and a depression which had weighed upon the whole household completely disappeared.

Once more I was the lighthearted girl that I had been before the foreigner's arrival. Even the Colonel forgot to mourn over his absence, owing to the all-absorbing interest in the coming competition in which his son was engaged.

It was our main subject of conversation, and bets were freely offered by the gentlemen on the success of the Roborough team, though no one was unprincipled enough to seem to support their antagonists by taking them.

Jack Daseby ran down to Plymouth, and "made a book on the event" with some officers in the Marines, which he did in such an extraordinary way that we reckoned that in case of Roborough winning, he would lose seventeen shillings; while, should the other contingency occur, he would be involved in hopeless liabilities.

Charley and I had tacitly agreed not to mention the name of Gaster, nor to allude in anyway to what had passed.

On the morning after our scene in the garden, Charley had sent a servant up to the Swede's room with instructions to pack up any things he might find there, and leave them at the nearest inn.

It was found, however, that all Gaster's effects had been already removed, though how and when was a perfect mystery to the servants.

I know of few more attractive spots than the shooting range at Roborough. The glen in which it is situated is about half a mile long and perfectly level, so that the targets were able to range from two to seven hundred yards, the farther ones simply showing as square white dots against the green of the rising hills behind.

The glen itself is part of the great moor, and its sides sloping gradually up, lose themselves in the vast rugged expanse. Its symmetrical character suggested to the imaginative mind that some giant of old had made an excavation in the moor with a titanic cheese scoop, but that a single trial had convinced him of the utter worthlessness of the soil.

He might even be imagined to have dropped the despised sample at the mouth of the cutting which he had made, for there was a considerable elevation there, from which you looked down on the long, straight glen.

It was upon this rising ground that the platform was prepared from which the riflemen were to fire, and thither we bent our steps on that eventful afternoon.

Our opponents had arrived there before us, bringing with them a considerable number of naval and military officers, while a long line of nondescript vehicles showed that many of the good citizens of Plymouth had seized the opportunity of giving their wives and families an outing on the moor.

An enclosure for ladies and distinguished guests had been erected on the top of the hill, which, with the marquee and refreshment tents, made the scene a lively one.

The country people had turned out in force, and were excitedly staking their half crowns upon their local champions, which were as enthusiastically taken up by the admirers of the regulars.

Through all of this scene of bustle and confusion we were safely conveyed by Charley, aided by Jack and Trevor, who finally deposited us in a sort of rudimentary grandstand, from which we could look round at our ease on all that was going on.

We were soon, however, so absorbed in the glorious view, that we became utterly unconscious of the betting and pushing and chaff of the crowd in front of us.

Away to the south we could see the blue smoke of Plymouth curling up into the calm summer air, while beyond that was the great sea stretching away to the horizon, dark and vast, save where some petulant wave dashed it with a streak of foam, as if rebelling against the great peacefulness of nature.

From the Eddystone to the Start the long rugged line of the Devonshire coast lay like a map before us.

I was still lost in admiration when Charley's voice broke half-reproachfully on my ear.

"Why, Lottie," he said, "you don't seem to take a bit of interest in it!"

"Oh, yes, I do, dear," I answered. "But the scenery is so pretty, and the sea is always a weakness of mine. Come and sit here, and tell me all about the match and how we are to know whether you are winning or losing."

"I've just been explaining it," answered Charley. "But I'll go over it again."

"Do, like a darling," said I; and settled myself down to mark, learn, and inwardly digest.

"Well," said Charley, "there are ten men on each side. We shoot alternately: first, one of our fellows, then one of them, and so on—you understand?"

"Yes, I understand that."

"First we fire at the two hundred yards range—those are the targets, nearest of all. We fire five shots each at those. Then we fire five shots at the ones at five hundred yards—those middle ones; and then we finish up by firing at the seven hundred yards range—you see the targets far over there on the side of the hill. Whoever makes most points wins. Do you grasp it now?"

"Oh, yes; that's very simple," I said.

"Do you know what a bull's-eye is?" asked my lover.

"Some sort of sweetmeat, isn't it?" I hazarded.

Charley seemed amazed at the extent of my ignorance. "That's the bull's-eye," he said; "that dark spot in the center of the target. If you hit that, it counts five. There is another ring, which you can't see, drawn round that, and if you get inside of it, it is called a 'center,' and counts four. Outside that, again, is called an 'outer,' and only gives you three. You can tell where the shot has hit, for the marker puts out a colored disc, and covers the place."

"Oh, I understand it all now," said I, enthusiastically. "I'll tell you what I'll do, Charley; I'll mark the score on a bit of paper every shot that is fired, and then I'll always know how Roborough is getting on!"

"You can't do better," he laughed as he strode off to get his men together, for a warning bell signified that the contest was about to begin.

There was a great waving of flags and shouting before the ground could be got clear, and then I saw a little cluster of red coats lying upon the greensward, while a similar group, in gray, took up their position to the left of them.

"Pang!" went a rifle shot, and the blue smoke came curling up from the grass.

Fanny shrieked, while I gave a cry of delight, for I saw the white disc go up, which proclaimed a "bull," and the shot had been fired by one of the Roborough men. My elation was, however, promptly checked by the answering shot which put down five to the credit of the regulars. The next was also a "bull," which was speedily canceled by another. At the end of the competition at the short range each side had scored forty-nine out of a possible fifty, and the question of supremacy was as undecided as ever.

"It's getting exciting," said Charley, lounging over the stand. "We begin shooting at the five hundred yards in a few minutes."

"Oh, Charley," cried Fanny, in high excitement, "don't you go and miss, whatever you do!"

"I won't if I can help it," responded Charley, cheerfully.

"You made a 'bull' every time just now," I said.

"Yes, but it's not so easy when you've got your sights up. However, we'll do our best, and we can't do more. They've got some terribly good long-range men among them. Come over here, Lottie, for a moment."

"What is it, Charley?" I asked, as he led me away from the others. I could see by the look in his face that something was troubling him.

"It's that fellow," growled my lover. "What the deuce does he want to come here for? I hoped we had seen the last of him!"

"What fellow?" I gasped, with a vague apprehension at my heart.

"Why, that infernal Swedish fellow, Gaster!"

I followed the direction of Charley's glance, and there, sure enough, standing on a little knoll close to the place where the riflemen were lying, was the tall, angular figure of the foreigner.

He seemed utterly unconscious of the sensation which his singular appearance and hideous countenance excited among the burly farmers around him; but was craning his long neck about, this way and that, as if in search of somebody.

As we watched him, his eye suddenly rested upon us, and it seemed to me that, even at that distance, I could see a spasm of hatred and triumph pass over his livid features.

A strange foreboding came over me, and I seized my lover's hand in both my own.

"Oh, Charley," I cried, "don't—don't go back to the shooting! Say you are ill—make some excuse, and come away!"

"Nonsense, lass!" said he, laughing heartily at my terror. "Why, what in the world are you afraid of?"

"Of him!" I answered.

"Don't be silly, dear! One would think he was a demigod to hear the way in which you talk of him. But there! that's the bell, and I must be off."

"Well, promise, at least, that you will not go near him?" I cried, following Charley.

"All right—all right!" said he.

And I had to be content with that small concession.

The contest at the five hundred yards range was also a close and exciting one. Roborough led by a couple of points for some time, until a series of "bulls" by one of the crack marksmen of their opponents turned the tables upon them.

At the end it was found that the volunteers were three points to the bad—a result which was hailed by cheers from the Plymouth contingent and by long faces and black looks among the dwellers on the moor.

During the whole of this competition Octavius Gaster had remained perfectly still and motionless upon the top of the knoll on which he had originally taken up his position.

It seemed to me that he knew little of what was going on, for his face was turned away from the marksmen, and he appeared to be gazing abstractedly into the distance.

Once I caught sight of his profile, and thought that his lips were moving rapidly as if in prayer, or it may have been the shimmer of the hot air of the almost Indian summer which deceived me. It was, however, my impression at the time.

And now came the competition at the longest range of all, which was to decide the match.

The Roborough men settled down steadily to their task of making up the lost ground; while the regulars seemed determined not to throw away a chance by overconfidence.

As shot after shot was fired, the excitement of the spectators became so great that they crowded round the marksmen, cheering enthusiastically at every "bull."

We ourselves were so far affected by the general contagion that we left our harbor of refuge, and submitted meekly to the pushing and rough ways of the mob, in order to obtain a nearer view of the champions and their doings.

The military stood at seventeen when the volunteers were at sixteen, and great was the despondency of the rustics.

Things looked brighter, however, when the two sides tied at twenty-four, and brighter still when the steady shooting of the local team raised their score to thirty-two against thirty of their opponents.

There were still, however, the three points which had been lost at the last range to be made up for.

Slowly the score rose, and desperate were the efforts of both parties to pull off the victory.

Finally, a thrill ran through the crowd when it was known that the last red coat had fired, while one volunteer was still left, and that the soldiers were leading by four points.

Even *our* unsportsmanlike minds were worked into a state of all-absorbing excitement by the nature of the crisis which now presented itself.

If the first representative of our little town could but hit the bull's-eye the match was won.

The silver cup, the glory, the money of our adherents, all depended upon that single shot.

The reader will imagine that my interest was by no means lessened when, by dint of craning my neck and standing on tiptoe, I caught sight of my Charley coolly shoving a cartridge into his rifle, and realized that it was upon his skill that the honor of Roborough depended.

It was this, I think, which lent me strength to push my way so vigorously through the crowd that I found myself almost in the first row and commanding an excellent view of the proceedings.

There were two gigantic farmers on each side of me, and while we were waiting for the decisive shot to be fired, I could not help listening to the conversation, which they carried on in broad Devon, over my head.

"Mun's a rare ugly 'un," said one.

"He is that," cordially assented the other.

"See to mun's een?"

"Eh, Jock; see to mun's moo', rayther! Blessed if he bean't foamin' like Farmer Watson's dog—t' bull pup whot died mad o' the hydropathics."

I turned round to see the favored object of these flattering comments, and my eyes fell full upon Doctor Octavius Gaster, whose presence I had entirely forgotten in my excitement.

His face was turned toward me; but he evidently did not see me, for his eyes were bent with unswerving persistence upon a point midway apparently between the distant targets and himself.

I have never seen anything to compare with the extraordinary concentration of that stare, which had the effect of making his eyeballs appear gorged and prominent, while the pupils were contracted to the finest possible point.

Perspiration was running freely down his long, cadaverous face, and, as the farmer had remarked, there were some traces of foam at the corners of his mouth. The jaw was locked, as if with some fierce effort of the will which demanded all the energy of his soul.

To my dying day that hideous countenance shall never fade from my remembrance nor cease to haunt me in my dreams. I shuddered, and turned away my head in the vain hope that perhaps the honest farmer might be right, and mental disease be the cause of all the vagaries of this extraordinary man.

A great stillness fell upon the whole crowd as Charley, having loaded his rifle, snapped up the breech cheerily, and proceeded to lie down in his appointed place.

"That's right, Mr. Charles, sir—that's right!" I heard old McIntosh, the volunteer sergeant, whisper as I passed. "A cool head and a steady hand, that's what does the trick, sir!"

My lover smiled round at the gray-headed soldier as he lay down upon the grass, and then proceeded to look along the sight of his rifle amid silence in which the faint rustling of the breeze among the blades of grass was distinctly audible.

For more than a minute he hung upon his aim. His finger seemed to press the trigger, and every eye was fixed upon the distant target, when suddenly, instead of firing, the rifleman staggered to his knees, leaving his weapon upon the ground.

To the surprise of everyone, his face was deadly pale, and perspiration was standing on his brow.

"I say, McIntosh," he said, in a strange, gasping voice, "is there anybody standing between that target and me?"

"Between, sir? No, not a soul, sir," answered the astonished sergeant.

"There, man, there!" cried Charley, with fierce energy, seizing him by the arm, and pointing in the direction of the target. "Don't you see him there, standing right in the line of fire?"

"There's no one there!" shouted half a dozen voices.

"No one there? Well, it must have been my imagination," said Charley, passing his hand slowly over his forehead. "Yet I could have sworn—Here, give me the rifle!"

He lay down again, and having settled himself into position, raised his weapon slowly to his eye. He had hardly looked along the barrel before he sprang up again with a loud cry.

"There!" he cried; "I tell you I see it! A man dressed in volunteer uniform, and very like myself—the image of myself. Is this a conspiracy?" he continued, turning fiercely on the crowd. "Do you tell me none of you see a man resembling myself walking from that target, and not two hundred yards from me as I speak?"

I should have flown to Charley's side had I not known how he hated feminine interference, and anything approaching to a scene. I could only listen silently to his strange, wild words.

"I protest against this!" said an officer, coming forward. "This gentleman must really either take his shot, or we shall remove our men off the field and claim the victory."

"But I'll shoot *him!*" gasped poor Charley.

"Humbug!" "Rubbish!" "Shoot him, then!" growled half a score of masculine voices.

"The fact is," lisped one of the military men in front of me to another, "the young fellow's nerves ar'n't quite equal to the occasion, and he feels it, and is trying to back out."

The imbecile young lieutenant little knew at this point how a feminine hand was longing to stretch forth and deal him a sounding box on the ears.

"It's Martell's three-star brandy, that's what it is," whispered the other. "The 'devils,' don't you know. I've had 'em myself, and know a case when I see it."

This remark was too recondite for my understanding, or the speaker would have run the same risk as his predecessor.

"Well, are you going to shoot or not?" cried several voices.

"Yes, I'll shoot," groaned Charley—"I'll shoot *him* through! It's murder—sheer *murder!*"

I shall never forget the haggard look which he cast round at the crowd. "I'm aiming *through* him, McIntosh," he murmured, as he lay down on the grass and raised his gun for the third time to his shoulder.

There was one moment of suspense, a spurt of flame, the crack of a rifle, and a cheer which echoed across the moor, and might have been heard in the distant village.

"Well done, lad—well done!" shouted a hundred honest Devonshire voices, as the little white disc came out from behind the marker's shield and obliterated the dark "bull" for the moment, proclaiming that the match was won.

"Well done, lad! It's Maister Pillar, of Toynby Hall. Here, let's gie mun a lift, carry mun home, for the honor o' Roborough. Come on, lads! There mun is on the grass. Wake up, Sergeant McIntosh. What be the matter with thee? Eh? What?"

A deadly stillness came over the crowd, and then a low incredulous murmur, changing to one of pity, with whispers of "Leave her alone, poor lass—leave her to hersel'!"—and then there was silence again, save for the moaning of a woman, and her short, quick cries of despair.

For, reader, my Charley, my beautiful, brave Charley, was lying cold and dead upon the ground, with the rifle still clenched in his stiffening fingers.

I heard kind words of sympathy. I heard Lieutenant Doseby's voice, broken with grief, begging me to control my sorrow, and felt his hand, as he gently raised me from my poor boy's body. This I can remember, and nothing more, until my recovery from my illness, when I found myself in the sickroom at Toynby Hall, and learned that three restless, delirious weeks had passed since that terrible day.

Stay!—do I remember nothing else?

Sometimes I think I do. Sometimes I think I can recall a lucid interval in the midst of my wanderings. I seem to have a dim recollection of seeing my good nurse go out of the room—of seeing a gaunt, bloodless face peering in through the half-open window, and of hearing a voice which said, "I have dealt with thy so beautiful lover, and I have yet to deal with thee." The words come back to me with a familiar ring, as if they had sounded in my ears before, and yet it may have been but a dream.

"And this is all!" you say. "It is for this that a hysterical woman hunts down a harmless *savant* in the advertisement columns of the newspapers! On this shallow evidence she hints at crimes of the most monstrous description!"

Well, I cannot expect that these things should strike you as they struck me. I can but say that if I were upon a bridge with Octavius Gaster standing at one end, and the most merciless tiger that ever prowled in an Indian jungle at the other, I should fly to the wild beast for protection.

For me, my life is broken and blasted. I care not how soon it may end, but if my words shall keep this out of one honest household, I have not written in vain.

Within a fortnight after writing this narrative, my poor daughter disappeared. All search has failed to find her. A porter at the railway station has deposed to having seen a young lady resembling her description get into a first-class carriage with a tall, thin gentleman. It is, however, too ridiculous to suppose that she can have eloped after her recent grief, and without my having had any suspicions. The detectives are, however, working out the clue.—EMILY UNDERWOOD

**Other rediscovered classics
by Sir Arthur Conan Doyle
available from Chronicle Books:**

The Lost World & The Poison Belt
The Professor Challenger Adventures: Volume I
Introduction by William Gibson

When the World Screamed & Other Stories
The Professor Challenger Adventures: Volume II

Round the Fire Stories

**A forgotten classic
about the French Revolution
available from Chronicle Books:**

Scaramouche
by Rafael Sabatini

Dad's Guide to Pregnancy FOR DUMMIES®

by Matthew M. F. Miller
and Sharon Perkins

WILEY

Wiley Publishing, Inc.

Dad's Guide to Pregnancy For Dummies®

Published by
Wiley Publishing, Inc.
111 River St.
Hoboken, NJ 07030-5774
www.wiley.com

WILEY

About the Authors

Matthew M. F. Miller is a dad to one, an uncle to ten, and a "father" to anyone who will listen to his countless nuggets of unsolicited advice. Author of the book *Maybe Baby: An Infertile Love Story*, Matthew is a graduate of the University of Southern California's Master of Professional Writing program.

Matthew lives in Chicago where he is a full-time work-at-home dad, providing childcare for his daughter while working as the health-and-wellness editor for a national newspaper syndicate. In his spare time (because there's just so much of that!), Matthew is a musician, runner, tennis enthusiast, and baker.

Sharon Perkins has never been a dad, but she's had lots of experience on the mom side of parenting, with five children and three grandchildren. Almost 25 years as a registered nurse in fertility, labor and delivery, and neonatal intensive care have also taught her a thing or two about pregnancy and babies.

Sharon lives in New Jersey with her husband but would live in Disney World if it were legal. The opportunity to write about what she does for a living has been a dream come true.

Dedications

From Matt: Whether writing this book, watching tennis, or taking a nap, I am inspired, awed, and grateful for the love and support of my wife, Constance, and our beautiful daughter, Nola. Thank you for a charmed life.

From Sharon: This book is dedicated to my three grandchildren, Matthew, Emma, and Jessica, who keep me current on what's going on in the world of kids.

Authors' Acknowledgments

From Matt: Writing about family takes a deep, rich understanding of what it means to be a good person, and I am grateful to my mom, dad, sisters, nieces, and nephews for teaching me how to be one. Also, a very special thanks to my favorite doula, Holly Barhamand, for teaching and empowering me to explore and educate myself about what childbirth means to me.

As this is my first *For Dummies* tome, I am particularly grateful to the folks at Wiley, but also to Sharon herself. She took me under her wing and made this one of the most rewarding, fun experiences of my writing career. To my agent, Grace Freedson, you are a joy to work with and I look forward to the next amazing opportunity you bring my way.

Finally, thank you to my wife and, most importantly, to our daughter, an IVF baby born after nearly three years of waiting. And although we waited a long time for you, every day since your birth has been counted among the best of my life.

From Sharon: Wiley took a chance on me with my first book, *Fertility For Dummies,* almost ten years ago, and I've been extremely grateful ever since. In particular, Lindsay Lefevere, Erin Mooney, Chrissy Guthrie, and Caitie Copple have been the usual pleasure to work with throughout this book's creation.

Matt Miller has been the easiest coauthor ever! From day one, our writing styles meshed, and this book just flowed. Thanks, Matt, for making this a piece of cake.

And, last but not least, I thank my family for giving me so much raw material to work with over the years!

Publisher's Acknowledgments

We're proud of this book; please send us your comments at http://dummies.custhelp.
com. For other comments, please contact our Customer Care Department within the U.S. at
877-762-2974, outside the U.S. at 317-572-3993, or fax 317-572-4002.

Some of the people who helped bring this book to market include the following:

Acquisitions, Editorial, and Media Development

Senior Project Editor: Christina Guthrie

Executive Editor:
Lindsay Sandman Lefevere

Copy Editor: Caitlin Copple

Assistant Editor: David Lutton

Technical Editor: Jared Beasley

Editorial Manager: Christine Meloy Beck

Editorial Assistants: Rachelle S. Amick,
Jennette ElNaggar

Art Coordinator: Alicia B. South

Cover Photos: © iStock / Terry J Alcorn

Cartoons: Rich Tennant
(www.the5thwave.com)

Composition Services

Senior Project Coordinator: Kristie Rees

Layout and Graphics: Samantha K. Cherolis

Proofreaders: John Greenough, Toni Settle

Indexer: Becky Hornyak

Illustrator: Kathryn Born

Publishing and Editorial for Consumer Dummies

    Kathleen Nebenhaus, Vice President and Executive Publisher

    Kristin Ferguson-Wagstaffe, Product Development Director, Consumer Dummies

    Ensley Eikenburg, Associate Publisher, Travel

    Kelly Regan, Editorial Director, Travel

Publishing for Technology Dummies

    Andy Cummings, Vice President and Publisher

Composition Services

    Debbie Stailey, Director of Composition Services

Contents at a Glance

Introduction.. 1

Part I: So You Want to Be a Dad 7
Chapter 1: Fatherhood: A Glorious, Scary, Mind-Boggling,
and Amazing Experience.. 9
Chapter 2: Beyond the Bed: Conception Smarts 23

Part II: Great Expectations:
Nine Months and Counting.............................. 45
Chapter 3: Surviving Sudden Doubts and Morning Sickness:
The First Trimester.. 47
Chapter 4: Growing Into the Second Trimester.................... 65
Chapter 5: The Fun Stuff: Nesting, Registering, and Naming 79
Chapter 6: Expecting the Unexpected 95
Chapter 7: In the Home Stretch: The Third Trimester 113
Chapter 8: The Copilot's Guide to Birthing Options...................... 129

Part III: Game Time! Labor, Delivery,
and Baby's Homecoming.................................. 149
Chapter 9: Surviving Labor and Delivery 151
Chapter 10: Caring for Your Newborn 173
Chapter 11: Supporting the New Mom................................. 197

Part IV: A Dad's Guide to Worrying 217
Chapter 12: Dealing with Difficult Issues after Delivery.................. 219
Chapter 13: Daddy 911: Survival Tips for Bumps, Lumps,
and Scary Moments 233
Chapter 14: Time and Money: The High Cost of Having a Baby...... 255
Chapter 15: Planning for Your New Family's Future..................... 277

Part V: The Part of Tens.................................. 293
Chapter 16: Ten Things She Won't Ask for but Will Expect............. 295
Chapter 17: Ten Ways to Be a Super Dad from Day One................. 301

Index.. 307

Table of Contents

Introduction.. *1*

About This Book 1
Conventions Used in This Book.................................. 2
What You're Not to Read 2
Foolish Assumptions 3
How This Book Is Organized 3
   Part I: So You Want to Be a Dad 3
   Part II: Great Expectations: Nine Months
      and Counting 4
   Part III: Game Time! Labor, Delivery,
      and Baby's Homecoming 4
   Part IV: A Dad's Guide to Worrying 4
   Part V: The Part of Tens.................................... 4
Icons Used in This Book... 4
Where to Go from Here 5

Part 1: So You Want to Be a Dad 7

**Chapter 1: Fatherhood: A Glorious, Scary, Mind-
Boggling, and Amazing Experience 9**

Looking at the Concept of Fatherhood 10
   A father? Who, me?...................................... 10
   Reacting to a life-changing event.................... 10
   Dealing with fears of fatherhood 11
   Debunking a few myths of fatherhood.............. 12
Becoming a Modern Dad.. 14
   Changes in your personal life......................... 15
   Changes in your professional life 15
   Lifestyle changes to consider 16
Deciding to Take the Plunge (Or Not) 17
   Determining whether you're ready 17
   Telling your partner you're ready 18
   Telling your partner you're not ready 18
   Being patient when one of you is ready
      (and the other isn't) 19
   Dealing with an unexpected pregnancy............. 19
   Welcoming long-awaited pregnancies............... 20
Glimpsing into the Pregnancy Process Ahead 20
   First trimester 21
   Second trimester... 21
   Third trimester... 21
While You Were Gestating....................................... 22

Chapter 2: Beyond the Bed: Conception Smarts 23

Understanding Conception... 23
   Baby making 101 23
   Conception statistics... 27
   Answering commonly asked questions
      about getting pregnant... 27
Evaluating Health to Get Ready for Parenthood.................. 28
   Uncovering female health issues that
      impact conception... 29
   Recognizing issues that cause
      fertility problems in men 30
   Assessing lifestyle choices that affect
      eggs and sperm 31
Keeping Sex from Becoming a Chore 33
   Choosing the best time for conception 33
   Looking at do's and don'ts for scheduling sex 35
Taking a Brief Yet Important Look at Infertility.................. 36
   Knowing the facts about infertility.............................. 36
   Checking on potential problems when
      nothing's happening... 37
   Working through it when your
      partner needs treatment.. 38
   Exploring solutions when your sperm
      don't stack up.. 39
   Deciding how far to go to get pregnant 42
Sharing Your Decision to Have a Baby.................................. 42
   Considering the pros and cons of spilling the beans...43
   Handling unsolicited advice about reproduction...... 43

Part II: Great Expectations:
Nine Months and Counting................................... 45

Chapter 3: Surviving Sudden Doubts and
Morning Sickness: The First Trimester 47

Baby on Board: It's Official! 47
   Reacting when your partner breaks the news 48
   Making the announcement to friends and family...... 48
   Overcoming your fears of being a father.................... 49
Finding a Practitioner Who Thinks Like You........................ 50
   Finding a doctor who works for both of you.............. 50
   Attending the first of many prenatal visits................ 52
   Going to the first ultrasound.. 52
Baby's Development during the First Trimester 53
   He may not look like much now, but 53
   Amazing changes in weeks 7 to 12 54

Dealing with Possible Complications in
the First Trimester 55
Miscarrying in early pregnancy 55
Understanding ectopic pregnancy 57
Coping with pregnancy loss 58
Common First Trimester Discomforts — Yours and Hers ... 58
Helping your partner cope with the symptoms
of early pregnancy 59
Getting used to strange new maternal habits 60
Taking on your emerging support role 62

Chapter 4: Growing Into the Second Trimester 65

Tracking Baby's Development during
the Second Trimester 65
Growing and changing in months four and five 66
Refining touches in the sixth month 67
Checking Out Mom's Development in
the Second Trimester 67
Gaining weight healthfully 68
Looking pregnant at last! 70
Testing in the Second Trimester 71
Preparing for the risks of tests and ultrasounds 72
Understanding blood test results 72
Following up on the test results 73
Scrutinizing ultrasounds 73
Having Sex in the Second Trimester 75
Maintaining a healthy sex life during pregnancy 75
Addressing common myths and concerns 76
Exploring Different Options for Childbirth Classes 77

**Chapter 5: The Fun Stuff: Nesting,
Registering, and Naming 79**

Preparing the Nursery and Home, or "Nesting" 79
Making the house spic and span — and then some ... 80
Setting up the nursery 81
Arranging the nursery for two or more 83
Baby-proofing 101 83
Understanding the Art of the Baby Registry 85
Doing your homework ahead of time
to get exactly what you want 85
Finding out what you need — and what you think
you won't need but can't live without! 86
Discovering five things you don't
have to have but will adore 89
Checking out five things you don't have
to have and will never adore 90

Surviving the Baby Shower..90
Naming Your Baby...91
Narrowing down your long list 92
Reconciling father/mother differences of opinion 92
Discussing choices with friends and family 93

Chapter 6: Expecting the Unexpected 95

Managing Pregnancy-Related Medical Issues......................95
Pregnancy-induced hypertension...............................95
Gestational diabetes...96
Placenta previa 97
Mandatory bed rest...98
Handling Abnormal Ultrasounds 100
Birth defects 100
Fetal demise..101
Preparing Yourself for Preterm Labor and Delivery 102
Recognizing the risks of preterm delivery 102
Handling feelings of guilt 103
Navigating the NICU 103
Knowing what to expect with a preemie 105
Clarifying common problems.....................................105
Learning the ropes — er, wires...................................106
Preparing for preemie setbacks.................................107
Taking baby home 107
Hi, Baby Baby Baby: Having Multiples 108
Multiple identities: What multiples are
and who has them..108
Health risks for mom 109
Risks for the babies 110
Keeping Cool in Monetary Emergencies 111
Checking out your insurance limits 111
Covering the cost of unexpected
medical expenses...112

Chapter 7: In the Home Stretch: The Third Trimester ...113

Tracking Baby's Development during
the Third Trimester 113
Adding pounds and maturing in
the seventh and eighth months 114
Getting everything in place in the ninth month.......114
Finding Out What Mom Goes Through in
the Third Trimester 116
Understanding your partner's physical changes 116
Heeding warning signs 118
Bracing for your partner's emotional changes 118

Sympathizing with her desire
to have this over, already 120
Dealing with tears, panic, and doubts...................... 120
Getting Your Paperwork in Order.................................... 122
Understanding your insurance 122
Preparing for the costs if you don't
have insurance 124
Guaranteeing a smooth admissions
process at the hospital... 125
Whose Baby Is This, Anyway? Dealing with
Overbearing Family Members 126
Picking a Pediatrician 126

Chapter 8: The Copilot's Guide to Birthing Options. . . 129

Making Sure Your Birth Practitioner Is a Good Fit 130
Screening potential practitioners.............................. 130
Working with a midwife 131
Getting some additional help with a doula................ 132
Choosing Where to Deliver... 133
Delivering at a hospital 134
Exploring alternative options:
Using a midwife at home 135
Looking at Labor Choices 136
Going all natural or getting the epidural 137
Taking it to the water 138
Creating a Birth Plan.. 138
Visualizing your ideal experience............................. 139
Drafting your plan.. 140
Sharing your birth plan with the world 143
Picking the Cast: Who's Present, Who Visits,
and Who Gets a Call.. 145
Deciding who gets to attend the birth...................... 145
Planning ahead for visitors....................................... 146
Planting a phone tree 146

**Part III: Game Time! Labor, Delivery,
and Baby's Homecoming... 149**

Chapter 9: Surviving Labor and Delivery............151

When It's Time, It's Time — Is It Time?............................. 151
Avoiding numerous dry runs (yes, it's us again)..... 152
Knowing when it's too late to go 153
Supporting Your Partner during Labor............................. 154
Figuring out how she wants to be supported 154
Not taking the insults seriously 154

Looking at What Happens during and after Labor 155
    First stage 155
    Second stage... 156
    Wrapping things up after the birth............................. 157
    Helping baby right after delivery................................ 158
Undergoing Common Labor Procedures 159
    Vaginal exams 159
    IVs.. 159
    Membrane ruptures... 160
    Fetal monitoring.. 161
Coping with Labor Pain... 163
    Enduring it: Going natural 163
    Dulling it: Sedation (No, not for you)........................ 164
    Blotting it out: Epidurals... 164
Deviating From Your Birth Plan/Vision............................. 167
Having a Cesarean.. 168
    Scheduled cesarean section.. 168
    Unplanned cesarean delivery....................................... 169
    What to expect before the operation......................... 170
    What to expect during the surgery 171
    Getting past disappointment.. 172

Chapter 10: Caring for Your Newborn 173

Knowing What to Expect When Baby's Born 173
    Looking at newborns... 173
    Rating the reflexes 175
Feeding a Newborn 176
    Choosing to breast-feed... 176
    Bottle-feeding basics 179
Changing Diapers 181
    Cleaning baby boys 182
    Cleaning baby girls 183
Bathing Basics 183
Holding Your Baby.. 185
Cosleeping Pros and Cons 186
Back to Sleep: Helping Baby Sleep Safely
   and Comfortably.. 187
    Coping if baby hates being on his back.................... 187
    Swaddling your little one.. 188
    Preventing the flat head look 188
Soothing Baby Indigestion 190
    Crying with colic 191
    Gas 191
    Reflux... 192
Scheduling Immunizations... 193
    Skipping some shots?... 194
    Spreading them out 194

Chapter 11: Supporting the New Mom **197**

Handling Housework during Recovery 198
Getting the house in order 198
Taking care of meals.. 202
Calling in backup 203
Supporting a Breast-Feeding Mom................................... 204
Making the decision to breast-feed 204
Offering lactation support 206
Including yourself in the process 207
Dealing with Postcesarean Issues................................... 208
Helping with a normal recovery 208
Knowing when to call the doctor.............................. 209
Riding the Ups and Downs of Hormones 209
Thinking before speaking in the sensitive
postpartum period.. 209
Shedding light on physical symptoms 210
Supporting her baby blues 211
Recognizing postpartum depression 211
Sleeping (Or Doing Without) 212
Coping with Company 213
Dealing with grabby grandmas 214
Managing unsolicited advice..................................... 214
Handling hurt feelings when you want to be alone....215
Approaching Sex: It's Like Riding a Bicycle...................... 216

Part IV: A Dad's Guide to Worrying................. *217*

**Chapter 12: Dealing with Difficult
Issues after Delivery** **219**

Coping with Serious Health Problems.............................. 219
Congenital defects 219
Developmental delays... 220
Illnesses.. 222
SIDS.. 222
Watching Out for Postpartum Issues 224
Getting through the "baby blues".............................. 224
Taking a look at postpartum depression.................. 224
Acting fast to treat postpartum psychosis............... 227
Managing Grief 228
Going through the stages of grief 228
Why, why, why? Getting past the question 229
Grieving together and separately.............................. 229
Determining when grief has gone on too long 230
Talking to Other People about Your Child 231
Telling other people 231
Handling insensitive remarks.................................... 232

Chapter 13: Daddy 911: Survival Tips for Bumps, Lumps, and Scary Moments 233

Handling Inevitable Illnesses 233
  Nursing baby through common
    childhood diseases 234
  Staying alert for scarier diseases..................... 239
Protecting Baby from Common Accidents and
  What to Do When They Happen........................ 240
  Taking care of baby after a fall....................... 240
  Staying safe in the car 241
Managing Medical Crises at Home........................ 243
  Don't panic! Don't panic!............................. 243
  Calling the doctor 243
Open Wide, Baby! Administering Medicine 244
Taking a Baby's Temperature 245
  Choosing a thermometer 246
  Taking a rectal temperature........................... 247
  Recognizing fevers..................................... 248
Deciphering Diaper Contents 249
  Knowing what's normal 249
  Checking out color changes 250
Teething Symptoms and Remedies 250
Reacting to Medicines and Vaccines...................... 251
  Vaccination reactions — yours and your baby's 252
  Medications that cause reactions...................... 252
Dealing with Food Allergies 253
  Introducing new foods 253
  Recognizing allergic reactions 254
  Preventing allergic reactions 254

Chapter 14: Time and Money: The High Cost of Having a Baby...........................255

Creating a New Work/Life Balance with Baby.................... 255
  Taking time off with paternity leave.......................... 256
  Managing sick time when you're back at work........ 258
  Dealing with after-work expectations 259
  Reprioritizing your commitments 260
Readjusting When and If Mom Goes Back to Work 262
  Making going back to work easier on mom.............. 262
  Deciding to be a stay-at-home parent 264
  Helping mom adjust if she doesn't
    go back to work... 266
  Becoming a stay-at-home dad 267

Exploring the Expected (And Unexpected)
Costs of Baby.. 268
Deciding what baby really needs........................... 268
Bracing yourself for the costs of
must-have baby supplies................................ 269
Comparing childcare options and costs.................. 271
Managing Your Money 273
Prioritizing your needs 274
Determining where to cut costs............................ 275

Chapter 15: Planning for Your New Family's Future . . .277

Securing a Financially Sound Future 277
Prioritize your expenses.. 278
Create a budget (and stick to it).............................. 279
Pay down your debt 280
Create an emergency fund..................................... 281
Buy disability insurance 281
Contribute to a retirement account 282
Work with a financial advisor 282
Mind your credit score 282
Saving Money for Your Child's Education 283
Getting the Lowdown on Life Insurance 284
Making sure you and your partner have
adequate life insurance................................. 284
Considering a policy for your baby........................... 285
Health Insurance Options for Newborns 286
Adding baby to an existing work-paid plan.............. 286
Buying coverage just for baby 287
Obtaining free and low-cost care
for uninsured kids...................................... 288
Taking Care of Legal Matters................................... 288
Creating a will... 288
Establishing power of attorney.............................. 291

Part V: The Part of Tens................................... 293

Chapter 16: Ten Things She Won't Ask for but Will Expect 295

Keep It Complimentary 295
Start a Baby Book.. 296
Disguise Fitness as Fun 296
Curb Your Advice.. 297
Attend Prenatal Appointments 297
Plan a Getaway... 298

Register for a Prenatal Parenting Class.............................. 298
Do Your Homework and Spread the Word 299
Learn Prenatal Massage 299
Clean High and Low 300

**Chapter 17: Ten Ways to Be a Super Dad
from Day One 301**

Overcome Fragility Fears 301
Trust Your Instincts.. 302
Bond Skin-to-Skin, Eye-to-Eye 302
Manage Frustrations... 303
Embrace Your Goofy Side 304
Get Out 304
Teach Baby New Tricks.. 305
Roughhouse the Safe Way 306
Read Aloud . . . and Not Just from Baby Books.................. 306
Send Mom Away... 306

Index.. *307*

Introduction

*W*elcome to impending fatherhood! Being a dad is better than you can ever imagine and far less scary than you're probably believing it to be. One of the main reasons we wrote this book was to empower men to get actively involved in every aspect of the childbirth process, as well as the care, feeding, and loving of newborns. Most dads-to-be have only a dim idea of what parenthood is going to be like, and their excitement mixes liberally with sheer terror and trepidation. We hope this book will spare you some of that fear and trepidation by giving you the knowledge you need to feel confident.

Traditionally, men have been removed from the processes of pregnancy, labor and delivery, and raising children. On TV, fathers have long been portrayed as emotionally distant, bumbling fools incapable of changing diapers, getting kids to go to bed, or handling any of the routine tasks that mothers seem to do with ease. In reality, today's dad is confident, capable, and totally in love with his children — and not afraid to let it show. Not that it all comes easily and naturally. Learning how to support your pregnant partner and, subsequently, to care for a newborn, takes time, effort, and education.

Most men in the world will become fathers at some point, and most will enter the experience without much knowledge of how babies develop, how to be a supportive partner, or what their role should be in the process. But not you. The savvy readers of this book will be prepared for just about anything — and will know exactly what it takes to be an equal partner on the pregnancy (and parenting) journey.

About This Book

This book answers all the burning questions you have about the impact your partner's pregnancy will have on your life. We tell you how your sex life will change, because we know that's at the top of your list. But we also explain everything you ever wanted to know about how a fetus develops, what it's like to live with a pregnant woman, and how your pocketbook will be hit by adding a new member (or members) to your family.

We also delve a little into what to expect the first six months or so after the baby arrives. We walk you through the ins and outs of feeding, changing diapers, dealing with common illnesses and emergencies, and how to stay sane and true to yourself through it all.

In short, you will close this book feeling completely prepared for fatherhood. You won't be, because no one ever is, but you'll at least feel like you are until the baby comes.

Conventions Used in This Book

Following are a few conventions we used when writing this book:

✓ We don't know if your baby is a boy or girl — you may not even know that yourself. So we use *he* and *she* interchangeably throughout.

✓ Because we also don't know if your medical practitioner is a doctor or midwife, or a pediatrician or nurse practitioner, we use the term *medical practitioner* when we talk about anyone medical.

✓ We call your partner your partner, because that's what she is, in every sense.

✓ We use *italic* font to highlight new terms, and we follow them up with a clear definition.

✓ **Boldfaced** font indicates keywords or the action in numbered steps.

✓ Monofont is used for Web addresses.

What You're Not to Read

If you decide this book is too long, you may decide to skip some of it, so you want to know what's not very important. Naturally, we think every word we've written is not only essential but brilliant, so we're the wrong people to ask. However, info marked with the Technical Stuff icon may be more than you want to have to think about. Information marked with this icon is certainly interesting and helpful, but skipping it won't impede your understanding of the topic in the slightest.

Also, we've included sidebars throughout the book (look for gray-shaded boxes) that often contain interesting but nonessential information and personal stories, and we give you permission to skip them if you really have to.

If your partner is already pregnant, congratulations! That means you can skip Chapter 2, which discusses conception. And we hope everyone will be able to skip reading Chapter 12, which discusses problems that can come up after delivery. However, you may still want to skim this one so you'll know where to turn in the unfortunate event of complications.

Foolish Assumptions

If you picked up this book, we assume you fall into at least one of the following categories:

- ✔ You don't know much about pregnancy.
- ✔ You're an expectant dad.
- ✔ You're hoping to become an expectant dad.
- ✔ You are already a father but are looking to learn new tricks for the next go-round.
- ✔ You know an expectant dad and would like to get into his head and understand why he's behaving the way he is.

Expectant dads are often the forgotten partner in the new family-to-be, and they need all the understanding they can get.

How This Book Is Organized

This book starts with the process of getting pregnant and ends with practical information on day-to-day dad stuff. However, we know you may not be interested in reading about the journey straight through from beginning to end. So feel free to start wherever you want. If tomorrow is your first ultrasound appointment, jump right into that section so you know what to expect. If your partner isn't pregnant yet but you want to read about labor, go right ahead. Every chapter of this book is modular, which means you can understand it without reading other chapters first.

Part 1: So You Want to Be a Dad . . .

Becoming a dad is one of the most exciting times of a man's life, but that doesn't mean you don't also have concerns and questions. This part dives into the normal fears and frustrations associated with deciding to start a family and the actual process of getting pregnant — and no, you don't already know it all!

Part II: Great Expectations: Nine Months and Counting

Your partner may be the one who's pregnant, but you're in it for the ride, too. From morning sickness to labor, we tell you exactly what happens during pregnancy, from your perspective as well as hers and the baby's. We also talk about the fun stuff, like baby showers (okay, maybe not so fun for you) and naming, and the not fun stuff, like potential health issues for mom and baby. We also give you an overview of birthing options so you can talk knowledgably with your partner about what she wants to do.

Part III: Game Time! Labor, Delivery, and Baby's Homecoming

No one ever said labor and delivery are fun, but they are interesting, and you have a lot to learn if you want to win the supportive partner of the year award. This part covers everything about actually having the baby, from the first contraction to the first all-night crying session — which just may come from an exhausted parent, not the baby!

Part IV: A Dad's Guide to Worrying

This part touches on all the things that keep you up at night worrying after the baby's born. We discuss possible postdelivery issues such as congenital defects and postpartum depression as well as baby's inevitable illnesses. If your worries are more monetary, we also advise you on handling your money with an expensive new baby and planning for your family's financial security. We also help you stay sane and happy with suggestions for managing your time so that you don't let the new baby take over your life.

Part V: The Part of Tens

The Part of Tens is just fun. We touch on how to be both a super dad and a super partner. We also talk about what it's like to be a stay-at-home dad.

Icons Used in This Book

Icons are another handy tool you can use as you work your way through this book. If you find the tips really helpful, for instance, you can skim through and search for that icon. Conversely, when you see a Technical Stuff icon, you can know that information is completely skippable (though certainly worth the extra time, if you have it).

Following is a rundown of the icons we use in this book:

The Remember icon sits next to information we hope stays in your head for more than two minutes.

TechnicalStuff goes into more detail than you really need to understand the facts, but you may find it interesting if you're an especially curious type.

The Tip icon gives helpful insider info that you may take years to learn on your own.

Whenever we use a Warning icon, you'd better sit up and take notice, because not heeding our warning could be disastrous for you or your loved ones.

Where to Go from Here

This is where we tell you to go read the book, already!

Although you can start absolutely any place and get the benefit of our expertise, if your partner isn't yet pregnant or is newly pregnant, we suggest starting at the beginning and reading right on through. It will calm your nerves, we promise.

If you're the last-minute type of guy and you're reading this book just a few months (or weeks!) before the impending birth, you can certainly skip the first trimester stuff (at least this time around) and start wherever makes the most sense for you.

And if you got this book at the beginning of the pregnancy but never got around to opening it until now, when baby has his first case of sniffles, that's okay too — we still have plenty of valuable information for you. Pregnancy is the start of the adventure, but the fun continues long after.

Part I
So You Want to Be a Dad . . .

The 5th Wave   By Rich Tennant

"I'm bonding with the baby. We're sharing an intimate moment with the Cleveland Browns on their 37 yard line."

In this part...

Chances are, the road to fatherhood wasn't something you dwelled on much in your earlier years. When you decide to begin a family, though, exciting thoughts about conception alternate with fears of not being a good dad and concerns about money, time, and a brand-new way of life. In this part we look at the doubts and worries that consume every new dad-to-be and explain the mechanics of getting pregnant. You may think this is one area where you need no help, but many couples find getting pregnant a frustrating struggle, and even those who don't can benefit from a refresher course on Conception 101.

Chapter 1

Fatherhood: A Glorious, Scary, Mind-Boggling, and Amazing Experience

In This Chapter

▶ Exploring what it means to be a father today

▶ Understanding what will change in your life

▶ Facing the decision of whether to have a baby

▶ Looking down the long road ahead

Apparently congratulations are in order: Either you're going to be a father sometime within the next nine months or you're in the planning stages of becoming a dad. Either way, you've come to the right place. You'll face no bigger life decision than choosing to become a parent (and no bigger jolt than being told baby is coming if you didn't expect it!), and the best gift you can give to your soon-to-be child is confidence. And the only way to feel confident before you've ever been a parent is to get yourself prepared for the unknown journey that lies ahead.

Perhaps you've already been floored by equal doses of joy and fear, which is a good sign that you recognize the magnitude of the change but you're up for the challenge of fatherhood. Emotions run deep when confronted with the prospect of raising a child, mainly because it's a huge commitment and responsibility that, unlike a job, never has off-hours. Babies are expensive, confusing, time consuming and, for many fathers, they represent the end of a carefree "youth" that extends well into adulthood.

Experiencing a jumble of feelings is normal, and the more you take those emotions to heart and explore what fatherhood means to you — and what kind of father you want to be — the easier the transition will be when baby arrives.

Looking at the Concept of Fatherhood

What exactly does it mean to be a father? The answer depends on the kind of father you want to be for your child. In recent years, movies, TV, and even commercials have begun to transition from the bumbling, know-nothing father of yore to the modern dad who is just as comfortable changing a diaper as he is fixing a car. Fathers today range from traditional to equal partners in every aspect of parenting.

The majority of parents today don't adhere to the traditional masculine and feminine roles that our parents and grandparents grew up with. Women work, men work, and caring for the home — inside and out — is both partners' responsibility. Today, fatherhood is a flexible word that's defined by how involved you want to be in the rearing of your child, but the more involved you are in your child's upbringing, the more likely he is to be a well-adjusted, loving, and confident person.

A father? Who, me?

Yes, you. As strange as it sounds, you are going to be a father. A great one at that, because just through the mere act of reading this book, you're taking the proverbial bull by the horns and doing your homework to learn what it takes to be a good dad from day one. As they say, anyone can be a father, but it takes someone special to be a dad.

Even if you've never held a baby before, don't let self-doubt rule the day. Being a good father isn't about knowing everything about everything; it's about loving and caring for a baby to the best of your abilities. So don't be afraid. Yes, that's easier said than done, but being fearful of what lies ahead doesn't change the fact that you've got a baby on the way, however far off.

You may feel silly, but start by saying the words "I'm going to be a father" out loud a few times. Maybe even look into a mirror while you say it. If the thought of fatherhood scares you, you need to get used to the label, and the more you say and internalize it, the more it will become you.

Reacting to a life-changing event

Devolving into a tearful, slobbering mess upon finding out that you are going to be a father isn't unusual. Neither is throwing up, passing out, laughing, swearing, or any of the normal, healthy reactions people have upon receiving life-altering information.

If your reaction isn't 100 percent positive, that's okay, too. Just remember that your partner likely won't be particularly thrilled if you get upset, defensive, or angry when she tells you she's expecting. As best as you can, react to the news with all the positivity you can muster. You'll have plenty of time to revisit any concerns or frustrations after you've given the situation some time to sink in.

Some dads-to-be go into fix-it mode upon hearing the news, ready and eager to crunch budget numbers, baby-proof the entire home in a single night, begin make college plans 18 years in advance, and so on. Feeling like you need to get everything in order before baby arrives is normal, but remember that you can't do it all in a day, and take some time to celebrate before you dive into the practical side of life with baby. (Turn to Chapter 3 for more on handling the news.)

Dealing with fears of fatherhood

Even men who have been lucky enough to be surrounded by positive male role models for their entire lives still find themselves doubting whether or not they have what it takes to be a dad. It's like the fear of starting a new job amplified by 100. Part of being a good father is taking the time to confront these fears so that when baby comes, you won't be parenting with fear.

Following are some of the common fear-based questions men ask themselves in regard to fatherhood:

- Am I ready to give up my present life (free time, flexibility, freedom) to be a dad?
- Will I have time for my pastimes and friends?
- Will I ever sleep again?
- Is this the end of my marriage and sex life as I know it?
- Do we have enough money to raise a child?
- Do I know enough about kids to be a good dad?
- Am I mature enough to be a good role model for my child?
- What if the baby comes and I don't love him?

Your head may be spinning with all of the questions you ask yourself, and although you can't answer them all right away, you need to address them at some point. However, plenty of men have felt unprepared and unwilling and turned out to be great dads, so don't despair if your initial answers to the questions above are mostly negative.

Parenthood involves a lot of sacrifice, but it doesn't have to sound the death knell for your identity or happiness. Talk with your partner, a trusted friend, or a therapist — anyone who will listen to you and support your concerns without getting defensive — about the questions you have. Some of your fears, as you will find, have no basis in reality. Others, such as the fear of losing yourself and your free time, will require you to prioritize your time and energy.

Regardless of what your fears may be, don't let them fester. No man is an island, and you can't effectively deal with all those emotions by yourself. Starting an open dialogue with your partner will keep you both on the same page, which is a good start toward making you an effective parenting duo.

Debunking a few myths of fatherhood

Many of the concerns or fears you likely have originate from the many long-standing myths of what a father's role should be in the life of a child. Not all that long ago, men stood in the waiting room at the hospital during delivery and returned to work the next day. The landscape of fatherhood has changed quickly, leaving the modern dad wondering where he fits in the parenting scheme.

Following are some of the most common misconceptions about fatherhood. We debunk those myths to help you understand how to be a more-involved father.

Myth #1: Only the mom-to-be should have input about labor and delivery

While the focus is on your partner — she is, after all, the one carrying your child — you also matter, and you have the right to voice your opinions along the way. Throughout the pregnancy, share what you're experiencing and let her know what you're afraid of. She has a lot to think about and worry about, too, but the more you deal with those issues together, the stronger your relationship will become.

If you have thoughts and opinions about what kind of delivery option you're most comfortable with, share those with her as well. Although ultimately you need to let your partner pick the childbirth option that's best for her, she deserves to know your feelings on the matter. Getting involved in the decision-making process isn't just your right; it's the right thing to do. You can turn to Chapter 8 to start getting informed on the options and many decisions to be made.

Myth #2: Men aren't ideal caretakers for newborns

Boobs are generally the issue at the forefront of this myth. No, you won't be able to breast-feed your child or know what it's like to give birth. Because they don't have that initial connection, a lot of fathers wonder what exactly they're supposed to do.

Mother and baby are attached to each other for nine months, but after baby arrives, it's open season on bonding and caretaking. When your partner isn't breastfeeding, hold, rock, and engage in skin-to-skin contact with your baby. Changing diapers, bathing, and changing clothes are just a few of the activities that you can do to get involved. And the more involved you get, the less likely you are to feel left out of the equation. Chapter 10 provides tips for caring for your new baby so you can feel confident in your abilities.

Myth #3: You will never have sex or sleep ever again

Good things come to those who wait, and you will have to wait. Sex won't happen for at least six weeks following delivery, and even then you have a long road back to normalcy. For many couples, a normal sex life following childbirth isn't as active as it once was, but you can work with your partner to make sure both of your needs are being met.

One need that will deter your sex life — and override the sex need — is sleep. Babies don't sleep through the night. They wake up hungry and demand an awake parent to feed them, burp them, and soothe them back to sleep. Some babies begin sleeping through the night at six months while other kids won't until the age of 3. The good news is that they all do it eventually, and when you begin to understand your baby's patterns, you'll be able to figure out a routine that allows you to maximize the shut-eye you get every day.

Myth #4: Active fathers can't succeed in the business world

Unless work is the only obligation you've ever had in your adult life, you're probably used to juggling more than one thing. Fathers who are active in the community or fill their schedules with copious hours of hobbies will have to reevaluate their priorities. Family comes first, work comes second, and with the support of a loving partner and a few good baby sitters, you'll be able to continue on your career trajectory as planned.

In fact, being a dad may just make you a more effective worker. Having so many demands on your time will make you better at time management and maximizing your workday. Focus on work at work and home at home, and you'll succeed in both arenas.

Myth #5: You're destined to become your father

Destiny is really just a code word for the tendency many men have to mimic the patterns and behaviors that are familiar because they grew up experiencing them. However, if you didn't like an aspect of your father's parenting or don't want to repeat a major mistake or flaw that he perpetrated, talk about it with your partner. The more you talk about it, the less likely you are to repeat that mistake because you'll engage your partner as a support system working with you to help you avoid it.

But don't forget to replicate and celebrate the things your father may have done right. You'll be chilled to the bone the first time you say something that your father used to say, but remember that repeating the good actions isn't a bad thing. Don't try to be different from your father "just because." Identify what he did that was right, what was wrong, and use that as a blueprint for your parenting style.

Myth #6: You will fall in love with your baby at first sight

Babies aren't always so beautiful right after being born, but that's to be expected, given what they've just gone through to enter the world. Don't feel guilty if you look at your baby and aren't immediately enamored with him. Emotions are difficult to control, and for some fathers — and even mothers — falling head-over-heels for your baby may take some time.

Childbirth is a long, intense experience (as we describe in Chapter 9), so allow yourself adequate time to rest and get to know the new addition to your family. If you suffer from feelings of regret, extreme sadness, or experience thoughts of harming yourself or the baby, seek immediate medical assistance.

Becoming a Modern Dad

Dads today are involved in every aspect of a child's life. They're no longer relegated to teaching sports, roughhousing, and serving as disciplinarians. Modern fatherhood is all about using your strengths, talents, and interests to shape your relationship and interactions with your child.

Modern dads change diapers, feed the baby, wake up in the middle of the night to care for a crying child, and take baby for a run. They do not "baby-sit" their children; they're capable parents, and no job falls outside of the realm of a modern father's capabilities. Though all that involvement does mean you're going to put in far more effort and time than previous generations, it also means that you're bridging the gap of emotional distance that used to be so prevalent in the father-child experience.

In addition to reading the sections below, you can flip to the chapters in Part IV for information and advice on making changes and stepping into the practical role of daddy.

Changes in your personal life

If what you fear most is losing the freedom to spend as much time as you want engaging in leisure activities, then you are in for some mammoth sacrifices. Babies require you to say no to a lot of commitments that the prebaby you would have agreed to partake in. Don't make a lot of outside-the-home plans that you consider optional, at least at first.

For the first six months, going out at night will be challenging, especially if your partner is breast-feeding, and even more so if you don't live near family. However, as your baby ages, leaving him with a baby sitter becomes more feasible and less stressful.

Perhaps what you fear the most is the impact baby will have on your relationship with your partner. This fear is valid, given that you will scarcely find time for the two of you to be alone. But that doesn't mean you won't have time to connect.

Just because going out as a couple is tough to manage doesn't mean you can't have ample one-on-one time. Plan stay-in dates that start at baby's bedtime. Order food or make a fancy dinner, queue up a movie, or bring out your favorite board game. Try not to talk about baby. Rather, focus on each other and talk about topics that interest you both.

Changes in your professional life

Depending on the requirements of your job, your daily routine may go completely unchanged aside from the uptick in yawns due to late-night feedings and fussiness. Thoughts of your new family may make focusing difficult, especially when you first return to work following any paternity leave or vacation you take. In time, you'll settle back into a normal routine, and work just may become the one arena of your life that provides a respite from parenting duties.

Workaholics, however, will find themselves at a crossroads. Some will choose to cut back on hours spent at the office while others, hopefully with the full support of their partners, will proceed with business as usual. There is no right or wrong way to balance a demanding job with a new baby as long as you and your partner both are comfortable with the arrangement and you spend enough quality time with your child.

What is quality time? It's time you spend with your child, focusing *on* your child. Some people say quality time has nothing to do with the quantity of time you spend with your child, but we feel it is affected by the amount of time you devote to your child. Give as much as you can, because the old adage is true — they grow up so fast.

Some dads even leave the workforce altogether or take work-at-home positions in order to provide full-time childcare for their newborn. If you choose this route, make sure to check out Chapter 14, where we discuss some important considerations of being a stay-at-home dad.

Lifestyle changes to consider

Bad habits are hard to break, but when you have the added stress of a child, those bad habits can be even harder to conquer. That said, you're about to have a child — a sponge that will soak up your every word and action — so it's time to clean up your act.

Following are a few lifestyle alterations to consider making so you can lead by example without reservation:

- ✔ **Quit smoking/drinking too much/taking recreational drugs.** Second-hand smoke increases the risk of illness for your child, as well as the likelihood that she will become a smoker as an adult. Frequent overconsumption of alcohol makes you less likely to be a responsible parent capable of making good, safe decisions for baby. In fact, alcohol and drugs often lead to harmful and neglectful decisions that can land you in legal trouble and your child in the foster care system.

- ✔ **Start an exercise regimen.** Physically active, healthy parents get less run down and are less susceptible to illness. Plus, you'll want to live a long life with your children.

- ✔ **Lose weight.** If you're heavily overweight, you're more susceptible to illness and a shortened lifespan, and furthermore, children of obese parents are more likely to be obese. Kids learn nutrition and lifestyle habits from their parents, so set a good example and give your child a fair shot at a long, healthy life.

- ✔ **Eat healthier.** Your partner needs to be extremely diligent about eating pregnancy-positive foods, so use this time as an opportunity to get your diet in order. Soon enough, you'll be cooking for three, and if you're already in the habit of preparing healthy foods, you'll have no trouble providing proper nutrition to your child.

- ✔ **Control your anger/censor your potty mouth.** Kids learn how to treat and interact with others at a very young age. Start revising your behavior now and get used to swearing less, before your kid picks up some nasty communication habits.

- ✔ **Spend less money on nonessential items.** Teaching kids fiscal responsibility is just as important as teaching them social responsibility. Plus, kids aren't cheap, so stop spending $50 per week on beer and start banking your savings to provide a sound, secure future for your family.

✔ **Organize and de-clutter your home.** Create a safe, livable place for your new addition, which also helps decrease the amount of stress in your life.

✔ **Develop routines.** Be it running errands, cooking, phone calls, or paying the bills, get systems in place to ensure that everything gets done with the least amount of hair pulling. Knowing who does what when keeps you on track when baby throws a wrench into everything.

Deciding to Take the Plunge (Or Not)

For some of you, the question of whether or not you're ready for fatherhood comes too late. Others may be reading this book as a first step in planning for the future. Deciding the right time in life to have a baby isn't an easy task, especially because circumstances change on a seemingly daily basis.

However, family planning is an essential step that can minimize what ifs, frustrations, and regrets. Once you have a baby, you can't take it back. Knowing when you're ready to be parents and then trying to conceive means that when you actually do get pregnant, the time will indeed be right. Or at least as right as any time can be, as you have such little control over life's variables.

Determining whether you're ready

How does it feel when you know you want to be a father? And how can you know when you're actually ready to start trying for a baby? Those questions have no simple answers, because the feeling is different for everyone, but suffice it to say, you'll know when you know.

One sign to look for is a prolonged interest and fascination with the babies of friends and family members. Women call the growing desire for a baby a *biological clock,* and many men experience similar feelings. The desire to procreate, to have your genes carried on in the species, can be powerful.

Just make sure it's a desire that lasts more than a day. Also, make sure that you take the time to analyze the impact baby is going to have on your life. If you're in the final two years of a college program, it may be in your best interest to wait. If you're unemployed, perhaps you want to put off trying until you find a job you like that can support a family.

Just because you're ready doesn't make now the right time. Don't decide to have a baby on an impulse. Think about the impact a child will have on your time, money, and home, and if you don't see any major obstacles, then by all means, proceed. Obviously you can choose to proceed even if having a baby now doesn't make sense on every level, but please make sure first that you can provide a loving, safe home and can pay for all the things baby needs to thrive.

Telling your partner you're ready

You can tell your partner anytime and anyplace that you're ready to take the plunge into parenthood, but however you broach the subject, remember that she may not be as ready as you. A good way to introduce the subject is by asking her questions about her feelings on when the right time is to have a baby.

Let her know how excited you are, but also let her know that you've thought about the finances and logistics of having a baby, too. Fatherhood involves a lot more than choosing a name and a nursery theme. A big part of feeling ready is knowing that the person you're going to have a baby with isn't just enamored with the idea of a baby but is also prepared for the practicalities of responsibly starting a family.

You don't have to outline every aspect of how and why you're ready, but treat the idea with respect and let your partner know you're sincere by proving that you've actually thought it through.

Telling your partner you're not ready

If your partner is already pregnant, do not under any circumstances tell her you're not ready. If, however, the two of you simply are exploring the idea of having a child, now is the perfect time to speak your piece and let her know that you're just not prepared for fatherhood.

Reasons for not being ready vary from practical (not enough money or time) to logistical (still in school, caring for a sick parent) to selfish (not ready to share the Xbox). No reason to not be ready is wrong, but if your partner is ready for a baby, don't expect her to be fully supportive.

Regardless, don't agree to have a child before you're up for the challenge just so your partner doesn't get angry with you. Be honest, because when she's pregnant, you can't do anything to change the situation. If you're uncertain now, be honest and speak up!

Being patient when one of you is ready (and the other isn't)

Being on different pages can be an uncomfortable position for any couple, especially when it comes to the kid issue. Men have long been saddled with the Peter Pan label whenever they announce they aren't ready to "grow up" and have kids. Women are unfairly chastised for choosing career over family if they aren't ready to have a child.

Everyone has his reasons for wanting or not wanting to have a baby, and every one of them is valid — at least to the person who isn't ready. Attempting to persuade your partner, or vice versa, to have a baby is not recommended. Having a child with someone who isn't ready is setting up your relationship — and your relationship with the child — for failure.

If one of you isn't ready, try to work out a timeline as to when the wary party will be ready. If you can't set a definitive date, choose a time when you will revisit the topic. Check in with each other on the topic at least every six months. Nagging the other person isn't a good idea, but if it's something one of you wants, then you should continue to work toward a solution.

Seek counseling at any point if you and your partner are fighting about the issue frequently, or if one of you makes the decision that you never want children. Couples who find themselves at an impasse about whether or not they will have children often need the guidance of a trained professional.

Dealing with an unexpected pregnancy

Unplanned pregnancies aren't uncommon, and, for the majority of people in a committed relationship, adjusting to the surprising news is often no more than a minor bump in the road. If you unexpectedly find out that you're going to be dad, do not get angry with your partner. Blaming the other person is easy when emotions run high, but don't forget how you got into this situation in the first place. It does, indeed, take two.

Birth control and family planning are the responsibility of both the man and the woman, and accidents sometimes happen. The best thing you can do in this instance is to talk with your partner about your options and start making a plan about how to give that child the best life you possibly can. Having a child unexpectedly is not the end of the world, and you don't have to feel ready to have a baby to be a good father.

Welcoming long-awaited pregnancies

Getting pregnant isn't always as easy as they make it look in the movies, as the millions of infertile couples know all too well. (And if you and your partner are dealing with infertility, turn to Chapter 2 for help.) Finding out that you're pregnant after a long wait brings a mixed bag of emotions, most of which are joyful.

If you and your partner have been struggling to get pregnant, you likely feel relieved that you're about to get the gift you've been working so hard to find, but don't be surprised if you have difficulty adjusting to life outside of the infertility world. After months and years of scheduled sex, countless doctor visits, and suffering month after month of disappointment, not everyone transitions into the pregnancy phase with ease.

You also may struggle with a hypersense of fear due to previous miscarriages, close calls, and years of disappointment. Make sure to allow yourselves the opportunity to gripe, complain, worry, and grieve for a process that took a lot of patience and energy. Frustrations that were bottled up for the sake of optimism may finally surface, which is absolutely healthy.

 Just because you've finally achieved your goal doesn't make all the feelings of sadness and frustration suddenly disappear. If you and/ or your partner are having trouble letting go of the feelings that gripped you during your fertility struggle, you can find countless support groups, online communities, and blogs that provide both of you a place to talk about what you've been through. You can also learn transition tips from others who have been through the same thing. Moving forward will get easier, but it can take time — and a heaping helping of support.

Glimpsing into the Pregnancy Process Ahead

When you get used to the idea of being a father (which you hope-fully will), you may wonder what comes next. For the uninitiated, first-time dad, the nine months of pregnancy are a whirlwind of planning, worrying, parties, nesting, name searching, doctor visits, and information gathering as you move toward baby's birth. In the following sections we lay out what you can expect in each trimester (period of three months).

First trimester

In the first trimester, which encompasses the first three months of pregnancy, your partner suffers from the majority of pregnancy symptoms, such as nausea, intense sleepiness, unexplained tears, and the all-important cravings.

By the end of the first trimester, your baby grows to be about 3 or 4 inches in length and weighs approximately 1 ounce. At that time your baby's arms, legs, hands, and feet are fully formed, and your baby is able to open and close her fists. The circulatory and urinary systems are fully functional. Secondary body parts, such as fingernails, teeth, and reproductive organs, begin developing. Turn to Chapter 3 for more information on what happens during the first trimester.

Second trimester

During the second trimester, most of your partner's early pregnancy symptoms disappear, but her body undergoes visible changes. She begins to look and feel pregnant, and may begin struggling with the not-so-fun aspects of carrying a child, such as weight gain and forgetfulness.

This is also the time when the fun stuff begins. Around week 20, your partner has the ultrasound that can determine the sex of the baby — if you choose to find out and if the baby allows the ultrasound technician a clear view. It's also the time when you register for your baby shower, prepare the nursery, weed through countless baby names, attend birthing classes, and baby-proof your house.

By the end of the second trimester, your baby is roughly 14 inches long and weighs approximately 2 pounds. Her skin is still be translucent, but her eyes begin to open and close, and your partner likely starts feeling movements and even baby's tiny hiccups. Check out Chapter 4 to find out more about the second trimester.

Third trimester

Assuming all goes according to plan and your baby goes full-term (isn't premature) or somewhere close to it, the third trimester is one of the longest three-month periods of your life. Your partner begins to feel uncomfortable as her body makes it difficult to move and sleep in a normal way, and you both get antsy about the impending arrival.

To make the most of the time, you and your partner need to take care of business, mainly picking a pediatrician who you're comfortable with and has a similar parenting philosophy as you and your partner, crafting your birth plan, hiring a doula if you want one, getting your maternity and paternity leave squared away, ensuring that you understand your insurance benefits, creating a phone tree to announce baby's arrival, and finishing up any odd projects around the house that need to be done prior to baby's arrival.

During the third trimester, your baby is fully developed and focused on growing larger and stronger for life on the outside. This is also the last time for many, many years that you and your partner exist solely as a couple, so be sure to take the time to indulge yourselves in the things you love to do together. Life may feel like it's on pause for at least the first six months of baby's existence, so get out now and enjoy the freedom of childlessness. Soon enough, your life will be a lot more complicated and busy — and happy, too. Very, very happy. Chapter 7 gives you more information on what to expect and do in the third trimester.

While You Were Gestating

Because the first few weeks of pregnancy will probably be rather uneventful, now is a good time to start a time capsule for the year your baby will be born. Many years down the road, when your child is an adult, it will be a touching, informative look back at the time when he entered the world. For you and your partner, it will be a fun, celebratory action to kick off the pregnancy festivities.

Keep movie tickets stubs, take-out menus, a newspaper from the day you found out your partner was pregnant (as well as clippings of the most important headlines of the year), favorite ads, magazine clippings, and so on. Make a mix CD of the most popular songs, as well as one of your favorite music.

As you choose names, add the list of all potential names into the time capsule. When you choose a paint color for the nursery, put in the paint color card. Any decision you and your partner make for the baby is a good candidate for inclusion. It may seem silly now, but in 20 years it will be the best gift you can give your child.

Chapter 2

Beyond the Bed: Conception Smarts

In This Chapter

▶ Finding out why getting pregnant is harder than it looks sometimes

▶ Improving your health and lifestyle to help your chances

▶ Determining the right time for fertilization (and making it a good time)

▶ Understanding and dealing with infertility issues

▶ Talking to your family about your baby plans

*Y*ou may have spent years trying not to get pregnant, so the change from not trying to trying can be mind boggling. Something even the most clueless people manage to do effortlessly can cause you to lose sleep at night and turn sex into a job. Getting pregnant is hard work sometimes.

In this chapter we tell you how to make the getting pregnant process not just painless, but fun, even if it takes longer than you expected.

Understanding Conception

You can't get pregnant any old time you want; your partner has to be ovulating and releasing an egg, and you have to be sending some good swimmers her way. The whole baby-making process can be so complex that it seems like a miracle people are on earth at all. This section tells you about the mechanics of how eggs and sperm actually get together and what they need from the two of you.

Baby making 101

Getting pregnant requires that several players be on the scene at the right time: namely, good sperm and a mature egg. If the two meet in the fallopian tube, which is the conduit from the ovary down to the uterus, join together to form a fertilized egg, and then float down to a uterus with a lining that's exactly the right thickness to facilitate implantation, pregnancy occurs. If any of those factors are amiss, well, that's when things get complicated.

Producing a mature egg

Before she's even born, a woman has all the eggs she'll ever have. Unlike sperm, no new eggs are being produced; the original eggs are just matured, usually one at a time. Mature eggs are produced from immature ones (called oocytes), located in the ovaries, through a complex interaction of three hormones during the menstrual cycle. Those hormones — estradiol (a form of estrogen), follicle stimulating hormone (FSH), and luteinizing hormone (LH) — work like this:

1. FSH stimulates the ovaries, which produce estrogen.

2. Estradiol production starts to mature a number of egg-containing follicles, small cystlike structures that contain the immature eggs.

3. One follicle, called a lead follicle, continues to develop while the rest atrophy.

4. Around day 14 of the menstrual cycle, LH kicks in to mature the egg and move it to the center of the follicle so it can release.

5. The egg releases from the follicle and begins to float down the fallopian tube. This is where you come in.

Figure 2-1 shows the events of a menstrual cycle when pregnancy does not occur.

Sending in some good sperm

Sperm can only fertilize an egg that's mature, so you need to either have sperm waiting in the tube when the egg is released or get some there within 12 to 24 hours after ovulation, because that's how long the egg can live. Sperm (shown in Figure 2-2) live for at least a few days, so having sex the day before ovulation, or even two days before, is usually adequate. If your partner is monitoring her ovulation, give it one more shot the day of ovulation.

Making the journey and attaching to the uterus

After fertilization, the new potential life has to make it down the tube to the uterus, where it implants. The journey from fallopian tube to uterus takes between five to seven days, on average, and implantation normally occurs seven to ten days after conception. The fallopian tube is normally a fairly straight tube, but if it's been damaged by infection so that it's twisted or dilated, the embryo may wander around in the crevasses and never get to the uterus.

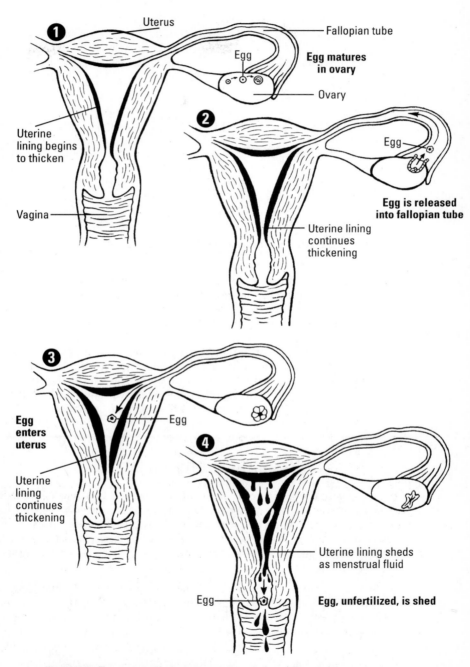

Figure 2-1: Every event in the menstrual cycle has a purpose.

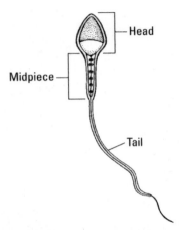

Figure 2-2: Sperm are compact swimming machines.

Even worse, it may implant in the tube, which is an *ectopic pregnancy*. The tube has no room for a developing fetus, so an ectopic pregnancy is doomed from the start and can cause serious, life-threatening bleeding if the tube ruptures.

Even after the embryo reaches the uterus, it's not always clear sailing. The uterine lining has to be just right for implantation. Estrogen thickens the lining before ovulation, and progesterone released from the corpus luteum, the leftover shell of the follicle that contained the egg, prepares the lining after ovulation.

Why so many sperm?

Women produce one egg a month, most of the time, and men produce millions of sperm. You may wonder, why the huge disparity? Because of the inability of one sperm to do the honors. Only one sperm makes it into the egg, but it takes many sperm to break down the coating that surrounds the egg. And while eggs get to drift downward from the ovary to the fallopian tube, sperm have to swim upstream. Needless to say, some fall by the wayside.

Sperm also are produced in large quantities because many are abnormal, having two tails, no tails, round tails, small heads, large heads, or abnormally shaped heads. Abnormal tails make navigation difficult, and abnormal heads often indicate chromosomal abnormalities.

Only 50 to 60 percent of sperm need good motility, or movement, for a sperm sample to be considered normal, so lots of sperm don't make the grade, creating a need for more numbers.

If either of these hormone levels are low, the lining may not be able to support a pregnancy. Your partner's doctor can assess the uterine lining by ultrasound and prescribe extra progesterone if needed to achieve pregnancy.

After the embryo reaches the uterus and implants, the implanting embryo begins to produce human chorionic gonadotropin, or hCG, the hormone that pregnancy tests measure. hCG levels aren't detectable until the embryo implants, or around the time of the first missed period.

Conception statistics

If you don't get pregnant the first month you try, the wheels in your head may start turning as you obsess about why this is taking so long. Pregnancy is by no means a sure thing, even when you do everything right and have no major fertility issues. In any given month, statistics say that:

- Out of 100 couples under age 35 trying to get pregnant in a given month, 20 will achieve their goal, but 3 will miscarry.

- If your partner is in her late 30s, you have a 10 percent chance of pregnancy each month, but a 34 percent chance of miscarriage.

- If she's older than 40, you have only a 5 percent chance of pregnancy each month, and more than a 50 percent chance of miscarriage.

The good news is that 75 out of 100 30-year-olds trying to get pregnant will become pregnant within a year of trying, and 66 percent of 35-year-olds will get pregnant in a year. Around 44 percent of 40-year-olds become pregnant within a year. Over age 40, variables such as hormone levels affect pregnancy rates, and generalizations are hard to make.

Answering commonly asked questions about getting pregnant

Getting pregnant may seem straightforward, but what exactly does it take? Here are some answers to the most common concerns:

- **How long does it take?**

   On average, more than half of couples get pregnant within the first six months of trying and four out of five are pregnant within one year.

✔ **Does having more sex increase the chances of pregnancy?**

No. In fact, due to the amount of time it takes for semen volume to build back up to normal levels following ejaculation, overdoing it around ovulation time by having sex several times a day can deplete your sperm count, which probably won't be a problem if you have a normal sperm count, but can be if your count is low.

✔ **Should we only have sex with my partner on her back and me on top?**

It's a myth that this standard position is the best way to get pregnant. While it may help the semen stay in better, there is no scientific proof that the sexual position you choose has any effect on conception rates.

✔ **Does my partner's past use of the birth control pill mean it will take longer?**

It varies from person to person. One woman can miss a single pill and end up pregnant while others may take a little longer. Just remember, the chances of getting pregnant the first month are small, but the average couple is pregnant within a year regardless of past birth-control usage.

✔ **Is it okay to drink and smoke when trying to conceive?**

If you're ready to be pregnant, you should give up smoking immediately. Occasionally having a drink or two when you're trying to become a mom or dad won't likely produce a negative outcome, but the general rule of thumb is to live as though your partner is pregnant from the moment you begin trying to conceive. Check out the next section for more tips on getting healthy to improve the odds of conception.

Evaluating Health to Get Ready for Parenthood

Some health issues and bad habits can make it harder to get pregnant. A few months before trying to get pregnant, take inventory of behaviors and health issues and get yourselves into the best shape possible, not only so that you can get pregnant without difficulty but also so you'll be healthy new parents.

Checking out your physical health before trying to get pregnant isn't difficult. See your doctor, let him know you're trying to get pregnant, change any medications that may impact fertility, and run some blood tests.

Uncovering female health issues that impact conception

Many female health problems can cause fertility difficulties. Some affect egg production and the menstrual cycle; others affect egg transport and implantation, like fibroids and fallopian tube damage. Many can be improved after you identify them.

Sexually transmitted diseases

One of the biggest fertility busters in the age of sexual freedom is sexually transmitted diseases, or STDs. The following STDs can affect female fertility in these ways:

- Chlamydia, if not treated promptly, increases by 40 percent the risk of pelvic inflammatory disease, which damages the fallopian tubes. Women with PID are seven to ten times more likely to have an ectopic pregnancy. Eighty percent of women who have had chlamydia three or more times are infertile.

- Gonorrhea also increases the risk of PID and ectopic pregnancy.

- Syphilis can cause miscarriage, stillbirth, and developmental delays and blindness in your unborn child.

STDs need to be treated early with antibiotics before damage is done to the tubes. Having a hysterosalpingogram (HSG), a dye test to assess the patency of the tubes, is a good idea if your partner has any concerns about whether her tubes have been damaged in the past.

Endometriosis

Endometriosis, implantation of the tissue that lines the inside of the uterus in places it doesn't belong, is common; 5.5 million women in the United States suffer from it, and 40 percent of women with endometriosis have fertility issues.

Endometriosis tissue bleeds at the time of the menstrual period and leads to scarring and pain. Endometrial implants can be removed in some cases, but they tend to recur. Most endometriosis is found in the pelvis, near the uterus, but it can turn up in some odd places, like the lungs. In vitro fertilization (IVF) can increase the chances of pregnancy in women with endometriosis.

Polycystic ovary syndrome

Polycystic ovary syndrome, PCOS, affects between 5 to 10 percent of women of childbearing age, and can cause *anovulation,* or failure to produce a mature egg. PCOS is associated with an abnormal rise in male hormones, called androgens; all women have some male hormones, but women with PCOS have more than normal. They're often overweight and have excess body and facial hair, thinning head hair (just like some men), and acne. Women with PCOS also have a higher rate of type 2 diabetes, heart disease, high cholesterol, and high blood pressure. Fertility medications may be needed for women with PCOS to get pregnant.

Thyroid problems

Thyroid problems are common in women of childbearing age and can cause anovulation (failure to recruit and develop eggs). A simple blood test checks for thyroid function. Low thyroid levels can raise prolactin levels, which can also interfere with ovulation.

Fibroids

Fibroids are common uterine growths (rarely cancerous) that occur in up to 75 percent of women and often cause no problems with conception. However, fibroids can grow big enough to interfere with embryo implantation or to cause preterm labor in some women. See Figure 2-3.

Fibroids are easily seen with pelvic ultrasound, and can be removed surgically if they appear to be interfering with pregnancy.

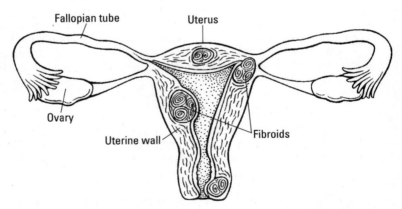

Figure 2-3: Fibroids grow into the uterine lining and occasionally interfere with pregnancy.

Recognizing issues that cause fertility problems in men

Sperm take a long time to make. Sperm you ejaculate today have been three months in the making, so if you're working on health problems or making lifestyle changes, give them enough time to take effect.

While male health issues may seem less important to a quick conception, your health problems can interfere with conception. Here are a few examples of potentially problematic issues:

✔ Diabetic men often have problems with erection and ejaculation. Presumably if you have a problem with erection, you're already well aware of it, but ejaculatory issues may not be quite as obvious. Retrograde ejaculation, where sperm get pushed into the bladder rather than out through the urethra, can affect diabetic men.

✔ Men who take high-blood-pressure medications called calcium channel blockers may have sperm that don't penetrate eggs well; other blood pressure medications may cause retrograde ejaculation.

✔ Toxins common to the workplace, such as lead, X-rays, inhaled anesthetics in the operating room, and a host of other environmentally damaging substances can also be damaging your internal plumbing if you work with them frequently.

✔ STDs can also take their toll on the male reproductive system. Chlamydia and gonorrhea can cause an infection and inflammation in the epididymis, part of the testes where sperm develop. Syphilis can cause low sperm count and poor motility.

Assessing lifestyle choices that affect eggs and sperm

You can impact your chances of pregnancy every month with your lifestyle choices. Yes, giving up bad habits is painful, but not getting pregnant month after month is pretty painful, too. Take the step of cutting the following bad habits out of your life before you start trying to get pregnant.

Smoking

Smoking can affect sperm and eggs and increase miscarriage rates. Nearly one in four adults smoke in America. If either of you is a smoker, quit for at least a few months before trying to get pregnant. It may help you avoid these pitfalls:

✔ Smokers have sperm that are less motile (capable of moving spontaneously). They have a long way to go to reach the egg, so they need all the motility they can get.

✔ Smokers have lower sperm counts and more abnormally shaped sperm, which are chromosomally abnormal.

✔ Female smokers have more eggs that are chromosomally abnormal.

✔ Female smokers have a 50 percent higher rate of miscarriage.

✔ Smokers are two to four times more likely to have ectopic pregnancy, pregnancy that implants outside the uterus.

Drinking alcohol

Alcohol has far-reaching issues for the fetus long past the moment of conception, so cutting out alcohol before trying to get pregnant and avoiding it like the plague after getting pregnant are essential for your partner. It won't hurt you, either. Heavy drinking, three or more drinks a day for a guy, can decrease sperm quantity and quality. And a drink doesn't have to be hard liquor; one beer is a drink.

Using drugs

Two commonly used drugs can affect male fertility: marijuana and anabolic steroids. Marijuana lowers testosterone levels in males, and testosterone is the male hormone responsible for male sexual functioning and sperm production. Sperm counts are lower and sperm is less motile in men who use marijuana regularly.

Steroid use is more common than you may think: 6 to 7 percent of all men have used steroids to build muscle mass. Steroids suppress testosterone production and can cause irreversible damage to the sperm production line. Avoid anabolic steroids at all costs.

Maintaining an unhealthy weight

Unfortunately, being overweight is a huge problem, and it's getting bigger all the time. Around 20 percent of women of childbearing age in the United States are obese. Women who are overweight may not ovulate, and if they don't ovulate, they can't get pregnant. One Australian study showed that obese women were only half as likely to get pregnant as normal-weight women.

However, being underweight can also interfere with ovulation. Overall, 12 percent of infertility issues are related to being over- or underweight. Fortunately, either losing or gaining weight in these cases results in pregnancy 70 percent of the time.

Issues that may never have crossed your mind

Sometimes behaviors you may never have considered can negatively impact your chances of pregnancy. Here are a few:

✔ **Douching:** Although between one-third to one-half of child-bearing age women do it, it's not only unnecessary, it's potentially harmful. Women who douche are 73 percent more likely to have pelvic inflammatory disease, which can seriously damage the fallopian tubes and increases the chance of ectopic pregnancy by about the same percentage.

And because you want your partner around for a long time, remind her of this statistic: Women who douche are 80 percent more likely to develop cervical cancer.

✔ **Not sitting on the couch enough:** No, not really — some exercise is definitely good for you. But some sports, like bicycling, may cause testicular damage from the pressure of the bike seat. Women who exercise too heavily may stop having periods (called *amenorrhea*), and good luck getting pregnant without them.

✔ **Spending time in hot tubs and other heat sources:** Hot tubs, tight underwear, saunas, steam rooms, and anything else that raises the temperature of the testicles is bad for the boys. Hot tubs may also damage eggs and increase miscarriage rates, so neither of you should be lolling in the hot tub.

Keeping Sex from Becoming a Chore

As unfathomable as it seems, sex while trying to conceive isn't always fun. Couples often begin to feel a sense of duty and pressure when they segue from spontaneity to planning exactly when to have sex to increase chances of conception. Monitoring rises in body temperature, charting mucus, and even lying down afterward to give the semen time to do its job are just a few of the unromantic actions that can take your sex life from crackin' to clinical.

Pleasure may seem to take a back seat to the goal of having a baby, and nothing takes the "sexy" out of sex faster than making it feel like work. In fact, if the sex becomes solely about trying to conceive, you may begin to feel a bit like a sperm-producing machine that's only needed during ovulation, and performance issues can arise (no pun intended).

If for some reason conception takes a while, this feeling will only increase as you both grow impatient. If you begin to suffer these feelings, share them with your partner immediately. Plan "sex dates" that don't revolve around conception time and discuss ways to create a more relaxing, less stressful, romantic environment.

Choosing the best time for conception

We're not talking about the phase of the moon or the alignment of the stars here; we're talking about planning to have sex at certain times to increase the odds that you'll hit the day when an egg is present and ready to be fertilized. Not all women have 28-day menstrual cycles, and ovulation doesn't always occur on day 14 of the cycle. Ovulation does always occur 12 to 14 days before the next period is due, or, to be more accurate, your partner's period starts 12 to 14 days after ovulation occurs. You can figure out the best timing for your conception efforts in several ways, which we explore in the following sections.

Monitoring ovulation with a kit

Predicting ovulation doesn't take mind-reading abilities. Simple observation and a few ovulation predictor kits from the pharmacy are all you need to pinpoint the big day. Ovulation predictor kits (OPK) pinpoint the rise in luteinizing hormone that occurs just before egg release. Your partner urinates into a cup, and then dips the test stick into the urine and reads the results.

The only drawback to OPKs is that women who have high levels of LH normally, like women in or near menopause and women with PCOS, may not get accurate results.

Watching for physical signs of ovulation

Your partner may also be able to tell when ovulation occurs by these signs:

- ✔ Cervical mucus becomes more copious, thinner, and more slippery and stretchy as ovulation approaches.
- ✔ She may have *mittelschmerz,* a pain on the left or right side as the egg releases from the ovary.
- ✔ Her temperature drops slightly right before ovulation and rises afterward.

Ovulation can be tracked by keeping a monthly temperature chart, but it can be a real pain because she has to take her temperature first thing in the morning, before she gets out of bed, uses the bathroom, or has a cup of coffee.

Catching ovulation with a regular visit

If you don't want to closely monitor ovulation, you can take the easy way and simply have sex on a frequent, regular schedule. Doctors seem to have differing opinions on how much sex is enough when you're trying to get pregnant. Some say every other day helps build up a good supply of sperm; some say every day is okay starting a few days before ovulation and continuing (if you're not dead yet) until the day after ovulation.

The most sensible schedule suggests having sex every other day, all month if you're up for it, starting right after her period ends. Since sperm live for up to 5 days, having sex the day before ovulation or the day of gives you a good shot at fertilization, and if you're aiming for every other day, you're bound to hit one or the other.

Looking at do's and don'ts for scheduling sex

Just because you've written sex down on your calendar doesn't mean it's just another obligation that eats up your time and lacks excitement. After all, this appointment has a far bigger upside than the average visit to the dentist.

Since you have only a few ideal times each month to conceive, you need to make time for sex on those days, which requires planning ahead. Follow these do's and don'ts to make sure your sex life doesn't suffer for the sake of conception.

Do:

- ✔ **Put it on your calendar.** While it may seem unsexy, it can be very exciting to look forward to intercourse all week. In fact, verbal foreplay leading up to intercourse will only increase the excitement.

- ✔ **Plan a date that night if possible to make it a full-fledged romantic evening.** Making it just about the sex will increase the pressure to perform.

- ✔ **Engage in foreplay.** On TV and in movies, you often see the ovulating woman demand sex the minute her body temperature leads her to believe it's the best time. Make sure to keep it romantic and intimate. Some light massage, touching, and kissing should do the trick.

- ✔ **Mix it up.** Remember that though some positions are supposed to be better when trying to conceive, that doesn't mean you have to stay in the same one the whole time.

- ✔ **Keep it spontaneous.** Knowing the exact date you're going to have sex doesn't mean the setting has to stay the same. Play music, light candles, take a warm bath (not too hot — remember, you don't want to overheat the boys!), or even play out a fantasy if your partner is onboard.

- ✔ **Help make the aftermath enjoyable.** Your partner may want to elevate her legs and stay in bed for a while after intercourse to give the semen the best chance to stay put. Help her elevate her legs, and then put on her favorite show or read to her from a book. Don't just get up and leave her alone.

- ✔ **Have unscheduled sex.** Letting nature run its course every once and a while is okay, even when your road to conception is more like driving in bumper-to-bumper traffic than the autobahn. After ejaculation, sperm can live in a woman's reproductive tract for up to five days.

Don't:

✔ **Try too hard.** Sex carries its own set of complex, anxiety-inducing expectations, but now that the expectations include creating a baby, the pressure can become downright overwhelming. If you experience performance issues, either mental or physical, due to the stress of the moment, talk it out with your partner. You won't do anyone a favor by having sex as if you're taking the SAT.

✔ **Talk about the baby.** Unless talking about getting her pregnant is a turn-on to your partner, keep the baby discussion out of the sex equation. Although trying to have a baby does indeed require sex, talking about getting her pregnant while engaging in intercourse likely won't set your bedroom on fire.

✔ **Drink before you have sex.** Alcohol can cause performance issues, and the last thing you want to do is let your partner down because you had one too many beers.

✔ **Assume your partner isn't interested in both pleasure and conception.** In fact, studies show that women who orgasm have a greater chance of conceiving than those who don't.

✔ **Make her laugh afterward.** Keeping a good sense of humor during sex is always a good thing, but after you ejaculate keep the comedy to a minimum. Laughing tenses muscles that cause the semen to come out, reducing the chance of conception.

Taking a Brief Yet Important Look at Infertility

Infertility is an issue that affects more than 7 million people in the United States, but not getting pregnant within a month or two doesn't necessarily mean you're infertile. Couples under the age of 35 are diagnosed with infertility following 12 months of attempted reproduction that do not yield a pregnancy.

Knowing the facts about infertility

Imagine 100 average couples under the age of 35 trying to get pregnant — the following outcomes are expected:

✔ 75 couples are pregnant within a year.

✔ 10 couples are pregnant after two years of trying without medical intervention.

✔ 10 couples need treatment from an infertility specialist in order to conceive.

Causes of infertility can be complex and often hard to diagnose. Some are related to health and lifestyle issues discussed in the section "Evaluating Health to Get Ready for Parenthood" in this chapter. Despite treatments and diagnostic practices that primarily focus on women, the statistics paint a different picture:

- One-third of infertility is diagnosed as female-factor.
- One-third of infertility is diagnosed as male-factor.
- Between 10 and 15 percent of infertility cases are diagnosed as a combination of male- and female-factor.
- About 20 percent of infertility cases are unexplained following diagnostic testing.

For women, the main causes of infertility are

- **Ovulatory disorders:** No ovulation or ovulation on an irregular schedule
- **Tubal disorders:** Fallopian tubes are blocked or have an infection that interferes with ovulation or sperm travel
- **Uterine issues:** Fibroids (noncancerous tumors in the uterus) and polyps (growths that can cause blockages)

For men, the main causes of infertility are

- **Low sperm count:** Not enough guys to get the job done
- **Decreased sperm motility:** The sperm has trouble moving forward into the fallopian tubes
- **Abnormally shaped sperm:** Abnormal shapes usually indicate chromosomal abnormalities
- **No sperm present in the ejaculate:** A blockage somewhere in the reproductive tract or hormonal disorders can cause an absence of sperm

Checking on potential problems when nothing's happening

For many couples, the first step toward fixing infertility is admitting that you're having a problem. It's not an easy revelation to make, because it means that at some basic level your bodies are failing you. Fertility problems aren't fair, they're not fun, and they can be cause for a wide array of emotions, frustrations, and outright anger.

The good news is that we live in an age in which getting pregnant doesn't have to be a simple matter of the birds and the bees.

Throw in a doctor or two, and you may be well on your way to conceiving in no time flat.

If you're not getting pregnant after a few months, especially if your partner is older than 35, it's time to check things out — for both of you. For her, this may involve the following tests:

✔ **Blood tests:** These check hormone levels, including follicle stimulating hormone, or FSH. FSH levels are normally below 9 mIU/ml on day two or three of the menstrual cycle; higher levels indicate decreased ovarian reserve and the possible need for medical intervention.

✔ **Hysterosalpingogram (HSG):** This test injects dye into the uterus through a catheter placed through the cervix. The dye outlines the shape of the uterus and fallopian tubes. HSG can identify blockages in or dilation of the fallopian tubes that interferes with embryo transport, and it also shows fibroids and polyps in the uterus, which may interfere with implantation.

✔ **Hysteroscopy:** This test uses an endoscope, a sort of mini-telescope, to evaluate the uterus for fibroids or polyps, small growths that can interfere with implantation. Small fibroids and polyps can also be removed at the time of the test.

For you, it's a quick trip to the urologist for a full physical, blood work, and a semen analysis. This is the only way you can find out your sperm count and the quality and motility of your sperm.

Collection of semen is just as uncomfortable as it sounds, but it must be done. Just keep your expectations to a minimum and forget all of those movie scenes showing posh rooms, dirty magazines, and absolute privacy. If you have to produce in the doctor's office or a hospital lab, you may very well find yourself in a bathroom, unable to escape the distractions of screaming children and the witty banter of the nursing staff.

 Some offices allow specimens to be collected in the privacy of your home and then delivered to the lab within an hour. Ask your doctor about this alternative, as well as any special instructions for collection and transportation.

Working through it when your partner needs treatment

Some female fertility issues are easily dealt with by simply taking a pill that induces ovulation. But female infertility can also lead to daily injections of fertility medications, uncomfortable vaginal ultrasounds to assess egg development, painful surgeries to remove fibroids or repair damaged fallopian tubes, and frequent blood tests.

Fixing female fertility issues can be a drawn-out affair that combines inconvenient and uncomfortable procedures with medications that manipulate hormones, a difficult combination if there ever was one. And if she suddenly views childbearing as a woman's most important prerogative, her seeming inability to accomplish it and subsequent emotions can make fertility treatment a tough time for both of you.

Even though you may have your own stresses when dealing with fertility issues, remember that at least you aren't dealing with a barrage of excess hormones, and keep your cool if conversations get complicated.

Exploring solutions when your sperm don't stack up

A count of less than 20 million is considered a low sperm count. Although that may sound like a large number, due to the number of abnormal sperm in the normal sample as well as the distance required to reach the egg, it takes a lot of good sperm to achieve conception.

Sperm is produced on a cycle, so the semen you produce now actually was created three months ago. If your sperm count is low, start by thinking back to what was going on then. An illness, medications, or a hot-tub vacation may be the culprit.

Learning the components

What exactly makes a semen specimen normal? The following guidelines from the World Health Organization (WHO) are deemed the ideal for baby making:

- ✔ **Volume:** About 1.5 to 5 milliliters of semen should be present in a single ejaculate, equaling about a teaspoon.

- ✔ **Concentration:** Strength in numbers is key. You'll need at least 20 million sperm per milliliter of ejaculate to hit the normal range.

- ✔ **Motility:** For every man, an average ejaculate contains dead, slow, and immobile sperm. However, at least 40 percent of your sperm in a single sample should be moving.

- ✔ **Morphology:** Shape is also important to reproduction, and the lab technician examining your sample takes a close look at how many of your swimmers are normally shaped. A normal amount of normally shaped sperm is considered to be anything above 30 percent.

✔ **Trajectory:** Graded on a four-point scale, this test determines how many of your sperm are moving forward. You're looking for a score of 2+ to be considered normal.

✔ **White blood cells:** Too many white blood cells can indicate an infection in your groin. A passing grade is no more than 0 to 5 per power field.

✔ **Hyperviscosity:** Your semen sample should liquefy within 30 minutes after ejaculation. If it takes longer, it reduces the chances for sperm to swim before being expelled from the vagina.

✔ **pH:** Like a AA battery, your semen needs to be alkaline in order to avoid making the vagina too acidic and, ultimately, killing the sperm.

In addition to the above, a semen analysis evaluates the following:

✔ **Head quality:** The head of the sperm contains all of the genetic material, so if the head is misshapen, it won't be capable of fertilizing an egg.

✔ **Midsection malaise:** Believe it or not, this part of your sperm contains fructose, which gives your sperm energy to swim. If the levels are low, it can account for slow swimmers.

✔ **Tail troubles:** Much like a fish, a good tail is required for the sperm to swim forward. If too many of your sperm have no tail, multiple tails, or tails that are coiled or kinked, they won't reach their destination.

A low sperm count may have you feeling, well, downright low. Feeling embarrassed is completely natural but also completely unnecessary. Infertility has no correlation to a man's masculinity, nor does it have anything to do with the size of his penis. Having a low sperm count is no different than having asthma — it's a medical condition that requires treatment.

Identifying and treating the causes

Because sperm counts are created months out, you'll need to have a follow-up semen analysis to see if the issue is corrected by lifestyle changes. Although you won't be in a rush to do it all again anytime soon, whether your results are good or bad, schedule a follow-up analysis four to six weeks after the first one to get a better, more complete picture.

The most common cause of a low sperm count is a *varicocele,* an abnormality in the vein in your scrotum that drains the testicles. Varicoceles can cause decreased fertility in the following ways:

- Increasing temperature in the testes
- Decreasing blood flow around the testicles
- Slowing sperm production and motility

Varicoceles are treatable in the following ways:

- **Surgery:** An outpatient procedure during which an incision is made just above the groin and the swollen vein is "tied off." Recovery takes seven to ten days and requires minimal activity and no heavy lifting. Risks are minimal and include infection, nerve injury, and the collection of fluid around the testicles.

- **Radiographic embolization:** Also an outpatient procedure, this requires the insertion of a catheter through the femoral vein in the groin. Dye is injected to show where the problem is located and, when isolated, it's blocked so blood flow to that vein stops.

Other less-common male-fertility issues include the following:

- **Hormone imbalances:** Medications to adjust hormone levels may improve sperm quantity.

- **Chromosomal abnormalities:** One such problem is sperm that lack part of the Y chromosome, the male chromosome. *In vitro fertilization* (IVF) and *intracycloplasmic sperm injection* (ICSI), where the best-looking sperm are injected directly into your partner's egg in the lab, can help overcome abnormal sperm issues. (See the following section for more info.)

- **History of cancer:** Having treatment for cancer, including lymphoma and testicular cancer, can kill or damage sperm. Many men freeze sperm before undergoing cancer treatment for this reason.

- **Various diseases:** Diabetes, sickle cell disease, and kidney and liver diseases can cause problems. Treatment depends on your individual issues.

Even if your ejaculate has no sperm at all, a procedure called a *sperm aspiration* in conjunction with an IVF cycle may be able to remove sperm directly from the testicles.

Deciding how far to go to get pregnant

Deciding what steps you're willing to take in order to get pregnant will be easier after you have a better understanding of the infertility issues you and your partner are facing. Most infertility treatments can be quite expensive, so check with your insurance company to see what is covered. Making the decision based on finances seems heartless, but if your insurance doesn't cover a treatment or medicines, you can be looking at bills in the thousands of dollars.

The most common procedures to aid in pregnancy are the following:

- **Intrauterine insemination (IUI):** A lab tech takes your sperm sample, pulls out the best of the best, and adds it to a saline solution, which then is inserted past your partner's cervix. This gives the sperm a far shorter distance to travel and a greater chance for success.

- **In vitro fertilization (IVF):** Sperm meets egg in a lab, and then the fertilized embryo is placed into the womb. Fertilization can take place by either placing a concentrated semen sample in a dish with the egg or via *ICSI*, intraycloplasmic sperm injection. In ICSI, a single sperm is injected directly into a mature egg. Even with ICSI, fertilization may not occur, because the egg or sperm may be chromosomally abnormal, which in some cases isn't evident just by looking at it.

Try not to make too many long-term decisions about how far you're willing to go, because undergoing fertility treatments is like riding a roller coaster, and once you're on, it becomes harder to get off. Especially when it feels like your baby could be just around the next corner. Make decisions month-to-month and procedure-to-procedure to avoid stress and allow for an open, ever-changing dialogue with your partner.

Sharing Your Decision to Have a Baby

Deciding to try to have a baby is a very big, very exciting step for most couples, and increasingly it is something many people choose to share with a select group of friends and family members. News of an expanding family is usually met with joy, cheers, and even a few inappropriate jokes about your sex life. But although sharing good news is fun, you also need to be prepared for people in the know to ask nosy questions and offer unwanted advice.

Considering the pros and cons of spilling the beans

Sharing the news means that you're turning your quest to have a baby into a mini-reality show that your loved ones are going to closely follow. Having a well of support during this time can be great, but having your mom and dad hinting for info every time you talk on the phone also can feel intrusive.

If getting pregnant takes longer than expected, you're also setting yourself up to have to deal with the inevitable questions about the delay. On the plus side, if you and your partner must deal with infertility, you'll need all the support you can muster.

Just make sure you're both ready to continue sharing information and dealing with questions from the people you tell. Once their curiosity is piqued and their excitement sparked, there's no turning back. (Especially for a first-time grandmother-to-be.)

Handling unsolicited advice about reproduction

You may think you've got a handle on lovemaking, but after you announce to the world that you're trying to have a baby, it may seem like all the folks in your life suddenly morph into Dr. Ruth.

Now that reproduction is fodder for morning news programs and countless blogs and Internet sites, more people have more sound bites and nuggets of wisdom to offer you and your partner than ever before. If your mother tells your partner she shouldn't be eating that grilled hamburger because the *Today* show said so, or telling you that you really should be wearing boxers instead of briefs, you may find yourself at wit's end before you even make it to the bedroom.

If your loved ones start interfering or offering advice that you don't want, thank them for their excitement and interest, but reassure them that you have the situation under control. Remind them that people have been having babies forever and let them know that being bombarded with all this information, be it from them, the TV, or the newspaper, stresses out you and your partner, and that can decrease your chances of conception.

Not all unsolicited advice is about the act of having sex. Some people may think you're too young or too old to have kids. Your parents may chime in about how expensive kids are, implying that you're not financially ready to have a baby. Perhaps your stressed-out brother (and father of three) tells you to enjoy your freedom while you still can.

Whether somebody thinks you're too immature to be a father because you still play Xbox or that your wife's job is too demanding for her to be a mother, remember that the only voices that matter are yours and your partner's.

Part II

Great Expectations: Nine Months and Counting

By Rich Tennant

"We're going to stick to a more traditional name for the baby-'Chuckles,' 'Zippy,' something like that."

In this part...

After you've gotten past conception, a whole new field of emotions, experiences, and concerns pops up. From the sometimes uncomfortable moments of early and late pregnancy to the thrills of hearing the baby's heart-beat and seeing the first ultrasound pictures, pregnancy is a roller coaster ride like no other. This part takes you from the positive pregnancy test to delivery options, covering every aspect of fetal and maternal growth as well as the all-consuming questions of what kind of stroller and car seat to buy.

Chapter 3

Surviving Sudden Doubts and Morning Sickness: The First Trimester

● ●

In This Chapter

▶ Getting the news that your partner is pregnant

▶ Finding a doctor and attending important appointments

▶ Taking a look at fetal growth in early pregnancy

▶ Understanding the complications that can arise

▶ Taking on the role of a supportive partner

● ●

ew new fathers-to-be actually pass out when they get the big news that there's a baby in their future, despite what you see on old television shows. That's not to say you may not feel a bit blown away by the news, though. Whether you've been trying for ten years or just met your partner last month, hearing that you're about to be a dad is life changing.

Early pregnancy is not without its physical, mental, and emotional challenges, and although your partner bears the brunt of it, you can expect to experience a few symptoms, too. In this chapter we tell you what happens in the first few months and help you adjust to one of the biggest events in your life.

Baby on Board: It's Official!

Nothing is more momentous than hearing from your partner, "It's positive! I'm pregnant!" If you've been trying to get pregnant for a while, these words are your cue to breathe a sigh of relief — your boys can swim! In fact, you may feel more relief than excitement at first. Trying to get pregnant can be quite stressful, as we discuss in Chapter 2, and the news that your worst fears can be put aside is reason for relief.

On the other hand, if this was a big "oops" on your part — and many pregnancies are, even in this day and age — your first reaction may be more like, "Oh . . . heck," or worse. Don't feel guilty if your first reaction is negative; most of the world's babies were an "Oh, heck" at one time. In many cases pregnancy takes time to get used to.

Reacting when your partner breaks the news

When your partner tells you the big news, try to mirror her reaction, at least outwardly. If her reaction is, "Oh . . . heck," you can go along in that vein also, at least for a minute or two. Remember, though, that she is gauging your reaction to the news, and if you act like having a baby is a huge imposition in your life, she's going to be really upset, even if she just said the same things five minutes before.

So try to throw in a few encouraging statements about how you wanted kids eventually, having a baby will be fun in the winter when there's nothing else to do, or whatever encouraging babble you can come up with at a stressful time.

Some women get very creative with their announcements, from filling the living room with balloons to baking a cake with a pair of booties inside. Just try to not choke on one, literally or figuratively. If she's gone all out to break the news, you can safely bet that she's really excited, so make sure she knows you feel the same way.

Even if you've been trying to conceive forever, an initial fear reaction isn't uncommon. Remember that your partner may also be feeling some sudden doubts and fears, and allow her to express them. Under no circumstances is "We spent $20,000 for fertility treatments and now you're not sure this is the right time?!" the right response to her feelings of concern.

Making the announcement to friends and family

Deciding when to tell family and friends is tricky. On one hand, telling on the first day of the missed period makes the pregnancy seem about 15 months long, and telling early means you'll need to go through the grief of telling everyone if a miscarriage occurs, which happens in around 20 percent of pregnancies.

On the other hand, you may have told people you're trying, and they may be obsessively counting the minutes until your partner can take a pregnancy test, too. If that's the case, saying, "Gee, we don't know yet; we forgot to do the test" is going to come across as a big insult, and "We've decided not to tell anyone" will probably get you thrown out of the will. If you've been going through fertility treatment, you may feel the need to tell your fertility friends right away, because they know exactly when your embryo transfer and pregnancy test took place.

If you've already had to deal with a miscarriage, you may be understandably more reluctant to tell people in the first trimester. Nearly all miscarriages occur in the first 12 weeks of pregnancy, and most of those occur before 8 weeks, so waiting until you're pretty sure the pregnancy is going well may be prudent.

Whenever and whoever you decide to tell, realize that keeping news this big to yourself is hard. Even if you and your partner make a solemn pact not to tell a soul until after the first ultrasound, don't be shocked and disappointed to find out she's already told her best friend, mother, and entire online support group. In fact, she may have told them before she told *you*. Be understanding, and sheepishly admit you secretly told your parents, the guys at the gym, and half your co-workers, too.

Overcoming your fears of being a father

You have a lot of time to get used to the idea of being a dad, so don't worry if you have a lot of fears at first. Even if you aren't sure you're ready to become a father, you'll be surprised how quickly you come around to the idea. Besides, the baby will be here before you know it, ready or not.

When to tell work

For you, letting your work know that you're a father-to-be may not be such a big deal, because many workplaces still don't have any sort of daddy maternity plan. If yours does, though, let your boss know after the first three months, when you're reasonably sure things will go well with the pregnancy.

If your partner is working and dealing with a lot of nausea or other pregnancy issues, the secret may be out earlier. The boss may not figure it out, but her co-workers may.

It's important, however, to use this time to confront any fears about parenting that you may have. Spend time with the male role models from your past (and present!) and use them as learning tools. Ask them what they did right, what they would change, and what advice they have for you when raising your own child. It may feel like you're the first father ever, but you don't need to reinvent the wheel when it comes to parenting. If you admire someone else's skills, monitor and mimic their behaviors.

Working on overcoming your fatherhood fears is doubly important if the father in your life wasn't the best role model for the type of dad you want to be to your son or daughter. To attempt to come to terms with any wrongdoings your father may have committed, talk with a counselor or therapist, or even a trusted friend, about your relationship with your father and try to identify the mistakes you don't want to repeat. Talking about your experience with your own father can also help heal some of the emotional wounds. Being a father is hard work, and you don't want to wait until after the baby arrives to start overcoming your fears or past traumas.

Finding a Practitioner Who Thinks Like You

When we talk about finding the right medical practitioner, we're not talking personality, although that's important, too. Finding the right pregnancy "partner" primarily means finding someone whose basic philosophies on pregnancy and birth are similar to yours, so that you don't find yourself debating every single pregnancy and birthing decision with your partner's practitioner.

Medical practitioners' views can vary tremendously on every facet of pregnancy, from medication in labor to the vitamins your partner should take, so make sure you're all in agreement on the biggies before signing up for nine months of visits.

Finding a doctor who works for both of you

Finding a medical practitioner who both of you like and trust isn't as easy as looking in the phone book for the first obstetrician listed under *A*. For one thing, many women already see a gynecologist for routine care. However, not all gynecologists deliver babies; as they age, they often choose to stop doing the middle-of–the-night phone calls and races in to the hospital and just do gynecology.

The situation can get sticky if your partner's gynecologist doesn't do OB (obstetrics) but her partners do, and your partner can't stand the gynecologist's partners. Or you're thinking about a hospital birth, but you find out her gynecologist has the highest cesarean section rate in the city. Or, in some cases, you and your partner may opt for a low-tech birth and want to use a midwife for the pregnancy and delivery. If your partner has been seeing her current gynecologist since she was 13, she may be concerned about hurting his feelings by seeing someone else during her pregnancy.

Your partner and you, if you go to the appointments, will be seeing a lot of the person who's going to deliver your baby over the next eight months, so being comfortable with each other is essential. Chapter 8 contains a list of interrogations — err, questions you want to ask your prospective medical partner before planning on spending the most important occasion of your life with her. In addition, keep the following tips in mind:

- **Doctor shopping is not a sin.** Your insurance company may refuse to pay for visits to several doctors, but if you can afford it, you may want to see a few to decide who works best for you. The office mood, the length of time you wait, and the answers you get to your pointed questions can give you a much better idea of who to choose than just going with a friend's recommendation or the information you find on the Internet.

- **Find out where your practitioner delivers.** Next to how much you like your practitioner, how much you like the birthing facility is the most important thing.

- **Ask who covers when your practitioner is off.** Even the best doctors and midwives take vacation and get sick, and getting the partner you really dislike for your delivery can make the birth a bit stressful (although in the end you'll have the same baby you were going to end up with anyway, no matter who delivers him).

- **Discuss birthing options right upfront.** While this conversation may seem premature, the day your partner's water breaks is no time to find out that bed rest–labor induction–epidural and a 50 percent rate of cesarean sections is your practitioner's standard labor plan. Asking about a doctor's rate of cesarean, for example, can give you insight into his practices. Throwing out a few questions about water birth or unmedicated delivery can also allow you to gauge his feelings by his response.

If you want a midwife delivery, you may be extremely limited in choices if you don't live near a large city. Some hospitals have midwives who run clinics but don't do private practice, which may not be what you want. If you can't find a midwife, look for an obstetrician who treats childbirth more like a natural event than a pathology.

While you want to be involved, this is not your show. Let your partner ask the questions and remember that she makes the final decision on who she feels most comfortable spending the next nine months with.

Attending the first of many prenatal visits

Many dads now attend prenatal visits, in stark contrast to the dark ages before 1970 when fathers never went near the obstetricians — or the labor room, either.

This is what you can expect during the first prenatal appointment:

- ✔ **A vaginal exam:** Many guys are not comfortable watching their partner undergo a vaginal exam. Discuss this with your partner before you go, because it will definitely happen.

- ✔ **A pregnancy test:** Blood may be drawn for specific pregnancy levels, or a simple urine test may be done, even if she's already had a positive home test.

- ✔ **Blood tests:** Your partner's blood will be drawn to determine the blood type and check for certain diseases, such as HIV and syphilis, which can impact the baby. A complete blood count, or CBC, to check for anemia will also be done.

- ✔ **Time to talk:** Your practitioner or the ancillary staff will go over the prenatal schedule, prescribe vitamins, and discuss your specific concerns. Because obstetricians, like other doctors, often seem to have one foot out the door even in the middle of important discussions, make sure you pipe up and ask about what's important to you.

The first prenatal appointment is the longest one and is probably the most important one for you to attend, so if you're going to have trouble getting to a lot of appointments, make sure you're at this one if at all possible. The later appointments are often so short you may wonder why she has to go at all, but rest assured that doing a few simple tests can prevent big-time problems.

Going to the first ultrasound

Your partner's practitioner may decide to do an ultrasound in the first few weeks, often as part of the first OB appointment, especially if she has any vaginal bleeding, the time of conception hasn't been determined, or if your partner did fertility treatments. Ultrasounds are done at the doctor's office, hospital, or radiology office. Even though you won't see much, seeing that "something" is in there is still a thrill! If you can get to this appointment, go. You may even get to see the tiny heartbeat flicker if your partner is six-plus weeks pregnant.

Baby's Development during the First Trimester

When the embryo first implants in the uterus, about a week before a menstrual period is missed, it's too small to be seen without a microscope. Within a week, though, the first signs of pregnancy can be seen via vaginal ultrasound. While the embryo still isn't discernable, the gestational sac that surrounds him shows up as a small black dot. From this point on, fetal growth is an astounding miracle.

He may not look like much now, but . . .

In six weeks your baby embryo grows from a ball of cells to a recognizable creature, although the exact species is difficult to define. Following are the changes that occur in the first six weeks of pregnancy, which include the first four weeks, the time from the last menstrual period to the first missed period.

- **Week 2:** Egg and sperm meet, usually in the middle of the fallopian tube. The zygote formed by the union of egg and sperm drifts down to the uterus over several days.

- **Week 3:** Implantation occurs 7 to 12 days after fertilization. There may be a small amount of *implantation bleeding* as the embryo burrows into the uterine lining.

- **Week 4:** The menstrual period is missed. A pregnancy test, which detects minute amounts of *human chorionic gonadoptropin,* or hCG, may be positive as early as week 4. On ultrasound, a small dark spot, the gestational sac, may be seen. The embryonic cells divide into two sections during this week, one that will become the embryo and one that will become the placenta.

- **Week 5:** The yolk sac, which nourishes the embryo before the placenta forms, may be visible next to the gestational sac on ultrasound. The embryo now consists of three layers that will develop into different areas of the body.

✔ **Week 6:** During this week, the embryo looks like a bent-over bean with a slight curve at the end. The heart is still a primitive tube, but a flickering heartbeat can be seen on ultrasound as blood begins to circulate. Arm and leg buds are sprouting, and the eyes, ears, and mouth begin to form, although they're still a long way from a finished product at this point.

Amazing changes in weeks 7 to 12

Although few people would says, "Yes, sir, that's my baby" by week 6, between weeks 7 and 12 the embryo really starts to look human (take a look at Figure 3-1).

✔ **Week 7:** In week 7, the baby is huge — around the size of a blueberry! At least he's something you could see with your own two eyes, and it's a 10,000-times increase over his original size. The brain and the internal organs are all growing, and the arms and legs have primitive hands and feet.

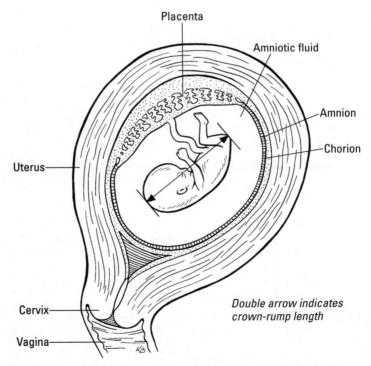

Figure 3-1: By the end of 12 weeks, the fetus actually looks like someone who just may be related to you.

✔ **Week 8:** Fingers and toes start to form, and the nervous system is starting to branch out. Those new limbs are moving, although it will be weeks before your partner can feel movement, even if she swears she's feeling it already.

✔ **Week 9:** The baby's heartbeat may be audible using a Doppler, which amplifies sound. You'll never forget the first time you hear that rapid beat and realize there's a real human attached to it.

✔ **Week 10:** The kid doesn't even have knees yet, and he's already forming teeth in his gums! He does have elbows, though, and knees aren't far behind.

✔ **Week 11:** Your 2-inch bundle of joy is beginning to look like a real miniature person, one who has brand-new fingernails and an admittedly large head.

✔ **Week 12:** The internal organs are growing so much that they protrude into the umbilical cord (they'll start moving back into the abdominal cavity shortly), and the baby is making urine.

Dealing with Possible Complications in the First Trimester

Although the majority of pregnancies really do go like clockwork, things can and do go wrong. In early pregnancy, the biggest threat is that of miscarriage. One in four women has a miscarriage at some point in her reproductive life. Another less common threat is an ectopic pregnancy. We discuss both miscarriages and ectopic pregnancies in this section and provide some tips for coping if you experience either of these complications.

Miscarrying in early pregnancy

Miscarriage is more common as women age, and though you may not consider your partner "old" if she's older than 40, Mother Nature does, at least for childbearing purposes. In fact, doctors used to refer to pregnant women older than 35 as "elderly." The reason that miscarriage increases with age is that her eggs, which have been hanging around since before she was born, have aged, and you can't put face cream on eggs and have them look younger. The good eggs get used up first, so the ones left are more likely to be chromosomally abnormal. Miscarriage rates by age break down like this:

✔ **Under age 35:** 15 percent

✔ **36 to 40:** 17 percent

✔ **41 to 45:** 34 percent

✔ **Older than 45:** 53 percent

Keep in mind that these are averages and that a woman's actual risk depends on many other health factors. These numbers describe the potential risk *after* a pregnancy is diagnosed. Before the first missed period, many pregnancies are lost when they start to implant but then stop growing, usually because they're chromosomally abnormal.

The symptoms of miscarriage are bleeding that becomes heavier over time, passing clots, and abdominal cramping. If your partner is newly pregnant, she may just have what seems like an unusually heavy period around the time of her period or shortly afterward. Pregnancies that end this early are often called *chemical pregnancies*.

Some women have spotty bleeding that isn't continuous, sometimes called a *threatened abortion*. (Abortion is the medical term for a miscarriage.) Some medical personnel still prescribe bed rest for women with spotting, although studies show it really doesn't change the risk of miscarriage.

The overwhelming number of miscarriages are caused by chromosomally abnormal embryos. You and your partner didn't cause the miscarriage, and you couldn't have prevented it. But although miscarriage is a natural event, it's still an emotional loss (to varying degrees for different people) and talking about how you feel is an important part of coping. Allow yourself and your partner to mourn the loss of the baby, no matter how early in the pregnancy it occurs.

Having one or two miscarriages doesn't increase the risk of it happening again, but women with three or more miscarriages should see a fertility specialist to determine the cause, if possible. Following are some of the possible causes of recurrent miscarriage (three or more losses):

✔ **Uterine abnormalities:** Fibroids, polyps, scar tissue, or congenital uterine malformations can prevent the pregnancy from implanting properly in 15 to 20 percent of recurrent miscarriage cases. Surgical correction of the abnormality may help.

✔ **Incompetent cervix:** An incompetent cervix dilates prematurely because it's been weakened by trauma or congenital deformities. Women whose moms took DES to help prevent miscarriage may have incompetent cervices. Miscarriage usually occurs after 12 weeks. Incompetent cervices cause around 5 percent of recurrent miscarriages and can be treated by placing a stitch in the cervix to hold it closed.

- ✔ **Chromosomal abnormalities:** You or your partner may carry genes that are causing recurrent miscarriage. Genetic testing can help determine the cause.

- ✔ **Immune system problems:** Women who have autoimmune disease can have recurrent miscarriages. Treatment with medication may reduce pregnancy loss.

- ✔ **Low progesterone levels:** Sometimes progesterone levels are too low to sustain a pregnancy, and supplementation helps.

After a miscarriage, many women pass all the tissue and need no further medical care. Others need tissue surgically removed so it doesn't cause infection or continued bleeding. This procedure, called a *dilatation and curettage,* or D&C for short, is done as an outpatient procedure.

If your partner passes tissue, be sure to save it and take it to your medical practitioner so she can see that everything's been passed and possibly test to figure out what happened. When cramping intensifies, keep a clean container with a lid in the bathroom so you can collect any tissue as it passes. Take the tissue to your practitioner's office as soon as possible; keep the container in the refrigerator or follow your practitioner's instructions on where to take it if a miscarriage occurs during the weekend.

The miscarriage may be diagnosed afterwards as a *blighted ovum,* a pregnancy where the embryo stops developing and only the placenta grows. Blighted ovum is the most common type of chromosomally abnormal pregnancy. It can't be predicted or prevented; a certain percentage of embryos are chromosomally abnormal, and one blighted ovum doesn't mean problem will recur in the next pregnancy.

Understanding ectopic pregnancy

Sometimes a pregnancy implants in the fallopian tube, or rarely, in another location, such as the ovary, abdominal cavity, or cervix. A pregnancy that implants outside the uterus is called an *ectopic pregnancy.* Ectopic pregnancies are more common in women who have damaged fallopian tubes and occur in 1 in 100 pregnancies.

An ectopic pregnancy usually seems to be developing normally up until around seven weeks. An early pregnancy test is positive, but if an ultrasound is done, nothing shows up in the uterus. If the embryo is in the fallopian tube, the tube may appear distended.

If an ectopic is diagnosed early enough, medication to stop the pregnancy from growing can be given, which saves the tube or other implantation sites from being removed. The products of conception are absorbed naturally and don't need to be surgically removed if the drugs are given early enough and are effective.

Rarely, abdominal pregnancies have continued to the point where the baby reaches viability and can survive after delivery, but such cases are very rare.

When the ectopic pregnancy gets too far along, bleeding starts, and the tube is in danger of rupture. At this point, removal of the fallopian tube is the only way to prevent serious blood loss that may threaten the mother's life. An ectopic pregnancy cannot be removed and replanted elsewhere, so the embryo will be lost.

Signs of ectopic pregnancy in danger of rupture include slight bleeding, abdominal pain on one side, lightheadedness, shoulder pain, or passing out. Ectopic pregnancy is a life-threatening emergency. Get to the hospital immediately!

Coping with pregnancy loss

Losing any pregnancy can be devastating. Many people you tell won't make coping with the loss any easier with comments suggesting it was "for the best" or that "you'll have another one," either. Many people don't really see early pregnancy loss as something to grieve over and may not understand it's hitting you or your partner so hard.

In fact, one of you may not understand why the other is taking it so hard. Whether you're on the same page or not, be respectful of each other's feelings and give yourselves time to grieve. It can be gut-wrenching to attend christenings, family gatherings with lots of kids running around, or children's birthday parties during this time.

Don't try to handle what you're really not up for. If your partner doesn't want to go see your sister's new baby right now, run interference for her. Hopefully your sister will understand that this is a temporary situation, not a permanent rejection of her and your new niece or nephew.

Common First Trimester Discomforts — Yours and Hers

Early pregnancy can be uncomfortable — for both of you. Though your partner bears the brunt of it, the first three months of pregnancy may bring some unwelcome changes into your life as well. Hang in there, though — it'll all be worth it in the end!

Helping your partner cope with the symptoms of early pregnancy

Early pregnancy brings extreme fatigue and the overwhelming desire to take a nap, food cravings, food aversions, nausea, vomiting, and a constant need to urinate. Not to mention hormonal changes that cause pendulum-like mood swings, from crying to euphoria almost before you can ask what's wrong.

Knowing the symptoms ahead of time helps you keep your cool when all around you seems to be falling to pieces. Following are more things you can do to help your partner through these first topsy-turvy months of pregnancy:

- **Let her rest.** Although sitting at home all weekend watching her take two naps a day may not seem like a whole lot of fun, use this time to get projects done around the house or catch up on your parenthood reading.

- **Help her.** Shoulder some of her chores for now, especially the ones that make her nauseated, such as cooking, garbage patrol, dishing out the dog food, and cleaning toilets. Remember that handling cat litter is strictly verboten for pregnant women, so that's your job, too.

- **Accept her limitations.** Maybe you went out to eat several times a week and now the sight of restaurants makes her sick. Hang in there. By the middle trimester she'll be eating everything in sight, and the Szechuan restaurant will still be there.

- **Don't take emotional outbursts seriously.** Not letting her outbursts get to you is hard when they're pointed at you and all your shortcomings, but listen to what she says, accept what may actually be true, and disregard the rest. Don't forget to fix any shortcomings you can, though.

- **Satisfy her cravings.** Not that many pregnant women really want pickles and ice cream, but if your partner does, get some for her. Try not to gag as you watch her eat them; you may have to leave the room yourself.

- **Plan pit stops.** If you're the type of driver who doesn't stop the car unless the road abruptly ends before you reach your destination, realize that pregnant women really do have to pee every five minutes; she's not making up an excuse to go in to the gas station shop for a frozen custard. Also, because blood volume increases during pregnancy, blood clots can develop if she doesn't move her legs regularly. Let the woman get out of the car every few hours!

Getting used to strange new maternal habits

At times, you may look at your partner and wonder who this woman actually is. The sweet-tempered woman you once knew may have been replaced by someone whose head appears to be rotating at times, and the woman who used to party all night long barely makes it into the living room to collapse on the couch after work. You knew having a baby was going to change your life, but you probably didn't expect things to change this much so early in the game.

Take heart: These are temporary changes. After her body adjusts to the new hormone levels, many of the symptoms will decrease, and your original partner will start to emerge again.

In the meantime, some of her new habits may be impacting you in a big way, and you may need to find ways to cope with them. The following sections help you deal with a few of your least favorite early pregnancy things.

Vomiting

Although she's the one vomiting, sometimes you may not be far behind. Many people have a hard time dealing with vomit, whether it's their own or someone else's. If you have a sensitive stomach, hearing her heave may inspire the same reflex in you. Staying supportive while holding on to your own cookies can be difficult. You may want to try the following tips if the sight, sounds, and smell of vomiting are getting to you:

- ✔ **Dab something under your nose that smells good to you.** This really helps. Peppermint oil can get you through some tough moments. Nose plugs may also work, if your partner doesn't take offense at them. She probably doesn't want you to start vomiting too, so she may be okay with them.

- ✔ **Stay cool.** People are less likely to vomit when cool air is blowing on them, so turn the fan all the way up and get a small fan that can blow right on you. This may help keep your partner from vomiting, too.

- ✔ **Avoid trigger foods.** If certain things really get to her, make sure they don't enter your house, no matter how much you crave them.

Gaining weight

While weight gain isn't such a problem during the vomiting weeks, when the nausea ends, your partner may start eating like food is going to be taken off the market next week. This can be bad for her waistline, sure, but it can also be not so good for yours, since you may find yourself overeating just to keep up with her and matching her weight gain pound for pound. The woman who never let a chocolate-covered donut in the house may now be eating them by the cartload.

For both of your sakes, try to put a stop to the madness. You don't have to remind her how hard this weight is going to be to lose later; just talk about your own weight gain and how you're afraid you're not going to play frisbee on the beach with the kid if you keep eating like this. Don't turn into the food police; no one responds well to being told what they should and shouldn't eat.

Even if your pleas for healthier food choices don't get her out of the junk food aisle and back into the vegetable section, force yourself to cut back on the unhealthy foods. She's eating for two, but you aren't, although you may look like you are about halfway through the pregnancy. And, all kidding aside, that extra weight will interfere with your ball-playing and horsey-back-ride abilities down the road.

Coping with your cravings

If an active sex life was part of your semiweekly (or more) agenda, you may be in for a rough few weeks. Sex may be the last thing on her mind in the first trimester. And some types of sex may trigger her gag reflex, which is the last thing you want to associate with a previously enjoyable activity! While turning into a monk may not be on your list of fun things, you can cope with the words "Not tonight, honey" by

- ✔ **Experimenting with touching.** Depending on how open your partner is to experimentation, you can do a lot to pleasure each other that doesn't involve intercourse. In fact, this may be a great time to start understanding your partner sexually more than ever before. Find out what she's up for by taking it slow, working together to find comfortable positions and techniques, and by being supportive if at any moment she needs to stop.

- ✔ **Practicing self-release.** Masturbation isn't something most adults like to talk about, but if you have a voracious sexual appetite and both you and your partner are okay with the idea, there's no shame in taking the matter into your own hands, so to speak.

✔ **Watching her patterns.** If morning sex used to be your thing but her new thing is promptly vomiting every time she wakes up, shake things up. Try to engage in sexual activity at times of day when she's generally not tired, nauseated, or weepy.

✔ **Being flexible — this too shall pass.** Some women are ready for sex sooner than others, and for some, when the sex drive returns, it's strong. It may come and go throughout the day. Be ready to perform when your partner is ready, because the window of opportunity can be slammed shut before you've had a chance to look outside.

A desire to have sex is normal, and becoming frustrated during the time she isn't up for it doesn't make you a pig. Don't push the issue or make your partner feel bad about the lack of sex, but do let her know that you miss being with her and look forward to when she's up for having sex again. In the meantime, work off that extra steam with a nice run or a game of tennis.

Taking on your emerging support role

Don't think of yourself either as your partner's personal assistant or as the pregnancy police. She may become a diva in her pregnancy, but it's not your responsibility to do it all. And try to avoid becoming overprotective of your partner's physical capabilities, especially early in the pregnancy. If everything goes well with the pregnancy, she won't have many restrictions on her activities. But that doesn't mean she's going to be up for taking care of everything she's always managed.

For the first several months — and for the last few — your partner may be too tired/nauseated/hot/and so on to make dinner, walk the dog, or perform many of the household chores you used to split. Pick up the slack until she feels good enough to contribute again. When she's back in the swing of things, she can move around and help again. Physical activity is beneficial for both mom and baby.

One of your main roles is ensuring that she eats healthfully and exercises if and when possible, but the way to do this is by example, not with a whip and chain in hand and bathroom scales placed in front of the refrigerator. Ask her to take walks with you and help by preparing meals that will settle her stomach and feed baby's growing systems.

Pregnancy does not turn your partner into a child, even though she's carrying one around with her. She still gets to make her own choices about what she eats and when, or if, she exercises, and you may have to bite your lip if she starts exceeding the weight limit for your delicate Queen Anne chairs.

In addition to supporting your partner physically, you need to support her emotionally. She will likely be weepier and more sensitive than normal. If you're not the kind of guy who likes to talk about feelings, I suggest you become that guy for a month or so.

As hormones surge and wane, roll with the punches. Let the little things go without a struggle, because your partner won't always be able to control her reactions the way she used to. Let her dictate what's for dinner, and if her stomach turns when you plate the exact dinner she asked for, don't take it personally.

Being a rubber wall isn't easy, but the more you can let things bounce off you, the easier this time is for everyone. Supporting your partner throughout pregnancy is a constant game of choosing your battles and helping her make healthy decisions for her and the baby. Don't tell her what she should do — lead by example. It's good practice for when you have a kid in the house.

Chapter 4

Growing Into the Second Trimester

In This Chapter
▶ Watching baby's growth in the second trimester
▶ Helping your partner through physical and emotional changes
▶ Understanding prenatal ultrasounds and blood tests
▶ Finding a childbirth class that suits your style

*W*elcome to the best three months of pregnancy, for both you and your partner. The second trimester is universally regarded as the "golden era" of pregnancy — she's big enough to look pregnant and not just pudgy, morning sickness is left in the dust, and the aches and pains of late pregnancy are still in the distant future. Enjoy these three months, because the next three will bring much more upheaval into your partner's life — and consequently into yours!

In this chapter we walk you through the garden of the second trimester, with your first exciting look at your baby, finding out the sex (if you want to), and few emotional upheavals.

Tracking Baby's Development during the Second Trimester

By the end of the first trimester, your baby's vital parts are all in place and beginning to perform the functions they'll carry out for the next 80 or so years. By the end of the second trimester, the baby's lungs, one of the slowest organs to mature, are almost capable of supporting life with assistance if he's born very prematurely (23 to 24 weeks is considered the earliest that a fetus can survive if born early). But the lungs aren't the only area experiencing change; every body system is becoming more refined with each passing day.

Growing and changing in months four and five

Even though the basic structures are in place, they undergo further refinement in months four and five:

- **Week 14:** The baby's eyes close for several months while they develop on the inside.

- **Week 15:** Some women may start to feel flutters when the baby moves; many women, especially those in their first pregnancy, don't feel movement for several more weeks.

- **Week 16:** By week 16, hair (including eyebrows) begins to grow.

- **Weeks 17–18:** Air sacs start to form in the lungs, but the lungs won't be able to support life for another six weeks or so.

- **Week 19:** The permanent teeth form in the gums. The baby can swallow.

- **Week 20:** By this week, the midpoint of pregnancy, the fetus is around 6.5 inches long and weighs around 10 ounces.

- **Weeks 21–22:** The fetus now has a functioning tongue! A baby girl's ovaries contain all the eggs she'll ever have in life, around 6 million.

- **Week 23:** The baby can now hear, but more importantly, if born now, she has around a 15 percent chance of survival.

Figure 4-1 gives you an idea of what these changes look like.

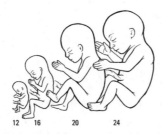

12   16   20   24

Figure 4-1: Months four and five of pregnancy.

Refining touches in the sixth month

The sixth month continues the refining process; all the major components are in place, and all the baby has to do is grow and mature.

- ✔ **Week 24:** Your baby has around a 50 percent chance of survival if born at this point. She now weighs around 1.3 pounds.

- ✔ **Weeks 25–26:** The spinal cord and lungs are forming more completely, and the eyes reopen at last!

- ✔ **Week 27:** At the end of the second trimester, your baby approaches 2 pounds and 14.4 inches. The lungs, spine, and eyes continue their refinement process. Every week increases the odds of survival if born early.

Check out Figure 4-2 to see how much baby has developed by the end of the sixth month.

Figure 4-2: By the end of month six of pregnancy, the fetus is likely to survive if born early.

Checking Out Mom's Development in the Second Trimester

The middle trimester of pregnancy may be the best time of your partner's life: She feels good, looks "cutely" pregnant, and usually enjoys these three months, which means that you get to enjoy them, too! It's also the time when her sex drive may return and the urge to begin getting the home ready for baby kicks in.

During this time, make the most out of your waning days as a twosome. Later in the pregnancy, your partner may not be up for doing as much, and after baby arrives all bets are off. So get out now! Go on dates, take a vacation, or just indulge in all the things that you and your partner enjoy doing one-on-one.

Now also is the time when your partner's body goes through a lot of changes, which means that your support is more important than ever. Giving up her body for a baby isn't easy, and the more you help her deal with the ups and downs of pregnancy, the easier it will be for everyone.

Gaining weight healthfully

One of the most overwhelming concerns for many pregnant women is weight gain: They're afraid they're gaining too much, aren't sure how much they should gain each month, and are desperately afraid that extra weight will be with them for a lifetime.

It's not unusual for dads-to-be to begin packing on the pounds, too. Perhaps you also indulged in your partner's first-trimester cravings. Maybe she wasn't feeling up for those long walks you used to take after dinner so you skipped it, too. If you're gaining right along with her, you may have some concerns in this area, too! The following info may help you help her (and yourself) with weight gain issues:

- ✔ After the first trimester, a weight gain of around a pound a week is considered normal.

- ✔ Total weight gain, on average, should be between 25 to 35 pounds, with underweight women gaining a little more (28 to 40 pounds), and overweight women less (15 to 25 pounds).

- ✔ Pregnant women need only an extra 100 to 300 calories a day.

- ✔ The baby contributes around 8 pounds to the total weight; amniotic fluid, placenta, breast tissue, an increase in uterine muscle each add another 2 to 3 pounds. The rest is stored fat and increased blood, each adding around 4 pounds.

Keeping the emphasis on eating well during pregnancy helps you and your partner ensure that the baby grows well — and that your partner won't end up with 40 extra pounds after the pregnancy. Focus on eating plenty of fresh fruits, vegetables, and healthy protein sources and limiting junk food, rather than focusing on the daily weigh-in numbers. Pregnancy is not the time to keep an obsessive weight chart; even if you fear that she'll never get back to her normal weight, rest assured that she most likely will.

Foods to avoid during pregnancy

In the second trimester, a pregnant woman's first-trimester distaste for food and often decreased appetite seem to vanish in the wind. Your partner may now seem to be chowing down on anything and everything with gusto. Although a healthy appetite is good for her and the baby, pregnant women must avoid certain foods that can be harmful to the growing fetus or to their own health. Some of the listed no-nos aren't good for you, either, so you can stop eating them together.

Mercury can affect fetal brain, nervous system, and visual development. Most fish contain some mercury, but some have very high levels of mercury and should be completely avoided by pregnant women, including the following:

- Grouper
- Mackerel
- Marlin
- Orange roughy
- Shark
- Swordfish
- Tilefish

The following fish also have high amounts of mercury, but fish from this group can be eaten up to three times a month:

- Bluefish
- Halibut
- Lobster (Maine)
- Tuna

Following are some other foods to avoid, or at least limit, during pregnancy:

- **Deli meats:** Deli meats may contain listeria, bacteria that can cross the placenta and cause pregnancy loss.

- **Soft-serve ice cream/frozen yogurt:** Listeria is also the concern here as the machines used to make the equipment can be magnets for bacteria.

- **Imported soft cheeses:** Soft cheeses can also contain listeria if made from unpasteurized milk. Brie, Camembert, feta, Roquefort, and Mexican-style soft cheeses should be avoided unless made from pasteurized milk.

- **Raw eggs:** Raw eggs can contain salmonella, a bacterial infection that can cause severe vomiting and diarrhea.

- **Raw meat:** Raw meat can contain a number of harmful pathogens, including coloform bacteria, salmonella, and toxoplasmosis, which can cause severe fetal complications.

- **Unwashed vegetables:** Unwashed vegetables can also transmit toxoplasmosis as well as salmonella.

Pregnancy is also not a time to lose weight or avoid gaining it, unless she's very overweight and is working with a medical practitioner. If she's really cutting down on food intake, she may need some help dealing with her fear of weight gain. Talk to her medical practitioner about how to handle the issue, because it's a pretty sure bet she'll take her practitioner's advice over yours when talking about weight gain.

And remember, leading by example is always the best option. The healthier you both are during this time, the more likely you are to continue those healthy eating habits after baby comes. Don't wait to start living healthy until baby arrives, because it won't happen. Soon enough, it will be your responsibility to teach your child how to eat as well as you.

Looking pregnant at last!

One annoying aspect of early pregnancy is looking not quite pregnant enough and worrying that you look pudgy instead of pregnant. Thankfully, by the end of the second trimester, most women definitely look pregnant, although if your partner is overweight, it may still be difficult to tell, something that may frustrate her to no end.

The days of voluminous maternity wear are, for the most part, long gone, although most women will invest in a few pairs of maternity pants with an elastic tummy and a few shirts either in a larger size than they normally wear or made of a stretchy fabric. Women who have to dress well for work will probably break down and buy actual maternity clothes so they don't look sloppy if their clothes are just overall too big for them or to avoid the skin-tight "hey, I'm pregnant, look at my belly!" look that may be considered out of place in an office.

Many pregnant women today do accentuate their bellies with tight T-shirts, hip-hugger pants, and two-piece bikinis (not on the streets of Manhattan, hopefully, although stranger things have happened). If you're extremely conservative, the "let-it-all-hang-out" look may bother you.

Approach your partner carefully with any suggestions as to how she should dress in pregnancy. Pregnancy hormones may be under control in this trimester, but they make an immediate reappearance under duress. There's really no nice way to say "I hate the way you're dressed," so you may just need to keep your opinions to yourself.

You can try buying her a few articles of clothing that fit your image of what a well-dressed pregnant woman should wear. She may just wear them, if for no other reason than that she doesn't want to hurt your feelings!

Figure 4-3 shows where the uterus is during the fourth, fifth, and sixth months of pregnancy, as well as where you can expect it to go throughout the rest of the pregnancy. You can see why pregnancy gets really uncomfortable in the third trimester.

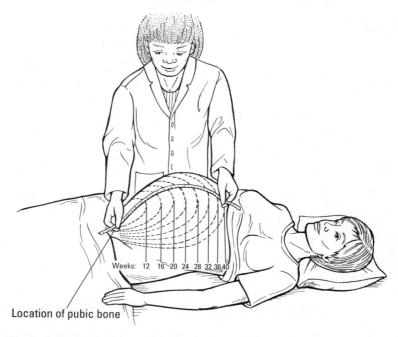

Weeks: 12 16 20 24 28 32 36 40

Location of pubic bone

Figure 4-3: Uterine height changes during pregnancy.

Testing in the Second Trimester

The second trimester is often the time for blood tests and ultrasounds that show the baby's development is on target and no major problems exist. Blood tests to assess the risk of genetic defects are usually done between weeks 11 to 13 or 15 to 20, depending on the tests being done, and screening ultrasounds, which look at the baby's major organs for anomalies and often can determine the baby's sex, are done around week 20.

Some babies are extremely reluctant to show their private parts on ultrasound, so not all parents learn their baby's sex at the first ultrasound, and insurance may not pay for a second without good medical cause. If you can't find out the sex of your child, don't stress about it. Buying gender-neutral clothing and nursery décor is easier than ever. Greens and yellows work for boys and girls, and you'll always have time to add touches of gendered colors after baby comes home.

Preparing for the risks of tests and ultrasounds

Having screening blood work and an ultrasound done bring risks of a kind, as well as benefits. Neither procedure carries any significant physical risk to either mom or baby, but the procedures do carry a risk of finding out that something is wrong with the baby. This is knowledge some parents would rather not have.

Most parents prefer to know if the baby has problems so they can consider their options and prepare for potential difficulties, but others would not consider terminating the pregnancy under any conditions and prefer not to know. This is a personal issue that every parent has to consider for him or herself.

If you are opting not to undergo testing, make sure that your partner's OB/GYN is supportive of that decision. Be upfront about your preferences so that you don't feel pressured by your medical provider down the road. Most midwives will allow you to make special considerations so long as those decisions pose no risk to the baby or mother.

Understanding blood test results

Although some prenatal screening tests are for your partner's overall well-being and check for potentially harmful medical conditions, second-trimester triple- and quadruple-screen blood tests are aimed at determining the risk of genetic anomalies in the fetus.

Also used in conjunction with second-trimester ultrasound, quadruple screens help predict the risk that the fetus has Down syndrome, trisomy 18, or neural tube defects such as spina bifida or anencephaly, where part of the brain is missing.

Quadruple screens test the blood for four things:

- ✔ **Alpha feto-protein, produced by the fetus:** High levels of AFP may indicate neural tube defects, abdominal wall defects, or multiple pregnancy.

- ✔ **hCG, produced by the placenta:** hCG levels may be higher than normal in Down syndrome pregnancies.

- ✔ **Estriol, a form of estrogen made by the placenta and liver of the fetus:** Estriol levels are low in Down syndrome pregnancies.

- ✔ **Inhibin A, produced by the placenta:** Inhibin A levels are elevated in cases of Down syndrome.

Following up on the test results

 Remember that first and second-trimester blood tests are screening tests only. They do not diagnose congenital defects; they only indicate the odds that a congenital defect exists. The risk also varies with maternal age: The older your partner is, the more likely you are to have a child with a genetic defect, although the risk is still low.

If your partner's screening test comes back abnormal, the most important thing to do is stay calm. An abnormal result only indicates a need for further testing. Try hard to keep both of you thinking positive until you have a clear answer on what, if anything, is wrong.

 The March of Dimes reports that 5 percent of screening tests are abnormal, but only 4 to 5 percent of fetuses with abnormal test results actually have Down syndrome. This is a very small percentage, so stay optimistic; the odds are highly in your favor for a good outcome.

In the second trimester, amniocentesis may be done between weeks 15 and 20, when amniotic fluid is easily accessible. A thin needle is inserted into the fluid through the abdominal wall, and the fetal cells in the fluid are analyzed. Amniocentesis comes with a slightly increased risk of miscarriage afterward, so most medical practitioners don't recommend doing an amniocentesis routinely.

Women older than age 35, who have a higher risk of having a child with chromosomal abnormalities, and those with a family history of genetic problems may consider doing amniocentesis, which can determine if chromosomal defects such as Down syndrome, hemophilia, cystic fibrosis, and other genetic disorders are present.

Scrutinizing ultrasounds

As excited as you both are for the first prenatal ultrasound, the actual event can sometimes be a bit of a letdown. Reading ultrasounds is an art, and unless the ultrasonographer is really patient about pointing things out, you may be unsure of whether you're viewing the baby's head or its tush.

Much depends on the direction the baby's facing. You may get a somewhat frightening straight-on face shot, which looks far more like the creature from *Alien* than any relative of yours, or you may get a front-on foot view that looks like nothing more than five round balls. You may be happy to know the baby has five toes on each foot, but that's usually not the main information parents-to-be want. The next section describes what the ultrasonographer is trained to look for.

Measuring growth

First and foremost, your medical practitioner wants to know that the baby is growing as he should. Some of the measurements taken to check for normal growth include

- ✔ **The length of the longest leg bone, called the femur**
- ✔ **The head circumference**
- ✔ **The head diameter, called the biparietal diameter**
- ✔ **The abdominal circumference**

Comparing these measurements to standards assures your practitioner, and you, that the fetus is growing as he should.

Checking for genetic markers

Genetic markers indicate an increased risk of congenital problems, but as with blood tests, genetic markers only indicate the risk potential; they don't diagnose the disease. Some ultrasound markers are known as "soft" markers because they're often misinterpreted and not as diagnostic as other signs. Soft markers may also be transient and no longer seen in later ultrasounds. Following are genetic markers, including soft markers:

- ✔ **Thickness of the skin on the back of the neck:** Called nuchal translucency, thicker-than-normal neck skin indicates an increased risk of Down syndrome.
- ✔ **Cardiac defects:** Around 50 percent of Down syndrome babies have cardiac defects, which may be visible via ultrasound.
- ✔ **Bowel abnormalities:** Around 12 percent of Down syndrome babies have gastrointestinal defects that may also be spotted on ultrasound.
- ✔ **Shortened arm and leg bones:** Children with congenital abnormalities often have arms and legs that are shorter than normal.
- ✔ **Missing nasal bone:** Failure to see the nasal bone or a shortened nasal bone on ultrasound may indicate Down syndrome.
- ✔ **Polyhydramnios:** An increased amount of amniotic fluid may be associated with congenital defects.
- ✔ **Kidney abnormalities:** Dilated kidneys, missing or small kidneys, and other anomalies may indicate genetic disorders.

Determining the sex on ultrasound . . . or not

While the ultrasonographer's priority is looking for information that shows the baby is growing properly, your consuming interest during the first prenatal ultrasound may be the baby's sex.

Ultrasonographers who do prenatal ultrasounds are well versed in not blurting out the sex of the baby and usually ask if you want to know. Most generically use *he* or *she* to avoid calling the baby *it* if you don't want to know, so don't assume anything by the choice of words if you've requested that you not be told. You can feel legitimately concerned if she starts using the term *they,* though!

Ultrasounds are generally not done just to satisfy parental curiosity, but rather to catch any potential problems early on. If the baby's sex can't be determined in the first ultrasound and you absolutely must know in advance, your insurance will likely require you to pay out-of-pocket for another ultrasound.

If you had your heart set on a girl and it's as plain as the nose on your face, even to your untrained eyes, that a little boy is on the way (or vice versa), remember that it's normal and okay to feel a twinge of disappointment. Try to keep it to yourself and concentrate on what you're probably seeing — a healthy, normally developing child.

If one of you really wants to know and the other doesn't, strategize before the appointment so you're not arguing in front of the ultrasonographer. One method of keeping the news to just one person is to have the ultrasonographer write down the sex and put it in an envelope. That way, one of you can look and find out, and the other person doesn't have to.

This tactic also works if neither of you want to know at the moment, but you're concerned that your curiosity may get the better of you later. If you have the answer, you can look at it any time, but you don't have to.

Having Sex in the Second Trimester

For many women, the libido is back on the ascent during the second trimester, which will be a big sigh of relief for any guy who has patiently waited through nausea, exhaustion, discomfort, and a lack of sexual energy for some long-awaited sex. In fact, some women become very sexual during this time because they're flush with hormones and feeling in touch with their bodies.

Maintaining a healthy sex life during pregnancy

Forget what you may have heard — sex during pregnancy is safe as long as your partner is having a normal pregnancy. Her desire to have sex may change by the day due to fluctuating hormones, tiredness, or body aches. She also may struggle with being a sexual being as she transitions into the role of mother.

The most important thing to do is to keep talking about sex. As you get back into the swing of things, be open and honest about what you both need. Explore ways to satisfy each other's romantic and physical needs, even if your partner isn't up for sex.

Don't be surprised if your partner needs to take it slowly in the beginning. Stop at any signs of discomfort. As the baby bump continues to expand, you'll likely find yourselves exploring new positions that offer support for your partner's stomach. Many women are most comfortable on their sides or even up on their knees, and can use pillows for stomach support.

If your partner desires oral sex, it is absolutely safe. Just make sure not to blow air into the vagina because this can cause an embolism, which can be fatal for the baby and the mother-to-be.

Addressing common myths and concerns

We'll just get the myths out of the way right now: Your penis is not long enough to hit or poke the baby during sex. The baby cannot see your penis when you're having sex, and he isn't afraid of your penis during sex. Your semen will not get all over the baby upon completion of sex.

Sex is perfectly healthy during pregnancy. Your baby is protected by an amniotic sac that's sealed tightly by a thick mucus plug, which keeps out foreign and unwanted intruders. In a few instances, however, sex during pregnancy isn't recommended. Talk with your partner's doctor or midwife prior to having sex if your partner has dealt with any of the following issues:

- **Miscarriage:** If your partner has ever had one, or a medical professional has said she is at risk for having one, check before sex.

- **Bleeding:** Sometimes vaginal bleeding ranging from normal to potentially life threatening can occur during the early months of pregnancy. Sex can cause the cervix to bleed, which can be alarming if you're already worried about bleeding.

- **Preterm labor:** If your partner gave birth to a previous child prematurely, get clearance to make sure having sex is safe.

✔ **Leaking amniotic fluid:** Any time amniotic fluid is leaking, the sterile barrier between the baby and the outside world is broken, and infection can enter into the uterus and infect the baby. No sex after her water breaks!

✔ **Placenta previa:** With the placenta close to or overlying the cervix in placenta previa, having sex can cause life-threatening bleeding.

✔ **Weakened cervix:** Sometimes called an *incomplete cervix,* this condition means the cervix dilates before full term, which can lead to miscarriage. A stitch is often placed into the cervix to keep it closed. Sex can cause uterine contractions that disrupt the stitch.

✔ **Pregnant with multiples:** Because multiples often deliver early, you need to avoid anything that can upset the delicate balance between no children and two — or more — children, sex included. Semen contains substances that may bring on labor if the tendency for preterm delivery exists. Besides, your partner probably has enough going on in there already.

A female orgasm during low-risk pregnancy will not cause your partner to go into labor prematurely. Contractions of the uterus associated with sex are not the same as those experienced during labor (and your partner is *very* thankful for this!). However, orgasm achieved by any method can start contractions that can lead to preterm labor in high-risk pregnancy, so put the vibrator away for the duration as well.

Some doctors recommend avoiding sex during the final weeks of pregnancy due to the prostaglandins in semen, which are hormones that can stimulate contractions. On the flipside, if your partner is overdue, your doctor may "prescribe" sex as a means to jump-start the contractions.

Exploring Different Options for Childbirth Classes

Yes, you are expected to attend childbirth classes. The good news is that today's market offers a variety of choices that are welcoming to both mother and father. And they aren't just about learning how to breathe! These classes are an opportunity to ask questions, build confidence, and connect with other couples going through the same experiences you are at the exact same time.

Regardless of the type of class you sign up for, you'll be taught the basics in the following areas:

- ✔ Techniques for coping with labor and delivery pain
- ✔ Your role in assisting your partner
- ✔ What labor feels like/signs of labor
- ✔ When to call your doctor/midwife/doula
- ✔ Choosing the birthing option that's right for you and your partner

Selecting the class that's right for you has a lot to do with the kind of childbirth experience you and your partner want to have. Whatever class option you select, make sure to meet with the instructor prior to signing up (and paying the fee!) to make sure he's the right teacher for your needs. Ask what is covered in the class, how many couples are in the class, where the class is held, and how many weeks the class runs.

Following are the most popular types of classes offered:

- ✔ **Lamaze:** Developed in the 1940s by a French obstetrician, Lamaze focuses on empowering women to be confident in their abilities to birth children. Its teachings are rooted in natural childbirth options, and it follows the philosophy that women shouldn't be required to have routine medical intervention in childbirth.

- ✔ **HypnoBirthing:** Sometimes called the Mongan Method, this class teaches couples how to use relaxation and visualization — self-hypnosis — to have a natural, intervention-free childbirth when possible.

- ✔ **The Bradley Method:** Also focusing on medication-free, natural childbirth, this class focuses on the roles diet and exercise play in childbirth, as well as breathing techniques. Generally includes heavy emphasis on the father's role.

- ✔ **International Childbirth Education Association (ICEA) classes:** Although they don't adhere to a particular philosophy, these classes offer certified instructors. Check with the teacher to find out what to expect.

- ✔ **BirthWorks:** The philosophy of this program is that women instinctively know how to give birth and that they can be empowered to understand their bodies and respond accordingly to their own labor experience.

- ✔ **The Alexander Technique:** These classes focus on utilizing techniques that reduce tension in the body and offer the mother-to-be freedom of movement during childbirth.

Chapter 5

The Fun Stuff: Nesting, Registering, and Naming

In This Chapter

▶ Preparing your home for baby's arrival

▶ Registering for what you really need to survive

▶ Having fun at the shower (if you choose to attend)

▶ Getting your lengthy baby-name list narrowed down to one

As the calendar inches closer to baby's arrival, usually around month five of the pregnancy, many soon-to-be parents get the urge to bring order to the home. What may start as getting the nursery ready often triggers an avalanche of do-it-yourself projects and more items added to the ever-growing registry list.

And to make this whole baby thing even more real, this is the time to think about names. In this chapter we tell you how to get through the planning and preparing without any major blowups.

Preparing the Nursery and Home, or "Nesting"

Put down the twigs and leaves — it's not that kind of nesting. This nesting is all about making the concept of baby a real thing in your everyday life.

Nesting can give you a sense of progress in the seemingly endless pregnancy and serves as the first of many acts of giving and loving that you will show your baby. It can also be a great motivator for finally getting the kitchen cabinets repainted and replacing the broken bathroom tile.

Making the house spic and span — and then some

For many pregnant women, the biological need to nest can be powerful. It can also veer into the seemingly irrational as your partner donates or trashes perfectly good linens, rugs, and towels because they may have unseen germs. Some women even get the urge to grab a toothbrush and some disinfectant and literally scrub the house top-to-bottom. This is perfectly normal.

Try your best to be supportive without breaking the bank on unnecessary purchases. If your towels aren't in need of replacing, suggest having them professionally cleaned instead. Sometimes, however, the best thing to do when your pregnant partner is going through a bout of nesting-induced hysteria is to just let her do it. It's a natural process, and, as with all things, this too shall pass.

However, don't just sit back and watch. She may not ask, but she definitely wants you to help with the cleaning and organizing. Even if you don't think everything she's doing is necessary, she may be unable to see why it's not as important to you as it is to her. Simply ask her how you can help or just join in with the express knowledge that this is a fleeting phase of late pregnancy.

This is also a time when your partner feels the need to launch a new set of rules regarding safety and cleanliness, such as no more shoes in the house or no more dogs allowed on the sofa. If your partner feels very strongly about something you disagree with, work together to find a compromise.

Some pregnant women are so bothered by the idea of pet hair, cat litter, and the suspect grooming habits of animals that they may start talking about re-homing the family pet. As best as you can, try to delay any decision-making regarding your pet's future until after the baby arrives. Hormones change following pregnancy, and the last thing you want is a crying partner feeling guilty about giving up Rover in the heat of the moment. Offer to take over the duties of pet maintenance for the remainder of the pregnancy and reevaluate monthly.

Pregnant women have to be a little more cautious than normal while doing work around the house. Take note of the following household projects and their do's and don'ts:

> ✔ **Painting:** Pregnant women should avoid the urge to paint the nursery — or any wall, for that matter — because among other potentially harmful chemicals, latex paint may contain mercury, and old paint may contain lead; both of which can

cause birth defects. Sanding and breathing in particles are also no-no's. If your partner is going to be around while you coat the walls, make sure the room is well ventilated and that no food or beverages are consumed in the room where you're painting.

✔ **Cleaning:** Using eco-friendly cleaning products is always better, so start during pregnancy. Not only will your partner avoid exposure to harsh chemicals, but you'll already be prepared for the day when baby is crawling around and putting everything in his mouth.

✔ **Lifting:** It's a myth that lifting heavy objects lowers a baby's birth weight or causes birth defects. (Also, raising her hands over her head doesn't cause the baby to become tangled in the umbilical cord.) But a woman's center of gravity changes as her stomach grows and her tendons and ligaments soften. Lifting objects heavier than 25 pounds in the last few months of pregnancy can throw off her balance and result in a fall, so have her leave the heavy lifting to you.

✔ **Pet care:** According to the U.S. Centers for Disease Control & Prevention, pregnant women should not clean a cat's litter box due to the risk of toxoplasmosis, a parasite in cat feces that can cause congenital defects in the baby. To further decrease the chance of toxoplasmosis, make sure you clean the litter box frequently, keep your cats indoors, and avoid adopting new cats during pregnancy.

Setting up the nursery

Fun *should* rule the day when it comes to setting up the nursery, but overanxious parents-to-be often try to tackle too much at once. Begin your nursery designing with a planning session. Draw a bird's-eye floor plan of the room and start filling in the space with all the things you need. Decide the placement of all of the furniture, and before you run out and start buying, measure the allotted spaces to make sure you don't end up with an overstuffed debacle à la the Griswold family Christmas tree.

Clearing and painting the room

Unless you're starting with an empty space, the next step is to empty the room and find a home for all of your displaced things. This chore is the least fun thing to do, but don't put it off. Having an organized room just for your baby will make you feel less anxious about bringing him home.

When the room is empty, painting is a cinch. Since pregnant women shouldn't paint, this is your job. If you don't have the time or desire to paint, find a friend, family member, or local painter to do it for you.

After the room is painted, have the carpets and rugs deep cleaned, or refinish the floors if they need it.

Buying and assembling the furniture

When the paint's dry and the floors are ready, it's all about shopping and assembly.

Budget some alone time for assembly if possible. Cribs often come with instructions that seem to be written in Swahili, and they don't just pop together. They're solidly constructed, which is good for baby's safety but bad for your frustration threshold. Take your time and figure on spending a few hours on assembly. Lay out all of the parts and read through the instructions (yes, actually read through the instructions!).

Most of today's instructions offer picture-only guidance, which can be quite vague and frustrating. If you can't understand what you should do based on the company's illustrations, don't just do what you think should be done. Take the time to call. Not only is the safety of your child at stake, but your warranty, too!

Assemble the crib in the nursery because many cribs are too wide to fit through doorways, and won't you be frustrated if you have to take it apart and do it all over again!

Opinions differ on bumper pads, the quilted bands that are strung around the bottom of the crib. The Canadian government discourages their use due to the chance of suffocation, and a 2007 study in the *Journal of Pediatrics* determined them to be unsafe. Others believe that with the use of a crib positioner, which keeps baby sleeping on his back, bumper pads cause little increased risk.

Whether or not it's worth the risk is up to you and your partner, but it is a risk. If you use bumpers, make sure you remove them if you notice your baby creeping toward the bumper in his sleep. Another option is to use mesh bumpers, which are not padded but do offer a breathable barrier between baby and the crib's slats.

Some parents opt to use cosleepers, which are small, three-sided cribs that butt up to your bed, keeping the baby very close at hand. This arrangement is ideal for late-night feedings but less ideal when considering the amount of your personal space you have to sacrifice.

Arranging the nursery for two or more

Not all nurseries accommodate just one little baby. Whether welcoming multiples or adding a second child into a preexisting nursery, creating a space that works for more than one takes a little extra effort.

Multiples

The only real challenge in accommodating multiples is making room for them to sleep. Changing tables, dressers, and closets can easily be shared when you invest in closet organizing systems to allow more items to be stored in less space.

For twins, some people opt to use a single crib with a crib divider that literally splits the bed down the middle. It's great for space-limited parents, and research shows that twins sleep better when placed near one another as they were in utero. However, crib dividers are a short-term solution because as the babies grow, each needs more space.

If money and space allow, you have many options for twin cribs that are smaller versions of full-sized units and are generally built side-by-side. And if you're having more than two, you may want to look into bunked cribs, which offer an individual space for each baby. Most are not notably stylish, but if you're having more than two babies, stylish cribs are probably the least of your worries.

Separate-birth siblings

If you're going to have an older child cede space to the newborn, the situation won't be all that different from having multiples. Most of your work concerns organization and maximizing storage space with closet organizing systems, baskets, and bins. However, investing in a cosleeper (a three-sided crib that attaches to the side of your bed) or a portable crib can be a lifesaver when the older child and the baby aren't on the same sleep schedules. And if your older child is still a baby, it also allows for a secure place for the older child when you're tending to the newborn.

Baby-proofing 101

You have some time before baby starts getting into things, but that doesn't mean that the nesting period isn't the perfect time to baby-proof. In fact, doing it early allows you plenty of time to adjust to the complicated life of cabinet locks, outlet covers, and doorknob locks.

To make sure your baby's safe, take the following precautions:

✔ Get down on the floor, look at the room from baby's level, and clear all potential hazards.

✔ Install rubber stoppers at the top of doors to keep baby's fingers from being pinched.

✔ Remove rubber tips from doorstoppers at floor level because they're choking hazards.

✔ Install mesh baby gates in dangerous locations.

✔ Plug in outlet covers on all outlets below waist level.

✔ Install cabinet locks.

✔ Add a toilet-lid lock.

✔ Make sure all rugs and mats have slip-proof pads underneath.

✔ Add foam coverings to the edges and sides of sharp furniture.

✔ Apply doorknob covers to keep toddlers from being able to open doors.

✔ Find an out-of-reach location for pet supplies and the cat litter box.

✔ Remove any toxic plants or chemicals that are within baby's reach.

✔ Cover the bathtub waterspout with a plastic cover to avoid head injury.

✔ Put your trash cans in an inaccessible place — to baby, not to you.

✔ Keep bags and purses off the floor.

Monitoring options

Baby monitors have come a long way in the past few years. Your options range from hi-def, flat-screen video units to the classic walkie-talkie-like models. If you live in a larger home, a video monitor may make more sense to save you a lot of trips to the nursery to check on noises. Even in smaller homes, it can be useful to have a video screen to check if that little noise was a minor disturbance or something requiring your immediate attention.

Regardless of your choice, make sure that the unit you purchase can effectively communicate at the distance between the nursery and the other rooms of your home. Many monitors now can transmit up to 400 feet.

When in doubt, move it or remove it. Get into the habit of looking for small items on the floor, closing doors, putting the toilet seat down, and putting all potential choking hazards out of baby's reach. After years of not having to think about where you throw your keys, retraining your brain takes a while, so start now.

Understanding the Art of the Baby Registry

If the mere suggestion of free stuff has you lacing up your sneakers to run out to the nearest baby goods store, slow down. Registering isn't as easy as it sounds. Babies need a lot of gear, but they don't need everything, so you need to think through your particular wants, needs, and style before you point the scanner and click.

When you get into the store, registering can be an overwhelming, almost paralyzing experience. Some parents-to-be first realize how unprepared to care for baby they feel when forced to choose between different styles of bottles, diapers, and baby monitors. Some couples enter panic mode and just start registering for one of everything because they feel like their baby *might* need it.

You only get free stuff once, so be sure to make the most of it by getting prepared before you register. The more online research you do about the differences between various products, the more competent and confident you will begin to feel about your parenting duties to come. Registering is the perfect opportunity to familiarize yourself with exactly what it takes to raise a baby.

Doing your homework ahead of time to get exactly what you want

When it comes time to register, everyone who has been a parent will tell you the things that you won't be able to live without. In truth, you *have* to have very few items in order to raise a baby, but a lot of modern inventions can make raising a baby easier.

First, consider your space. If your nursery is too small to fit an entire bedroom set and a glider, you and your partner need to prioritize. The size of the room helps dictate the size and number of items you can add to it, as well as the style of crib, dresser, changing table, curtains, and every other accoutrement you can imagine. If a rocking chair is the one thing you must have, plan the rest of the room around that to make sure you have enough space.

Register for the essentials first and don't make your registry too long, or you run the risk of not getting everything you need. Also, don't register for too many clothes, because although clothes are necessary, everyone will want to buy clothes first, and you may not get other more vital things. People often throw in an outfit along with whatever registry gift they purchase, anyway.

Spend time thinking about how you're going to use your stroller. If you're a runner, do your homework about the best running stroller for you and try them at the store. If you live in a city, make sure the stroller is durable enough to handle bumpy, uneven sidewalks, but not too big to make you the enemy of your fellow pedestrians. If you drive a lot, make sure the stroller folds up small enough to fit in your car and still leave room for shopping bags.

And before you register for anything, check safety ratings and parent reviews online. Visit Consumer Reports' baby section (`www.consumerreports.org/cro/babies-kids/index.htm`) for recalls and safety information.

Finding out what you need — and what you think you won't need but can't live without!

When you've never before had to care for a baby, knowing what you need — and how many of each thing — is nearly impossible. Use the basic checklist in this section as your guide.

A system for travel

Travel systems that offer a compatible stroller, infant car seat, and car seat base in one package are a popular option for new parents. If you're on a tight budget, a travel system is an ideal solution to get everything you need for less than $200. However, many are quite bulky, and the included strollers generally aren't top-of-the-line quality.

Travel systems come in many styles, so start by picking the car seat of your choice. Make sure it has a five-point harness system and that it's the appropriate size for your vehicle. Consider the size of the stroller, too, and make sure it fits comfortably in your trunk. Make sure to collapse the stroller in the store before you buy it to see how small (or big) it is when not in use.

Note: We don't mention certain items, such as a high chair, jumpers, and play mats, because you don't need them right away. However, if you have room to store them, pick the ones you want and register for them. Remember, though, that when you meet your baby and get to know him, your idea of what he might like may change. The play gym you picked out before you met him may not really suit him. It's kind of like signing him up for college before he's born; you may think Harvard is the best, but he may not like it.

Following are the items you absolutely must include on your registry (in our opinion, at least).

Sleeping and changing essentials:

✔ Cradle/bassinet/cosleeper/crib

✔ Two to four fitted sheets

✔ Crib mattress

✔ Two to four swaddling blankets

✔ Nursery monitor

✔ Changing table or station

✔ Two to three changing pad covers

Furniture:

✔ Nursery seating

✔ Baskets/bins for closet organization

Clothing:

✔ Eight to ten onesies

✔ Six pairs of socks

✔ Three to six newborn hats

✔ Four to six warm, footed pajamas

✔ Two to six bibs

✔ Six to eight burp cloths

✔ Hangers

Toiletries:

✔ Diapers (As many as you have room to store!)

✔ Wipes

- Diaper cream
- Baby powder
- Baby shampoo
- Baby lotion
- Infant manicure set
- All-natural hand sanitizer

Just in case:

- Digital thermometer
- Dye-free infant Tylenol
- Dye-free gas relief drops
- First-aid kit

On-the-go goodies:

- Infant car seat
- Stroller
- Backseat mirror
- Car window sun shades
- Diaper bag
- Portable baby wipe container
- Travel-size hand sanitizer

Feeding:

- High-quality breast pump (if breast-feeding)
- Milk storage bags (if breast-feeding)
- Nursing pads (if breast-feeding)
- Boppy support pillow
- Lanolin and/or gel nursing pads
- Bottle brush
- Bottle drying rack
- One each of six different kinds of BPA-free bottles
- Four nipples for each type of bottle

Not all babies take to every type bottle; you may end up trying many different brands before you find the right one. Avoid registering for too many of the same brand in case your baby refuses to use them. You can always return any unopened bottles and nipples if your baby takes to the first or second brand you try.

Discovering five things you don't have to have but will adore

Yes, some things are luxuries, but they can become necessities if you use them every day and they save your sanity. These five items may well fit into your "don't need it, gotta have it" category:

✔ **Ergonomic bouncy chair:** Not all bouncy chairs are created equal. Finding one that sits baby upright (great for gas relief) and allows him to grow with the chair will save you down the road — but not upfront. A bouncy chair is a perfect sanity-saver for the shower-starved parent and a great place for naps and playtime for baby.

✔ **Hands-free baby carrier:** Whether in a sling, a front carrier, or a pouch, carrying your baby in a hands-free carrier allows you to get work done around the house and move about more freely. Most babies love the body-to-body contact. Make sure to try them on first to make sure the carrier you're getting fits your body.

Recent recalls of baby slings have called their safety into question, so make sure you get a model that keeps the baby upright and able to breathe freely. When a baby slumps in a curled position, her airway can be compressed.

✔ **Snap-and-go stroller:** This stroller provides only the skeleton of a traditional stroller with no seat. Instead, it has bars for a car seat to snap into, as well as a bottom basket. Infants aren't in the bucket-style car seat for very long, which makes the idea of having a second dedicated stroller seem a bit extravagant. But it's the smallest stroller on the market, which makes it ideal for car travel and easy use. You literally snap the car seat into the stroller and you're ready to roll.

✔ **Wipe warmer:** This may seem unnecessary, and in reality, it probably is. A lot of babies, however, cry less during diaper changes when the cold, wet wipe straight from the package is replaced by the warm, cozy wipe straight from the warmer. It also helps keep the wipes from drying out when accidentally left open.

✔ **Yoga ball:** All babies are gassy, and nothing helps get the gas out better than bouncing. Save your legs and back a lot of undue stress by sitting on a yoga ball and bouncing the burps right out of your baby. It's also a great alternative to a nursery chair for those with space limitations and a great late-term pregnancy chair for the woman who can't get comfortable.

Checking out five things you don't have to have and will never adore

Some things, luxurious or otherwise, are just downright unnecessary. Especially the items that don't actually make a new parent's life any easier. Here are five things you should consider omitting from your registry:

- ✔ **Baby DVDs/CDs:** Before your child has the ability to ask for the latest Jonas Brothers album/Baby Einstein DVD to be played ad nauseum, why on earth would you voluntarily spend your time engaging with this entertainment? Babies shouldn't be watching TV, and your child will be just as happy listening to music from your collection.

- ✔ **Crib mobile:** It only takes one time of knocking into a crib mobile while putting your sleeping baby down to realize that it's more of a nuisance than it's worth. Instead, opt for a natural sounds teddy bear or other system that attaches to the side of the crib.

- ✔ **Infant shoes:** If your child gestates for 18 months and comes out walking as nimbly as a newborn horse, you will need lots of for fancy footwear. For the rest of you, forgo the shoes. Most babies are annoyed by socks, let alone shoes, and for the most part, babies under the age of 6 months will spend most of the time in sleepers with attached feet.

- ✔ **Car-charger bottle warmer:** If your baby is breastfed, the milk will most likely be frozen or straight from mom, and the warmer won't help. If your child is formula fed, you will be making bottles as needed. Either way, how often will you need warm milk in the car? Most babies will be just as happy with room-temperature milk. Unless you plan on using it for your coffee, skip this one!

- ✔ **Baby bathtub:** Why exactly does your baby need a smaller version of the same device you already have in your home? Many parents opt to bathe with newborns and most others use a clean sink in lieu of the tub. As baby grows, your existing tub will work just as well. Besides, it's not like you're going to give baby his bath-time privacy while you read *Sports Illustrated* on the back patio.

Surviving the Baby Shower

These days, baby showers often aren't just for the mom-to-be and the other women in your life. If you want to be involved, by all means, tell the people planning your shower that you want it to be a unisex affair. If you don't want to attend, that's okay, too, as long as your partner is fine with that decision. Deciding how much you want to be involved is up to you and your partner, but don't forget that the more involved you are on the front end, the more connected to and involved with that baby you will be down the road.

Traditional showers are female-centric and a bit on the cheesy side. Men often don't go because they aren't really welcome. So if you don't want to spend an afternoon sniffing diapers filled with melted candy bars, let the planners know what kind of shower you and your partner desire. It can be anything from a lunch at a nice restaurant to a traditional streamers-and-balloons affair and anything in between.

If you opt to have a coed shower, make sure that everything about the event is inclusive to people of both sexes. Here are some simple ideas to make your shower welcoming to all:

- ✔ Send invitations that are gender neutral.

- ✔ Invite all of the fathers you know to ensure there are more men than just you at the shower.

- ✔ Pick a fun, unique setting or theme, such as a park or a back-yard barbeque.

- ✔ Plan some separate men-only and women-only activities.

- ✔ Open gifts with your partner. It's awkward to send her up there alone and for you not to be part of the fun.

- ✔ Set up an assembly station where the new gifts can be put together after they are opened (this idea works best if you have the shower at your home).

- ✔ Play a creative game, such as constructing babies out of clay or holding a diapering competition to see who can wipe, powder, and diaper a doll the fastest.

- ✔ Have guests write down a funny story from their childhoods and then try to match the guest to the story.

Naming Your Baby

When people find out you're having a baby, the first thing they ask is, "Is it a boy or a girl?" Question number two is inevitably, "Do you have names picked out?"

Choosing a name for your baby is one of the most fun and most challenging decisions you'll ever make in your entire life. Soon-to-be parents spend hours upon hours combing through books and Web sites, searching for the perfect name and making lists of their top choices. And with so many options, the list can easily become mind-numbingly long and a point of contention. Getting two people to agree on the same first and middle name for a baby can devolve from a congenial conversation into something resembling a Congressional hearing.

The following section helps you and your partner choose the perfect name for your baby with as little stress as possible.

Narrowing down your long list

Just like a to-do list at work or that never-ending list of weekend projects you've been meaning to tackle for years, a long list of baby names will only distract and overwhelm you. Keeping the list at a reasonable length makes you more likely to engage in a meaningful conversation about the names that truly are in play.

Remember that you're not really choosing between 30 names. Just because you really like all of them doesn't mean you don't like some more than others — you just may not realize it yet. Stop trying to choose between Evan, Graham, Dexter, and Jude all at the same time. Instead, pit two names against each other at a time and choose one. It's like filling out your March Madness bracket; you don't pick the champion without first picking the winners of the early rounds. This tactic allows you to begin crossing some names off the list while continually pitting new names against the winner of the previous round.

At this point, you and your partner shouldn't take the opinions of others into consideration. The name is your choice, and unless you're ready to justify your choices, get frustrated with other people's input, and stand up in the face of criticism, keep the contenders to yourselves until you've made a final choice.

Reconciling father/mother differences of opinion

In a perfect world, your favorite name is also your partner's top choice. The chances of that happening, however, are slim to none. When differences of opinion arise, don't get defensive. Be able to articulate why you like the name, and even do your research about the history of the name, the name's popularity, and any family history regarding the name.

If your partner still doesn't like it, or you don't like a name she adores, allow each other absolute veto power. With so many names from which to choose, don't waste your time fighting a losing battle. And besides, do you really want your partner to cave in and name your child something she despises?

For more background information on baby names, check out the following resources:

✔ **Social Security Administration's Popular Baby Names** (www. ssa.gov/OACT/babynames): For some people, the relative popularity of a name can have a huge impact on the decision-making process. The SSA provides a comprehensive look at the top 1,000 names from 1880 to the present year and can help you keep your kid from being one of 17 others in her kindergarten class with the same name — if that's important to you.

✔ **The Baby Name Wizard** (www.babynamewizard.com): This interactive site takes the info from the SSA site, pumps it into an innovative chart and provides site-user input about how names are perceived, an encyclopedia-like "Namipedia" entry for each name, and a "Namemapper" that charts the popularity of names by state.

✔ **Baby Names Country** (www.babynamescountry.com): This site is an exhaustive resource for unique baby names and their meanings from around the world.

✔ **Baby Namer** (www.babynamer.com): An encyclopedic reference of names that allows you to create a digital list as you find names, as well as offering similar names, famous people with the same name, and possible drawbacks of using the name, including bad nicknames.

Discussing choices with friends and family

If you think it's hard talking about names between the two of you, just wait until your loved ones start offering their two cents' worth. No matter what name you choose — be it classic, modern, or something in between — someone you know is going to tell you she doesn't like it. You'll probably hear it from multiple people, friends and strangers alike.

Don't feel the need to defend your choice. In fact, the more you defend it, the more likely the person is to continue to challenge you on your choice. Instead, focus on why you chose that name and don't be afraid to let other people know the matter is not up for debate. A playfully delivered, "I guess it's a good thing this is my baby and not yours" can put them in their place without too many hurt feelings.

Even after the baby is born, the name will be under scrutiny. From co-workers to cashiers at the supermarket, everyone will inquire about your baby's name, and you'll be confronted with a variety of reactions. Remember that everyone has his own association with the name of your child, but at the end of the day, your only association with the perfect name you choose will be the perfect baby on whom you bestow that name.

Some people are reluctant to share baby names with others for fear that they may get "stolen" by another friend or family member. If your partner has this concern and you do not, be very careful about sharing the name you choose. Though you may think it's silly, she won't take it lightly.

Chapter 6

Expecting the Unexpected

In This Chapter

▶ Handling maternal medical issues

▶ Dealing with difficult ultrasound discoveries

▶ Knowing what to expect if baby comes early

▶ Managing multiples

▶ Resolving money matters without panicking

*Y*ou may assume that things will go off without a hitch during pregnancy and childbirth, but the fact is that many pregnancies experience some sort of complication. Complications may be related to your partner's health, the baby's well-being, or to the pregnancy itself. Some complications are relatively minor, but others can pose a serious threat.

In this chapter we look at some of the things that can go wrong in pregnancy and guide you through to supporting your partner while dealing with your own fears.

Managing Pregnancy-Related Medical Issues

Problems that affect your partner's health sometimes develop with frightening speed. Other times problems develop insidiously and build to a crisis point. Neither is easy for a dad-to-be to deal with, especially when you have to keep your own fears under control so you can help your partner deal with hers. We take a look at some of the most common maternal pregnancy problems in the next sections.

Pregnancy-induced hypertension

Pregnancy-induced hypertension, often called PIH, is a newer term for elevated blood pressure in pregnant women. It is closely related to a long recognized disease, *preeclampsia,* also called *toxemia.* PIH is elevated blood pressure that develops in 5 to 8 percent of women after the 20th week of pregnancy. The signs of PIH are hypertension, retained fluid in the face and extremities, and protein in the urine.

Your partner is more likely to develop PIH if:

- ✔ This is her first pregnancy.
- ✔ She's older than 40.
- ✔ She had high blood pressure before she got pregnant.

PIH is dangerous because it reduces blood flow to the baby and also to the mom's major organs, including the liver, kidneys, and brain. In severe cases of PIH, decreased blood flow to the baby can cause *intrauterine growth retardation,* known as IUGR, which means low birth weight or stillbirth. Your partner may experience

- ✔ Severe headaches
- ✔ Blurred vision
- ✔ Light sensitivity
- ✔ Abdominal pain
- ✔ Decreased urine output

New onset of any of these symptoms requires a call to your medical practitioner. Women with PIH often end up on modified or complete bed rest (see the section "Mandatory bed rest") or may at least have to stop working or work a reduced schedule. Resting on the left side increases blood flow through the placenta, and decreasing sodium intake can help lower blood pressure. Blood pressure medications may be prescribed if pressure rises too high. She will probably need more frequent doctor visits and possibly more frequent ultrasounds to check on the baby's well-being.

Rarely, women with PIH need hospitalization to control the symptoms and decrease the chance of eclampsia, which is severe PIH with seizures. Eclampsia can be life threatening for your partner and the baby and may require immediate delivery even if the baby is premature. Part of your job is to watch for changes in your partner's mental status, such as confusion, irritability, or disorientation, because these changes may precede a seizure.

Gestational diabetes

Gestational diabetes, high blood sugar that develops during pregnancy and disappears after delivery, affects 2 to 5 percent of pregnancies. Glucose testing for gestational diabetes is normally done in the second trimester. Women who are diagnosed may be treated with insulin injections to lower blood-sugar levels.

The problem with high blood sugar in pregnancy is that it affects the baby, who will also develop high blood-sugar levels. Gestational diabetes can affect the baby (and you) in several ways:

- ✔ The baby may grow larger than normal, which can make for a difficult delivery and increase the chance of a cesarean delivery.

- ✔ Babies whose moms have gestational diabetes are more likely to be born early and can have a severe and potentially dangerous drop in blood-sugar levels after the delivery.

- ✔ The baby may have to be monitored in the neonatal unit for a short time until his blood sugars stabilize, which is probably not the way you envisioned your time in the hospital.

If your partner is older than 35, is overweight, or has a family history of diabetes, she's more likely to develop gestational diabetes. Studies indicate that gestational diabetes is often a sign that she may develop type 2 diabetes later in life.

The introductions of daily injections and monitoring can add a whole layer of annoyance to pregnancy, for both you and your partner. If she cooks, her cooking will probably become a whole lot healthier, which you may or may not appreciate. If you're the chef, you may be expected to devise a new repertoire of healthy yet appealing meals. The bonus is that you both probably will be healthier by the end of pregnancy if you follow her new diet.

Placenta previa

Placenta previa is a condition in which the placenta implants too low on the uterine wall (see Figure 6-1). Usually the placenta, which transports nutrients to the baby, implants near the top of the uterus. If too low, all or part of the placenta can cover the opening to the uterus, the cervix, and cause bleeding.

Bleeding from placenta previa is painless, can happen without warning, and can be severe enough to require immediate delivery. A known placenta previa can necessitate bed rest and possibly a prolonged hospital stay to try and hold off delivery until the baby is less premature.

A marginal placenta previa, one that's near but not covering the cervix, may allow for a vaginal delivery, but most of the time a cesarean will need to be done. And sex is out of the question, since anything that causes contractions or any cervical movement can start heavy bleeding. Your partner is more likely to have a previa if

> ✔ She's had a previous cesarean delivery.
>
> ✔ She's older than 35.
>
> ✔ She smokes.
>
> ✔ She's of Asian descent.
>
> ✔ She's having more than one baby.

Mandatory bed rest

If your partner has a risk of early delivery or other problems, your medical practitioner may put her on bed rest. Bed rest can mean anything from not going to work and taking it easy to not getting out of bed at all, even to go to the bathroom, depending on the seriousness of the medical condition.

Having your partner on bed rest is difficult for both of you. However, if bed rest is advised, take it seriously. Bed rest brings its own risks, mostly the risk of blood clots from inactivity, so doctors don't suggest it lightly.

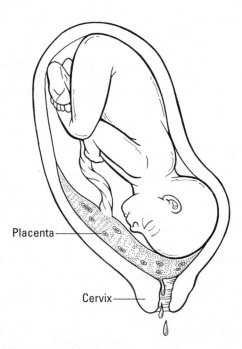

Placenta

Cervix

Figure 6-1: Placenta previa.

And while bed rest may sound like fun, especially if you're running around trying to cook, clean, take the dog out, run errands, and set up the nursery, trust us, she's not happy that she's unable to help put away the freshly washed baby clothes and hang the pictures on the wall.

Setting up a bed rest station

Your bedroom may not contain all the elements needed to entertain a sometimes bored, often dejected woman who's just itching to get up and paint the nursery. But any space can be turned into a home inside your home, or inside the hospital, if necessary. Make sure her living space has all the following comforts:

✔ **A method of communication:** Unless your house is really small, yelling back and forth isn't the best method of communication. Walkie-talkies are great, and cellphones work too.

✔ **A table to hold food and drink:** A drawer for snacks means she won't have to call for help every time she's hungry, and a cooler filled with drinks by the bed also gives her a little independence. Some tables fit over the bed, but a table next to the bed works fine, too.

✔ **Entertainment:** A TV, reading material, cards, games, puzzles, and a computer all help pass the time.

✔ **Extra pillows:** Spending time in bed is really hard on your back, especially when you're pregnant! Invest in extra pillows to facilitate position changes. And take the Star Wars pillowcase off, too; give her something pretty and cheerful.

✔ **Space to work and something to do:** No, she can't load the dishwasher from the bed, but she'd probably love to fold baby clothes!

✔ **Pen and paper for shopping ideas and other thoughts:** She may see something on TV or think of something she'd like to try for dinner, so give her a way to write down ideas as they come to her.

✔ **Exercise ideas:** Even if she can't run around the bed, she needs to keep the blood flowing to prevent blood clots in the legs. Depending on what her doctor says is okay, encourage position changes, ankle circles, and calf flexes several times a day. Discourage a cross-legged position, which decreases blood flow.

✔ **Venting room:** In this context, *venting* has nothing to do with fresh air and everything to do with letting her get frustrations off her chest. Constant negativity should be discouraged, but frustrated people need to express their aggravation, and better she vents to you than to her doctor — or her mother! So be available to her, not only just to keep her company, but also to let her vent when she needs to.

Many women on prolonged bed rest get depressed, especially if they have to stay in the hospital rather than at home. Make sure to keep her in the loop of baby stuff; if it's okay with her doctor, have friends visit regularly. You can even suggest that her baby shower be held while she's on bed rest, to give her something to look forward to. (See the sidebar "Setting up a bed rest station" for more ideas on helping her through the restrictions of bed rest.)

Her job is vital, though, and it's simple — stay put so the baby stays put for as long as possible. So make her feel like she's pulling her weight, because she is. In case you've never noticed until now, women often feel guilty even when they have no reason to. If your partner has to worry about how all the extra work is affecting you, she won't be resting peacefully, and staying calm and relaxed is essential on bed rest.

Handling Abnormal Ultrasounds

Many couples don't really relax about a pregnancy until they see the baby on ultrasound. But some couples don't come away from the ultrasound appointment with reassuring news. While ultrasounds aren't perfect and can miss some abnormalities, they recognize many problems.

In most pregnancies the ultrasound isn't done until the second trimester, usually around 18 weeks. By this time all the major structures of the baby are in place and can be evaluated. Ultrasounds may be done earlier if your partner is bleeding or if her doctor has any other concerns about the pregnancy. If your medical practitioner sees anything suspicious on ultrasound, she may schedule a level 2 ultrasound, which is done in the same way as a regular ultrasound but takes a more detailed look at the fetus.

Always research your insurance company's policy on ultrasounds during pregnancy, because some may not cover routine ultrasounds or repeat ultrasounds done just to find out the baby's sex. Knowing what's covered and what isn't prevents shocks to your pocketbook when an unexpected bill arrives in the mail.

Birth defects

Hearing that your baby has a problem is devastating. Even if a birth defect is minor, you or your partner may mourn the loss of the "perfect child." This reaction is normal, and neither of you should feel guilty. If a serious defect is found, you'll need to make decisions together about what to do.

Following are some of the most common birth defects in the United States, according to the March of Dimes:

- ✔ **Heart defects:** 1 in 115 births

- ✔ **Musculoskeletal defects:** 1 in 130 births

- ✔ **Club foot:** 1 in 735 births

- ✔ **Down syndrome:** 1 in 900 births; risk increases with age of mother

- ✔ **Spina bifida (abnormal opening in the spine):** 1 in 2,000 births

- ✔ **Anencephaly (lack of part of the brain):** 1 in 8,000 births

The most important thing to do when you get bad news is to find out exactly what you're dealing with. You may need to see a perinatologist, a doctor who specializes in complicated pregnancies, and possibly a genetic counselor.

You and your partner may not be on the same page when it comes to making decisions about birth defects. One of you may be more optimistic about the situation and the other more pessimistic. Your feelings will be a jumble, and emotions will run high. Try to support your partner in whatever she's feeling, but don't discount your own feelings and grief, and don't feel like you can't let your feelings show. No one expects you to be emotionless at a time like this, and crying with your partner can be a bonding experience.

Expect to go through the five stages of grief: denial, anger, bargaining, depression, and acceptance. Getting to acceptance can take a long time and a lot of anger. Give yourself the time you need.

Talking to someone outside the situation who listens and doesn't tell you what to do, like a friend, religious advisor, or relative, can be a godsend. And most important of all, don't play the blame game. Congenital birth defects are rarely anyone's fault.

Fetal demise

Even more devastating than the discovery of birth defects on routine ultrasound is the discovery of a fetal demise. The term *fetal demise* is usually used to describe the death of the fetus in utero after 20 weeks. There are many potential causes of fetal demise, and few if any can be anticipated or avoided.

Fetal demise may be discovered because the baby doesn't seem to be moving much, bleeding starts, or amniotic fluid begins to leak, but it can also be found during a routine gynecological check up. Fetal demise occurs in 6.8 per 1,000 pregnancies overall.

Most fetuses are delivered vaginally after labor induction. Parents are encouraged to hold their baby and give him a name, but at no time will this be forced on you if you don't feel it's the right thing for you to do. Your partner will be given medication to dry up her milk supply and will be put in a room off the maternity floor in most hospitals. Most hospitals will let her go home as soon as she's physically stable.

In many cases parents are better able to get though a fetal demise if they know exactly why it occurred, but sometimes the reason isn't obvious. Not knowing why can be very difficult. Again, blame has no place in the aftermath of a fetal demise.

Preparing Yourself for Preterm Labor and Delivery

More than 12 percent of all deliveries in the United States are preterm, which means they occur before 37 weeks. Of those:

- ✔ 70 percent are born between 34 and 36 weeks.
- ✔ 12 percent are born between 32 and 34 weeks.
- ✔ 10 percent are born between 28 and 31 weeks.
- ✔ 6 percent are born before 28 weeks.

The chances of delivering a very small preemie are low. Babies born between 28 weeks and term may require prolonged hospital stays, but most ultimately do well.

Recognizing the risks of preterm delivery

Many preterm deliveries occur without any known cause, but in a good percentage of cases, doctors can pinpoint the reason. The following situations all increase the risk of preterm delivery:

- ✔ **Structural abnormalities:** An abnormally shaped uterus or an *incompetent cervix,* one that starts to dilate from the increase uterine weight, can cause labor.
- ✔ **Multiple birth:** A large percentage of twin, triplets, and other multiples deliver before 37 weeks.

✔ **Infections:** Urinary tract infections can start uterine contractions if not promptly treated.

✔ **Hypertension:** High blood pressure can reduce blood flow through the placenta to the baby, causing poor growth that may necessitate early induced delivery.

✔ **DES exposure:** Diethylstilbestrol (DES) was a drug given to millions of women to prevent miscarriage between 1938 and 1971. Women whose mothers took the drug may have structural abnormalities that cause preterm delivery.

Handling feelings of guilt

Guilt is common after a preterm delivery, just as it is after any other setback in pregnancy. Again, don't get caught up in what you and your partner could have done to prevent it, or whose fault it is that you went for that long walk the day before the delivery. Even if one of you did something foolish, rehashing it now is pointless.

Put your energies into working with your partner to help your baby get healthy as quickly as possible. Visit often, and if support groups are available, get involved; studies show that parents involved in support groups have less anxiety, anger, and depression.

Navigating the NICU

The neonatal intensive care unit (NICU) is like nothing you've ever seen before. Although hospitals put more emphasis than they used to on keeping NICUs quiet and more like the womb, they are, by necessity, fairly noisy, with alarms going off, lights on day and night so hospital personnel can see what they're doing, and at the center of it all, your little baby. She may be hooked up to just a single monitor, or perhaps so laden down with medical equipment and IV lines that you can scarcely find the baby, as shown in Figure 6-2.

The best way to deal with the NICU is to focus on your little part of the world. Get to know your baby's nurses, and stay near your own baby's isolette. Asking what's wrong with other babies is really bad etiquette, and the nurses won't (or shouldn't) tell you, anyway.

Preterm babies are often moved from the hospital where they're born to a level 3 nursery, a nursery with advanced technology to handle complicated preterm issues. This can make your life complicated, especially if the new hospital is some distance from your house, but your baby's care is ultimately worth it.

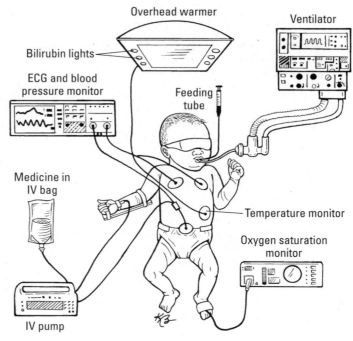

Figure 6-2: A preemie baby in the NICU.

Some hospitals with large regional NICUs have facilities that allow parents to stay overnight for a small charge or for free. Ronald McDonald houses are examples of facilities available near some hospitals.

If your partner is still in the hospital and can't see the baby right away, make sure you take lots of pictures, not just of the baby, but also of the neonatal unit and, if possible, of the people taking care of her. This way she can get a real sense of where the baby is and picture her in an actual place.

Some regional NICUs provide video feed to community hospitals so that moms who are separated from their babies can still maintain a connection until they have a chance to see the baby in person.

Expect the first time you hold your baby to be extremely awkward; she may be festooned in IV lines, and you'll probably be scared to death of her. Don't worry; it gets easier with time. She'll have less equipment attached, and you'll get to be a pro at dealing with dangling wires.

Knowing what to expect with a preemie

Preemies don't exactly look like the babies you have pictured in your mind, especially if they weigh less than 5 pounds. If your baby is born before 35 weeks, this is what she may look like:

- ✔ **Skinny:** Babies born before 35 weeks often don't have a good layer of fat.

- ✔ **Big eyed:** The lack of fat in her face gives your preemie a wide-eyed look.

- ✔ **Thin skinned:** The blood vessels are more visible in a preemie's skin.

- ✔ **Hairy — except on her head:** Preemies often are still covered with *lanugo,* a fine downy hair that helps keep her warm before she develops enough subcutaneous (under-the-skin) fat. Babies born before 26 weeks, on the other hand, may have no hair anywhere, and may have very red, gelatinous looking skin.

- ✔ **Boys may have underdeveloped genitalia:** Don't worry, dad — they'll grow.

If you think the baby looks really odd, check with the nurses for reassurance that everything's okay, but not within your partner's earshot. No matter what she looks like, she's going to think she's the most beautiful person on the planet.

Parents often have a sixth sense or are just more observant of the little changes in their babies and may notice a change in their baby's condition before the staff does. Don't be afraid to speak up if you feel something's not right!

Clarifying common problems

Premature babies often have respiratory problems because their lungs aren't well developed. Artificial ventilation may be started almost immediately and will gradually be decreased as the baby tolerates the decrease in extra oxygen. Some babies need special types of ventilation to overcome resistance in their lungs.

Most premature babies have feeding problems. Tiny babies, under 28 weeks, may not be fed by mouth for weeks or months, because their digestive systems are too immature to handle food. Intravenous feeding is given instead, and as the baby grows, tube feeding is started. Nippling is begun very slowly, because it can tire a preemie and use up her energy stores.

Many babies grow very slowly in the NICU. Infections, stress, and any number of complication can slow growth. Reading the weight chart and seeing the weight increase by a few grams can be the highlight of a NICU parent's day.

Learning the ropes — er, wires

Sometimes knowing what's what when it comes to the wires and machines attached to your baby can calm your anxiety. Your average preemie may sport the following wires and attachments.

Breathing apparatus

If the baby can't breathe on his own, he may be attached to a ventilator via a tube that goes through his mouth or nose down to his lungs, which delivers a certain number of breaths per minute, or to nasal prongs, which deliver extra oxygen to his lungs via — naturally — prongs that fit into his nose. Try very hard not to do anything that may dislodge the breathing tubes.

Monitoring equipment

Since preemies have an unfortunate habit of forgetting to breathe, often even babies who don't need breathing equipment are hooked up to a monitor that flashes a series of incomprehensible numbers, some with little flashing hearts next to them. The monitor is attached to the baby by wires that lead from the baby's chest, and possibly also from his hand or foot, or even from his umbilical cord if a line was placed there right after birth.

The machines monitor pulse (that's the flashing heart), respiration, (the number of times the baby breathes each minute), and oxygenation levels. Preemie heart rates are from 110 to 160 beats per minute, on average. Respirations are 40 to 60 per minute. Oxygenation in the 90s is good. Blood pressure may also be continuously monitored in very sick babies.

The baby's temperature may also be monitored frequently, if not continuously. Because preemies have little in the way of fat stores, they get cold easily, and stress and the extra work of being sick and trying to grow can use up energy that may otherwise help keep them warm. The incubator or bed the baby's laying on also has its own thermometer to make sure it doesn't get too hot or too cold.

Intravenous lines

Most NICU babies receive intravenous medications and nourishment, at least at first. IV lines can be very precarious in preemies and need to be replaced frequently. The medications infused are sometimes hard on the veins, which "blow," necessitating a new IV. The NICU nurses don't do it on purpose, believe us; spending time putting a new IV in a preemie is rarely on the "fun things to do in the NICU" list.

If your baby has an umbilical line, he may not have a peripheral line (a line in the extremities or head), but umbilical lines can't be used for very long because they're a potential source of infection.

Preparing for preemie setbacks

Just when you think things are finally moving in the right direction, your preemie may get sick. Because preemies have decreased ability to fight off infection, and because they're attached to invasive equipment that can serve as a portal into the body, infections are very common among preemies. Some common NICU complications include the following:

- ✔ **Respiratory infection:** The tubes allow entry of germs into the lungs; pneumonia may develop and need antibiotic treatment.

- ✔ **Respiratory disease:** Long-term ventilation can save your baby's life but can also contribute to bronchopulmonary dysplasia, damage to the lungs that can take months or years to fully heal. This problem is more common in tiny babies known as micropreemies. Some babies with respiratory disease are discharged to home while still receiving oxygen, which is decreased gradually as they develop the ability to breathe better on their own.

- ✔ **Necrotizing enterocolitis:** Called *NEC* by the NICU staff, this inflammation of the immature digestive system usually occurs after feedings are started. NEC can seriously damage the intestines. Feedings are temporarily stopped so the gut can heal, and IV feedings are given instead.

- ✔ **Intraventricular hemorrhage (IVH):** IVH is a bleed into the brain that can range from mild (graded I) to very serious (graded IV). Around a third of babies born between 24 and 26 weeks have a bleed, but any baby born before 34 weeks can have an IVH. Bleeds may occur at the time of delivery or afterward.

Taking baby home

Preterm babies don't always have to stay in the hospital until they reach their original due date, and they don't always have to weigh 5 pounds before being discharged, either. NICUs generally assess the baby's condition, the parent's ability to handle possible problems, and the parent's willingness to learn the baby's care so they can do it at home.

Many parents take home babies who are still being tube fed or who are on monitors to make sure they keep breathing. Others don't feel at all comfortable with technical equipment and would rather have their child in the hospital for a little longer to be monitored. In fact, feeling completely unprepared to take home a preemie who has spent weeks or months in the NICU is very common.

 If you or your partner starts to go into panic mode about homecoming, get involved with a preemie support group if you haven't already. Knowing that other families have done this and the whole family has survived is very reassuring. And seeing a former 2-pounder tooling around the block on his bike is the best possible assurance that most preemies come through their early trauma just fine.

Seriously, going home with the inept pair of you is not the worst thing your baby will have to face in life, so just do it. Keep that NICU number on speed dial for a while, though!

Hi, Baby Baby Baby: Having Multiples

The birth rate of twins, triplets, and more has exploded with the advent of in vitro fertilization (IVF) and other advanced reproductive technology. Seventeen percent of twins and 40 percent of triplet births are results of infertility treatment. In 2006 the multiple-birth statistics in the United States broke down as follows:

- ✔ Twin births occurred in 3,200 per 100,000 deliveries.
- ✔ Triplets comprised 143 per 100,000 births.
- ✔ Quadruplets occurred in 9.89 of 100,000 births.

 If you're expecting multiples, find a support group pronto. Not only are they a great source for used twin or triplet baby paraphernalia, which can be extremely expensive, but they're also a source of a lot of practical info on how to handle more than one baby.

Multiple identities: What multiples are and who has them

Although infertility treatments are the largest risk factor for multiples, you're more likely to have multiples if

✔ **Your partner is black.** Black women have the highest natural twinning rate of the different racial groups; Asian women have the lowest.

✔ **Your partner is older than 35.** Twins occur naturally around 3 percent of the time in women 25 to 29, and 5 percent of the time in women 35 to 39.

✔ **Fraternal twins (nonidentical) run in her family.** Your family history doesn't seem to have any bearing on the statistics. If she's a fraternal twin, she has a 1 in 17 chance of having fraternal twins.

Twins can be either fraternal or identical. Fraternal twins are created from two different eggs and are no more similar than any other two siblings. Identical twins are the result of one embryo splitting into two at a very early stage of development. Siamese twins, also called conjoined twins, are always identical twins who didn't completely split as embryos. Conjoined twins are usually identified on ultrasound before delivery.

Obviously, boy-girl twins are always fraternal, but if you have two of the same sex, it may be difficult to tell at first whether they're identical or fraternal. The majority of twins, especially twins from IVF cycles, are fraternal, although IVF also increases the risk of having identical twins. DNA testing is the only definite way to determine if twins are identical or fraternal, although sometimes it's obvious twins are fraternal, if they look quite different.

Many IVF parents who implanted only two embryos have been surprised to find themselves carrying three fetuses. If this happens to you, don't accuse the doctor of putting in an extra embryo he had lying around! What happened was that one of the embryos split into identical twins.

Health risks for mom

All the usual pregnancy complaints are intensified during a multiple pregnancy. Annoying issues such as morning sickness, weight gain, heartburn, constipation, shortness of breath (especially on any type of exertion), urinary problems, and hemorrhoids are all likely to be magnified.

Many of the health risks of pregnancy for your partner increase with the number of fetuses she's carrying. Multiple pregnancies are more often medically complicated by:

✔ **Gestational diabetes:** The increased placental size and hormone production may raise the risk of gestational diabetes in multiple pregnancies.

- **Pregnancy-induced hypertension:** High blood pressure after 20 weeks of pregnancy. One in three mothers of multiples develops PIH.

- **Anemia:** Maternal low red blood cell count.

- **Hemorrhage:** Severe blood loss at the time of delivery.

- **Placental abruption:** Women with multiples are three times more likely to have the placenta come off the uterine wall prematurely, possibly resulting in severe hemorrhage.

- **Cesarean deliveries:** Cesarean deliveries are pretty much a given in higher order multiple births because it's unlikely all the babies will be head down, and high order multiples are so small that even if they're all head down before birth, one or more are very likely to flip as soon as the first baby is delivered and the rest have more room, possibly necessitating an emergency cesarean.

For high-order multiples (triplets or more), bed rest during pregnancy is very likely.

Risks for the babies

Twins are five times more likely than single babies to have problems at birth or to die before or soon after delivery. Multiple pregnancies often deliver early, since the womb has less room for all the occupants, and preterm babies are known to have more complications, so these factors account for some but not all of the risks multiples face. Statistics show that

- Approximately 60 percent of twins deliver before 37 weeks.

- Thirty-six percent of triplets deliver before 32 weeks.

- Eighty percent of quads and more deliver before 32 weeks.

Twins are also more likely to have the following complications:

- Twin-to-twin transfusion syndrome can occur only in identical twins who share the same placenta. One twin receives too much blood, the other too little. Both can cause problems.

- Birth defects such as cerebral palsy are much more common in multiples, and the risk increases with the number of fetuses.

- Cord accidents can occur, such as knots in the cord or entanglement in a cord. Cord accidents reduce blood flow to the fetus. Identical twins, who develop in one amniotic sac, are more likely to become entangled in their own or their twin's cord.

Your medical practitioner may well suggest that you deliver at a medi-cal center equipped for high-risk births, but if she doesn't, you should still plan to do so. Knowing that your babies will have all the techno-logical advances that may be needed in place from the moment of delivery can really reduce the stress you and your partner feel.

Babies can be transported, if necessary, but it's stressful for the babies and for the parents. And if one baby is transported and the other isn't, you'll be trying to split your visiting time between two hospitals, which is unnecessarily stress inducing.

Keeping Cool in Monetary Emergencies

Not all pregnancy emergencies involve medical crises: Some are all about cold, hard cash, or the lack of it. You may have taken a quick glance at your health insurance policy before you got pregnant, just to make sure you had the sterling coverage you thought you had, and you may have even checked the limits of coverage, with-out ever dreaming that you might rack up a hospital bill of more than a million dollars for one little baby.

Worse, you may have let your policy lapse just before getting pregnant — surprise! With unemployment around 10 percent in 2010, many people have no insurance coverage.

It's possible (probable, even, if you're normally a healthy two-some) that you have no idea what your insurance actually covers. Take time to dig through the drawers and find that policy, because pregnancy illnesses and hospitalization costs can blow your socks off. Many hospitals today have counselors who help educate you on your fiscal responsibilities before they let you walk out the door, but it's nice to know your coverage ahead of time.

If you find yourself without insurance or with minimal coverage, ask your healthcare provider or your local hospital about your options sooner rather than later, so you know ahead of time what your options are. Community resources are likely available to help with prenatal care or baby's care if you are experiencing financial hardship, and you may get the most benefit from them if you look into these resources ahead of time.

Checking out your insurance limits

Most insurance policies have their limits clearly listed, includ-ing an amount listed as a lifetime benefit. Insurance policies also may list your maximum obligation, or deductible, for the year; for example, you may have a yearly cap of $5,000 on your out-of-pocket expenses for a year, meaning your insurance company pays everything else. However, you may have to pay every penny of your deductible before benefits kick in.

Covering the cost of unexpected medical expenses

Even the best insurance plans leave you footing a certain portion of the medical expenses. Over the next six months, don't be surprised to receive separate bills from every wing and department of the hospital in which you stayed.

A 2001 study reported that as many as one third of bankruptcies are related to medical debt. Even if you have insurance, using up your limits can leave you with a hefty bill. Most hospitals have a social worker or debt counselor who will work with you on bills that result from being underinsured or if you have no insurance. Most have debt repayment plans, and many will reduce the bill in some circumstances.

You may be able to get some aid from the hospital's charity program or, if your child has an unusual medical condition, from a foundation involved in the disease.

 The main thing to do when faced with a bill that equals the national debt is not to panic. You have options, and you need to investigate them. You also need to be upfront with the hospital from the beginning about your coverage, so you have time to resolve things before the hospital threatens to hold your partner or baby hostage. (Don't worry, they won't.)

 Parents of newborn baby girls have been charged for circumcisions — mistakes happen, and they can be difficult to find. At the grocery store, you may not be overly pleased if your receipt only listed your total charge and not each item individually, but that will be the case with your hospital bills. If at any point your bill doesn't make sense — or it seems like you are paying for the same thing twice or for something you didn't receive — ask your hospital's billing department for an itemized receipt. It will be a lengthy document to comb through, but it allows you to challenge mistakes and suspect charges, and it may save you money.

Chapter 7

In the Home Stretch: The Third Trimester

In This Chapter

▶ Seeing how baby gets ready for delivery in the third trimester

▶ Putting on weight and dealing with hormones: Mom's last three months

▶ Understanding your insurance benefits

▶ Choosing a pediatrician early

*T*he last three months of pregnancy are when reality hits like a ton of bricks and you and your partner realize, albeit still rather dimly, that a real baby is coming to live with you. A baby with her own personality, a separate person who is developing definite likes and dislikes even before birth and will be able to express them even when she can't say a word.

In the third trimester, all the major organs and appendages are in place, and all the baby has to do is grow. Mom is also doing her own growing, with an attendant list of common discomforts and complaints that you'll become well acquainted with. In this chapter we look at baby's growth, mom's growth, and your part in dealing with your family's expansion.

Tracking Baby's Development during the Third Trimester

At the start of the third trimester, your baby is fully formed, although you wouldn't think so if you got a look inside the womb. The eyes are still fused, the skin is gelatinous, and the body fat is nonexistent, but everything that the baby needs to develop into a normal newborn is present and accounted for. The following sections provide the highlights of fetal development in the last three months of pregnancy.

Adding pounds and maturing in the seventh and eighth months

Week 27 starts off the final trimester of pregnancy, and don't think your partner will let you forget for one minute that she's been hauling this child around for six months already. While week 27 marks the beginning of the end of a full-term pregnancy, it also marks the end of the "easy" trimester.

So if you thought you heard lots of complaints in months four, five and six, you ain't seen nothin' yet! And her complaints are justified. The baby grows from around 10 inches long and 1.5 pounds at week 27 to around 18 inches long and 4 to 6 pounds by week 36. That's a lot of growth in just nine weeks, and your partner will be feeling it.

In the seventh and eighth months, the baby develops in the following ways:

- ✔ **Fully develops the lung tissue necessary to breathe outside the womb:** By 36 weeks, most babies can breathe independently without oxygen supplementation.

- ✔ **Matures the digestive tract and kidneys:** The ability to breathe, suck, swallow, and eliminate in tandem is essential for life outside the uterus.

- ✔ **Begins to see:** The eyes open around week 31, and the baby begins to perceive light and darkness.

- ✔ **Jumps in response to loud noises and recognizes familiar voices:** Go ahead, talk just to him — he'll turn toward your voice after he's born if he's familiar with it, and "Honey, get me a beer" aren't the only sounds you want him to associate with you.

- ✔ **Puts on some fat:** Your baby gains weight in these nine weeks (and so does your partner) because the baby is both growing and developing fat stores to help him regulate his temperature after birth.

Figure 7-1 shows the development of your baby in these final weeks.

Getting everything in place in the ninth month

The ninth month is the home stretch. In these four weeks the baby assumes the head-down position for good — at least you hope she does. After 36 weeks, she's usually too big to go flipping around, although some babies do manage to turn themselves right-side up, which, for birthing purposes, is upside down, or *breech*. (See Chapter 9 for more about breech deliveries.)

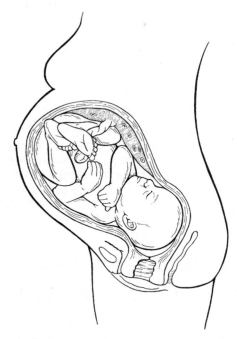

Figure 7-1: The fetus looks more and more like a fully developed person in the third trimester.

Your baby doesn't have much left to do in the last four weeks but grow and perfect already-in-place systems. In the last month, your baby will:

- ✔ **Have descended testicles, if he's a boy:** Earlier in pregnancy, the testicles develop in the abdomen and descend gradually into the groin before assuming their final position outside the body. Boys whose testicles don't descend by the time of birth are evaluated periodically. Surgery may be required if they don't descend by a certain age because the increased body temperature can damage reproductive organs in males.

- ✔ **Start to develop wake-sleep patterns:** Most babies seem to be more active at night, which may give you some idea of what you're in for.

- ✔ **Shed body hair and gain some head hair:** Lanugo, the soft downy hair that covers the fetus earlier in pregnancy, starts to disappear. Hair on the head may be abundant or nonexistent.

Dark-skinned babies often have more hair at birth than future blondies.

✔ **Swallow amniotic fluid, urinate, and practice breathing:** Babies get ready to eat by swallowing amniotic fluid, which also gives the kidneys practice in elimination as urine is excreted into the amniotic fluid.

✔ **Be active:** Some babies are thumb suckers even before birth. She may yawn, grimace, and grab the umbilical cord in her hand. Kicking gets harder as space becomes tighter, and she's likely to stay in position — hopefully head down — without turning during the last month.

✔ **Drop lower into the pelvis:** In anticipation of labor, the baby may drop down so that her head is pressing more directly on the cervix. This pressure helps thin and dilate the cervix, and also helps prevent the umbilical cord from falling below her head if your partner's water breaks, a dangerous situation known as a cord prolapse. (See Chapter 9 for more about cord prolapse.)

Finding Out What Mom Goes Through in the Third Trimester

The baby isn't the only one who changes in these final months, of course. Although your partner's changes on the outside are obvious, if somewhat unnerving at times (Can she really get any bigger than this? Won't her skin break apart?), the changes on the inside are just as dramatic, if not more so.

Getting acquainted with your "new" partner, now known as mother-to-be-with-a-vengeance, can be as complicated as getting to know the baby after he's born. Keep in mind at all times that she's going though physical and emotional upheavals the likes of which you will never be able to fathom, but you need to try.

Understanding your partner's physical changes

A pregnant woman at the end of the second trimester still looks pretty much like her normal self. Your partner may not even be wearing maternity clothes at this point, letting large shirts (yours, probably) and pants a size or two larger than her normal size cover her cute little belly. All that changes in the third trimester for most women, although some lucky women never look all that pregnant, even when delivering 8-pound babies.

Between the seventh and ninth months, expect these changes in your partner's physique and physical condition:

- ✔ **The uterus can be felt** a few inches above her belly button at the start of the third trimester, and up under her ribs by the end.

- ✔ **Legs cramps** occur because of nerve compression by the growing uterus.

- ✔ **Backache** is common because of the strain from the additional weight in front.

- ✔ **Constipation and hemorrhoids** can occur due to sluggish, compressed bowels. Pain and rectal bleeding can accompany hemorrhoids. Stool softeners and lots of roughage can help.

- ✔ **Urination** becomes almost a full-time job. She may need to get up in the night to urinate.

- ✔ **Varicose veins** may pop out on her legs; they may itch or ache. Spider veins, small broken capillaries, may also occur on her face, neck, and arms.

- ✔ **Itchy skin** is a huge problem for some pregnant women in the third trimester. Creams help keep the skin moisturized and decrease itching.

- ✔ **Heartburn** becomes more severe, but despite old wives tales, it's in no way related to the amount of hair the baby will have!

- ✔ **Feet and ankles often swell,** especially if you're having a summer baby. Encourage her to rest with feet up as much as possible.

- ✔ **Her center of gravity shifts,** making falls more likely. Hide her high heels and, if she'll let you, take her arm when walking, like a proper gentleman.

- ✔ **Shortness of breath comes with exertion,** because the baby is pressing on her lungs. When the baby drops, she may feel relief, but the tradeoff is increased frequency of urination.

- ✔ **She may have trouble sleeping,** even though she's always tired. Try tying a 6-pound, baby-shaped weight to your abdomen and you'll quickly understand why.

- ✔ **Breasts may start leaking** a few drops of colostrum, the first fluids produced after birth. They may also look humongous, since they contain around 2 pounds of extra weight — each!

- ✔ **Vaginal discharge increases,** so expect the reappearance of sanitary pads in the linen closet.

- ✔ **Interest in sex** may be at either extreme; it may be the last thing she's interested in, or one of the things that interests her most. Hormones are funny that way. (See Chapter 4 for more about sex during pregnancy.)

Contractions may also begin to occur on and off, starting first with Braxton-Hicks contractions, which don't change the cervix and are felt mostly in the front of the abdomen rather than in the back.

As the due date approaches, more contractions may come and go, usually with just enough frequency to have you leaping for the suitcase and putting it in the car before they peter out. Don't worry, the real thing will start soon enough!

Heeding warning signs

Though many complaints of late pregnancy are normal and expected, some are not. Make sure your partner contacts her medical provider if she experiences any of the following symptoms:

- **Vaginal bleeding:** In the last few weeks of the pregnancy, her doctor should be told about any type or amount of bleeding, with the exception of *bloody show* (blood-tinged mucus). Bleeding can indicate a placental detachment, called a placental abruption, or placenta previa, a low-lying placenta. (See Chapter 6 for more about both conditions.)

- **A sudden severe headache:** Strong headaches can be a sign of preeclampsia. (See Chapter 6 for more on the risks of preeclampsia.)

- **Severe abdominal pain:** This can be a sign of placental abruption, the premature separation of the placenta from the uterine wall, which can be life threatening for mother and baby.

- **Swelling of her face, hands, and feet:** Some swelling at the end of pregnancy is normal, but facial swelling can also be a sign of preeclampsia, especially if accompanied by sudden weight gain, headache, or a rise in blood pressure.

- **Leaking fluid:** This symptom usually indicates the bag of waters has broken. This is normal at the end of pregnancy, but not in the seventh or eighth month. Always call if she notices more discharge than normal or is leaking fluid. After the water breaks, the baby is more susceptible to infection because its protective sac is breached. If labor doesn't begin with 24 hours, her medical practitioner may consider inducing labor.

Bracing for your partner's emotional changes

Hormone levels are very high in the last few months of pregnancy, and, for many women, with hormones come mood swings. Be prepared for the following emotional changes in the last trimester:

- ✔ **Irritability:** When you don't feel your best physically, every-thing irritates you. Try not to be one of the "everythings" that drives her crazy.

- ✔ **Weepiness:** Women find many reasons to cry in the last few months of pregnancy. They cry because they're happy, or sad, or frustrated, or angry. They cry for reasons they can't even express to you, which can, of course, be frustrating to you, but you'll get over it.

- ✔ **Self-image issues:** Pregnancy changes a woman's body image, sometimes for the better, sometimes not. Some women resent the loss of the perfect figure, while others are happy that pregnancy provides an excuse for the extra weight that's always bugged them. Expect to hear her make negative com-ments, and don't respond to them in kind. The answer to "Do I look fat?" is never "Yes."

Some degree of moodiness, sadness, or depression is normal, but mood changes in late pregnancy should be fleeting, not permanent. As many as 10 percent of women become clinically depressed during pregnancy and need medical intervention, and up to 20 per-cent develop some depressive symptoms that may also need medi-cal treatment.

Symptoms of clinical depression include sadness that doesn't lift, feelings of hopelessness or guilt, difficulty sleeping, constant fatigue, or behavior not typical for her. Don't ignore depression that seems extreme or that doesn't lift after a few days. (See Chapter 12 for more on depression after pregnancy.)

Pregnant dad symptoms: Couvade syndrome

In the past few years, some attention and study has been given to the idea that expectant dads may develop symptoms similar to those of their partners. This phenomenon, known as *couvade syndrome,* may affect as many as 90 percent of dads-to-be. Weight gain, nausea, backache, and other pregnancy symptoms may be experienced by dad as a psychological or physical reaction to his own weight gain, which may be due to eating more from stress or just from keeping up with his partner. Whatever the reason, rest assured in the third trimester that if you have "pregnancy pains," they too will soon be coming to an end.

Antidepressant medications can be given in pregnancy if her medical practitioner feels the benefits outweigh the risks. Because certain antidepressant known as *selective seratonin reuptake inhibitors* may increase the risk of heart defects, respiratory problems, low muscle tone, irritability, and eating difficulties in the newborn, the Food and Drug Administration issued a warning about the use of SSRIs in pregnancy in 2004.

Sympathizing with her desire to have this over, already

Around the seventh month, many women start expressing a strong desire to have this pregnancy over and done with. Before you jump in with long-winded explanations of how the baby isn't fully developed yet, it's too early, and other pompous statements about why being pregnant for just two more months is a good idea, realize that she isn't really wanting to have the baby early (well, maybe she is, a little); she's just tired and frustrated with being pregnant.

The last few months of pregnancy are no picnic, and unfortunately, you can't truly understand what she's going through. When she starts talking about getting this baby out by hook or crook the minute she hits 37 weeks, take it with a grain of salt. She's every bit as concerned about the welfare of this baby as you are, and she's not going to do anything rash.

Let her vent without giving her a lecture, and in five minutes, she'll probably be telling her mom how pregnancy has been the best time of her life. That's how hormones go sometimes.

Dealing with tears, panic, and doubts

Doing anything for the first time can be stressful, overwhelming, and scary. Facing labor, delivery, and motherhood for the first time certainly qualifies. Yes, you're also facing fatherhood for the first time, and dealing with the prospect of labor, seeing your partner in pain, and a host of doubts and fears, but her concerns are fueled by hormones and the knowledge that some form of delivery, be it labor or surgery, is the only way to emerge with a baby after nine months of pregnancy. The inevitability of the end of pregnancy can be overwhelming at times.

Your partner won't be the first woman to ever express the feeling that she can't do this, that having a baby was a mistake, or that she's changed her mind about the whole thing and wants to call it off. These feelings will intensify when she's in labor, so if you deal with them rationally now, you'll be better prepared for them then.

These feelings are temporary, but they're overwhelming when they hit. All new parents fear they won't be good at their new role. The two of you can approach this fear together by taking the following practical steps:

- ✔ **Read baby books and online pediatric sites.** You'll still go to pieces during the first colic episode, but if you know what to expect, it's a little easier to handle.

- ✔ **Take a class.** Most hospitals offer pregnancy classes that touch on at least the basics of breast-feeding and newborn care.

- ✔ **Visit friends with babies.** If you have friends or relatives with infants, hang out with them and pick their brains, if you trust their judgment.

- ✔ **Talk to your mom and dad.** Although time dims the memories of parenting, your own parents may be able to vaguely recall their early parenting days and give you some advice based on their own experiences. After all, you turned out okay, didn't you? If you didn't, don't ask them.

- ✔ **Talk it out.** Experience may change your mind about a number of parenting issues, but you'll feel more prepared if the two of you try to set out some basic ideas about how you want to raise the baby. This helps avoid drama-filled discussions when one of you wants to put the baby in your bed at 3 a.m. and the other doesn't, and also gives you the sense of having some grasp of what parenthood is all about. Expect your ideas to change frequently in the first actual weeks of parenthood, though.

Facing your own fears about fatherhood

Today's new dads may not have had involved fathers as role models as they were growing up, which can lead to uncertainty about exactly how to approach the fatherhood thing. The idea that dad should be as involved in child rearing as mom is a fairly new one, and you may feel uncertain about what your role is.

Because no two families are alike, you and your partner will design your own family model. You set your own standards here, so don't worry about what a "good" dad does or how other people approach fatherhood. You're going to be a "good" dad, so however you decide to embrace the parenting role will be the right thing for you and your partner.

Allow your partner to vent and express doubts and concerns, but never fail to reassure her that you know she'll be a great mom, that she was born to do this, and that you'll be helping her every inch of the way. Feel free to express your own fears and doubts about being a really good parent, but never in a "Can you top this" way.

Many women at the end of pregnancy have very vivid dreams about the baby or develop fears that something may be wrong with him. You can't do much about these fears except let her talk them out and reassure her that no matter what happens, you're there for her and the baby. However, if your partner becomes fixated on thoughts that she may harm the baby, or that something is wrong with the baby, she may be experiencing a severe depressive disorder. Make sure she sees her medical practitioner promptly.

Getting Your Paperwork in Order

Filling out forms and investigating your insurance benefits aren't ideal ways to spend a Saturday afternoon, but when the alternative is trying to fill in the blanks while your partner is enduring the beginning states of a painful labor, well, doing them now is a no-brainer! The more prepared you are from the business end of having the baby, the smoother the admissions process at the hospital will go.

Likewise, the better you understand your insurance coverage, the less likely you are to receive an unexpected (and unexpectedly large) hospital bill upon your return home.

Understanding your insurance

Although navigating your insurance plan may sound as impossible as understanding your income taxes, it's an important predelivery step for couples. Talk with someone from your human resources department at work as well as with your insurance company to fully understand your coverage.

Unites States law says that pregnancy cannot be deemed a pre-existing condition by insurance companies, so if you or your partner switched jobs or insurance plans in the middle of pregnancy, you're probably still covered. However, the law is limited to group policies, not individual policies, and has multiple loopholes, so be sure to carefully research your coverage.

Your personal insurance plan dictates the following factors:

- ✔ **Length of stay in the hospital:** The Newborns' and Mothers' Health Protection Act is a U.S. federal law that requires all insurance companies to cover the hospital stay for 48 hours after a standard delivery and 96 hours after cesarean. It does not, however, require that insurance companies cover any or all of the birth itself.

- ✔ **Where you can give birth:** Unless you want to get stuck footing a huge portion of the bill, make sure that the hospital or birthing center of your choice is an approved facility by your insurance company.

- ✔ **Who can attend your birth:** Not all doctors are covered by your insurance, either, so make sure that yours is. If you're opting for a midwife, investigate the coverage your insurance provides and make sure your midwife is willing to work with your insurance company. In rare cases, some insurance plans cover part of a doula's fees.

- ✔ **What drugs are covered:** It may seem like your insurance is obligated to fully cover any drug or medicine your doctor provides your partner, but that's not always the case. Find out how much of the total cost of an epidural will be covered, because they're quite expensive, and you may need to plan ahead for the costs you may incur.

- ✔ **Elective procedures:** Whether it's a scheduled cesarean or a circumcision, not all insurance companies cover procedures that can be deemed as elective.

- ✔ **Percentage of total cost:** 80 percent coverage may seem like an awesome deal, until you realize your entire stay cost $10,000 and you're now on the hook for two grand. Knowing what to expect allows you to save ahead so when the bills start arriving, you won't have to scramble.

Midwives are generally less expensive to employ than a doctor, and if your insurance covers the cost of a midwife, you likely will save money going that route. Many midwives even deliver in hospitals and partner with a doctor to ensure emergency care when needed.

Home births are the cheapest option of all options but are generally recommended only for women who fall into the low-risk pregnancy category. However, if you and your partner are opting for a home birth, check with your insurance provider to find out how it handles such situations and what is covered in case of an emergency.

In the case of multiples, the cost will increase by a great deal because the babies are more likely to stay in the neonatal intensive care unit. Again, assuming 80 percent coverage, you could be responsible for 20 percent of a bill that quickly escalates into the six figures. Also, keep in mind that after mom is discharged, the costs of travel and staying at or near the hospital while your baby/babies are in the NICU are up to you.

Here are some other important questions to ask your health insurance provider:

- ✔ Do you need to notify the provider upon admission into the hospital?
- ✔ Are childbirth classes covered by your plan?
- ✔ Will any portion of a doula's services be covered?
- ✔ Is lactation consultation covered?
- ✔ What newborn care is covered in case of emergency?
- ✔ Are any prescriptions or medications not covered?
- ✔ Are any procedures (circumcision, scheduled C-section), or prenatal tests (amniocentesis) not covered? Are there exceptions?

During benefits open season at your work, which usually occurs sometime around the end of the year, check into the labor and delivery coverage of any alternative insurance plans offered by your company and consider switching plans or providers to one that best suits your needs. It may save you thousands of dollars in hospital bills.

Preparing for the costs if you don't have insurance

Under no circumstances is living without health insurance a preferable idea, especially if you're pregnant or have children. However, due to myriad reasons, ranging from job loss to self-employment, a small portion of people find themselves pregnant without coverage.

The costs of all of the tests, ultrasounds, and doctor visits leading up to and following childbirth are an enormous expense, and many medical providers won't even accept you as a patient if you're paying out-of-pocket. However, others are happy to work out a payment plan, which may require a larger upfront deposit. Your provider options may be limited, but with a little legwork you can find someone.

Aside from the cost of your partner's doctor, you have to make similar arrangements with the hospital for your stay and any medicines, procedures, or operations you may undergo. The same goes for the anesthesiologist, who may require that you pay the fee for an epidural upfront, running you between $1,000 and $2,000, depending on the provider. And after baby is born, he'll need more checkups and vaccinations, and you'll have to find a pediatrician who accepts patients without insurance.

With all those expenses, an insurance plan you buy on your own will probably pay for itself. In the case of job loss, pay for COBRA coverage for as long as it's offered to your family. *Note:* Some states also offer low- to no-cost healthcare for low-income families that covers the majority of childbirth costs.

Guaranteeing a smooth admissions process at the hospital

Think back to the last time you arrived at a crowded shopping mall with a parking lot packed to the gills with cars and you ended up walking ten minutes just to get to your store of choice. Now imagine that you drive right in and, miracle of miracles, the parking spot closest to the door is waiting for you.

If you want that experience upon arriving at the hospital when your partner is in labor — and believe us, you do — you need to make sure you fill out all of the preadmissions paperwork at your hospital or birthing center. This keeps you from having to fill out forms and answer an endless array of questions when you should be focused on the woman in pain.

A good time to make sure everything is in order is during your prenatal visit to the birthing center. The visit is not only a chance to get to know a few of the faces you may be seeing, but also the perfect firsthand opportunity to make sure that your partner is in the system.

Also, you want to make sure that you contact your delivery doctor or midwife prior to going to the hospital. Many doctors want a call as soon as labor begins; others just want a 30- to 60-minute heads-up before you head to the hospital. And because many labors begin (and end!) in the middle of the night, you want to give your doctor or midwife ample time to wake up before heading out the door.

At some point during the admissions process, you may be asked to leave the room so the nurse can talk to your partner alone. Although it may seem off-putting at first, this procedure is very important. Unfortunately, domestic violence is far too common, and one of the nurse's duties is to ensure that the woman in labor and the baby she's bringing into the world are in a safe environment during labor and delivery. Don't take it personally!

Whose Baby Is This, Anyway? Dealing with Overbearing Family Members

From the time you share the news of your coming baby, you'll be inundated with advice and visitors. Nobody will want to be more hands-on than your family, and it may grow tiresome and become a source of angst very quickly the closer to labor and delivery your partner gets, and especially when you get home from the hospital and crave some family time.

Mothers, grandfathers, aunts-to-be — they all get nervous, too. Unfortunately, their offers of assistance and their constant presence can keep you and your partner from some much-needed quiet bonding time before baby arrives. Your lives are about to change forever, for the better (baby, baby, baby!) and for the worse (goodbye sleep and frequent sex!), and you need time to enjoy the waning bits of childlessness you have left.

Your families love you, and their well-meaning, obtrusive advice, visits, and purchases are the only way they know how to show you just how excited they are to meet the new little person you're bringing into the family. However, if members of your family are becoming too involved or over-the-top for your tastes, be sure to thank them for the love and support and simply let them know that you and your partner need to take some time for yourselves before the baby comes.

Depending on how big and how emotionally connected your family is, consider starting a phone tree to share news earlier in your pregnancy to save you from having to call every single relative in your phone book every time you go in for an ultrasound (see Chapter 8 for details on creating a phone tree). Telling the same story over and over to 13 aunts, cousins, and neighbors may take the fun right out of your fun news. That said, don't cut off communication altogether. Make sure to call the most important people in your life as frequently as you see fit. It's an exciting time for everyone, and you won't want to tarnish a loved one's joy by letting him get all the news secondhand.

Picking a Pediatrician

Choosing a pediatrician before the baby arrives may seem unnecessary, but with so much going on in the weeks before and after delivery, you want to get it checked off the list in the third trimester.

It may take more time than you think to find someone who agrees with your stances on breast-feeding, vaccinations, and the necessity of certain in-hospital procedures.

Also, your baby will need to be cleared for checkout from the hospital by a pediatrician, and the sooner you start working with the doctor of your choice, the better. Building a relationship between a pediatrician and your baby increases the likelihood that your child will get the care she needs. And what better time to start than in the hospital?

Get a list of approved pediatricians from your insurance company and start your research. Talk to other parents in your neighborhood, as well as friends who live close by. As best you can, choose a pediatrician who is close to home, because you will be making the trip many times during the first year. Research feedback the doctor has received online, too. Considering the sheer number of hateful things people are willing to post online, take nasty reviews with a grain of salt, but do take note if a doctor has an overwhelming amount of negative feedback.

Next, schedule an interview with two or three doctors of your choosing. Here's a list of questions that you should ask any potential pediatrician to ensure you get the care you want for your baby, both during your hospital stay and beyond:

- ✔ How long have you been a pediatrician?

- ✔ How many doctors are part of your practice?

- ✔ What are your hours on the evenings and weekends?

- ✔ Is there an on-call doctor at all times? Is there a charge for after-hours calls/services?

- ✔ Are you a family practice doctor or solely practicing pediatrics?

  New parents may find it easier for the whole family to be treated by the same doctor. If you and your partner have strong feelings about this, make sure to ask if you can be seen too.

- ✔ Do you offer same-day appointments for illness?

- ✔ Are you often double booked?

- ✔ How long is the average wait?

- ✔ Will I always see you at each visit, or will my baby be seen by other doctors, nurses, or junior staff members?

- ✔ What is your stance on formula feeding? How long should our baby be breast-fed? What formulas do you recommend?

  Whatever decisions you and your partner make about feeding your child, it's vital that you have a pediatrician who will support your choices.

✔ Are you flexible with immunization schedules?

Some parents choose to delay vaccinations or use alternate schedules. Make sure your pediatrician is onboard with your immunization wishes.

✔ When do you recommend beginning to feed solid foods?

Depending on the doctor, you may be told to start feeding your child solid foods beginning at 4 months or as late as 6 months. Research varies on what is best, so get educated and make sure your pediatrician will support your feeding schedule.

✔ Do you require breast-fed babies to take vitamin D supplements?

Breast-fed babies are often prescribed a supplement for vitamin D, however, not all pediatricians and parents agree that it's necessary. Do your research on what feels right to you and make sure your pediatrician agrees with your decision.

✔ Do you employ a lactation consultant or offer lactation support?

✔ What is your stance on use of antibiotics in children?

✔ How often are the play facilities cleaned?

Also, feel free to show your potential pediatrician your birth plan. Her reaction to your decisions, such as whether or not to give the baby a vitamin K shot right after birth or whether or not a baby needs erythromycin on his eyes, may help guide your decision. (See Chapter 8 for more on the choices detailed in a birth plan.)

Choose a doctor who most closely aligns with your wants and desires for your baby. You don't want to have to start the search all over again just because a pediatrician doesn't agree with your decision to delay vaccinations or give your child formula.

Chat up the other parents in the waiting room to find out the real dish on how long they have to wait at each visit, how often they actually see the doctor, and their overall impressions of her caregiving style. Parents are brutally honest, and they are your best source of information.

If you have a long-time family physician with whom you have a personal relationship and you don't plan to have be your child's pediatrician, let him know before the baby arrives. Not only is it respectful, it will help you avoid the awkwardness of having both your family doctor and your pediatrician show up at the hospital.

Chapter 8

The Copilot's Guide to Birthing Options

In This Chapter

▶ Making basic decisions about labor: Who, what, how, and where

▶ Creating a birthing plan

▶ Picking the people who get to be at the birth

*L*abor is nothing like it used to be. From the au naturel days when biting down on a bullet was the "medication" and the 1950s when every woman was sedated up to her eyeballs while dad spent the night in the bar, labor has evolved into a family event that involves medications that really take the pain out of labor, sleepovers for dad, and champagne dinners the night before discharge.

One thing about having a baby is sure: There's no one right way to do it. For every person who wants to deliver at home on her grandma's favorite quilt, another person feels that *epidural on demand* is the best phrase in the English language. Whatever you and your partner dream up as the ideal labor experience, rest assured it probably won't be the weirdest idea your birthing practitioner has ever heard.

You have more childbirth options today than ever before. Natural deliveries, home deliveries, and give-me-everything-you've-got deliveries are all possible. And the good thing is, no one is going to hold your partner to the ideas you both thought sounded good before labor started. If she decides she wants an epidural after all, all she has to do is scream — er, say so.

Although the number of options is much larger than in previous years, some of them may not be feasible in your situation. For instance, if your partner has certain medical conditions, such as preeclampsia, or if the baby has congenital birth defects, they really need to be under a doctor's care in a hospital, even if your partner had her heart set on a home delivery. Be sure to talk to the doctor early in the pregnancy about your plans so that she can advise you on their feasibility and safety and let you know if circumstances change.

In this chapter we review the options that are available and help you decide what works best for you and your partner. We also provide tips on crafting a birth plan and deciding who's allowed in the delivery room.

Making Sure Your Birth Practitioner Is a Good Fit

Discussing your plans with your current birth practitioner as soon as you figure out what they are is important. For one thing, he may not be interested in participating if you're planning something out of his comfort zone, and you may need time to find someone who thinks childbirth in the backyard sounds like fun. If your midwife balks at assisting you during a delivery that features a medically unnecessary planned cesarean, you need to find one who doesn't.

Though many doctors are more flexible about childbirth options than they used to be, most doctors still have a fairly narrow comfort range, one that likely includes fetal monitoring, intravenous infusions, and limited time in the hot tub. The practices used by midwives, on the other hand, have become more mainstream in many areas, and a midwife may practice only slightly differently than an obstetrician.

Screening potential practitioners

Whichever birth practitioner you choose, the best way to know if you're in the right place is to ask. Both you and your partner should be there when discussing options, because if the practitioner isn't on board with your plan, he may think he can just wait and talk some sense into the absent parent. Presenting a united front, especially on non-negotiable items (such as home birth, for example) is best done as a couple. Consider asking these questions:

  ✔ **Where do you deliver?** Most doctors only deliver at one or maybe two hospitals. It wouldn't be practical for them to run around from place to place. If you choose a midwife, find out whether she delivers at homes only or also at hospitals, and make sure she can do it where you want to be.

✓ **What's your cesarean rate?** The cesarean rate in the United States and other developed countries is appallingly high. While cesarean sections are often necessary and lifesaving, they have a higher risk of complications for your partner and the baby. A significantly higher rate than your area's average is a warning sign that your doctor may be too quick with the knife.

✓ **How many inductions do you do?** Nobody wants to be pregnant forever, or even nine months, but pregnancies were designed to end naturally. Some doctors do way too many inductions, especially on Friday mornings. Your convenience isn't always the goal when the doctor offers to induce labor, and induced labors have a higher cesarean rate, and cesarean deliveries cause more maternal and fetal complications.

✓ **Who's on call?** Does the doctor come in when her patients go into the hospital, or is labor managed by residents? Early in labor, some doctors have the resident check their patient and call them for instructions; this isn't necessarily a problem, but knowing it ahead of time will keep you from badgering the nurses about when your doctor's coming in. For midwives, find out if she has an assistant or backup person to cover for her if she can't attend.

✓ **How do you feel about [fill in the blank]?** If you have an unusual request, politely approach your practitioner with this line, rather than demanding, "We want [whatever]." If you want to both spend labor in the hot tub naked, now would be a good time to get your practitioner's feedback on this idea.

Make sure you and your partner are agreed on what you want before discussing plans with your practitioner, and discuss it well before labor starts. Arguing in front of the nurses and trying to talk her out of an epidural at 6 centimeters is considered really bad form by the hospital staff, and they may not let you use the coffee machine or show you their hidden stash of emergency snacks for fainting fathers if they don't like the way you talk to your partner!

Working with a midwife

A midwife delivery in the hospital or birthing center can be a wonderful option. Midwives really are committed to fewer interventions in labor and give much more personal care. However, your partner may become so attached to her that you feel a little left out. Don't let that happen unless you're fine with being the third man; go to appointments and get to know the midwife yourself so she knows you're interested in being a real part of the partnership.

If you and your partner are thinking about delivering with a midwife, check the American College of Midwives (`www.midwife.org`) or Midwives of North American (`www.mana.org`) for options in your area. Using a search engine or checking chatboards on sites such as `www.mothering.com` for information is often the best way to get other people's opinions and experiences on what using a midwife or having a home birth is like.

A personal interview is always the best way to get a feel for not only the nuts-and-bolts information about education and experience, but also a sense of whether your personalities will "mesh" for the next nine months. When you interview your prospective midwife, ask the following questions:

- ✔ **What's your training?** Some midwives have nearly as many degrees as your doctor, and others have no formal training at all. But don't necessarily reject a midwife because of a lack of diplomas: Some people have a natural ability to deliver babies, love the work, and have all the knowledge necessary for a safe outcome, as long as there's medical backup nearby.

- ✔ **How long have you been doing this?** The longer the better. You see everything if you work in obstetrics long enough.

- ✔ **What's *your* backup plan?** If she says it isn't necessary to have a backup plan, reconsider this person. Having a backup plan is always necessary.

Getting some additional help with a doula

Although the word *doula* may have you picturing some sort of metal-studded medieval torture device, a doula actually can be a soon-to-be dad's secret weapon — one that can take some of the pressure off your very tense shoulders. A doula is a person, generally a woman, with a comprehensive understanding of the birthing process. She is hired by the couple to provide emotional and physical support throughout labor. Think of her as your very own in-hospital, labor-specific Google search/motivational speaker. Services doulas offer include:

- ✔ Allowing you to participate in labor and delivery as much or as little as you are comfortable

- ✔ Assistance in creating a birth plan

- ✔ Staying with you and your partner throughout labor and delivery (the doctor and nurses will not be present the whole time)

✔ Facilitating communication of the birth plan and the decisions of the mother and father to the doctor/midwife and nurses

✔ Giving light massage to both you and your partner during labor and delivery

✔ Postpartum education and assistance with newborn care, breastfeeding, and adjusting to family life

If you think doulas are only necessary for deliveries in which the father isn't involved, think again. Labor is a complex process, and as it progresses you and your partner will be asked to make many decisions about procedures and medications for which you may not feel fully prepared. A doula can inform you about both the risks and benefits involved, as well as help you explore other options that may better suit your birth plan.

Doulas also provide your partner constant support while giving you the opportunity to step out of the room to grab a quick snack or take a breath of fresh air. For long labors, a quick 15-minute nap can make the difference for a worn-out dad-to-be. Doulas ensure that someone who understands the process and your birthing choices is with your partner at all times — even when your eyes are closed.

And doula-ing has a medical benefit, too. Research shows that couples who have a doula present during childbirth tend to have shorter labors with fewer complications as well as a reduction in the use of labor-inducing medications, forceps, vacuum extractions, and cesarean sections.

After your new family returns home, most doulas make a postpartum visit that provides support for mom and baby, and she also provides telephone support for a specified duration following birth.

Not all doulas are created equal. Make sure to interview multiple candidates and ensure that they're certified by Doulas of North America (DONA). Make sure that she has had a criminal background check. For more information about hiring a doula, visit the DONA Web site: www.dona.org.

Choosing Where to Deliver

A century ago, everyone delivered at home. Fifty years ago, everyone delivered in the hospital. Today parents can choose either option, or may deliver in a special birthing center designed to mimic the comforts at home while still providing cutting-edge medical treatment if needed.

Delivering at a hospital

Hospitals today love to stress how much like home they are while still having all the most up-to-date equipment at their fingertips. And though hospitals have come a long way in improving the overall birthing experience, they're still not home. Some, however, are better than others at creating a welcoming, open-door policy for family, so check out the local possibilities, keeping in mind that your doctor can only practice where he has privileges and that in the long run a doctor you trust is far more important than lavender quilts and a pull-out sleeper chair. Here's what to look for when you visit different hospitals:

- **Is it secure?** Most hospitals have beefed up security, especially around the maternal and child health area. Hospital bracelets are embedded with alarm triggers, codes have to be activated to enter certain areas, and the staff all dresses in one color so you know who belongs there. It should *not* be possible to just walk onto a maternity floor without a pass. You want security to be tight, even if it's a pain in the neck.

- **What are visiting policies?** What you're looking for depends on your preferences. Do you want your entire family and a three-piece band present, or are you hoping to have just the two of you at the delivery and in the mother-baby unit afterward? Keeping family out is much easier if you can quote "hospital rules."

- **How much access does dad have?** Many places allow dad 24-hour visiting privileges, but some don't. Find out the rules ahead of time so security isn't called to remove you.

- **Is the staff helpful?** You can tell a lot by the attitude of the staff even on a short visit. Do they smile and say hello, or run over your foot with a gurney without even an "excuse me"? You're going to spend way more time with the nurses than with your doctor in labor — in fact, she's in and out so fast you may not be quite sure she was there at all — so your experience will be more pleasant if the nurses are good. Although you may still draw Nurse Ratched for your labor nurse, it's less likely at a hospital with a mission statement and policies that promote a positive atmosphere. If you're planning to use a midwife, find out how the staff will work with her.

- **Is anesthesia in house all night?** Surprising as it may be, some small hospitals don't have an anesthesiologist in the hospital all night. The anesthesiologist may have to be called in from home if your partner wants an epidural during the night. And if the hospital has only one on staff, she may be doing an appendectomy just as your partner starts getting really uncomfortable. Know ahead of time so you can ask for an epidural early, if need be.

✔ **How's the décor?** Consider the appearance of the hospital room after everything else has been taken into consideration. Pretty surroundings are nice, but you'll be too busy to notice them. And that pretty quilt will be removed from the bed, because the staff doesn't want anyone bleeding — or worse — all over it.

After you make your decision, visit the hospital again. Knowing exactly what your room will look like and even recognizing some familiar faces removes a layer of stress as you get ready for delivery. Most hospitals and birthing centers offer tours, but you can call and schedule a private tour of the facility as well.

While you're there, take note of the eating options, parking guidelines, and prenatal and postpartum classes offered by your hospital or birthing center. This allows you to plan ahead and offer your well-wishers the information they need as well as make full use of the facilities' offerings.

Many hospitals offer prenatal lactation classes that are taught by the on-staff lactation consultant who will visit your room after delivery. The classes are usually free and quite short. Encourage your partner to attend a class in order to learn the basics of breast-feeding as well as to initiate a face-to-face relationship prior to the consultant's postpartum visit. Your partner will be much more comfortable asking questions and discussing any issues she and baby are having if she has met the consultant previously.

Exploring alternative options: Using a midwife at home

The idea of having your baby at home may appeal to you and your partner. Home delivery may be an option for you if you meet all the following strongly suggested guidelines:

✔ You have found a midwife who's willing to deliver at your home.

✔ You live fairly close to a medical facility in case of emergencies.

✔ You're not delivering in Montana in January or any other area where roads are impassable during the part of year you're due.

✔ You're both calm, sensible people who are really committed to the idea of home birth.

The trouble with labor is that while 99 out of 100 times everything goes perfectly, you need to be prepared for that one time when things go bad so quickly you can't believe your eyes. Having nearby medical help is really essential, unless your midwife can do a cesarean in under 30 minutes in an emergency.

Make sure your midwife has a backup plan to cover contingencies such as sudden illness or other problems that would prevent her from getting to you for the delivery. Does she have a partner or someone who covers her? Discuss circumstances that may cause you to change your mind about home delivery, from ominous weather to last-minute cold feet.

If you plan to use a midwife at home, be sure to get good answers to the following questions (in addition to the questions listed in "Working with a midwife" earlier in this chapter):

  ✔ **What type of equipment will you bring with you?** You can be sure a ventilator and fully equipped operating room won't appear out of her black bag, but basic medications like intra-venous fluids and Pitocin to prevent heavy bleeding after delivery and oxygen, plus equipment like an ambu bag to breathe for the baby in case of problems after birth, should be in every midwife's bag.

  ✔ **How long do you stay?** "As long as you need me" is a good answer. She should stay at least an hour or two to make sure your partner and the baby are behaving normally and to get nursing started. On the other hand, you may not want her moving in with you — that's your mother-in-law's role. She should also visit for the next few days to recheck both mother and baby in case of any late-developing problems.

Looking at Labor Choices

Standard labor practices vary depending on who is delivering and where you deliver, but no matter the situation, you and your partner will have to make a number of decisions and can opt to make dozens of others if you have preferences. Educate yourselves on common procedures and their pros and cons by talking with the doctor and doing some reading. One of the biggest issues for women in labor is deciding whether or not to have an epidural or other pain medication. In this section we discuss that as well as another big issue, water births.

Going all natural or getting the epidural

The decision about pain medication is one area where, although you're welcome to have your say — if you say it nicely — the decision is really up to your partner. As long as she's not planning to do anything unsafe, she's the one who has to go through labor, not you, so the drug decision should be hers.

The *all-natural* method of childbirth, which avoids unnecessary pain medication and medical interventions such as episiotomies, seems to have peaked about the time the hippie movement went mainstream and started buying BMWs, but letting nature take its course in childbirth still has many proponents. Women have been having babies naturally since forever, and many women find going through labor without any medication empowering.

Classes that teach breathing and relaxation techniques as a natural way to deal with pain, such as the Bradley Method (see www. bradleybirth.com for classes near you), are available. A doula, midwife, or obstetrician who's supportive of natural childbirth can also be a good source of information on the pros and cons of delivering naturally and the classes available in your area. Some classes focus on specific breathing patterns (can you say, "Hoo hoo hee"?), while others stress learning to listen to your body, relaxation methods, and the benefits of staying upright during labor.

Around 50 percent of women in labor these days have *epidurals,* an injection that numbs the nerves from the abdomen down to the thighs. Epidurals are usually given when labor is well established, around 4 centimeters, because contractions can slow down if it's given too early. Some doctors, though, order epidurals earlier and then start Pitocin, a labor-induction drug, if contractions slow down.

Epidurals are better than they used to be; they can be run as a continuous infusion on a pump so they don't wear off and need to be re-injected. Some hospitals offer "walking epidurals," where the dose given still allows patients to walk, which is better for keeping labor going than lying in bed.

Some women turn down the epidural but are given intravenous pain medications to help with labor pains. One problem with IV medications is that they can depress the baby's ability to breathe after birth, so they can't be given too close to the time of delivery.

Taking it to the water

Water birth is delivery of the baby while the mother is in a large tub of water. The baby is delivered while under the water, which is considered by proponents of the practice to be less traumatic to him because he's spent nine months in water. Although water birth sounds like a warm, back-to-nature experience, no cultures actually practice water birth. This fact doesn't mean that water birth doesn't have some appealing possibilities, mostly for mom-to-be, who gets to spend most of her labor floating in a tub of water. Many women find spending some time in labor in water reduces pain and aids in relaxation.

Babies have never been traditionally born into a vat of water, and although most babies don't breathe until they're out of the water, a few baby deaths have been related to water birth. Laboring in water and getting out for the actual delivery may be a safer option to consider.

Some women absolutely should not have a water birth. The list includes:

- ✔ Women giving birth prematurely. (See Chapter 6 for more on preterm delivery.)
- ✔ Women with genital herpes.
- ✔ Women whose babies have passed *meconium,* the first stool, before delivery. These babies need their mouth and nose suctioned as soon as the head is delivered, to help prevent meconium aspiration into the lungs.

Creating a Birth Plan

A birth plan is a document that outlines the procedures, medications, and contingency plans that you and your partner are comfortable with throughout labor and delivery. It details your ideal birth experience while acknowledging the unpredictability of the process.

A birth plan is not a set of marching orders for your nurses, doctor, or midwife, so keep it simple and friendly. You share this document with your entire birthing team, and not all doctors and nurses are thrilled at the prospect of a couple telling them how to do their jobs.

Creating a birth plan requires that you and your partner discuss what you're comfortable with and make many important decisions prior to your arrival at the hospital. The last thing you want to do is to leave life-altering, labor-changing decisions to be made during an emotionally wrought time.

Visualizing your ideal experience

Labor and delivery are like reading a choose-your-own-adventure novel; every decision you make can lead you to a slightly different outcome.

As corny as it may sound, you and your partner should spend some time with your eyes closed trying to picture what your perfect experience would look like. Try to be realistic — a pain-free, 60-minute labor is highly unlikely, and making that dream a reality is beyond your control. Instead, focus on the things you can control.

When creating a birth plan, consider the following basic questions:

- What types of medication is your partner willing/wanting to have administered?

- Do you want to cut the umbilical cord? Do you want to bank the cord blood? (See the sidebar "To bank or not to bank" for more information.)

- Does your partner want final approval before the doctor performs a vacuum extraction? This involves a suction device that helps pull the baby out, which can cause painful tearing of the vagina as well as temporarily misshapen baby heads. It is a safe and, in some cases, necessary procedure, but many women want to have the choice as to whether or not it is performed.

- Does your partner want constant or intermittent fetal monitoring? Fetal monitoring tracks baby's stress levels during childbirth, and constant monitoring will limit your partner's ability to move freely during labor.

- Does your partner want to veto an episiotomy? An episiotomy is a surgical incision that enlarges the vaginal opening to allow the baby to come out more easily. It used to be a common procedure, but most studies show that letting the body tear naturally is a better option. An episiotomy is quite painful during recovery and not an attractive option for most women unless absolutely necessary for the health of the baby.

- Does your partner want to be able to get up and walk around while laboring?

- Are you opting to forgo circumcision?

To bank or not to bank

Cord-blood banking is the freezing of the blood in the umbilical cord, which is full of your baby's stem cells and can be used to treat disease (80 serious diseases including leukemia, other cancers, and blood disorders) down the road. It's becoming more popular in the United States, but is it necessary?

To purchase the collection kit (which you take with you to the hospital in order to collect the cord) and the first year storage fee will cost you between $1,000 and $2,000, with an annual storage fee of at least $100. Some research shows that using a matching donor's stem cells is just as effective as the stored blood, but due to the raging debate about how stem cells are collected, this is an effective way to ensure access.

In addition, your baby's cord blood can be used to treat other stem-cell matches in your family. It's more or less an insurance policy that, most likely, you'll never have to use. If banking the blood is outside of your financial possibilities, don't sweat it. Some research even suggests that letting all the blood from the cord flow into the baby before cutting is better for the baby's health, in which case, the blood isn't available to be collected, anyway.

In order to make sure you both feel positive about your childbirth experience, you need to prepare answers to these important questions. Many procedures may be done as a matter of course that might not jive with you and your partner's desires, so invest the time beforehand in order avoid any regrets that you could have prevented.

Many prenatal classes include exercises that help you visualize your ideal experience, and some even offer help developing your birth plan. When selecting a class, ask the instructor if these activities are included as part of the course. Having a third party involved, be it a doula or your prenatal instructor, may help you and your partner narrow down your list of what's truly important and turn those priorities into a cohesive, effective birth plan.

Drafting your plan

After you and your partner have decided what your ideal birth looks like, you need to put it into writing. Try to use language that's friendly, concise, and represents your flexibility.

Births don't usually go exactly according to plan, so allow wiggle room for the unexpected to make sure the nurses and doctors know that your priority is having a healthy baby at the end of the day. Here are some basic tips for writing your birth plan:

- ✔ Write a nice, short introduction that introduces who you are and thanks your team in advance for following your plan.

- ✔ Include a brief overview that states your basic, overall desires for the kind of labor and delivery you and your partner want.

- ✔ Break the main body into three sections: labor, delivery, and postdelivery.

- ✔ Under each heading, make the major points into a bulleted list for easy reading.

Keep it to one page unless you know ahead of time that your labor and delivery are going to be complicated and therefore require more steps.

Since the majority of what's being outlined in the birth plan is up to your partner to decide and ultimately undergo, get involved in this project by taking the lead. Make her favorite dinner and start a dialogue. Ask her questions about what she wants and tell her what you want, too. Take notes during your discussion and then start composing your birth plan. It won't happen overnight, but it will let her know how involved you want to be.

Use the following birth plan as an outline for creating an effective, concise document for your team:

The Johnson Family Birth Plan

The Midwives at Methodist Hospital Family Center

Parents: Rachel & Evan Johnson

Doula: Holly Barhamand

We're looking forward to having our baby at Methodist Hospital with the midwife group and staff! We know you see a lot of birth plans and we thank you for reading ours.

We anticipate a normal birth and would like to allow the process to unfold naturally. However, in the unlikely event of a complication, we will cooperate fully after an informed discussion with the birth team has taken place. We are also willing to sign release forms if legally required in order to avoid "routine" procedures we opt against.

Overall, we would like no medication, exam, or procedure to be administered to mother or baby until it is explained to us and we have given our consent. Thank you in advance for all of your hard work and excellent care!

Labor:

✔ I would like to attempt labor without pain medication — I will ask (loudly, I'm sure!) if I feel I need something.

✔ We prefer intermittent, external fetal monitoring to continuous or internal. We consent to admission strip monitoring.

✔ I decline all vaginal or other internal exams except with my expressed consent at the time.

✔ I prefer to avoid IV. If IV is necessary, please use a saline lock.

Delivery:

✔ I would like to have freedom of movement and position during delivery — squatting, hands and knees, and so on.

✔ I very strongly prefer natural tearing to an episiotomy.

✔ We very strongly prefer delaying cord cutting until the cord has stopped pulsating (consent for exception will be considered if baby is in distress or excess meconium is present).

✔ We decline Pitocin, uterine massage, and pulling the cord.

✔ If surgery is required, Evan and Holly (our doula) need to be present. I prefer regional anesthesia rather than general, except in case of an emergency. Please use double-layer sutures when repairing my uterus.

Postdelivery:

✔ Please place baby on mother's abdomen immediately. We would like the baby to remain with parents at all times. We would like to start breast-feeding as soon as possible and delay potential interruptions.

We respectfully request the following:

✔ No routine suctioning of the baby's mouth and nose (unless needed)

✔ No erythromycin eye ointment

✔ No vitamin K injection (unless there is bruising or birth trauma)

✔ No vaccinations are to be given at this time

✔ No blood to be drawn from baby. We consent to PKU test and are happy to discuss desired timing of this test with nursing staff.

Thank you for your sensitivity to our preferences and for bringing your knowledge and care to this great event in our lives.

As important as this day is, you are not a celebrity, and your unrealistic demands won't be met with a smile and a nod. Nor will your team take any unnecessary risks that could harm mother or baby just to meet the requirements of your birth plan. Keep your birth plan focused on the elements of the birthing process that can be controlled, take each hurdle one at a time, and if and when things begin to deviate from the plan, help your partner to make the best decisions possible by getting as much information about the risks and benefits from the knowledgeable members of your team.

Sharing your birth plan with the world

Unfortunately, labor usually doesn't begin on that imprecise due date you've been hanging your hat on for the last nine months. Babies can come early, and with so much to get ready for, you may find yourself putting off creating and sharing your birth plan. Make time to write your birth plan toward the beginning of the third trimester, which will give you plenty of time to share it with your birthing team and any inquiring relatives and friends.

Going over your plan with the birthing team

Have your birth plan in place far in advance of your due date so that you can share it with your doctor or midwife during the seventh or eighth month of pregnancy. That gives you time to discuss the plan and address any concerns he may have. If you're hiring a doula, schedule a prenatal visit to go over the document.

Upon arrival at your delivery room, give a copy of your birth plan to the nurse assigned to your room. Hang a copy on the front of your door if permitted, as well as on the wall in your room, preferably near where your partner will deliver.

Getting off on the right foot is always a good first step. Deliver your birth plan to the nurses on duty with a plate of fresh-baked goodies. Making cookies or cupcakes can be a welcome distraction during early labor at home and can make the overworked, underpaid nurses more welcoming of your birthing decisions.

Informing family and friends of your plan

Choosing not to have an epidural, opting to use a midwife, or allowing a doula into your birthing room and not your partner's mom/sister/best friend can cause quite a stir. Anything you choose to do or not do that departs from other people's birthing experiences not only is "new and weird," but also can make them feel like you think the way they did it was wrong.

Conveying your plans early and often is key to getting everyone on the same page — or at least reading the same book — by the time the big day rolls around. Even if you can't get everyone to agree with your decisions, don't sweat it. Thank everyone for their concerns, but assure them that you would never make a decision that wasn't both educated and in the best interest of your partner and child. And, at the end of the day, when the baby arrives nobody will care how he got here.

Unless you're openly soliciting advice from others in your lives, talk about the plan as if it were a done deal. Talking about considerations and decisions you're making with a larger group of people means that although you may get a wide spectrum of opinions, you'll also get an even wider spectrum of criticism when your decision doesn't adhere to everyone else's recommendations. However, you and your spouse have the right to decide the birthing option that works best for you. When your plan is in place, simply tell the people in your lives where, when, and how you plan on having the baby.

If you and your partner are worried about the reaction your mother-in-law will have to the news of your plans to have an at-home water birth, don't be afraid to share the news of your personal birth plan via e-mail. That way she's allowed to have her reaction without making you feel judged. Also, the more unconventional your birth plan is, the more information your family and friends will want about your choices. In those instances, it is best to formulate a detailed, concrete birth plan before sharing the information.

Many people are quite opinionated when it comes to whether or not to have a medicated labor as well as whether or not you plan to circumcise. Don't feel the need to argue your position; the decision is ultimately yours, and what you want most is to do what's best for mother and baby in your eyes. Consider telling people that you plan on seeing how the events unfold and that you'll address mom's and baby's needs as you see fit on delivery day. After all, nobody knows what your partner will need or want until she needs it.

Get educated on your options and be honest with your friends and family. If all else fails and someone still insists you're wrong, have a confrontation. Arguments aren't enjoyable, but you'll be happier if you have it hashed out before the big day arrives.

Picking the Cast: Who's Present, Who Visits, and Who Gets a Call

Labor and delivery aren't the times for a family reunion. Having a baby is exhausting, emotional, and the one time in your lives when you need to focus on each other and your baby more than anything else in the world. Which means that you and your partner probably won't want many people in the room with you. To avoid any arguments or awkwardness at the hospital when you should be focusing on other matters, decide in advance who you'll allow in the room for delivery, who can visit at the hospital, and how you're going to spread news of the birth to everyone who isn't present.

Deciding who gets to attend the birth

Deciding who gets to be in the room is a big decision that's not yours to make. Your partner's the one nearly naked under a spotlight in a room of people, so she gets to make the call on who is allowed to be in the room during labor and delivery. And gentlemen, let's face it — she just may not want your mother there, no matter how much your mother would like to be present. As labor progresses, most women won't care who sees what because they will be so focused on birthing the baby, but it's still best for her labor to have only the people she wants to have present. Any stress or distraction in early labor can slow down the process.

In addition to you, the doctor or midwife, a doula (if applicable), and nurses, some women opt to have a sister or close friend in the room who can provide her with much-needed emotional support. Other women decide to have one or both parents present. Again, check with your hospital or birthing center to see who (and how many) they allow to be present for a birth.

Telling family members or friends that they need to leave isn't easy, but if your partner doesn't want someone in the room, it's your job to politely ask him or her to exit. For instance, if her father won't stop offering unsolicited stories about how painful his foot surgery was in comparison to her labor and she's on the verge of clobbering him with forceps, pull him aside, thank him for being there to support you both, let him know that your partner sends her love, and then firmly explain that she's feeling the need to have silence in the room for the remainder of the delivery.

Of course this message won't go over well, but it's not about other people at this point. Put your partner's needs first and worry about hurt feelings later. Besides, the moment baby arrives, nobody will remember anything other than how perfect and amazing your new bundle of joy is.

Planning ahead for visitors

Many people opt to have no friends or family members present in the delivery room. But it also goes beyond that. Being inundated with visitors at the hospital may seem like a nice thing in theory, but in practice it can become overwhelming in a snap. You will be tired, and your partner and baby will need rest, so make sure to take enough time for yourselves.

Also, having too many people handle your newborn only increases the risk of spreading illness. Invite only the most important people in your lives to the hospital and save the rest for a home visit in the following weeks. Thank anyone who offers to come and tell them that you look forward to spending time with them in the coming weeks. Simply telling someone that your new family will need rest, not visitors, should do the trick.

However, if someone shows up unannounced who you would rather not have at the hospital, don't be afraid to tell her that you have to keep visits short, say five minutes or so, because your partner and baby need time to rest. Schedule a follow-up visit if you wish. If there is someone who you don't want allowed into your room, for safety reasons or otherwise, be sure to alert the staff of the person's name and description.

There's never been a better time in your life to focus inward, so don't spend time worrying about what other people will think about your decisions. You can always make up later if someone is offended.

Planting a phone tree

Spreading the news far and wide can be both exhausting and time consuming, and after a delivery you and your partner likely won't be up for talking to everyone you know. Nor will you have the time! Nonetheless, everyone you know will request to be alerted within seconds after baby's arrival into the world.

Here are some simple tips to make a phone tree, which will require you to make only one call in order for the news of baby's arrival to begin branching out into the world.

1. **Start by gathering all the names and phone numbers of people you want contacted after your baby is born.**

2. **Start a list, with the first person as your primary contact.** He or she will be the one person you call upon baby's arrival.

3. **Write two names side-by-side under the primary contact.** These are the people your primary contact will call.

4. **Branching off those two people, write two more names under each.** The two people your primary contact calls will each have these two phone calls to make. Continue making the phone tree, assigning each person two calls.

5. **Pass out copies of the phone tree to everyone on the list and instruct them that when they get the call, they're responsible for calling the next two people right away.**

   The phone tree still works if your callers have to leave phone messages, but the delay will slow down the rest of the communication.

If your list of contacts is short, consider having each person call just one other person.

Social network announcements

Sending an update to 500 of your nearest and not-so-nearest friends every time you have a witty musing about your favorite celebrity may be fun on the average day, but it may not be appropriate during labor and delivery.

Your partner may want you to keep the world abreast of the baby developments while she's in labor, but the most women will prefer that your focus be on soothing her and not navigating your smart phone.

A word of warning: As easy as it is to communicate using social networking sites, sharing major news, such as the birth of your child, via Facebook or Twitter will be offensive and hurtful to some of the more important people in your life. Finding out your best friend's baby arrived via a status update that already has 75 comments will leave those who truly love you feeling a bit cold. Take their feelings into consideration when making announcements throughout the pregnancy process. Make sure to hold off any major announcements until your phone tree has been initiated.

However, after news of the baby has spread through the appropriate channels to the appropriate people, social networking sites are a great way to show off your new bundle of joy to the adoring masses. It may cut down on the number of visits and phone calls you will receive when you're basking in the glow of new fatherhood.

Part III

Game Time! Labor, Delivery, and Baby's Homecoming

The 5th Wave

By Rich Tennant

"They said we might notice some changes a week before she went into labor. Sure enough, 5 days ago, gas prices went up 6 cents at the pump, my lawn mower stopped working, and the guy across the street had his house painted."

In this part...

If you want to be prepared for labor and delivery as well as the first hectic days at home, this part gives you all the necessary details. From knowing what to do when labor starts to feeding concerns and understanding the contents of the baby's diaper, the chapters in this part equip you to handle the big and little events and changes that take place in all your lives in a very short time span.

Chapter 9

Surviving Labor and Delivery

● ●

In This Chapter

▶ Determining when labor is really happening

▶ Providing the best support possible

▶ Understanding the normal physical and medical aspects of labor

▶ Dealing with labor pain

▶ Needing a cesarean section

● ●

*N*o matter how many birth plans you write (refer to Chapter 8 for more on writing a birth plan), and how many times you suffer through your relative's birth stories, labor always comes as a surprise. For many guys, it's the first time you see your partner in real pain. Even worse, you know it's your fault — because she reminds you of that fact every five minutes. The end result will be worth it, though, so fasten your seat belt and get ready for the roller-coaster ride of labor and delivery.

No two labors are alike, so we can't say exactly what will happen in your partner's labor. The only thing most labors have in common is a beginning and an end, and still, labor can begin in a number of ways and can end in an operating room, birthing center, back seat of the car (not to scare you), or in your own bedroom. Although details differ, knowing approximately how labor will go can reduce your anxiety by, well, maybe a little bit.

When It's Time, It's Time — Is It Time?

Although you may think you won't have trouble telling when your partner is in labor, you may. Contractions often get closer as labor progresses, but sometimes they don't. Some women are in a lot of pain in labor, and some aren't.

All this confusion over the start of labor may have you leaping into the car every time your partner sighs during the last month of pregnancy; an actual moan may have you reaching for the phone to call 911. Take 911 off speed dial, though; labor isn't always clear cut, but you can follow a few general rules when it comes to heading for the hospital:

✔ **If her water breaks, call your medical practitioner.** If you're having the baby in the hospital, they'll probably want her to come in, even if she isn't having contractions. However, many women prefer to go through early labor at home, even after the water breaks. Discuss this with your medical practitioner. After the water breaks, she has an increased risk of infection and a small chance that the umbilical cord can *prolapse,* or fall below the baby's head.

✔ **If your partner's a beta strep carrier, go to the hospital as soon as her water breaks.** During pregnancy, women are tested for beta strep, a common bacteria that can be carried in the vagina. The bacteria normally causes no harm in healthy women, but after the water breaks, beta strep can ascend up to the fetus and cause serious infection, so intravenous antibiotics need to be started right away.

✔ **If your partner's in severe pain, even if the contractions are not regular, call your medical practitioner.** Pregnancy complications such as the placenta separating from the uterine wall, called *placental abruption,* can cause severe pain and can be life threatening.

✔ **If bleeding like a menstrual period occurs, call your medical practitioner.** A small amount of blood-tinged mucus is common when the mucus plug is passed, but heavier bleeding needs medical evaluation.

✔ **When contractions are regular and getting closer, call your medical practitioner.** They don't have to be — and may never be — five minutes apart.

Avoiding numerous dry runs (yes, it's us again)

Calling your medical practitioner before going to the hospital and following his advice can save you many embarrassing excursions in and out of the labor and delivery ward. Think no one ever gets sent home without a baby? Think again. Think no one has ever gotten sent home ten or more times in a single pregnancy? Think again, again. And yes, the staff will remember you from last week, and the week before, et cetera, et cetera.

Many women have contractions in the last month of pregnancy. If your partner's contractions aren't becoming stronger or getting closer together, this probably isn't the real deal. Unless her water breaks, she's in severe pain, or she's bleeding, wait until contractions get stronger and closer together. Just being in the labor and delivery ward really doesn't speed up the birthing process.

Knowing when it's too late to go

When your partner can't walk or talk through contractions that are progressively stronger and closer together, it's really time to go to the hospital. You'll know this instinctively when she says, "It's time to go *now*." But if by some chance she's a woman with short labors and says she feels pressure, has to have a bowel movement, or starts to push, dial 911, unless you personally want to deliver the baby in the back seat or the hospital lawn. (Coauthor Sharon has seen both situations.) Most emergency medical technicians have delivered babies before, or at the very least have read the manual that tells them what to do.

If the EMTs don't arrive in time, get your medical practitioner (or anyone's medical practitioner, actually) on the phone and follow her instructions. Rapid deliveries are usually uncomplicated, and your job may consist of calming your partner and not letting the baby fall on the floor.

In addition:

- ✔ **Don't pull on the cord or cut it.** Cutting the cord, dealing with the placenta, and worrying about vaginal tears can be done by people more schooled in such things than you.

- ✔ **Dry the baby off and keep him warm.** Skin-to-skin contact with mom is ideal.

- ✔ **If the baby isn't breathing, flick his heels.** Don't slap him or turn him upside down, even if you've seen it in the movies.

Don't dwell too much on the possibility of an unexpected home delivery. The odds are very small that a first labor will progress so quickly that the baby delivers at home.

Supporting Your Partner during Labor

Women in labor need lots of support. Your partner needs to hear that she's doing well, that things are progressing as they should, and that she really can do this. Even if her mother, sister, doula, and five of her dearest friends are with her, she needs *you*. Support means different things to different women, though, and your job is to figure out what she needs while in labor and do it.

Figuring out how she wants to be supported

Your partner may not be in a very talkative mood during labor, so asking her what she wants you to do may get you kicked right out of the room. This is one time in her life when she wants you to think for yourself and take action without being told what to do. Take the lead by offering choices. Ask her if she wants

- A back rub
- A massage
- A hand to hold
- You to sit behind her and support her back
- An epidural
- You to kick her mom out of the room
- Ice chips
- To get in the tub
- Any of the other labor options you discussed before today

Not taking the insults seriously

Women are not responsible for anything they say during labor, but you are, so don't get upset with any suggestions she makes about your anatomy or comments on your ancestry. And she doesn't really mean what she said about your mother, either.

Pain makes people say things they don't mean and may not even remember, so don't file away her remarks for another day. Vocalizing the pain in this way is both healthy and normal.

Looking at What Happens during and after Labor

Although childbirth classes and books do their best to tell you what will happen in labor, the reality is hard to describe in a book. But since it's our job to give you all the facts you can handle, the following sections describe what the normal stages of labor look like.

First stage

The first stage of labor encompasses the time between the first labor pain and complete dilation, when your partner will begin to push. Because quite a few things happen during the first stage of labor, it's further broken down into early, active, and transition stages of labor.

Early labor

Early labor is defined as the time between the start of labor and dilation of the cervix to 3 centimeters. This is the longest part of labor, sometimes lasting a day or two. During the early stage, contractions are often far apart and irregular. These early contractions thin and dilate the cervix. In late pregnancy, the cervix is thick, and the opening between the uterus and vagina is closed.

Normally the cervix thins before it begins to dilate, but there are no hard and fast rules. Many women are already somewhat thinned and dilated before labor begins.

Active labor

Things really start to move along during active labor, which is defined by regular contractions that become stronger and dilate the cervix from 4 to 10 centimeters. Active labor takes four to eight hours on average, although subsequent labors are often much shorter. A woman in active labor usually can't walk or talk through her contractions. She also may become a creature you haven't met before, one who knows words that may totally surprise you.

You need to be active in active labor, too. If your partner is doing natural childbirth, she needs help staying focused and breathing through the contractions. Don't just tell her to breathe; breathe with her. Some women want you to count off the seconds, others don't. Be guided by her responses, even if they're a little impolite at the height of a contraction.

If she's having an epidural, your help will also be appreciated. See the section, "What to expect during epidural placement" for the do's and don'ts.

Transition labor

Transition, the hardest stage, is the last part of active labor. Transition lasts from 7 centimeters to full dilation, or 10 centimeters. If your partner has a good epidural, this stage will probably breeze by, but if she's going natural, transition can be difficult. Transition can last anywhere from a few minutes in someone having a second or subsequent baby to a few hours in a woman having her first child. Typical side effects of transition include

- Shaking
- Vomiting
- Intermittent urges to push

Second stage

Second-stage labor lasts from the first push to the final delivery. Second-stage labor lasts anywhere from two minutes to three-plus hours. Women with epidurals often push less effectively, and medical practitioners may let the baby "labor down" without pushing if she's comfortable and the baby is doing okay.

Push, push, push!

Active pushing requires help from you, but don't actually push along with her, or you may have hemorrhoids almost the size of the baby after delivery. The nurse may ask you to help support your partner's legs or to support her back slightly.

The people in attendance at the delivery usually do lots of enthusiastic cheering when mom starts pushing. You'll find it easy to be enthusiastic when the baby's head finally begins to appear, although a little apprehension about how that big thing is going to make its way out of your partner's body is also normal.

Not all women are into the cheerleading scene, though, and actually prefer just to hear a single voice (yours) offering encouragement, or perhaps prefer no loud noises at all. If she looks aggravated during the cheers (beyond the effort of pushing), ask her what she wants. Then do it, and ask everyone else to comply.

Most delivery rooms have mirrors near the foot of the bed so that your partner can see what's going on. When your medical practitioner takes her seat at the end of delivery bed or table, she may block the mirror, but most mirrors can be adjusted so your partner has a better view if she wants it. Pushing is difficult with your eyes open, so she may not see much of the actual birth.

If you want to cut the cord, make your wishes known, although many practitioners will ask you automatically. If you're turning a little green, don't feel like you have to cut the cord. In fact, if you're turning a little green, please go sit on the floor, or in a chair, so the staff doesn't have to tend to you.

Getting a little lightheaded during delivery is not a sign of weakness. Many guys don't eat enough while their partner's in labor, and you may be standing for several hours helping her push. Deliveries are very messy; vomit, poop, and blood can make a pungent odor that can be hard to deal with, even for the most experienced labor and delivery staff. Try not to add to the mess by passing out and taking the delivery tray with you.

It's a miracle!

Birth is miraculous. There's no other way to put it. Even practitioners who have seen thousands of births are still awed by it at times. Watching a new human being come into the world is an amazing privilege, especially when he's *your* new human being.

Crying at deliveries is not unusual. Of course the baby usually cries and family members often do too, but sometimes even the staff cries if they've gotten really attached to a particular couple. Don't expect your doctor or midwife to get all teary eyed, although it does happen in some cases.

Don't be surprised if your first feeling upon seeing your baby is dismay, either. New babies are not always the most beautiful of creatures. (We discuss newborn peculiarities in Chapter 10.)

If the baby is okay, your practitioner may give your partner the baby to hold and possibly to try to nurse, if she wants to try immediately. Some centers prefer to dry off, weigh, and assess the baby before bringing him back to mom to nurse. Either way, within the first 15 minutes, the baby will be dried off, weighed, and wrapped up so one or both of you can hold her or your partner can start nursing.

Wrapping things up after the birth

The placenta is delivered usually within 15 minutes of the birth. Contractions may accompany the loosening and passage of the placenta, but if your partner had an epidural, she may not notice.

If the placenta doesn't pass within 15 minutes, some medical practitioners give additional medication to help loosen the placenta or gently tug on it. Both the medication and tugging can cause uncomfortable cramping. Other practitioners give the placenta more time to release on its own before starting more medical interventions.

Very rarely, a condition called placenta accrete occurs in which the placenta can't be removed from the uterine wall. In severe cases, a hysterectomy is done because the placenta can't be removed and severe bleeding often develops.

If your partner has a tear, or if an episiotomy was cut to give the baby a little extra room and avoid a tear, the wound needs to be closed after the placenta is delivered. It normally takes about 15 minutes to stitch everything back together. An injection of numbing medication is given before stitches are put in unless your partner's still completely numb from the epidural. If she didn't have an epidural, passing the placenta and stitching may be mildly uncomfortable or annoying.

Many facilities now do delivery and recovery in the same room, so the bed will be refreshed and your partner's gown changed after the mechanics of the delivery are all taken care of. And she can eat! If she wants something special, you may be sent out to get what she wants, or, better yet, send one of her friends or her mom out so you can stay to admire your new family.

Helping baby right after delivery

If the baby doesn't breathe well at first (many don't, so don't panic), she may be taken right over to the warmer to be given a little oxygen. Don't worry; the staff will bring her back to your partner as soon as she's stable.

As normal as it is to ask a lot of questions and want to know exactly what's happening, try to stay to the sidelines so you're not interfering with your baby's care. You want the staff to focus on taking care of the baby, not talking to you.

Most issues that affect babies right after delivery are related to breathing. Not breathing inside the womb to breathing on one's own is a big transition, and some babies take a few minutes to get the hang of it.

Oxygen may be given by *blow by*, which means a tube is placed near the baby's nose but not too close to her eyes. If she needs extra help, oxygen is given with a bag and mask connected to an oxygen source; the mask fits over her mouth and nose, and the staff squeezes the bag to force oxygen into the lungs.

If the baby doesn't pink up and start crying quickly, she may be taken to the special-care nursery for further evaluation. You will usually be welcome to accompany her and find out what's happening, but don't forget your partner, still lying on the table feeling as confused and upset as you are and possibly getting stitches in her bottom at the same time. Make sure you keep her informed about what's happening and let her know you haven't forgotten about her. She may want you to follow the baby so you can report back and tell her what's going on.

Undergoing Common Labor Procedures

In the interests of making you familiar with all possible aspects of labor and delivery, some of the procedures you can expect to see during labor are detailed in the next sections.

Vaginal exams

Vaginal exams are often uncomfortable, especially when they're done during a contraction, but they're the only way to tell what's happening during labor. The cervix is checked for dilation, which is the only way to assess labor progression. Although your partner may not be overly fond of vaginal checks, you may love them because they give you new information to convey to friends and family in the waiting room or on the other end of the phone.

IVs

If you're delivering in a hospital in the United States, your partner will most likely have an *intravenous infusion,* or IV for short. The IV serves the following purposes:

- **Supplying fluids:** Many hospitals restrict fluids when labor begins, and getting dehydrated is easy when you're working extra hard and not taking anything in. If an epidural is given, prehydration is necessary to avoid a drop in blood pressure, which can decrease oxygen flow to the baby.

- **In case of cesarean delivery:** With the percentage of cesarean deliveries now more than 30 percent in the United States, there's a very good chance your partner will end up with a cesarean. If the surgery is done as an emergency, with time being of the essence, having an IV already in place saves time.

~ **Covering the hospital's legal obligations:** If a woman has serious bleeding, an emergency cesarean, or just about any complication, an IV is necessary to give fluids to replace possible blood loss and maintain normal blood pressure, which often drops if spinal anesthesia is given for the surgery. Many hospitals routinely give IVs before they are really needed because, unfortunately, we live in a litigious society, and in the case of a malpractice suit, the lawyers will want to know if she had an IV in place for just such possible emergencies.

After an IV is in place it shouldn't be terribly uncomfortable, so if it is, let your partner's nurse know. Sometimes just retaping the catheter so it's at a different angle helps with the discomfort. Women who want to walk without dragging around an IV pole or spend time in the hot tub can have the IV hep-locked, which means the end is capped off and the bag of fluid detached. If needed, the hep-lock is flushed with solution to make sure it's still working before the bag is reattached.

Membrane ruptures

Although many women fear that their water will break someplace embarrassing, like in church or in the middle of aisle three at the grocery store, only around 10 percent of women's membranes rupture before labor starts. Often the membranes are broken by medical personnel using what looks like a crochet hook to snag the membranes and tear them. This procedure isn't painful for your partner or the baby.

Membranes are ruptured if your practitioner wants to check the fluid inside the sac for the presence of meconium, a sign of potential stress, sometime before or during labor. Between 6 to 25 percent of babies pass meconium before delivery; the older the meconium, the yellower and less particulate the fluid is. Newer meconium may be dark green, sticky, and form particles that can be sucked into the baby's lungs, causing respiratory problems at birth. The presence of either old or new meconium can cause respiratory problems at birth, so the fluid is always checked for meconium as soon as the membranes rupture.

If meconium is present, your practitioner will suck out the baby's nose and mouth as soon as the head is delivered to decrease the chance of inhalation. Keep in mind, however, that meconium can be inhaled before birth; there's no way to prevent this from happening because babies take practice breaths while still in the womb. Most of the time, the baby clears the meconium from the lungs, and no problems ensure, but it can cause severe lung infection and problems with circulation that require mechanical ventilation until the lungs heal, usually within a few days.

The membrane may also be ruptured to try to speed up labor, although labor doesn't always go faster after the membranes are ruptured, or so internal monitoring devices can be placed. (See "Fetal monitoring" for more about the ways your baby's heartbeat can be monitored before birth.)

Rupturing membranes can lead to harder, more painful contractions that don't actually speed up the process, so ask your medical practitioner why he wants to do this if you have concerns about it.

Fetal monitoring

Fetal monitoring devices record the fetal heart rate and the frequency and duration of the contractions. Don't let yourself become so enamored with the technology that you forget about the person at the other end! Many men love gadgets and start watching the monitor like it was the educational channel. (See the sidebar "Understanding fetal heart rates" in this chapter for more on what's normal and what's not.)

Monitoring your partner and the baby externally

External monitoring systems consist of two recording devices fastened around your partner's stomach and plugged into a fetal monitor, which provides a continuous printout of the fetal heart rate and the contractions. The monitor records the duration of contractions and the time between them but doesn't tell you the strength of the contraction. Each contraction resembles a hill or a bell-shaped curve, starting low, rising slowly, and then returning to baseline. Because the device sits on your partner's abdomen, attached with a belt, her body shape and position can affect how the contractions look on the monitor. Contractions that look like very large mountains on the monitor don't always indicate really strong contractions, and tiny hills don't mean the contractions aren't very strong.

The external fetal heart monitor tracks and records the fetal heart rate but has some limitations as well. It doesn't record the baby's exact heartbeat, but an average of beats. Variability, the difference in heart rate over a certain time period, can't be determined by external monitors, and beat-to-beat variability can help ascertain how well the baby is handling labor.

A heartbeat that stays the same with little variation may indicate that the baby is stressed. Short periods of decreased variability also occur when the baby is asleep. (And yes, babies do take short naps during labor!) The fetal heart rate may also have a short period of minimal beat-to-beat variability if your partner gets a dose a narcotic pain medication.

Understanding fetal heart rates

A normal fetal heart rate ranges from 110 to 160 beats per minute (BPM). Variations in the heart rate often occur for a short period of time before returning to baseline. Babies all have different baselines, so a heart rate of 115 BPM may be normal for one baby, but *bradycardic,* or unusually slow, for one whose baseline is 160 BPM.

Brief increases in the heart rate are called accelerations. They occur when the baby moves, if he runs a fever, or if he develops an infection. If the baby's heart beats too fast, your medical provider may say the baby is *tachycardic,* or *tachy.* Tachycardia can become dangerous because less oxygen is pumped out of the heart with each beat.

Brief drops in the heart rate often occur at the peak of the contraction and are caused by temporary pressure on the baby's head during active labor as the baby's descends into the birth canal. Bradycardia may also be caused by cord compression, if the baby compresses the cord with some part of his body and oxygen flow is temporarily decreased.

Bradycardia that lasts just a few seconds is not considered alarming, but bradycardia that lasts after the end of a contraction or that starts after the peak of the contraction, recovering shortly after the end of the contraction, can indicate decreased blood flow through the placenta.

Any unusual change in the fetal heart rate can be better assessed with continuous monitoring with an internal fetal monitor, which records an exact representation of the baby's heartbeat.

The external monitor also can't always distinguish between mom's heart rate and baby's. If your partner has a rapid heartbeat because of fever, anxiety, or other reasons, or if the baby has bradycardia, an extremely low heart rate, it may not be obvious that the external monitor isn't recording the right heartbeat.

Monitoring internally

Internal monitors resolve the shortcomings of external monitors by giving more accurate information. Internal contraction monitors are inserted directly into the uterus, which makes them able to record the exact strength of each contraction. You may be disappointed to watch those huge mountains that appeared to be very strong contractions shrink down to little blips on the monitor, indicating that the uterus is contracting only mildly, or you may be excited to see the opposite.

Internal fetal monitors fasten a tiny wire into the baby's scalp that records the exact fetal heart rate. This ensures that variability displayed is an accurate representation of the fetal heartbeat. An internal monitor can also differentiate maternal and fetal heart rates, if it's difficult to tell whose heart rate is recording on the external monitor.

Some centers use internal monitors routinely, while others use them only if they're having trouble picking up the heart rate or assessing the contractions. Internal monitor complications occur rarely, and include infection at the site of insertion or hematoma, a large bruise.

Coping with Labor Pain

Although you and your partner discussed pain medication options before the big day (and we discuss making the decision on pain medication in Chapter 8), nothing is written in stone when labor actually starts. A staunch au naturel supporter may find herself asking for an epidural the minute she hits the labor floor, and a woman who was sure she's epidural material may find herself breathing through labor and deciding she'd rather do without one. Don't ever be surprised by the decisions of a laboring woman.

Enduring it: Going natural

Going natural was all the vogue in the 1970s but fell out of favor when epidural anesthesia became available in all but the smallest hospitals. Natural delivery still does have some advantages, and there are good reasons to consider an unmedicated delivery. Your partner may decide to go natural for the following reasons:

- ✔ Babies whose moms haven't received medication may be more alert and may nurse better. Medication does cross the placenta to the fetus before delivery.

- ✔ Moving around during labor is easier if you're not medicated. Epidural anesthesia usually keeps you in bed, although "walking epidurals" are offered by some centers.

- ✔ Pushing is easier without an epidural, although some centers let an epidural wear down enough for mom to be able to push.

- ✔ Water therapy can't be utilized if you have epidural anesthesia.

- ✔ Going through labor unmedicated can be an empowering experience.

- ✔ Some women have bad reactions to medications in general and don't want to take anything they don't really need.

One good thing about going natural is that with a first labor, it's almost never too late to change your mind and request an epidural. If she decides she want an epidural at 9 centimeters, in many centers, she can have one.

Dulling it: Sedation (No, not for you)

Sedation takes the edge off labor without numbing the lower part of the body. Typical sedatives given in labor include Demerol, Nubain, or Stadol, which can be given intramuscularly or intravenously. IV administration takes effect quickly and lasts one to two hours.

Sedation may be given if it's too early in the labor to give epidural anesthesia. Sedation can take the edge off the pain and help your partner get a little sleep, but it can also slow contractions in some cases.

Because sedation can reach the baby, narcotics and narcotic-type medications often are not given if delivery is expected within the hour because the baby may not breathe well.

Blotting it out: Epidurals

Epidural anesthesia consists of medications given through a catheter placed in the spinal canal. The pro of epidurals is obvious: They decrease pain. They do have other benefits as well, in some cases. For example,

- Epidurals can help a tense mom relax. Tension can slow labor; women who are especially tense may benefit from an epidural to help them relax.
- Epidurals provide continuous pain relief. In many cases, a continuous infusion of medication prevents the medication from wearing off.

Medications used in epidurals

Several different types of medication are used in epidural anesthesia. Anesthetics such as lidocaine or bupivacaine may be combined with narcotics such as fentanyl or morphine. Narcotics decrease the amount of local anesthetics needed to achieve adequate comfort. Narcotics given in an epidural don't cause drowsiness the way sedatives do.

What to expect during epidural placement

An epidural can be given at any stage of labor, but usually isn't given in very early labor because it can slow progress. Some doctors will start Pitocin, a drug to induce labor, when epidural anesthesia is given in early labor.

A large amount of IV fluid, approximately one bag, is infused rapidly to offset the drop in blood pressure that may occur with epidural anesthesia. This infusion can be uncomfortable because the fluid is at room temperature and feels cold.

Dads are very much in demand during epidural placement to give mom a person to lean on so she can get into the proper "curled shrimp" position for catheter placement (see Figure 9-1). The epidural catheter is placed into the epidural place on the midback by inserting a metal needle into the epidural space and then threading the catheter through the needle. Only the soft plastic catheter remains in the back. She must remain sitting up and still, even through contractions, for a period of five to ten minutes while the catheter is placed.

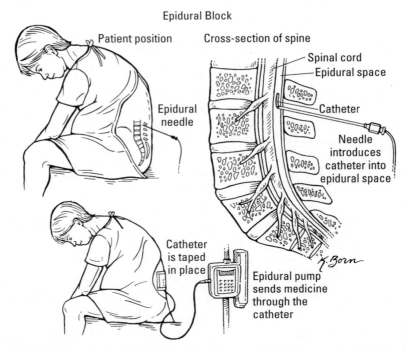

Epidural Block

Patient position · Cross-section of spine

Spinal cord
Epidural space
Epidural needle
Catheter
Needle introduces catheter into epidural space
Catheter is taped in place
Epidural pump sends medicine through the catheter

Figure 9-1: Placement of the epidural catheter requires remaining curled up and still for a short period.

After the catheter is taped in place, the anesthesiologist assists her back to a lying down position and assesses her blood pressure and comfort level for several minutes. In many centers, the epidural catheter is attached to an infusion pump that delivers a continuous infusion during labor to help maintain adequate pain relief.

 If you feel at all shaky or nervous while your partner receives the epidural, or if you start to get lightheaded from standing in one position too long, ask someone else to take over supporting mom so you can sit down before you fall down.

Sometimes placing the catheter is difficult due to your partner's anatomy, and more than one needle stick may be necessary. This isn't anyone's fault, and getting the catheter correctly placed is important, so you can help by staying calm and keeping your partner calm, too.

When the catheter is in place, a test dose is given, and your partner's blood pressure is carefully assessed, because epidural anesthesia can cause blood pressure to drop. She has to wear an automatic blood-pressure cuff on her arm for a short period, and she may find this very uncomfortable. If her blood pressure is low, she may be tilted slightly to her left side.

Possible side effects of an epidural

Following are some of the side effects of epidural anesthesia:

- ✔ **A rise in temperature:** It's difficult to tell whether infection or the epidural is causing a rise in temperature, so intravenous antibiotics must be given to avoid complications in case an infection is present. Any time mom runs a fever, the fetus may also develop one, from the increase in womb temperature.

- ✔ **Nausea and/or vomiting:** These symptoms may also occur in labors without epidurals.

- ✔ **Shivering:** The fluid infusion or the epidural can cause shivering. Your partner will appreciate extra blankets, especially if they're straight out of the warmer.

- ✔ **Hot spots:** Sometimes women have an area that doesn't "take" to the epidural, and they need to change positions so that the anesthesia goes to a different area and numbs the nerves that haven't been numbed well. In the worst-case scenario, the epidural may need to be re-placed.

- ✔ **Difficulty urinating:** Most women can't urinate well after the epidural is given, and a full bladder can get in the way of the baby's head and slow the pushing stage of labor. A Foley catheter may be placed to drain urine, or the bladder may be emptied intermittently.

Deviating From Your Birth Plan/Vision

Everyone has some vision of how labor is going to go, even if it isn't committed to paper. But most labors don't follow the book, or the birth plan. Knowing this ahead of time helps you avoid serious disappointment. Consider the birth plan as a guideline of what you would like to happen, with the proviso that mom's and baby's well-being come first.

Some women feel guilty about taking pain medication in labor if they were gung-ho to go natural before delivery. If your partner wants to take pain medication but is hesitating because she feels like she's letting the birth plan — or you — down, encourage her to follow her instincts. Remind her that no one knows what labor is like until she's in it, and that most women do end up taking pain medication in labor. After all, labor hurts!

On the other hand, your partner may have gone from au naturel woman to "give me the drugs!" seemingly in the blink of an eye, and you may be the one having a hard time with it and try to encourage her to stick to the plan. Don't do it. Encouragement is fine if she's just going through a rough spot in transition, for example, but if she's made her decision, your job is to support her in it. You may have devised the birth plan together, but she's the one going through labor, not you.

If your practitioner participates in a call group and baby comes at night or on the weekend, you may have a different practitioner for the actual delivery. After having established a relationship with a doctor over the past nine months, having a stranger do the delivery can be frustrating, especially if your partner specifically chose a doctor for his approach to labor. However, rest assured that whoever delivers your baby will do everything he can to ensure a safe and smooth delivery. Discuss this possibility with your practitioner in advance to find out what to expect.

If your partner ends up having a cesarean section or if the baby has any type of problem, large or small, she may feel that something she did in labor caused the problem. Assure her that this is not the case (because it won't be). Things go wrong in labor that are no one's fault; they can't be predicted or, in most cases, prevented. Your job is to tell her that she did exactly what she should have and that she has no reason for regrets. And if you have any niggling doubts about the wisdom of her labor choices, keep them to yourself.

Having a Cesarean

Cesareans now comprise more than 30 percent of all deliveries in the United States, so the odds of having one are high. Although cesareans are major surgeries, they're generally safe for your partner and the baby. However, babies born by cesarean section may retain more fluid in the respiratory tract than babies born vaginally, and the fluid can be aspirated into the lungs, causing breathing difficulties.

Maternal complications such as infection, anesthesia complications, blood clots, and excessive bleeding can also occur, as with any surgery.

Scheduled cesarean section

Cesareans may be scheduled ahead of time if you know your partner's going to need one. Knowing she's going to have a cesarean ahead of time helps you to get things ready for her homecoming, knowing that she's going to be extremely sore as well as tired. Your partner may not want to navigate stairs for the first week afterward, and won't be able to drive for several weeks.

Reasons for planned cesareans

Reasons for a scheduled cesarean include previous cesarean delivery and abnormal fetal position, such as breech (feet first) or transverse (sideways) lie. Most of the time, but not always, these are determined ahead of time, but babies have been known to switch positions just a few days before delivery.

Occasionally, women ask for a medically unnecessary cesarean delivery. Some doctors will perform these procedures, but having surgery you don't need is never a good idea. Cesarean delivery is riskier for the baby because fluid doesn't get squeezed out of the lungs before delivery, setting up potential respiratory difficulties.

Multiples are almost always delivered by cesarean, even though twins who are both vertex (head down) can certainly be delivered vaginally. However, after the first twin is delivered, there's an abundance of room in the womb, and the second twin may flip or turn sideways with the joy of having all that space to himself, necessitating a cesarean for baby B. No mother wants to experience both a vaginal delivery and a cesarean with all the attendant discomforts on the same day, so most twins are scheduled for C-sections.

Setting the date

Choosing your baby's birth date can be exciting, but consider the following caveats:

- ✔ Don't choose a weekend day. Most practitioners won't schedule surgery for the weekend.

- ✔ Don't expect to bypass the last three weeks of pregnancy with an early delivery date. More practitioners are trying to schedule cesareans no earlier than 38 weeks, to avoid preterm (before 37 weeks) delivery and potential complications.

- ✔ Understand that the baby may come before your scheduled date. The baby hasn't read your birth plan and doesn't know that you want him to be born on an auspicious date, and he may decide to show up a week earlier.

- ✔ Realize that having an 8 a.m. surgery time scheduled doesn't always mean your surgery will be at 8 a.m. Emergency cases can bump you off the schedule, which is understandable, so don't get too upset if you're delayed because someone else's cesarean needs to be done first.

- ✔ You don't have to set a date. Some couples decide not to schedule their delivery but to have the cesarean done when labor begins so that the baby chooses the time. Your practitioner may not be quite as happy to see you at 3 a.m. as she is at 8 a.m., though.

Unplanned cesarean delivery

A large percentage of cesareans are unplanned, with the most common reason cited for an unplanned C-section as "failure to progress," which means labor wasn't progressing as expected. This can mean a baby too large for the pelvis, an unusual maternal anatomy, or a practitioner who's getting antsy about how things are going.

If labor goes on too long, complications such as infection become more likely, and doing a C-section is often less stressful than waiting for the situation to possibly deteriorate. And as all too many practitioners are well aware, the decision to do a C-section is less likely to be attacked in court than a delay in action that leads to problems with the mother or baby.

Fetal distress is an undeniable reason for an unplanned C-section, although true fetal distress is different from potential fetal distress that could possibly worsen if labor goes on. True fetal distress is marked by a run down the hall at top speed, minimal surgery prep, and often general anesthesia, because it's the quickest way to put mom to sleep.

Potential fetal distress or mild distress usually results in a more leisurely trip to the operating room and a much calmer atmosphere, because the baby isn't in any real danger yet. And because you don't want him to reach that point, a C-section can be the best option. Trust your practitioner; if she says you need to do a C-section, do it.

Choosing a medical practitioner whose philosophy on cesareans as well as other medical interventions fits with yours is essential. Doctors do have different tolerance levels for deviations from the norm, and doctors who have a low tolerance for deviance generally have higher cesarean rates because they're less likely to watch and wait for a short time before performing surgery.

What to expect before the operation

Certain procedures must be done before cesarean delivery. Normally, a Foley catheter is placed to keep the bladder empty so it won't be injured during the surgery. If your partner already has an epidural, she won't even feel the catheter placement; if she doesn't, she may be mildly uncomfortable during the procedure.

A preparatory mini-shave is done (if she hasn't already done it herself) to eliminate hair where the incision goes. Most cesarean scars are known as a bikini cut, a horizontal lower abdominal incision (see Figure 9-2). Occasionally a vertical skin incision is done if the baby or babies lie in a position that makes her — or them — difficult to reach, or if the surgery has to be done very rapidly.

Your partner may be given medications to reduce the chance of nausea and to neutralize stomach acids in case of vomiting and possible aspiration into the lungs. She will also be given an intravenous line if she doesn't already have one. If spinal anesthesia is used for the procedure, fluid will be quickly infused, which can feel very cold. Also, an adequate amount of fluid is necessary to keep blood pressure from dropping after the cesarean.

Your partner may be taken into the operating room by herself while you get dressed in a sterile outfit. When you're allowed in, you'll probably be given a seat right near her head so you can talk to her and support her without getting in anyone's way. Keeping the operative area sterile is extremely important during surgery, and the staff will take care to make sure you don't inadvertently contaminate anything.

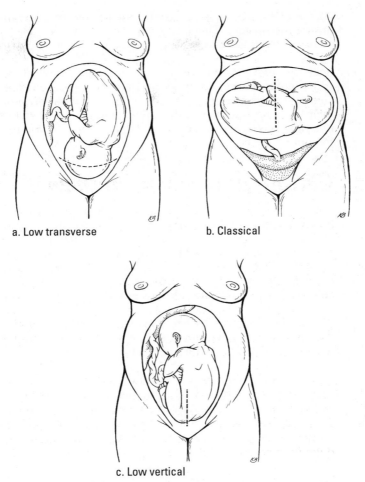

a. Low transverse   b. Classical

c. Low vertical

Figure 9-2: Most cesarean incisions are done just above the pubic hairline.

What to expect during the surgery

When the surgery actually gets underway, removing the baby takes between five and ten minutes. You won't be able to see much, because a sterile drape is placed between your partner's head and the rest of her body. When the baby is delivered, he may be brought close to your wife so she can see him, but she won't be able to nurse immediately or do any type of skin-to-skin contact due to the sterile operating field.

If general anesthesia is not used, your partner may feel tugging during the surgery. This is normal, but she may need lots of reassurance that it is okay.

Because babies born during cesarean sections have an increased risk of complications, a pediatrician or special-care nursery personnel may be present for the delivery. You'll be allowed to walk over to the warmer to see the baby, and in many hospitals, after the baby is weighed and cleaned, he'll be given to you to hold next to your partner.

Getting past disappointment

When you have the baby, you have her; it doesn't really matter how she got here. Your partner may not see it that way, though, and she may mourn the loss of the "perfect" labor and delivery and feel like she failed the labor test. With so many women having cesareans today, this feeling of failure is less common than it used to be, but if you and your partner had your hearts set on a certain labor scenario, a deviation from the script can be upsetting.

You can be a big help by accentuating the positives in the situation, by reminding her how well she handled the change in plans and how she put the baby's needs before her wishes.

Understanding why certain procedures were necessary can be very important in helping new mothers "grieve" the loss of a perfect delivery. Request a time to speak with the person who delivered your baby so that you and your partner can ask lingering questions about why the delivery went the way it did.

Chapter 10

Caring for Your Newborn

• •

In This Chapter

▶ Getting to know your newborn

▶ Deciding on breast- or bottle-feeding, or both

▶ Cleaning up your baby and putting him to bed

▶ Alleviating your baby's discomfort from indigestion

▶ Preparing for first immunizations

• •

*W*alking out the hospital door with a newborn who is still basically a stranger to you can be a scary experience. Getting to know your baby is a process that takes time. Fortunately you'll be putting in lots of time with this demanding stranger, and before you know it, you'll feel as if you've known this marvelous little person all your life. In this chapter we talk you through the seemingly mundane tasks that help you build a lifetime relationship with your new baby.

Knowing What to Expect When Baby's Born

Newborns don't look anything like the smooth-skinned, dimpled, smiling babies on TV. A new baby emerges from nine months in a dark, watery environment, and her skin shows it. She squints like she's just emerged from a cave. Although your newborn may not look exactly like the baby in your idealized dreams, she'll look perfect to you — at least after you get used to her in a day or two.

Looking at newborns

What should you expect when your newborn is put into your arms for the first time? Not the Gerber baby, that's for sure — although your baby will be, your partner will assure you, the most beautiful creature she's ever seen. You may seriously wonder about her taste in human beings. Newborn babies have the following characteristics:

- **Small:** The average baby is around 7 pounds and 20 inches long. The reality of how small and fragile a newborn seems won't hit you until the first time you hold him.

- **Red and covered with — what's that white stuff?** Newborns are amazingly red. They come out a dark red and then turn a lighter red, which gradually fades to a normal skin color over a few days. Many newborns are coated, especially in the creases, with *vernix,* a creamy substance that protected newborn skin in water.

- **Wrinkled and peeling:** Since he just spent nine months immersed in water, his entire skin has the equivalent of dishpan hands, and as soon as he begins to dry out, his skin wrinkles because it's no longer waterlogged. His skin will crack and peel, especially around the bendable joints like the ankles and wrists.

- **Cone headed:** You thought the Coneheads weren't real, until you met your new baby. If your partner pushed for any amount of time, or if the baby was delivered by vacuum extraction, the baby's head may be pointed at the back, or she may have a little cone cup, like a jaunty little hat, to the side of her head. The baby's head will become round in a week or so. Cesarean babies usually escape the cone-head look.

- **Spotted, dotted, and blotched:** Newborns often have a variety of blotches, splotches, whiteheads and other marks that will fade over time. *Milia* look like little whiteheads on the baby's nose, chin and forehead. Don't squeeze these; they'll disappear on their own. The majority of black, Indian, and Asian babies have what look like black and blue marks on their legs or buttocks, called *Mongolian spots,* which fade with time. Red blotches on the back of the neck, eyelids, and between the eyes, called *stork bites,* are immature blood vessels that also disappear with time.

- **Not very well put together:** Newborns often seem like they may fall apart if a strong wind comes along. Their heads wobble alarmingly, and their arms and legs shoot off in all directions when they're startled. No wonder nurses wrap them up tight in blankets.

- **A bit, uh, out of proportion:** You may be saying, "That's my boy!" but baby boys may have overlarge genitals due to fluid retention, trauma during delivery, and hormonal influences. This condition is temporary. Girls often have swollen genitalia as well, but it's less noticeable. Also, girls may pass a few drops of blood from the vagina.

✔ **Swollen breasts:** Because of maternal hormones, both baby boys and girls often have swollen breasts that may actually produce a few drops of milk. This condition disappears within a few days.

✔ **May have no family resemblance:** Before you accuse your partner that the baby isn't yours, rest assured that many newborns look slightly Asian, even if their parents aren't. Puffiness and swelling around the eyes make them appear Asian, and the yellow tinge of jaundice that many babies have after the first day or two may have you convinced that someone has a lot of explaining to do. Puffiness will improve daily, and by the end of the week, you won't be able to stop telling everyone how much the baby looks like you.

Rating the reflexes

Newborns are active from the minute they're born. Your baby will yawn, grimace, and even seem to smile a little. (Yes, the smiles are really caused by gas at this stage, just like your mother says.) Babies also have certain reflex actions that are normal at birth. Your medical practitioner will assess the baby to make sure these reflexes are present. Lack of normal reflexes can indicate a problem that should be investigated. They include the following tests:

✔ **Babinski reflex:** When the bottom of her foot is stroked, the big toe rises and the other toes fan out. The Babinski reflex lasts for around two years.

✔ **Grasp reflex:** If the baby's palm is stroked, she closes her fingers, a reflex that lasts several months.

✔ **The Moro, or startle, reflex:** Your baby tremors slightly, throws back her head, and flails her arms and legs away from her side in response to a sudden movement or a loud noise. The Moro reflex lasts five or six months before disappearing.

✔ **Rooting reflex:** Stroking the corner of the baby's mouth makes her turn toward the touch; this helps her find the breast or bottle for feeding.

✔ **Step reflex:** When her foot touches a solid surface, she appears to step, lifting one foot and then the other.

✔ **Sucking reflex:** When an object touches the roof of the baby's mouth, she begins to suck. This reflex doesn't develop until around 32 weeks of pregnancy and isn't fully developed until 36 weeks.

✔ **Tonic neck reflex (TNR):** If the baby's head turns to the side, her arm on that side stretches out and the opposite arm bends at the elbow, which makes her look like she's fencing. The TNR lasts six to seven months.

Feeding a Newborn

Every baby needs to be fed, but the sheer number of choices to be made about feeding may have you begging your partner to consider nothing but breast-feeding for at least the next year. However, though breast-feeding is best for the baby, it may not be best for your partner.

While your opinion is probably valued, the final decision about breast-feeding is absolutely, unquestionably, your partner's. Many women just aren't comfortable with breast-feeding, and a woman who isn't comfortable usually won't do it well. Sure, breast is best, but bottle-feeding is a perfectly adequate method of feeding.

A number of considerations go into the decision to breast- or bottle-feed. If your partner has even the slightest interest, breast-feeding for the first few days so the baby receives *colostrum,* the first fluids produced, is a good way to start. Colostrum contains many nutrients and antibodies that are good for the baby. If your partner hates it, she can stop at any time, but she may love it! If she stops breast-feeding, though, it's hard, but not at all impossible, to get the milk flowing again. See Chapter 11 for more on making the decision to breast-feed.

Choosing to breast-feed

If your partner decides to breast-feed, you may be breathing a sigh of relief that the nighttime duties won't fall to you, but not so fast! Breast-fed babies usually eat more frequently than bottle-fed babies because breast milk is more easily digested. If you're cosleeping, or even if the baby is across the room, you'll probably be awake at 12 a.m., 3 a.m., and 6 a.m., too.

Even if you normally sleep like the dead and wouldn't wake up if the Titanic floated through your bedroom, getting up and offering support for at least one of the night feedings can be a wonderful contribution to your partner and make you feel closer to your baby. Get your partner a drink, help her get into a comfortable position, and talk to her if she wants conversation. Late-night talks are conducive to confidences and discussions you may not have time for during the day.

If you're working full-time, getting up in the night is hard but worth it. Getting to know your new little person and your partner better is worth the sacrifice, and this time too shall pass, faster than you can imagine.

Getting started

Although breast-feeding seems like it should be easy and natural, it isn't always. Many women today have no role models for breast-feeding; their moms may not have breast-fed, their friends may not be doing it, and you're not much help, either. Most hospitals have lactation consultants to help new moms get started breast-feeding. Some also offer at-home visits if needed. If you have a doula, she will also be invaluable in helping with issues that arise.

And of course, books like *Breastfeeding For Dummies* (Wiley) cover everything you need to know and are available for consultation day and night! The most common problems with breast-feeding include:

✔ **Latch-on problems:** Women with large or flat nipples often have a difficult time getting the baby to latch on. This is frustrating for mom and baby alike, and often ends with both in tears. If the baby isn't properly latched, he won't get a good milk supply. Patience, and in some cases, using a nipple shield, which fits over the nipple to give the baby something to grasp onto if nipples are very flat, can conquer latch-on problems.

✔ **Supply issues:** Most women have ample milk supply starting around the third day after delivery, but some need supplements to increase milk supply. Drinking plenty of fluids, getting enough rest, and eating herbs like fenugreek can help increase supply. Before a good milk supply is established, supplementing the baby's diet with formula or pumping rather than nursing is discouraged, because sucking increases the supply. Pumping isn't as effective as a baby's suck at stimulating milk supply. Breast milk is the original supply-and-demand system.

✔ **Parental anxiety:** Many new parents are obsessed with their baby's weight. Breast-feeding can frustrate parents who want to know how much milk the baby is getting at each feeding. However, you can still measure his intake if you have a baby scale; just weigh the baby before and after a feeding and compare. Don't change his clothes, not even his diaper, or the weight won't be accurate. A baby scale can save the sanity of weight-obsessed parents.

Supplemental bottles

After the milk supply is well established, supplemental bottles of formula or pumped breast milk can be given. Bottle-feeding is a nice way for you to be able to feed and bond with the baby occasionally, and it gives your partner a chance to get out of the house or actually take an uninterrupted shower. Decreasing the number of nursing times a day reduces the milk supply, though, so don't overdo the supplemental bottles.

Don't be surprised if the baby doesn't quite understand what to do with the bottle at first. Bottle-feeding and breast-feeding require completely different tongue positioning and techniques on the baby's part. Some babies refuse supplemental bottles, which can be a problem if your partner gets sick or for some reason can't breast-feed. While you can feed a recalcitrant breast-feeder with an eyedropper, it certainly isn't fun for either of you. Some medical practitioners recommend an occasional supplemental bottle after nursing is well established so the baby gets used to taking an occasional bottle.

Many dads are a little envious of the closeness of the breast-feeding relationship and enjoy skin-to-skin contact while they feed the baby. Others find this just too weird. Whichever camp you're in, supplemental bottles can give you time to study your baby's face in detail and revel in the miracle you've created.

Pumping

Pumping to fill a supplemental bottle or if your partner goes back to work is easier than it used to be. Your partner can use an electric pump that's more efficient than the old bicycle-horn-type pumps. A really good pump can be really pricy but is worth it if your partner is going to use it a lot. Pumping is nowhere near as efficient as nursing is, so the amount produced may be much less than you think it should be. This difference is normal and not a sign that the baby isn't getting enough milk.

Pumped milk should be stored in feeding sized amounts, especially if you're freezing it, because you don't want to thaw out more than you'll use at one time. Use plastic or glass containers with well-fitted tops, but avoid anything containing bisphenol A (BPA). Collection bags made specifically for freezing breast milk are ideal.

Don't use plastic baggies or bags from disposable bottles, which may leak or contain substances that affect the nutrients in breast milk.

Breast milk can be stored at room temperature for up to six hours, in the refrigerator for up to eight days, and in the freezer for up to 12 months.

Bottle-feeding basics

Bottle-feeding has never been more complicated. Not only do you have to choose a formula and a nipple type, you have to worry about the materials the bottle is made of. Recent reports about the high levels of BPA (a chemical used in plastics) released when bottles are heated in the microwave or dishwasher has made choosing a bottle type more difficult. At least bottles no longer need to be sterilized on top of the stove: Ask your mom or grandma about how much fun that used to be!

Winning the bottle battle

Once upon a time, all baby bottles were made of glass. Then parents got tired of being beaned with glass bottles, and everyone worried about glass bottles breaking when the baby threw it out of the crib, so plastic bottles were invented about two minutes after the invention of plastic. Not only were they lighter and unbreakable, but they also came in pretty colors.

Then bottle manufacturers decided to mix things up a bit. Now bottles and nipples are no longer interchangeable, and bottle "systems" sometimes include plastic liners and inserts that reduce air intake and, hopefully, colic. Every bottle has to be used with its own system, and parents have to decide which works best for their baby.

Studies have shown cause for concern about plastic bottles releasing the harmful chemical BPA when heated. Some parents have switched back to glass, but manufacturers now create BPA-free plastic bottle systems. If you have older bottles and they're not BPA free, get rid of them. Spending more money on another whole bottle system is painful, but it's better than worrying about poisoning your child every time you warm a bottle in the microwave.

Choosing a formula

After you pick your bottles, you can start worrying about which formula to use. The array is truly formidable. For starters, you have to consider powder versus concentrate versus readymade. Following are the advantages and disadvantages of each type:

- ✔ **Ready to serve** can be very convenient for travel, if you use one can at a feeding. However, it's out of the question for everyday use for most people, because a month's supply is equal to the national budget of a small European country.

- ✔ **Concentrate** comes in small cans, and you dilute it with water before feeding. It's easy to use but more expensive than powder, though it's cheaper than ready to serve.

 ✔ **Powder** is the cheapest of the three options. If you're out of the house, it's easy to put the powder in a bottle and just fill with warm water when the baby's ready to eat. However, it comes in ginormous cans that take up half your kitchen countertop. It also clumps and takes more effort to shake smooth, a consideration at 4 a.m. when any effort seems like too much. Shaking the bottle to mix increases the bubbles and air inside the bottle, which can cause gasiness, so if your baby is already prone to gas, powder formula may not be for you.

After you decide on the form of your formula, it's time to choose one. This will not be easy; about a hundred different formulas are on the market, all claiming to be the best (although most grudgingly acknowledge that breast-feeding is also very good). Following are the general categories of formulas:

 ✔ **Regular:** Regular formula is made from cow's milk and contains 20 calories per ounce. Regular formula is usually fortified with iron. Some are also fortified with long-chain polyunsaturated fats that they claim enhance eye and brain development, but these claims are not well substantiated.

 ✔ **Enhanced:** Enhanced formula, often used for premature or failure-to-thrive babies, contains 24 calories per ounce.

 ✔ **Soy:** Soy-based formulas may be used by parents wanting to avoid animal proteins. However, soy contains estrogen, and some studies show that too much soy can be harmful to infants and children. Make sure to do your research before you switch to soy.

 ✔ **Hypoallergenic:** Babies who are allergic to lactose or soy may need protein hydrolysate formulas, which are easier to digest. Nutramigen, Pregestamil, and Alimentum are examples of protein hydrolysate formulas.

Preparing a bottle

The hardest part of preparing some bottles is putting the "system" together. Some bottles have inserts to put in, and others have little bags to put in place that hold the formula.

To make a bottle, read the instructions on the formula label. For powder, you mix a certain number of scoops with a certain amount of water, sometimes a foggy concept in the middle of the night. Concentrates are usually diluted 1:1, and ready-to-serve formulas don't get diluted at all.

Never try to "stretch" formula by adding more water than usual or by adding water to ready-to-serve formulas. You may deprive your baby of essential nutrition by doing so.

Many parents prefer to use distilled water, sometimes labeled as *nursery water,* rather than tap water, but if you have city water, it's probably not necessary. Boil the water from the tap if you're concerned about it, and use cold water rather than hot, which may contain more lead from the pipes. Let the water run for 30 seconds to reduce lead and other mineral contamination.

If you want to use well water, have a sample of it tested to make sure it doesn't contain high levels of nitrates or other minerals. Boiling well water concentrates nitrates instead of removing them, so it isn't recommended.

Knowing how much formula is enough

When your baby is brand new, he probably won't take more than 2 or 3 ounces at a time. The most important thing about bottle-feeding is to not try to force the last drop down your child's throat. With childhood obesity at an all-time high and a major health concern, the last thing you want to do is overfeed your child from an early age.

On the other hand, if he drains the bottle and acts like he's still hungry, give him a little more. Babies aren't machines, and they don't take the same amount of formula at each feeding. When he stops sucking and tries to push the bottle out of his mouth, he's had enough.

Changing Diapers

Changing diapers is the task new parents are probably least excited about. If you and your partner find yourselves playing "rock, paper, scissors" to determine which of you gets stuck changing the runny yellow poop that has overflowed out of the diaper and on to the sleeper, your shirt, and the new leather sofa, you're normal.

Diaper duty isn't fun, but it is necessary an appalling number of times a day when your baby is new, so rest assured you'll both get plenty of experience.

Circed or uncirced? Making the decision

Circumcision is a procedure in which the foreskin of the penis is removed. For Jewish parents, circumcision is a religious ritual usually done in a ceremony called a bris. For other parents, whether or not to have your baby boy circumcised is a personal choice. Twenty years ago, nearly all baby boys were circumcised, but today, more parents are questioning whether a surgical cosmetic procedure is necessary in a baby's first days of life. Around 50 percent of baby boys are now circumcised each year in the United States.

The main benefit to circumcision is ease in cleaning and avoiding the need to have the foreskin removed at a later date for medical reasons, but boys who are circumcised also have fewer urinary tract infections. Uncircumcised males are also more likely to contract sexually transmitted diseases later in life. Some dads just want their son circumcised so they'll "look the same."

Cleaning baby boys

Boys and girls really are different when it comes to diaper changing. When dealing with a baby boy, the worst part is projectile urination. You can easily avoid it if you remember to keep the penis covered at all times. A few good shots to the eye will reinforce your memory quickly.

Boys who have been circumcised (see Figure 10-1a), which means that the foreskin covering the tip of the penis has been removed, need extra TLC at first. You may need to wrap Vaseline-coated gauze around the tip for the first few days, depending on your practitioner's instructions. The gauze needs to be changed every time you change his diaper.

 When you remove the gauze around the circumcision, you may be horrified to see that the skin is a yellowish color. This is normal healing for a mucus membrane. If the area is oozing or has pus or a foul odor, call your practitioner.

Uncircumcised boys are a little harder to clean, and the foreskin (see Figure 10-1b) needs to be kept loose. The foreskin doesn't retract, or pull back easily, before the age of 1 year or even longer. Up to this point, only the outside of the foreskin should be cleaned. When it can be retracted, gently push it back as far as it will go, which isn't be very far, and clean with only water. Return the foreskin to its normal position afterward. If the foreskin becomes red or swollen, have your medical practitioner take a look to make sure he doesn't have an infection.

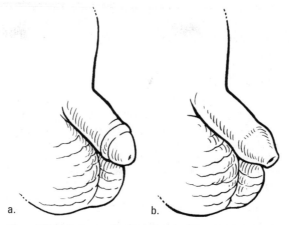

Figure 10-1: A circumcised penis (a) and an uncircumcised penis (b).

Cleaning baby girls

Baby girls aren't likely to spray the room when you remove their diaper, but they have their own set of problems. Keep these points in mind when changing a baby girl:

- ✔ Girls have lots of cracks and crevasses, and getting all of them clean is difficult. A runny, poopy diaper goes everywhere. Use moistened wipes or cotton balls to make sure you remove all the stool.

- ✔ Girls are more likely to have urinary tract infections because of the proximity of the anus and vagina to the urethra, so it's really important to make sure the whole area is clean.

- ✔ Always wipe from front to back. Doing so helps to avoid introducing fecal matter into the vaginal area, which can cause infections.

- ✔ Don't be too gentle. Make sure to thoroughly wipe the opening of the vagina or it can close up. If that happens you will have to apply a steroid cream to help reopen it, or, even worse, have it surgically reopened.

Bathing Basics

Few things strike fear into the hearts of inexperienced parents like the first bath. Take a squirmy baby, soap him all over to make him incredibly difficult to hold on to, and then put him in a tub of water. Sounds like a recipe for disaster, or at the very least, parental heart failure, but it doesn't have to be. Many hospitals now do a "trial run" bath to make sure you won't drown the poor child right off the bat, but even the least experienced new dad can learn to give the bath. Remember these suggestions when getting ready for baby's first bath:

1. **Get your supplies ready first.**

   Nothing makes a bath more difficult than getting the water drawn, the baby undressed, and the towel laid out and realizing you forgot to get the soap, or the lotion, or the diaper. No, the baby doesn't wear the diaper into the bath — you need it ready the minute you take him out, though, especially if your baby's a boy, unless you want an eyeful of urine.

2. **Put the baby in a comfortable spot.**

   Undressing him on the toilet lid may seem like a good idea if you're bathing him in the sink, or on the counter if you're bathing him in a little baby bath, but those surfaces are cold and hard, even with a towel over them, and they may be riddled with germs. Get him ready on the changing table or bed; take off everything except the diaper (urine, remember?) and bring him into the bathroom wrapped in the towel.

3. **Hold the baby and fill the tub, or have your partner handle one of those jobs.**

   Bath water for the baby should be 90 to100 degrees F. You can monitor the temperature to make sure it isn't too hot or isn't getting too cold with cute little floating bath toys that have built-in thermometers. If you're using a sink, pad it by lining it with a towel. A towel also helps reduce the slipperiness of a baby bathtub.

4. **Before putting the baby into the bath, wet a washcloth and squirt the baby soap onto the washcloth.**

   This way you don't have to do it while you try to hold the baby in the water at the same time.

5. **Undo the diaper tabs, then whip off the diaper and put the baby in the water.**

   Don't give him time to do anything dastardly.

6. **Don't expect the baby to enjoy this new experience at first.**

   Yes, he spent 9 months in water, but he's forgotten already, and your inexperienced hands aren't supporting him as well as the womb did. Some baby tubs have a little sling or are curved to support the baby. Otherwise, support his head and neck with your hand, or the crook of your arm, if you're well coordinated.

7. **Wash the baby with the soapy washcloth, starting at his head and working your way down.**

   Yes, just like you'd wash the wall, or the car. The genitalia should be the last part you wash. When you get to the bottom (literally), use a clean washcloth if it seems more hygienic to you.

8. **Rinse him off with a clean washcloth.**

9. **Lift him out of the water and wrap the towel around him.**

   A towel with a little hood help keep him warm and makes him look like an adorable elf. Don't admire him too long, because you need to get his diaper back on — quickly.

10. **Carry him to the changing surface, where the fresh diaper is already laid out. To keep him warm, keep the towel over the top half of his body while you put the diaper on.**

11. **Dry him off gently and dress him.**

    Babies have delicate skin, so don't rub too hard with the towel.

12. **Now collapse on the couch — you've earned it!**

Holding Your Baby

You're going to find yourself carrying the baby around quite a bit during the first few weeks. Babies who are colicky (cry a lot) are often more comfortable if you keep moving, and moving will help dispense your tension and anxiety when you're on hour two of a colic episode. Babies can be held in several ways, and yours may have a definite preference. Try these tried-and-true baby holds:

- **Cradle position:** Cradle the baby's head in the crook of your arm. Most people hold the baby on the left side, but go with what works for you.

- **Over the shoulder:** Some gassy babies feel better with pressure on their abdomen, so slinging them up onto to your shoulder may help get the gas out. However, spit-up-prone babies and vomiters also like this position, so have a burp cloth on your shoulder at all times.

- **Football hold:** The baby's head rests on your hand looking up, while her body lies on your arm, with her feet pointed at your elbow.

Whichever position you choose to hold your baby in, use it often! Nothing is better for dad and baby bonding than time spent in close proximity.

Cosleeping Pros and Cons

Cosleeping, or sleeping with the baby in your bed, goes in and out of vogue. Right now cosleeping is popular with many parents, although it comes with a twist in some cases: The baby may sleep in a little sidecar, or cosleeper, that attaches to your bed. You get the whole bed to yourself, but the baby is right nearby.

Traditional bassinets or small playpens or baby beds also work well, if you're not comfortable sharing the bed with the baby. If you're still debating about keeping the baby in your bed, or even in your room, consider the following advantages:

- ✔ **Cosleeping is convenient if your partner is breast-feeding.** Breast-feeding is much easier if you don't have to get out of bed to get the baby.

- ✔ **You hear the baby as soon as she starts stirring.** While this itself has pros and cons, the benefit is that she doesn't have a chance to work herself into a crying frenzy before a feeding.

- ✔ **It can give you a sense of closeness as a family.** To hear your baby's soft breathing is reassuring and also enjoyable.

Also consider the following disadvantages:

- ✔ **Very light sleepers, especially light sleepers with a baby who is also a light sleeper, may find the whole family awake most of the night.** If you're keeping the baby awake, or she's keeping you awake, you're all going to be excessively cranky.

- ✔ **You may be too worried about rolling over on the baby to enjoy cosleeping.** If you sleep very soundly, and the baby is right next to you, this can be a concern, but most parents are very aware of the baby's presence. If it worries you, a bassinet or other sleeping arrangement in the room may be better for you.

- ✔ **If one of you works odd shifts, you may find getting in or out of the room without waking the baby difficult.**

- ✔ **When you put the baby in your bed, you eventually have to put her out.** While your child may prefer to stay in your bed until she goes to college, you may want your bed back in a few years. Some children don't go quietly into the dark night and put up quite a fight about sleeping in their own rooms.

Remember that even if you don't want the baby in your room with you, baby monitors make it possible to hear the slightest stirring from another room.

Back to Sleep: Helping Baby Sleep Safely and Comfortably

Once upon a time, almost all babies slept on their stomachs. The babies preferred it, they had less gas, and if they spit up or vomited, they were less likely to choke. Then, in 1992, the American Academy of Pediatricians released new recommendations about placing babies on their backs rather than stomachs to sleep, claiming that babies were less likely to die of sudden infant death syndrome (SIDS) if they slept on their backs.

The "Back to Sleep" campaign went into full swing in 1994, heavily promoted by pediatricians. Within a few years, almost all babies were put to sleep on their backs, at least while they were in the hospital. Since the back sleeping movement was launched, the incidence of SIDS-related deaths has dropped by more than 50 percent, from 1.2 deaths per 1,000 live births in 1992 to 0.55 in 2006. Studies in 2006 showed that overall in the United States, 75 percent of babies slept on their backs.

A baby who is used to sleeping on his back but is placed prone (on his stomach) to sleep, possibly by a caregiver not familiar with the benefits of back sleeping, has an 18-fold increased risk of SIDS, according to the American Academy of Pediatricians (AAP).

Side positioning was originally considered a viable alternative to back sleeping, but more recent recommendations from the AAP are that side sleeping also increases the risk of SIDS, as well as the risk of the baby moving from a side to a prone position. To further reduce the risk of injury or death, keep soft fluffy blankets, pillows, and mattress pads out of the crib as well. A firm sleeping surface is best.

Coping if baby hates being on his back

Many babies truly hate sleeping on their backs. They don't sleep well, their parents don't sleep well, and everyone is miserable. What should you do if you and your baby are both desperate to get some sleep?

✔ **Tough it out.** This is really hard to do, but a good night's sleep is not worth the risk of SIDS.

✔ **Rock the baby to sleep first.** If she's asleep before you lay her down, she may stay asleep when you place her on her back.

✔ **Use a pacifier.** Even if you hate them, pacifiers really do soothe some babies. The American Academy of Pediatricians (AAP) recommends using one at bedtime because pacifier use also decreases the risk of SIDS.

Swaddling your little one

Some parents find their babies are calmer and sleep better when they're tightly wrapped in blankets so their arms and legs can't go flying off in every direction whenever they're startled. Nurses swaddle babies in the hospital for this reason (and because it makes them look adorable). Even the most fumble-fingered dad can do this at home, even though it won't look at all like the nurse's version at first. To swaddle, follow these instructions and also refer to Figure 10-2:

1. **Put the blanket on a flat surface like a diamond, with a point up.**

2. **Fold the pointy end at the top down about 6 inches.**

3. **Put the baby on the blanket, with his head just above the folded-down edge.**

4. **Pull one of the pointy ends on the side across the baby, covering his arms, and tuck it behind his back.**

5. **Bring up the bottom point to the baby's chin.**

6. **Repeat Step 4 using the remaining point of the blanket**

    Make it tight enough to make the baby feel secure, but not tight enough to cut off his circulation!

Realize that the baby is not going to lay perfectly still during this procedure. It will take you at least a few tries to get it right.

Preventing the flat head look

Babies now sleep on their backs and also spend hours with their heads back in swings, bouncy seats, and car seats. No wonder so many of them have flat heads. A flattened back or side part of the head, called plagiocephaly, can be more than just a cosmetic problem. Though 20 percent of infants today have flat heads, according to the AAP, all but 8 percent will round out naturally without treatment by 24 months.

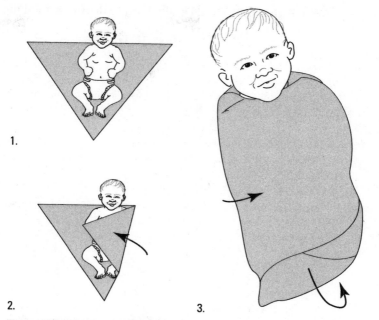

1.

2. 3.

Figure 10-2: How to swaddle a baby.

You can help prevent plagiocephaly by following these suggestions:

- ✔ **Have tummy time:** Babies need to spend some time on their stomachs when they're awake to strengthen their neck muscles. This time also gives the back of the head a chance to round out!

- ✔ **Carry the baby:** Don't always plop the baby in a swing or bouncer when he's awake; carry him around with you so he gets to see more of the world and he doesn't put pressure on his head. Figure 10-3 shows you how to carry your baby in a carrier, if you're interested in doing so.

- ✔ **Change the room around:** If possible, move the crib from one side of the room to the other from time to time so the baby sleeps with his head turned a different way. Or leave the crib in place and turn the baby, moving him from one end of the crib to the other.

Plagiocephaly is treated by molding a custom helmet that exerts pressure on the baby's head and gradually changes the shape as the baby grows. The helmet is worn 23 hours out of the day and is adjusted as the baby's head begins to round out.

Deciphering cries

Every baby cries a little differently, and every baby has different cries for different occasions. Differentiating the "I'm hungry" cry from the "I have a gas bubble"
or "I'm all alone and need company" cry takes practice, but eventually you'll
be like the Amazing Kreskin, able to decipher your baby's every need from two
rooms away.

And if you have no idea what the kid wants, even when you've had her home for a few
months? Do what other parents do: Fake it and try everything until something works.
Some parents resort to teaching sign language to babies who can't articulate yet so
they'll have at least some notion of what she wants. Anything is worth a try.

Front pack   Sling   Backpack

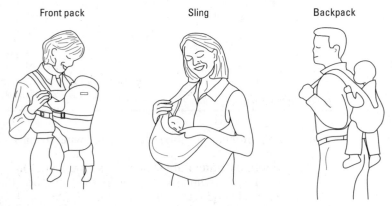

Figure 10-3: A baby carrier lets your baby see more of the world and keep your
hands free in the process.

Having your baby wear a helmet 23 hours a day for several months
is understandably upsetting for parents. It's possible to make
helmet wearing more fun — for you, not the baby — by painting
the helmet or applying decals to cute it up. The babies don't seem
to mind wearing them; having the plaster mold of their head done
will probably annoy your child far more than the helmet will.

Soothing Baby Indigestion

All babies fuss from time to time, and many have a short fussy
period every single day, usually around the time when you're the
busiest and have the least patience for it. Although all screaming
seems pretty much the same to you, fussiness can be caused by
one end or the other of the gastrointestinal tract.

Crying with colic

Colic can send a parent around the bend in no time at all. Colic, defined by the Mayo Clinic as three hours of crying a day at least three days a week for three weeks or more in a well-fed, healthy baby, affects around 40 percent of infants. Colic generally starts between 3 and 6 weeks of age and ends by 3 months of age. They may seem like the longest three months of your life.

No one really knows what causes colic, but colicky babies often pull their legs up to their stomach and act as if they have a belly ache, so perhaps they do. Breast-fed and bottle-fed babies both get colic, and changing the formula rarely helps. Things that help calm a colicky baby include:

✔ **Car rides:** The motion of the car calms down many colicky babies. With the price of gas, this can be an expensive solution, but believe us, you'll try anything after the first two hours.

✔ **Vibration:** Vibrating chairs or swings calm some colicky babies. If you don't have either of these, you can do what many a desperate parent has tried: putting the infant seat on the dryer and turning it on. Whether it's the motion or the noise, something about it calms some babies. (Make sure to remain next to the baby to make sure she doesn't fall off of the dryer.)

✔ **Position changes:** Some babies like pressure on their abdomen, so letting her dangle over your arm while you walk around may work. Putting her over your knee, face down, and patting her back may work, too. See Figure 10-4 for help.

✔ **Decrease the stimulation:** Some babies can't handle any handling or stimulation when they're colicky and do better in a quiet, dark room.

Gas

Babies often need help to get gas out of their stomachs after they eat. Some babies burp it up spontaneously, but others need to be patted between the shoulder blades for a few minutes to get the gas out.

If the baby falls asleep at the end of a feeding without burping, don't put the baby down without getting a burp up. He'll give you just enough time to fall asleep or get involved with something before he wakes up with that piercing cry that means a bubble is stuck. Take a few extra minutes and get him to burp; you'll be glad you did.

Figure 10-4: Try this position if your baby is colicky.

Reflux

Although many babies spit up after feedings, gastrointestinal reflux disease (GERD) is a whole different entity. Gastrointestinal reflux (GER — not the same thing as GERD), or normal spitting, occurs in over half of all babies, but usually is worse between the ages of 1 and 4 months and disappears by 6 to 12 months.

Keeping the baby in an upright position for half an hour or so after feedings helps reduce GER, and then keeping her at a 30 degree angle for sleep may help. Some parents elevate one end of the crib to keep the baby's head higher than her feet.

Despite what you may be told, studies show that thickening the formula with cereal does not help, and it may worsen respiratory problems in children with GERD.

GER is annoying and potentially ruinous to your clothing and the baby's, but GERD is a more serious problem. Babies with GERD fail to gain weight, may have respiratory difficulties from milk aspiration, and may have feeding aversion, which is understandable since food so often brings them discomfort.

Keeping your cool during baby meltdowns

Babies sense stress, and an already stressed out, screaming baby will be made more unhappy by a stressed out, screaming parent. To help maintain control in difficult situations, try these ideas:

✔ **Leave the house:** You and your partner can take turns getting out of Dodge for a short time.

✔ **Close the door:** For periods of time when you can't leave the house but truly can't take it anymore, put the baby in his room and close the door for a few minutes.

✔ **Get help:** When a crying baby brings you to the brink, you may be shocked at how quickly your anger escalates. Anger management courses can help you tame an out-of-control temper. Learning to do it now rather than later is beneficial, because this child will be doing things to drive you crazy for the next 50 years. (No, parenthood isn't easier when your children are adults!)

Breast-fed babies are less likely to develop GER or GERD, because breast milk digests more easily and empties out of the stomach twice as fast as formula. Medications to reduce stomach acid or to keep stomach acid from entering the esophagus may be prescribed to treat GERD.

Scheduling Immunizations

Immunizations are a very hot topic today, and one that many parents have vehement opinions about. Although studies have not supported fears that immunizations are responsible for the increase in children diagnosed with some form of autism, a brain disorder that now affects 1 in 105 babies in the United States, many parents believe the increase in immunizations and increase in autism are tied together.

The number of injections a baby receives in her first year can seem overwhelming. Table 10-1 shows the average newborn schedule of immunizations (some of the series are continued after the first birthday):

Table 10-1   Average First-Year Immunization Schedule

Vaccine	Before Leaving Hospital	2 Months	4 Months	6 Months	1 Year
Hepatitis B	x	x		x	
Rotavirus		x	x	x	
Diphtheria/Tetanus/Pertussis		x	x	x	
Haemophilus influenzae type B		x	x	x	x
Pneumococcal		x	x	x	x
Inactivated Poliovirus		x	x	x	
Influenza				x	
Measles/Mumps/Rubella					x
Varicella					x
Hepatitis A					x

Skipping some shots?

Immunizations are so controversial in some circles today that you may consider giving the baby some but not all of the recommended vaccines, possibly skipping influenza, hepatitis, and chicken pox vaccines and splitting the measles-mumps-rubella injection into three separate shots. Talk seriously with your pediatrician about the advisability of this, and check with your local board of education, because some schools may require certain immunizations before your child is allowed to start school.

Spreading them out

Many parents compromise on the immunization question by spacing the immunizations over a longer time period than that recommended by the American Academy of Pediatricians. Taking more time may necessitate more visits to the pediatrician than are normally scheduled but can make it easier to determine which injection is causing a reaction if a problem occurs.

Pediatrician Robert Sears published an alternative vaccination schedule in his book *The Vaccine Book* (Little, Brown and Company). Be aware, however, that the American Academy of Pediatrics has vigorously protested his alternative schedule and continues to support the current guidelines. Discuss alternative schedules and the pros and cons thoroughly with your medical practitioner before making up your mind about vaccinations.

Marking the milestones

Baby books are a wonderful invention; it's a shame more parents don't use them throughout their child's infancy. Nearly every baby shower includes one as a gift, and most parents start out with great enthusiasm, recoding every pregnancy symptom, movement, and ultrasound. But when the actual baby arrives, time is precious, and the baby book often is neglected, although an occasional guilt trip may result in copious recording for a week or so.

Make every attempt to record your baby's milestones somewhere. You don't have to use a baby book; baby calendars, your own journal, or a blog can be used to keep track of your baby's first tooth, word, or step. You may think now that you could never forget such important milestones, but the sad truth is that you can, very easily. And if you have more than one child, trying to remember who had croup and who had chickenpox gets to be impossible. And when you have grandchildren, many years from now, you can prove to their parents how much more advanced the grandchildren are compared to them at the same age!

Chapter 11

Supporting the New Mom

● ●

In This Chapter

▶ Helping your partner by doing the dirty work

▶ Providing emotional assistance when her hormones are haywire

▶ Recognizing signs of postpartum problems

▶ Dealing with changes and establishing a new "normal"

● ●

A new baby is a celebrity, with every coo, smile, and gurgle met with a flash of the camera. A doting parent or grandparent is always ready to meet baby's every whim, and your protective nature makes you feel like you could uproot a mighty sequoia if it somehow threatened the well-being of your baby. Unfortunately, that limelight is taken away from the woman who just spent the better part of a year carrying that child and hours (or days!) in labor. She suddenly goes from living as an A-list celebrity to feeling like an out-of-work actress working for tips at the local diner.

This is your chance to step up and shine, new dad, by making sure your partner feels every bit as adored, pampered, and attended to as that new bundle of joy. This means taking care of tangible needs, like making sure the litter box is clean and dinner's on the table, and also less-tangible needs, like emotionally supporting your partner, limiting guests, and getting by on less sleep.

We know that the upheaval of a new baby can be a difficult adjustment for new dads, too, but rising to these challenges has long-term benefits for the health and happiness of your whole family. The following sections help guide you through the postpartum needs of your partner and teach you how to be a hero for the new mom in your life.

Handling Housework during Recovery

New moms and dad both experience the stress of adapting to a new little person who's still a stranger to you, but moms have the added burden of uncontrolled hormones and physical recovery from the delivery. Your partner's energy needs to be directed at keeping herself together right now, not worrying about the house — or you.

While your partner recovers, gets her hormones back together, and works into her new routine as a mom, she needs you to pick up the scut work around the house without being told what to do. You may not know exactly what that entails, but that's why we're here: to help you with all the things that need to be done. The following sections may look like a list of chores, but remember that a happy mom means a happy baby — and a happy next six months for your new family.

Getting the house in order

TV commercials make it appear that men are only good for making messes and that women derive joy from cleaning up after them, but in the real world, making sure the home is in tip-top shape is everyone's job. Except that now that your partner's limited to lifting nothing heavier than a baby for the next six weeks, cleaning has just become fully your responsibility.

You don't have time to clean every part of the house every day, so ask your partner point-blank what tasks are most important to her; then carry out her requests word for word — even if it seems irrational. For example, if she wants the bathroom cleaned every day, then grab your toilet brush and get scrubbing. She'll be spending a lot more time in there following labor due to postpartum bleeding, which can last anywhere from two to eight weeks, so a clean environment may help her relax and keep her from feeling embarrassed when visitors unexpectedly appear.

Speaking of visitors, well-wishers come bearing a lot of stuff, which means that clutter can get out of control very quickly. Because mom is trapped indoors with a baby who's feeding around the clock, feeling suffocated by balloons, flowers, and stuffed animals may only increase her anxiety. Make sure to find a new home for everything that comes into the house.

In addition, doing the dishes, vacuuming, and taking out the trash are some of the obvious tasks that need regular attention. The following sections guide you through some of the more unexpected tasks you're about to become intimately acquainted with.

Battling baby's bottomless laundry basket

Laundry may seem straightforward, but like all things related to babies, it's complicated. If you're already accustomed to the ins and outs of laundry, you'll have ample opportunity over the next few weeks to put these basic skills into action. But laundering baby's things is a bit different. We break down the important points for you here:

- ✔ **Wash brand-new infant clothes prior to first use to remove any chemicals or germs in the fabric.** As new clothes arrive, be sure to remove all price tags, stickers, and plastic tag holders.

- ✔ **To avoid exposing your baby to dyes and chemicals that can irritate his delicate skin, wash baby clothes in dye- and chemical-free detergent.** Generally, any detergents labeled as dye- and chemical-free are okay to use. Using organic is always best but can be quite pricey. Several detergents, such as Dreft, are designed specifically to wash baby clothes.

- ✔ **Use the delicate cycles on your washer and dryer.** Using the delicate cycle helps keep the materials used in baby clothing from shrinking, which they tend to do. And baby clothes are outgrown fast enough without adding shrinkage to the mix.

- ✔ **Be sure to treat stains — and you'll have stains — prior to washing.**

Couples opting to take the eco-friendly route of cloth diapers find the mounting laundry pile an even taller task. Follow these steps to take care of this particularly dirty laundry:

1. **Rinse the diapers.**

   Solid poops can be shaken off into the toilet and flushed. Consider installing a sprayer attachment on your toilet to help with loose stools and urine. It allows you to rinse the diapers and flush without having to dunk the diaper into the toilet.

2. **Pretreat cloth diapers by placing them in a pail, sprinkling stains with baking soda, and covering the pail to keep smells at bay for no more than three days.**

   Place an air freshener inside the pail to help control odors, too.

3. **Gather a load of no more than two dozen diapers, fastening all tabs on each diaper to keep them from sticking to each other.**

4. **Use a quarter to half the amount of laundry detergent you would for a normal load.**

   Using a normal amount can lead to detergent buildup in the fabric. Diapers are designed to absorb, after all, and they're not discriminating about it.

5. **Wash on a cold/cold cycle.**

6. **Wash a second time, using a hot/cold cycle to kill any remaining bacteria.**

Dealing with pet duty

Animals require a delicate transition when the baby arrives. To help reduce the shock of a new human roommate, prior to bringing baby home from the hospital, wash your pet's bed or favorite toys in baby laundry detergent to get her used to what baby will smell like. You can also prepare your pets by inviting over friends with babies so your animals adjust to the sounds of babies. Enroll your dogs in an obedience course to make sure they are well trained and will lie down on the floor next to you on command.

No matter how well trained or prepared your pets are, take care when introducing your baby. When baby comes through the door, be prepared to deal with any jumping, clawing, growling, or rough-housing your pet may want to engage in with both mom and baby. Keep animals separated from mom until she's healed enough to endure any unexpected pet reactions. When you trust that your pet won't react wildly, have the animal sit next to you while you hold the baby. Reward your pet with treats as you interact with the baby to begin making a positive connection between the two. Never hold your baby in your pet's face as this can cause a possibly dangerous reaction from the animal.

In addition to mediating interactions between your partner and rambunctious pets and baby and *all* pets, it's also your responsibility to complete all pet-related tasks. That means changing the kitty litter, taking the dog for walks, grooming, and playing. Making sure your pet's life stays as normal as possible eases everyone's transition. For example, if your dog enjoys playing catch, make sure to play catch with him as often as you did before so he doesn't make a negative association between the new baby and your lack of attention.

After contact with your pets, make sure to wash your hands with soap and water before handling the baby.

The weight game

Your partner may not be ready to get back into her pre-pregnancy jeans the moment she gets home from the hospital. Some women do lose a considerable amount of weight shortly after delivery, but some actually put on weight due to fluid retention. And as with all weight loss, unfortunately, losing pounds put on during and after pregnancy requires time and hard work.

Exercise helps the body recover from pregnancy (and has also been linked to decreased occurrence of depression), but even with exercise, it takes an average of two or three months before a woman gets back to her normal body weight. And even then, things will have changed. Stomachs are softer, body parts seemingly have shifted, stretch marks will have appeared, and she's likely to feel like a stranger in her own body.

You can help your partner improve her body image and fitness by reminding her how beautiful you think she is and planning activities that get you both moving together. A nice walk around the park or the neighborhood is always an enjoyable activity for the whole family, and following a normal childbirth, women can begin light walking a few days after returning home. If the gym is her scene, ask her if she'd like you to hire a personal trainer with knowledge of post-pregnancy fitness. If the yoga studio is her style, she may enjoy a mom-and-baby yoga class.

Whatever her desires, make sure she has been cleared by her OB-GYN prior to beginning any workout routine, and she'll likely be advised to stick with activities that she engaged in before having the baby. She needs to start small, and you need to make sure your partner is comfortable. Remind her to exercise at a slow pace with moderate effort, especially during the first weeks. If she experiences an increase in bleeding, shortness of breath, or extreme fatigue, have her wait a few days before trying again.

Most importantly, let any new exercise regimen be her idea. Suggesting that a new mom join a gym will put you squarely in the doghouse.

Becoming the errand boy

Grab the keys and get rolling, because driving duties are up to you for a while. Doctors recommend that women who have a vaginal birth don't drive for two weeks following delivery. That time increases to six weeks for a cesarean delivery.

Use the hours you spend driving to the grocery store and the post office (to mail thank-you notes, of course!) to recharge your batteries. Alone time is hard to come by these days.

Don't forget to extend an invitation to mom and baby, too. Many women will begin to feel trapped in the house, so as soon as your partner is up for it, begin including her in outings whenever she feels up to it. If she doesn't feel up for it or can't come along for the ride, bring her back some flowers or another favorite treat to make her feel loved and cared for.

Taking care of meals

For the first few weeks following delivery, you need to manage the meals, because your partner is likely too physically drained — and too busy feeding baby — to think about cooking. Whether you're the guy who likes to take charge in the kitchen or the type who routinely forgets to add the cheese packet to macaroni and cheese, making sure you and your partner are well nourished is one of your most important roles.

Understanding what she needs

Breast-feeding women need to consume an additional 400 to 600 calories more than they would when eating a normal diet. That's because breast-feeding burns about as many calories as a 30-minute run. New moms need to eat energy-packed, nutritious foods. And with all the extra work you're doing on reduced sleep, you do too! Keep the following nutrition do's and don'ts in mind when grocery shopping and preparing meals:

- **Do** stock up on milk, yogurt, and other dairy products. Vitamin D and calcium are especially important for new moms. Some women are forced to eliminate dairy from their diets because it can cause excess gas and fussiness in the nursing baby. In order to get her the nutrients she otherwise would get from dairy, stock-up on plant-based milk substitutes, such as soy or almond milk, which have been fortified with vitamins.

- **Don't** bring home a lot of foods that are high in sugar, carbohydrates, and fat. Nothing is forbidden here, but don't go overboard. Not only is it bad for her waistline, but all the refined sugars, flours, and artificial fats are hard to digest and aren't ideal postpartum nutrition for baby or mom As hard as it is to deny a new mother anything, try to talk her out of those cravings for fried food.

- **Do** make sure she's getting enough water. If she's breast-feeding, she needs to drink at least 72 ounces of water each day to aid in milk production. If your tap water doesn't taste good, pick up a filtration pitcher or faucet attachment.

- **Don't** let her (or you!) drink too much alcohol. A glass of wine or a beer is okay, especially as a way for the new mom to clear her head and relax. But nursing moms should keep in mind that what goes in ends up in the breast milk, so moderation is essential. Non-nursing moms, and dads for that matter, still must be responsible caregivers, and alcohol lowers inhibitions and decreases sound judgment. Always drink very responsibly.

In addition to taking her nutritional requirements into account, make sure to ask her what sounds good before doing any grocery shopping. Just like during pregnancy, many women find certain foods unappetizing and/or nauseating following childbirth.

Putting food on the table

Since you're going to be getting less sleep and doing more work around the house, you may not be eager to strap on the apron three times a day. To make the task easier on yourself, cook meals that can be eaten multiple times or frozen for future consumption, such as easy-to-assemble casseroles or pots of soup. If time allows, this can be a great nesting activity with your partner prior to delivery, too.

Another great idea that only requires a little work on your end is to make a bunch of peanut butter sandwiches, put them back in the bread bag, and store the bag in the fridge, so that she can just grab one quickly. This would be especially helpful for a mom who's going to be home alone during the day when making good eating choices may be next to impossible with a baby whose needs come first.

 Make sure mom has plenty of nutritious foods around that she can just grab and eat without either of you having to prep. Yogurt, nuts, fruit, and precut, precleaned raw veggies should be on hand as quick energy boosts that require no cooking.

When friends and family ask you what they can do to help, ask them to bring you a meal in a freezer-safe storage container in lieu of flowers. Having prepared homemade meals on-hand will help you avoid the temptation to order takeout or fast food, which is high in sodium and fat and not the most nutritious for mom and baby.

Calling in backup

Not every new dad has the luxury of taking ample time off work to attend to the needs of his partner, which means your partner may be facing a lot of alone time with baby at a very early stage.

 Leaving a new mom alone while you're off at work isn't a good idea. Many women, especially those who delivered via cesarean section, need physical and emotional support during the daytime for several weeks following delivery.

Talk to your partner about the needs and desires she has while you're at work, then help her find the appropriate support from friends, family, and neighbors. Make chore lists for daytime help-ers so your partner won't feel burdened by having to ask for help.

If financially viable, hire a cleaning service. It will be the best gift you can give to your partner . . . and yourself.

Following the birth of their grandchild, your parents and partner's parents may want to visit during this time in order to help, especially when you go back to work. Before agreeing to visits, however, make sure your partner wants them around. All of the advice and constant companionship from a parental figure may cause her more stress. She also may want a chance to go it alone without anyone's help.

If she does want them around, try to stagger the visits to provide a longer duration of coverage — and a little more sanity for you and your partner.

Supporting a Breast-Feeding Mom

Breast-feeding is a full-time job, especially in the first few months, and although it may be more fun and rewarding than changing poop-filled diapers, it's still a lot of responsibility. To the untrained eye, it may look like your partner is simply sitting in a rocking chair holding your baby, but she's actually working very hard to develop a complicated feeding relationship. This section shows you how you can help mom and baby be as successful as possible.

If you feel really lost on this subject, check out *Breastfeeding For Dummies* (Wiley) for more in-depth encouragement.

Making the decision to breast-feed

If your partner is physically capable of breast-feeding (some medical conditions prevent women from doing so), the decision is ultimately hers. It's her body, her time, and her commitment. Prior to the arrival of baby, discuss this topic so you both can research the benefits of breast-feeding and decide whether or not to do it and, if so, for how long.

According to the U.S. Department of Health and Human Services, breast-feeding is an important health choice, and it recommends that any amount of time a mother and baby can do so benefits both. Breast-feeding is a natural process, and the milk contains disease-fighting cells that help protect infants from germs, illness, and even SIDS (sudden infant death syndrome — turn to Chapter 12 for more info). Infant formula, while meeting the requirements of basic nutrition, does not include the human cells, hormones, or antibodies that fight disease.

For the new mother, breast-feeding is a wonderful bonding experience that has been shown to decrease the risk of postpartum depression and lessen its impact. It also causes more afterpains, which are spasms that help shrink the uterus back down to normal size. Producing milk also burns anywhere from 200 to 500 calories a day. Studies also show it reduces a woman's risk of breast cancer and increases her bone density after baby is weaned, reducing her chances of developing osteoporosis in the future.

The health benefits for baby and mom are good reasons to breast-feed, but be sure your partner considers the following details when making the decision:

- **Convenience:** Breast-feeding is much more convenient at home than bottle-feeding, but it can be awkward when you're out and about. Although many shopping centers, museums, and amusements parks have nursing stations, not all do, and your partner may not be comfortable nursing in public. That's why supplemental bottles were invented.

- **Comfort:** Some women are not comfortable with the idea of breast-feeding. Don't blame your partner. This discomfort may be due to a culture that makes breasts into sex objects rather than feeding machinery.

- **Ability:** Breast-feeding is not possible if breast reconstruction surgery that cuts the ducts has been done.

- **Schedule:** If your partner is going back to work in a few weeks, establishing nursing may seem like too much trouble. But nursing for even a short time is better than not nursing at all. Encourage her to try, for even a short time. Just don't be pushy about it.

The American Academy of Pediatrics recommends breast-feeding for the first year of a child's life, and the World Health Organization recommends breast-feeding for the first two years. However, the benefits of breast-feeding continue for as long as mother and baby do it, whether it be three days or three years. The more you support your partner in breast-feeding, the more unparalleled health benefits your baby will receive.

Whether you start off baby with formula or switch after a period of breast-feeding, do your research about the best, safest formula for your child. Many breast-fed babies resist the transition, so be patient. Then again, you're probably used to that by now.

Offering lactation support

LeBron James makes dunking a basketball look as simple as flushing a toilet, but that doesn't mean you can do it. If your partner chooses to breast-feed, keep in mind that it's not as easy as it looks, especially at first. Issues will arise, and although you can't be the one to solve those issues, your support is a major factor in her success. Be positive and upbeat, listen to your partner when she talks, and thank her profusely for making such a wise decision for both the baby's health and hers.

The most important role for dad is to stay informed about the process of breast-feeding. Many complications can arise, and the more you know about how to help your partner through those issues, the more likely mom and baby will be able to work through them. One of the most common reasons women have for ceasing breast-feeding is that it is uncomfortable or painful. Breast-feeding *should not hurt* after mom and baby establish the correct feeding positions and latches (how baby attaches his mouth to the nipple).

Some of the most common breast-feeding issues are

- **Sore nipples:** This problem is usually temporary during the first few days as mom adjusts to breast-feeding. For some women the pain increases, and the nipples become chapped or cracked. This is most commonly a result of a bad latch and can be treated by correcting the latch.

- **Pain from breast engorgement:** Engorgement occurs when the breasts fill up with milk, and can be eased by massage, milk expression, and warm compresses.

- **Clogged ducts:** This occurs when the breast has not been completely emptied and it becomes clogged, causing a small lump to form inside the breast. Heat packs, massage, and increased feeding from the clogged breast can treat it.

- **Mastitis:** Mastitis is a breast infection that a small percentage of breast-feeding women get. It can cause fevers, tiredness, and a hard lump in the breast. Treat with warm compresses, acetaminophen (Tylenol), and a trip to the doctor for a round of antibiotics.

Remember that it's the mother's decision to quit breast-feeding if she so chooses and should never be your suggestion. If lactation issues arise, don't tell her to throw in the towel and go buy some formula, no matter how frustrated or tearful she becomes. Listen to her concerns, help her find resources to correct problems and, ultimately, be supportive no matter what she decides.

Breast-feeding 911

If your partner is experiencing discomfort or suffering from a low supply, know where to go to get her the help she needs. Many hospitals employ lactation consultants and may also provide free breast-feeding support groups your wife can attend. Some lactation consultants also make home visits to help mom and baby work out their issues. Here are a few resources to contact when your partner needs guidance:

✔ The La Leche League International, phone 800-LA-LECHE; Web site www. llli.org.

✔ International Board of Lactation Consultant Examiners; phone 703-560-7330; Web site www.iblce.org.

✔ International Lactation Consultant Association; phone 919-861-5577; Web site www.ilca.org.

✔ Doulas of North America International, phone 888-788-DONA; Web site www.dona.org.

Whenever your partner decides for any reason to stop breast-feeding, thank her for the time she has invested in doing so and congratulate her for her achievements. You both should be proud of the hard, rewarding work you've done.

Including yourself in the process

Just because mom does the actual breast-feeding doesn't mean that you can't be involved, too. An important role for dad is to serve as mom's arms and legs while she breast-feeds, especially in the early stages while your partner's mobility is severely limited by a baby who eats at frequent intervals all day long. Let your partner know that you're happy to get her anything she needs and thank her for breast-feeding the baby. The more you can anticipate her needs, the better. Always have a drink and snack at hand, as well as the TV remote and something to read.

Many women feel frustrated by not being able to do things for themselves. Reassure her that baby's constant eating schedule is only temporary and that it won't be long before he eats less often and her mobility returns. Until then make sure to bring your partner everything she asks for without hesitation.

Sometimes fathers of breast-fed babies feel as though they're missing out on an important, unparalleled bonding opportunity. Remember that breast-feeding is about the well-being of your child, and although you can't ever experience what your partner does, you can join in on the skin-on-skin bonding by letting baby rest on your bare chest. You can also occasionally give baby supplemental bottles of pumped milk. (See Chapter 10 for more on supplemental bottles.)

Dealing with Postcesarean Issues

Not only is the hospital stay longer for a cesarean section than that of a vaginal delivery — two to four days total — but the recovery time upon returning home is extended as well. A cesarean delivery is classified as a major surgery, which means that even if everything goes smoothly, you have to care for a woman who has been through nine months of pregnancy followed by a serious operation. You also will need to be on the lookout to make sure that no complications arise while your partner is recovering.

Helping with a normal recovery

Give your partner additional physical support for the first few weeks. She shouldn't engage in vigorous exercise or household chores or even climb a lot of steps. If you have to go back to work during the first two weeks postdelivery, find a family member or friend who can come to your home and provide all-day support for your partner.

Emotionally, it's important for the new mom to sit and bond with her baby following a cesarean procedure. Some women experience feelings of disappointment and can even struggle to bond with a newborn when unable to give birth vaginally. Most, however, have no trouble bonding after spending some time together.

If the operation was unexpected, many new dads and moms need some time to decompress following the stress of the situation. Following the birth, discuss the events leading up to the cesarean with your partner. Some new parents find it helpful to discuss the events with the obstetrician to help deal with any negative feelings they have about their birth procedure.

Pain management is important following a cesarean, and when not properly managed it can reduce the chances of successful breast-feeding and increase the chances of postpartum depression. Encourage your partner to ask her doctors about appropriate pain relief medication and how it will affect her breast milk.

Knowing when to call the doctor

Most women who deliver via cesarean recover quickly and without incident. However, watch out for these warning signs and contact a physician immediately if your partner

- ✔ Incurs a fever in excess of 100 degrees Fahrenheit

- ✔ Notices pus discharge from the incision

- ✔ Suffers a swollen, red, painful area in the leg or the breast, possibly accompanied by flu-like symptoms

- ✔ Complains of a painful headache that does not subside

- ✔ Experiences abrupt pain in the abdomen, including abnormal tenderness or burning

- ✔ Has a foul-smelling vaginal discharge

- ✔ Experiences an unusual amount of heavy bleeding that soaks a sanitary pad within an hour

- ✔ Feels abnormally anxious, panicky, and/or depressed

Riding the Ups and Downs of Hormones

If feeling physically normal while exhausted and still carrying a few pounds of extra baby weight wasn't hard enough for a new mom, along come the hormones to make it all even worse. As the body recovers from childbirth, several months are needed for a woman's hormone levels to completely even out. This section overviews the many changes your partner may experience and how to deal with them.

Thinking before speaking in the sensitive postpartum period

If you've ever put your foot in your mouth, then you know that you can accidentally hurt your partner's feelings via your own thoughtlessness. After delivery you need to be even more careful of what you say, because for most new dads, your partner's emotional sensitivity will feel like uncharted shark-infested waters.

Avoid using leading statements, such as "why don't you just" and "why didn't you" when your partner is upset. You don't have all of the answers, and she's not looking for answers, anyway. What she's likely seeking is a listening ear and an understanding hug.

The last thing you ever want to tell a tearful new mother when she confesses feelings of isolation is, "Why didn't you just go out today?" She likely has worked very hard all day taking care of herself and the baby, and by flippantly suggesting that she should have done more than she did can make her feel like a failure.

To show support, ask her questions that show you're listening, such as "What would make you feel better?" and "What can I do to help you?" If your partner responds with "I don't know" or "Nothing will help until the baby is older/sleeps more/cries less," then tell her you want to help in any way possible. If she has trouble expressing what she needs, you may find yourself becoming frustrated with your inability to fix the problem. Until she can express her needs, plan some time away for her that doesn't force her to make any decisions but instead pampers and caters to her needs and shows her how much you care.

When your partner is upset about something you said, keep in mind that hormones are at play, but don't suggest to her that hormones are the reason she's being sensitive. (That will go over about as well as telling her she's moody because "it's that time of the month.") The last thing you want to do is imply that her feelings aren't legitimate. Simply apologize for any and all offending statements and let her know that you understand where she's coming from.

Many new moms also become sensitive to anything involving hurt or neglected children, which can make TV programs, movies, and books potential minefields. To the best of your abilities, do research about the contents of your entertainment. If the movie you want to watch involves a child death, botched childbirth, kidnapping, or the destruction of Earth, put it on your queue for later viewing.

Shedding light on physical symptoms

Body-drenching night sweats are very common for new moms, and you can't do much to help except to set up a fan near the bed. Sudden hair loss is another physical effect of surging hormones. In the first few months following delivery, most women begin to notice a lot more hair coming out in the shower and on the hairbrush. Reassure your partner that this is normal and that it usually goes back to normal by nine months after delivery. If it doesn't, have her seek treatment from a dermatologist.

Supporting her baby blues

Happiness is only one of the complex emotions you and your partner will feel following baby's arrival. The most common and complicated issue for new mothers is the baby blues, feelings of exhaustion, insomnia, irritability, nervousness, panic, and that she will never be a good mother, which usually occurs during the first few weeks following delivery. Studies show that nearly 80 percent of women suffer feelings of sadness and loss postdelivery.

Experts believe that shifting hormone levels are partly to blame but that it's also a difficult for a woman who has been focused on giving birth for nine months to suddenly switch gears and focus on nurturing a newborn. Caring for a child stirs strong emotions and can make new parents feel an overwhelming sense of responsibility and fear, both of which are perfectly normal.

Talk openly with your partner about her feelings, as well as any sad feelings you may be experiencing. Keep reading to find out how to determine if her baby blues are something more serious that needs treatment.

Recognizing postpartum depression

While most new mothers experience some feelings of sadness that eventually pass, 10 to 15 percent of all new mothers suffer from depression during the first six months postdelivery, and depression requires some care and treatment. Distinguishing between the baby blues and postpartum depression is not as difficult as you may think, especially for you. Your partner may not be able to put her feelings into words or admit she's depressed, but you can be alert for signs of depression and have a discussion with her if you recognize any symptoms. Common symptoms include

- Lack of interest in caring for self or child
- Loss of appetite
- Relentless unhappiness
- Incapable of being happy while spending time with baby
- Sudden arrival of anxiety and panic attacks
- Hearing voices
- Disturbing thoughts about harming self or baby

If you believe your partner is depressed, tell her that you're concerned about her health, allow her to discuss her symptoms and how she's feeling, and let her know that what she's dealing with is a serious medical condition. It doesn't mean she's a bad mother or a weak person. Good people can suffer from postpartum depression. Don't let her brush the issue aside by saying that it's just a matter of feeling sad and that she'll "snap out of it," because she won't.

A depressed new mom needs to be treated by a medical professional immediately, so work with your partner to schedule a session with her doctor. Counseling and antidepressants are very effective treatments.

Sleeping (Or Doing Without)

Surprise! It's a baby who doesn't sleep through the night. Depending on your newborn, you may be woken every hour on the hour for feedings and comforting. Or you may be one of the lucky parents catching hours and hours of uninterrupted sleep. Every baby is different, but one thing is constant: Sleep is a precious commodity for new parents.

Babies' sleeping habits change frequently, but the average newborn sleeps about eight hours during the day, waking up every hour or so to eat. They generally sleep another eight hours during the night, again waking frequently to eat. Newborn sleep cycles are shorter than those of adults, and they spend more time in light sleep than adults do, which accounts for the frequent disturbances.

The common rule of thumb is to sleep when your baby sleeps. A million chores may need to be done around the house, and you may enjoy an hour watching tennis in peace, but close your eyes instead. If you nap during the day when you have a chance, you'll be in much better shape to deal with a baby who's ready to party when you're ready for pillow time at night. You can take turns with your partner throughout the night, alternating who gets up each time or switching nights. Use a schedule that works for you both.

Many babies wake up for good before the sun has a chance to hit the horizon. If you're routinely jarred from sleep at an obscenely early hour, alternate days of getting up early with your partner so at least one of you can get some additional sleep. That way, when the early riser's energy wanes later in the day, the other partner can step up to help out.

A baby's internal sleep clock begins to mature between the ages of 6 and 9 weeks and starts to become constant between 3 and 5 months. By 10 months, the average baby's sleep cycle is constant, and he will go to bed and wake up at the same time every day. If you're still awake by that time and haven't become addicted to caffeine, congratulations. Your sleep cycle will start getting longer, too.

Ferber versus no-cry

Different schools of thought have varying theories about how to help a baby sleep through the night. Many parents opt to use the Ferber method, created by Dr. Richard Ferber. Commonly referred to as *Ferberizing* your baby, this is the classic cry-it-out system that offers limited comforting for a baby in an effort to teach him how to fall asleep by self-soothing. An increasing number of parents are beginning to use alternative no-cry methods that address an individual baby's sleep issues and offer parents tools to help babies put themselves to sleep without so many tears. Generally, a no-cry method encourages a slow, steady process to segue from cosleeping to crib sleeping that involves building a positive association with the crib for your baby instead of letting her cry until she falls asleep. Research all of your options and decide which method suits your parenting style.

Many babies begin sleeping through the night between 4 and 6 months. Then again, many babies begin sleeping through the night at 1 year of age. Both are normal. Consult your pediatrician if your baby's sleep pattern is unmanageable for you and your partner.

Coping with Company

Family and friends will be vying for any opportunity to get their hands on your baby. Being surrounded by love is important at this time, but mom, dad, and baby also need to get plenty of rest and to have sufficient time to bond as a family. And getting plenty of rest and private family time will help keep you from lashing out at your mother when she offers yet another "helpful pointer" about the proper way to fold bath towels.

Try not to schedule multiple visitors at a time, and limit the number of visits to two or three per day. Now is also the time in your life when it's okay to cancel or say no to visits. If Aunt Sarah is scheduled to drop by in the evening and your partner just needs to catch some shut-eye, put your partner's needs first. Reassure Aunt Sarah that she will get to see the baby in due time. If she's offended, she'll get over it the moment she holds your baby for the first time.

You and your partner should decide together when it's a good time to have people over and when you need some peace and quiet. However, she may feel guilty about saying no even when you know very well that having an empty house is in all of your best interests. Don't be afraid to turn people away without asking your partner so she doesn't always have to feel like the "bad guy."

As visitors cycle through your home, make sure they all wash their hands or use an alcohol-free hand sanitizer to avoid spreading germs. If someone is sick, it is your duty to keep him out of your home. Thank him for his support but let him know that exposing newborns to illness is dangerous.

Baby will be passed around a lot when company is visiting and often only handed back to the new mom for feedings. Make sure that your partner gets plenty of nonfeeding time with the baby to avoid having her feel like a dairy.

Dealing with grabby grandmas

Sharing isn't easy — especially for new grandmas. And as they will gladly tell you (again and again), someday you'll understand when you have a grandchild of your own. Until then, you need to manage everyone's needs for the next 20-plus years without offending anyone.

The best way to handle a too-hands-on grandma is to be honest and respectful. If you want to hold your baby and your mother or mother-in-law is reluctant to give up the wheel, reach for the baby and say something such as, "I just can't hold this little one enough. I've been waiting for this moment my whole life." There's nothing like a display of paternal love to remind a grabby grandma how important bonding is between parent and child.

Don't be passive-aggressive in your approach. Avoid asking questions like, "Mom, do you think I could hold the baby now?" You don't want to imply you think grandma is being overbearing, thoughtless, or disrespectful of your time.

If the problem persists, speak to the offending parent in private. Thank grandma for her love and support, and use only *I* statements (such as, "I have really been feeling the need to spend more time bonding with my baby right now, and even though it may not be what everyone would want, I really need this time") to convey how much you want to spend time with your baby.

Managing unsolicited advice

One of the first things to raise the ire of a new parent is a pushy, well-meaning advice giver. It makes parents feel like they're the heroes in a zombie movie who turn around and see a horde of the undead ready to rip then to shreds. Everyone seems to have opinions when it comes to how to care for your baby, and if you start paying attention to everyone, it will completely overwhelm you. So just run. Run far, far away and don't look back.

Whether the advice is on how to hold him, how to burp him, or even how to soothe him when he's on a crying jag, try to internalize the fact that most people are reaching out with advice because of the love they feel for your newborn. When advice comes across as criticism of your parenting skills, shrug it off. You and your partner know your baby's needs and preferences better than anyone else. Defer to your instincts. Every baby is different, and what works for one may cause another one fits of hysteria.

That being said, you may find some advice helpful, so be open to listening to what others who have parented before you have learned. Don't be afraid to reach out to others if you have questions, but never take someone's advice as gospel. Take the time to do your own homework and decide what works best for your family.

Don't feel the need to explain yourself, however. If your Uncle Robert thinks you're somehow failing your child by picking him up every time he cries, don't be afraid to push back. Say something like, "I guess the beauty of being a parent is getting to decide how you want to raise your own child."

Handling hurt feelings when you want to be alone

Inevitably at some point you'll need time to yourself. So will your partner. Baby love is all encompassing, but you can't let it overtake your individuality. Even though visitors have traveled from afar and people want to shower your new family with affection, you have to put on your own oxygen mask first, so to speak. Whether you're a runner or an avid video gamer, don't feel guilty about taking time to do what you need to relax.

Never under any circumstances utter the phrase, "I just need a break." Your partner will not like to hear that, because nobody deserves a break more than a new mom. Let her know that you really need to blow off some steam in order to continue being the best caregiver you can be. If she's angry, tell her you understand how she feels and offer her the same amount of time upon your return. Even the breast-feeding mom can enjoy a brief walk or a quick run to the store just to have some time to be on her own again.

Make sure to schedule time for your mental well-being, because it probably won't seem like a priority until you're raving like a madman because you just need a second of solitude. Keep a calendar and block out times in different colors for family time, dad time, mom time, and visiting hours.

If family or friends take offense when you say no to a visit or an invitation to attend a family function, don't change your mind to save their feelings. You deserve time to bond as a family and time to unwind and just be yourself. Thank them for the offer, be honest about why you can't commit to that time, and plan a get-together for a later date that suits everyone's schedule.

Approaching Sex: It's Like Riding a Bicycle

Hang tight, fellas. It's gonna be a while. The earliest a woman can have sex is six weeks following delivery, and that's only after getting clearance from her doctor. Your hormones may be raging, but you need to remember that your partner's genitalia have been through the wringer, so to speak, and intercourse can severely jeopardize her healing process.

In addition to needing time for physical healing, most women won't be feeling all that sexy for a while. Hormones are the major culprits, but a lack of sleep, breast-feeding, and the difficulty of straddling the roles of mother and sexual being are also hurdles. As hard as it is to internalize, remind yourself that her lack of physical interest in you has nothing to do with her feelings toward you. Her absence of desire isn't personal; it's physical.

Some women find their sexual desires return by the time their doctor okays sex, but for many it can take between 6 and 12 months. Some new fathers also experience a diminished interest in sex when adjusting to the role of dad.

Even after your partner has healed and desire returns, she may experience discomfort when returning to a normal sex life. Be prepared to take it slow. You may need several attempts before you actually have sex to completion. Time will also be at a premium and baby just may wake up before you finish.

Time will also be at a premium as you work around baby's schedule, so as unromantic as it sounds, schedule sex with your partner and slowly ramp up to a frequency that works for both of you. With so much on your plates, it will give you both the security of knowing the "when" and the excitement of thinking about the "how."

Birth control also needs to be a talking point for you and your partner. Many people believe that breast-feeding women cannot get pregnant, but although breast-feeding does often delay a return to regular ovulation, some women do ovulate while nursing. Many breast-feeding women prefer not to go on birth control pills due to changes in milk supply, so condom usage is common for new parents returning to active sex lives. You can speak with a doctor to help you both determine a birth control option that fits your needs.

Part IV

A Dad's Guide to Worrying

The 5th Wave   By Rich Tennant

DURING LABOR, THE HUSBAND SHOULD DO WHATEVER HE CAN TO MAKE HIS WIFE FEEL BETTER

She always liked my slight-of-hand.

In this part...

This part is designed to keep you from staying up all night worrying about all the things new dads worry about, from colic to college. We discuss possible complications and newborn concerns, and we devote a whole chapter to being a supportive partner, lest you forget the person who gave birth to your progeny. We also help you plan for your child's future financial security.

Chapter 12

Dealing with Difficult Issues after Delivery

. . . .

In This Chapter

▶ Learning that your baby has problems

▶ Coping with serious postpartum issues

▶ Grieving together and separately

▶ Telling other people when your baby has problems

. . . .

*N*ot everyone goes home to perpetual roses and lollipops after their baby is born. In fact, hardly anyone does. But serious issues in baby or mom are rare, so when they occur, they can really knock you for a loop. In this chapter we discuss some of the serious complications that can arise after delivery and how to handle them. This is a chapter you can skip if you don't need it — and we hope you never will.

Coping with Serious Health Problems

Approximately 1 in 33 babies born in the United States has a congenital birth defect, according to the Centers for Disease Control. Developmental delays, serious illnesses, and sudden infant death syndrome are problems no one wants to contemplate when having a baby, but they can and do happen. The following sections give you an overview of the most common serious health problems.

Congenital defects

Congenital defects, defects that exist at birth (also simply called *birth defects*), are common. Some are minor issues that no one but the parents would ever notice; others are more serious. The most common birth defects include

✔ **Heart defects:** One in 100 to 200 babies born has a heart defect, which can range from mild to severe. Heart defects comprise one-quarter to one-third of all birth defects.

✔ **Down syndrome:** One in 800 babies is born with Down syndrome, which causes distinct physical features and mental retardation. The percentage is higher in older mothers and lower in those younger than 35.

✔ **Neural tube defects:** One in 1,000 infants has neural tube defects, which affect the brain and spinal column. They include spina bifida, an abnormal opening in the spine, and anencephaly, an absence of part of the brain.

✔ **Cleft lip and/or palate:** One in 700 to 1,000 babies has deformities of the lip and hard palate.

Sixty percent of the time, the reason for the birth defect is unknown. Inherited disorders, on the other hand, may be suspected ahead of time if a family history of a genetic disorder exists.

Some of the most common inherited genetic disorders include

✔ **Cystic fibrosis:** A disorder that causes thick secretions in the respiratory and gastrointestinal tract, cystic fibrosis is the most common inherited genetic disorder in Caucasians in the United States, affecting 1 in 3,000 babies. Both parents must carry the defective gene for a child to have the disease; it's estimated that 12 million people in the United States are carriers.

✔ **Sickle cell anemia:** An autosomal recessive disease causing deformities of the red blood cells, sickle cell anemia affects mostly people of African and Middle Eastern descent. Approximately 2 million African Americans carry the sickle cell gene.

Minor birth defects are much more common than serious defects. Eye, ear, and limb defects; extra digits; abnormal development of the intestines; and birthmarks may not be life threatening in most cases, but they can still be devastating for parents. Being concerned about birth defects, especially visible ones, is normal for parents.

Developmental delays

Many parents keep baby books that chronicle their baby's progress, and eagerly await each milestone: the first smile, the first step, the first word. When milestones aren't met when books say they should be, or when your friend's babies are meeting them but your baby isn't, doubt, concern, frustration, and a cold fear may begin to creep into your days.

Moms are usually the first ones to recognize a problem, so if your partner voices concerns, don't belittle them, even if the baby seems fine to you. Verbalizing fears about your baby's development takes a lot of courage.

When babies are very young, physical milestones are very important. Babies, after all, don't dazzle you with their small talk or charm you with their recitation of *The Iliad*. If they lift up their head, it's a big deal. Rolling over for the first time merits phone calls to relatives all over the country, and the first gurgle — the one that startles the baby almost as much as it does you — earns your undivided attention for the next hour as you try to catch a command performance on video.

When your baby isn't keeping up with the other babies on the block (whether in your mind or in fact), discuss it with your doctor, who may tell you that all babies are different and that you're making yourself crazy. Or he may nod and take notes, which is really frightening, because even when you know something's wrong, having someone else verify it makes it all too real.

If you suspect that your baby isn't meeting developmental milestones, take a deep breath and consider the following facts:

- ✔ **Babies really do develop at different rates.** Milestones happen at an average age, and an average is just that: 50 percent of babies achieve the goal at a younger age, and 50 percent don't meet it until they're past that age.

- ✔ **Babies all have different abilities.** Some are more physically oriented; others are more verbally inclined. Since physical milestones are all you have to go on at a young age, children who will shine verbally later may seem to be behind early on.

However, talk to your doctor if your baby doesn't meet the following milestones:

- ✔ Turns her head in the direction of a voice or sound shortly after birth

- ✔ Smiles spontaneously by 1 month

- ✔ Imitates speech sounds by 3 to 6 months

- ✔ Babbles by 4 to 8 months

If your baby does have developmental delays, she'll need your help to achieve normal milestones. Getting help early is the best thing you can do for her.

Illnesses

Infant illness can be *acute* (severe but brief) or *chronic* (long last-ing or recurring). Both are terrifying, especially if your baby has to be hospitalized. A sick baby, especially a chronically sick baby, changes your family dynamic in major ways and can come become the unhealthy focus of the entire family. The following suggestions can help you deal with an illness in your infant, whether acute or chronic:

✔ **Absolutely, positively avoid any hint of the "blame game."** Even if anything either of you did caused the baby to get sick, it's over and done with, so pinning blame on someone will only make everyone feel worse. Babies can't be raised in a bubble, so getting sick is, unfortunately, a fact of life.

✔ **Don't let yourselves get overtired.** Especially if your partner delivered not too long ago, she really needs to get enough rest. Take turns staying at the hospital or being up with the baby at home, or one of you could get sick, too.

✔ **If your partner is breast-feeding, keep pumping.** Stress is hard on milk supply, and pumping isn't nearly as effective as a nursing baby for stimulating the supply, but encourage your partner to do her best. As long as she keeps it going in the interim, the supply will build up when the baby is nursing again.

SIDS

Sudden infant death syndrome, or SIDS, has decreased since pedia-tricians began recommending that babies sleep on their backs with the "Back to Sleep" campaign, but it's still the third most common cause of death for infants up to 1 year old. More than 7,000 babies in the United States succumb to SIDS each year.

Identifying the causes and debunking myths

The causes of SIDS still are not clear. However, doctors know that the following are *not* causes of SIDS:

✔ Suffocation

✔ Choking

✔ Vomiting

✔ Infections

✔ Immunizations

SIDS is considered to be multifactorial, meaning that it doesn't have just one cause. Several factors must all be present for SIDS to occur, including abnormalities in the brain, respiratory system, and possibly the heart.

Understanding what increases the risks

The following factors increase the likelihood of SIDS:

- The baby was born premature.

- The baby is male.

- The baby is of black, Native American, or Native Alaskan ethnicity.

- The baby is between 2 and 3 months of age

- The baby is overheated or overdressed. Too many clothes or an overly heated room may increase the risk of SIDS. SIDS occurs more often in cooler fall and winter weather when babies get bundled up.

- The baby has a sibling who died of SIDS.

- The baby was/is exposed to tobacco. SIDS rates are higher in babies whose moms smoked during pregnancy or who smoke around the baby.

- The mother used cocaine, heroin, or methadone during pregnancy.

- The baby recently had a respiratory infection.

- The baby sleeps on his stomach, especially if he's switched from back to stomach sleeping or is overheated and sleeping on his stomach.

Research also indicates that babies who are breast-fed and those who suck on pacifiers may have a lower risk of SIDS. Side sleeping may seem like a compromise if your baby hates being on his back, but back sleeping is still safer, and many side sleepers roll over onto their stomachs.

Placing a fan in the window, or even just opening a window, also has been shown to decrease the risk of SIDS in at least one study. SIDS deaths dropped more than 70 percent when a fan was placed in a window and dropped 36 percent when the window was opened. Better ventilation may decrease carbon dioxide buildup.

Watching Out for Postpartum Issues

Female hormones are a jumbled mess right after delivery, which is why women are so emotionally fragile after birth. Add sleep deprivation and insecurities about parenting ability, and it's amazing that your partner can function at all.

Mood swings and depression are normal for the first few weeks or even months after having a baby, but sometimes more serious problems can arise. One of your jobs is being aware of the signs of a serious problem and making sure your partner gets help if needed.

Getting through the "baby blues"

Nearly every new mom experiences the "baby blues," emotional mood swings and mild depression triggered by hormone changes after delivery. Symptoms of baby blues include

✔ Anxiety or feelings that she's not doing things "right"

✔ Crying for no reason — at least, for what seems like no reason to you

✔ Difficulty concentrating

✔ Irritability

✔ Mood swings

✔ Periods of sadness

✔ Trouble sleeping

Baby blues normally last just a few weeks after giving birth, so if symptoms last longer or seem more severe, get your partner to her medical practitioner for help. Many women don't recognize the severity of their own symptoms or don't have the emotional energy to deal with them.

Taking a look at postpartum depression

Postpartum depression, a more serious form of the typical "baby blues," occurs in up to 10 percent of women. Some of the symptoms of baby blues and postpartum depression overlap, but postpartum depression is more pronounced, lasts longer, and includes serious signs that need immediate medical evaluation.

Recognizing the symptoms

Women with postpartum depression may have the following symptoms:

- ✔ **Difficulty bonding with the baby:** This is a major red flag. If your partner pushes the baby off on you or says she's not a good mom or that the baby would be better off without her, get medical help.

- ✔ **Thoughts about harming herself or the baby:** She may not verbalize these thoughts, so they may be hard to recognize. She may want other people to handle the baby because of her fears that she will hurt him, accidentally or on purpose.

- ✔ **Guilt and shame over her negative thoughts:** Again, because she may not verbalize her thoughts, recognizing what's going on may be difficult. Statements like "I'm no good" or "Someone else would be a better mom to this baby" are warning signs.

- ✔ **Sleep difficulties:** She may not be able to sleep, or she may want to do nothing but sleep.

- ✔ **Disinterest in normal activities, including sex:** Seeing old friends, going out, even everyday activities like cleaning the house, doing laundry, and watching TV may all go out the window. While you may at first think she's just tired, a deeper reason may be at the root of her continued lack of interest in life that lasts for several months after delivery.

- ✔ **Loss of appetite:** Losing interest in eating is often an early sign of depression.

- ✔ **Anger and irritability:** Her anger may go far beyond a few swear words when she drops a quart of milk, and can be frightening.

Postpartum depression usually is not a short-lived disorder, so don't try and wait it out, thinking she'll get over it in a week or two. Postpartum depression can last up to a year, which can interfere with maternal-child bonding and seriously disrupt your family.

Children of moms with untreated depression also suffer the consequences, with a higher incidence of behavior problems, sleeping disorders, feeding problems, hyperactivity, and language delays.

Knowing who's more at risk

Any woman can have postpartum depression, but the chances of this developing increase if

- ✔ **She has a history of depression.**

- ✔ **She's recently undergone major life changes.** These changes can include a move, a death, job loss, illness, pregnancy complications, or trouble between the two of you.

- ✔ **She doesn't have a good support system.** Family and friends make a big difference in the life of a new mom. Postpartum depression makes it difficult to reach out to others, so a woman who doesn't have pushy friends and family who will check in on her even if she doesn't call them is very isolated.

- ✔ **The pregnancy was unplanned or unwanted.**

Treating the disease

Treatment for postpartum depression may include

- ✔ **Antidepressants:** Make sure the doctor knows if she's breast-feeding so he can prescribe an antidepressant safe for use by breast-feeding moms.

- ✔ **Hormone therapy:** Estrogen replacement to offset the rapid drop in estrogen after giving birth may be helpful for some women.

- ✔ **Counseling:** Talking things out with a professional is very helpful for some women.

Taking care of yourself

If your partner is suffering from postpartum depression, a large part of her normal chores and responsibilities may fall on you. If you're trying to hold down a job, make sure your partner's okay, make sure the baby's okay, and run the household on top of it all, you may start to feel a little stressed yourself.

While rushing in to take over a short-lived crisis is easy, a situation that drags on for months can take its toll on your mental and physical well-being. Take care of yourself by making sure you

- ✔ **Get enough sleep.** Sleep deprivation makes everything look worse. The very worst time to pore over your worries is the middle of the night; everything looks insurmountable at 3 a.m.

- ✔ **Eat right.** You'll feel better and be better able to handle situations if you're not eating junk food.

- ✔ **Call in the troops to help.** You may not have readily available family and friends, but if you do, enlist their aid. Send them to the store, or have them come over and clean. This is a fine line, because you don't want to give your partner the impression that she can't do all this stuff, even when she can't. If you call in your mom to clean or cook, your partner may view it as a judgment against her abilities and a sign that you feel your mom is more capable than she is. Sometimes hiring help for household chores is a better idea.

✔ **Consider taking a leave of absence from work.** Some companies offer paid time off for dads or will let you use vacation or sick time. You can also use Family Medical Leave Act (FMLA) time for up to 12 weeks of time off, but this will probably be unpaid time, unless you work for an extremely generous company. Dipping into savings or borrowing from your 401(k) isn't ideal, but if it gets your family through a difficult time, it's worth it.

Acting fast to treat postpartum psychosis

Postpartum psychosis is an extremely dangerous psychiatric disorder that occurs in around 1 to 2 percent of women, usually in the first few weeks after giving birth. Women with bipolar disease or previous history of postpartum psychosis are more likely to develop the condition. Onset is sudden and includes the following symptoms:

✔ Paranoia

✔ Hallucinations

✔ Delusions

✔ Insomnia

✔ Irritability

✔ Restlessness

✔ Rapidly changing moods

✔ Bizarre thinking

Left untreated, postpartum psychosis can be lethal; the risk of suicide or infanticide is high. If your partner displays any of these symptoms, don't try to talk her out of it or persuade her to see her doctor. She almost certainly won't recognize her behavior as abnormal and in fact will probably consider you to be an adversary. Call 911 immediately.

Managing Grief

Grief is intense sorrow due to loss. The loss of the perfect child, the perfect partner, or perfect family can cause grief. The most important thing to remember about grief, no matter what the cause, is that it takes time to work through. Don't be hard on yourself or your partner when you're grieving, and don't expect you'll be in the same stages at the same time. Everyone works through grief differently.

Going through the stages of grief

Grief can be caused by many different scenarios, but the widely acknowledged five stages of grief, described by Elisabeth Kübler-Ross, include similar phases whatever the cause.

Whether you've found out that your baby has a long-term problem, your partner if suffering from serious postpartum illness, or your baby has to be hospitalized, expect to experience the five stages of grief:

1. **Denial:** The first stage of grief is often a feeling of "This can't be happening to us."

2. **Anger:** The second stage of grief is anger, often directed at God or other people.

3. **Bargaining:** Trying to make secret deals — "I'll donate our savings to this hospital if my baby's heart surgery saves him" — often with God (even if you don't believe in God!) is common in the bargaining stage.

4. **Depression:** When reality sets in and you realize that this is happening to you, fair or not, depression often follows.

5. **Acceptance:** Eventually you get through the other stages and settle down to dealing with what you have to deal with, but you may still go in and out of earlier grief stages at different times.

Stages may not follow this exact pattern, and not everyone goes through every stage. Yo-yoing back and forth between several stages is also common.

Grieving is important during the entire pregnancy process. Even if your baby is born without incident, you will be going through a lot of changes. Allow yourself and your partner to discuss the many things you're giving up in order to bring this child into the world.

Even something as silly as giving up your daily latte in order to buy diapers can become a source of resentment over time. As a general rule, talk openly and honestly about the changes that affect you and support each other.

And cut yourself a break — parenting isn't easy, and it's perfectly natural to miss having nights out with friends or even being able to eat an entire meal before it gets cold. Grieving the little things doesn't mean you don't love your baby — it means you're dealing with change in a healthy manner.

Why, why, why? Getting past the question

When grieving, getting bogged down in why a particular thing has happened to your partner or child is easy to do. However, it's not particularly good for you, especially if there's no way of deciphering exactly why something happened and most of your thoughts are purely speculative.

Unless knowing the reason why your problem happened can prevent a recurrence or change a situation, asking "why" doesn't help. Wanting a reason is a way of imposing control on a situation, but it doesn't help you move forward in helping your child.

Grieving together and separately

Everyone needs time to grieve a loss in their own way. Grieve together with your partner, certainly, but take time to grieve separately as well. Don't feel bad about needing to be alone with your thoughts sometimes. At the same time, the following tips can help you and your partner get through your grief, both together and on your own:

- ✔ **Stay physically close.** It helps you feel less alone, keeps you centered on still being a couple, and helps keep your relationship going in a situation that could easily break it apart. Even if you don't feel like it, make the effort to hold hands, cuddle on the couch watching TV, and have sex regularly.

- ✔ **Expect to be discouraged at times.** Everyone has moments when things look much worse than they really are, usually because they're tired, hungry, or just plain stressed. Identify it for what it is: temporary discouragement, not a new permanent negative outlook on life.

✔ **Don't get upset with your partner.** One day you or your partner may be raging at the world, and the next day the other one may take a turn. Listen to each other without taking things personally, trying to make it all better, or reproving them for their feelings.

✔ **Arm yourself with knowledge.** Knowledge really is power. Especially if your baby has a genetic or long-term condition, learning all you can about it helps you be your baby's best advocate and can help you and your partner feel like you're doing something productive in a frustratingly out-of-control situation.

✔ **Keep a journal, if the thought appeals to you.** Journals are not only good for privately venting feelings and fears that you and your partner don't want to share with each other; they're also good for looking back later and realizing how far you really have come.

✔ **Find a support group.** If you're coming to terms with a birth defect, your child or partner is ill, or you're dealing with a loss, talking to other parents dealing with the same thing can be a lifesaver. When relevant, it can also be a really good source of information on specialists, educational programs, and other outside help.

✔ **Get help for yourself.** If you find yourself mentally overwhelmed, seek counseling, either with your partner or alone. Often just being able to talk through a situation with a person not involved helps you sort things out.

✔ **Tell people when you're not up to something.** Another baby's christening, a big family party, or a holiday celebration may all be beyond your or your partner's ability to handle at first. Don't be afraid to say no to things that you feel would strip you raw right now. People who love you will understand, even if they're disappointed.

Determining when grief has gone on too long

Grieving can take a long time. But sometimes grief takes on a life of its own, and a situation called *complicated grief* can become permanently entrenched in your or your partner's life. While everyone has times when the sadness of circumstances becomes overwhelming, normally these feelings don't affect every aspect of life after the first few weeks or months. Complicated grief may be taking over your life or your partner's after a period of time if

✔ You still feel numb and detached.

✔ You're preoccupied and bitter about what's happened.

✔ You can't perform normal tasks, go to work, or participate in normal social functions.

✔ You feel life has lost its meaning.

✔ You're unusually angry, irritable, or agitated most of the time.

✔ You make rash decisions or do things you normally wouldn't do, such as drinking too much.

When grief becomes complicated, it becomes self-perpetuating. This is a time for intervention, either with medication or therapy. Talk to a grief counselor, psychologist, psychiatrist or other mental health personnel about your feelings and symptoms. Antidepressants have been found to help in some cases.

Talking to Other People about Your Child

Accepting a child's health problems is challenging enough for parents, and an emotionally sensitive situation is made even more difficult by the fact that eventually you need to inform other people of the problem. In time you may become accustomed to the comments of well-meaning but blundering family members and rude strangers, but at first you will likely be uncomfortable and upset. The following sections give you guidelines for getting through these situations.

Telling other people

Telling other people that your child has a problem can be gut wrenching; verbalizing to other people can be almost like hearing it for the first time yourself. When you tell other people your child has a problem, try the following tips:

✔ **Keep it simple.** Especially if your child has an ongoing medical problem, giving out information a little at a time may make it easier for others to digest.

✔ **Keep it positive.** Maybe your child isn't going to be able to be all you ever hoped for him. Actually, no child ever can! Remember that your child will be able to have a happy life, no matter what his disability, and you can enjoy him no matter what his issues. That positive outlook will express itself in your message.

✔ **Keep it straightforward.** You may be tempted to sugarcoat a situation when explaining it to others, but there's no reason to give them hope that a child will grow to be something he won't. Be honest about the situation from the beginning.

Handling insensitive remarks

Unfortunately, people do notice when a child has a birth defect or development delay and sometimes your hear them whispering to each other or pointing at your child. As devastating as this is, use it as a teaching experience if you can. If your child has a visible birth defect, comments *are* going to come your way — and your child will hear and understand those comments as she gets older.

Openly discussing your child's disability as something not to be hidden or ashamed of sets a positive example for your child. This doesn't mean that you have to freely discuss your child with every obnoxious person who asks pointed questions. But addressing questions with an open, accepting, positive attitude tells your child — and everyone else — that he's a great kid and that you're happy with him just the way he is.

Sometimes you won't have the patience to deal with questions, and you don't have to educate every person who crosses your path. But when your mood allows it, try the following suggestions when confronted with insensitive remarks:

✔ **Answer a small child's questions.** Children, having no discretion at all, often ask their parents about people with visible problems at the top of their lungs. Introduce yourself and use this opportunity to teach others about your child's disability.

✔ **Address an adult's comments in a nonjudgmental way, if you're up to it.** Most insensitive remarks are made out of ignorance, not malice, and even if they were made out of malice, addressing them politely can take the wind of a person's puffed sails and, with any luck at all, shame them into better behavior in the future.

✔ **When your own relatives are saying inappropriate things, address it firmly and in a non-negotiable way.** Offer to teach them anything they'd like to know, but let them know in no uncertain terms that this is your child and certain comments will not be tolerated.

Chapter 13

Daddy 911: Survival Tips for Bumps, Lumps, and Scary Moments

- -

In This Chapter

▶ Surviving the illnesses and accidents

▶ Staying cool and handling emergencies

▶ Giving medicine, taking temperatures, and monitoring diapers

▶ Helping your child through teething

▶ Taking a look at reactions to vaccines, medications, and food

- -

*N*othing in fatherhood gets your adrenaline flowing like a "thump" from the other room, followed by a scream, or worse, by silence. Nothing, that is, except endless vomiting, a seizing child, or a fender bender with baby in the car.

Fatherhood is full of frightening moments, but most of the time, babies survive parental ineptitude and concern. No one gets through babyhood and early childhood without a few accidents, sicknesses, and spills and thrills along the way. If your child never has a bruise or bump, you're probably protecting him too much, and a child who never gets sick never develops a good immune system. So take heart when dealing with heart-stopping situations: They're an inevitable part of parenthood. In this chapter we review the most common sources of parental anxiety, tell you what to do when they occur, and reassure you that, 99 times out of 100, baby — and you — will be just fine.

Handling Inevitable Illnesses

Most babies are now vaccinated against the most common illnesses, but plenty of illnesses can still infect your baby. And no matter how hard you try to protect your baby from illness-causing germs, you can't protect him from them all — and that's okay. Although hand washing, careful food handling, and cleanliness do help reduce germs, some germs are necessary. In fact, recent studies indicate that people who keep the bacteria around them at too much of a minimum are more likely to get sick than people who share their abode with a few stray germs. Go figure.

You can be sure that your baby will catch something in his first year, no matter how carefully you clean the shopping cart handles. In the following sections we tell you the symptoms, causes, and treatments of common illnesses so you'll feel prepared when the inevitable happens.

Nursing baby through common childhood diseases

Babies have immunity to many illnesses for their first six months because of antibodies passed on during pregnancy, but after six months, it's open season for germs. Following is a rundown on the most likely candidates for first illness to infect the baby.

Common colds

The common cold is so common that it comes in more than 100 varieties, which is why having a cold this month doesn't mean you won't get another one next month. And because your baby has never had any of them, she's likely to have at least one case of the sniffles in the first year. In fact, the Mayo clinic says that the average baby has eight to ten colds in the first two years of life, and each one lasts seven to ten days, no matter how many decongestants you buy. You may want to consider buying stock in facial tissue.

For most babies, colds aren't serious, although they are messy. Typical symptoms of a cold include:

✔ Runny nose, which may start with clear, thin secretions that turn thicker and yellow or green

✔ Sneezing

✔ Coughing

✔ Decreased appetite (young babies may find it hard to nurse or drink from a bottle because of nasal stuffiness)

✔ Low-grade fever up to 100 degrees

✔ Irritability

Babies under the age of 3 months should not be given decongestants at all, and infants younger than 6 months should be given them
only if congestion interferes with breathing or sleeping. Infant acetaminophen or ibuprofen are fine to help the baby feel better.

Although colds aren't usually serious, babies younger than 3
months old who develop cold symptoms need to visit a medical
practitioner. Babies that young are more likely to develop
pneumonia or other complications from a cold.

Ear infections

Between 5 and 15 percent of babies with colds develop an ear
infection, which just prolongs the misery. Contrary to popular
opinion, tugging on the ears doesn't always indicate an ear infection, although it can. Other ear infection symptoms include:

- ✔ Irritability
- ✔ Head shaking
- ✔ Refusal to nurse or take a bottle
- ✔ Mild fever
- ✔ Trouble sleeping

Breast-feeding when mom is sick

Moms aren't allowed to get sick — it's in the code of parenthood. But if your partner does get sick while breast-feeding, you both may wonder about the wisdom of
continuing to nurse.

If she's already sick, the baby's already been exposed to the germs before the sickness became evident, so there's no reason to avoid the baby. Very few illnesses
require her to stop breast-feeding. In fact, moms who develop colds and other
common illnesses develop antibodies that they pass on through the breast milk, so
nursing when sick may actually help the baby. Toxins such as E. coli, salmonella,
botulism, and other gastrointestinal bugs stay in the GI tract and don't affect the
milk, so breast-feeding is safe.

Your partner should check with the baby's doctor if she's taking heavy-duty cold
medication that has a sedative effect, and she should avoid cough syrups with
alcohol contents over 20 percent. Nasal sprays for sinus congestion can dry up
her milk, so use sparingly.

When your partner's sick, she's likely to require higher than usual amounts of fluid
to stay hydrated — and a double dose of TLC to keep her going through nighttime
nursing sessions. Getting up yourself and giving a bottle of pumped breast milk for
a night or two so she can sleep will buy you bonus points as a helpful dad.

The thinking on treating ear infections has changed during the last few years; ear infections may not require antibiotic treatment, because more than eight out of ten heal without treatment. Some doctors treat, and others wait, depending on the severity of the infection and the symptoms. Pain relievers help with discomfort.

Respiratory syncytial virus (RSV)

Respiratory syncytial virus (RSV) is a lower respiratory illness that infects most children at least once before age 2. Symptoms include lethargy, poor feeding, cough, difficulty breathing, and fever. While most cases are mild, severe illness requiring hospitalization can occur in small babies and premature or otherwise compromised infants.

For less severe cases, which occur far more frequently, acetaminophen or ibuprofen help with discomfort. Like most viruses, this one needs to run its course.

Vomiting

Small children and babies vomit more easily than adults when they're ill. Vomiting once at the beginning of an illness is common and requires no special treatment, but repeated vomiting requires medical evaluation because of the risk of dehydration.

Signs of serious dehydration require medical treatment. A sunken fontanel, the soft spot on the top of an infant's head, extreme lethargy, sunken eye, or sunken skin that remains raised after you pinch it deserve an immediate call to the baby's doctor.

Pediatricians often recommend giving vomiting children younger than 6 months an oral balanced-electrolyte solution such as Pedialyte in place of formula, starting with a few teaspoons or half an ounce every 15 minutes or so. Don't give plain water to any child younger than age 1 unless your pediatrician specifically recommends it. A medication syringe often works better than a spoon for this if your baby refuses to drink. Gradually increase the amount you give each time if the baby isn't vomiting it back up.

Don't give a volume more than you normally would: for example, if you normally give 4 ounces of formula every four hours, don't exceed that amount.

If no vomiting occurs after 12 hours, slowly start to reintroduce formula, but stop if vomiting occurs again. Breast-fed babies should continue to nurse, because breast milk is more digestible than anything on the planet. However, if vomiting continues, call your doctor.

Some medical personnel recommend following the BRAT (bananas, rice, applesauce, and toast) diet during and after a vomiting illness for children older than 1 year, after they haven't vomited for eight hours or so, because these foods are easily digested. Go slowly with foods and don't introduce any new foods until all vomiting and stomach upset have passed.

Babies who suddenly start vomiting after every feeding even though they appear healthy and still have an appetite may have *pyloric stenosis,* a narrowing between the stomach and small intestine. Pyloric stenosis requires surgery but has no aftereffects; when it's fixed, it's fixed.

Wheezing

Wheezing often follows a cold and doesn't always mean a baby is going to have asthma. Children younger than age 2 who wheeze with respiratory infections are no more likely to develop asthma than children who don't wheeze, according to a study published in 2002 in the *American Journal of Respiratory and Critical Care Medicine.* Children who start wheezing at an older age are more likely to develop asthma.

Wheezing can be scary for parents, and may require prescription bronchodilators that are breathed in as a mist, using a nebulizer, to open the narrowed airways and make it easier for the baby to breathe. Wheezing always requires a call to the pediatrician, especially if the baby doesn't have a cold or cold symptoms. An object stuck in the throat or more serious medical conditions can also cause wheezing. Some children wheeze with every upper respiratory treatment and may need nebulizer treatments whenever they have bad colds.

A child who is limp and exhausted, who has a bluish tinge around the lips, or who is struggling to breathe needs immediate medical attention.

Infectious diseases

Many infectious diseases of old (30 years ago!) have been eradicated, or nearly so, due to vaccines (see the later section "Reacting to Medicines and Vaccines"). However, vaccines haven't been developed for everything, and sometimes a baby is exposed to an infectious disease before she gets the vaccine. Chicken pox, measles, mumps, and rubella (German measles) vaccines, for example, aren't given until age 1, and roseola, a common infectious disease in infants, has no vaccine.

Being viruses, most common childhood diseases have no specific treatment beyond treating the symptoms and keeping the child comfortable. Aspirin should never be given to treat fever or discomfort, due to the possibility of Reye's syndrome. Acetaminophen or ibuprofen are fine if your child is uncomfortable; follow your pediatrician's instructions on dosing.

Many infectious diseases are accompanied by rashes, so any time your child has a rash and fever, call your medical practitioner for advice. He may want to see your child, but then again, in some cases, he may not want you bringing your infectious child into the waiting room! If the disease is highly contagious and fairly evident from the type of rash, such as chicken pox, he may give instructions over the phone without seeing the child. Following are some common infectious diseases with rashes:

- **Roseola:** Roseola has few complications but often results in frantic calls to medical personnel because the first symptom, which lasts for several days, is a high fever. Around day four the fever breaks and a rash appears. A telltale sign of roseola is that even with a fever as high as 104 degrees, the child doesn't appear ill. Roseola has no treatment and generally doesn't cause a great deal of discomfort.

- **Chicken pox:** Chicken pox is unmistakable: small red spots that form blisters that break and crust. A mild temperature and respiratory symptoms often accompany chicken pox. In rare cases, chicken pox can cause encephalitis, brain inflammation that can have long-term consequences. There's no way to shorten the duration of the disease, but cool baths and anti-itch lotions help with discomfort.

- **Hand, foot, and mouth disease:** Although this sounds like some ghastly disease only ranch hands would catch, hand, foot, and mouth disease is a common virus that causes blisters on the — yes, you guessed it — hands and feet and in the mouth. Mild fever can also occur, and the mouth sores can make it hard for a child to eat.

- **Measles:** Also called rubeola, measles was once a common disease. From 2000 to 2007, an average of only 63 cases occurred each year in the United States, but in the first half of 2008, 131 cases were reported, with most cases not vaccinated or with unknown vaccination status. Measles rarely occurs before age 6 months, due to maternal immunity being passed to the fetus. Children with measles usually appear quite ill and have a rash and high fever.

- **Rubella:** Rubella, sometimes called German measles, is a mild infection that causes a rash. While not serious for infected children, rubella poses serious risks for pregnant women, causing a number of birth defects as well as pregnancy loss. Rubella has become rare in the United States due to vaccination.

✔ **Mumps:** Mumps causes pain and swelling in the parotid glands, resulting in the classic "chipmunk" appearance. Mumps, like measles and rubella, has become rare in developed countries with the mumps vaccine. Mumps can cause painful testicular infection in males and affects sterility less than previously believed.

Staying alert for scarier diseases

Some major-league bacteria and viruses can infect infants, but the signs are usually pretty obvious: Your baby looks and acts sick, refuses to eat, cries, and sleeps too little or too much. Rest assured that if your baby is seriously ill, you'll recognize the signs. In the following sections we tell you what to watch for.

Meningitis

Meningitis, an inflammation of the tissues that cover the brain, can require hospitalization. Meningitis can be bacterial or viral and is caused by a number of organisms. Vaccination for *Haemophilus influenzae* type B, also known as Hib, reduces the chance of meningitis. Symptoms include fever, irritability, poor feeding, rash, seizures, a high-pitched cry, and stiff neck. In infants, the soft spot at the top of the head, the fontanel, may be bulging rather than flat. Signs of meningitis need immediate treatment to prevent complications.

Diarrhea

Although diarrhea may seem like more of a nuisance than a serious disease, severe diarrhea can cause life-threatening dehydration in an infant within a day or two. Diarrhea accompanied by fever, vomiting, or refusal to drink fluids needs immediate treatment. Diarrhea is most often caused by bacterial or viral illnesses including food poisoning.

The following symptoms indicate serious dehydration that needs a doctor's treatment:

✔ Extreme lethargy

✔ Sunken fontanel (the soft spot on top of baby's head)

✔ Sunken eyes

✔ Sunken skin that remains raised after you pinch it

Loose, frequent stools aren't always diarrhea; see the section "Deciphering Diaper Contents" in this chapter for ways to distinguish diarrhea from normal stool.

Protecting Baby from Common Accidents and What to Do When They Happen

You may not think newborns have a lot of accidents, since they're not all that mobile, but they do. In this section we go over the most likely scenarios and tell you how to handle them.

Taking care of baby after a fall

Even a newborn can scoot himself enough to fall off the changing table or bed, which is why you're not supposed to leave a baby unattended, without your hand on him, for even a second. Babies usually bounce pretty well and rarely break bones in a fall, but the parental guilt may be enough to put you in a rest home for a week.

Even worse is the "I was holding the baby on the couch and the next thing I knew there was a thump" fall. Most common in the first sleep-deprived weeks of parenthood, the "I dropped the baby" fall devastates guilty parents. Avoid the guilt by not lying down on the couch holding the baby — and don't sit up holding her if you're feeling really sleepy, either.

Parents rarely drop babies when they're walking, but a trip on the sidewalk or over a misplaced toy can send you and baby sprawling. Whenever the baby goes to ground, watch for these signs that a medical evaluation is in order:

- **Prolonged crying:** Every baby cries after a fall, if for no other reason than that landing on the ground is startling. Besides, you're crying, so baby thinks she should be, too. However, crying that lasts more than a few minutes may indicate an injury that should be checked out.

- **No crying:** Obviously, if your baby is completely unresponsive after a fall, call 911 immediately. Give him a minute, though; he may be too stunned to cry for a few seconds.

- **Repeated vomiting:** A baby who falls with a full stomach may spit up, but repeated vomiting can indicate a head injury.

- **Sleepiness:** This is one of the trickiest judgment calls of parenthood: What do you do when the baby falls right before bedtime? Keeping a tired baby awake is nearly impossible, and you shouldn't wake him up every few minutes just to make sure he's still responsive. Watch him for an hour and keep him awake if possible, but don't stress if it's not. If it's naptime or the middle of the night, let him sleep, but assess his breathing and color for any changes every few hours and watch to make sure he's moving normally in his sleep. Breathing that becomes very heavy or deep may indicate a problem.

✔ **Inability to move a body part:** Babies bones are still made of mostly cartilage, which bends easily, so she's unlikely to break a bone in a fall. If a mobile baby refuses to crawl or use an extremity, have it checked out.

✔ **Gaping cuts:** If he falls on a metal object and comes up bleeding, see if the wound's edges are close together or gaping. Gaping wounds usually need stitches, glue (no, this is not a do-it-yourself project!), or butterfly bandages. Take your baby to a doctor or hospital.

✔ **Huge bruises:** Foreheads are famous for developing immense bruises after a bump. Bruises alone aren't concerning, unless they're accompanied by other signs, such as sleepiness, or if they keep growing. Bruises that bleed excessively can be a sign of other diseases, such as hemophilia, and need to be evaluated.

Staying safe in the car

Car accidents are a fact of life, and you can't always prevent other drivers from driving badly or from running into your rear end at a stop light. This is why a properly fitted, age-appropriate, approved car seat is absolutely essential.

A newborn should never, never, never be held in a moving vehicle. Not in the front seat, the back seat, or anywhere else. Numerous studies have proven you cannot hold on to an infant in an accident; the baby will fly out of your arms and straight out the front or side window into the street, or will be tossed around the car like a rag doll.

Yes, this warning is meant to create a vivid picture that will scare you into never riding with your child in your arms. Babies die this way every year because they were taken out of the car seat to be fed or soothed for a moment. A moment is all it takes.

Following is essential car-safety information for your baby:

✔ **Put newborns and small infants in a car seat designed for their weight.** Never put a newborn in a seat designed for an older child, or vice versa.

✔ **Never put infants and small children in the front seat, even if they're in an approved car seat.** The front seat is much more dangerous for your child if you're in an accident. Getting them in and out of the car is easier in the front seat, but put them in the back. Please.

✔ **Use rear-facing car seats for infants up to at least 12 months and 20 pounds at a minimum.** Riding facing backwards is safer in the event of a crash, and pediatricians now recommend keeping children rear facing to the weight limits of the seat they're in. Children do not mind riding backwards, even up to age 2 or longer, and you can place a mirror so you can see them.

✔ **Don't use a car seat beyond its expiration date.** Yes, car seats have expiration dates, usually on a sticker on the side of the seat. The plastic can degrade over time, making the seat unstable in a crash.

✔ **Don't reuse a car seat that has been in an accident**. The car seat may have been weakened or damaged in the accident and may not perform as expected if you have another accident. It's worth the extra money to get a new one

✔ **Don't borrow a car seat unless you know the expiration date and know it's never been in an accident.** Don't take chances on a car seat that may be damaged in any way, even if it looks fine.

✔ **Read the instructions so you install the seat correctly.** A huge percentage of car seats are found to be incorrectly installed when checked at car seat clinics.

✔ **Don't carry dangerous loose items in the car, like shovels.** They become missiles in an accident.

✔ **Always wear your own seatbelt!** It sets a good example and helps you maintain control of the car in an accident, not to mention keeps you from flying around the car, possibly landing on the baby.

If you are in an accident, check the baby carefully for bruises and cuts, especially if the car seat is dented or banged up at all. Remove the car seat from the car with the baby in it if you can so you can check for signs of injury without causing more injury to the neck or back.

Be assured that if your child is in a safe car seat, the chances of his getting injured in an accident are low. If you don't think you can afford a car seat, talk to your medical provider or health department; some organizations offer help with money for car seats.

Managing Medical Crises at Home

Staying calm while talking about what to do in an accident is much easier than staying calm if your child actually gets hurt. In the next section we give you hints on how to stay calm and effective if your child needs help.

Don't panic! Don't panic!

Panic is inevitable when your child is injured, but try not to show it, because even babies can sense your alarm and respond to it with a few alarms of their own. Try to remember the following guidelines when your child crashes into the coffee table or experiences some other medical crisis:

✔ At first glance, it always looks like more blood than it actually is. Because blood is red, you notice it immediately. The injury probably isn't as bad as it first looks.

✔ Head and face wounds can bleed copiously because of the large number of blood vessels there. Clean up the area, and you may find just a tiny cut or scrape.

✔ Spurting blood can indicate a cut artery. Hold firm pressure over the wound with something clean. This injury requires medical attention, because arteries, unlike veins, do not stop spurting on their own quickly enough to prevent significant blood loss. Call 911.

✔ Any injury to the eye should be seen by an ophthalmologist. If your child has something stuck in his eye, don't pull it out; you may make things worse. Call 911.

✔ If you suspect a neck injury, don't move your child. Call 911 for help.

Calling the doctor

In an emergency, thinking clearly is very difficult. Sometimes you may even have trouble remembering your doctor's name, much less his phone number. To save yourself from fumbling through the phone book when you want to call your doctor, post the following information on your refrigerator in bold print so it's visible not only to you, but to the baby sitter, relative, friends, or anyone else who may be watching the baby:

✔ **Your baby's doctor's name and phone number:** Even you probably won't remember this information in an emergency.

✔ **Your baby's full name and date of birth:** Yes, we're sure you'll remember your baby's name. But today, with hyphenated last names and moms who keep their maiden names, don't be so sure your sitter knows your baby's last name! And it's a pretty safe bet she doesn't know his date of birth, unless she's closely related to you.

✔ **Your address:** Believe it or not, people tend to go blank on this kind of information in an emergency. You may not forget where you live, but your mother-in-law may.

✔ **Your phone number:** Ditto the above. Everyone's on speed dial now; your mother may not even know your phone number!

Taking the precaution of writing down important information may seem a little silly until you're actually in an emergency and can't seem to remember your own name, much less the baby's birth date.

When you get the doctor or emergency personnel on the phone, speak clearly and slowly enough so she can understand you the first time and not waste time asking you to repeat yourself.

If you have the presence of mind to do so, jot down a few notes about exactly what happened, because, believe it or not, the actual details get very jumbled in a crisis, which is why eyewitness stories never jibe.

Open Wide, Baby! Administering Medicine

Getting a baby to take medicine isn't as easy as it seems. Even small babies seem to have an uncanny sense that you've spiked their evening bottle with medicine, and if your partner is breast-feeding, spiking the boob with baby Motrin just isn't going to work.

When drawing up a dose of medication, remember that a kitchen teaspoon is not always a teaspoon; it can range from half a teaspoon to two or more. One U.S. teaspoon equals 5 milliliters or cubic centimeters, usually abbreviated to cc. Milliliters, known as ml, and cc are the same thing. So if the dose for your child's age is half a teaspoon, it's 2.5 ml or cc. To measure these miniscule amounts, you need a specially marked syringe, which pharmacies often provide with medication. If yours doesn't, beg for one.

Since a wrestling match will end up with far more medication on your shirt and on the floor than in the baby, try the following tips when you really need your baby to take medicine:

- ✔ **Mix the medicine with a small amount of a sweet-tasting food like baby applesauce.** Unfortunately, even small amounts of medications often change the flavor of the food, so don't put a tiny bit of medicine into a large amount of food hoping to dilute the taste enough so that baby will eat it. Chances are, he won't eat all the food, and you won't know how much medicine he actually got. Mix the medication into just a few bits of food he likes, and you may have a fighting chance of getting it into the baby.

- ✔ **If you mix medication into formula, don't spike the whole bottle, because this will be the first time in your baby's entire life that he doesn't chug down an entire 6 ounces of formula.** Mix it into 1 ounce, so he finishes it before he realizes there's something rotten in Denmark.

- ✔ **Use a syringe to squirt the medicine into the baby's mouth.** Insert the syringe gently into the corner of her mouth; don't try to force her mouth wide open, unless you want to wear cherry-flavored Tylenol for the rest of the day. Push the syringe plunger down slowly but steadily, gently holding her lips closed, and hope for the best.

- ✔ **Some medications can be given in rectal suppositories.** This may not sound like a really great solution, but inserting a suppository into the rectum is easier sometimes than getting medicine into a recalcitrant mouth. Just don't put a suppository into the child's mouth.

- ✔ **If your child is not an infant, firmly tell him he has to take his medicine.** You may not believe this now, but kids often know when you really mean business, and they comply. It's a miracle when it happens.

Taking a Baby's Temperature

Taking a baby's temperature is much easier now than it was a few years ago. You no longer have to stick a rigid glass thermometer into a flailing child's behind and hold it there for three minutes — in fact, there are very good reasons not to! You can measure temperatures even in tiny babies much easier today.

Choosing a thermometer

When standing in the big-box baby store looking for items to add to your baby registry, the sheer number of thermometer types may stagger you. Talking to friends who have babies may not clarify the thermometer choices, because everyone seems to have a favorite method, and hardly anyone agrees with anyone else. Following is a list of different types of thermometers and their pros and cons:

- **Digital rectal thermometers:** These are the gold standard for temperature taking, especially for infants younger than 3 months. Rectal thermometers measure internal temperature, the most accurate way to determine a child's temperature, and they have a flexible tip that gives if your child squirms. They're accurate and easy to use on some babies, although others hate them.

- **Digital oral thermometers:** These aren't practical or accurate until your child is 3 or 4 years old, because they can't hold them properly under their tongue and may bite and break them.

- **Axillary thermometer:** You can use a digital rectal or oral thermometer under the arm as an axillary thermometer, but this method gives the least accurate reading and normally registers as much as 2 degrees lower than a rectal temperature.

- **Tympanic thermometers:** These thermometers, shown in Figure 13-1a, are used in the ear canal and aren't appropriate for use in children younger than age 3 months because their ear canals are too small to properly insert the cone-shaped tip. They also may not be accurate for temperatures higher than 102.

- **Forehead thermometers:** These register temperature as you roll the tip across the forehead, but they're not very precise.

- **Pacifier thermometers:** If your baby will suck a pacifier for three minutes, a pacifier with a built-in oral thermometer (see Figure 13-1b) may be the way to go.

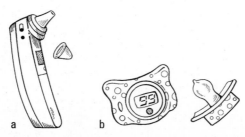

a   b

Figure 13-1: A tympanic ear thermometer (a) and pacifier thermometer (b).

Taking a rectal temperature

Taking a rectal temperature is much easier if the baby is lying face down. Inserting the thermometer while the baby is on his back is possible, but you'll have much more difficult keeping him from flailing around and possibly hurting himself. To take a rectal temperature, follow these steps and also check out Figure 13-2:

1. **Put a little Vaseline or other lubricant on the thermometer to make it less uncomfortable to insert.**

2. **Place the baby over your lap, with his head slightly down over your thigh.**

   This brings his rear end up slightly, making the anus, the opening to the rectum, easier to find.

3. **Locate the anal opening visually before you start prodding around with the thermometer tip.**

4. **Hold the thermometer the entire time that it's in the baby's bottom, to avoid injury.**

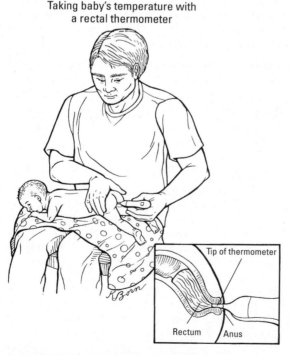

Taking baby's temperature with a rectal thermometer

Figure 13-2: Taking a baby's rectal temperature.

If you still have an old mercury thermometer lying around the house, get rid of it. Don't just throw it in the trash. The Environmental Protection Agency recommends taking it to a hazardous waste dump, and throwing them in the trash is actually illegal in some states.

Recognizing fevers

So when is a fever a fever? It can be hard to know, especially when you're juggling half a dozen methods of temperature taking in an attempt to get an accurate reading. The following guidelines explain what your medical practitioner means when he talks about a fever:

- **In an infant up to age 3 months, a rectal temperature of 100.4 (or oral pacifier temperature of 99.5) or higher needs immediate evaluation.** Small babies don't normally run fevers, so even these seemingly low temperatures need attention.

- **Between ages 3 months and 3 years, a rectal fever of 102 or higher should be reported to your medical practitioner.** Although fever is important, the way your child is behaving is equally important. A child who is still eating, drinking, and playing happily with a high fever is less concerning than a lethargic child with a lower fever.

- **An axillary temperature of 99 or higher may be a fever.** Confirm the exact reading rectally, if at all possible.

- **Ear temperatures are roughly equivalent to rectal temperatures.** If you're sure the tip is properly inserted into the ear, call your doctor for a temperature of 100.4 for infants and 102 for ages 3 months to 3 years.

Febrile seizures

Febrile seizures, or convulsions, are extremely scary for parents, although the child probably won't remember it. Most febrile seizures occur when the temperature rises suddenly, but the exact degree of fever isn't the determining factor of whether a child has a febrile seizure. Around 3 to 5 percent of children experience febrile seizures, usually between the ages of 5 months and 5 years.

Don't try to do anything while your child is having a seizure, other than trying to cool her off by sponging her down with cool water. Don't put anything into her mouth or try to restrain her; more damage is done by these attempts to prevent damage.

Move any hard or sharp objects away from the child during a seizure to prevent injury. Remember to move the objects away from the child; don't try to move the child away from the objects.

 Most febrile seizures last only a few minutes, but your child may be limp and lethargic afterward. Follow up with medical personnel immediately after a seizure; your doctor may want you to bring the baby in immediately or may be okay with a visit the next day to determine the cause of the fever. Be guided by his advice. Most parents who have just experienced an infant seizure want the reassurance of a visit.

 If your child's seizure lasts 15 minutes or more, she starts to turn blue, or she remains unresponsive after a seizure, call 911 immediately.

Treating a fever

Fevers of 100.2 or less don't always need treatment. Fever is the body's way of fighting off infection, so giving your child medication at the first sign of a fever doesn't help her immune system to develop. Aspirin is no longer recommended for children, due to the possibility of developing Reye's syndrome. Infants can be given children's Tylenol or ibuprofen in recommended doses.

Deciphering Diaper Contents

Some parents are inordinately interested in their offspring's waste products (mostly parents who were raised to be inordinately obsessed with their own). But even parents who are pretty casual about the contents of a diaper can sometimes be concerned about what appears there.

Knowing what's normal

Breast-fed babies normally have frequent stools that are often looser than those of bottle-fed babies. Breast-fed babies' stools are often yellow and seedy, whereas bottle-fed babies' stools may be tan and firmer.

Babies frequently poop after every feeding in the first month or so, and then slow down production. Some babies may only "produce" every few days, which is fine as long as the stool is soft. At the same time, they may begin to squirm, cry, grunt, and make faces when pooping, worrying parents that they're having a hard time passing stools. What they're actually doing is becoming aware of their own bodily sensations.

However, if stool is hard, comes out in pellets, or if the baby doesn't go for several days, call the pediatrician for advice.

Checking out color changes

Stool is usually yellowish or tan in babies who are exclusively breast-fed and/or formula-fed. When unusual-colored poop makes an appearance, parents are understandably concerned. Changes in stool color can be perfectly normal or a sign of a problem, so keep the following information in mind when deciding whether to call the pediatrician:

- ✔ If your baby is on iron-fortified formula, she may have green or dark stools.

- ✔ Green stools can indicate an imbalance of foremilk, the first milk released, and hindmilk, which has a higher fat content. Too much foremilk and not enough hindmilk can produce green stools and upset the stomach. Allowing the baby to nurse long enough on one side — ten minutes or longer — to get a good dose of hindmilk corrects the problem.

- ✔ If blood is on the outside of the stool, the baby may have a small fissure and may need a stool softener, but ask the pediatrician. Make sure the baby doesn't have a diaper rash that's causing the blood.

- ✔ Bloody, mucousy stools need immediate attention, as they can indicate intestinal problems.

- ✔ Dark, tarry stools can indicate intestinal bleeding and should be evaluated.

Teething Symptoms and Remedies

Parents peer into their infant's mouths looking for teeth like gold miners sifting through the silt for nuggets of gold. When it comes to teeth, the best thing you can do is relax. All children, with very few exceptions, get teeth eventually, and prying your kid's mouth open to search for a pearly white doesn't make them come in any faster.

Keeping in mind that these guidelines have many exceptions, you generally can expect teeth to appear in this order and at these times:

- ✔ The first tooth appears between 4 and 7 months.
- ✔ The two lower middle teeth usually come in first.

> ✔ The two upper middle teeth follow next.
>
> ✔ The back teeth are the last to come, usually around age 2; you probably won't be all that excited by new teeth by then and may not even notice.
>
> ✔ By age 3, your child will have 20 teeth, 10 on each level.

After you get over the thrill of finding a new tooth, you may be consumed with ways to ease the discomfort of teething. Although alcohol, an old-fashioned remedy for easing the pain of teething, should not be applied to baby's gums, it may help to apply it to *yours*. You can decrease teething discomfort in your baby with:

> ✔ Pain medication such as Tylenol or ibuprofen
>
> ✔ Teething gels applied to the gums
>
> ✔ Chilled teething rings or other items for baby to bite down on

Teething tablets are popular over-the-counter mixtures of homeo-pathic medications but should always be cleared by your baby's doctor before using them. Teething does not normally cause a fever higher than 100 degrees, so a fever still needs investigation, even if your baby is breaking in a full set of choppers all at once. (Not likely, by the way — teeth tend to trickle in in groups of no more than two at a time.) Teething can cause:

> ✔ Drooling
>
> ✔ Irritability
>
> ✔ Swollen gums
>
> ✔ Difficulty sleeping
>
> ✔ Difficulty nursing or taking a bottle
>
> ✔ Biting on everything within reach

Whether or not teething causes diarrhea, vomiting, and rashes other than the rashes associated with constant drooling is debat-able. Kids can get sick while teething, so don't assume that teeth-ing is responsible for sudden signs of illness.

Reacting to Medicines and Vaccines

Giving a child any type of foreign substance can trigger allergic or hypersensitivity reaction. New foods are actually the biggest cul-prit, but medications and vaccinations can also cause reactions.

Vaccination reactions — yours and your baby's

Many parents have concerns about the number of vaccinations given to infants and worry about which ones their child should have, when to give them, and possible consequences of vaccinations. Remember that vaccines are given to prevent *serious* illness; they're not given to prevent diseases that aren't potentially harmful for your child.

Giving two or three injections at one visit, especially when each one contains more than one vaccine, is concerning to many parents. But the American Academy of Pediatrics stands by the current vaccination schedule recommendations (which you can find in Chapter 10) and states that giving a number of injections at one time does not overwhelm the immune system, as some opponents suggest. They state that children are exposed to 2,000 to 6,000 antigens every day, as opposed to the 150 antigens introduced in vaccines during the entire vaccination schedule.

While there's no proof that vaccines are responsible for the increase in autism and similar issues, vaccines can cause complications in some children. Typical symptoms include fever, pain at the injection site, redness, or rash. Approximately 3 out of 10,000 children have febrile seizures (see the section "Recognizing fevers" for more on febrile seizures) after getting the measles-mumps-rubella (MMR) vaccine, the Merck Manual reports.

The debate about how to spread out vaccines and which ones are really necessary could fill books — and undoubtedly has — and every couple has their own feelings about vaccines. The most important thing in deciding on how, when, and what to vaccinate is to find a medical practitioner whose opinion you trust, discuss the pros and cons, and follow her recommendations.

Because many children do run fevers after vaccinations, premedicating your child with Tylenol or ibuprofen before the doctor visit can prevent a few hours of misery after the injection. Usually fever is a short-term reaction, so if your child is still feverish and miserable the next day, let the doctor know.

Some children develop a rash after vaccinations. Again, if it lasts more than a day, ask the doctor about it.

Medications that cause reactions

Any medication can cause allergic reactions, but some are more likely to cause a reaction than others. Antibiotics are more likely to cause an adverse reaction than other medications. Typical offenders include:

- Penicillin or any of the same family, such as amoxicillin or ampicillin (Penicillin causes more allergic reactions than any other antibiotic.)
- Sulfa medications
- Cephalosporins

Drug allergies can cause a variety of skin reactions, including

- Rashes
- Hives, small welts that move around from one area to another
- Erythema multiforme, a moving bull's-eye-patterned rash with a fever, joint pains, itching, and a overall sick feeling, as well as painful eyes and sore mouth.

Notify your child's doctor if any reaction occurs after taking any medication. Children's diphenhydramine helps control itching and swelling in most cases, but follow your pediatrician's advice. Severe reactions may require steroids.

Dealing with Food Allergies

Food allergies affect around 1 in 18 babies before age 3. As with many facets of baby raising, the thinking on solid food introduction and allergies has completely changed since you were a baby, a fact that can result in heated discussions between you and your parents.

Introducing new foods

At one time, introducing solids early was all the rage in parenting, as if having your 2-month-old chow down pureed carrots merited some sort of parenting prize. Today, pediatricians recommend waiting until a baby is 4 to 6 months old to introduce new foods to reduce the chance of developing food allergies, especially the five most common food allergens, which are:

- Cow's milk
- Eggs
- Peanuts
- Soy
- Wheat

An almost unbelievable 90 percent of food allergies are caused by one of the big five, which is why the American Academy of Pediatricians recommends introducing new foods one at a time. Age at the time of introduction is no longer considered a factor in whether a child develops allergies after age six months.

Recognizing allergic reactions

Parents who have allergies themselves may be looking for signs of allergies in their children, and allergic tendencies do run in families. Some common reactions, like reddened cheeks after eating tomatoes or citrus fruits, aren't allergies, and lactose intolerance, caused by a missing enzyme that breaks down milk products, also isn't an allergy. Irritability, skin rashes, and intestinal upsets are the most common signs of food allergy in infants.

Colic, skin rashes, and stomach upsets such as loose stools are the most common signs of food allergy, but severe anaphylactic reactions with difficulty breathing, hives, and loss of consciousness can also occur, often within minutes of eating the offending food. Get medical help immediately if this occurs.

Having previously eaten a food without a reaction is no guarantee that an allergic reaction won't occur; reactions don't occur the first time a person is exposed to a substance. Always call your baby's doctor if a significant reaction occurs and follow his recommendations on treatment.

Preventing allergic reactions

The best prevention for allergy development is exclusive breast-feeding for at least the first 4 to 6 months of life. Some evidence exists for prevention of wheezing in infancy and early childhood by exclusive breast-feeding for the first 3 months of life. There's no proof that use of soy formulas prevents allergies compared to cow's-milk-based formulas; in fact, many children with cow's-milk allergies are also allergic to soy.

Cook fruits and vegetables for your infant rather than serving them raw, because cooking appears to decrease the risk of allergic reactions. Processed foods, including junior baby foods, contain a number of ingredients, which makes it hard to tell what an infant is reacting to if he develops an allergic reaction.

If your child has severe allergies, your pediatrician may recommend carrying an auto-injector containing epinephrine in case of serious allergic reaction. Fortunately, around 20 percent of children outgrow allergies to foods by the time they hit school age.

Chapter 14

Time and Money: The High Cost of Having a Baby

In This Chapter

▶ Balancing work and life with baby

▶ Going back to work, or deciding not to

▶ Preparing for unexpected baby expenses

▶ Spending your money wisely

*E*ven before baby arrived you probably never felt like you had enough time in the day or money in the bank for everything you wanted to do. Money concerns aren't a new worry in the lives of most new parents, but with diapers, baby wipes, and the cutest clothing you've ever seen in your life added to your weekly expenses, even financially sound parents can quickly begin to feel strapped for cash.

The only thing in shorter supply than money may be your time. Sometimes just finding the time to shower in the morning may feel like a major accomplishment, but keeping your life and self in order is important for your entire family. Adjusting to a new life in which baby comes first is a challenge, and even the most organized parents will find that tasks that used to require minimal effort are now a major undertaking. In this chapter we take a look at how to juggle your new responsibilities with your old ones — with a little fun mixed in to boot.

Creating a New Work/Life Balance with Baby

Unfortunately, bliss doesn't pay the bills, which means that unless you're embarking on a new journey as a stay-at-home dad or you win the lottery while on paternity leave, you will find yourself back in the throes of work in what feels like the blink of an eye. Don't be surprised if for the first few days you find yourself disinterested, distracted, or bored on the job, especially if your partner is still at home. In the beginning your mind will be more focused on the amazing event you've just experienced, and the fatigue your brain may be feeling as a result of less sleep won't help any.

When you're working full time again, winding down after a hard day won't be as easy as it once was now that you have to help with baby's bath time, night feedings, diaper changes, and endless chores. Congratulations — you now have another full-time job awaiting you when you get home.

Striking an ideal work/life balance is a major challenge for all parents, and it takes a lot of negotiating, planning, and sacrifice. From work to home to play, everything becomes a little more complicated to juggle. In the following sections we help you make the best of a very full plate.

Taking time off with paternity leave

Not so very long ago, new dads were expected back on the job the day after welcoming a baby into the world. And although we're still a long way from equal time off for both mother and father, strides have been made to allow new dads time to bond with their new family.

Looking at possible time-off options

When planning your time off, consider the following options that may or may not apply to your employment situation:

- **Parental leave:** A benefit offered by many companies, parental leave is time off that may be paid, unpaid, or a combination of both. Companies usually require that you be employed there at least 12 months in order to qualify. Parental leave usually applies to maternal, paternal, and adoption leave, and policies vary by company. Speak with your human resources manager to find out your company's policy — or lack thereof.

- **Family medical leave:** In the United States, the Family Medical Leave Act of 1993 requires companies that employ more than 50 people to allow up to 12 weeks of unpaid leave in a given year for certain medical reasons, including caring for a new child.

- **Vacation time:** Is there a better way to use your vacation time than to bond with your new baby? If you don't qualify for any of the above time-off options, or the parental leave offered by your company is insufficient for your needs and wants, most companies allow you to use vacation days at the end of the leave in order to extend your time off. If your company allows you to use vacation days for emergencies and illnesses, be sure to save a few days in case you don't have enough sick time to get you through the rest of the year.

✔ **Sick time:** Some companies permit you to use sick time as part of your leave. Using sick time can be especially beneficial to hourly workers and unsalaried employees who don't accrue time-off benefits at a rapid pace or may not be eligible for all of a company's benefits, as well as for employees who haven't worked for their company long enough.

Just remember not to use it all — babies tend to come down with all sorts of bugs. And with all of the extra responsibilities and late nights involved in parenting, you may find yourself in dire need of a sick day for your own use. Instead of using all your sick time, inquire about the possibility of using unpaid time off so you can save those sick days for when you really need them. Your boss will probably be more willing to give you unpaid time off for baby's arrival than for your stuffy nose.

✔ **Flextime:** Perhaps your company really needs you back ASAP. Talk with your boss and HR representative about temporarily working flexible hours or even part time from home. You may be expected to meet daily and weekly goals and complete all of your work, but the non-nine-to-five schedule can be helpful for numerous reasons, especially if baby or mom has health concerns that require extra care or help.

Discussing your leave options

Before meeting with your employers to find out what arrangements for leave you can make, speak with other recent fathers in your company about their experiences to get a better idea of what to expect. Their information can provide you an opportunity to craft a plan that meets your needs and adheres to your company's policies. Some great questions to ask other fathers are:

✔ What was the company's paternity leave policy at the time you became a new dad?

✔ How did your boss react to your paternity leave inquiry?

✔ How much time off did they grant you? How much of it was paid?

✔ Did you use the Family Medical Leave Act, and if so, what was your boss' reaction?

✔ How did you structure your paternity leave?

✔ Did you ask about using flextime before or after baby's arrival? If so, what was their response?

✔ How much responsibility did you have to take for covering your job in your absence?

✔ What is the one thing you wish you would have done differently in arranging your time off?

When meeting with your boss and/or HR representative, make sure to take notes of everything that is said and get any policy-related statements in writing. In addition to asking about some of the issues in the questions above, be sure to ask about the company's policy regarding additional time off in case of complications with mom or baby. Also find out if the leave will cause delays in future raises and how you will pay your share of health insurance if you're taking unpaid leave.

Getting all your paperwork in order

Be sure to get the necessary time-off paperwork in order prior to heading to the hospital. Don't get defensive if your employer requires a doctor's note regarding your leave — nobody is questioning the fact that you're a new parent, but rules must be followed.

Keep a folder with all of the paperwork and forms you need to secure your time off. Following are some of the forms and papers to have on hand:

✔ **Family and Medical Leave Act application.** Your HR office can give you a copy.

✔ **State-sponsored family-leave applications.** You need these forms only if your state's regulations differ from federal.

✔ **Medical time-off verification forms.** Include any forms your family doctor or pediatrician needs to fill out for your HR department.

✔ **Your company's family-leave policy.**

✔ **Copies of all e-mail and letters sent to or received from your boss or HR department regarding your time off.**

✔ **Vacation time request.** This form needs to be approved and signed by your boss and/or HR representative.

Managing sick time when you're back at work

When both parents head back to work, sick time suddenly becomes a hot commodity. Between baby's multitude of doctor appointments, vaccination reactions, fevers, and diarrhea, as well as your sitter's unexpected life moments, you will be required to leave work more frequently than you used to do pre-baby.

Check with your employer several weeks prior to the beginning of your leave to find out if flextime or work-at-home days are allowed in case of child illness or childcare gaps. If they aren't, stay honest. Don't start coughing and sneezing or fabricate some family emergency as a front to mask the real reason you have to leave.

Ask for a performance evaluation a month or so after returning from paternity leave. If you're be experiencing bouts of insecurity and anxiety about how you're perceived and performing on the job now that you're a dad, or feel intimated or scared about asking for days off because of the new baby, a performance review gives you an opportunity to address any minor issues that have arisen before they become full-fledged annoyances for your boss. Be sure to let your boss know that you're aware that your schedule is trickier than normal, and that you appreciate her/his flexibility as you adjust to a new schedule. Letting your boss know that you're open to criticism and want to fix any problems will make you look like the responsible new parent you have become.

Dealing with after-work expectations

Depending on the business you're in, you may be used to participating in after-work activities and commitments. However, after baby arrives, it quickly becomes clear that you no longer have the ability to attend happy hour three nights a week. Although nobody wants to be seen as the new dad who suddenly says no to everything and isn't the same fun, karaoke-loving guy he used to be, a certain amount of reality will dictate your ability to party instead of heading straight home to take care of business and spend time with your family.

Evaluate any after-work requests with the following guidelines to help you determine the appropriate way to handle them:

- ✔ **Mandatory engagements:** Sometimes meetings run late, business dinners take priority, and your boss asks you to work overtime on a very important project. Always say yes to anything that's important to the function and maintenance of your job, and work with your partner to find help for her at home if needed.

- ✔ **Occasionally important dates:** A beer isn't always just a beer. Sometimes going to a bar after work is an important networking opportunity or even where important business decisions and advancement opportunities are made. Try not to commit to quasi-important after-work requests more than a few times each month unless you can arrange for (and afford) childcare during that time.

✔ **Optional events:** Sometimes a beer *is* just a beer — and there's nothing wrong with that, as long as you keep in mind that you can say yes only so many times without annoying your partner and it's best to save those for when it really counts. If you perceive an after-work event to be merely for sport, pass unless you need a mental-health night out. Just remember that every time you say yes, you're giving your partner the opportunity to say yes to an activity of her own down the road. It doesn't take too many commitments to severely diminish that all-important family time.

Be proactive in scheduling out-of-the-office social events over lunch. If you take the lead, you will have control over when they're held and won't feel the need to justify your inability to commit to activities after work.

If a co-worker challenges your decisions to not attend after-work events that you perceive to be nothing more than social calls, don't feel the need to defend your decision. Let him or her know that you spend eight hours a day with your co-workers and you like to spend the rest with your family.

Reprioritizing your commitments

With so much on your plate, you may wonder when you'll have time to hit the gym, go to the movies, take your partner on a date, volunteer at the local farmer's market, or engage in any of the myriad activities you enjoy doing. The bad news is that there isn't time in the day/week/month to do everything you've always done on top of caring for baby. The good news is that you'll still have time to have fun despite your overfull schedule.

Make sure to keep yourself high on the list of priorities, because you can't manage work, family, and your social life if you're run down, sick, or depressed. If you try to do it all, you won't do anything very well because you'll be spread too thin. To have more energy and stave off illness, take your vitamins, get as much sleep as possible, eat healthy foods, and continue to make exercise a priority.

Just as you wouldn't skip a doctor appointment or just not show up at work one day, you have to schedule your personal commitments as well. Whether that's a stroll through the park with your family, sex with your wife, or time to sit and watch a tennis match on TV, don't make your personal time optional, or the balance between work and life can easily become off kilter.

How do you make the work/life balance stay in balance? Keep a calendar and write down everything, even blocking out time you set aside for fun. Try as best as you can to separate your commitments by focusing on work at work, family during family time, and you during your scheduled personal time. You can't make the most of your time if you're mentally juggling too many tasks and people.

Figuring out what's most important to you

Because thinking about everything you need and want to do at the same time is impossible, make a list of all of your commitments and activities. You list may include the following activities:

- Spending time with your family
- Working overtime
- Exercising
- Socializing with friends
- Engaging in hobbies, such as fixing cars or reading
- Traveling
- Maintaining a healthy relationship with your partner
- Doing community service
- Participating in clubs, groups, and intramural sports

When you complete your list, ask yourself, "If I could only give my attention to one thing in life, what would that be?" After you pick the most important thing in your life, choose the next four so you've designated your top five priorities. As your child grows and your life changes, frequently revisit this priority list. What's important to you now may not be as important four months from now.

Figuring out what can go, at least for now

After you set your priorities, drop any unnecessary activities from your to-do list — at least the ones that require a major time commitment. Sure, a twice-weekly euchre league may be a fun getaway, but is it really vital to your well-being and that of your family? How much TV can you cut out of your week and still feel entertained? Any activity that eats up copious amounts of your time without much reward should be removed from your regular routine.

Work with your partner, as well as baby sitters and family members, to help you adhere to your priority list. Couples often tag-team to great effect: Mom watches baby while dad attends guitar lessons, and dad watches baby while mom goes to yoga. And when your friends and family members offer to baby-sit, try not to always use that time for errands. Instead, take your partner out for a night — or an afternoon, which is sometimes easier with babies — on the town.

Readjusting When and If Mom Goes Back to Work

Not every mother (or father, for that matter!) decides to go back to work. Others have to do so for financial reasons even when their hearts and tear ducts tell them otherwise. And some mothers and fathers are excited to get back to the daily routine and job they love. Everyone's experience is different, but regardless of what choice you and your partner make, the transition is challenging.

Making going back to work easier on mom

Mom gets far more time off work after baby is born than you will (usually 6 to 12 weeks), which only makes the going-back process more difficult and emotional for her. There may be tears, running mascara, threats of quitting her job — lots of them — and it's your job (on top of everything else!) to support her through this difficult transition.

Mom's innate protective instincts will be at an all-time high the moment she's forced to put her 3-month-old baby into full-time daycare for 40-plus hours every week. When you went back to work, you had the benefit of transitioning back when baby was at home with the only other person you trust as much as yourself to care for your child. Under most circumstances, mom doesn't get that luxury, and taking the leap back into business-as-usual won't be easy for her.

Try these techniques to ease your partner's return to the workplace:

- **Practice in advance:** Getting out the door won't ever be the same again, and the last thing you want is a panicked, rushed mom on her first day back. Much like you did with the trial run to the hospital before baby's birth, take the time go through a trial run for mom's first day back to work. It will benefit you, too, since you'll be involved in the process of getting baby fed and clothed and delivered to the sitter *and* still making it to work on time.

- **Provide mommy alone time:** It's not so unusual for new moms to cling to their newborns, and in some cases, going back to work is your partner's first separation experience after giving birth. Start slowly by giving your partner blocks of time to be alone on the weekends or evenings during which she can practice doing things without baby around.

✔ **Get comfortable with childcare:** Trusting someone else to care for your fragile baby isn't easy, but the sooner you start, the easier it will be when that care becomes more frequent. Start letting friends and family take short shifts watching the baby, and even ask your future childcare provider to take on a shift before your partner goes back to work. Also, feel free to ask your provider for time to observe his or her interaction with your child on-site.

✔ **Stagger the return:** Going from full-time mom to full-time employee overnight can be a major shock to the system. Have your partner talk to her employer about the possibility of a staggered return. If the first week back she only works one day, and then the following week she works three, and so on, the transition will be much smoother.

✔ **Plan ahead for morning:** Mornings are tough for everyone, so don't leave anything other than showering and getting dressed for the a.m. because you now have to factor in getting baby ready for the day and travel time to the sitter. Take time the night before to make lunches, pick out clothing, pack baby's diaper bag, and so on to create a calmer mood in the morning.

If your partner is threatening to quit her job the first day back, don't panic and certainly don't try to change her mind. The best thing to do is listen to her concerns and give her all the bonding time she needs with baby upon returning home from work. Tell her to take it day by day, and that at the end of every week you will reevaluate the situation. There's nothing wrong with her making the decision to stay home, but making the decision when her emotions are heightened isn't a good idea.

Following are some thoughtful ways to improve your partner's emotional state during the transition back to work:

✔ **Digitize baby:** Buy your partner a digital picture frame for her desk at work, or even a pocket-sized device if she works in a nonoffice environment. Add new pictures every day to give your partner a daily visual jolt of baby, which will help her feel more connected.

✔ **Free nights for bonding:** Though you won't want to shoulder the chore burden all by yourself forever, consider giving your wife a get-out-of-jail-free card during her first week back. Allow her to spend every waking moment with baby to give her the opportunity to reconnect with her child and not feel like she's missing out on everything.

✔ **Shower her with gifts and praise:** You don't have to go overboard, but some flowers on her first day back may go a long way toward making her smile, at least for a second, during that first week back. Be sure to tell her how well she's doing at adjusting to the changes and that you think she's a wonderful mother.

✔ **Don't try to fix it:** Let her cry and validate her experience, even if you don't understand why it's so hard. Mothers give birth to the babies, and as deep as the bond between fathers and kids can run, it's still different for mom. Call her throughout the day to check in and let her know that what she's experiencing is normal.

Deciding to be a stay-at-home parent

Making the decision to be a stay-at-home parent can be the fulfillment of a lifelong dream for some parents and a total surprise to others. If you and your partner make the decision that one of you will stay at home to care for the baby, thus begins another exciting, challenging chapter in your new parenthood experience. However, it isn't a decision that should be taken lightly. If you've been used to income from both yourself and your partner, losing half that income will make a profound difference in your lives, and you and your partner need to carefully consider whether or not you can make it work.

Considering whether your partner can stay home

Some women know in advance that they don't want to go back to work after having a baby, and some come to that decision after baby arrives. If you can make it work financially and your partner is refusing to budge, do your best to make arrangements for her to stay at home that work for both of you. She may have loved her job before and you thought the routine you'd established as a family was working fine, but while you don't always need to understand why your partner feels the way she does, it is vital that you respect her right to feel that way.

Take plenty of time to talk it over and make sure staying home is really a feasible option. When choosing to stay at home, many costs beyond salary must be considered. If your insurance coverage comes from your partner's employer and she decides to stay home, you will have to opt-in to your company's plan, which will reduce the size of your check. Also, most companies have an open season at the beginning of each year during which you can enroll for insurance. If the decision is made outside of the open-season period, you will either be without insurance or forced to pay for private insurance until that time arrives.

Looking at options when you can't afford to lose the income

Sometimes the desire to stay home won't subside, and you and your partner may be at odds as to what is best for your family. If your financial situation doesn't allow for your household income to be reduced by tens of thousands of dollars annually, stand your ground. Be understanding to her concerns and desires, but don't put your livelihoods at risk in order to make her happy. Most importantly, don't rule it out forever. Make a savings plan that you both can work toward in order to achieve her goal of staying at home. Encourage your partner to seek out work-at-home opportunities. Work with your partner to create a tangible goal that will keep your finances in the green and eventually allow your partner to stay home.

Sometimes both parents want to quit their jobs to stay home and care for the child. Unless you and your partner are independently wealthy, this won't be an option. As unfortunate as it is, the decision will probably come down to money. If you can only afford for one person to stay home, the logical choice is for the person with the larger salary to continue working. It's possible, however, that the person who makes more money is working long hours and traveling frequently. Sometimes the decision is better made from a work/life balance standpoint rather than salary. In this case, lifestyle changes have to make up for the loss of salary, but it can be done.

Some companies are adapting to the push for flexibility by allowing new parents the opportunity to spend some or all of their work hours at home. This arrangement can ease your partner's pain if she really wants to stay at home with baby but you can't afford to lose her income. However, working at home doesn't eliminate the need for childcare; you still need someone in the home to help while your partner gets work done, unless your partner is willing to work nights and weekends while you take over childcare duties. Even then, having baby sitters at the ready is a must for busy times, meetings, and phone conferences.

If you and your partner can both work from home, you may be able to stagger your work hours so that you take turns caring for the baby. These kinds of alternate work arrangements can vary widely; your company may have guidelines in place for such arrangements, or you may have to renegotiate your own plan. Ask your boss or human resources manager about this option if you're interested.

Helping mom adjust if she doesn't go back to work

The adjustment to being a stay-at-home mom can be just as challenging as heading back to work, only in different ways. As wonderful as it is to have the opportunity to raise your own child during the day, it can be an isolating experience. Some women will find themselves a bit stir-crazy from all of the indoor time and begin to crave adult interaction.

Here are some ways to help your partner transition to staying at home:

- ✔ **Repeat after us: Raising a child is a job.** Sure, staying at home may seem at times like a dream gig — access to the TV all day, no more commuting — but resist the thought that she's got it made. As you know full well by now, taking care of a baby is exhausting. Babies require full-time attention and are the most demanding bosses on earth.

- ✔ **Remember that her office is your home.** If your partner suddenly has higher standards for the cleanliness and tidiness of your home, help her keep it that way. She's now in the house all day, every day, and as strange as it may sound, you need to treat your home as her office, too.

- ✔ **Encourage hobbies.** Mental boredom is inevitable, no matter how much you love your child. Stacking blocks, reading books, and taking long walks can be fun, but urge your partner to take up a hobby that's just for her that works her mind and gives her something to focus on other than baby.

- ✔ **Give her personal time.** When you get home from work, you'll both need some time to decompress from a long day. Make sure to give her as much time off from baby duty as she needs. Plan relaxing surprises for her, such as a massage, every once in a while to make sure her emotional needs are being met. Work together to create an evening schedule that allows both parents ample baby-free time. Alternate being responsible for bath time, reading, the bedtime routine, and so on, to give both of you free time to do relaxing things. Just because you're away from baby all day doesn't mean that you should be the sole caregiver once you get home.

- ✔ **Ask her about her day.** Just because she's not in meetings and dealing with bosses doesn't mean she won't need to talk about the challenges and events of the day. Be sure to ask how she's doing — it's easy to do, but easy to forget.

✔ **Don't think of her as your maid/errand girl.** Just because she's home all day doesn't mean picking up your dry cleaning, making dinner, grocery shopping, and vacuuming are all her responsibilities. She has more time to do things around the house, but don't give her a list of things to do for you. Being a stay-at-home mom doesn't mean you're her boss. Thank her profusely for everything she does do, which benefits the both of you every day.

Some days you hate your job, and the same rings true for the stay-at-home parent. Imagine how you'd feel if you never got a day off from your job. A stay-at-home parent works every day, nights and weekends, too, so if your partner reaches the boiling point, don't hesitate to offer her a day off. Either take a vacation day to stay home with your child or encourage her to find alternate childcare for the day.

You may be surprised how much stress will be removed from your life when your partner transitions to full-time childcare and can take care of some of the chores and tasks that eat up your precious weekend, but don't have unrealistic expectations. Taking care of a baby is a full-time job as it is. To help both of you adjust to her stay-at-home schedule, sit down together and work out what her new role will look like so that you expect the same things. Create a "job description" that will benefit the entire family and help avoid frustration down the road, and be open to modifying it if she discovers that, say, doing all the laundry and cooking in addition to her childcare duties is exhausting her.

Becoming a stay-at-home dad

By no means is the stay-at-home dad a norm in our society. As of 2008 there were roughly 140,000 stay-at-home dads in the United States, a number that has grown slowly every year in the past decade. If you decide to stay at home, remember that the rules outlined for the stay-at-home mom are no different than the rules for you.

Following are some special considerations for the stay-at-home dad:

✔ **Fight for your right to "daddy."** If you've never experienced sexism in your lifetime, get ready for an onslaught. As a stay-at-home dad, at every turn you will be confronted by people who are surprised at your choice, concerned that you don't know what you're doing, and judgmental of your decision to "throw away" your career. Strangers, especially women, will fawn over you and even say that it's so nice of you to "baby-sit" for mom. Be confident in your decision and let the world know that you're excited about your new career and that men are capable of more than changing a diaper. Taking care of a baby is a lot of hard work, but it's not rocket science — you can do it!

✔ **Make friends with other parents.** Be it moms at the park or daddy playgroups, reach out to other stay-at-home parents in your neighborhood even before the baby comes. You will need friends to lean on for advice and last-minute baby-sitting, and the more you help out your new-parent friends and neighbors, the more options for help you'll have when you need it.

✔ **Utilize your unique skills.** Babies are mesmerized by everything, so use your stay-at-home time as an opportunity to play guitar, further your baking skills, or even start an out-of-the-home business. Having a daytime activity will provide you a much-needed creative outlet, and down the road, your kid will learn to appreciate (and mimic) your skills.

✔ **Turn off the TV.** It's tempting to keep ESPN on in the background all day, but too much TV isn't good for babies and children. Limit your TV time to two hours or less a day while baby is awake. Naptime is all yours.

Exploring the Expected (And Unexpected) Costs of Baby

One of the first things you'll hear from other parents is how expensive it is to have and raise a child in today's high-cost world. According to the U.S. Department of Agriculture, you can expect raising your child to the age of 18 to cost between $125,000 and $250,000, and possibly more.

Some costs of having a child are fixed and can't be avoided. Babies need food, clothes, diapers, wipes, and a safe, warm place to sleep. Babies don't need an entire closet jam-packed with enough designer-label clothing to make Suri Cruise weep with envy. You and your partner need to control the urge to shower your baby with every possible toy or accessory.

The following sections help guide you in spending your money wisely on only the things baby truly must have.

Deciding what baby really needs

Experts estimate that baby's first year of life, including daycare, diapers, clothing, and medical expenses just to name a few, will cost you about $11,000 — and far more if you live in a city where childcare costs alone can exceed $11,000 annually. You'll find quickly that the choices you make with your cash have to count. Some costs arrive early: The average hospital delivery costs between $7,000 and $11,000, and even with a great insurance plan you will still be getting hit with a portion of the bill.

Contact your insurance company in advance of baby's birth to verify what is covered and up to what cost. This information gives you a rough idea of how much of the medical bills will be your responsibility and may even help you make some decisions based on what you want versus what is covered.

After you bring baby home, his needs are rather modest, but the costs will add up very quickly if you don't stick to the basics. Before you run out and buy the baby bouncy chair, swing, play mat, and so on, spend some time getting to know what your baby likes so you won't be stuck with a lot of unused toys that cost you a lot of dough.

Most towns have a vibrant baby resale shop or, if not, a hopping garage sale culture. One thing you'll learn quickly is that the life span of baby goods long outlasts the amount of time your child will actually use it, and there is nothing wrong with buying used items instead of new. Just make sure that what you buy is clean, in good condition, and meets current safety standards. Buying secondhand is a great way to get inexpensive clothing, toys, and strollers, especially since your baby will grow out of all of them before you know it.

Network with the other parents you know, especially those with older babies or toddlers born in the same season as your baby. Many parents will happily pass along or sell you the things they no longer use, which frees up space in their home and cuts down on the cost for you.

Whenever possible, before you buy anything, give your child the chance to try it out. Pull down the floor sample or take it out of the box to make sure your child is engaged with what you're about to buy. You may think all bouncy chairs are the same, but your baby inevitably will like one more than another. To make sure you get your money's worth, buy what your baby shows interest in.

Bracing yourself for the costs of must-have baby supplies

Babies don't need a lot of stuff, but what they do need tends to be a bit on the expensive side. If your partner isn't breastfeeding, you'll have to spend a great deal of money on formula, which is quite expensive. Parents opting to use only organic, chemical-free goods for their baby will find the costs increase as well.

Every choice you make will change the weekly amount you spend, but here is a basic look at what to expect:

- **Diapers and wipes:** If you develop an allegiance to a national brand of disposable diapers, you're going to spend $12 to $15 every week. Many big-box stores offer their own brands, which can cut the cost in half. Baby wipes present the same conundrum, with the name-brand options costing $10 to $15 for a month's supply.

  For both diapers and wipes, the cost-per-unit goes down when you buy a larger-sized box. You're going to be using wipes for the foreseeable future, but baby will outgrow diapers, so make sure not to buy a box that may go to waste. Also, buy only what you have room to store — it's worth a little extra to not have a house overfilled with diapers and wipes.

  Upfront costs are higher for cloth diapers than dispos-able, but you will save money in the long run. Expect to pay about $200 for the diapers, sized for up to age 6 months, and another $200 for diapers sized up to age 2. Cloth diapers increase your energy and water use as well as the amount of baby-safe laundry detergent you must buy. Total cost for babies' first two years in cloth diapers will be about $500. Bonus: you can use the same cloth diapers for any subse-quent children you have, which makes the cost extremely low. Cloth diaper services are also available, which provide fresh, clean diapers in exchange for your dirty ones. It cuts out the hassle of cleaning but does increase the cost.

- **Feeding supplies:** Whether your partner breast-feeds or uses formula, you'll have costs to meet.

  - **Breast-feeding supplies:** Breast milk may be free, but you still need supplies, especially if mom is going back to work. Aside from a decent breast pump (a one-time cost of $150 to $400), you need freezer storage bags ($8 to $12 for a two-week supply), as well as nursing pads for a while ($8 to $12 for a two- or three-week supply).

  - **Formula:** Expect to spend between $150 and $200 per month on formula, depending on the brand and formula you choose to purchase. Specialty formulas, including those for sensitive systems and organic brands, cost even more. Also, if you use bottles with liners, expect to spend another $15 to $20 per month.

- **Insurance and medical expenses:** Adding baby to your insur-ance plan increases the monthly amount withdrawn from your paycheck. The change in policy must be completed within 30 days of baby's birth and generally increases the amount by

$50 to $100 per month, depending on the quality and cost of your insurance plan. Account for one doctor visit per month in the first six months to be on the safe side, with the only cost being the amount of your copay.

✔ **Clothing and laundry:** Baby-safe laundry detergent costs more than the stuff you buy for your own clothes, and you will have to use it for the first 18 to 24 months of baby's life. Expect to pay between $8 and $15 for a month's supply. And, seeing as babies grow at a rapid pace, you need to allot anywhere from $50 to $100 per month on clothing, which includes hats, shoes, sleepers, coats, socks, onesies, and outfits so cute they could make a puppy bark with jealousy.

Some parents opt to use dye-free detergents, such as Tide Free or All Free and Clear, which are intended for adult use. Using these detergents for the whole family will simplify the laundry process and save you money. Make sure to read the label of any product to make sure it is nontoxic. Also, for babies with sensitive skin, use 1/2 cup of vinegar in the wash cycle in lieu of fabric softener.

You can save money on clothing by checking out consignment shops and garage sales and asking for hand-me-downs from friends with older children. All babies outgrow clothes before they're worn out, so you can find a lot of perfectly nice used items at a fraction of the cost of new.

College may seem a long way away, but it's never too early to start saving for your kid's education. However, if you don't have a retirement fund or an emergency fund for your own future survival, start there. You have to take care of your future first, and that responsibility sets a good example for your child. And if you can't pay for that college education someday, well, that's what student loans are for!

Comparing childcare options and costs

Paying someone else to care for your child 40 to 50 hours each week will become your new number-one expense. In fact, depending on where you live, it very well may cost you more than your mortgage or rent. Taking care of a baby is big business, but it's also a huge responsibility, so it comes with an equally huge financial burden.

Like when shopping for cars, you have many options when choosing childcare. Depending on whether you're looking to buy a luxury car (an in-home nanny) or a two-door compact (your neighbor's in-home daycare) or something in between, the costs will vary depending on the services you are promised.

Regardless of which option you choose, create a contract (unless the provider has one of his own) to make sure you're getting what you expect and that you won't have unexpected costs when you pay the bill. Go over the following questions with your daycare provider and get the answers in writing:

- ✔ Are you licensed to provide childcare in this state?
- ✔ What training have you received in childcare and education? What about your staff?
- ✔ Are you insured in case of accident?
- ✔ Who is providing the food?
- ✔ How often and on what day are you expected to pay?
- ✔ Do you need my permission to take my child in a car?
- ✔ How much notice do you need to give in order to terminate the agreement?
- ✔ Do you frequently have visitors? Are they allowed to interact with the children?
- ✔ Will my child always be under your care, or will your spouse/ child/friend/family member be helping?
- ✔ Do I have to pay when my child is sick or we are on vacation?
- ✔ How do you discipline children?
- ✔ What do you charge for days I need to drop my child off early/ pick him up late?
- ✔ What security provisions are in place?
- ✔ Are you certified in both infant and child CPR?

Outlining your expectations in writing will reduce your fears and help prevent any unexpected surprises or litigation down the road.

If after you check out the costs of daycare you're reconsidering quitting your job (or having your partner quit her job) and staying at home, be sure to carefully weigh the points outlined earlier in "Deciding to be a stay-at-home parent." Staying at home is expensive in its own way and isn't a decision to be made lightly.

Private in-home daycare

A friend, neighbor, or local daycare provider who operates a facility out of the home likely will be your cheapest option, depending on the sophistication level of the facility. Expect to pay between

$150 and $300 per week depending on your location. Many providers who work in their own homes are also watching their own children, which can reduce the cost to you.

Be sure to visit this type of daycare on a regular weekday during business hours to see how things function during "high-volume times." Some states require certifications for any daycare providing care for a certain number of children, and you should research the regulations in your state and make sure the provider is compliant.

Daycare center

A daycare center, also sometimes called corporate daycare, is any facility that accommodates many children and employs multiple staff members to care for a wide age-range of children. Depending on the facility and the qualifications of the people it employs, this service can cost between $200 and $500 per week. For instance, if the daycare has child-development specialists on-staff and a play facility that pulls all the punches, costs will be higher than at a basic facility.

Make sure the child-to-adult ratio at the facility meets accepted guidelines. The U.S. Department of Health and Human Services recommends a 3:1 ratio for babies age 0 to 24 months; 4:1 for 25 to 30 months; 5:1 for 31 to 35 months; 7:1 for 3-year-olds; and 8:1 for 4- to 5-year-olds.

Your own in-home nanny

Paying someone to come into your home to provide full-time childcare for your child and your child alone is a custom and very expensive option. For many parents, the peace of mind involved in this setup is worth every penny, especially when you factor in the time, gas, and stress saved by not having to take your child to the sitter every day. Costs typically range from $400 to $800 per week, depending on your location, expectations of the care provider, the provider's experience level, and the number of hours the provider is expected to be in your home.

Managing Your Money

Regardless of your financial situation, the impact of a baby will be felt early and often. Aside from the frightening amount of supplies, toys, doctor visits, and clothing, the enormous cost of childcare will leave you with a lot less cash — and financial freedom — than you had in the past. Depending on where you live and the option you choose, you may be paying your childcare provider the same amount you'd pay for a car payment — every week!

So perhaps your days of three-dollar lattes are behind you. Maybe you'll be buying one less album online each month. Regardless of your vices and other financial obligations, you'll need to get your spending habits in tip-top shape to absorb the high cost of having children.

Prioritizing your needs

The difference between what you want and what you need is a gulf roughly the size of the Grand Canyon. The same can be said for what you want for your baby and what your baby actually needs in order to thrive. As a parent you have to get the needs of your entire family in check to secure a financially sound future for all.

Every family's situation and needs are different, but one rule is universal: Make a budget. Start by taking a realistic look at where your money goes. Call your credit card company and ask for an analysis of how you spent your money in the past year (some companies send you this statement automatically each year), and look at your bank statements from the same time period, If you struggle to make cuts, consider meeting with a financial planner. Figuring out how to spend, save, and survive is a big job, and you don't have to go it alone.

Factor in the monthly costs of housing, food, transportation, investments, insurance, and any medicines you take regularly. You also have to plan for the unexpected, and with a baby in the equation you'll have a lot of unexpected. Starting an emergency fund is easier said than done, but it's a must. When you have a kid, absorbing an unexpected job loss, income reduction, or family emergency can be debilitating. Try to slowly work your way up to having six months' expenses set aside just in case life throws you a curveball.

As unpleasant as thinking about tragedy is, now is the time to make sure you have sufficient life insurance coverage for you, your partner, and your baby. Work with a reputable insurance agent to make sure that your family will be provided for if the worst were to happen. Also, make sure that you have short- and long-term disability coverage through your employer. If not, consider buying your own policy. Missing even one paycheck can spell disaster for some families, so try to be overprepared for emergencies. See Chapter 15 for more on insurance and disability coverage.

Determining where to cut costs

Giving up things you love isn't easy, but it's a must now that you have someone to provide for. Consider cutting costs in the following areas:

✔ **Food:** Prepackaged and/or snack foods tend to be expensive. Items such as chips, ice cream, candy, beer, frozen dinners, and soda are not only bad for your body, but also bad for your budget. You may not be willing to give them up all together, but try to cut down on the number of purchases of these high-cost, low-nutrition foods. Also, consider making a big casserole or stew to eat for numerous meals, which will reduce both your time in the kitchen and your grocery bill.

✔ **Utilities/bills:** Take a long, hard look at your monthly expenses. Do you need both a cellphone and a home phone? Can you downgrade any of your plans to a lower-cost option that still suits your needs? If you live in a cold-weather climate, can you go on a monthly payment plan to evenly spread out the costs of heating your home throughout the year? Are you in good standing with your credit card company? If so, ask to reduce your interest rate. Call every insurance company you do business with and see if you can get a lower rate. Don't be afraid to ask all of the companies that you do regular business with for a financial break.

✔ **Entertainment:** Take a look at the last six months of expenses and try to cut or reduce the monthly cost of these nonessential items, which are the biggest expendable category for cost savings. Cable is not a utility, and if you're struggling to make ends meet, consider cutting your package down to basic or even getting rid of cable altogether, even just for a little while. If you have both cable and a mail-based movie subscription, do you truly need both? Baby will automatically limit the days you can go out to dinner, catch a movie, or get tickets to a football game, but monitor and limit these expenses, too, especially if you have to pay for a baby sitter when you go out.

✔ **Convenience purchases:** Sure, buying lunch is simpler than getting up early to make it in the morning. Same goes for coffee. If you find yourself a constant consumer of takeout food, taxis, dry cleaning, bottled water, and other nonessential costs that simply make your life easier, cut back. Even one less purchase per month can make a major impact on your bank account.

Turn to Chapter 15 to find out more about budgeting and cutting costs.

Chapter 15

Planning for Your New Family's Future

In This Chapter

▶ Organizing your finances and putting safety nets in place

▶ Saving for your child's education

▶ Buying life insurance for worst-case scenarios

▶ Choosing the right health insurance

▶ Creating a will and designating a guardian for your child

*D*uring this time of immense joy, you probably resist worrying about the ifs, ands, or buts that could bring all of that happiness to a screeching halt. You may also think it seems a bit premature to begin squirreling away cash for her education when your baby hasn't even mastered the art of sitting up. But, as the time-honored, cliché goes, they grow up so fast.

Planning for the future, whether for planned events or unexpected ones, is the least enjoyable part of being a parent because it reminds you just how fleeting life can be. And nobody wants to think about what would happen if they died, especially with a newborn just beginning to enhance life. However, now is the time to make sure your child will be taken care of, regardless of the circumstances.

Securing a Financially Sound Future

New parents are saddled with an enormous uptick in caretaking responsibilities. In fact, your role as caretaker now involves getting your financial life in order so that you can properly care for your child today, tomorrow, and even after you and your spouse die.

It's not the cheeriest item on the new-parent to-do list, but it's one of the top priorities.

In this section we share some financial tips that will help to ensure a bright (and green!) future for your entire family.

Prioritize your expenses

Singling out purchases that you can — and should — live without can be a real buzzkill. Giving up the little things in life can be a difficult adjustment, especially for new parents who are already sacrificing sleep and freedom. For most new first-time parents, the financial strain of having a child means looking at where you can cut down on your own expenses. If you fall into this category, this section helps you make some tough choices.

Your fixed costs are food, housing, electricity, heat, and transportation. The rest is a mix of choices made by you and your spouse about how to live your lives. There are no hard-and-fast rules about what to axe from your life, but depending on your particular needs and your income, the following areas are good places to cut back:

- ✔ **Entertainment:** This category includes movie tickets, concerts, cable, magazine subscriptions, music, books, DVDs, hobbies, sporting events, and so on. With baby occupying most of your free time, time constraints will help you cut way back on sporting events, movies, and concerts. And instead of spending money on some of the other items, get a free membership to your local library; most have extensive DVD and CD collections as well as books and magazines. Borrow movies from your friends, too, or host a movie night and share in the rental and food expenses.

- ✔ **Food:** Whether you eat out often, always dine in, or regularly grab coffee, you can make a change in your food spending. Look at your past expenses and find places to save. Even choosing to eat out one less time each month or spending $10 less per week at the grocery store will save you big over the long haul.

To replace the fun of eating out, host a dinner party or start a rotating dinner club with a group of friends. Assign each attendant a different course so you can drink and dine in style at a fraction of the cost.

- ✔ **Luxury:** New clothing, spa visits, hair care, skin-care products, and new jewelry are a few items that can be downgraded, reduced, or perhaps axed altogether.

✔ **Interest rates:** If you have high interest rates, you're essentially spending money on nothing — clearly a spending habit you won't mind changing! Refinancing your home can save you a bundle in the long run, and if you have good credit, try to negotiate down your interest rate with your credit card company. It's not always easy or possible, but it's always worth a call to find out if — and how — you can save.

Create a budget (and stick to it)

After you put your expenses under the microscope and find places to cut back, make a plan and stick to it. Knowing what you plan to spend each month allows you to explore savings options, such as setting up a college account for your baby. Saving money can be a fun game. The more you save, the more thrilling it becomes to push yourself further and watch your personal worth rise.

 If you find yourselves struggling to spend only what you have designated for each item in your monthly budget, use cash. If you take $100 to the grocery store, you have exactly that much to spend. Calculating what you can buy takes more time, but before long you'll be able to eyeball what you can and can't afford.

To make a budget, start by breaking down your finances into the following categories, placing a monthly spending allotment next to each:

✔ Mortgage/rent

✔ Home/rental insurance

✔ Electricity

✔ Gas

✔ Cable

✔ Water, sewage, trash

✔ Phone

✔ Internet

✔ Home maintenance

✔ Car payment, insurance, and gas

✔ Childcare

✔ Groceries

✔ Entertainment

Parenting on the cheap

People tell you that babies are expensive, and, for the most part, they're right. All of the things that babies need to survive add up quickly, especially over time, which is why buying only what you need is of the utmost importance.

Baby stuff is cuter and more expensive than ever before, and more and more parents are buying high-end goods. If you don't have the money for the $1,000 stroller that all of the other parents in your neighborhood seem to have, don't buy it. Your baby doesn't need — and won't remember having — an expensive crib, stroller, or bassinet, and he certainly doesn't need nicer clothes than you wear.

Create a monthly budget for your baby expenses. Buy the essentials first and use any leftover money to buy secondary items, such as new toys. Babies don't need a lot to play with; in fact, your tot will probably like the packaging the toy came in better than the toy itself.

Resale shops aren't just for hipsters and low-income families. Buying lightly used goods will save you a fortune, and, considering that babies grow in and out of clothes, toys, and furniture very quickly, you're likely to find exactly what you want at a fraction of the cost. You can also utilize online sites such as Craigslist, eBay, and Freecycle to get what you need for cheap or even free!

Many excellent software programs, books, and Web sites can help you make and maintain a monthly budget. QuickBooks is one of the most popular computer programs for managing your personal finances and even paying your taxes, and www.mint.com offers a popular (and free!) online service. For the Dummy-phile, check out *Personal Finance For Dummies,* 6th Edition, or *Managing Your Money All-in-One For Dummies* (both published by Wiley) for everything you need to know to get your finances in order.

Pay down your debt

Not all debt is equally bad. Some debt, such as student loans and real estate mortgages, tends to have low interest rates and build future value. Bad debt is anything with a high interest rate; mainly credit cards, and especially credit cards used to purchase unnecessary or disposable goods and subsequently not paid off every month.

Pay off your high-interest debt first, which is most likely your credit card bills, and do so as aggressively as your finances allow. Don't use your cards until all of your debt is paid down and after that, only use your card for emergencies and essential expenses, such as groceries. Using it for limited, essential items (that you've budgeted for) will ensure that you can pay off the balance every month. Pay for nonessential items with cash, or you'll end up paying even more for them if you don't pay off your balance each month.

After your credit cards are paid off, start paying off your debt with the next highest interest rate, likely a car loan. Also, paying one additional mortgage payment every year can take years off of the length of your loan. Remember, this isn't about getting rid of debt altogether. Everyone has debt, and it helps build your credit score. The goal is to get rid of unnecessary and high-interest debt.

Create an emergency fund

An emergency fund can be a lifesaver for a number of reasons. Job loss happens when you least expect it. Family members get sick and require your time and attention. Houses and cars break down all too often. Whatever life throws at you, it's going to cost you some dough. The rule of thumb changes all the time, but most experts advise saving enough money to cover anywhere from 6 to 12 months of expenses.

If you managed to read that and not faint, take heart — most people don't have that much money tucked away, and a lot of folks never will. However, you have to start somewhere, and the less you spend, the more you can save. And now that you have a baby to care for, being able to handle the unexpected expenses is more important than ever.

Make a plan that works for you and your family. If it's easier to start a savings account and slowly move over money each month after bills are paid, go for it. For some, having a set amount or percentage of salary automatically moved into an account each month is easiest. To begin saving, try putting 5 percent of your paycheck into a separate savings account. If after a few months you find you still have extra money in your primary checking account, start saving more.

Buy disability insurance

Most companies provide employees the option to buy short- and long-term disability coverage, which generally pay 60 percent of your salary in the event that you are injured and unable to work. If you haven't signed up for that coverage, do so immediately. You are far more likely to get injured than die, and the loss of a salary can sink your family into financial ruin in no time. Short- and long-term disability can provide a source of income for around two to five years if you're unable to work.

If you're self-employed or your company doesn't offer coverage, contact a local life-insurance representative or financial advisor to help determine the right amount of coverage for you. It's essential to have a policy that can cover your family's expenses if you're out of commission.

Contribute to a retirement account

Taking care of yourself first means ensuring that your kids won't have to in the future. It is vital that new parents begin saving for their own retirement. As your kids grow, so will your financial needs, which means you need to start saving when you're young in order to have enough to live the way you want to when you retire.

If your work has a 401(k) or a similar program, make sure you contribute the maximum amount allowed each year, especially if your company matches that amount. Consider opening a Roth IRA account, which allows you to contribute a certain amount of your earnings to the account each year while making tax-free withdrawals when necessary.

For all of the information you need to establish your retirement security, check out *Retirement For Dummies* (Wiley).

Work with a financial advisor

If numbers make your head spin or if you're not sure you that you have the right kind or enough of the savings, insurance, and retirement accounts you need for your lifestyle, you may benefit from working with a financial advisor. Consultations are free, and the advisors work on commission from sales (of life insurance, investments, and so on), so it won't cost you anything except your time.

If your advisor is unnecessarily pressuring you into buying her company's wares, beware. Her main role is to help you prosper financially, and if you are not interested in or in the position to buy something she's pushing, seek counsel from someone else. Yes, she has a job to do, but don't get suckered into something you don't want. Always take a day or two to think about a financial advisor's advice before committing to anything and, when possible, seek a second opinion.

Mind your credit score

If the only scores you keep track of involve the doings of professional athletes, you're probably long overdue for a check of your credit scores. Your credit scores change all the time, so periodically check to make sure you're on track and your credit history has no mistakes. Your credit score affects the interest rates of every line of credit you have, and a mistake may be costing you on your mortgage, car payment, credit cards, and student loans.

Credit scores range from 350 to 850. A very low credit score is any number below 600. An average credit score is between about 650 and 700. An excellent credit score is anything above 700. Your credit score is reported by three different agencies that provide three different scores. Checking all three is important so that you can clear up any mistakes. You can request your free credit report once a year from each of the following:

- ✔ Equifax: www.equifax.com
- ✔ Experian: www.experian.com
- ✔ TransUnion: www.transunion.com

Saving Money for Your Child's Education

Every parent wants his child to get the best college education money can buy. Not all parents, however, can afford that education, nor do they want their children to accrue mass amounts of student loan debt.

If you have the luxury of being able to save some money for your child's education, you have a number of options. Following are a few common savings options (check out *529 & Other College Savings Plans For Dummies* [Wiley] for more specifics):

- ✔ Parents can invest money in a Coverdell Education Savings Account (CESA), which allows you to save $2,000 a year tax-free. However, CESA funds are considered student assets and can reduce the amount of student loans available to your child.

- ✔ Every state offers at least one 529 plan, a state-sponsored college savings plan that allows you to choose the aggressiveness and amount of money you want to invest. It grows tax-free and it only requires you to fill out an easy form, usually available on your state's Web site. After you file the paperwork, you begin depositing money according to the plan you chose. The investments are even managed by a professional. Plus, you can begin saving before your child is born.

✔ You can save in a personal investment account — that is, a savings, stock, bond, or mutual fund account. These accounts give you more control to add or remove money, and you earn capital gains, interest, or dividends. You pay taxes on the income each year you earn it, but these accounts give you more freedom to use the savings when and how you see fit. Depending on what level of access you want your child to have to the money, set it up to as a trust that can be accessed with conditions, or simply pay the tuition bills yourself.

If you don't want a college fund to go to a child if he decides not to attend college, or you don't want him to coast through high school knowing he doesn't need scholarships, set up a personal investment account in your own name. If your child doesn't go to college, you'll be able to dispense the money at your discretion or keep it for yourselves. If he does go to college, you can reward your child for his hard work when the time arrives.

For parents looking to save for college, make sure first that you have an emergency fund in place and your own future is secure with retirement savings. Don't prioritize your kids' education above these other crucial savings. After all, you don't want your money tied up in a college savings account if your house burns down, and although there's no such thing as a retirement loan, kids for generations have been taking out student loans to pay for college.

Getting the Lowdown on Life Insurance

Purchasing life insurance policies in the event that you or your child dies couldn't be more outside the spirit of happiness that comes along with welcoming of a newborn. However, tragedy can strike in many ways and at any time, and although it's not pleasant to think about, life insurance is a must.

Making sure you and your partner have adequate life insurance

Ensuring your child is well cared for in the event of an emergency means confronting your own mortality as well. Buying life insurance for both you and your partner provides a security policy that will allow your family to continue living the life you're all accustomed to without financial ruin in the event one or both of you were to die. Now that you're a parent, it's your responsibility to make sure that bills can be paid and food can be put on the table — even in the event of your death.

Policy needs vary based on your financial circumstances, but the amount you buy should be enough to cover not just funeral costs, but a few years of your current income and expenses, as well as funds to pay off any bad debt you currently have. This safety net will keep your family financially sound while they deal with their grief.

Considering a policy for your baby

Buying life insurance for your baby is a controversial and unsavory topic. Many financial experts say it's a waste of money because a life insurance policy is necessary only when the death of the individual will cause financial stress on a family. For many lower- and middle-income families, however, a policy that would cover the cost of the funeral is well worth the monthly payment.

Whole-life coverage versus term

Not all life insurance policies are the same. Some policies are "rentals," covering a child through a certain age and then offering no more benefit. If you elect to go the "buying" route for a policy, it will start your child on the right track to financial security for retirement. You can choose between two basic types of policies that determine the price, coverage level, and longevity of the policy:

- ✔ **Whole-life coverage:** As the name implies, a whole-life policy stays with your child for his or her entire life. This permanent insurance has a fixed premium that never increases as your child ages and offers the policy owner a guaranteed cash value against which the owner can borrow money in case of emergency.

  The coverage is generally between $25,000 to $150,000. Buying whole-life coverage for your baby usually doesn't require a medical checkup. One of the more popular plans is available through Gerber, but most life insurance providers offer competitive plans, too. It is important to speak with a professional before purchasing. You will not be able to cash out the whole-life policy at any time for full value, and depending on your financial situation, saving money in an interest-yielding account may be a better idea. That way, you can always access the money you have invested.

✔ **Term coverage:** Term insurance is sometimes referred to as a "rental policy" because the named person on the policy will never own it like one does with whole-life coverage. Think of it as magazine subscription with huge financial benefits: As long as you have a subscription, you're covered. But when the subscription runs out — the policy expires — you stop getting coverage.

The money you invest is simply going toward "what if" protection. The cost is generally a fraction of the price of whole-life coverage, which is why it's such an attractive option for some parents. Plans generally come in 10- to 30-year terms, with coverage ranging from $25,000 to $150,000. However, premiums are not fixed and do increase as your baby ages.

How much coverage is enough?

Determining how much coverage you should buy depends on your budget. Buy only what you can afford. The more payout benefit you purchase, the more you pay each month. If you're purchasing term insurance, you don't need to buy a policy that will exceed the costs of a funeral and, perhaps, any wage losses due to unpaid leave during your grieving period.

Buy only what you can afford to pay every month. Talk with a financial planner to determine if a whole-life policy is actually the best investment for your child or if another form of savings would yield bigger rewards for him down the road — and still provide you a safety net in case of death.

Health Insurance Options for Newborns

Navigating the health insurance mélange has always been a bit of a headache. HMO, PPO, what does it all mean? For the most part, your insurance won't be any different after you have a baby. The only thing that definitely changes is the cost. For those parents without insurance — or those who can't afford it — the process is a bit more complex.

Adding baby to an existing work-paid plan

Don't worry if baby doesn't arrive during your company's insurance open season. Whenever a major life event occurs, such as the birth of a baby, you're allowed to change your insurance coverage.

Check with your HR department to get the proper paperwork for adding baby.

You won't actually add baby until after he is born. Your insurance company will need his name, sex, and birth date in order to issue a policy. However, baby's medical expenses will be covered according to your current plan's postnatal coverage. Policies are retroactive back to birth, but won't continue to cover baby's expenses forever. Most plans require you to add baby within the first month of life or your child will not be covered under your plan.

The most important thing to consider when adding a baby to your insurance is the cost of plans. If you purchased your company's top-notch insurance plan, the cost may skyrocket out of your price range with the addition of a child. Don't just add baby to your existing plan without first looking at the price of all of the family plans your company offers. A different plan may save you hundreds of dollars every month.

Look for the plan that offers the highest level of coverage that you can afford. Also be sure to choose a plan with a reasonable copayment, because your child will be going to the doctor frequently.

Be sure to call your insurance company to add your child to your plan as soon as possible. Some companies give you as little as 30 days to make the change following the birth of a baby, and because you'll be going to the doctor multiple times in those early weeks, you want to get the changes made ASAP so you won't be on the hook for some huge expenses. When you add a child to a plan, the insurance company usually has a time limit for submitting proof of birth, such as a copy of the birth certificate, to make it official. Check with your insurance company for the deadlines and paperwork specific to your plan.

Buying coverage just for baby

Statistics show that more than 46 million Americans live without health insurance. That number includes 9 million children. If you are living without health insurance and are about to have a baby, you're facing the high costs of labor and delivery, but the money hemorrhage won't stop after baby arrives. Your child must have wellness checks and vaccination appointments frequently, which means you'll be shelling out a large portion of your hard-earned cash to your child's pediatrician.

Consider buying a health insurance policy for your child. Even if you can't afford to buy them for you and your partner and have to pay for labor and delivery out of pocket, coverage for your baby is essential. Policies generally start around $100 per month, and, ultimately, you'll spend much less than if you pay 100 percent of the bills yourself.

Obtaining free and low-cost care for uninsured kids

If you do not have a work-sponsored health insurance program and can't afford to buy a policy for your child, but earn too much to qualify for Medicaid, explore the free or low-cost coverage options provided by both the federal and state governments. Your child may qualify for coverage if you meet certain low-income standards. Visit insurekidsnow.gov to see if your family qualifies for federal coverage and to find a provider in your state.

If you don't meet the low-income guidelines, many state-sponsored programs offer coverage. For the contact in your state, visit the National Association of Insurance Commissioner's Web site: www.naic.org/state_web_map.htm.

Taking Care of Legal Matters

Arranging legal matters is an important step in ensuring your child's well-being in the case of your early death. As unpleasant as the topic may be, you need to sit down with your partner as soon as possible and make decisions about what will happen to your assets and who will take care of your child if you die, and what should happen if either of you is incapacitated. Then make those decisions legally binding by creating a formal will and establishing power of attorney. These tasks aren't fun, but the peace of mind you'll have is worth it.

Although most of the forms you need to make these decisions and declarations are available for free online, the only way to make sure that your forms are valid and written in accordance to state and federal laws is to have them reviewed by a lawyer. It's an added expense, but it's worth the money to know your family will be taken care of in the event you are no longer around.

Creating a will

Drawing up a will doesn't have to be as macabre as reading a Stephen King novel. As a soon-to-be or new parent, having a will can bring you peace of mind by leaving no question about what will happen to your possessions (and children!) when you die. A will includes three provisions:

> ✔ **Who will inherit your bank accounts, real estate, vehicles, and personal property when you die.** Most dads have simple wills that leave everything to their partners and, in the event they both die, to their children.
>
> ✔ **Who will be your children's guardian in case you and your partner are incapacitated or die.** This is your chance to make sure your child will be cared for by the person of your choice and not put into foster care.
>
> ✔ **Who will manage any property and money you leave to your child until she reaches a designated age.** Most people name a single executor of their will who is charged with carrying out their wishes. However, some people are more comfortable having the person responsible for carrying out the will's commands to be separate from the person who controls the money.

A will doesn't trump the beneficiaries listed on life insurance policies. Make sure to contact your life insurance company to make the desired changes to those policies, such as adding your new child as a beneficiary.

Making your will

You don't have to go the lawyer route to make a will. Several do-it-yourself computer programs and books (such as *Wills and Trusts Kit For Dummies* [Wiley]) provide simple step-by-step instructions for arranging what happens after you die.

Filling in the blanks and hitting print doesn't automatically offer you the protection you need. Any will not made with a lawyer still has to be notarized in order to be valid in the eyes of the law. Leave a copy of your will with your executor as well as in a safe-deposit box.

Make a separate will for each parent. A joint will is binding after the death of even one person, and that makes it difficult for the surviving parent to make changes that may better suit his changed circumstances. Separate wills are especially important when kids are involved, because finances change and you want your partner to have access to funds in order to care for your kids. Name your spouse or partner as the sole beneficiary to ensure that she has 100 percent control of your assets, and have concrete, detailed discussions about how you want the dispersing of money and property, as well as your funeral and burial, handled in the event of your untimely demise.

Appointing guardians

If you have children, guardianship should be addressed when you create a will. If you work with a lawyer, she will be able to help you fill out all the necessary paperwork. However, if you use an online form or a software program, be sure that it includes the appropriate form for your state.

If you are unsure of the legal requirements, consult your state's courts Web site to find the necessary forms. Most forms require a signature from both parents and the appointed guardian as well as notarization.

A will allows you to designate temporary guardianship in the case that your named guardian lives a few states away or can't come for your child immediately until the new guardian arrives. This temporary situation will keep your child out of the foster care program and in the loving home of your choice.

Guardianship is a huge responsibility for the person you ask. When approaching him, keep in mind that you may not get an immediate yes. In fact, if the person you ask needs some time to think it over, it's a good sign that he understands the responsibility and won't make rash decisions he may later regret. This person will not only be in charge of your child but will also have to cover any of the financial gaps not covered by the money you set aside to be used for your child's upbringing.

If the person you ask declines, ask for more information about why he refused. Perhaps you have information that can assuage any fears he may have about the job. However, if the person you ask (even after further discussion) isn't up for the job, find someone else. Yes, it will be disappointing, but respect that person's honesty and forthrightness in admitting he is the wrong person for the job. And when it comes down to it, finding the right person is most important.

Appointing an executor

The person you appoint as executor is in charge of *executing* your will, or making sure that taxes and debts are paid and your estate is distributed according to your will. Avoid appointing someone as an executor who is also a beneficiary of your will. You can name coexecutors if you want one person to manage your money and the other to manage, say, your property. It can be good to utilize different people's skills and gives you backup if one person drops the ball.

You designate an executor using the same online or software program you use to make a will, or when creating a will with your lawyer. Make sure that the person you designate is willing and able to perform the role. Most forms that designate an executor for your will require you to provide one or two contingency executors in case the first named executor cannot perform the job. Some states only recognize executors who live in the same state as the deceased. Check your states rules before you designate.

Questions to ask yourself when choosing a legal guardian

When deciding who would make the best guardian for your child in case of your death, consider the following questions:

✔ Does the person love my child?

✔ Is the person good with children in general?

✔ How important is it that my child's guardian be family?

✔ Will my child be uprooted from his/her home to move in with the guardian?

✔ Does the person have the same parenting philosophies I have?

✔ Is the person going to raise the child with the same religious beliefs?

✔ Does the person have any medical conditions that would prevent him from being a long-term, able-bodied guardian?

✔ Will your child cause too big of a personal, professional, or financial strain for the person?

✔ Does the person have a stable home life and career?

✔ Will this person guarantee your child has access to family?

✔ Does this person value the same things I do (education, music, community, and so on)?

When there's no will

State laws vary, but if you don't have a will, less than half of your property and money will go to your spouse and the rest will be divided among your children. If your children aren't 18, all money and property will be managed by a state-appointed trustee until that time arrives, which means your partner won't have access to your money in order to raise your children.

In the event that both parents die without a will, the state will designate a guardian for the children, which likely will be the most closely related family member willing to accept the job. While guardianship is arranged, your child will enter the state's foster care program.

Establishing power of attorney

Granting power of attorney to someone gives that person the power to make decisions — both legal and medical — in the event that you're incapacitated. The person you name will be able to make important decisions about life support and control of your bank accounts.

Knowing your options

You can designate four main types power of attorney. Not everyone appoints a person for each, and appointing the same person to serve in multiple roles is common:

- **Limited power of attorney:** The person you designate will only be allowed to act on your behalf for a specified amount of time. This, most likely, will not be helpful when creating a will that covers the care and guardianship of your children.

- **General power of attorney:** The American Bar Association refers to this person as your *agent,* and she has the power to act on your behalf in every capacity that you did prior to your incapacitation. This person literally becomes you in the legal sense until you are capable again of handling your own affairs.

- **Durable power of attorney:** Granting someone this power means his authority ceases to be recognized by the law after you pass away, except in the areas you give him control.

- **Healthcare power of attorney:** This person is empowered to make important medical decisions but has no control over your finances.

Appointing a power of attorney

Generally included as part of the will-making process, appointing power of attorney takes only a simple form that usually must be signed by you and the named power of attorney and then notarized.

Experts suggest choosing someone you trust but who isn't a close friend or family member. After all, even if you've made it clear that you don't want to be on life support for an extended period of time, your mother may have difficulty pulling the plug. Select a person who you can trust to follow through with your wishes.

The power of attorney should follow what you outline in your will, so go over your will with that person to make sure he is comfortable following your orders. If not, find someone else, or complications may arise that will cause added stress for everyone involved. What's most important is finding a person you can trust who will be informed about your wishes and make sure they're followed.

Part V
The Part of Tens

The 5th Wave   By Rich Tennant

"I'm looking for a rattle that both informs and entertains."

In this part...

The Part of Tens provides practical tips on everything from reading your partner's mind to being a super dad. We also look at the wonderful world of stay-at-home fatherhood, should you be considering that increasingly common route.

Chapter 16

Ten Things She Won't Ask for but Will Expect

In This Chapter

▶ Showing your excitement about being a father

▶ Helping your partner with emotional and physical support

*D*uring the course of your partner's pregnancy — and many months thereafter — she will expect myriad tasks, words of comfort, and loving gestures from you without her having to ask for what she wants. Sadly, you weren't born with advanced psychic aptitude, and therefore you'll have to infer a few *musts* to keep peace around the house.

Follow these ten simple tips to make sure your partner gets everything she needs.

Keep It Complimentary

Face it — you'll never know what it's like to give up your body so that someone else can grow inside of you. That said, it probably isn't too hard to remember the last time you got a new haircut or lost ten pounds and then waited around for someone to tell you how nice you looked.

Going fishing for compliments is never a fun or fruitful excursion, so try to spare your partner from going to that length. When her hormones and ever-increasing waistline are waging a full-fledged attack on her insecurities, remind her early and often exactly how beautiful she looks. And the best part is, you won't have to lie. It may be hard to imagine finding your partner gorgeous when she's carrying around 30 to 40 extra pounds, but pregnant women glow, and knowing that she's having your baby can be extremely attractive.

When she asks you how she looks or if she has gotten fat (and she will ask you!), flatter her to no end, deny it vehemently, and thank her for her sacrifices.

Start a Baby Book

Baby books, with their endless pages of blank space calling out for someone to fill in the missing data, can be a daunting undertaking, especially when chronicling the journey is left solely to the mom-to-be/new mommy. Most women won't admit it, but during pregnancy they're looking for constant signs that you're just as committed to raising a child together as she is. Filling out a baby book together can be the perfect way to put into words just how ready you are for baby.

A great way to exhibit your commitment and excitement to the baby she's carrying is to buy the best baby book on the market that suits your styles. If you and the mom-to-be are the long-form journaling types, pick one that offers lots of space to write about how you're feeling during each trimester and your thoughts about becoming a parent. If you fall into the less-is-more crowd, choose a book that adheres to a mostly fill-in-the-blank format. Many themed books are available, running the gamut from religious to hipster chic, so choose one that represents both parents.

The baby book is a time-honored time capsule that chronicles the pregnancy and early days of your baby's life, and like any good time capsule it should be something fun to put together as a couple that captures the time and place. Someday that book will mean the world to your child, so make sure to buy one that you'll realistically finish.

Disguise Fitness as Fun

Exercise is of the utmost importance to both baby and mommy, but try telling your partner to get up off of the sofa and go for walk without having something hard thrown at your head. Getting a loved one involved in fitness is never easy to do without hurt feelings, so instead of telling her that she needs to exercise, help her exercise without making it personal.

Turn fitness into a social activity: Plan walks with friends and family members, or schedule errands together that require you to get up and move around. Plan a "treasure hunt" date to local baby stores to scope out the latest gear, or even a hunt with a romantic bent. Even a trip to the mall can be good exercise so long as you steer clear of the food court.

If your partner has a particular interest in a certain type of exercise, give her a free pass as a gift. Be it yoga, spinning, or running, most fitness clubs or personal trainers offer prenatal versions of their classes. Many classes welcome partners, too, and by making it a couples' affair it won't send the message that you think she's fat.

Curb Your Advice

Never has there been a better time to let go of your desire to be right at all costs than now, even if you really *do* know best. Let your partner complain about her job, her body, the mere fact that she's pregnant, or whatever, and don't take her complaints, gripes, or outbursts personally. Now, that doesn't give her free reign to be a raving lunatic just because she's pregnant, but don't try to solve her problems with your sage wisdom unless she specifically asks for it. Listen to her and validate what she's feeling, but don't tell her how to fix it.

Also, avoid telling her what to eat, when to exercise, that she needs to sleep more, and so on. Instead, lead by example. If you think she should eat more fruits and vegetables, buy more fruits and vegetables. Or better yet, make meals packed with pregnancy power foods. If you think she needs to rest more, ask her to sit down and do a crossword with you. Telling her what to do will not go over well, so don't waste your breath.

Attend Prenatal Appointments

Repeat after me: Prenatal appointments aren't just for the mothers. Yes, she is carrying the baby, but that baby didn't get there on its own. You're in this together, and if she has to make time in her schedule to attend countless appointments, ultrasounds, and tests, so should you. It will demonstrate to her that you're a team in the raising of this baby, and you'll be much more excited and invested in the process by being just as involved as your partner.

Childbirth is an empowering experience for both mother and father, and the more appointments you attend, the more knowledgeable you'll be about the entire process. Being an involved father starts long before the baby arrives. In fact, if you plan on being a 50-50 partner in the raising of your child, it's won't just happen overnight. You wouldn't play a baseball game without practice, and you shouldn't enter into parenthood without practicing the type of dad you want to be.

If your work schedule doesn't allow for you to attend every appointment, go to as many as possible. Follow up with her immediately after each appointment you miss and ask her for a recap. Ask lots of questions; your partner will be grateful to know you care. Many important decisions and discussions occur during prenatal visits, and even if you can't be present, make sure you remain part of the discussion.

Plan a Getaway

After baby arrives it won't be easy to abandon ship and head for the hills when you need a relaxing reprieve from life. And as the long wait for baby drags on and you both begin to realize how much is going to change in your personal lives after he comes, you may find yourselves looking for one last couples retreat.

Take the lead and plan a trip. Keep in mind that the later she is in her pregnancy, the closer to home you'll want to be in case she goes into labor. Also, her body (and especially her bladder) won't be up for sitting in a plane or in the car for long periods of time. Wherever you go, make the trip romantic, personal, and quiet. Make it a time to focus on your relationship — just the two of you — because it won't be the focus of your lives for some time to come.

If you plan something during the third trimester, keep in mind that many airlines have restrictions about how close to her due date your partner can travel. Check with your airline before booking tickets, because many require a doctor's note for travel.

Register for a Prenatal Parenting Class

The days of prenatal parenting classes that focus solely on breathing and birthing techniques are over. Today's classes offer opportunities for parents-to-be to explore birthing options, relationships, the type of parents they want to be, CPR, and infant care. Find a class that's welcoming to both mother and father and register, either through your local hospital or birthing center, or by searching online.

Many communities have fatherhood experts that offer a new brand of class just for fathers-to-be that explores the myths of fatherhood, what it means to be a father, and male bonding exercises. It allows men to confront their fears of fatherhood and any issues they have in regards to their own fathers. Putting in the work before baby comes only increases the odds that you'll be the best dad you can be.

Do Your Homework and Spread the Word

Clearly, if you're reading this book, then you've already done the majority of your homework. Congratulations — you're going to be a great dad. Now don't be afraid to toot your own horn. Not every dad-to-be is as equipped and awesome as you, and you deserve credit. Make a point of telling your partner how much you've found out in these pages. Ask her, "Did you know . . . ?" and "Have you thought about . . . ?" Who knows, you just may teach her something she didn't know. And is there any better feeling in the world than feeling accomplished?

At the very least, you'll set a good example of your own involvement in the future of your relationship. In the past, fathers weren't expected to know anything about pregnancy, and it wasn't all that long ago that the majority of men stayed out of the delivery room and returned to work the day after delivery. The more you know, the more your partner will trust you to care for the baby. Trust is earned, and by getting educated about babies, you're earning that trust that many fathers of the past forfeited.

Learn Prenatal Massage

Pregnancy puts stress on all the body's joints and ligaments as muscles (and even bones!) shift and expand, causing mothers-to-be to walk, stand, sit, and sleep in ways that often are at odds with their normal movements and positions. Add an additional 30 to 40 pounds hanging off her front, and it's no wonder that your average pregnant woman gets achy, tired, and downright sore.

Learning the basics of massage can help you help her alleviate many of those aches and pains — and will make you her hero after a long day of carrying around your child. Many hospitals and birthing centers offer prenatal massage classes. Doulas often are trained in light massage, and if you hire one, be sure to learn techniques from her. If you can't find someone to learn from, buy or rent a DVD about prenatal massage, or even buy a book that offers ample illustrations so you'll know what to do.

While you're at it, consider learning the ins and outs of infant massage. Research shows that infant massage can help babies digest foods and sleep better, and helps prevent and treat colic. Check with your hospital or birthing center for more information.

Clean High and Low

The closer you get to delivery time, the more likely your partner is to desire a clean, tidy home. Limited by a rather large belly and an unflinching tiredness, your partner won't always feel like cleaning or be able to do it. Areas that fall below your partner's knee level and things out of her reach are particularly difficult for her during the latter stages of pregnancy.

But her limitations don't mean that you have to clean everything all by yourself. In fact, the exercise involved in cleaning can be beneficial for her. However, assign yourself the job of picking up everything from the floor on a frequent basis. Clutter-free floors and walkways will prevent her from falling and will keep her from pulling a muscle in her back trying to reach down.

While you're down there, you have a good view of what baby will see when he's crawling around your home. You can always begin baby-proofing your abode; the extra time you give yourself will let you get used to the new limitations and restrictions.

Though it's a myth that a pregnant woman will strangle the baby if she raises her arms above her head, it may be a rather uncomfortable experience. Take the lead on cleaning the blinds, putting away dishes in the cupboards, changing light bulbs, and dusting.

Chapter 17

Ten Ways to Be a Super Dad from Day One

In This Chapter

▶ Learning how to bond with your baby

▶ Reading, teaching, and playing for fun and for learning

▶ Mastering the art of baby-and-daddy time

*W*hen it comes to parenting, what you don't know won't kill you, but it sure can keep you from making the most of the greatest, most joyous time in your life. After nearly a year of waiting for baby to arrive — or longer in some cases — don't forget that now is the time to have fun. Yes, bringing a teeny, tiny baby into your home evokes a great deal of worrying, but babies aren't as fragile as you may think. If you want to be a super dad, try to follow these tips on how to be a confident, loving, and cool father from day one.

Overcome Fragility Fears

Animals can sense fear, and when they know you're afraid, they exploit your weakness at every turn. The same goes for babies, albeit without the evil ulterior motive. If you're afraid of holding your baby, you probably aren't providing a solid, sturdy base for him, and he'll fuss and cry until somebody who is confident takes over the reins. The same holds true for diapering, feeding, and cuddling.

Repeat after us: I am not going to break my baby. He's designed to survive a first-time parent like yourself, and as long as you're not trying to juggle knives while burping him, chances are that you're both going to be just fine. Babies are small, but so long as you take reasonable safety precautions like never leaving him unattended, always securing him in a car seat, and listening closely to the baby monitor during sleep time, you aren't going to hurt him.

The most important tip is to take deep, steady breaths and hold your baby in the same casual-yet-protective way you grasp your iPad. Don't fumble with the baby as you lift him up onto your shoulder. Use firm, fluid movements. The more you act like you know what you're doing, the more the baby will like what you're doing.

Trust Your Instincts

Because babies are designed to be cared for by people who don't have any education in the raising of children, you have no choice but to follow your instincts. Babies have been around since, well, the dawn of man, and all the parents since that time have raised them their own way. It wasn't all that long ago that parents and parents-to-be told stories of their experiences around the campfire instead of relying on modern inventions such as parenting classes and Lamaze. We are born with the instinct to care for our children, and so long as you don't have mental or emotional impediments (such as postpartum depression), you'll just know what to do.

Just remember that nobody can know your baby better than you do, and despite the seeming lack of faith others may show toward your judgment (how warmly you dress him, how often you feed him, how you hold him, and so on), the only truly vital task of the parent is to ensure safety. Trust yourself, educate yourself, and you will not steer that little one wrong.

Bond Skin-to-Skin, Eye-to-Eye

Mothers get an amazing opportunity to spend skin-to-skin time with baby while breast-feeding. This sensory bond is so important that mere moments after the baby is born, the doctor or midwife will often place her on mom's bare chest. Studies show that skin-to-skin contact increases the bond that both mother and child feel, as well as the soothing feeling babies experience from listening to mom's heartbeat. Also, a newborn's eyesight is just powerful enough to see the distance from the breast to mom's eyes.

You won't be breast-feeding, so you have far fewer opportunities to experience the same closeness. Yes, baby's head will rest on your hands and arms, and you can get close and make eye contact, but that doesn't provide the same bonded feeling. When baby is only in her diaper, take off your shirt and place her on your chest. It may sound a little cheesy, but it's an important bonding experience for every parent, not just mothers, and it gives you and baby the opportunity to meet skin-to-skin and eye-to-eye for the first time.

Manage Frustrations

Admit it — your son or daughter is the most beautiful sight you've ever seen. As you stare into the wondering eyes of your newborn you may think it impossible to ever feel anything but absolute adoration for this child. However, babies often are exhausting and unmanageable beings who wake you up in the middle of the night, cry endlessly without giving you a clue as to what's wrong, and require 100 percent of your attention.

Feeling frustrated is okay, because parenting, especially when you're brand new at it, can and will be a frustrating experience from time to time. In preparation for when that cute bundle of joy becomes an obstinate teen, here are some simple ways to manage your frustration:

- ✔ **Control the controllable.** It's easier said than done, but some things you can change and some things you can't. Babies do not sleep through the night. Babies spit up. Babies cry for no good reason. Don't waste your time trying to solve problems that aren't really problems. If your baby has a clean diaper, a full belly, and a gas-free stomach, yet still continues to fuss, just put on some noise-canceling headphones and let him cry. Unless something is wrong, don't worry about him.

- ✔ **Monitor baby's routine.** Keep a log of when baby sleeps, wakes, eats, poops, and pees. Understanding his routine takes a lot of the guesswork out of determining what he needs at any given time. If you discover that your little one starts getting fussy after being awake for 90 minutes, you'll know how to structure your day to make sure that everyone — including you — gets what they need to function.

- ✔ **Blow off steam.** Pick your poison — running, video games, bowling, reading — whatever it is that puts your mind at ease, and make sure you take time to continue engaging in it. If you find yourself getting frustrated, spend five minutes doing your favorite activity. Even a walk around the block can be a great way to hit your reset button.

- ✔ **Lean on your support system.** When the going gets rough and you feel like you need to get out of Dodge, do it! Call a sitter, a friend, or a family member to fill in for you, even if it's just for an hour so you can run to the grocery store in peace. Don't discount the benefits of time alone or with your partner to make your frustrations dissipate.

- ✔ **Sleep in shifts.** Sleep is a hot commodity among the parenting set, and before long you'll be coveting every available minute of shut-eye. However, if baby is constantly waking during the night, both you and your partner will quickly lose patience in the wee hours of the morning. Though it's not the ideal situation, try taking turns sleeping for blocks of time in the night and throughout the day while on leave (or the weekends). You need to get as much sleep as possible, even if those hours aren't consecutive. The key to keeping your frustrations in check just may be two hours of peaceful slumber.

Embrace Your Goofy Side

By now you've probably made a list of all of the things you're not going to do as a parent. For many too-cool-for-school dads, that list includes such things as baby talk, funny faces, and the pure lunacy of dress up, tea parties, and dancing that requires dads to check traditional masculinity at the door in favor of fun.

Do all the things on that list. Don't feel stupid and don't feel restrained by how you think men should behave. Babies (and kids, for that matter) love expressive faces, singing, and goofy voices, and while acting silly may leave you in a shroud of self-consciousness, you'll get over it the instant your baby laughs or smiles at your goofball antics. Allow yourself to have fun, and you'll reap the rewards for life.

Get Out

Going to work doesn't qualify as getting out of the house. Yes, it may be a nice change of pace to spend time doing things that don't require baby wipes and a Pee-Pee Teepee, but the kind of getting out you need is of the date variety.

You may be surprised to know that getting out of the house is easier when your baby is younger. Make sure to schedule a date within the first month of baby's arrival. Start slowly — new moms (and many dads) find it hard to leave baby for the first time. Ask a trusted friend or family member to watch baby while you grab a quick bite to eat at your favorite restaurant.

Ground rules? Don't talk about the baby. You may not achieve this almost impossible goal, but shoot for the stars. You need to connect as adults again, not just as parents, and that brief time away will remind you why you love your partner so much. And, upon returning home, you'll have a welcome reminder of just how much you love that baby.

Teach Baby New Tricks

You may think babies discover the world of their own volition, but the truth is that you need to give your little one a push. In fact, the more time you put into teaching and nurturing your baby, the prouder you will be when she learns to roll over, clap, wave bye-bye, or play with a toy. Bonding happens daily with babies, and a child's way of thinking is practically set in stone by age 3. You can have a huge influence on the rate at which your child develops, but more importantly, you can have a huge influence on your child's entire life by getting involved in playtime and the open expression of love.

Following are some milestones you can help baby achieve in the first six months:

- **Tracking objects:** Slowly move a colorful object back and forth and up and down in front of baby's eyes. This activity helps the brain begin to follow movement. Sound tracking can also be done in the same way.

- **Making sounds:** Your baby makes a lot of strange sounds, and a supremely important part of language development is hearing you repeat those sounds back to her. Babies have their own language that you don't understand, and the more they hear it the more they will talk, which aids in language development down the road.

- **Reaching and grabbing:** Dangle colorful toys and baby-safe objects in front of your child and wait for her to reach for them. Encourage gripping by wrapping baby's hand around the object and letting go.

- **Peek-a-boo:** Babies will laugh as you disappear and reappear time and again, all while beginning to understand the idea of cause and effect. Showing baby the mirror is also a fun, mind-expanding game.

- **Rolling over:** Lay your baby on her back on a play mat or a colorful rug to encourage her to turn over and begin to explore. When she can support her own head, give her plenty of tummy time on her belly, which develops the stomach muscles and allows her to roll over.

- **Crawling:** New studies show that the way babies' brains react during crawling (the right brain controls the left side of the body and vice versa) is an important milestone that can help reduce behavioral and mental disorders in children. Help ensure your child can crawl by putting a coveted toy just out of reach and waiting for her to come and get it.

Roughhouse the Safe Way

Though we don't want to engage in gender stereotyping, fathers are often more likely to get physical during playtime with their kids. And although you probably won't be wrestling with your newborn (please, don't wrestle your newborn!), go ahead and swing him in your arms, hold him up high over your head, rub your scratchy face into his belly, tickle him, and chew on his feet. Mom may think it's too much, but more than likely, baby will think it's hysterical. As long as you're being safe, have fun.

Read Aloud . . . and Not Just from Baby Books

Read to your baby every single day. Not only will she love the sound of your voice, but she'll also learn to speak from hearing the constant repetition of speech patterns. And the more you read to baby, the more likely it is that she will develop a strong vocabulary and the ability to speak at a younger age.

While baby is too young to truly enjoy kid's books, don't be afraid to read her passages from the novels you want to read. It's a good way to engage in adult activities while also helping your baby grow smarter every single day.

Send Mom Away

Unless you're fortunate enough to be a work-at-home dad like coauthor Matthew, you'll need to make sure that you block off some one-on-one time with your baby. Finding your own way as a parent and learning how capable you are are important steps in feeling empowered as a new dad. Which means that mom needs to go away for a while.

Book an appointment at the spa for your partner and spend the afternoon doing everyday things with just you and your baby. Take him for a walk, feed him, change him, or even go out to the coffee shop and read the paper with him. Regardless of the activities you do together, this time establishes one-on-one intimacy with your child and proves to yourself and your partner that you are capable of taking care of your child on your own.

Index

• A •

accidents
  in cars, 241–242
  falls, 240–241
active labor, 155
administering medications, 244–245
admissions process at hospitals, 125
advice
  curbing, 297
  unsolicited, handling, 43–44, 214–215
after-work requests and expectations,
    259–260
age, and miscarriages, 55–56
alcohol
  after childbirth, 202
  conception and, 28, 32
  overconsumption of, 16
Alexander Technique classes, 78
allergies
  to food, 253–254
  to medications, 252–253
all-natural childbirth method, 137,
    163–164
American College of Midwives, 132
amniocentesis, 73
anemia, 110
anger, controlling, 16, 193
antidepressant medications, 120
anxiety with breast-feeding, 177
aspirin, 238
assembling furniture for nursery, 82
asthma, and wheezing, 237
axillary thermometer, 246

• B •

babies. *See* newborns
Babinski reflex, 175
baby blues, 211, 224
baby books or calendars, 195, 296
baby carriers, 89, 189, 190
baby monitors, 84
baby registries. *See* registering at
    stores
baby showers, coed, 90–91
baby sitters, cost of, 273

baby-proofing living areas, 83–85
"Back to Sleep" campaign, 187
backpacks for carrying newborns, 189,
    190
backs, positioning newborns on for
    sleep, 187
backup, calling in, 203–204, 226–227
banking cord blood, 140
bathing newborns, 183–185
bathtub, baby-sized, 90
bed rest
  mandatory, 98–100
  multiple births and, 110
  placenta previa and, 97–98
  pregnancy-induced hypertension and,
    95–96
beta strep carriers, 152
bills, itemized, asking hospitals for, 112
biological clocks, 17
birth control, 216
birth defects, 100–101, 110, 219–220.
    See also chromosomal
    abnormalities
birth plan
  attendance at birth, 145–146
  description of, 138–139
  deviations from, 167
  sharing, 143–144
  visualizing ideal experience, 139–140
  writing, 140–143
birthing options. *See also* cesarean
    delivery; epidural
  discussing with practitioner, 51–52
  location for delivery, 133–136
  natural methods, 137, 163–164
  practitioner, 130–133
  water birth, 138
BirthWorks classes, 78
bisphenol A (BPA), 178
bleeding
  at delivery, 110
  during labor, 152
  from placenta previa, 97–98
  during third trimester, 118
blighted ovum, 57
blood pressure medication, 31
blood tests in second trimester, 71–73
bonding with newborns, 302, 306

bottle warmer for car, 90
bottle-feeding
  formula, choosing, 179–180
  preparing bottles, 180–181
  supplemental, while breast-feeding,
    177–178
  systems for, 88–89, 179
bottles, plastic, 88, 178
bouncy chairs, 89
bowel movements, changes in, 249–250
boys, changing diapers of, 182–183
BPA (bisphenol A), 178
Bradley Method classes, 78, 137
bradycardia, 162
BRAT diet after vomiting, 237
Braxton-Hicks contractions, 118
breast-feeding
  birth control and, 216
  cosleeping and, 186
  decision about, 176, 204–205
  as full-time job, 204
  getting started with, 177
  illness in mother and, 235
  involving father in, 207–208
  latch-on problems in, 177
  nutritional issues with, 202
  prenatal lactation classes, 135
  prevention of allergic reactions and, 254
  pumping, 178
  reflux and, 193
  resources on, 207
  supplemental bottles and, 177–178
  support for, 176, 206–207
  vitamin D supplements and, 128
breasts of newborns, 175
breathing issues
  after delivery, 158–159
  of premature babies, 105
breech position, 114–115
bronchopulmonary dysplasia, 107
budget
  for childcare, 273
  creating, 279–280
  cutting costs in, 275
  debt, paying down, 280–281
  for deliveries, 269
  for first-year necessities, 268–269
  for preterm labor and deliveries,
    111–112
  prioritizing needs in, 274, 278–279
  resources for, 280
  spending less, 16
  for supplies, 269–271, 280

bumper pads in crib, 82
burp cloths, 185
burping
  by bouncing on yoga ball, 89
  to prevent gas, 191
business world. *See* work

• *C* •

car seats, 86, 241–242
carriers, hands-free, 89
carrying babies around, 189, 190
car
  bottle warmer for, 90
  safety in, 86, 241–242
cat litter, 81
CDs for babies, 90
cervical mucus, and ovulation, 34
cesarean delivery
  emotions related to, 172
  IVs during, 159
  multiple births and, 110
  placenta previa and, 99
  planned or scheduled, 168
  procedures during, 171–172
  procedures prior to, 170
  rate of, 131
  recovery from, 208–209
  types of, 171
  unplanned, 169–170
chairs, ergonomic bouncy, 89
changing diapers
  for boys, 182–183
  essentials for, 87
  for girls, 183
chemical pregnancy, 56
chicken pox, 238
childbirth classes, 77–78
childbirth costs, 111–112, 122–125, 269
childcare options and costs, 271–273
chlamydia, 29, 31
chromosomal abnormalities. *See also*
    birth defects
  as male-fertility issue, 41
  miscarriage and, 56, 57
circumcision, 182–183
classes
  birth plans developed in, 140
  childbirth, 77–78
  prenatal lactation, 135
  prenatal parenting, 298–299
cleaning house, 80–81, 198–201, 300

cleft lip/palate, 220
clothing for babies
  cost of, 271
  essential, 87
coed baby showers, 90–91
colds, common, 234–235
colic, dealing with, 191, 192
colostrum, 176
commitments, reprioritizing, 260–261
complicated grief, 230–231
complications. *See* medical issues
compliments, giving, 295–296
conception. *See also* infertility
  basics of, 23–28
  best time for, 33–34
  common questions about, 27–28
  female health issues that affect, 29–30
  lifestyle choices that affect, 31–33
  male health issues that affect, 30–31
  sex life and, 33–36
  statistics about, 27
congenital defects, 100–101, 110,
    219–220
conjoined twins, 109
Consumer Reports, baby section of, 86
contractions
  fetal monitoring and, 161–162
  membrane ruptures and, 161
  regularity of, 152
  during third trimester, 118
  vaginal exams during, 159
convenience purchases, 275
convulsions, 248–249
cord accidents, 110
cord prolapse, 116, 152
cord-blood banking, 140
cord, cutting, 157
cosleeping, 82, 83, 186–187
costs, cutting, 275. *See also* budget
couples, finding time to interact as
  after birth of baby, 15, 304
  in second trimester, 68
  in third trimester, 22
couvade syndrome, 119
Coverdell Education Savings Account,
    283
cravings in early pregnancy, 59
credit scores, 282–283
crib
  assembling, 82
  bumper pads for, 82
  mobiles for, 90
  for multiples, 83

crying
  dealing with, 193
  deciphering meaning of, 190
cry-it-out sleep method, 213
C-section. *See* cesarean delivery
cutting costs, 275. *See also* budget
cystic fibrosis, 220

● *D* ●

daycare centers, 273
D&C (dilatation and curettage), 57
death of fetus in utero, 101–102
debts, paying down, 280–281
decongestants, 226
dehydration, signs of, 236, 239
delivery. *See also* cesarean delivery;
    preterm labor and delivery
  attendance at, 145–146
  birth plan and, 138–144
  cost of, 269
  helping babies after, 158–159
  hemorrhage at, 110
  insurance coverage for, 122–124
  lightheadedness during, 157
  location for, 133–136
  of placenta, 157–158
  practitioner, choosing for, 130–133
  pushing during, 156
  rapid, 153
  voicing opinions about, 12
depression
  postpartum, 211–212, 224–227
  during pregnancy, 120, 122
  risk factors for, 225–226
  support role in, 226–227
  symptoms of, 225
  treatment for, 226
  while on mandatory bed rest, 100
detergents, choosing, 199, 271
development of babies
  delays in, 220–221
  in first trimester, 53–55
  in second trimester, 65–67
  in third trimester, 113–116
  ultrasounds and, 74
diabetes
  ejaculatory issues and, 31
  gestational, 96–97, 109
diapers
  cost of, 270
  interpreting contents of, 249–250
  laundering, 199–200

diapers, changing
  for boys, 182–183
  essentials for, 87
  for girls, 183
diarrhea, 239
differences in readiness for
    parenthood, 19
digital thermometer, 246
dilatation and curettage (D&C), 57
disability insurance, 274, 281–282
discussing names with friends and
    family, 93–94
distilled water for formula, 181
doctor shopping, 50–52
douching, 32–33
doula, 132–133
Doulas of North America, 133
Down syndrome, 220
dress during pregnancy, 70
drugs, using
  impending fatherhood and, 16
  SIDS and, 223
  sperm quantity and quality and, 32
DVDs for babies, 90

• *E* •

ear infections, 235–236
early labor, 155
eating. *See* food; healthy eating
eclampsia, 96
ectopic pregnancy, 26, 32, 57–58
education, saving money for, 283–284
eggs
  mature, production of, 24
  smoking and, 31–32
embryo
  in first trimester, 53–55
  implantation of, 27
  journey of down fallopian tubes, 26
emergencies
  funds for, 274, 281, 284
  handling, 243–244
emotions
  about birth defects, 100–101
  about cesarean delivery, 172, 208
  about fragility of newborns, 301–302
  about pets, 80
  after childbirth, 14
  anger, 16, 193
  at announcements of pregnancy,
      47–48
  dealing with, 120–122
  at delivery, 157

in early pregnancy, 59, 63
  frustration, 303–304
  grief, 228–231
  with infertility, 37
  during labor, 154
  at learning sex of baby, 75
  with miscarriages, 56, 58
  postpartum, 209–212, 224–227
  with preterm labor and delivery, 103
  at prospect of fatherhood, 9, 10–12,
      49–50
  in third trimester, 118–120
  when babies cry, 193
  when mother returns to work,
      263–264
  while on mandatory bed rest, 99
employment. *See* work
endometriosis, 29
engorgement of breasts, 206
entertainment costs, 275, 278
epidural
  medications used in, 164
  placement of, 165–166
  side effects of, 166
  types of, 137
episiotomies, 139, 158
ergonomic bouncy chairs, 89
errands, running, 201
estradiol, 24
executor of will, appointing, 290
exercise
  after birth of baby, 201
  conception and, 33
  disguising as fun, 296–297
  starting, 16
  while on mandatory bed rest, 99
external fetal monitoring, 161–162

• *F* •

"failure to progress" and cesarean
    delivery, 169
fallopian tubes
  in conception, 25, 26
  ectopic pregnancy and, 57–58
falls, 240–241
family
  dealing with, 126, 203–204, 213–214
  discussing names with, 93–94
  phone tree for, 126, 146–147
  resemblance of newborns to, 175
  sharing information on readiness for
      parenthood with, 42–43

Family Medical Leave Act, 227, 256
family planning, 17–20
fatherhood
  conceptions of, 10
  description of, 14
  emotions at prospect of, 9, 10–11
  fears of, dealing with, 11–12, 49–50, 121
  lifestyle changes and, 16
  myths of, 12–14
  personal life changes and, 15
  professional life changes and, 15–16
  readiness for, 17–18
  stay-at-home parenting and, 267–268
fatigue during early pregnancy, 58–59
fears
  of fatherhood, 11–12, 49–50, 121
  of fragility of newborns, 301–302
febrile seizures, 248–249
feeding babies
  bottle-feeding, 179–181
  breast-feeding, 176–178
  cost of, 270
  essentials for, 88–89
  overview of, 176
  when premature, 105–106, 107
  solid foods, 128
feelings. *See* emotions
female health issues that influence
    conception, 29–30
female infertility issues, 37, 38–39
Ferber method, 213
fetal demise, 101–102
fetal distress and cesarean delivery,
    169–170
fetal monitoring, 139, 161–162
fevers
  recognizing, 248–249
  treating, 249
fibroids, 30, 37
financial advisor, 282
financial planning. *See also* budget
  disability insurance, 274, 281–282
  life insurance, 274, 284–286
  retirement accounts, 282, 284
  saving for education, 283–284
first stage of labor, 155–156
first trimester
  complications in, 55–58
  development of baby during, 53–55
  discomforts of, 58–66
529 plans, 283
flat head, preventing, 188–190
flextime, taking advantage of, 257

follicle stimulating hormone, 24
food
  allergic reactions to, 253–254
  to avoid during pregnancy, 69
  cutting costs on, 275, 278
  solid, feeding, 128
forehead thermometer, 246
foreskin of penis, 182–183
formula
  choosing, 179–180
  cost of, 270
  "stretching," 181
fraternal twins, 109
frequency of sex, and conception, 28,
    34
front packs for carrying newborns, 189,
    190
frustrations, managing, 303–304
furniture, buying and assembling, 82, 87

• *G* •

garage sales, 269
gas, dealing with, 191
gastrointestinal reflux disease (GERD),
    192–193
genetic disorders, 220
genetic markers, 74
genitals of newborns, 174
GERD (gastrointestinal reflux disease),
    192–193
gestational diabetes, 96–97, 109
getaways, planning, 298
gifts, registering for. *See* registering at
    stores
girls, changing diapers of, 183
gonorrhea, 29, 31
goofy side, embracing, 304
grandparents, visits by, 204, 214
grasp reflex, 175
grief
  after cesarean delivery, 172
  complicated, 230–231
  partner and, 229–230
  stages of, 228–229
guardians, appointing, 289–290, 291

• *H* •

Haemophilus influenzae type B
    vaccination, 239
hair loss after delivery, 210
hand, foot, and mouth disease, 238

hands-free baby carriers, 89
heads of newborns
  flat, preventing, 188–190
  shape of, 174
health care for uninsured children, 288
health insurance. *See* insurance
  coverage
healthy eating
  after childbirth, 16
  in first trimester, 61
  foods to avoid, 69
  in second trimester, 68
heart defects, 220
heart rate, fetal, 161–162
hemorrhage at delivery, 110
holding newborns, 185–186, 301–302
home, working from, 265
home birth, 123, 135–136
hormones
  after delivery, 209–212
  in conception, 24
  in implantation, 27
  infertility and, 38
  in third trimester, 119
hospital
  admissions process at, 125
  asking for itemized bills from, 112
  delivery at, 134–135
  discharge of premature babies from,
    107–108
  neonatal intensive care unit, 103–104
hot tubs, 33
household projects, 80–81
household tasks, 198–201, 300
human chorionic gonadotropin, 27, 53
hypertension
  pregnancy-induced, 95–96, 110
  preterm deliveries and, 103
HypnoBirthing classes, 78
hysterosalpingograms, 29, 38
hysteroscopies, 38

• *I* •

identical twins, 109
illnesses
  dealing with, 222
  fevers, recognizing, 248–249
  handling, 233–239
  medications, administering, 244–245
  of mothers, and breast-feeding, 235
  preventing exposure of newborns to,
    214

serious, 239
teething and, 250–251
temperature, taking, 245–248
immunizations
  Haemophilus influenzae type B, 239
  reactions to, 252
  scheduling, 193–195
implantation of embryos, 27, 53
in vitro fertilization
  abnormal sperm issues and, 41
  description of, 42
  multiple births and, 108, 109
incompetent cervix, 102
indigestion, soothing, 190–193
induction, 131
infants. *See* newborns
infections
  in premature babies, 107
  preterm deliveries and, 103
infectious diseases, 237–239
infertility
  admitting to problem of, 37–38
  deciding on treatment for, 42
  female treatment for, 38–39
  male treatment for, 39–41
  statistics on, 36–37
insensitive remarks, handling, 232
instincts, trusting, 302
insurance coverage
  checking on, 111–112, 122–124
  co-payments and, 112
  cost of, 270–271
  for newborns, 286–288
  questions to ask about, 124
  for ultrasounds, 100
interest rates, 279, 280–281
internal fetal monitoring, 162–163
International Childbirth Education
    Association classes, 78
interviewing
  birth practitioners, 130–131
  childcare providers, 272
  pediatricians, 127–128
intrauterine growth retardation, 96
intrauterine insemination, 41
intravenous lines for premature babies,
    106–107
intraventricular hemorrhage in
    premature babies, 107
irritability during third trimester, 119
IV (intravenous infusion) during labor,
    159–160

• J •

job. *See* work

• L •

labor. *See also* preterm labor and delivery
  birth plan and, 138–144
  common procedures during, 159–163
  coping with pain during, 163–166
  determining when not to go to hospital, 153
  determining when to go to hospital, 151–152
  first stage of, 155–156
  insurance coverage for, 122–124
  orgasm and, 77
  practitioner, choosing for, 130–133
  second stage of, 156–157
  support role during, 154
  types of, 136–138
  voicing opinions about, 12
lactation. *See* breast-feeding
Lamaze classes, 78
lanugo, 105, 115–116
latch-on problems in breast-feeding, 177
laundering baby items, 199–200, 271
leaking fluids during third trimester, 118
leave options, 256–258
legal matters, arranging, 288–292
life insurance, 274, 284–286
lifestyle changes to consider making, 16
lifting, 81
lightheadedness
  during deliveries, 157
  during epidural placements, 166
listeria in food, 69
living areas, baby-proofing, 83–85
luteinizing hormone (LH), 24, 34

• M •

male health issues that influence conception, 30–31
male infertility issues, 37, 39–41
massage, learning, 299–300
mastitis, 206
meal management, 202–203

measles, 238
meconium, 138, 160
medical crises at home, managing, 243–244
medical issues. *See also* cesarean deliveries
  abnormal ultrasounds, 100–102
  with breast-feeding, 198
  conception and, 29–31
  gestational diabetes, 96–97
  grief over, 228–231
  insensitive remarks about, handling, 232
  mandatory bed rest, 98–100
  with multiple births, 109–110
  of newborns, 219–223
  placenta previa, 97–98
  pregnancy-induced hypertension, 95–96
  sharing information about, 231–232
  in third trimester, 118
medical practitioner. *See also* midwife; pediatrician
  from call groups during delivery, 167
  doula, 132–133
  finding, 50–52
  perinatologist, 101
  philosophy on cesareans of, 170
  screening, 130–131
medications
  administering, 244–245
  antidepressants, 120
  for blood pressure, 31
  in epidurals, 164
  during labor, 137
  reactions to, 252–253
membrane ruptures, 160–161
men as caretakers for newborns, 12–13, 267–268
meningitis, 239
menstrual cycle, 25
mercury in food, 69
mercury thermometer, 248
midwife
  delivery by, 51–52, 123
  home delivery and, 135–136
  interviewing, 132
Midwives of North America, 132
milestones
  delays in reaching, 221
  helping babies achieve, 305
  recording, 195, 296
milia, 174

miscarriage
  in first trimester, 55–57
  frequency of, 48
  timing of, 49
mistakes of father, repeating, 13–14
mittelschmerz, 34
mobiles for crib, 90
Mongolian spots, 174
monitoring equipment for premature
    babies, 106
monitors, video, 84
Moro reflex, 175
multiple births
  arranging nurseries for, 83
  cesarean deliveries and, 168
  health risks for babies with, 110–111
  health risks for mothers with, 109–110
  hospital costs and, 123–124
  preterm deliveries and, 102
  risk factors for, 108–109
  statistics on, 108
mumps, 239
myths of fatherhood, 12–14

• *N* •

names, choosing
  discussing with friends and family,
      93–94
  narrowing down long lists, 91–92
  reconciling differences of opinion,
      92–93
nanny, cost of, 273
natural childbirth methods, 137,
    163–164
nausea in early pregnancy, 59
necrotizing enterocolitis, 107
neonatal intensive care units (NICUs),
    103–104
nesting
  baby-proofing, 83–85
  cleaning and, 80–81, 198–201, 300
  description of, 79
  setting up nursery, 81–82
neural tube defects, 220
newborns. *See also* development of
    babies
  bathing, 183–185
  bonding with, 302, 306
  changing diapers of, 182–183
  cosleeping with, 82, 83, 186–187
  fears of fragility of, 301–302
  feeding, 176–181
  flat head, preventing, 188–190

health problems of, 219–223
holding, 185–186, 301–302
indigestion of, soothing, 190–193
looks of, 173–175
love at first sight of, 14
men as caretakers for, 12–13, 267–268
pets and, 200
positioning for sleep, 187
preventing exposure to illnesses, 214
reflexes of, 175
sleep cycles of, 212–213
swaddling for sleep, 188, 189
Newborns' and Mothers' Health
    Protection Act, 123
NICU (neonatal intensive care unit),
    103–104
night sweats after deliveries, 210
no-cry sleep method, 213
nursery
  arranging for multiple babies, 83
  setting up, 81–82
  size of, and registering for gifts, 85
nursery water for formula, 181
nutritional issues with breast-feeding, 202

• *O* •

obesity, and conception, 32
one-on-one intimacy with newborns, 306
oocytes, 24
oral sex, 76
organizing and de-cluttering home, 17
orgasm and labor, 77
overfeeding, 181
ovulation
  infertility and, 37
  monitoring, 34
  pregnancy and, 24

• *P* •

pacifier thermometers, 246
pacifier at bedtime, 188
pain
  after cesarean deliveries, 208
  during labor, 163–166
painting house or nursery, 80–81
parenting classes, prenatal, 298–299
paternity leave, 256–258, 259
pediatrician
  choosing, 126–128
  discussing immunization schedule
      with, 194–195

pelvic inflammatory disease (PID), 29, 32
penis, circumcision of, 182–183
performance issues when scheduling sex, 36
perinatologist, 101
personal investment accounts, 284
personal life, changes in, 15
pets
  caring for, 81, 200
  feelings about, 80
  introducing to newborns, 200
phone tree, 126, 146–147
PID (pelvic inflammatory disease), 29, 32
Pitocin, 137, 165
placenta previa, 97–98
placental abruption, 110, 118, 152
placenta, delivery of, 157–158
plagiocephaly, 188–190
planning for future. *See also* budget; financial planning
  health insurance, 286–288
  legal matters, 288–292
plastic bottles and BPA, 178
playing with newborns, 306
polycystic ovary syndrome, 29–30
polyps, 37
positions for sex, and conception, 28
postpartum period
  emotions during, 224–227
  hormones during, 209–212
power of attorney, establishing, 291–292
practitioner. *See* medical practitioner; pediatrician
preeclampsia, 118
pregnancy
  first trimester of, 21
  long-awaited, 20
  second trimester of, 21
  third trimester of, 21–22
  unexpected or unplanned, 19
pregnancy-induced hypertension, 95–96, 110
pregnant dad syndrome, 119
premature babies (preemies)
  common problems of, 105–106
  look of, 105
  preparing for setbacks with, 107
  taking home, 107–108
  wires and machines attached to, 106
prenatal visits
  attending, 52, 297–298
  to birthing centers, 125, 135

preparation for mother's return to work, 262
preterm labor and delivery. *See also* premature babies
  guilt with, 103
  look of preemies, 105
  medical bills from, 111–112
  neonatal intensive care unit, 103–104
  risks of, 102–103
  statistics on, 102
private in-home daycare, 272–273
psychosis, postpartum, 227
pumping to fill supplemental bottles, 178
pushing during delivery, 156
pyloric stenosis, 237

• **Q** •

quality time, spending
  as couple, 15, 22, 68, 304
  with infant, 15, 302, 306

• **R** •

radiographic embolization, 41
rapid delivery, 153
rashes, 238
reactions
  to medications, 252–253
  to news of pregnancies, 48
  to vaccinations, 252
readiness for parenthood
  determining, 17–18
  differences in, 19
  evaluating health and, 28–33
  sharing with family and friends, 42–43
  telling partner about, 18
reading to newborns, 306
recovery from cesarean deliveries, 208–209
rectal temperature, taking, 247–248
reflexes of newborns, 175
reflux, 192–193
registering at stores
  doing homework before, 85–86
  essential items, 86–89
  nonessential but nice-to-have items, 89
  unnecessary items, 90–91
reprioritizing commitments, 260–261
resale shops, 269, 280

respiratory infections or diseases in
    premature babies, 107
respiratory syncytial virus, 236
retirement accounts, 282, 284
retrograde ejaculation, 31
Reye's syndrome, 238
risks of tests and ultrasounds, 72
rooting reflex, 175
roseola, 238
roughhousing, 306
routines, developing, 17
rubella, 238

• S •

safety
    in cars, 241–242
    Consumer Reports, baby section of, 86
    of hospital maternal and child health
        areas, 134
    of living areas, 83–85
    of slings, 89
    of visitors, 146
salmonella in food, 69
saving
    for education, 283–284
    for emergencies, 274, 281, 284
scheduling
    immunizations, 193–195
    sex for conception, 35–36
Sears, Robert, *The Vaccine Book,* 195
second stage of labor, 156–157
second trimester
    development of baby during, 65–67
    sex life during, 75–77
    testing during, 71–75
    women during, 67–71
second-hand smoke, 16
sedatives during labor, 164
seizures, febrile, 248–249
self, taking time for, 215–216, 260, 303,
    304
self-image issues during third trimester,
    119
semen analysis, 39–40
sex life
    after childbirth, 216
    conception and, 33–36
    in early pregnancy, 61–62
    following childbirth, 13
    placenta previa and, 97
    in second trimester, 75–77

sex of baby, determining from
    ultrasound, 71, 74–75
sexually transmitted diseases (STDs),
    29, 31, 182
sharing information
    about birth plan, 143–144
    about decision to have baby, 42–43
    about health problems, 231–232
    about pregnancy, 48–49
    about readiness for fatherhood, 18
    with partner, 299
    by phone tree, 126, 146–147
    by social networking sites, 147
shoes for infants, 90
showers, 90–91
Siamese twins, 109
siblings, arranging nurseries for, 83
sick time
    managing, 258–259
    taking after birth of baby, 257
sickle cell anemia, 220
SIDS. *See* sudden infant death
    syndrome
skin of newborns, look of, 174
skin-to-skin contact with newborns, 302
sleep
    breast-feeding and, 176
    cosleeping, 82, 83, 186–187
    essential items for, 87
    Ferber method and, 213
    following childbirth, 13, 212
    frustrations over, managing, 303–304
    of newborns, 212–213
    positioning newborns for, 187, 223
    swaddling newborns for, 188, 189
slings, 89, 189, 190
smoking
    after childbirth, 16
    conception and, 28, 31–32
    SIDS and, 223
Social Security Administration, Popular
    Baby Names Web site, 93
solid foods, feeding, 128
sperm
    collection of for analysis, 38
    conception and, 24
    diagram of, 26
    infertility and, 37, 39–41
    life of, in reproductive tract after
        ejaculation, 35
    quantity of, 26
    smoking and, 31
startle reflex, 175

stay-at-home parenthood
  decisions about, 264–265
  fathers and, 267–268
  mothers and, 266–267
STDs (sexually transmitted diseases),
    29, 31, 182
step reflex, 175
steroids, using, 32
stitches after tears or episiotomies, 158
stomach sleeping, 223
stool, changes in, 249–250
stores. *See* registering at stores
storing pumped breast milk, 178
stork bites, 174
strollers, 85, 86, 89
sucking reflex, 175
sudden infant death syndrome (SIDS)
  back sleeping and, 187
  breast-feeding and, 204
  myths about, 222–223
  pacifiers and, 188
  risk factors for, 223
  side positioning and, 187
supply issues in breast-feeding, 177
support groups
  for grief, 230
  for multiple births, 108
  for premature births, 103, 108
support role
  for breast-feeding, 176, 206–207
  for deviations to birth plan, 167
  of doulas, 132–133
  in early pregnancy, 62–63
  in grief, 229–230
  household tasks and, 198–201
  during labor, 154
  meal management and, 202–203
  with nesting tasks, 80
  overview of, 197–198
  postpartum depression and, 226–227
  in postpartum period, 209–210
  for return to work, 262–264
  for stay-at-home mothers, 266–267
  in third trimester, 120–122
swaddling newborns for sleep, 188, 189
swearing, 16
syphilis, 29, 31

• *T* •

tachycardia, 162
teaching newborns, 305

teething, symptoms of and remedies
    for, 250–251
temperature
  ovulation and, 34
  rectal, taking, 247–248
  teething and, 251
term life insurance, 286
testicles, descended, 115
thermometer, choosing, 246
third trimester
  development of baby during, 113–116
  emotional changes in women during,
    118–120
  physical changes in women during,
    116–118
threatened abortion, 56
thyroid problems, 30
time alone, needing, 215–216, 304
time capsule, starting, 22
toiletry essentials, 87–88
tonic neck reflex, 175
touring birthing centers, 125, 135
towels for newborns, 185
toxins in workplace, 31
toxoplasmosis, 81
transition labor, 156
travel essentials, 88
travel systems, 86
trips, planning, 298
twins, types of, 109
twin-to-twin transfusion syndrome, 110
tympanic thermometers, 246

• *U* •

ultrasound
  abnormal, 100–102
  determining sex of babies from, 71,
    74–75
  first, attending, 52–53
  results of, 73–75
  risks of, 72
uninsured
  costs of labor and delivery for,
    124–125
  health care for, 288
unsolicited advice, handling, 43–44,
    214–215
urination
  frequent, during pregnancy, 59
  projectile, of baby boys, 182
utilities, cost of, 275

• V •

vacation time, taking, 256–257
The Vaccine Book (Sears), 195
vaccines
  Haemophilus influenzae type B, 239
  reactions to, 252
  scheduling, 193–195
vacuum extraction, 139
vaginal exams during labor, 159
vagina, openings of, 183
varicoceles, 41
ventilation
  for premature babies, 105, 106, 107
  in rooms, and SIDS, 223
vernix, 174
video monitors, 84
visitors
  coping with, 213–215
  planning for, 146
vitamin D supplements, 128
voices, recognition of, 114
vomiting
  of babies, 236–237
  in early pregnancy, 60

• W •

water
  for baths, 184
  birth in, 138
  for formula, 181
water breaks, 152, 160–161
Web sites
  for breast-feeding, 207
  for credit rating agencies, 283
  for doulas, 133
  for midwives, 132
  for names, 93
  for social networking, 147
  for uninsured, 288
weepiness during third trimester, 119
weight gain
  in early pregnancy, 61
  in second trimester, 68–70
weight loss
  after birth of baby, 201
  in preparation for fatherhood, 16
well water for formula, 181
wheezing, 237
whole-life insurance coverage, 285
wills, creating, 288–291
wipes
  cost of, 270
  warmers for, 89
work. *See also* workplace
  adjusting when mother returns to,
    262–264
  calling in backup for return to, 203, 208
  from home, 265
  juggling fatherhood and, 13, 15–16
  taking leave from, 227
work/life balance
  after-work requests and expectations,
    259–260
  overview of, 255–256
  paternity leave, 256–258, 259
  reprioritizing commitments, 260–261
  sick time, managing, 258–259
  stay-at-home parenting, 264–268
workplace. *See also* work
  announcing pregnancies at, 49
  toxins in, 31

• Y •

yoga ball, 89
yolk sacs, 53